NEW TOEIC
多益 13 大情境全拆解

單字・聽力・閱讀一書搞定！ 解析本

TOEIC is a registered trademark of Educational Testing Service (ETS).
This publication is not affiliated with, endorsed, or approved by ETS.

CONTENTS 目錄

- NEW TOEIC 測驗　分數換算表　2
- 13 回單元測驗簡答表　3
- NEW TOEIC 模擬測驗 Test 01 簡答表　5
- NEW TOEIC 模擬測驗 Test 02 簡答表　6

- **Chapter 01**　7
  Corporate Development:（企業發展）
  research, product development

- **Chapter 02**　26
  Dining Out:（外出用餐）
  business and informal lunches, banquets, receptions, restaurant reservations

- **Chapter 03**　46
  Entertainment:（娛樂）
  cinema, theater, music, art, exhibitions, museums, media

- **Chapter 04**　67
  Finance and Budgeting:（財務預算）
  banking, investments, taxes, accounting, billing

- **Chapter 05**　88
  General Business:（一般商業）
  contracts, negotiations, mergers, marketing, sales, warranties, business planning, conferences, labor relations

- **Chapter 06**　107
  Health:（健康）
  medical insurance, visiting doctors, dentists, clinics, hospitals

- **Chapter 07**　126
  Housing / Corporate Property:（房屋 / 企業財產）
  construction, specifications, buying and renting, electric and gas services

- **Chapter 08**　144
  Manufacturing:（製造業）
  assembly lines, plant management, quality control

- **Chapter 09**　163
  Offices:（辦公室）
  board meetings, committees, letters, memoranda, telephone, fax and e-mail messages, office equipment and furniture, office procedures

- **Chapter 10**　182
  Personnel:（人事）
  recruiting, hiring, retiring, salaries, promotions, job applications, job advertisements, pensions, awards

- **Chapter 11**　201
  Purchasing:（採購）
  shopping, ordering supplies, shipping, invoices, inventory

- **Chapter 12**　221
  Technical Areas:（技術領域）
  electronics, technology, computers, laboratories and related equipment, technical specifications

- **Chapter 13**　241
  Travel:（旅遊）
  trains, airplanes, taxis, buses, ships, ferries, tickets, schedules, station and airport announcements, car rentals, hotels, reservations, delays and cancellations

NEW TOEIC 測驗　分數換算表

聽力測驗 答對題數	估計分數範圍	閱讀測驗 答對題數	估計分數範圍
96 － 100	475 － 495	96 － 100	460 － 495
91 － 95	435 － 495	91 － 95	425 － 490
86 － 90	405 － 470	86 － 90	400 － 465
81 － 85	370 － 450	81 － 85	375 － 440
76 － 80	345 － 420	76 － 80	340 － 415
71 － 75	320 － 390	71 － 75	310 － 390
66 － 70	290 － 360	66 － 70	285 － 370
61 － 65	265 － 335	61 － 65	255 － 340
56 － 60	240 － 310	56 － 60	230 － 310
51 － 55	215 － 280	51 － 55	200 － 275
46 － 50	190 － 255	46 － 50	170 － 245
41 － 45	160 － 230	41 － 45	140 － 215
36 － 40	130 － 205	36 － 40	115 － 180
31 － 35	105 － 175	31 － 35	95 － 150
26 － 30	85 － 145	26 － 30	75 － 120
21 － 25	60 － 115	21 － 25	60 － 95
16 － 20	30 － 90	16 － 20	45 － 75
11 － 15	5 － 70	11 － 15	30 － 55
6 － 10	5 － 60	6 － 10	10 － 40
1 － 5	5 － 50	1 － 5	5 － 30
0	5 － 35	0	5 － 15

估計分數試算範例：

	答對題數	估計分數範圍
聽力測驗	50	190-255
閱讀測驗	64	255-340
TOEIC 估計得分範圍		445-595

＊上表僅供參考用。資料來源為日本 ETS 出版的 TOEIC 測驗官方指南：《公式 TOEIC Listening & Reading 問題集 10 別冊「解答‧解說」》, 2023, 頁 4。

13回單元測驗簡答表

Chapter 01
1.B	2.D	3.C	4.A	5.D	6.C	7.C	8.D	9.B	10.C
11.C	12.A	13.A	14.C	15.A	16.D	17.C	18.D	19.B	20.D
21.A	22.C	23.A	24.C	25.B	26.B	27.A	28.B	29.C	

Chapter 02
1.C	2.D	3.C	4.A	5.C	6.B	7.D	8.A	9.C	10.B
11.B	12.D	13.C	14.B	15.C	16.D	17.C	18.C	19.D	20.B
21.A	22.C	23.C	24.D	25.D	26.A	27.B	28.C	29.B	30.D

Chapter 03
1.B	2.C	3.B	4.C	5.B	6.D	7.A	8.C	9.C	10.D
11.A	12.A	13.B	14.B	15.A	16.C	17.B	18.C	19.D	20.C
21.A	22.C	23.D	24.C	25.A	26.A	27.D	28.C	29.B	30.D
31.C									

Chapter 04
1.C	2.D	3.B	4.B	5.D	6.D	7.C	8.D	9.C	10.B
11.C	12.B	13.D	14.B	15.B	16.D	17.B	18.D	19.D	20.A
21.B	22.C	23.A	24.C	25.B	26.C	27.C	28.A	29.A	30.C

Chapter 05
1.B	2.B	3.C	4.C	5.A	6.A	7.D	8.A	9.D	10.B
11.C	12.B	13.D	14.D	15.C	16.B	17.B	18.C	19.A	20.D
21.B	22.B	23.B	24.C	25.A	26.C	27.B	28.B	29.A	30.D

Chapter 06
1.B	2.C	3.C	4.C	5.A	6.B	7.D	8.B	9.C	10.A
11.D	12.A	13.C	14.B	15.D	16.C	17.C	18.B	19.B	20.D
21.C	22.D	23.B	24.D	25.A	26.B	27.C	28.B	29.D	30.C
31.C	32.D								

13回單元測驗簡答表

Chapter 07	1. D	2. C	3. A	4. B	5. A	6. B	7. C	8. D	9. C	10. B
	11. B	12. D	13. C	14. C	15. C	16. A	17. D	18. D	19. C	20. A
	21. C	22. D	23. B	24. A	25. C	26. C	27. D	28. A	29. C	30. A

Chapter 08	1. B	2. C	3. A	4. A	5. C	6. A	7. B	8. B	9. A	10. D
	11. D	12. A	13. C	14. C	15. B	16. D	17. C	18. B	19. D	20. A
	21. C	22. B	23. D	24. D	25. D	26. D	27. D	28. B	29. D	30. A

Chapter 09	1. C	2. B	3. B	4. A	5. A	6. B	7. C	8. C	9. D	10. B
	11. C	12. D	13. D	14. B	15. A	16. B	17. C	18. A	19. D	20. B
	21. B	22. D	23. B	24. B	25. C	26. B	27. C	28. A	29. C	30. C

Chapter 10	1. A	2. C	3. A	4. B	5. A	6. B	7. B	8. B	9. D	10. C
	11. C	12. A	13. C	14. D	15. C	16. A	17. D	18. D	19. D	20. B
	21. C	22. B	23. A	24. A	25. C	26. B	27. B	28. B	29. D	30. A

Chapter 11	1. B	2. C	3. B	4. C	5. A	6. B	7. D	8. B	9. C	10. A
	11. C	12. D	13. D	14. D	15. D	16. B	17. B	18. C	19. B	20. D
	21. A	22. A	23. A	24. D	25. D	26. C	27. D	28. D	29. D	30. B

Chapter 12	1. D	2. B	3. C	4. C	5. B	6. B	7. C	8. B	9. C	10. C
	11. B	12. A	13. C	14. C	15. A	16. D	17. D	18. B	19. A	20. A
	21. D	22. D	23. D	24. C	25. B	26. A	27. D	28. B	29. C	30. B

Chapter 13	1. D	2. B	3. A	4. B	5. D	6. C	7. D	8. C	9. B	10. D
	11. B	12. A	13. B	14. C	15. B	16. D	17. C	18. C	19. B	20. D
	21. A	22. A	23. C	24. D	25. C	26. D	27. C	28. D	29. B	30. A

NEW TOEIC 模擬測驗 Test 01 簡答表

PART 1
1. C 2. B 3. D 4. A 5. D 6. B

PART 2
7. A 8. B 9. B 10. C 11. A 12. B 13. B 14. C 15. C 16. A
17. B 18. A 19. C 20. A 21. C 22. B 23. C 24. C 25. B 26. B
27. C 28. C 29. A 30. B 31. A

PART 3
32. B 33. C 34. B 35. A 36. A 37. D 38. B 39. C 40. B 41. B
42. D 43. C 44. C 45. B 46. D 47. D 48. A 49. D 50. C 51. B
52. C 53. D 54. D 55. C 56. B 57. B 58. B 59. C 60. C 61. B
62. C 63. D 64. A 65. C 66. B 67. A 68. B 69. B 70. D

PART 4
71. D 72. B 73. A 74. C 75. B 76. A 77. B 78. D 79. D 80. B
81. A 82. C 83. D 84. B 85. C 86. A 87. D 88. D 89. B 90. D
91. B 92. A 93. C 94. C 95. C 96. D 97. C 98. A 99. C 100. D

PART 5
101. B 102. D 103. A 104. C 105. B 106. C 107. C 108. A 109. D 110. D
111. B 112. C 113. C 114. A 115. C 116. B 117. D 118. C 119. D 120. B
121. B 122. A 123. D 124. D 125. B 126. C 127. A 128. C 129. B 130. D

PART 6
131. D 132. C 133. B 134. D 135. D 136. A 137. C 138. B 139. B 140. C
141. B 142. D 143. A 144. D 145. B 146. C

PART 7
147. B 148. C 149. B 150. D 151. B 152. C 153. D 154. B 155. C 156. A
157. D 158. C 159. D 160. B 161. D 162. B 163. C 164. B 165. C 166. B
167. D 168. D 169. D 170. A 171. C 172. B 173. D 174. C 175. C 176. B
177. D 178. A 179. B 180. C 181. D 182. C 183. A 184. C 185. B 186. B
187. C 188. A 189. C 190. D 191. B 192. C 193. B 194. C 195. A 196. C
197. D 198. D 199. B 200. C

NEW TOEIC 模擬測驗 Test 02 簡答表

PART 1
1. D 2. B 3. C 4. C 5. A 6. D

PART 2
7. A 8. C 9. C 10. C 11. B 12. A 13. A 14. B 15. A 16. C
17. B 18. B 19. B 20. A 21. B 22. C 23. B 24. C 25. B 26. B
27. B 28. C 29. C 30. A 31. C

PART 3
32. A 33. B 34. D 35. D 36. B 37. C 38. C 39. C 40. A 41. B
42. A 43. D 44. C 45. A 46. B 47. D 48. A 49. D 50. C 51. B
52. C 53. D 54. C 55. C 56. C 57. C 58. C 59. B 60. C 61. D
62. B 63. D 64. C 65. B 66. B 67. D 68. C 69. A 70. D

PART 4
71. A 72. C 73. A 74. A 75. C 76. B 77. D 78. C 79. C 80. B
81. D 82. D 83. D 84. C 85. A 86. B 87. C 88. B 89. B 90. B
91. C 92. D 93. C 94. B 95. D 96. A 97. B 98. C 99. B 100. C

PART 5
101. C 102. D 103. B 104. D 105. B 106. A 107. B 108. C 109. D 110. A
111. C 112. C 113. A 114. B 115. D 116. C 117. D 118. B 119. B 120. D
121. A 122. C 123. B 124. D 125. D 126. B 127. B 128. A 129. C 130. C

PART 6
131. C 132. C 133. A 134. D 135. B 136. D 137. A 138. C 139. D 140. C
141. C 142. B 143. B 144. D 145. B 146. C

PART 7
147. C 148. B 149. B 150. D 151. A 152. B 153. B 154. C 155. C 156. B
157. B 158. C 159. C 160. D 161. D 162. B 163. A 164. B 165. C 166. B
167. D 168. D 169. A 170. C 171. B 172. D 173. C 174. B 175. C 176. A
177. B 178. D 179. D 180. B 181. A 182. D 183. D 184. B 185. B 186. C
187. B 188. D 189. D 190. A 191. B 192. B 193. B 194. D 195. D 196. D
197. B 198. C 199. A 200. B

Chapter 01 Listening Test

Part 1 Photographs

B **1** 🔊 017 🇨🇦

(A) They're closing the curtains.
(B) They're looking at some prototype devices.
(C) One of the women is moving a table.
(D) One of the women is switching on a huge machine.

(A) 他們正把窗簾拉上。
(B) 他們正看著某些裝置的原型機。
(C) 其中一個女的正在搬桌子。
(D) 其中一個女的正打開某大型機器的開關。

重要單字片語

1. **curtain** [ˈkɝtn̩] *n.* 窗簾；(舞臺上的)布幕 & *vt.* 給……裝窗簾
   open / close the curtains
   拉開 / 拉上窗簾
   curtain sth off / curtain off sth
   用簾子遮住某物
   Part of the meeting room was curtained off, but the employees were unsure why.
   員工們不知道為何部分的會議室被簾子遮住了。

2. **look at...** 注視……；檢查……
   Jason asked the mechanic to look at his car's engine, which was making strange noises.
   傑森請修車師傅檢查他的汽車引擎，它發出異常的聲音。

D **2** 🔊 018 🇦🇺

(A) A man is putting on a lab coat.
(B) A woman is opening a drawer.
(C) People are mopping the floor.
(D) People are working in a research lab.

(A) 一名男子正穿上實驗袍。
(B) 一名女子正打開抽屜。
(C) 人們正在拖地板。
(D) 人們正在研究實驗室裡工作。

重要單字片語

1. **lab** [læb] *n.* 實驗室（= laboratory [ˈlæbrəˌtɔrɪ]）

2. **drawer** [ˈdrɔɚ] *n.* 抽屜
   a top / bottom drawer
   最上 / 下面的抽屜

Chapter 01　Listening Test

3. **mop** [mɑp] *vt.* 用拖把拖 & *n.* 拖把
   mop a floor　　拖地板

   Emma mops the kitchen floor twice a week.
   艾瑪一個禮拜拖廚房地板兩次。

Part 2　Question-Response

C　**3**　🔊 020

The product will be launched one month later than planned.
(A) No, it's not very innovative.
(B) Let's have lunch together.
(C) Yes, I'm aware of the delay.

這項產品會比原先計劃的晚一個月推出。
(A) 不，它沒有很創新。
(B) 我們一起去吃午飯吧。
(C) 是的，我有注意到延後的事。

重要單字片語

1. **plan** [plæn] *vi.* & *vt.* 計劃 & *n.* 計畫
   plan to + V　　計劃做⋯⋯
   = plan on + V-ing
   We plan to hold a farewell party for the manager.
   = We plan on holding a farewell party for the manager.
   我們計劃為經理辦一場歡送會。

2. **aware** [əˋwɛr] *a.* 察覺到的；知道的（與介詞 of 並用）
   be aware / conscious of...
   察覺到 / 知道⋯⋯
   Ted is not aware of the damage his excessive drinking has caused to his body.
   泰德沒有察覺到他酗酒對自己身體所造成的傷害。

A　**4**　🔊 021

We're going to need more electrical engineers on this project.
(A) I'll bring it up at the next meeting.
(B) Yes, they're doing a fine job.
(C) Be careful handling the equipment.

有關這份專案我們還得多找幾位電機工程師才行。
(A) 我會在下次會議上提出來。
(B) 是的，他們做得很出色。
(C) 操作那些設備時要小心。

重要單字片語

1. **bring sth up**　　提出某事
   bring up a question / a subject
   提出問題 / 話題
   = raise a question / a subject
   I was glad you didn't bring up the subject of money.
   我很高興你沒提到錢的事。

2. **handle** [ˋhændḷ] *vt.* 處理
   handle sth　　處理某事
   = cope with sth
   = deal with sth
   Be as careful as possible when you handle the problem.
   處理這個問題時要儘量小心。

🎧 Part 3 Conversations

Questions 5 through 7 refer to the following conversation. 🔊 023 M: 🇦🇺 W: 🇺🇸

M: I'm afraid that we are unable to develop our new insulating material any further. The project has run into some unexpected difficulties.
W: That's too bad. I thought things were coming along smoothly. What seems to be the problem?
M: Well, the material has to be strong enough to resist extremely high temperatures but light enough to reduce excess weight. After all, the product will be used in vehicles.

5 至 7 題請聽以下會話。

> 男：恐怕我們無法進一步開發這款新的絕緣材料了。這項專案遇到了一些意想不到的困難。
> 女：真不幸。我還以為事情進展得挺順利的。出了什麼問題嗎？
> 男：嗯……這個絕緣材料必須夠結實，才能耐得住極高溫，但同時又得夠輕，以減輕額外的重量。畢竟這產品主要是用在車輛上。

D 　5　🔊 024 🇨🇦

What are the speakers discussing?	說話者在討論什麼？
(A) A delayed flight	(A) 延誤的航班
(B) A new department	(B) 新的部門
(C) A hot climate	(C) 炎熱的天氣
(D) A developmental difficulty	**(D) 研發的困難**

C 　6　🔊 025 🇨🇦

What did the woman say about the project?	有關該專案，女子提到了什麼？
(A) She thought it was too difficult.	(A) 她以為太困難了。
(B) She underestimated the costs.	(B) 她低估了成本。
(C) She believed it was progressing well.	**(C) 她以為事情進展順利。**
(D) She was concerned with the quality.	(D) 她擔心品質。

C 　7　🔊 026 🇨🇦

What industry will the insulation be used in?	絕緣材料會用在哪種產業上？
(A) Construction	(A) 營造
(B) Education	(B) 教育
(C) Automobile	**(C) 汽車**
(D) Aeronautics	(D) 航空

Chapter 01 Listening Test

重要單字片語

1. **insulating** [ˈɪnsəˌletɪŋ] *a.* 絕緣的
2. **run into...** 遭遇（困難等）
   We ran into difficulties during the early phase of the project.
   我們在該專案初期階段便遭遇困難。
3. **unexpected** [ˌʌnɪkˈspɛktɪd] *a.* 意想不到的
4. **come along** 進展
   My French is coming along nicely because I'm constantly practicing.
   我的法文因為常練習所以進步許多。
5. **smoothly** [ˈsmuðlɪ] *adv.* 順利地；平穩地
   My first job interview didn't go smoothly.
   我第一次的工作面試進展得並不順利。
6. **resist** [rɪˈzɪst] *vt.* 抵擋
   resist + N/V-ing　抵擋……
   Nick couldn't resist showing off his new car.
   尼克忍不住炫耀起了他的新車。
7. **reduce** [rɪˈdus] *vt.* 降低，減少
   Lena reduced the amount of salt in her daily diet.
   莉娜減少了她在日常飲食中的鹽分攝取量。
8. **underestimate** [ˌʌndɚˈɛstəˌmet] *vt.* 低估
   Do not underestimate your abilities because everyone has unlimited potential.
   別低估自己的能力，因為每個人都有無限的潛力。
9. **aeronautics** [ˌɛrəˈnɔtɪks] *n.* 航空學

Questions 8 through 10 refer to the following conversation with three speakers. 🔊 027
M: 🇨🇦　W1: 🇬🇧　W2: 🇺🇸

M: Margie, the DNA analyzer we ordered hasn't arrived yet. We can't meet our deadline without it. It would really speed up our research results.
W1: I know. I called the supplier this morning to find out why there's a delay. The customer service rep assured me that she would personally deliver it to our lab early next week.
M: That's not good enough. We need it now.
W2: The lab on the fourth floor has a DNA analyzer. Maybe we could rent theirs until ours arrives. Shall I give them a call? What do we have to lose?
W1: Great idea, Kathy. It's worth a try.

8 至 10 題請聽以下三人的會話。

男：瑪姬，我們訂購的基因分析儀還沒送到。少了這項儀器，我們就無法趕在期限內完工。它真的可以加速完成我們的研究成果。
甲女：我了解。我今天早上打了電話給那家供應商，好了解延遲送達的原因。客服人員向我保證，下週初她會親自把分析儀送來我們的實驗室。
男：那樣沒有用。我們現在就需要。
乙女：四樓的實驗室裡有基因分析儀。在我們的送達前，或許我們可以租用他們的。要不要我打電話給他們？我們不會少一塊肉吧？
甲女：好主意，凱西。值得試試看。

D 8 🔊 028

What field do the speakers most likely work in?
(A) Accounting
(B) Retail
(C) Transportation
(D) Biology

說話者最有可能在哪個領域工作？
(A) 會計
(B) 零售
(C) 運輸
(D) 生物學

B 9 🔊 029

Why is the man concerned?
(A) He will be late for a meeting.
(B) Their work will fall behind schedule.
(C) The new equipment is too expensive.
(D) The supplier overcharged him.

男子為什麼擔心？
(A) 他開會會遲到。
(B) 他們的工作進度會落後。
(C) 新的儀器太昂貴。
(D) 供應商敲他竹槓。

C 10 🔊 030

What solution does Kathy propose?
(A) Selling redundant equipment
(B) Replacing a permanent staff member
(C) Renting a temporary replacement
(D) Ordering from a competitor

凱西提出什麼解決辦法？
(A) 出售多餘的儀器
(B) 替換某固定的職員
(C) 租用暫時的替代品
(D) 向競爭廠商訂貨

重要單字片語

1. **analyzer** [ˈænəˌlaɪzɚ] *n.* 分析器
   analyze [ˈænḷˌaɪz] *vt.* 分析

2. **deadline** [ˈdɛdˌlaɪn] *n.* 截止日期
   meet the deadline　　在截止日期內完成
   I'll send you an e-mail if I'm unable to meet the deadline.
   我若無法趕上截止日期，會寄一封電子郵件告知你。

3. **speed up...**　　加速……
   Can you try and speed things up a bit?
   你能不能設法加快一點事情的進度？

4. **delay** [dɪˈle] *n. & vt.* 延遲
   delay sth for + 一段時間
   將某事延後一段時間
   I apologize for the delay in answering your letter.
   我為延遲回信向你致歉。

   Today's meeting was delayed for half an hour.
   今天的會議被延遲了半個小時。

5. **representative** [ˌrɛprɪˈzɛntətɪv] *n.* 代表（人）
   sales representative
   業務代表（常簡稱為 sales rep）

6. **assure** [əˈʃʊr] *vt.* 向……保證
   assure sb of sth　　向某人保證某事
   assure sb + that 子句　　向某人保證……
   I can assure you (of the fact) that the workers are loyal to this company.
   我能向你保證這些員工對本公司忠心不二。

7. **personally** [ˈpɝsṇlɪ] *adv.* 親自地
   = in person

8. **deliver** [dɪˈlɪvɚ] *vt.* 運送

11

Chapter 01 Listening Test

9. **worth** [wɝθ] *prep.* 值得
   be worth + N/V-ing   值得……
   John thinks the matter is worth our attention.
   約翰認為該事情值得我們的關注。

10. **biology** [baɪˋɑlədʒɪ] *n.* 生物學

11. **overcharge** [ˌovɚˋtʃɑrdʒ] *vt.* 對……索價過高
    The store overcharged me for my computer.
    該店對我的電腦索價過高。

12. **redundant** [rɪˋdʌndənt] *a.* 多餘的

13. **permanent** [ˋpɝmənənt] *a.* 長久的，永久的
    反：temporary [ˋtɛmpəˌrɛrɪ] *a.* 短暫的，暫時的

Part 4 Talks

Questions 11 through 13 refer to the following talk. 🔊 032

I've called this meeting to discuss the XT-121 laptop upgrade project. Our target is to improve on the product while making sure it remains our top-selling item after we're done. Last week, I asked the marketing department to conduct a comprehensive customer survey, and they gave me a list of requested features. You'll be able to access an analysis of the survey results in an e-mail later on during the day. Now, here is a prototype that integrates the customer suggestions. Let's take a look at its capabilities.

11 至 13 題請聽以下談話。

> 我召開本次會議是為了討論 XT-121 型筆電的升級專案。我們的目標是要對它進行改善，但在完成後仍得確保它穩居本公司銷售冠軍的地位。上禮拜我叫行銷部做一輪全方位顧客調查，然後他們給了我一份功能需求的列表。今天稍晚你們會在電郵裡收到調查結果的分析報告。好，現在這裡有一臺整合了顧客建議功能的原型機。我們來看看它的功能。

C 11 🔊 033

What is the speaker discussing?
(A) Introducing a notebook computer
(B) Implementing a new sales strategy
(C) Improving a successful product
(D) Installing a piece of software

說話者在討論什麼？
(A) 推出一款筆記型電腦
(B) 實行一項新的銷售策略
(C) 改良一項熱門產品
(D) 安裝一個軟體

A 12 🔊 034

What will the listeners receive?
(A) A report
(B) A questionnaire
(C) A catalog
(D) A test

聽眾將會收到什麼？
(A) 一份報告
(B) 一份問卷
(C) 一本商品目錄
(D) 一項測驗

12

A `13` 🔊 035 🇺🇸

What will the speaker most likely do next?
(A) Use a computer
(B) Talk to the manager
(C) Call a customer
(D) Conduct a survey

說話者接下來最有可能做什麼？
(A) 使用電腦
(B) 與經理交談
(C) 打電話給顧客
(D) 進行一項調查

CH 01

🔍 **重要單字片語**

1. **upgrade** [ˋʌpˏgred] *n.* 升級
2. **conduct** [kənˋdʌkt] *vt.* 執行，實行
   conduct a survey　　進行調查
 = carry out a survey
   The company conducted a survey of the market before they launched their new product.
   這家公司在發表新產品前，先進行了一項市場調查。
3. **comprehensive** [ˏkɑmprɪˋhɛnsɪv] *a.* 全面的，廣泛的
   This dictionary is comprehensive and reader-friendly.
   這本字典內容豐富且方便使用。
4. **access** [ˋæksɛs] *vt.* 存取；使用 & *n.* 使用權
   have access to...　　可使用……
   You can access our library's database via the internet.
   你可以透過網路進入我們圖書館的資料庫。
   Students in this school have access to all the labs.
   這所學校的學生可以使用所有的實驗室。

5. **integrate** [ˋɪntəˏgret] *vt.* 整合；(使)融入/合併
   integrate A with B　　將 A 與 B 做整合
   integrate A into B　　將 A 融入 B
   It is essential that urban planning be integrated with energy policy.
   將都市計畫與能源政策做整合是非常必要的。
   The manager integrated Paul's ideas into our department's sales strategies.
   經理把保羅的點子納入我們部門的銷售策略中。
6. **capability** [ˏkepəˋbɪlətɪ] *n.* 功能；能力
7. **implement** [ˋɪmpləˏmɛnt] *vt.* 實施；執行
   The fast-food chain implemented a new way of cooking their French fries.
   那家速食連鎖店用了一種炸薯條的新方法。
8. **strategy** [ˋstrætədʒɪ] *n.* 策略；戰略
9. **instruction** [ɪnˋstrʌkʃən] *n.* 指示，說明（常用複數）
   The staff members need clear instructions on what to do next.
   針對下一步該做什麼，工作人員需要明確的指示。

Questions 14 through 16 refer to the following excerpt from a meeting. 🔊 036

Thank you all for coming to this meeting at such short notice. I know that you are all extremely busy now that we're in the final stage of the new Chocoramma Candy Bar project. Unfortunately, an unexpected issue has arisen. When we inspected the candy bars, we noticed that many of the wrappers were torn. We need to research why this happened and develop a new type of packaging as soon as possible. I don't need to remind everyone that <u>the product launch is in 14 days</u>.

Chapter 01 Listening Test

14 至 16 題請聽以下會議摘錄。

> 感謝諸位在臨時通知下前來本會。由於我們處在浪漫巧克力棒新專案的最後階段，所以我知道大家都很忙。但不幸的是，發生了一件沒預料到的事。我們在檢驗巧克力棒時，注意到有許多的包裝紙被扯壞了。我們得儘快研究事情發生的原因，並研發出一種新的包材。我不用提醒各位<u>十四天後產品就得上架了</u>。

C 14 🔊 037 🇬🇧

What department does the speaker most likely work in?
(A) Human resources
(B) Marketing
(C) Research and development
(D) Engineering

說話者最有可能在哪個部門工作？
(A) 人力資源
(B) 行銷
(C) 研發
(D) 工程設計

A 15 🔊 038 🇬🇧

What is the problem with the product?
(A) It was damaged.
(B) It was delayed.
(C) It was too sweet.
(D) It was spoiled.

產品出了什麼問題？
(A) 產品有損壞。
(B) 產品延期了。
(C) 產品太甜了。
(D) 產品變質了。

D 16 🔊 039 🇬🇧

What does the speaker imply when he says, "the product launch is in 14 days"?
(A) The deadline has been changed.
(B) Overtime is not required.
(C) Customers can enjoy the product soon.
(D) The situation is urgent.

說話者說「十四天後產品就得上架了」時，在暗示什麼？
(A) 結案期限被更改了。
(B) 不需要加班了。
(C) 顧客不久就能享用該產品。
(D) 狀況很緊急。

🔍 重要單字片語

1. **now (that)...** 由於……；既然……
   Lillian is enjoying the job now that she's got more responsibility.
   由於莉莉安承擔更多責任，所以她很喜歡她的工作。

2. **stage** [stedʒ] *n.* 階段；發展期間
   a(n) early / late stage of the disease
   病症初期 / 末期
   We are still in the experimental stage of the project.
   這個計畫我們仍在實驗的階段。

3. **arise** [əˋraɪz] *vi.* 產生，發生（三態為：arise, arose [əˋroz], arisen [əˋrɪzn̩]）
   Several problems arose, but I was able to handle them with ease.
   數種問題接踵而來，但我都能輕鬆應對。

Chapter 01 Reading Test

4. **inspect** [ɪnˋspɛkt] *vt.* 檢查；視察
   Nick inspected all of the windows before the typhoon hit.
   颱風來襲前，尼克檢查了所有的窗戶。
5. **wrapper** [ˋræpɚ] *n.* 包裝紙
6. **tear** [tɛr] *vt.* 扯破；撕破（三態為：tear, tore [tor], torn [tɔrn]）
   Tina tore up the letter that Peter sent her.
   蒂娜將彼得寄給她的信撕得粉碎。
7. **packaging** [ˋpækɪdʒɪŋ] *n.* 包裝材料（集合名詞，不可數）
8. **remind** [rɪˋmaɪnd] *vt.* 提醒；使想起
   remind sb of... 使某人想起⋯⋯
   Your voice reminds me of my junior high school teacher.
   你的聲音讓我想起國中老師。
9. **spoiled** [spɔɪld] *a.* 腐壞的
10. **overtime** [ˋovɚˏtaɪm] *n.* 加班

📖 Part 5 Incomplete Sentences

C **17**

Ms. Gilpin's team spent weeks troubleshooting the latest version of the app in order to ------- it before it was released to the public.

(A) abandon   (B) exchange   (C) optimize   (D) match

吉爾平女士的團隊花了數週時間對此應用程式的最新版進行故障排除，目的是為了讓它在公開發布前達到最優化。

（理由）

1. (A) **abandon** [əˋbændən] *vt.* 離棄；放棄
     When his car broke down in the middle of nowhere, Hank abandoned it and started walking.
     車子在荒郊野外拋錨後，漢克棄車步行離去。
   (B) **exchange** [ɪksˋtʃendʒ] *vt. & n.* 交換
     exchange sth with sb 和某人交換某物
     Kelly exchanged phone numbers with a handsome guy at the bar.
     凱莉在酒吧和一位帥哥交換了電話號碼。
   (C) **optimize** [ˋɑptəˏmaɪz] *vt.* 使最優化，使完善
     Through optimizing the process, we were able to increase our output by 20 percent.
     透過優化流程，我們得以將產量提高了 20%。
   (D) **match** [mætʃ] *vt.* 與⋯⋯匹敵 & *n.* 比賽（= game 美式英語）
     When it comes to sushi, no country can match Japan.
     講到壽司，沒有哪個國家比得過日本。
2. 根據語意及用法，(C) 項應為正選。

🔍 重要單字片語

app [æp] *n.* 應用程式（為 application [ˏæpləˋkeʃən] 的縮寫）

15

Chapter 01 Reading Test

D 18

Mr. Christiansen has ------- the customer feedback and will deliver a presentation on his findings at the next meeting.

(A) evaluate　　　(B) evaluates　　　(C) evaluating　　　**(D) evaluated**

克里斯汀森先生已對顧客回饋意見做出評估，將在下次會議上就他的心得進行簡報。

理由

1. 空格前有主詞 Mr. Christiansen（克里斯汀森先生）及現在完成式助動詞 has，得知空格內應置動詞之過去分詞 evaluated（評估）以與 has 形成現在完成式（has / have + 過去分詞）。
   Karen has prepared dinner for her family.
   凱倫已經為她的家人準備好了晚餐。

2. 根據上述，(D) 項應為正選。

重要單字片語

1. **presentation** [ˌprɛznˈteʃən] *n.* 口頭報告，簡報
   give / make / deliver a presentation (on...)
   （就……）做口頭報告 / 簡報
   Frank gave a very impressive presentation on the new product.
   法蘭克針對該項新產品做了十分精彩的簡報。

2. **finding** [ˈfaɪndɪŋ] *n.* 研究的結果；發現（常用複數）

B 19

After the company's application for a ------- was rejected, the R&D team began to brainstorm ways to adapt and modify the invention.

(A) newsletter　　　**(B) patent**　　　(C) portrait　　　(D) rival

在公司申請專利遭退件後，研發團隊開始腦力激盪，想找出改進和修改該項發明的方法。

理由

1. (A) **newsletter** [ˈnjuzˌlɛtɚ] *n.*（定期寄發給特定讀者的）通訊信函
   The organization's newsletter is read by thousands of people every week.
   該組織的通訊信函每個禮拜都有數千人看過。

   (B) **patent** [ˈpætn̩t] *n.* 專利（權）& *vt.* 取得專利 & *a.* 專利的
   apply for a patent (for...)　申請（……的）專利
   Mr. Johnson applied for a patent for the machine he had invented.
   強森先生替自己發明的機器申請專利。
   Kevin patented a new device that peels shrimp in an instant.
   凱文那個可瞬間剝掉蝦殼的新器具拿到了專利。

   (C) **portrait** [ˈpɔrtret] *n.* 肖像，畫像；人像照片
   Kyle asked the artist to paint a portrait of his wife.
   凱爾請這位藝術家為他的妻子畫一幅肖像。

   (D) **rival** [ˈraɪvl̩] *n.* 競爭者，對手 & *vt.* 與……匹敵
   have no rival / match / equal　無人能敵
   Sam is so good at sports that he has no rival at school.
   山姆在運動方面非常出色，以至於在學校無人能敵。

No one rivals my grandmother in baking.
在烘焙方面，沒有人能勝過我阿嬤。

2. 根據語意及用法，(B) 項應為正選。

重要單字片語

1. **R&D** 研究與開發（為 research and development 的縮寫）
2. **invention** [ɪnˋvɛnʃən] *n.* 發明物（可數）；發明（不可數）

D 20

The wonderful way the VR headset ------- the experience of a live concert really sets the benchmark for these kinds of devices.

(A) has been simulated　　　　(B) is simulated
(C) simulate　　　　　　　　　(D) simulates

此虛擬實境眼鏡唯妙唯肖地模擬現場音樂會的臨場感，給這類裝置樹立了一個標竿。

理由

1. 本句的主詞為 The wonderful way the VR headset... a live concert（此虛擬實境眼鏡……現場音樂會的臨場感），其中的 the VR headset... a live concert 為形容詞子句，修飾前方的名詞片語 The wonderful way。空格後的動詞 sets（樹立）實為本句的主要動詞，其後接受詞 the benchmark for these kinds of devices（這類裝置的標竿）。

2. 空格前有名詞 the VR headset（虛擬實境眼鏡），空格後有名詞片語 the experience of a live concert（現場音樂會的臨場感）作受詞。推知本句應在敘述虛擬實境眼鏡能「主動」模擬現場音樂會的一般特性，故空格內的動詞時態應為現在簡單式，且為主動語態。

3. 由於 the VR headset 為單數名詞，其後的動詞應搭配第三人稱單數變化。且根據上述，得知空格應置 simulates（模擬），故 (D) 項應為正選。

重要單字片語

1. **VR** 虛擬實境（為 virtual reality 之簡稱）
2. **headset** [ˋhɛdˌsɛt] *n.*（尤指附有麥克風的）耳機

A 21

If the company improved communication across departments, it ------- many obstacles and bring products to market faster.

(A) would overcome　(B) overcame　　(C) overcomes　　(D) will overcome

如果公司改善了部門間的溝通，就能排除許多障礙並加速產品上市了。

理由

1. 本題測試與現在事實相反的假設語氣，句型如下：

   | If + 主詞 + | 過去動詞
過去助動詞
were | ..., 主詞 + | would
could
might
should | + 原形動詞 ... |

   If Karen had enough money, she could buy that car.
   如果凱倫有足夠的錢，就可以買那臺車了。

2. 根據上述，(A) 項應為正選。

17

Chapter 01 Reading Test

重要單字片語

communication [kə,mjunəˈkeʃən] *n.* 聯絡,通訊;傳播,傳播學(恆用複數)

Part 6 Text Completion

Questions 22-25 refer to the following memo.

To:	All lab technicians
From:	Rebecca Anders, Lab Manager
Date:	July 1
Subject:	Meeting on lab safety procedures

　　Due to the unfortunate recent accidents in our organic chemistry laboratory ------- injuries to two lab technicians, I am calling a meeting to announce revisions to
22.
our lab safety procedures this Friday, July 4, from 3:00 to 5:00 PM. All lab technicians are required to attend. -------.
23.

　　"Safety First" should never be an empty slogan. Any injury ------- by our lab
24.
technician colleagues is unacceptable, however minor it is. Therefore, an updated handbook detailing our laboratory safety procedures will be distributed and discussed at the meeting. Attendees will be free to comment ------- any aspect of the proposed
25.
changes.

Sincerely,

Rebecca Anders

Lab Manager

---

22 至 25 題請看以下備忘錄。

收件者:所有實驗室技術員
寄件者:實驗室主任蕾貝卡‧安德斯
日　期:7 月 1 日
主　旨:實驗室安全程序相關會議

　　由於近日來本公司有機化學實驗室裡發生了幾起不幸的意外,<u>導致</u>兩名實驗室技術員受傷,所以我將在本星期五,也就是 7 月 4 日下午三點到五點召開會議,以宣達實驗室安全程序的修訂事項。所有實驗室技術員皆須出席。<u>實驗室主管須負責確保職員出席。</u>

「安全第一」不應只是空洞的口號。不論傷勢多輕微，實驗室的技術員同事受任何傷都是令人無法接受的。因此，我們將在會議上發放一份詳盡說明實驗室安全程序的更新手冊，並在會議上進行討論。會議上對於任何所更新方面的問題皆可隨意評論，請不用客氣。

順頌祺安

實驗室主任
蕾貝卡・安德斯　　上

C **22**

(A) bringing up　　(B) resulting from　　(C) resulting in　　(D) drawing up

理由

1. (A) **bring up sb**　　養育某人
    bring up sth　　提出某事
    Steven was brought up on the farm by his grandparents.
    史蒂芬由祖父母在農場上將他撫養長大。
    Please bring up this point at the next meeting.
    請在下次會議上提出這一點。

   (B) **result from + N/V-ing**　　起源於……
    David's illness resulted from eating bad food.
    大衛的病是由於吃了壞掉的食物。

   (C) **result in...**　　導致……
    = lead to...
    A moment of hesitation can result in missed opportunities.
    一時的猶豫會導致錯失機會。

   (D) **draw up...**　　擬訂……
    We need to draw up a budget before the next meeting.
    我們需要在下次會議前草擬預算案。

2. 根據語意，(C) 項應為正選。

A **23**

(A) Lab supervisors will be responsible for ensuring attendance.
(B) We specialize in all kinds of organic food.
(C) Please return the questionnaire as soon as possible.
(D) Efficiency has improved because of the regulations.

理由

1. (A) 實驗室主管須負責確保職員出席。　　(B) 我們專精於各種有機食品。
    (C) 請儘快繳交問卷。　　(D) 效率因該規定而有改善。

2. 空格前的句子 "All lab technicians are required to attend."（所有實驗室技術員皆須出席。）提及 are required to attend（須出席），選項 (A) 則提到 ensuring attendance（確保職員出席）。置入空格後語意連貫，故為正選。

Chapter 01　Reading Test

C **24**

(A) sustaining　　(B) were sustained　　(C) sustained　　(D) are sustained

理由

1. 原句實等於：Any injury which is sustained by our lab technician colleagues is
　　　　　　　　　　　　(1)　　　　　　　(2)　　　　　　　　　(3)
unacceptable,...
　　(4)
……，實驗室的技術員同事受任何傷都是令人無法接受的。
   (1) 本句主詞
   (2) 形容詞子句，which 在形容詞子句中作主詞，此處 sustained 表「遭受」。
   (3) 本句動詞
   (4) 本句形容詞

2. 本句測試將形容詞子句化為分詞片語。原則如下：刪除關代 which，之後動詞 is 改為現在分詞 being，而 being 可省略。因此空格內置過去分詞 sustained 即可。

3. 根據上述，(C) 項應為正選。

B **25**

(A) for　　　　　(B) on　　　　　(C) in　　　　　(D) before

理由

1. **comment** [ˈkɑmɛnt] *vi.* & *n.* 評論（皆與介詞 on 並用）
   comment on...　　對……進行評論
   = make a comment on...
   Gary always comments on what I'm wearing.
   蓋瑞總是對我穿的衣服有意見。
   I don't need any comments on my new haircut!
   對於我的新髮型我不需要任何評語！

2. 根據上述，(B) 項應為正選。

重要單字片語

1. **technician** [tɛkˈnɪʃən] *n.* 技術人員
2. **procedure** [prəˈsidʒɚ] *n.* 程序
   follow standard / normal procedures
   遵循標準／正常程序
   You must follow standard procedures when applying for a visa.
   你申請簽證時必須遵循標準程序。
3. **due to...**　　由於……
   = because of...
   The project was a failure due to lack of capital.
   該計畫因為缺乏資金而宣告失敗。

4. **unfortunate** [ʌnˈfɔrtʃənɪt] *a.* 不幸的
5. **organic** [ɔrˈgænɪk] *a.* 有機的
   organic food　　有機食物
6. **injury** [ˈɪndʒərɪ] *n.* 受傷
   sustain a minor / serious injury
   受輕／重傷
   Twenty train passengers sustained serious injuries in the crash.
   二十名乘客在這次火車事故中受重傷。
7. **require** [rɪˈkwaɪr] *vt.* 需要
   requirement [rɪˈkwaɪrmənt] *n.* 必要條件
   （常用複數）

meet / satisfy sb's requirements
滿足某人的需要
Anxiety is a kind of mental disorder that requires medication.
焦慮症是一種精神失調症，需要藥物治療。
The computers we sell will definitely meet your requirements.
我們所賣的電腦一定會滿足您的需要。

8. **attend** [əˋtɛnd] *vt.* 參加
attendance [əˋtɛndəns] *n.* 出席
be in attendance　　出席（某特別活動）
Jolin was happy because all her friends were in attendance at her wedding.
喬琳很高興，因為所有朋友都出席了她的婚禮。

9. **slogan** [ˋslogən] *n.* 標語；口號

10. **unacceptable** [ˏʌnəkˋsɛptəbl] *a.* 不能接受的

11. **aspect** [ˋæspɛkt] *n.* 方面
Alcoholism will affect all aspects of your life.
酗酒會影響你的生活各層面。

12. **supervisor** [ˋsupɚˏvaɪzɚ] *n.* 主管

13. **responsible** [rɪˋspɑnsəbl] *a.* 負責的
be responsible for + N/V-ing
負責……
Frank is responsible for supervising a staff of seven.
法蘭克負責監督七名職員。

14. **ensure** [ɪnˋʃʊr] *vt.* 確保（後接事物作受詞）
Hard work will ensure your success.
努力將確保你的成功。

📖 Part 7 Reading Comprehension

Questions 26-27 refer to the following advertisement.

> The *Journal of Medical Laser Technology* is now available online. The print version will continue to be made available by subscription to libraries, research centers, and university departments as well as to individuals. Subscription rates are identical for both versions. For more information, go to JMLT.com.
>
> The *Journal of Medical Laser Technology* will continue to inform and provide a forum for medical professionals. Subscribers will have the latest research findings at their fingertips. To remain a leader in your field, contact us today to subscribe to the online version.

26 至 27 題請看以下廣告。

> 《雷射醫療技術雜誌》現在已有線上版本。印刷版將繼續提供圖書館、研究中心、大學各系及個人訂閱。兩個版本的訂購價格相同。欲了解更多資訊，可上 JMLT.com 網站查詢。
>
> 《雷射醫療技術雜誌》將持續為醫療專業人士提供資訊及討論話題。訂戶將能輕易取得最新的研究發現。今天就和我們聯繫訂閱雜誌線上版，您就可以保持領域中的領導者地位。

Chapter 01　Reading Test

B 26

Why would people visit JMLT.com?
(A) To apply for a course
(B) To access further details
(C) To make an appointment
(D) To contact a library

人們為何要上 JMLT.com 網站？
(A) 報名課程
(B) 查看詳細資訊
(C) 約時間會見
(D) 聯繫圖書館

> 理由
>
> 根據本文第一段最後一句 "For more information, go to JMLT.com."（欲了解更多資訊，可上 JMLT.com 網站查詢。）得知，(B) 項應為正選。

A 27

What is being advertised?
(A) A publication
(B) Medical procedures
(C) Research data
(D) Health equipment

廣告刊登了什麼？
(A) 出版品
(B) 醫療程序
(C) 研究資料
(D) 健康器材

> 理由
>
> 根據本文第一段第一、二句 "The *Journal of Medical Laser Technology* is now available online. The print version will... to individuals."（《雷射醫療技術雜誌》現在已有線上版本。印刷版……個人訂閱。）得知，(A) 項應為正選。

重要單字片語

1. **available** [əˋvelәbḷ] *a.* 可買得到的；可提供的
   Is this jacket available in a larger size?
   這件夾克有大一點的尺寸嗎？

2. **subscription** [səbˋskrɪpʃən] *n.* 訂閱（與介詞 to 並用）
   subscribe [səbˋskraɪb] *vi.* 訂閱（與介詞 to 並用）
   subscribe to...　訂閱……
   To improve my English, I decided to subscribe to an English newspaper.
   為了使英文精進，我決定訂閱一份英文報。

3. **individual** [͵ɪndәˋvɪdʒʊəl] *n.* 個人
   The musical audition is open to both groups and individuals.
   這齣音樂劇試音會開放給團體及個人參加。

4. **rate** [ret] *n.* 價格

5. **identical** [aɪˋdɛntәkḷ] *a.* 相同的
   be identical to...　和……相同
   The tests are identical to those carried out last year.
   這些考試和去年考的相同。

6. **forum** [ˋfɔrəm] *n.* 論壇；討論機會

7. **have sth at one's fingertips**
   手邊有……（隨時可使用）；熟知……
   When Maria is cooking her famous pasta, she has many spices at her fingertips.
   當瑪莉亞烹煮她那有名的義大利麵時，她的手邊有很多的香料可用。
   I made sure I had all the facts at my fingertips before attending the meeting.
   參加會議之前，我確定自己對所有會議內容瞭若指掌。

8. **remain** [rɪˈmen] *vi.* 仍然是，保持不變（後接形容詞或名詞作補語）
   remain seated / silent / unchanged
   繼續坐著 / 保持安靜 / 保持不變
   Please remain seated until all the lights are on.
   所有燈亮之前請繼續坐著。

9. **appointment** [əˈpɔɪntmənt] *n.* 正式會面
   make an appointment 預約時間
   Jason made an online appointment to see a doctor at 7:30 p.m. today.
   傑森上網預約了今天晚上七點三十分看診。

10. **publication** [ˌpʌblɪˈkeʃən] *n.* 出版（物）

Questions 28-29 refer to the following text-message chain.

Brent Fargo (10:37 AM)
Hey, I just heard back from Jayden at Jay Corp. He thinks our proposal is viable. He wants to meet with us again ASAP!

Judi Walsh (10:38 AM)
Are you serious?! What did you tell him?

Brent Fargo (10:39 AM)
I said we would meet him in his office first thing tomorrow morning. He wants to see the prototype.

Judi Walsh (10:40 AM)
Great. Then we should get together this afternoon — we can put together a brief demonstration and work out exactly what to say.

Brent Fargo (10:41 AM)
I agree. How about I come over to your place at 2:30? I'll bring the prototype.

Judi Walsh (10:41 AM)
OK. I'll see you then.

Chapter 01 Reading Test

28 至 29 題請看以下簡訊討論串。

布蘭特‧法戈（上午 10:37）
嗨，我剛從傑伊企業的傑登那得到回應。他認為我們的提案是可行的。他想儘快再跟我們會面！

茱蒂‧沃爾什（上午 10:38）
真的假的？！你怎麼跟他說的？

布蘭特‧法戈（上午 10:39）
我說我們可以明天一早就到他的辦公室跟他會面。他想要看樣品。

茱蒂‧沃爾什（上午 10:40）
太棒了。那麼我們最好這下午見面 —— 我們可以整理出簡短的介紹，並想好到底要說什麼。

布蘭特‧法戈（上午 10:41）
我同意。我兩點半過去妳那好嗎？我會帶樣品。

茱蒂‧沃爾什（上午 10:41）
好。到時候見。

B **28**

At 10:38 AM, what does Ms. Walsh mean when she writes, "Are you serious"?
(A) She doesn't believe Mr. Fargo is telling the truth.
(B) She is excited by what Mr. Fargo wrote.
(C) She has more important matters to take care of.
(D) She thinks Mr. Fargo has a serious problem.

沃爾什女士於上午 10:38 寫「真的假的」時，是什麼意思？
(A) 她不相信法戈先生在說實話。
(B) 法戈先生所寫的留言讓她感到興奮。
(C) 她有更重要的事情要處理。
(D) 她覺得法戈先生遇到嚴重的問題。

> **理由**
>
> 根據法戈先生於上午 10:37 寫 "He thinks our proposal is viable. He wants to meet with us again ASAP!"（他認為我們的提案是可行的。他想儘快再跟我們會面！）得知法戈先生表達提案有所進展。又根據沃爾什女士於上午 10:40 寫 "Great...."（太棒了。……）得知沃爾什女士很興奮。根據上述，(B) 項應為正選。

C **29**

What does Ms. Walsh indicate they should do?
(A) Reschedule a meeting
(B) Contact a client
(C) Prepare a presentation
(D) Speak to the manager

沃爾什女士指出他們應該做什麼？
(A) 重新安排會議時間
(B) 與客戶連絡
(C) 準備口頭報告
(D) 向主管報告

> **理由**
>
> 根據沃爾什女士於上午 10:40 寫 "Then we should get together this afternoon — we can put together a brief demonstration and work out exactly what to say."（那麼我們最好這下午見面 —— 我們可以整理出簡短的介紹，並想好到底要說什麼。）得知，(C) 項應為正選。

重要單字片語

1. **put together... / put... together**
   整理出……；拼湊……
   put together a plan / proposal
   整理出一項計畫 / 提案
   John put together a proposal for the committee to consider.
   約翰整理出一項提案供委員會討論。

2. **demonstration** [ˌdɛmənˈstreʃən] *n.*
   示範，展示

Chapter 02　Listening Test

Part 1　Photographs

C　**1**　◀)) 041 🇺🇸

(A) A man is folding a serviette.
(B) The woman is adding condiments to her meal.
(C) The waitress is serving wine.
(D) The waitress has dropped the tray.

(A) 一位男子正在摺餐巾。
(B) 女子正在她的餐點上加調味料。
(C) 女服務生正在上紅酒。
(D) 女服務生弄掉了托盤。

重要單字片語

1. **serviette** [ˌsɝvɪˋɛt] *n.* 餐巾
2. **add** [æd] *vt.* 增加
   add A to B　將 A 添加在 B 上
   If you add five to six, you get eleven.
   五加六等於十一。
3. **condiment** [ˋkɑndəmənt] *n.* 調味料

D　**2**　◀)) 042 🇬🇧

(A) She is mixing the salad with a spoon.
(B) She is gathering some vegetables in a bowl.
(C) She is peeling different ingredients.
(D) She is pouring some dressing.

(A) 她用湯匙攪拌沙拉。
(B) 她把蔬菜放進碗裡。
(C) 她在削食材的外皮。
(D) 她把醬汁澆在上面。

重要單字片語

1. **peel** [pil] *vt.* 剝／削（外皮）& *n.* （蔬果的）外皮
   Carl never peels apples before he eats them.
   卡爾吃蘋果前從不先削皮。
2. **ingredient** [ɪnˋgridɪənt] *n.* （烹調用的）成分，食材

26

Part 2　Question-Response

C　**3**　🔊 044

May we see your menu, please?
(A) Remember to tip the waiter.
(B) We've run out of milk.
(C) Here's one for each of you.

麻煩請給我們看菜單好嗎？
(A) 記得要給服務生小費。
(B) 我們的牛奶用完了。
(C) 我這就給你們一人一份。

重要單字片語

run out of...　　用完……
run low on...　　快用完……
= run short of...
They ran out of gas on the highway last night.
他們昨晚在高速公路上開車開到沒油。
We're running low on milk. Could you buy some on your way home?
我們的牛奶快喝完了。你回家的路上可以買一些嗎？

A　**4**　🔊 045

Do you like the flavor of this dish?
(A) No, it's too bitter for me.
(B) Yes, I want to return the favor.
(C) The salt is in the kitchen.

你喜歡這道菜的味道嗎？
(A) 不喜歡，我覺得太苦。
(B) 對，我想報答你。
(C) 鹽在廚房裡。

重要單字片語

1. **bitter** [ˈbɪtɚ] *a.* （味道）苦的
2. **favor** [ˈfevɚ] *n.* 恩惠；幫助
   return the favor　報答某人，還某人人情

Thank you for giving me a ride to work; I'll return the favor someday.
謝謝你載我上班，這個人情是一定要還的。

Part 3　Conversations

Questions 5 through 7 refer to the following conversation.　🔊 047　M:　W:

W: Do you have any special requirements for the event to welcome the new staff into the company, sir?
M: Yes, I want us to hold an informal event so that people can get to know each other in a social setting. They should be able to wander around and mingle with the other guests rather than being confined to their seats for a sit-down meal.
W: I will select a venue and start arranging it right away.
M: Oh, and people should wear casual attire; there's no need for suits and ties.
W: Understood.

27

Chapter 02　Listening Test

5 至 7 題請聽以下會話。

> 女：老闆，關於公司的迎新活動，您有什麼特別要吩咐的嗎？
> 男：有的，我希望活動不要太正式，要讓大家在社交的氛圍當中彼此熟悉熟悉。我希望每個人都能自由走動，跟其他人打成一片，不要被釘在位子上純吃飯。
> 女：好，我去選場地，立刻做規劃。
> 男：喔，大家穿便服就可以了，不用穿西裝打領帶。
> 女：了解。

C 　**5**　🔊 048　🇬🇧

Who are the main guests of the event?
(A) Departing workers
(B) Important clients
(C) New employees
(D) Workers' families

這場活動的主客是誰？
(A) 離職員工
(B) 重要客戶
(C) 新進員工
(D) 員工家屬

B 　**6**　🔊 049　🇬🇧

What does the man say about the event?
(A) He hopes the food will be of good quality.
(B) He wants it to be relaxed and casual.
(C) He is unable to attend it himself.
(D) He hopes there will be enough seats.

對於這場活動，男子是怎麼說的？
(A) 他希望餐點的品質要好。
(B) 他希望活動的氣氛輕鬆自在。
(C) 他本人無法參加這場活動。
(D) 他希望現場有足夠的座位。

D 　**7**　🔊 050　🇬🇧

What does the woman indicate that she understands?
(A) The invitations will be sent out very soon.
(B) The party will be held during work hours.
(C) The organizational challenges will be great.
(D) The event's dress code will not be formal.

女子說「了解」時是針對哪件事？
(A) 邀請函很快就會發出。
(B) 派對將在上班時間舉行。
(C) 這場活動在籌備上相當有難度。
(D) 活動的服裝要求是休閒裝。

🔍 **重要單字片語**

1. **staff** [stæf] n.（全體）職員（集合名詞，不可數）& vt. 為……配備人員（一般用被動）
   a staff of thirty
   三十名職員（非 thirty staffs）
   This department is staffed with individuals from many different countries.
   這個部門的職員來自許多不同國家。

2. **wander** [ˋwɑndɚ] vi. 漫遊；閒逛 & vt. 漫步於 & n. 閒逛
   Sarah wandered around the department store to kill time.
   莎拉在百貨公司四處閒逛消磨時間。
   The children wandered the forest for a week before being found.
   那群小朋友在森林裡流浪了一個禮拜才被找到。

3. **confine** [kənˈfaɪn] *vt.* 限制；監禁
   be confined to... 被限制於……
   Evan was in a car accident and is now confined to a wheelchair.
   艾凡出了車禍，現在得坐輪椅。
4. **sit-down** [ˈsɪtˌdaʊn] *a.* 坐在桌前吃的
5. **casual** [ˈkæʒʊəl] *a.* 非正式的
6. **client** [ˈklaɪənt] *n.* 客戶
7. **relaxed** [rɪˈlækst] *a.* 輕鬆的；覺得放鬆的
8. **organizational** [ˌɔrɡənəˈzeʃənḷ] *a.* 籌備的；組織的
9. **code** [kod] *n.* 規範；密碼
   a dress code 服裝規定

CH 02

Questions 8 through 10 refer to the following conversation. 🔊 051 M: 🇨🇦 W: 🇺🇸

M: Thank you for suggesting this beautiful restaurant to celebrate the fact we've finally closed the deal! Do you come here often?
W: Yes, I patronize it regularly. If you're wondering what to order, I suggest their signature dish, which is the charcoal-grilled octopus with Mediterranean vegetables.
M: Actually, I'm not a fan of seafood, so I'm going to order the steak.
W: Fair enough! Shall we order a bottle of Champagne, too? We need to toast the deal.
M: I think that's a great idea. After all, <u>tomorrow is a holiday</u>!

8 至 10 題請聽以下會話。

> 男：感謝妳找了這麼讚的餐廳來慶祝我們搞定這筆生意！妳常來嗎？
> 女：對，我常來這家。如果你不知道該怎麼點，我推薦他們的招牌菜 —— 炭烤章魚配地中海蔬菜。
> 男：其實我沒有很喜歡海鮮，所以我打算點牛排。
> 女：也行！我們來叫一瓶香檳好不好？敲定交易一定得喝一杯。
> 男：好主意。畢竟<u>明天不用上班</u>！

A **8** 🔊 052 🇺🇸

What does the woman say about herself?
(A) She is a regular customer of the restaurant.
(B) She is a committed vegetarian.
(C) She is a part owner of the restaurant.
(D) She is a good friend of the chef's.

女子對於自己是怎麼說的？
(A) 她是這家餐廳的常客。
(B) 她嚴守素食的習慣。
(C) 她是這家餐廳的合夥人之一。
(D) 她是主廚的好朋友。

C **9** 🔊 053 🇺🇸

Why does the man not order the signature dish?
(A) He doesn't feel very hungry.
(B) He thinks it is too expensive.
(C) He does not really like seafood.
(D) He wants what the woman ordered.

男子為何不點招牌菜？
(A) 他沒有很餓。
(B) 他認為這道菜太貴。
(C) 他不大喜歡海鮮。
(D) 他想點女子點的菜。

Chapter 02 Listening Test

B 10 054

What does the man imply when he says, "tomorrow is a holiday"?
(A) They must close the deal today.
(B) They can enjoy some alcohol.
(C) They must finish the meal quickly.
(D) They don't have time for further talks.

男子說「明天不用上班」是在做何暗示？
(A) 他們一定得在今天把交易敲定。
(B) 他們可以痛快飲酒。
(C) 他們得趕緊吃完這頓飯。
(D) 他們沒時間再進一步討論。

重要單字片語

1. **charcoal** [ˈtʃɑr͵kol] *n.* 木炭
2. **grill** [grɪl] *vt.*（用烤架）烤 & *n.* 烤架
   The famous chef personally grills the restaurant's delicious steaks.
   此餐廳的美味牛排是由這位名廚親自烤炙。
3. **octopus** [ˈɑktəpəs] *n.* 章魚（複數形為 octopi [ˈɑktə͵paɪ] / octopuses [ˈɑktəpəsɪz]）
4. **Mediterranean** [͵mɛdətəˈrenɪən] *a.* 地中海的
5. **be a fan of...**
   喜歡……；是……的粉絲/迷
   Jennifer is not a fan of blind dates; she thinks it's better to meet people naturally.
   珍妮佛不喜歡相親，她覺得還是自然而然地認識人比較好。
6. **fair enough** 好的，沒問題；有道理
   Fair enough. Today, you choose the movie and I choose the restaurant.
   行。今天你選電影，我選餐館。
7. **Champagne** [ʃæmˈpen] *n.* 香檳酒（= champagne）
8. **committed** [kəˈmɪtɪd] *a.* 堅定的；盡力的
9. **chef** [ʃɛf] *n.* 主廚

Part 4 Talks

Questions 11 through 13 refer to the following talk. 056

I hope everyone's looking forward to tonight's formal banquet. In case some people have not attended this type of event before, I want to make a few points about dining etiquette. You should wait for the event host to indicate when to be seated, and wait for everyone to be served before you start eating. Your napkin should be placed on your lap when you are seated and then folded on the table at the end of the meal. As for silverware, this is arranged from the outside in. That means you should use the utensils on the outside first.

11 至 13 題請聽以下談話。

> 希望大家都很期待今晚的正式宴會。如果有人沒參加過此類的活動，讓我講一下幾個用餐禮儀的重點。大家要等主人示意後才能入座，並在所有人的餐點都上了以後才能開動。入座後要把餐巾鋪在腿上，並在用餐結束後把它摺好放回桌上。關於餐具，它們是由外到內排列的。意思是你應該從最外側的餐具開始用。

B **11** 🔊 057 🇨🇦

What is the speaker mainly talking about?
(A) The decline in table manners
(B) The rules when dining formally
(C) The difficulty of hosting an event
(D) The dishes on offer at a banquet

說話者主要是在說什麼事情？
(A) 餐桌禮儀的式微
(B) 正式宴會的用餐規矩
(C) 主辦活動的困難度
(D) 宴會供應的菜色

CH 02

D **12** 🔊 058 🇨🇦

According to the speaker, when can people start eating?
(A) When others leave the table
(B) When everyone raises their glasses
(C) When the host has given a speech
(D) When everyone is served their meal

根據說話者，大家何時可以開動？
(A) 其他人離開餐桌時
(B) 每個人舉起酒杯時
(C) 主人發表演說後
(D) 每個人的餐點都上桌後

C **13** 🔊 059 🇨🇦

What point does the speaker make about silverware?
(A) It should be wiped with a napkin.
(B) It should be taken from the left side first.
(C) It should be used in a certain order.
(D) It should be put on the plate after eating.

說話者對餐具有何說法？
(A) 應用餐巾擦拭餐具。
(B) 應先從左側拿取餐具。
(C) 應按特定順序使用餐具。
(D) 應在用餐過後把餐具放在盤子上。

🔍 重要單字片語

1. **look forward to + N/V-ing**
   期待……（此處 to 是介詞）
   We're really looking forward to working with your company on this project.
   我們非常期待與貴公司在此專案上的合作。

2. **in case** 假如
   In case you're hungry, we're ordering pizza for lunch.
   假如你餓了，我們中午會訂披薩來吃。

3. **napkin** [ˋnæpkɪn] n. 餐巾

4. **fold** [fold] vt. 摺疊 & n. 摺線
   The girl folded the colored paper to make a bird.
   小女孩把色紙摺成一隻鳥。

5. **decline** [dɪˋklaɪn] n. 沒落，衰退；下跌 & vi. 衰落；降低
   The quality of the company's products has recently declined.
   該公司的產品品質最近走下坡了。

6. **on offer** 可買的到的，提供的
   The products on offer in the store range from stationery to home appliances.
   店裡提供的產品從文具到家電都有。

7. **wipe** [waɪp] vt. 擦拭；消滅 & n. 擦，拭，抹
   The waitress wiped the spilled coffee off the table with a cloth.
   女服務生用布將桌上潑的咖啡擦掉。

Chapter 02 Listening Test

Questions 14 through 16 refer to the following telephone message and list.

Rosebud Restaurant	
Set Menu	Price per Person
A	$29.99
B	$39.99
C	$49.99
D	$59.99

Hi, this is Lyra Bradford calling from Gomez & Partners. I'd like to mention a couple of points about the retirement party we've booked there on June 4th. First of all, we will have 20 guests, not 25 as stated previously. Secondly, our budget per person is still $50, so we would like to choose the set meal option closest to that price. However, two of our employees are vegan, so we expect you to cater for their needs as well. Please call me back at 555-0167 to confirm you can do this. Thank you.

14 至 16 題請聽以下電話留言及表單。

玫瑰花蕾餐廳	
套餐組合	單人份價格
A	29.99 美元
B	39.99 美元
C	49.99 美元
D	59.99 美元

你好，我是 Gomez & Partners 公司的萊拉·布萊福德。關於本公司向貴餐廳預訂的六月四日退休派對，我有兩點事情要說明一下。第一點，客人總共是二十位，而不是之前所說的二十五位。第二點，我們的每人預算仍然是五十美元，所以將會選擇最接近這個價位的套餐選項。不過我們有兩個員工是吃全素，所以希望他們的需求也能被照顧到。請回電至 555-0167 與我確認你們這部分是 OK 的。感恩。

B 14

What has been changed for the party?
(A) The date of the booking
(B) The number of attendees
(C) The start time of the event
(D) The location of the restaurant

派對的哪方面有變動？
(A) 預訂的日期
(B) 出席人數
(C) 活動的開始時間
(D) 餐廳地點

C **15** 🔊 062 🇦🇺

Look at the graphic. Which set menu will the speaker most likely choose?
(A) Set Menu A
(B) Set Menu B
(C) Set Menu C
(D) Set Menu D

請看圖表。說話者最有可能選擇哪個套餐組合？
(A) A 組合
(B) B 組合
(C) C 組合
(D) D 組合

D **16** 🔊 063 🇦🇺

What does the speaker ask the restaurant to confirm?
(A) The total price for the booking
(B) The availability of certain wines
(C) The closing time on June 4th
(D) The ability to meet dietary needs

說話者請餐廳確認哪件事？
(A) 訂位該付的總金額
(B) 是否有某些種類的葡萄酒
(C) 六月四日的結束營業時間
(D) 是否能滿足特殊飲食需求

🔍 重要單字片語

1. **rosebud** [ˈroz͵bʌd] *n.* 玫瑰花蕾
2. **set** [sɛt] *n.* 一組 / 套
   a set menu　　套餐組合菜單
   a set meal　　套餐
3. **retirement** [rɪˈtaɪrmənt] *n.* 退休
4. **budget** [ˈbʌdʒɪt] *n.* 預算 & *vt.* & *vi.* 安排（開支）；規劃（時間等）
   on a tight budget　　預算吃緊
   Bruce had to live on a tight budget after taking out a loan to buy the apartment.
   布魯斯貸款買公寓後不得不緊縮荷包度日。
   Jerry budgets his money carefully so that he can retire when he's 50.
   傑瑞謹慎規劃自己的財務，以便能在五十歲時退休。
5. **option** [ˈɑpʃən] *n.* 選擇，選項
   have no option / choice / alternative but to + V　　除了……之外別無選擇
   After the flight was canceled due to the storm, Tom had no option but to stay overnight at a nearby hotel.
   該班機因為暴風雨被取消，湯姆只得在附近的旅館過夜。
6. **vegan** [ˈvigən] *n.* 全素食者 & *a.* 全素的
7. **confirm** [kənˈfɝm] *vt.* 確認；證實
   confirm a booking / reservation
   確認預約
   Emma called the restaurant to confirm a reservation for a table for three tomorrow night.
   艾瑪打電話給餐廳確認明晚三個人的訂位。
8. **attendee** [ə͵tɛnˈdi] *n.* 參加者，出席者
9. **availability** [ə͵velə'bɪlətɪ] *n.* 可得性；能出席
10. **dietary** [ˈdaɪə͵tɛrɪ] *a.* 飲食的

Chapter 02　Reading Test

📖 Part 5　Incomplete Sentences

C　**17**

After the guests have finished ------- at the industry event, there will be ample opportunities for networking.

(A) dine　　　　　(B) dines　　　　　(C) dining　　　　　(D) dined

這場業界活動的來賓在用完餐後會有充分的機會去建立人脈。

理由

1. 本題測試下列固定用法：
   finish + N/V-ing　　完成……
   Johnny has just finished doing the dishes.
   強尼剛剛洗完了碗盤。
   Sandy finished her report and handed it in on schedule.
   珊蒂完成了她的報告並按時交出。

2. 根據上述，(C) 項應為正選。

重要單字片語

1. **ample** [ˋæmpl̩] *a.* 充分的，充足的
   ample time / space / proof
   充足的時間 / 空間 / 證明

2. **opportunity** [͵ɑpɚˋtunətɪ] *n.* 機會
   a golden opportunity　千載難逢的良機

C　**18**

The Ocean View Restaurant, which provides a wide variety of both meat and vegetarian entrées, ------- a charming dining location.

(A) being　　　　　(B) be　　　　　(C) is　　　　　(D) are

「海景餐廳」提供多種肉類及素食主餐，是個頗有魅力的用餐地點。

理由

1. 空格前有前後以逗點隔開，由關係代名詞 which 引導的非限定形容詞子句 which provides a wide variety of both meat and vegetarian entrées（提供多種肉類及素食主餐），修飾先行詞 The Ocean View Restaurant（海景餐廳）。

2. 形容詞子句中的 provides（提供）為現在簡單式單數動詞，得知本句使用現在簡單式描述該餐廳的現況，且主詞 The Ocean View Restaurant 為單數，故本句主要動詞亦應為現在簡單式單數。

3. 選項 (A) being 為現在分詞無法作主要動詞，選項 (B) be 為原形動詞不符時態，選項 (D) are 為複數動詞。故 (C) 項 is 應為正選。

重要單字片語

1. **variety** [vəˋraɪətɪ] *n.* 變化；種類
   a (wide) variety of...　各式各樣的……
   = a (wide) selection of...

   The shopping mall sells a wide variety of goods.
   這座購物中心裡面有賣各種五花八門的商品。

2. **charming** [ˋtʃɑrmɪŋ] *a.* 迷人的

D **19**

The restaurant used to ------- only Japanese cuisine, but it has now branched out into Korean and Taiwanese dishes as well.

(A) serving　　　　(B) served　　　　(C) serves　　　　(D) serve

這家餐廳過去只提供日式料理，但現在也開始賣韓國及臺灣菜。

理由

1. 本題測試下列固定句構：
   used to + V　　過去經常（但現在不再）做……
   Laura used to go swimming on weekends.
   蘿拉以前經常在週末時去游泳。

2. 根據上述，(D) 項應為正選。

重要單字片語

branch out into + N/V-ing　　擴大（興趣、活動等的）範圍至……
The bookstore owner has decided to branch out into selling coffee and desserts.
這家書店的老闆決定擴展經營範圍，開始賣起咖啡與甜點。

B **20**

We kindly request that you ------- by January 31 to confirm your attendance at the party.

(A) garnish　　　　(B) RSVP　　　　(C) charge　　　　(D) treat

敬請您於一月三十一日前回覆請柬，以確認是否能參加派對。

理由

1. (A) **garnish** [ˈgɑrnɪʃ] vt. 給菜餚裝飾 & n.（食物上的）裝飾菜；裝飾品
    The cook garnished the steak with cherry tomatoes.
    廚師在牛排旁邊裝點了幾顆小番茄。

   (B) **RSVP** [ˌɑr ˌɛs ˌvi ˈpi] vi. 回覆請柬，確認是否參加
    Please RSVP by the end of the month.
    請在月底前回覆請柬。

   (C) **charge** [tʃɑrdʒ] vt. & vi.（向……）收費；充電 & n. 收費
    charge sb + 金錢 (+ for sth)　　向某人收取（某事物的）費用
    The repairman charged Kelly NT$600 for fixing the leaking pipe.
    修理師傅幫凱莉修水管漏水，收費新臺幣六百元。

   (D) **treat** [trit] vt. 對待；招待；治療 & n. 款待；樂事
    treat A like / as B　　把 A 當作 B 對待
    Peter is a nice guy and has always treated me like a friend.
    彼得是好人，一直當我是朋友。

2. 根據語意，(B) 項應為正選。

重要單字片語

attendance [əˈtɛndəns] n. 出席
be in attendance　　出席（某特別活動）

35

Chapter 02　Reading Test

A **21**

The celebrity couple has chosen the Bartle Hall Country Hotel as the venue ------- they will hold their wedding reception.

(A) where　　　　(B) which　　　　(C) who　　　　(D) what

這對名人情侶選定巴特霍爾鄉村飯店作為他們舉辦婚宴的場地。

理由

1. 空格前有表場所的名詞 the venue（舉辦場地），得知空格內應置關係副詞 where 來引導形容詞子句修飾先行詞 the venue，故 (A) 項應為正選。

2. 此處 where 即等於 in which，故本句也可改寫成：
The celebrity couple has chosen the Bartle Hall Country Hotel as the venue in which they will hold their wedding reception.

重要單字片語

celebrity [səˋlɛbrətɪ] *n.* 名人，明星；名流（可數）；名聲，名氣（不可數）

Part 6　Text Completion

Questions 22-25 refer to the following memo.

From:　　　HR Manager
To:　　　　All Employees
Subject:　　Cafeteria Improvements

Based on feedback from the recent staff surveys, the company is excited to announce improvements to the office cafeteria. This will primarily focus on ------- the menu.
　　　　　　　　　　　　　　　　　　　　　　　　　　　　22.
Beginning on July 1, a wider range of ------- will be served to better reflect our
　　　　　　　　　　　　　　　　　23.
diverse workforce. -------, there will be more dishes with spicier flavors and many
　　　　　　　　　24.
more vegetarian options available. -------. However, we remain committed to keeping
　　　　　　　　　　　　　　　　　　25.
our prices competitive. We appreciate your feedback and hope you enjoy the new dining experience.

---

22 至 25 題請看以下備忘錄。

寄件者：人資部經理
收件者：全體員工
主　旨：自助餐廳改善事項

公司根據最近員工意見調查的回饋，鄭重宣布將對員工自助餐廳進行改善，主要重點是在<u>增加</u>菜單上的選項。從七月一日開始，將會有更多樣化的<u>菜餚</u>以更好地反映本公司員工的多元性。<u>舉例來</u>

36

說，會有更多較辣的餐點以及更多素食選項。大家會注意到價格略有上漲，這是為了支應開發新菜單的成本。不過我們仍會盡力保持價格的競爭力。感謝大家的回饋意見，並希望大家滿意新的用餐體驗。

C 22

(A) expansively　　(B) expansive　　(C) expanding　　(D) expansion

理由

1. 本題測試下列固定句構：
   focus (one's attention) on + N/V-ing　（某人）把注意力集中在……
   The company's new management focused on improving employee efficiency.
   公司的新管理層專注於提高員工的效率。

2. (A) **expansively** [ɪkˋspænsɪvlɪ] *adv.* 友善健談地
   Marie talked expansively about her future career plans.
   瑪麗滔滔不絕地談論她未來的職涯規畫。

   (B) **expansive** [ɪkˋspænsɪv] *a.* 廣闊的；友善健談的
   The expansive wetlands are home to a variety of rare animals.
   那片廣闊的溼地是多種稀有動物的棲息地。

   (C) **expand** [ɪkˋspænd] *vt. & vi.* （使）（尺寸或數量）擴大；拓展
   Our company must expand its factory's production capacity to keep up with customer demand.
   我們公司必須擴大工廠的產能以順應客戶的需求。

   (D) **expansion** [ɪkˋspænʃən] *n.* 擴大
   Financial problems are interfering with the company's expansion plans.
   財務問題妨礙了公司擴大經營的計畫。

3. 空格前有介詞 on，其後須接名詞或動名詞。空格後有名詞 the menu（菜單）作動詞的受詞，得知空格應置動名詞，且根據上述，故 (C) 項應為正選。

C 23

(A) ballrooms　　(B) gourmets　　(C) cuisines　　(D) allergies

理由

1. (A) **ballroom** [ˋbɔlˏrum] *n.* 宴會廳，舞廳
   ballroom dancing　　交際舞
   George and Mary will hold their anniversary party in a hotel's ballroom.
   喬治和瑪麗會在一家飯店的宴會廳舉辦他們的週年紀念派對。

   (B) **gourmet** [ˋgʊrme / gʊrˋme] *n.* 美食家 & *a.* （食品）優質的；提供美食的
   gourmet food / coffee　　優質食品 / 咖啡
   Kyle is not very particular about food, while his wife is a gourmet.
   凱爾對食物不挑剔，但他太太是個美食家。

Chapter 02　Reading Test

(C) **cuisine** [kwɪˈzin] *n.* 菜餚
French / Chinese cuisine　　法國菜 / 中華料理
The cuisine in that Chinese restaurant is beyond compare.
那家中華料理餐館的菜餚無與倫比。

(D) **allergy** [ˈælədʒɪ] *n.* 過敏
have an allergy to...　　對……過敏
Jason has a severe allergy to pollen that causes him discomfort.
傑森有嚴重的花粉過敏，讓他很不舒服。

2. 根據語意，(C) 項應為正選。

B **24**

(A) By contrast　　(B) For example　　(C) Instead　　(D) Frankly

理由

1. (A) **by contrast**　　相較之下
This hotel is wonderful. By contrast, the one we stayed at last month was horrible.
這間飯店很棒。相較之下，我們上個月住的那間糟透了。

(B) **for example**　　舉例來說，例如
Jennifer has a lot to do this morning. For example, she has to do the laundry and clean the kitchen.
珍妮佛今天早上有很多事情要做。例如她又要洗衣服又要清潔廚房。

(C) **instead** [ɪnˈstɛd] *adv.* 作為替代，反而
Jason is not going home this weekend. Instead, he's going to Tokyo.
這個週末傑森不會回家，而是去東京。

(D) **frankly** [ˈfræŋklɪ] *adv.* 坦白說
Frankly, I don't think this plan will work.
坦白說，我認為這項計畫不會成功。

2. 根據語意，(B) 項應為正選。

D **25**

(A) The renovations are due to be completed by the first week in August.
(B) Employees voted this the tastiest dish on the cafeteria's updated menu.
(C) The surveys are completely anonymous, and the results will be compiled by an external company.
(D) You will notice a slight price increase to pay for the development of the new menu.

理由

1. (A) 裝修工程預計於八月的第一個禮拜完工。
(B) 員工票選這道菜為自助餐廳更新後菜單中最美味的一道。
(C) 調查是完全匿名的，結果將交由外部公司匯整。
(D) 大家會注意到價格略有上漲，這是為了支應開發新菜單的成本。

2. 空格前的句子 "... there will be more dishes with spicier flavors and many more vegetarian options available."（……會有更多較辣的餐點以及更多素食選項。）表菜單有所更新，空格後的句子 "However, we remain committed to keeping our prices competitive."（不過我們仍會盡力保持價格的競爭力。）表更新後的因應措施。(D) 項置入空格後語意連貫，故為正選。

重要單字片語

1. **feedback** [ˈfidˌbæk] *n.* 回饋意見 / 資訊（不可數）
   positive / negative feedback
   正 / 反面回饋

2. **reflect** [rɪˈflɛkt] *vt.* 反映，顯示；反射 & *vi.* 思考（與介詞 on 並用）
   reflect on / upon...　深思 / 反省……
   Paul's wine preferences reflect his unusual personality.
   保羅在葡萄酒上的偏好反映了他與眾不同的人格特質。
   The manager will reflect on your suggestion before making a decision tomorrow.
   經理會仔細考慮你的建議，明天做決定。

3. **diverse** [dəˈvɝs / daɪˈvɝs] *a.* 不同的，多元的

4. **workforce** [ˈwɝkˌfɔrs] *n.* 全體從業人員；勞動力 / 人口（常用單數）

5. **spicy** [ˈspaɪsɪ] *a.* 辛辣的；加香料的

6. **competitive** [kəmˈpɛtətɪv] *a.*（價格、服務等）有競爭力的；競爭的

7. **anonymous** [əˈnɑnəməs] *a.* 匿名的
   an anonymous letter / phone call
   匿名信件 / 電話

8. **compile** [kəmˈpaɪl] *vt.* 彙編（成冊）
   The scholars and their assistants spent nearly eight years compiling this dictionary.
   多位學者與其一眾助理花了近八年時間彙編這本字典。

9. **external** [ɪksˈtɝnl̩] *a.* 外部的

10. **slight** [slaɪt] *a.* 少量的，輕微的

Chapter 02 Reading Test

Part 7 Reading Comprehension

Questions 26-27 refer to the following letter.

Chinese Women's League of San Francisco
217 Baker Street
San Francisco, CA 94117
Tel: (415) 822-4719   Fax: (415) 822-8818

To Whom It May Concern: August 28

Double Star Restaurant is one of the Chinese Women's League's favorite eateries. On September 28, we will hold our 30th anniversary celebration at our headquarters. Your restaurant has been chosen as one of the possible caterers for the banquet. Would you kindly answer the following questions?

- Do you have enough seating for a 90-person party?
- Some of our members are senior citizens with disabilities. Therefore, we require additional staff to help. We are willing to spend extra for this special service.
- We prefer Chinese cuisine. Could we meet to discuss the party's menu?
- Finally, we require an estimate of the cost.

Please respond via e-mail at kayeliao@hotwire.com.

Sincerely yours,

Kaye Liao

Kaye Liao, President
Chinese Women's League of San Francisco

26 至 27 題請看以下信件。

舊金山中國婦女聯合會
加州舊金山市
貝克街 217 號
郵遞區號 94117
電話：(415) 822-4719　　傳真：(415) 822-8818

敬啟者：

雙星餐廳為中國婦女聯合會最喜歡的餐館之一。本聯合會將於九月二十八日在總部舉辦三十週年慶祝活動。貴餐廳獲選為本次宴會可能的酒席承辦商之一。您能否針對以下問題給予惠答？

- 貴餐廳是否具備足夠容納一行九十人的桌椅？
- 由於本會某些成員為高齡殘疾人士，所以我們需要餐廳額外職員的協助。本聯合會願意為此特殊服務另外付費。
- 我們偏好吃中國菜。能否見面討論宴會的菜單？
- 最後，我們要求估價。

請回信至電子郵件 kayeliao@hotwire.com.

舊金山中國婦女聯合會會長
凱・廖　敬上

八月二十八日

A 26

What is the main purpose of the letter?　　本信的主旨是什麼？
(A) To request information on a catering service　　(A) 詢問外燴服務的資訊
(B) To invite people to attend an annual celebration　　(B) 邀請群眾參加週年慶
(C) To compliment a restaurant　　(C) 讚美某家餐廳
(D) To confirm a restaurant's invoice　　(D) 確認餐廳開立的發票

理由

根據本文第一段第三、四句 "Your restaurant has been chosen as one of the possible caterers for the banquet. Would you kindly answer the following questions?"（貴餐廳獲選為本次宴會可能的酒席承辦商之一。您能否針對以下問題給予惠答？）得知，**(A)** 項應為正選。

Chapter 02 Reading Test

B **27**

What special request is made of Double Star Restaurant?
(A) That the banquet be held near the entrance
(B) That extra service personnel be available
(C) That a 30th anniversary discount be given
(D) That vegetarian food be provided

對雙星餐廳有什麼特殊要求？
(A) 宴會在入口處附近舉行
(B) 餐廳要提供額外服務人力
(C) 餐廳提供三十週年紀念折扣優惠
(D) 餐廳提供素食

理由

根據詢問問題的第二點第二句 "Therefore, we require additional staff to help."（所以我們需要餐廳額外職員的協助。）得知，(B) 項應為正選。

重要單字片語

1. **league** [lig] *n.* 聯盟
2. **To whom it may concern:**
   敬啟者：（信頭語）
3. **eatery** [ˈitərɪ] *n.* 小餐館；小吃店
4. **anniversary** [ˌænəˈvɝsərɪ] *n.* 週年紀念日
5. **headquarters** [ˈhɛdˌkwɔrtɚz] *n.* 總部
   （恆用複數）
   = head office
6. **citizen** [ˈsɪtəzən] *n.* 市民
   a senior citizen　　老年人（敬稱）
7. **disability** [ˌdɪsəˈbɪlətɪ] *n.* 缺陷，障礙
   learning disabilities　　學習障礙
8. **estimate** [ˈɛstəmət] *n.*（對數量、成本等的）估計
   estimate [ˈɛstəˌmet] *vt.* 估計
   estimated [ˈɛstəˌmetɪd] *a.* 估計的
   It is estimated + that 子句　　據估計……
   an estimated + 數字　　估計有……
   be estimated at + 數字　　估計有……
   It is estimated that three hundred people were killed in the air crash.
   = An estimated three hundred people were killed in the air crash.
   據估計有三百人在這場空難中喪生。
   The total cost of the project is estimated at US$500,000.
   該專案的總成本估計為五十萬美元。

9. **respond** [rɪˈspɑnd] *vi.* 回覆（= reply）；對……作出反應（= react）
   respond to...　　回答……；對……作出反應
   Sarah never responded to my letter.
   = Sarah never replied to my letter.
   莎拉從來不回我的信。
   How did your parents respond to the news?
   = How did your parents react to the news?
   你爸媽對這則消息的反應是什麼？
10. **via** [ˈvaɪə / ˈviə] *prep.* 透過，經由
    （= through）
    You can access our library's database via the internet.
    你可以透過網路進入我們圖書館的資料庫。
11. **compliment** [ˈkɑmpləmənt] *n.* &
    [ˈkɑmpləˌmɛnt] *vt.* 恭維
    compliment sb on sth　　就某事恭維某人
    I take it as a compliment when people say I look like my father.
    大家說我長得像老爸時，我把那當作是讚美。
    I complimented Judy on her excellent French.
    我讚美茱蒂流利的法文。

42

Questions 28-30 refer to the following Web page.

https://www.restaurate.com

Restaurate
Rate and review restaurants

| About Us | Sign Up or Log In | Read a Review | Write a Review |

For over eight years, Restaurate members' reviews and ratings have helped restaurant-goers choose the best meals at the best restaurants. — [1] —. From a humble start, operating from a laptop in Wellington, our site has grown to be an essential first stop for every serious foodie or casual diner planning to eat at an unfamiliar restaurant — no matter where they are on the planet. — [2] —. At the same time, Restaurate has become a hero for restaurants aiming for excellence and the enemy of poor-quality restaurants everywhere. — [3] —.

Restaurate is a free service. We do not charge subscription fees, sell products, or sell advertising. We do, however, pay full-time moderators. So, we ask those members that benefit from the site, and have the means, to donate through our tips page. — [4] —.

28 至 30 題請看以下網頁。

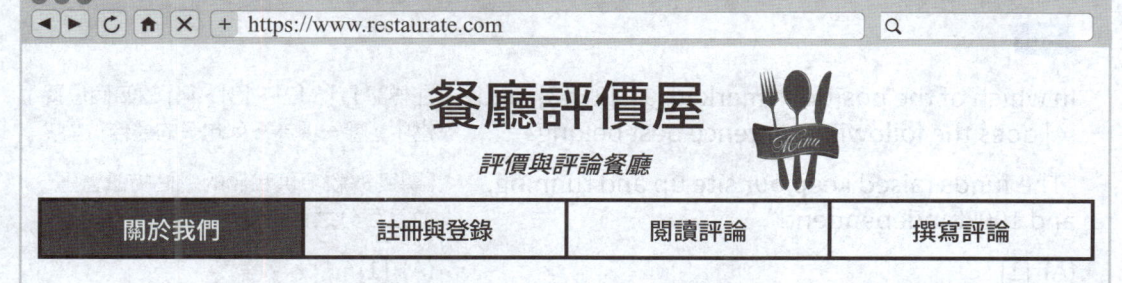

https://www.restaurate.com

餐廳評價屋
評價與評論餐廳

| 關於我們 | 註冊與登錄 | 閱讀評論 | 撰寫評論 |

八年多以來，餐廳評價屋會員的評論與評價，幫助了餐廳愛好者在最好的餐廳選擇最棒的餐點。— [1] —。從沒沒無聞地在威靈頓使用一臺筆記型電腦以來，我們的網站已發展成講究的老饕或是輕度食客打算在不熟悉的餐廳用餐前必造訪的首站 —— 不論他們身在世界何處。— [2] —。此外，對各地以完美為目標的餐廳而言，餐廳評價屋已成為英雄，而對劣質的餐廳而言，餐廳評價屋已成為痛恨的對象。— [3] —。

餐廳評價屋是免費的服務。我們不索取訂閱費、兜售商品或是銷售廣告。然而，我們還得花錢請全職控管人員。因此，我們懇求那些有財力且受惠於網站的會員們，透過打賞專頁捐款。— [4] —。

Chapter 02 Reading Test

B **28**

What do Restaurate members do?
(A) Train people to cook
(B) Comment on restaurants
(C) Work at restaurants
(D) Replace recipes

餐廳評價屋的會員在做什麼？
(A) 訓練民眾烹飪
(B) 評論餐廳
(C) 在餐廳工作
(D) 替換食譜

理由

根據本文第一段第一句 "…Restaurate members' reviews and ratings have helped restaurant-goers choose the best meals at the best restaurants."（……餐廳評價屋會員的評論與評價，幫助了餐廳愛好者在最好的餐廳選擇最棒的餐點。）得知，(B) 項應為正選。

B **29**

What is mentioned about Restaurate?
(A) It advertises extensively.
(B) It moderates reviews.
(C) It is only available in Wellington.
(D) It provides cooking advice.

關於餐廳評價屋，本文提及了什麼？
(A) 餐廳評價屋廣告氾濫。
(B) 餐廳評價屋管控評論。
(C) 餐廳評價屋只在威靈頓可看到。
(D) 餐廳評價屋提供烹飪建議。

理由

根據本文第二段第三句 "We do, however, pay full-time moderators."（然而，我們還得花錢請全職控管人員。）得知，(B) 項應為正選。

D **30**

In which of the positions marked [1], [2], [3], and [4] does the following sentence best belong?

"The funds raised keep our site up and running, and 100% independent!"

(A) [1]
(B) [2]
(C) [3]
(D) [4]

在標記 [1]、[2]、[3]、[4] 的四個位置當中，哪一項為下列句子的最佳位置？

「募到的款項供我們的網站持續營運，並且百分之百不受外力干預！」

(A) [1]
(B) [2]
(C) [3]
(D) [4]

理由

根據本文第二段最後一句 "So, we ask those members that benefit from the site, and have the means, to donate through our tips page."（因此，我們懇求那些有財力且受惠於網站的會員們，透過打賞專頁捐款。）此處提及捐款，與題目句中提的 The funds (which are) raised（募到的款項）產生關聯，故 (D) 項應為正選。

重要單字片語

1. **rate** [ret] *vt.* 評價
   rating [ˈretɪŋ] *n.* 等級，級數
   be rated (as) sth　被評價為……
   The 3D movie was rated a great success by critics.
   那部 3D 電影被影評評價為非常成功。

2. **review** [rɪˈvju] *vt. & n.* 評論
   The play was reviewed in the local newspapers.
   地方報紙都對這部戲劇作了評論。

3. **-goer**　常去……的人
   movie-goers　電影愛好者

4. **humble** [ˈhʌmbl̩] *a.* 不起眼的；謙虛的
   from humble beginnings　出身卑微
   The successful businessman emerged from humble beginnings.
   這位成功的生意人出身卑微。
   No matter how famous you become, you should still be humble.
   不論你變得多有名氣，你仍應該謙虛待人。

5. **essential** [ɪˈsɛnʃəl] *a.* 不可或缺的；絕對重要的
   be essential to...　對……是不可或缺的
   Clean water and air are essential to any species.
   乾淨的水源和空氣對任何物種而言都是不可或缺的。

6. **foodie** [ˈfudɪ] *n.* 美食家，美食主義者

7. **unfamiliar** [ˌʌnfəˈmɪljɚ] *a.* 陌生的，不熟悉的

8. **aim** [em] *vt.* 使對準 & *vi.* 瞄準
   aim for...　以……為目的
   We should aim for a bigger market share.
   我們應該以更大的市場占有率為目標。

9. **moderator** [ˈmɑdəˌretɚ] *n.*（網站）版主；仲裁者
   moderate [ˈmɑdəret] *vt. & vi.*（使）主持討論
   Jessica moderates our morning meetings.
   潔西卡主持我們的晨間會議。

10. **benefit** [ˈbɛnəfɪt] *vi.* 得益
    benefit from...　自……獲益
    Some of the patients will benefit from the new drug.
    這新藥有助於某些病患。

11. **means** [minz] *n.* 金錢，財富（= wealth）
    a man of means　富有的人
    live beyond / within one's means
    入不敷出 / 量入為出

12. **donate** [ˈdonet] *vt. & vi.* 捐獻
    donate sth to...　將某物捐給……
    Frank donated all his life savings to charity.
    法蘭克將他畢身的積蓄捐給了慈善機構。
    Everyone is encouraged to donate to the charity.
    每個人都被鼓勵捐款給該慈善機構。

13. **fund** [fʌnd] *n.* 資金（常用複數）

14. **raise** [rez] *vt.* 籌募
    raise funds / money　籌募資金
    They held a concert to raise money for charity.
    他們舉辦音樂會進行慈善募款。

15. **up and running**　運行，運轉
    The janitor soon got the air conditioner up and running again.
    工友很快就讓空調設備再次運轉了。

Chapter 03 Listening Test

🎧 Part 1 Photographs

B **1** 🔊 065

(A) He's painting streetscapes.
(B) He's exhibiting artwork.
(C) He's moving the chair.
(D) He's preparing a canvas.

(A) 他正在畫街景。
(B) 他正在展示畫作。
(C) 他正在移動椅子。
(D) 他正在準備一張畫布。

重要單字片語

1. **streetscape** [ˈstritˌskep] *n.* 街景
2. **canvas** [ˈkænvəs] *n.* 畫布；油畫

C **2** 🔊 066

(A) One of the men is conducting an orchestra.
(B) One of the men is holding a music stand.
(C) They are playing some instruments.
(D) They are putting violins in cases.

(A) 男子之一正在指揮管絃樂隊。
(B) 男子之一正拿著樂譜架。
(C) 他們在演奏樂器。
(D) 他們正將小提琴放入琴盒中。

重要單字片語

conduct [kənˈdʌkt] *vt.* 指揮（樂團）；處理 & [ˈkɑndʌkt] *n.* 行為（不可數）
The orchestra, conducted by André Previn, is performing *Boléro*.
由安德烈・普列汶指揮的樂團正演奏《波麗露舞曲》。

🎧 Part 2 Question-Response

B **3** 🔊 068

The first issue of the magazine sold out within two days.
(A) They were sold at the box office.
(B) It must be very popular.
(C) Tissues are in the cabinet.

該雜誌第一期在兩天內就銷售一空。
(A) 它們在售票處販售。
(B) 它一定很受歡迎。
(C) 衛生紙在儲藏櫃裡。

重要單字片語

1. **issue** [ˈɪʃu] *n.* （雜誌或報紙的）一期
2. **sell out** 銷售一空，售罄
   The concert tickets sold out within hours.
   那些演唱會的票在幾個小時內銷售一空。
3. **box office** （電影院、戲劇廳）售票處；票房
4. **cabinet** [ˈkæbənɪt] *n.* 儲藏櫃，櫥櫃；（英）內閣

C **4** 🔊 069 🇬🇧 🇦🇺

Did you read the review of the new comedy?
(A) It's renewed annually.
(B) It'll be released next summer.
(C) The critics say that it's very funny.

你看過那部新上映喜劇片的影評了嗎？
(A) 它每年都會更新。
(B) 那部片明年夏天會上映。
(C) 影評表示該片很搞笑。

重要單字片語

1. **comedy** [ˈkɑmədɪ] *n.* 喜劇
2. **renew** [rɪˈnu] *vt.* 更新
   My manager decided to renew my contract for another year.
   我的主管決定和我續簽一年的合約。
3. **annually** [ˈænjʊəlɪ] *adv.* 一年一度地
   annual [ˈænjʊəl] *a.* 每年的；年度的
4. **critic** [ˈkrɪtɪk] *n.* 評論家

🎧 Part 3 Conversations

Questions 5 through 7 refer to the following conversation. 🔊 071 M: 🇦🇺 W: 🇬🇧

M: Good morning. I'd like to purchase the painting by Johan Strahan, the one hanging on the back wall.
W: I'm sorry. All his artwork was bought by a collector at an exhibit held last week. I do have this three-piece collection by Jodie Dion — winner of this year's National Landscape Award. As you can see, the style is remarkably similar.
M: Are these paintings available individually, or would I need to purchase the entire collection?
W: I'm sorry; separating them is not possible. I do, however, have other paintings by the same artist available for sale individually. Would you like to see them?
M: Yes, thank you.

5 至 7 題請聽以下會話。

> 男：早安。我想要買掛在後面牆上的那幅約翰・斯塔漢的畫。
> 女：很抱歉。他所有的畫都被一位收藏家在上個星期舉辦畫展時買走了。我倒是還有這套三件式作品 — 出自今年度國家風景畫獎得主喬蒂・狄翁的手筆。您可以看得出來，他們的畫風像極了。
> 男：這些畫是獨立出售的，還是我得要全套都一起買下來？
> 女：很抱歉；這些畫是無法分開來賣的。不過，我倒是有這位畫家的其他幅畫是可以獨立出售的。您要不要看看這些畫呢？
> 男：好，謝謝妳。

Chapter 03 Listening Test

B 5 🔊 072 🇨🇦

Who most likely is the woman?
(A) An artist
(B) An art dealer
(C) A museum guide
(D) A headhunter

這名女子最有可能是誰？
(A) 畫家
(B) 藝術品經銷商
(C) 博物館導覽員
(D) 獵才顧問

D 6 🔊 073 🇨🇦

What does the woman say about Jodie Dion?
(A) She works at a local art center.
(B) She has planned an exhibition.
(C) She is a well-known art critic.
(D) She is an award-winning artist.

這名女子對於喬蒂・狄翁是怎麼說的？
(A) 她在本地的藝術中心上班。
(B) 她策劃了一個展覽。
(C) 她是知名的藝評人。
(D) 她是曾經得過獎的畫家。

A 7 🔊 074 🇨🇦

What does the woman offer to do?
(A) Present other artworks
(B) Paint a picture
(C) Provide a replacement
(D) Contact the artist

這名女子表示願意做什麼事？
(A) 介紹別的藝術作品
(B) 畫一幅畫
(C) 提供替代品
(D) 聯絡那位畫家

重要單字片語

1. **purchase** [ˈpɝtʃəs] *vt.* & *n.* 購買
   You can purchase the product online.
   你可以利用網路在線上購買這項產品。

2. **artwork** [ˈɑrtwɝk] *n.* 藝術作品
   Guests are welcome to admire the artwork in the hotel's private gallery.
   歡迎住客欣賞本飯店私營畫廊內的藝術品。

3. **landscape** [ˈlændˌskep] *n.* 風景畫；風景
   Alan achieved great fame as a landscape artist.
   亞倫成了聲名大噪的風景畫畫家。

4. **remarkably** [rɪˈmɑrkəblɪ] *adv.* 不尋常地；驚人地
   David performed remarkably well on the test.
   大衛這次考試表現得非常出色。

5. **individually** [ˌɪndəˈvɪdʒʊəlɪ] *adv.* 個別地
   The students performed as a group and then individually.
   學生們先進行團體表演，接著再進行個別表演。

6. **entire** [ɪnˈtaɪr] *a.* 全部的；整體的
   Johnny spent an entire night studying for the upcoming exam.
   強尼花了一整晚準備即將來臨的考試。

7. **for sale**　待售

8. **an art dealer**　藝術品經銷商

9. **headhunter** [ˈhɛdˌhʌntɚ] *n.* 以替公司物色人才為業的人
   The headhunter is finding new people to work in the international company.
   這位獵才顧問正在替那家跨國公司尋找新的人才。

10. **exhibition** [ˌɛksəˈbɪʃən] *n.* 展覽；展覽會
    be on exhibition　展出中
    = be on display

A guide showed us around the exhibition.
一位導遊帶我們參觀了展覽。

11. **award-winning** [əˈwɔrd͵wɪnɪŋ] *a.* 獲獎的
The award-winning magazine has a wide readership.
這本得獎雜誌有許多讀者。
   * readership [ˈrɪdɚ͵ʃɪp] *n.* 讀者群（集合名詞，不可數）

12. **present** [prɪˈzɛnt] *vt.* 介紹；出示；提出

Let me present Mr. White, one of today's greatest artists.
讓我來介紹懷特先生，他是當今最偉大的藝術家之一。

13. **replacement** [rɪˈplesmənt] *n.* 替代品；替代人選；替換物
   = substitute [ˈsʌbstə͵tjut]
It will be very hard to find a replacement for Jack in this company.
在這間公司裡很難找到能取代傑克的人。

CH 03

Questions 8 through 10 refer to the following conversation and leaflet. 🔊 075
M: 🇨🇦   W: 🇺🇸

M: Hey, I'm thinking of catching a movie after work. Would you like to join me?
W: It depends on what's showing. I'm not in the mood to watch anything too heavy or dramatic right now.
M: According to this leaflet, there's an old 1990s comedy playing at the Tivoli Vintage Movie Festival. It starts at 8:30.
W: Great! I'll meet you out front of the theater at, say, 8:15.
M: Better make it 8 o'clock. We'll need enough time to grab some junk food and soda.

Tivoli Movie Theater
Vintage Movie Festival

GENRE	MOVIE
Science fiction	War of the Planets
Bio-drama	Becoming Benjamin
Comedy	Randy Gupta's Road Trip
Horror	Monster Convention

8 至 10 題請聽以下會話及傳單。

男：嗨，我正在考慮下班後去看場電影。妳要不要跟我一起去？
女：那得要看現在演什麼電影？我現在可沒心情看太費神或太震撼的電影。
男：根據這張傳單所示，聚活力電影回顧展正在上映一部一九九〇年代的喜劇片。八點半開演。
女：太好了！這樣吧，八點十五分時我們在電影院正門的外面會合。
男：最好是在八點鐘見。我們需要有足夠的時間去買些垃圾食物和汽水。

Chapter 03 Listening Test

聚活力戲院
電影回顧展

類型	電影
科幻片	星球大戰
名人傳記片	成為班傑明
喜劇片	蘭迪‧古普塔的四輪長征
恐怖片	怪獸大集合

C 8 ◀) 076 🇬🇧

What is the woman invited to do?
(A) Have a picnic
(B) Review a movie
(C) Go to the movies
(D) Perform in a play

這名女子被邀請去做什麼事？
(A) 去野餐
(B) 寫影評
(C) 看電影
(D) 演話劇

C 9 ◀) 077 🇬🇧

Look at the graphic. Which movie will the man and woman most likely see?
(A) *War of the Planets*
(B) *Becoming Benjamin*
(C) *Randy Gupta's Road Trip*
(D) *Monster Convention*

請看圖表。男子和女子最有可能去看哪一部電影？
(A)《星球大戰》
(B)《成為班傑明》
(C)《蘭迪‧古普塔的四輪長征》
(D)《怪獸大集合》

D 10 ◀) 078 🇬🇧

What does the man suggest doing before the movie?
(A) Downloading a schedule
(B) Speaking to a coworker
(C) Dining at a restaurant
(D) Purchasing snacks

這名男子建議看電影前先做什麼事？
(A) 下載放映時間表
(B) 跟同事講話
(C) 在餐廳吃飯
(D) 買點心

重要單字片語

1. **leaflet** [ˋliflɪt] *n.*（單頁）傳單
   The kids were paid to circulate leaflets on the streets after school.
   這些孩子受僱在放學後到街上去散發傳單。

2. **catch a movie**　去看電影
   = go to a movie

3. **be not in the mood to + V**
沒心情做某事
I'm not in the mood to go to the movies with you.
我沒有心情跟你去看電影。

4. **dramatic** [drəˋmætɪk] *a.* 戲劇性的；強烈的
Dramatic changes have swept that country in the last twenty years.
那個國家在過去二十年來經歷了強烈的改變。

5. **vintage** [ˋvɪntɪdʒ] *a.* 經典的；老式（但質優）的；古典的；上等的
It's incredible that your vintage car goes so fast.
你的老爺車可以跑得這麼快真是令人難以置信。

6. **grab** [græb] *vt.*（因忙碌而）趕緊（吃或睡等）
grab a bite to eat
隨便抓東西吃；匆匆吃點東西
Jimmy grabbed a slice of bread and then rushed to work.
吉米抓了一片麵包就匆匆去上班了。

7. **science fiction** 科幻小說
8. **bio-drama** 名人傳記劇
9. **a road trip** 開車長途旅行
10. **convention** [kənˋvɛnʃən] *n.* 會議，大會
Attendees at the convention include congressmen, retired generals, and senior government officials.
大會的參加者包括國會議員、退休將領及政府高階官員。

11. **perform** [pɚˋfɔrm] *vi.* & *vt.* 表演；演出
Mary loves being on stage and performs in plays whenever she can.
瑪麗喜歡在臺上表演，只要有機會就在戲裡軋一角。

12. **download** [ˏdaʊnˋlod] *vt.*（電腦）下載
First, download these files and save them on the hard disk.
首先，下載這些檔案，接著把它們存在硬碟裡。

🎧 Part 4 Talks

Questions 11 through 13 refer to the following broadcast. 🔊 080

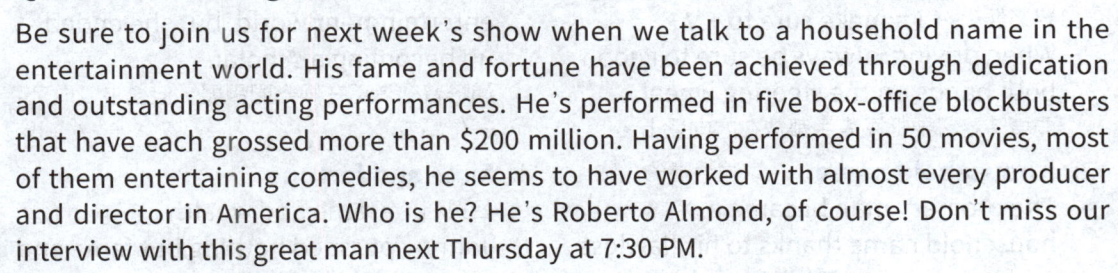

Be sure to join us for next week's show when we talk to a household name in the entertainment world. His fame and fortune have been achieved through dedication and outstanding acting performances. He's performed in five box-office blockbusters that have each grossed more than $200 million. Having performed in 50 movies, most of them entertaining comedies, he seems to have worked with almost every producer and director in America. Who is he? He's Roberto Almond, of course! Don't miss our interview with this great man next Thursday at 7:30 PM.

11 至 13 題請聽以下廣播。

下個星期我們將會請一位家喻戶曉的娛樂界人士來上節目，請大家屆時一定要收聽本節目。他對演藝事業的全心投入加上出色的演技，使他得以名利雙收。他參與演出了五部票房大賣的電影，這五部電影每部的票房總收入均超過兩億美元。他拍過五十部電影，其中大多為趣味性十足的喜劇，看來他幾乎已跟美國的所有製片人及導演都合作過。他是誰呢？沒錯，他就是羅柏托‧阿蒙德！下星期四晚上七點半千萬別錯過我們對這位大人物的專訪哦。

Chapter 03 Listening Test

A **11** 🔊 081 🇦🇺

Who is the speaker talking about?
(A) An actor
(B) A TV star
(C) A director
(D) A producer

說話者在談論誰？
(A) 某演員
(B) 某電視明星
(C) 某導演
(D) 某製片人

A **12** 🔊 082 🇦🇺

According to the speaker, how has Mr. Almond achieved his success?
(A) By performing in several movies
(B) By winning numerous awards
(C) By owning many large houses
(D) By hosting famous shows

根據說話者所述，阿蒙德先生是如何取得成功的？
(A) 在幾部電影中演出
(B) 贏得很多獎項
(C) 擁有許多間大宅
(D) 主持多個知名的節目

B **13** 🔊 083 🇦🇺

What does the speaker say will happen next Thursday?
(A) An audition
(B) An interview
(C) A premiere
(D) A lecture

說話者說下星期四將會有什麼事發生？
(A) 一個試鏡
(B) 一個專訪
(C) 一場首映
(D) 一場演講

重要單字片語

1. **be sure to + V**
   務必……（= make sure to + V）
   When driving, always be sure to keep both hands on the steering wheel.
   開車時務必要把兩隻手都放在方向盤上。

2. **a household name**　家喻戶曉的人物
   The ordinary man became a household name thanks to his flawless performance in a TV singing contest.
   那名男素人因在電視歌唱比賽中完美的表現而一夕爆紅，成為家喻戶曉的人物。

3. **the entertainment world**
   娛樂界；娛樂業（= the entertainment business）
   Rita used to aspire to a career in the entertainment world, but she ended up becoming a scholar.
   麗塔曾經渴望在娛樂圈發展，但後來變成了一位學者。

4. **fame and fortune**
   名與利（= fame and wealth）
   Johnny pursued nothing but fame and fortune all his life.
   強尼一生只追求名利。

5. **achieve** [əˋtʃiv] vt. & vi.（尤指經過努力）
   獲得；達到（= reach）
   Paul achieved the goal at the cost of his health.
   保羅達成了目標，卻犧牲了健康。

6. **dedication** [ˌdɛdəˈkeʃən] *n.* 全心投入；奉獻
Peter's dedication plays a crucial role in the success of our company.
彼得的全心投入對本公司的成功來說極為重要。

7. **outstanding** [ˌaʊtˈstændɪŋ] *a.* 出色的；傑出的
The young actor performed with such zest that he was awarded the prize for the most outstanding actor in the play.
這名年輕男演員的演出如此賣力，他因此獲頒此劇的最佳男演員獎。

8. **blockbuster** [ˈblɑkˌbʌstɚ] *n.* 賣座片；鉅片
This film successfully mixed historical facts with fantasy and became a blockbuster.
這部電影成功地把史實與幻想混雜在一起，成了一部賣座電影。

9. **gross** [ɡros] *vt.* 獲得……的總收入
The movie grossed almost US$100 million, but it still lost money.
那部電影的票房總收入雖有一億美元，但還是虧本。

10. **producer** [prəˈdusɚ] *n.* 製片人；製作人；監製

11. **director** [dəˈrɛktɚ] *n.* 導演

12. **interview** [ˈɪntɚˌvju] *n.* & *vt.* 採訪；訪談
Following the film, there will be an interview with the director.
電影結束之後，將會對導演做一個專訪。

13. **host** [host] *vt.* 主持；主辦
The upcoming program will be hosted by Jill Wood.
接下來的節目將由吉兒‧伍德主持。

14. **audition** [ɔˈdɪʃən] *n.* & *vi.* 試鏡；試演；試唱
George had a very good audition and landed a part in the movie.
喬治試鏡非常成功，在那部電影中軋上一角。

Questions 14 through 16 refer to the following voice message. 🔊 084 🇨🇦

Hello, this is Omar Abbasi from the Waterside Artists' Colony. I'm calling to thank you for the contribution you made during our recent fundraiser. I'd also like to ask if you would be our guest of honor at the opening of an exhibit by the one and only Travon Santos. I know that you wouldn't accept the request if he were a lesser-known artist, but let's face it, it is a Travon Santos exhibition. If you accept, we hope you will give a speech and introduce the artist. I'll arrange for a speech writer to prepare a speech for you. It goes without saying that you would have complete control of the content.

14 至 16 題請聽以下語音留言。

嗨，我是河濱藝術家聚居區的奧瑪‧阿巴西。我打電話給您是要來謝謝您在我們不久前的籌款活動中的捐款贊助。我同時也想要請問您可否來為特拉文‧山多士他獨一無二的展覽擔任開幕式的榮譽嘉賓。我知道假如他只是一個不太有名的藝術家您是不會接受這個邀約的，不過，說實話，這個展覽可是特拉文‧山多士的個展。如果您同意出席開幕式，我們希望由您來演講，介紹這位藝術家。我將會安排一位演講寫手為您撰寫演講稿。當然，對於演講內容您有全部的掌控權。

Chapter 03 Listening Test

B **14** 🔊 085 🇺🇸

What does the speaker thank the listener for?
(A) Attending an opening ceremony
(B) Donating money
(C) Purchasing artwork
(D) Writing an e-mail

| 說話者感謝那位聽語音留言的人什麼事？
(A) 參加開幕典禮
(B) 捐款
(C) 買藝術作品
(D) 寫電子郵件

A **15** 🔊 086 🇺🇸

What does the speaker imply when he says, "it is a Travon Santos exhibition"?
(A) Travon Santos is a renowned artist.
(B) It's Travon Santos's first exhibition.
(C) He forgot to mention the artist's name.
(D) He accidentally mispronounced the artist's name.

說話者說「這個展覽可是特拉文・山多士的個展」時，在暗示什麼？
(A) 特拉文・山多士是知名藝術家。
(B) 那是特拉文・山多士的首展。
(C) 他忘記提及那位藝術家的名字。
(D) 他不小心唸錯那位藝術家的名字。

C **16** 🔊 087 🇺🇸

What does the speaker ask the listener to do?
(A) Accept a gift
(B) Join a contest
(C) Make a speech
(D) Arrange an exhibition

說話者要求聽語音留言的人做什麼事？
(A) 接受一份禮物
(B) 參加一個比賽
(C) 做一場演講
(D) 策劃一個展覽

重要單字片語

1. **waterside** [ˈwɔtɚˌsaɪd] *n.* 水邊；湖邊；河邊

2. **colony** [ˈkɑlənɪ] *n.* 聚居地區；群體；殖民地

3. **fundraiser** [ˈfʌndˌrezɚ] *n.* 籌款活動；籌款者
   I'm happy to report that our fundraiser last month successfully raised over US$300,000.
   我很高興可以告訴大家，我們上個月的籌款活動已經順利募集到三十多萬美元了。

4. **guest of honor** 貴賓
   I was a bit nervous when they asked me to give a spontaneous speech as tonight's guest of honor.
   當他們要我擔任今天晚上的榮譽嘉賓做即席演說時，我有一點緊張。

5. **opening** [ˈopənɪŋ] *n.* 開幕式；開張

6. **the one and only**
   獨一無二的；唯一的

7. **request** [rɪˈkwɛst] *n. & vt.* 請求；要求
   The war-torn country made a request for international aid.
   那個飽受戰亂蹂躪的國家請求國際援助。

8. **an opening ceremony** 開幕典禮

9. **mispronounce** [ˌmɪsprəˈnaʊns] *vt.* 唸錯；讀錯
   David deliberately mispronounces Brian's last name every time they see each other because he thinks it's funny.
   每次大衛看到布萊恩時都故意把布萊恩的姓唸錯，因為大衛覺得這樣很好玩。

54

Chapter 03 Reading Test

Part 5 Incomplete Sentences

B 17

Many viewers ------- the final episode of the series for failing to satisfactorily resolve the show's central mystery.

(A) critic (B) criticized (C) criticism (D) critical

許多觀眾批評該影集的大結局那集，因為它未能圓滿解開劇中的核心謎團。

理由

1. (A) **critic** [ˈkrɪtɪk] *n.* 評論家；愛挑剔的人
   The new action movie received poor reviews from most critics.
   大部分影評人對這部新動作片給予了負面評價。

   (B) **criticize** [ˈkrɪtɪˌsaɪz] *vt.* 批評
   criticize... for + N/V-ing　　為某事批評……
   Some citizens criticized the mayor for not handling the situation properly.
   有些市民批評市長沒有妥善處理這個狀況。

   (C) **criticism** [ˈkrɪtəˌsɪzəm] *n.* 批評，爭議；評論（均不可數）
   There has been a lot of criticism from employees regarding the company's new policy.
   員工們對公司的新規定有很多批評。

   (D) **critical** [ˈkrɪtɪkl] *a.* 批評的；危急的
   be critical of...　　批判……
   Analysts are broadly critical of the government's new economic policies.
   分析師對政府的新經濟政策普遍持批評的態度。

2. 空格前有名詞詞組 Many viewers（許多觀眾）作本句的主詞，空格後有 the final episode of the series（該影集的大結局那集）作受詞，得知空格應置動詞，且根據上述，(B) 項應為正選。

重要單字片語

1. **viewer** [ˈvjuɚ] *n.* （電視）觀眾
2. **satisfactorily** [ˌsætɪsˈfæktərɪlɪ] *adv.* 令人滿意地
3. **resolve** [rɪˈzɑlv] *vt.* 解答，破解；解決；下決心 & *n.* 決心（不可數）
   resolve / solve a mystery　　解開謎團

Researchers finally resolved the mystery of the ancient civilization's sudden disappearance.
研究人員最終解開了該古代文明突然消失的謎團。

C 18

------- by the audience's positive reaction to their music, the rock band played well past midnight at the soccer stadium.

(A) Delight (B) Delights (C) Delighted (D) Delighting

該搖滾樂團對於觀眾的熱烈回應頗為歡喜，於是在足球場的這場演唱會超過半夜都還沒結束。

Chapter 03 Reading Test

理由

1. 本題測試副詞子句簡化為分詞構句的用法：
   當副詞子句和主要子句的主詞相同時，可使用「分詞構句」簡化句型。此處為簡化副詞子句的分詞構句，原句為：
   As they were delighted by the audience's positive reaction to their music, the rock band played well...
   將副詞子句中同樣指 the rock band（搖滾樂團）的主詞 they 刪除，並將其後的動詞 were 變成現在分詞 being 之後，予以省略，最後刪除引導副詞子句的從屬連接詞 as 形成以下句子：
   Delighted by the audience's positive reaction to their music, the rock band played well...

2. 根據上述，(C) 項應為正選。

重要單字片語

delighted [dɪˋlaɪtɪd] *a.* 感到高興的；滿意的
be delighted by / at / with...　對……感到高興
Frank was delighted by the prospect of becoming a father.
法蘭克一想到將為人父就滿心歡喜。
＊prospect [ˋprɑspɛkt] *n.* 前景

D 19

The publishing company ------- a best seller since Mike Borton's book, *The Nightfall*, was released five years ago.

(A) will not publish　(B) did not publish　(C) does not publish　(D) has not published

那家出版社自從五年前發行了邁可・波頓的《黃昏》以來就沒再出版過暢銷書。

理由

1. 句中的 since（自從）可作介詞或副詞連接詞，分別引導介詞片語或過去式副詞子句以修飾主要子句，而主要子句的動詞時態應採用現在完成式或現在完成進行式。
   I have lived here since 2008.
   　現在完成式　　介詞
   我自從 2008 年起就一直住在這兒了。
   Brian has been learning English since he entered junior high school.
   　　現在完成進行式　　　　連接詞
   布萊恩自從上國中以來，就一直研讀英文。

2. 根據上述，(D) 項應為正選。

重要單字片語

1. **a best seller**　暢銷書
2. **nightfall** [ˋnaɪt͵fɔl] *n.* 黃昏（= dusk [dʌsk]）

I wanted to be home before nightfall.
我想在天黑前回到家。

D **20**

After the fantastic performance by the renowned dance company, the audience erupted in -------.

(A) be applauded　　(B) applauded　　(C) applaud　　(D) applause

在該知名舞團的精彩表演過後，觀眾爆發出掌聲。

> 理由

1. 本題測驗下列固定句構：
   erupt in applause　猛地鼓掌
   applause [əˋplɔz] *n.* 掌聲
   The crowd erupted in applause after the magician performed the magic trick.
   魔術師表演完那個魔術後，觀眾爆發出掌聲。
2. 根據上述，(D) 項應為正選。

> 重要單字片語

1. **fantastic** [fænˋtæstɪk] *a.* 極好的；幻想的
2. **company** [ˋkʌmpənɪ] *n.* 劇團，歌舞團
3. **applaud** [əˋplɔd] *vi.* & *vt.* 鼓掌

After Dr. Johnson finished his speech, the audience applauded loudly.
強森博士演講完畢後，觀眾報以熱烈的掌聲。

A **21**

Those who present a valid identification card will receive a five percent discount on tickets to all theater -------.

(A) performances　　(B) perform　　(C) performs　　(D) performer

凡出示有效身分證件的人皆可獲得所有戲劇表演門票九五折優惠。

> 理由

1. 空格前有抽象名詞 theater 表「戲劇」，theater 為需經由人表演的一種娛樂形式，空格內若置入動詞不符語意，故 (B) 項複數動詞 perform（表演）及 (C) 項單數動詞 performs（表演）皆不可選。
2. 空格前提及 "… a five percent discount on tickets to all theater…"（所有戲劇……門票九五折優惠），(D) 項 performer（表演者）不符語意不可選。(A) 項名詞 performances（表演）置入空格與 theater 形成語意通順的名詞片語 theater performances（戲劇表演），故應為正選。

> 重要單字片語

1. **valid** [ˋvælɪd] *a.* 有效力的
   a valid credit card　有效的信用卡

2. **identification** [aɪˌdɛntəfəˋkeʃən] *n.* 身分證明（縮寫為 ID）（不可數）
   an identification card
   身分證（= an ID card）

Chapter 03 Reading Test

Part 6 Text Completion

Questions 22-25 refer to the following review.

Millie Simons has ------- an amazing voice that her phenomenal success comes
22.
as no surprise. And last night, she put on a concert that no one who attended will soon forget. From the flawless lights and sound to the creative staging, the concert easily ------- everyone's expectations.
23.

Supported on stage by eight energetic dancers and four backup vocalists, Millie Simons performed all of her hits, and her banter with fans was like a conversation with friends. However, the biggest highlight was near the end of the show when the dancers and backup vocalists left the stage, and Ms. Simons performed the national anthem ------- her own. -------.
24.　　　　　　25.

---

22 至 25 題請看以下評論。

米莉·西蒙斯的聲音是<u>這麼</u>令人驚艷，所以她獲致超凡的成功並不意外。她昨天晚上的那場演唱會，讓來赴盛會的樂迷都難以忘懷。從完美無瑕的燈光設計和音響效果，到具創意巧思的節目安排，讓樂迷輕易地就可感到這場演唱會<u>超出</u>他們預期的好。

在舞臺上，米莉·西蒙斯被八位活力四射的舞者和四位伴唱眾星拱月著，她演唱所有她自己的暢銷歌曲，而跟臺下粉絲互動時說的玩笑話就像是在跟朋友們談天說地。不過，在演唱會進入尾聲時的壓軸好戲是舞者和伴唱離開舞臺，獨留西蒙斯<u>一人</u>在臺上唱國歌。<u>她的國歌獨唱獲得全場觀眾起立為她鼓掌。</u>

C 22

(A) very　　　　(B) so　　　　**(C) such**　　　　(D) much

理由

1. 本題測試下列固定句構：
   so + 形容詞 / 副詞 + **that** 引導的副詞子句　　如此地……以致於……
   such + 名詞 + **that** 引導的副詞子句　　如此的……以致於……

   Peter is so <u>nice</u> that we all like him.
   　　　　　形容詞
   彼得人很好，所以我們都喜歡他。

   Peter studied so <u>hard</u> that he passed the exam.
   　　　　　　　　副詞
   彼得很用功，所以通過了考試。

   Peter is such a good <u>student</u> that all the teachers like him.
   　　　　　　　　　　名詞
   彼得是非常優秀的學生，所以所有老師都很喜歡他。

2. 根據上述，原句空格後有 that 引導的副詞子句，得知空格內應置 so 或 such，但空格後有名詞詞組 an amazing voice（令人驚艷的聲音），故得知空格應置 such，故僅 (C) 項為正選。若選 (B)，應採 "so + adj. + a / an + 單數可數名詞" 句構，即 so amazing a voice。

D **23**

(A) went　　　　(B) arrived　　　　(C) disappointed　　　(D) exceeded

理由

1. 本題測試下列固定用法：
   exceed sb's expectations　　超過某人的期望（此處 expectations 恆用複數）
   = surpass sb's expectations
   The album's huge success has exceeded everyone's expectations.
   這張專輯熱賣的程度超乎所有人的預料。
2. 根據上述，(D) 項應為正選。

C **24**

(A) in　　　　(B) for　　　　(C) on　　　　(D) at

理由

1. 本題測試下列固定片語：
   on one's own　　靠自己
   From now on, you'll have to be on your own, son.
   孩子，從此以後，你得一切靠自己了。
2. 根據上述，(C) 項應為正選。

A **25**

(A) Her solo performance received a standing ovation.
(B) The audience waited patiently for the show to start.
(C) Several VIPs also took to the stage.
(D) Tickets were soon sold out before the show.

理由

1. (A) 她的國歌獨唱獲得全場觀眾起立為她鼓掌。
   (B) 觀眾耐心地等著表演開始。
   (C) 幾位貴賓也上臺來表演。
   (D) 入場券在表演前很快就賣完了。
2. 根據空格前的句子 "However, the biggest highlight was near the end of the show when the dancers and backup vocalists left the stage, and Ms. Simons performed the national anthem on her own."（不過，在演唱會進入尾聲時的壓軸好戲是舞者和伴唱離開舞臺，獨留西蒙斯一人在臺上唱國歌。），得知此時臺上只剩下一人，若是後接 Her solo performance received a standing ovation. 可形成合理的脈絡，語意得以連貫。
3. 根據上述，可知 (A) 項應為正選。

59

Chapter 03 Reading Test

重要單字片語

1. **amazing** [əˈmezɪŋ] *a.* 令人驚奇的；令人吃驚的
   It's amazing that an ant can carry objects many times heavier than itself.
   螞蟻能搬得動比自己身體重好幾倍的東西真是令人驚訝。

2. **a phenomenal success**　　驚人的成功
   phenomenal [fəˈnɑmənḷ] *a.* 了不起的；令人印象深刻的
   I am impressed with Johnny's phenomenal achievements in that field.
   強尼在那個領域的了不起成就令我印象深刻。

3. **come as no surprise**
   不足為奇；一點也不意外
   The manager's resignation came as no surprise to me, for I knew about it ages ago.
   那位經理辭職對我來說一點都不驚訝，因為我老早就知道了。

4. **put on sth**　　上演（一齣戲）
   The drama club is putting on a play at the theater.
   那個戲劇社正在劇院演出一齣戲。

5. **attend** [əˈtɛnd] *vt. & vi.* 參加
   Few attended the concert because of bad publicity.
   這場音樂會因為宣傳不好，來聽的人並不多。

6. **flawless** [ˈflɔləs] *a.* 完美的（= perfect）
   Where did you pick up your English? It's almost flawless.
   你的英語近乎完美。你是在哪兒學的？

7. **staging** [ˈstedʒɪŋ] *n.* 舞臺演出

8. **energetic** [ˌɛnɚˈdʒɛtɪk] *a.* 精力旺盛的；精力十足的
   Modern women are energetic, ambitious and, most of all, persistent in the pursuit of their goals.
   現代女性有活力、有雄心，並且有毅力追求自己的目標。

9. **backup** [ˈbækˌʌp] *a.* 陪襯的

10. **hit** [hɪt] *n.* 成功的人或物
    The album was a smash hit in the 1960s.
    這張專輯在一九六〇年代紅極一時。

11. **banter** [ˈbæntɚ] *n.*（善意的）玩笑（不可數）
    Marty enjoys exchanging banter with his colleagues.
    馬蒂喜歡跟同事開玩笑。

12. **the national anthem**　　國歌
    anthem [ˈænθəm] *n.* 聖歌；國歌
    We should stand at attention when the national anthem is played.
    演奏國歌時，我們應該立正站好。

13. **solo** [ˈsolo] *a.* 單獨的 & *n.* 獨唱；獨奏

14. **a standing ovation**　　起立鼓掌
    ovation [oˈveʃən] *n.* 鼓掌
    Lang Lang's piano solo was so impressive that he received a standing ovation.
    郎朗的鋼琴獨奏非常精彩，獲得滿堂觀眾起立為他鼓掌。

15. **disappoint** [ˌdɪsəˈpɔɪnt] *vt.* 使失望
    disappoint sb
    使某人失望（= let sb down）
    My son disappointed me when he failed the test.
    我兒子考試沒及格，令我失望。

16. **exceed** [ɪkˈsid] *vt.* 超過
    Don't exceed the speed limit when driving.
    開車時千萬不要超速。

17. **take to the stage**　　登臺表演

📖 Part 7 Reading Comprehension

Questions 26-27 refer to the following email.

From: backstage@national-theater.com
To: backstage.subscribers@national-theater.com
Subject: "The Grandest Showman" Week 1

Hi!

You are receiving this email because you subscribed to the National Theater's backstage newsletter for the forthcoming production of *The Grandest Showman*. The first week of rehearsals is complete, and the cast are having a ball learning the songs. For a sneak peek at rehearsals and interviews with some of the cast members, click here. And, if you would like early access to tickets and other exclusive features, don't forget to enroll in the National Theater's VIP Membership Scheme.

See you again next week!

Malika Idrissi
Audience Engagement Coordinator
National Theater

---

26 至 27 題請看以下電子郵件。

寄件者： backstage@national-theater.com
收件者： backstage.subscribers@national-theater.com
主　旨： 《大表演家》排練首週紀實

您好！

您有訂閱國家劇院即將推出的《大表演家》舞臺劇的幕後花絮通訊，因此會收到此電子郵件。第一週的排練已經結束，演員們非常享受學唱歌曲的過程。欲搶先一睹排練實況及部分演員的訪談內容，請點擊此處。如欲享有提早購票及其他獨家好康，別忘了加入國家劇院的貴賓會員方案。

期待下週再與您分享最新花絮！

瑪莉卡・伊德里西
觀眾互動統籌
國家劇院

Chapter 03 Reading Test

A **26**

What is indicated about *The Grandest Showman*?
(A) It has just commenced rehearsals.
(B) It will premiere next weekend.
(C) It has received rave reviews.
(D) It will contain no music.

關於《大表演家》，本文指出了什麼？
(A) 該劇剛開始進行排練。
(B) 該劇將於下週末首演。
(C) 該劇已獲得極高評價。
(D) 該劇不會包含任何音樂元素。

（理由）

根據本電郵內文第二句 "The first week of rehearsals is complete, and the cast are having a ball learning the songs."（第一週的排練已經結束，演員們非常享受學唱歌曲的過程。），得知 (A) 項應為正選。

D **27**

According to the email, how would someone buy tickets early?
(A) Line up at the box office
(B) Reply to the email
(C) Click on a link
(D) Join a special program

根據本電郵，想要提早購票的人該怎麼做？
(A) 到售票處排隊
(B) 回覆該電郵
(C) 點擊某連結
(D) 加入某特別方案

（理由）

根據本電郵內文最後一句 "And, if you would like early access to tickets and other exclusive features, don't forget to enroll in the National Theater's VIP Membership Scheme."（如欲享有提早購票及其他獨家好康，別忘了加入國家劇院的貴賓會員方案。），得知 (D) 項應為正選。

重要單字片語

1. **showman** [ˈʃoˌmən] *n.* 表演家
2. **backstage** [ˈbækˌstedʒ] *a.* 幕後的；後臺的 & *adv.* 祕密地
3. **newsletter** [ˈnjuzˌlɛtɚ] *n.*（定期寄發給特定讀者的）通訊信函
4. **forthcoming** [ˌfɔrθˈkʌmɪŋ] *a.* 即將到來的
5. **have a ball** 玩得很開心
   Jerry promised that we would have a ball going camping with him.
   傑瑞向我們保證和他去露營一定會玩得很盡興。
6. **a sneak peek** 優先預覽
   sneak [snik] *a.* 偷偷的
   peek [pik] *n.* 匆匆看

7. **access** [ˈæksɛs] *n.* 接近或使用的權利或方法（不可數）& *vt.* 使用；存取（電腦資料）
   have access to sth
   可以接近 / 取得某物
   Children in that village don't have access to computers, not to mention the internet.
   那個村子裡的孩童沒有接觸電腦的機會，更不用說上網了。
   Soldiers at the military base can access the internet for only 30 minutes per day.
   該軍事基地內的士兵每天只能上網三十分鐘。
8. **exclusive** [ɪkˈsklusɪv] *a.*（新聞、商品）獨家的，專用的 & *n.* 獨家新聞

9. **scheme** [skim] *n.* 方案，計畫（英式英語）；詭計 & *vt.* & *vi.* 策劃，密謀
   scheme to + V　密謀要做……
   The company has been scheming to steal our market share.
   那家公司密謀搶走我們的市占率。

10. **coordinator** [ko'ɔrdn̩ˌetɚ] *n.* 協調者，統籌者

11. **commence** [kə'mɛns] *vt.* & *vi.* 開始
    commence + N/V-ing　開始……
    The city government will soon commence tearing down the old apartment building.
    市政府很快就會開始拆除這棟舊公寓大樓。

12. **rave** [rev] *a.* 大力稱讚的

Questions 28-31 refer to the following online chat discussion.

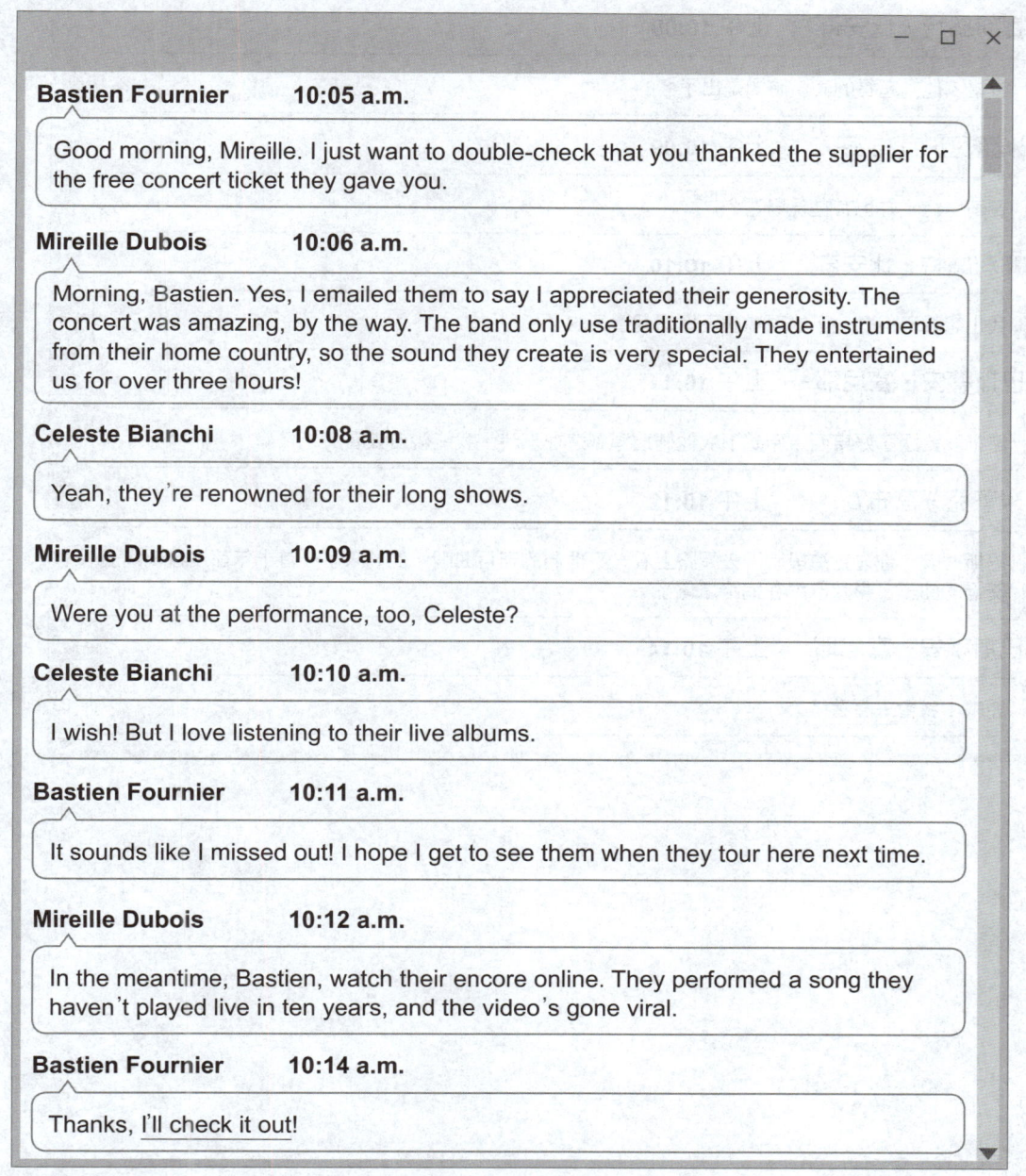

Bastien Fournier　　　10:05 a.m.

Good morning, Mireille. I just want to double-check that you thanked the supplier for the free concert ticket they gave you.

Mireille Dubois　　　10:06 a.m.

Morning, Bastien. Yes, I emailed them to say I appreciated their generosity. The concert was amazing, by the way. The band only use traditionally made instruments from their home country, so the sound they create is very special. They entertained us for over three hours!

Celeste Bianchi　　　10:08 a.m.

Yeah, they're renowned for their long shows.

Mireille Dubois　　　10:09 a.m.

Were you at the performance, too, Celeste?

Celeste Bianchi　　　10:10 a.m.

I wish! But I love listening to their live albums.

Bastien Fournier　　　10:11 a.m.

It sounds like I missed out! I hope I get to see them when they tour here next time.

Mireille Dubois　　　10:12 a.m.

In the meantime, Bastien, watch their encore online. They performed a song they haven't played live in ten years, and the video's gone viral.

Bastien Fournier　　　10:14 a.m.

Thanks, I'll check it out!

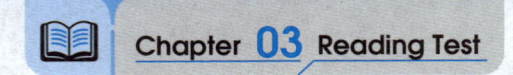

Chapter 03 Reading Test

28 至 31 題請看以下線上聊天內容。

巴斯蒂安・富尼耶　　上午 **10:05**

早,米蕾兒。我想再次確認妳有沒有對供應商送妳一張免費音樂會門票表達謝意。

米蕾兒・莒布瓦　　上午 **10:06**

早,巴斯蒂安。我有寄電郵去感謝他們這麼慷慨。順便告訴你,音樂會真讚!樂團只用了他們本國傳統工藝所製作的樂器,而其音色相當獨特。他們足足演奏了三個多小時呢!

賽莉絲特・比安奇　　上午 **10:08**

沒錯,他們超長的表演時間是出了名的。

米蕾兒・莒布瓦　　上午 **10:09**

賽莉絲特,妳也有在現場嗎?

賽莉絲特・比安奇　　上午 **10:10**

我也想啊!但聽他們的現場演奏專輯就蠻爽的了。

巴斯蒂安・富尼耶　　上午 **10:11**

看來我錯過了好東西!希望下次他們巡迴到這裡來時,我能親自去看。

米蕾兒・莒布瓦　　上午 **10:12**

巴斯蒂安,你先趁這段時間去網路上看一下他們的安可曲吧。他們來了一首十年都沒在現場演奏過的曲子,影片已經在網路瘋傳了。

巴斯蒂安・富尼耶　　上午 **10:14**

謝啦!我會去看看!

64

C **28**

Who gave Ms. Dubois the concert ticket?
(A) Her manager
(B) Her best friend
(C) A supplier
(D) A colleague

誰贈送音樂會門票給莒布瓦小姐？
(A) 她的經理
(B) 她的閨密
(C) 某供應商
(D) 某位同事

> 理由
>
> 巴斯蒂安・富尼耶於上午 10:05 表示 "I just want to double-check that you thanked the supplier for the free concert ticket they gave you."（我想再次確認妳有沒有對供應商送妳一張免費音樂會門票表達謝意。），故 (C) 項應為正選。

B **29**

What is suggested about the band?
(A) They never perform abroad.
(B) They play unique instruments.
(C) They formed three years ago.
(D) They typically play short concerts.

關於這個樂團，本文暗示了什麼？
(A) 他們從不出國演出。
(B) 他們演奏獨特的樂器。
(C) 他們是在三年前成立的。
(D) 他們的音樂會演出時間通常很短。

> 理由
>
> 莒布瓦小姐於上午 10:06 表示 "The band only use traditionally made instruments from their home country, so the sound they create is very special."（樂團只用了他們本國傳統工藝所製作的樂器，而其音色相當獨特。），故 (B) 項應為正選。

D **30**

What does Ms. Bianchi tell Ms. Dubois?
(A) She has no interest in the band.
(B) She has seen the band live before.
(C) She wishes the shows could be longer.
(D) She wishes she could have gone to the concert.

比安奇小姐對莒布瓦小姐說了什麼？
(A) 她對這個樂團不感興趣。
(B) 她以前看過這個樂團的現場表演。
(C) 她希望音樂會的時間能再長一些。
(D) 她真希望自己能夠去聽這場音樂會。

> 理由
>
> 比安奇小姐於上午 10:10 表示 "I wish!"（我也想啊！），推知她未能親臨音樂會現場。(D) 項使用「主詞 + wish (that) 主詞 + could + 原形動詞」（……希望／但願……）的假設語氣句型，表示不可能實現的願望，與上述內文語意相符，故 (D) 項應為正選。

Chapter 03　Reading Test

C **31**

At 10:14 a.m., what does Mr. Fournier most likely mean when he writes, "I'll check it out"?
(A) He will listen to a band's new album.
(B) He will read Ms. Dubois' email.
(C) He will watch a video on the internet.
(D) He will edit Ms. Dubois' report.

富尼耶先生於上午 10:14 表示「我會去看看」時，最有可能是什麼意思？
(A) 他會聽某樂團的新專輯。
(B) 他會讀莒布瓦小姐的電郵。
(C) 他會在網路上觀看一段影片。
(D) 他會校訂莒布瓦女士的報告。

理由

根據上午 10:14，富尼耶先生表示 "I'll check it out!"（我會去看看！）時，意思是說他會上網去看看莒布瓦小姐於上午 10:12 時推薦他看的一段已在網路上瘋傳的影片，故 (C) 項應為正選。

重要單字片語

1. **double-check** [ˌdʌbļˈtʃɛk] *vt.* 複查，複核
   The mechanic double-checked the car's engine to ensure that it was functioning properly.
   修車師傅再次檢查了汽車的引擎，以確保它運作正常。

2. **supplier** [səˈplaɪɚ] *n.* 供應商，供給者

3. **generosity** [ˌdʒɛnəˈrɑsətɪ] *n.* 慷慨，大方

4. **meantime** [ˈminˌtaɪm] *n.* 期間 & *adv.* 在此期間
   in the meantime　　同時；在此期間
   = in the meanwhile
   Mom will be back in an hour. In the meantime, let's prepare dinner.
   媽媽一小時後就會回來，這段時間我們來準備晚餐吧。

5. **colleague** [ˈkɑlig] *n.* 同事

Chapter 04 Listening Test

Part 1 Photographs

C **1** 🔊 089 🇬🇧
(A) She's removing her handbag.
(B) She's inserting a credit card.
(C) She's withdrawing some money.
(D) She's touching the keypad.

> (A) 她正在拿開她的手提包。
> (B) 她正在插入信用卡。
> (C) 她正在提領現金。
> (D) 她正在觸碰鍵盤。

重要單字片語

1. **insert** [ɪnˈsɝt] *vt.* 插入,放進
   Henry's manager inserted a new clause into his contract.
   亨利的經理在合約中加了一項新條款。

2. **keypad** [ˈkiˌpæd] *n.* 鍵盤

D **2** 🔊 090 🇺🇸
(A) The woman is fixing a computer.
(B) The woman is typing some data on the laptop.
(C) The woman is signing a document.
(D) The woman is examining some statistics.

> (A) 女子在修電腦。
> (B) 女子在筆電上打資料。
> (C) 女子在簽署文件。
> (D) 女子在檢查統計數字。

重要單字片語

1. **laptop** [ˈlæpˌtɑp] *n.* 筆電,筆記型電腦
2. **document** [ˈdɑkjəmənt] *n.*(書面或電腦)文件 & [ˈdɑkjəˌmɛnt] *vt.* 記錄

The TV show documents the process of making a traditional glove puppet.
這個電視節目記錄了傳統布袋戲偶的製作過程。

Chapter 04 Listening Test

Part 2 Question-Response

B 3 092

When will you file your income taxes?
(A) At the duty-free shop.
(B) By April 15.
(C) Form 1040.

你什麼時候會申報所得稅？
(A) 在免稅店。
(B) 四月十五日前。
(C) 1040 申報表。

重要單字片語

1. **file** [faɪl] *vt.* 申報
   file taxes　報稅
   Remember to file your taxes or you'll be fined.
   切記要報稅，否則會被罰錢。

2. **duty-free** [ˌdutɪˋfri] *a.* 免稅的
   duty-free shop　免稅店

B 4 093

Did you hear that Lola's company filed for bankruptcy?
(A) No, I deleted that file.
(B) Yes, it's very sad news.
(C) Yes, the bank is closed.

你有聽說蘿拉的公司提出破產申請了嗎？
(A) 沒有，我刪除了那個檔案。
(B) 有，好慘喔。
(C) 對，銀行關門了。

重要單字片語

1. **file for bankruptcy / divorce**
   提出破產申請 / 訴請離婚
   To Matt's disappointment, his wife still decided to file for divorce.
   令麥特失望的是，他太太仍決定訴請離婚。

2. **delete** [dɪˋlit] *vt.* 刪除，刪去（文字、檔案等）
   Tommy accidentally deleted the folder that contained many important files.
   湯米不小心刪除了那個存有許多重要檔案的資料夾。

Part 3 Conversations

Questions 5 through 7 refer to the following conversation. 095　M:　W:

M: I'm getting so little interest from my savings account that I went to see an investment broker today.
W: Yeah. With interest rates so low, it's hard to get a good return. What did the broker tell you?
M: It's all about risk. The higher the return, the higher the risk. I have a conservative attitude toward investments, so the broker advised me to diversify my portfolio. Now, I'm putting half into secured bonds and the other half into stocks. That way, I'm sure to come out ahead.
W: That sounds like a sensible strategy.

68

5 至 7 題請聽以下會話。

男：我銀行的儲蓄存款利息實在太少了，所以我今天去見了一位投資經紀人。
女：對呀。銀行的存款利率這麼低，當然就很難有好的利息收入。那位經紀人對你說了什麼？
男：都是說些跟風險有關的事。報酬越高，風險就越高。我對投資向來態度保守，所以那位經紀人建議我分散投資。現在，我把一半的錢投資公司債券，另一半則投資股票。這麼一來，我一定穩賺。
女：聽起來似乎是明智的策略。

D 5 096

What are the speakers mainly discussing?
(A) Broker fees
(B) Inflation
(C) Interest rates
(D) Investment strategies

這兩位說話者主要是在討論什麼事？
(A) 經紀費
(B) 通貨膨漲
(C) 利率
(D) 投資策略

D 6 097

What did the broker suggest the man do?
(A) Save more money
(B) Find another broker
(C) Sell his stocks and bonds
(D) Vary his investments

投資經紀人建議這名男子做什麼事？
(A) 再多存些錢
(B) 找別的經紀人
(C) 把股票和債券賣掉
(D) 做多元化投資

C 7 098

What does the woman imply about the new strategy?
(A) It will probably save time.
(B) It will probably have more risk.
(C) It will probably be profitable.
(D) It will probably reduce the service fees.

女子對此新策略有何暗示？
(A) 它可能可以節省時間。
(B) 它的風險可能會比較高。
(C) 它可能賺得到錢。
(D) 它可能節省服務費。

重要單字片語

1. **savings** [ˈsevɪŋz] *n.* 存款（恆為複數）
   open a savings account
   開儲蓄存款帳戶
   open a checking account
   開活期存款帳戶

2. **investment** [ɪnˈvɛstmənt] *n.* 投資
   make an investment in... 投資……
   I think you need a financial adviser to help you plan your investments.
   我想你需要一位理財顧問來幫你規劃你的投資。

3. **broker** [ˈbrokɚ] *n.* 經紀人；掮客
   As a stock broker, Johnny spends lots of time analyzing the stock market.
   身為股票營業員，強尼花很多時間分析股市。

4. **The + 比較級, the + 比較級**
   越……，就越……
   The more you think about it, the more depressed you will become.
   你越想這事就會越沮喪。

69

Chapter 04 Listening Test

5. **conservative** [kənˈsɝvətɪv] *a.* 保守的 & *n.* 保守派人士
Diana has a very conservative attitude towards marriage.
戴安娜對於婚姻的態度非常保守。

6. **attitude** [ˈætəˌtud] *n.* 態度（與 toward / towards 並用）
Jack has a positive attitude toward life.
傑克對人生抱持積極的態度。

7. **diversify** [dəˈvɝsəˌfaɪ / daɪˈvɝsəˌfaɪ] *vt. & vi.*（使……）多樣化 & *vi.* 進行多種投資

8. **portfolio** [pɔrtˈfoliˌo] *n.* 投資組合；有價證券組合
an investment portfolio　　投資組合

9. **secured bonds**　　有擔保品的公司債券

10. **sensible** [ˈsɛnsəbl̩] *a.* 明智的；理智的
That's a sensible approach to the problem.
那是一個解決問題的明智辦法。

11. **strategy** [ˈstrætədʒɪ] *n.* 策略
a promotional strategy　　促銷策略
We're working on new strategies to improve our share of the market.
我們正致力於新的策略以期能增進市占率。

Questions 8 through 10 refer to the following conversation with three speakers. 🔊 099
M:　　　W1:　　　W2:

M: Next on the agenda is last quarter's revenue. Indira, can you analyze the revenue from magazine sales and online subscriptions?
W1: Our total revenue was stable compared to the previous quarter. Given the problems we had with the new billing system, I think that can be regarded as a good result.
M: OK, thank you. Now, Alyssa, regarding the new Apple Mac computers for the graphics department, have they been recorded as fixed assets?
W2: Yes, they were a major expense and they'll be used long-term, so that's how they've been recorded.
M: Great, thanks. As far as liabilities go, Alyssa, I'll pick up that important issue with you in tomorrow's meeting. Thank you, everyone.

8 至 10 題請聽以下三人的會話。

男：接下來的議題是剛過去那一季的營收狀況。英蒂拉，妳可以分析一下我們的雜誌銷售加線上訂閱的營收狀況嗎？
甲女：與再前一季相比，總營收算是持平。考慮到我們新的收費系統有出問題，我覺得這樣的結果還算不錯。
男：好，謝謝。接下來，我要問艾莉莎：圖像設計部新買的蘋果麥金塔電腦，它們有被列認固定資產嗎？
乙女：有，它們屬於重大開支，而且使用期限長，所以已列認固定資產。
男：好，謝謝。至於負債部分，艾莉莎，我會在明天的會議上跟妳討論這個重要議題。謝謝大家。

D 8 🔊100 🇨🇦

What does Indira point out about the company's revenue?
(A) It has gone down sharply.
(B) It has increased significantly.
(C) It has not been analyzed.
(D) It has not changed.

英蒂拉對於公司營收狀況有何說法？
(A) 營收大幅下滑。
(B) 營收顯著成長。
(C) 營收還沒有被分析。
(D) 營收維持不變。

C 9 🔊101 🇨🇦

What has Alyssa noted down as fixed assets?
(A) Billing systems
(B) New printing presses
(C) Brand-new computers
(D) Book-binding machines

艾莉莎把什麼東西列認為固定資產？
(A) 收費系統
(B) 新的印刷機
(C) 全新的電腦
(D) 書本裝訂機

CH 04

B 10 🔊102 🇨🇦

What does the man say he will do tomorrow?
(A) Allocate resources to a department
(B) Talk about another subject
(C) Collect a package from a depot
(D) Read the latest magazine issue

男子說他明天會做什麼事情？
(A) 將資源分配給某個部門
(B) 討論另一個主題
(C) 從倉庫領取包裹
(D) 看最新一期的雜誌

重要單字片語

1. **agenda** [əˋdʒɛndə] *n.* 議程；工作事項
   on the agenda　　在議程 / 工作事項內
2. **subscription** [səbˋskrɪpʃən] *n.* 訂閱費；訂閱
   a subscription to sth　　訂閱某（刊）物
3. **given** [ˋgɪvən] *prep.* 考慮到，鑑於
   Given Emma's financial difficulties, the landlord did not increase her rent.
   考慮到艾瑪的經濟困窘，房東沒有漲她的房租。
4. **a billing system**　　收費系統
5. **graphics** [ˋgræfɪks] *n.* 圖像

6. **As far as sth goes, S + V**
   至於某事 / 就某事而言，……
   = As far as sth is concerned, S + V
   As far as hobbies go, Mike has something in common with his elder brother.
   在愛好方面，麥克和他的哥哥有些共同點。
7. **liability** [ˏlaɪəˋbɪlətɪ] *n.* 債務，負債（恆用複數）；（法律上的）責任，義務
8. **pick up sth / pick sth up**　　繼續……
   Let's pick up this conversation after my meeting.
   等我的會議結束後我們再來繼續談。
9. **brand-new** [ˏbrændˋnju] *a.* 全新的

71

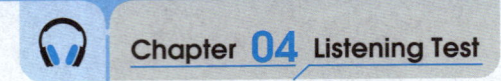

Chapter 04 Listening Test

10. **allocate** [ˈæləˌket] *vt.* 配給，分配；撥出（經費）
    allocate sth to... 將某物分配給……
    You shouldn't allocate the same amount of time to every question on the test.
    你在考試時不應該在每一道題目上分配相同的作答時間。

11. **depot** [ˈdipo / ˈdɛpo] *n.* 倉庫

Part 4 Talks

Questions 11 through 13 refer to the following excerpt from a meeting. 🔊 104

I'd like to talk about our financial goals for the coming year. As you are no doubt aware, for the second year in a row, we have struggled to remain profitable. Sales have been lower than expected, while at the same time, our tax bill has been higher than expected. To address the situation, I suggest we put all our efforts into advertising on social media. To get the ball rolling, this is what I'd like each of you to do. Find out which of our competitors advertise online and how much they are spending. I've sent you an e-mail outlining how to calculate a ballpark figure using an attached worksheet.

11 至 13 題請聽以下會議摘錄。

> 我想要討論我們明年財務上的目標。諸位肯定意識到，本公司已經連續第二年難以保持獲利。銷售量比預期差，同時，我們的稅單比預期高。為了解決該問題，我建議咱們將精力投入社群媒體上的廣告宣傳。一開始的動作就是，我想要諸位著手執行下列事項。了解我們的哪些競爭對手有在網路上宣傳，以及他們花費多少成本。我已經寄電子郵件給諸位，概述如何利用一份附件的計算表計算出粗略的數據。

C 11 🔊 105

What does the speaker want to focus on this year?
(A) Minimizing tax
(B) Reducing overheads
(C) Marketing online
(D) Purchasing equipment

說話者今年想關注什麼？
(A) 將稅賦減少到最少量
(B) 減少營運費用
(C) 網路行銷
(D) 採購器材

B 12 🔊 106

What does the speaker request help with?
(A) Producing a business plan
(B) Researching rivals
(C) Preparing a presentation
(D) Solving an accounting problem

說話者請求什麼方面的協助？
(A) 產出一份商業計畫
(B) 調查競爭對手
(C) 準備報告
(D) 解決會計上的問題

D **13** 🔊 107 🇺🇸

What will the listeners receive by e-mail?
(A) A budget
(B) An application form
(C) An invoice
(D) A spreadsheet

聽眾會透過電子郵件收到什麼？
(A) 預算案
(B) 申請表
(C) 發貨單
(D) 電子計算表

🔍 重要單字片語

1. **financial** [faɪˈnænʃəl] *a.* 財務的
2. **no doubt**　肯定；無庸置疑，毫無疑問
   （= doubtlessly = without doubt）
   This issue will no doubt be discussed at the next meeting.
   該問題毫無疑問會在下次會議上討論。
3. **in a row**　連續地
   John has been absent from work for three days in a row.
   約翰已經連續三天沒來上班了。
4. **struggle** [ˈstrʌɡl̩] *vi.* 掙扎；奮鬥
   After struggling for a few years, the restaurant finally closed down.
   經過幾年的艱困經營後，那間餐廳最後倒閉了。
5. **address** [əˈdrɛs] *vt.* 處理
   address an issue / a problem
   處理某問題（= deal with an issue / a problem）

6. **effort** [ˈɛfɚt] *n.* 努力；力氣
   put one's efforts into...　努力做……
   Kevin and his team put all their efforts into the new project.
   凱文與他的團隊投入所有精力進行新的計畫。
7. **get the ball rolling**　開始某事
   Let's get the ball rolling on this project by contacting the suppliers.
   咱們來從聯繫供應商開始進行這項計畫。
8. **outline** [ˈaʊtˌlaɪn] *vt.* 概述 & *n.* 大綱
   Brad outlined his proposal to his superiors.
   布萊德向他的上級概述他的提案。
9. **ballpark** [ˈbɔlpark] *a.* 大致正確的 & *n.* 棒球場
   a ballpark figure / estimate
   大致的數據 / 估計
10. **rival** [ˈraɪvl̩] *n.* 競爭者，對手

Questions 14 through 16 refer to the following announcement and schedule.　🔊 108
🇬🇧

Good morning, ladies and gentlemen, and welcome to the Northern Region Economic Forum. I'd like to begin by thanking the Northern Trade & Innovation Council for kindly sponsoring this event. Topics today will range from reforming tax systems to reducing the deficit. The most hotly anticipated speech, though, is about how to control the scourge of modern times: inflation. We expect the main hall to be packed for that one! Please remember that free refreshments are available throughout the day in the minor hall. Just show your badge to get into that room. Thank you, and enjoy!

Chapter 04 Listening Test

Northern Region Economic Forum	
Speaker	**Topic**
Ilya Morozov	Cutting the deficit
Kenji Takahashi	How to curb inflation
Sofia Márquez	Investment opportunities
Leila Farouk	Tax system reforms

14 至 16 題請聽以下宣布事項，並請看以下時間表。

各位女士先生早安，歡迎蒞臨北區經濟論壇。首先我要感謝北方貿易與創新委員會熱情贊助本次活動。今天的主題範圍包括稅制改革與減少財政赤字等多種議題。不過最令人期待的演講將會是如何抑制現代經濟的毒瘤，也就是通膨。我們預計大演講廳一定會爆滿！別忘了：小演講廳將全天供應免費茶點。只需出示您的識別證即可入場。謝謝，祝您有愉快的一天！

北區經濟論壇	
演講者	主題
伊利亞・莫羅佐夫	減少財政赤字
高橋健司	如何抑制通貨膨脹
蘇菲亞・馬爾克斯	投資時機
萊拉・法魯克	稅制改革

B **14** 🔊 109 🇨🇦

How does the speaker start the announcement?
(A) By outlining the order of speeches
(B) By offering his gratitude to a sponsor
(C) By introducing a keynote speaker
(D) By mentioning some security concerns

說話者在宣布事項的開頭說了什麼事？
(A) 簡介演講的排序
(B) 向贊助者表達感謝
(C) 介紹某位主題演講人
(D) 提出保安上的顧慮

B **15** 🔊 110 🇨🇦

Look at the schedule. Whose speech is most eagerly awaited?
(A) Ilya Morozov
(B) Kenji Takahashi
(C) Sofia Márquez
(D) Leila Farouk

請看時間表，哪位演講者的演說最受熱烈期待？
(A) 伊利亞・莫羅佐夫
(B) 高橋健司
(C) 蘇菲亞・馬爾克斯
(D) 萊拉・法魯克

Chapter 04 Reading Test

D **16** 🔊 111 🇨🇦

What does the speaker remind the listeners?
(A) That IDs must be worn at all times
(B) That the minor hall is not accessible
(C) That lunch will be served at 1:00 p.m.
(D) That free food and drink is available

說話者提醒聽眾什麼事？
(A) 必須隨時佩戴識別證
(B) 小演講廳不開放
(C) 午餐供應時間為下午一點
(D) 有免費食物與飲料

🔍 重要單字片語

1. **forum** [ˈfɔrəm] *n.* 論壇
2. **council** [ˈkaʊnsḷ] *n.* 委員會；議會
3. **sponsor** [ˈspɑnsɚ] *vt.* 資助，贊助 & *n.* 贊助商
   The company regularly sponsors charity events for the elderly of this community.
   公司經常贊助為本社區長者所舉辦的慈善活動。
4. **reform** [rɪˈfɔrm] *vt.* & *n.* 改革
   The new president has promised to reform the justice system.
   新上任的總統承諾改革司法制度。
5. **anticipated** [ænˈtɪsəˌpetɪd] *a.* 令人期待的
6. **scourge** [skɝdʒ] *n.* 苦難的根源；禍害
7. **refreshments** [rɪˈfrɛʃmənts] *n.*（會議或宴會時所供應的）茶點（恆用複數）
8. **badge** [bædʒ] *n.* 識別證，名牌；徽章
9. **curb** [kɝb] *vt.* 抑制 & *n.* 造成人行道與馬路間高度落差的緣石
   Jason successfully curbed his desire to drink alcohol.
   傑森成功抑制了他想喝酒的慾望。
10. **gratitude** [ˈɡrætəˌt(j)ud] *n.* 感激
11. **keynote** [ˈkiˌnot] *n.*（書、演說等的）要旨；主題
    a keynote speaker　主題演講人

📖 Part 5　Incomplete Sentences

B **17**

If you have a single source of income independent of interest or -------, you can fill out form W2EZ.

(A) divide　　　　　(B) dividends　　　(C) divided　　　　(D) divine

如果你僅有一個收入來源，且這份收入來源與利息或股息無關，便可填寫 W2EZ 表格。

理由

1. 空格前有名詞 interest（利息）及對等連接詞 or，得知空格應置與「利息」對等的名詞。
   選項中：

   (A) **divide** [dəˈvaɪd] *vt.* & *vi.*（使）分割 & *vi.* 分隔
       divide sth into...　　把某物分成……
       Mom divided the birthday cake into six equal pieces.
       媽媽把生日蛋糕分成六等份。

75

Chapter 04 Reading Test

(B) **dividend** [ˈdɪvəˌdɛnd] *n.* 股息
The company paid its shareholders a handsome dividend last year.
公司去年發給股東一筆可觀的股息。
＊ shareholder [ˈʃɛrˌholdɚ] *n.* 股東

(C) **divided** [dɪˈvaɪdɪd] *a.* 分歧的（與介詞 on / over 並用）
The team is divided over how to solve the problem of declining sales.
團隊對於如何解決銷量下滑的問題意見分歧。

(D) **divine** [dəˈvaɪn / dɪˈvaɪn] *a.* 神聖的，天堂般的
Maggie believed that some divine power had helped her survive the plane crash.
瑪姬相信有某種神祕的力量讓她在空難中生還。

2. 根據上述，(B) 項應為正選。

重要單字片語

1. **income** [ˈɪnkʌm] *n.* 收入
a source of income　　收入來源
What is their main source of income?
他們主要的收入來源是什麼？

2. **be independent of...**
獨立於…… / 與……不相關
The judiciary should be independent of the executive branch.
執法機關應獨立於行政系統之外。
＊ judiciary [dʒuˈdɪʃɪˌɛrɪ] *n.* 司法系統

D __18__
You are able to ------- money from your personal savings account using an ATM.
(A) deduct　　　　(B) fluctuate　　　(C) benefit　　　(D) withdraw
您可以去自動提款機從您的個人儲蓄帳戶當中提款。

理由

1. (A) **deduct** [dɪˈdʌkt] *vt.* 減去，扣除
deduct A from B　　從 B 中扣除 A
If you deduct expenses from your gross profit, the result is your net profit.
毛利扣除支出後的結果就是淨利。

(B) **fluctuate** [ˈflʌktʃuˌet] *vi.* 波動，震盪
The prices of fruits and vegetables often fluctuate due to extreme weather.
水果和蔬菜的價格經常受到極端天氣的影響而波動。

(C) **benefit** [ˈbɛnəfɪt] *vt.* 有益於 & *vi.* 獲益 & *n.* 利益
The government's new policy will significantly benefit low-income families.
政府的新政策將大大嘉惠低收入戶。

(D) **withdraw** [wɪðˈdrɔ] *vt.* 提（款）（三態為：withdraw, withdrew [wɪðˈdru], withdrawn [wɪðˈdrɔn]）
Linda withdrew $1,000 from her bank account to pay the rent.
琳達從銀行帳戶提領一千美元來付租金。

2. 根據語意，(D) 項應為正選。

> 重要單字片語

1. **a savings account** 儲蓄存款帳戶
2. **ATM** 自動櫃員機（為 automated teller machine 的縮寫）

D **19**

Please ask the accounting department to chase up the ------- payment from AlphaSource Industries.

(A) economic　　(B) wealthy　　(C) risky　　(D) outstanding

麻煩叫會計部門催促 AlphaSource 工業公司支付拖欠的款項。

> 理由

1. (A) **economic** [ˌikəˈnɑmɪk] *a.* 經濟上的，與經濟有關的
    The company didn't survive the global economic crisis and went bankrupt.
    該公司沒挺過全球經濟危機，破產了。
   (B) **wealthy** [ˈwɛlθɪ] *a.* 富有的
    The wealthy businessman has a mansion and two sports cars.
    那位富商擁有一棟豪宅和兩輛跑車。
   (C) **risky** [ˈrɪskɪ] *a.* 危險的，有風險的
    Walking alone through that part of town at night is very risky.
    城裡的那一區，如果晚上一個人走是相當危險的。
   (D) **outstanding** [autˈstændɪŋ] *a.* 未支付的；傑出的
    The restaurant still has over NT$1 million in outstanding debts.
    這家餐廳仍有新臺幣一百多萬元的未清償負債。

2. 根據語意，(D) 項應為正選。

> 重要單字片語

1. **accounting** [əˈkauntɪŋ] *n.* 會計（學）（不可數）
2. **chase up... / chase... up** 催促……

I need to chase up Tom about his section of the report.
我得追著湯姆要他負責的那一部分報告。

A **20**

Mr. Kwarteng advised Ms. Scott on the best investment ------- in which to place her money.

(A) funds　　(B) installments　　(C) hazards　　(D) transactions

夸滕先生向史考特小姐推薦了最適合她投資的基金。

> 理由

1. (A) **fund** [fʌnd] *n.* 基金；資金（複數）
    an investment fund　投資性基金
    The company contributed US$5,000 to the fund for the disaster victims.
    這家公司捐助了五千美元給災民救難基金。

(B) **installment** [ɪnˈstɔlmənt] *n.* 分期付款
by / in installments　　以分期付款方式
The car dealer allowed me to pay for the car in monthly installments.
車商讓我以月付方式買這輛車。

(C) **hazard** [ˈhæzɚd] *n.* 危險，隱憂
a health / safety hazard　　健康 / 安全隱憂
All drivers must be aware of the safety hazards of speeding.
所有駕駛人都該意識到超速駕駛產生的安全隱憂。

(D) **transaction** [trænˈzækʃən] *n.* 交易，買賣
Some people are worried about the safety of internet transactions.
有些人對網路交易的安全性感到擔憂。

2. 根據語意，(A) 項應為正選。

> 🔍 **重要單字片語**
>
> **advise** [ədˈvaɪz] *vt.* 建議；勸告
> advise sb on sth　　就某事向某人建議
> The consultant advised Kevin on some financial issues.
> 顧問為凱文提供了一些財務方面的建議。

B 21

The national cost-of-living index increased only 1.5% last year, ------- that inflation is now within an acceptable range.

(A) shows　　　　　　(B) showing　　　　　(C) to show　　　　(D) will show

去年全國生活成本指數只升高 1.5%，顯示通膨目前是在可接受範圍之內。

> 理由

1. 本題測驗非限定形容詞子句簡化為分詞片語的用法，原句實為：
The national cost-of-living index increased only 1.5% last year, <u>which shows</u> that inflation is now within an acceptable range.
上句中關係代名詞 which 為非限定形容詞子句 which shows that... 的主詞，代替作為先行詞的子句 The national cost-of-living index increased... 來引導該形容詞子句。劃線部分可簡化為分詞片語，即先刪除作主詞的關係代名詞 which，之後的動詞 shows 改為表主動的現在分詞 showing，即得原句。

2. 根據上述，(B) 項應為正選。

> 🔍 **重要單字片語**
>
> **acceptable** [əkˈsɛptəbl] *a.* 可接受的

📖 Part 6　Text Completion

Questions 22-25 refer to the following memo.

From:　　Head of Finance
To:　　　All Heads of Department
Subject: Next Year's Budget

For internal distribution only.

As you are aware, the country is experiencing economic challenges. Many businesses are struggling, and we are not immune to these difficulties. We have ------- decided to freeze departmental budgets for the next financial year. Despite this, departments will still be expected to ------- their operational commitments. Please submit proposals outlining how you intend to fund these commitments and if you plan to make cuts. -------. Late submissions may ------- a penalty. For any queries, please contact me or any senior manager on the finance team.

---

22 至 25 題請看以下備忘錄。

寄件者：財務長
收件者：所有部門主管
主　旨：明年度預算

僅供內部閱覽。

你們都知道國內經濟正經歷嚴苛的考驗。許多企業都風雨飄搖，本公司也未能倖免。<u>因此</u>，公司已決定要凍結各部門下一會計年度的預算。儘管如此，公司仍期待各部門<u>達成</u>既定的工作目標。請各位提出建議書，概述資金將如何運用在這些目標上，以及是否有削減開支的計畫。<u>建議書須於下星期的週末前交過來</u>。遲交可能會<u>導致</u>受罰。如有任何疑問，請與我或任何一位財務團隊的資深經理人聯繫。

C **22**

(A) moreover　　(B) although　　**(C) therefore**　　(D) even though

理由

1. 空格前有主詞 We 與完成式助動詞 have，空格後有動詞 decide（決定）的過去分詞 decided，得知本句的句型為現在完成式，空格應置副詞來修飾 decided。

79

Chapter 04 Reading Test

2. 選項中：

(A) **moreover** [mɔrˋovɚ] *adv.* 並且，此外
Kelly has decided to buy the scooter because it is affordable. Moreover, she loves its appearance.
凱莉決定要買那輛機車，因為價格她負擔得起。此外，她也喜愛它的外型。

(B) **although** [ɔlˋðo] *conj.* 雖然，儘管（= though）
Although Paul exercises a lot, he doesn't lose much weight.
雖然保羅經常運動，但他的體重並沒有減輕太多。

(C) **therefore** [ˋðɛr͵for] *adv.* 因此
Vincent had a tight budget; therefore, he could only afford a second-hand car.
文森的預算吃緊，因此他只買得起二手車。

(D) **even though** 雖然，儘管（視作連接詞）
Even though Laura did her best, she didn't pass the test.
儘管蘿拉全力以赴，她還是沒通過測驗。

3. (B)、(D) 項為連接詞均不可選。根據上下文及語意，得知 (C) 項應為正選。

A **23**

(A) meet   (B) fail   (C) live   (D) catch

理由

1. (A) **meet** [mit] *vt.* 符合，達到（條件、要求等）
Only by working hard can you meet your goals.
你唯有努力才能達成自己的目標。

(B) **fail** [fel] *vt. & vi.*（使）不及格 & *vi.* 失敗
If you don't study, you will surely fail the test.
你若不讀書，肯定會考不及格。

(C) **live** [lɪv] *vt.* 過著……的生活
live a(n) + adj. + life   過著……的生活
The old man lived a quiet life in the mountains.
那位老翁住在山上，過著平靜的生活。

(D) **catch** [kætʃ] *vt.* 吸引；抓住
catch one's eye   引起某人注意
The new smartphone really caught Owen's eye.
這款新智慧型手機著實吸引了歐文的目光。

2. 根據語意，(A) 項應為正選。

C **24**

(A) I went through the documents myself last night.
(B) We sincerely hope that next year is more profitable.
(C) These proposals are due by the end of next week.
(D) Many other countries are in a similar situation.

> 理由

1. (A) 昨晚我親自看過了這些文件。
   (B) 我們衷心盼望明年的獲利會更好。
   (C) 建議書須於下星期的週末前交過來。
   (D) 許多其他國家處在類似的狀況。
2. 空格前的句子 "Please submit proposals outlining how you intend to fund these commitments and if you plan to make cuts."（請各位提出建議書，概述資金將如何運用在這些目標上，以及是否有削減開支的計畫。）提及各部門主管要繳交關於資金運用的建議書，且空格後的句子提及 "Late submissions may..."（遲交……），選項 (C) 提到該建議書繳交的期限，置入空格後語意連貫，故應為正選。

B **25**

(A) agree with　　(B) result in　　(C) give up　　(D) glance at

> 理由

1. (A) **agree with...**　與……一致／相符
   Jeremy's description of the incident does not agree with mine.
   傑瑞米對該起事件的描述與我的描述不一致。

   (B) **result in...**　導致……
   = lead to...
   The earthquake resulted in the deaths of hundreds of people.
   這場地震導致數百人死亡。

   (C) **give up...**　放棄……
   No matter what you do, never give up hope, and you'll succeed.
   不論你做什麼，千萬別放棄希望，這樣你就會成功。

   (D) **glance at...**　匆匆一瞥……
   The shy girl didn't even dare glance at the boys at the party.
   在派對上，那個害羞的女生甚至不敢正眼瞧那些男生。

2. 根據語意，(B) 項應為正選。

重要單字片語

1. **memo** [ˋmɛmo] *n.* 備忘錄（為 memorandum [͵mɛməˋrændəm] 的縮寫）
2. **distribution** [͵dɪstrəˋbjuʃən] *n.* 散發；分配；分布
3. **immune** [ɪˋmjun] *a.* 不受影響的；免疫的
   be immune to...
   不受……的影響；對……免疫
   Hannah tried to get Paul to change his mind, but he was immune to her charms.
   漢娜想說服保羅改變心意，但他對她的魅力無動於衷。
4. **departmental** [͵dɪpɑrtˋmɛnt!] *a.* 部門的
5. **a financial year**　會計年度
6. **operational** [͵ɑpəˋreʃən!] *a.* 工作上的；操作上的
7. **commitment** [kəˋmɪtmənt] *n.* 承諾；奉獻（不可數）

Chapter 04 Reading Test

8. **submit** [səbˈmɪt] *vt.* 遞交，提出 & *vi.* 屈服，服從（三態為：submit, submitted [səbˈmɪtɪd], submitted）
submission [sʌbˈmɪʃən] *n.* 提交；屈服，投降

   All job applications must be submitted by May 31.
   所有的工作應徵文件都必須在五月三十一日前繳交。

9. **query** [ˈkwɪrɪ] *n.* 詢問

Part 7 Reading Comprehension

Questions 26-28 refer to the following document.

Angel Seed Company, Ltd.
Prospectus for Mom's Kitchen

Outline:

Welcome to Angel Seed Company, Ltd. The prospectus you are holding details a retail restaurant chain called Mom's Kitchen. There are currently several Mom's Kitchens throughout Oregon, and the chain is now expanding into other states. We believe that once our proposed funding goal is reached, all participants will achieve returns of at least 20% per annum. If you are interested in this exciting and profitable project after reading this prospectus, please fill out the form on page 17 and return it to us as quickly as possible.

Pages 3-6 show architecture diagrams for the layout of the standard Mom's Kitchen, though actual dimensions may be adjusted according to local conditions. All layouts conform to building, safety, and parking lot codes in the state of Oregon.

Pages 7-11 show more detailed floor plans for the lobby, dining areas, kitchen, restrooms, and parking lots.

Pages 12-16 show the monthly operating costs of each unit. We estimate a maximum number of guests at 120 per location, making each a medium-sized restaurant. We also estimate an entire staff of 20, including servers and chefs. These operating expenses include food and beverage costs, salaries, taxes, and other essential payments that a wise investor should be apprised of before investing.

We look forward to receiving your application and investment.

Brandon Ames
Senior Investment Consultant
Angel Seed Company, Ltd.

26 至 28 題請看以下文件。

天使種子股份有限公司
媽媽廚房招股章程

概述：

歡迎來到天使種子股份有限公司。諸位目前拿在手上的是詳載零售連鎖餐廳媽媽廚房的招股章程。目前在奧勒岡州有好幾家媽媽廚房，這間連鎖餐廳正將營業範圍擴展到其他州。我們相信，一旦能達成本公司提出的資金目標，所有參與者每年至少能拿到 20% 的利潤。諸位閱讀本章程後，若對此令人興奮的賺錢計畫感興趣，敬請填寫第十七頁的表格，並儘快繳交給我們。

第三至第六頁標示媽媽廚房的標準建築格局圖，不過實際尺寸可能會依當地情況做調整。所有格局皆符合奧勒岡州的建築、安全及停車場法規。

第七至第十一頁標示大廳、用餐區、廚房、洗手間及停車場更詳細的平面圖。

第十二至第十六頁標示各單位每月的經營成本。我們估計每家中型餐館的場地最多可容納一百二十位賓客。我們也估計每家餐館全體職員為二十人，包括服務生及廚師。這些營運開銷包括食品及飲料費用、薪資、稅收和其他必要支出，以上都是明智的投資者該在投資前要了解的。

我們期待收到諸位的申請及投資。

天使種子股份有限公司
資深投資顧問
布蘭登‧埃姆斯

C **26**

What is the purpose of the prospectus?
(A) To improve kitchen hygiene
(B) To train restaurant personnel
(C) To attract business partners
(D) To finalize a business loan

這份投資章程的目的是什麼？
(A) 改善廚房衛生
(B) 訓練餐廳員工
(C) 吸引生意夥伴
(D) 完成商業貸款

〔理由〕
根據本文第一段第四句 "We believe that once our proposed funding goal is reached, all participants will achieve returns of at least 20% per annum."（我們相信，一旦能達成本公司提出的資金目標，所有參與者每年至少能拿到 20% 的利潤。）可推測發文者希望藉獲利的誘因來吸引人投資，故 (C) 項應為正選。

C **27**

What will probably be found on page ten?
(A) An investment form
(B) Oregon state building codes
(C) Restroom floor plans
(D) Expected salaries for employees

在第十頁上最有可能找到什麼？
(A) 投資表格
(B) 奧勒岡州的建築法規
(C) 洗手間平面圖
(D) 員工預估薪資

Chapter 04 Reading Test

> **理由**
>
> 根據本文第三段 "Pages 7-11 show more detailed floor plans for the lobby, dining areas, kitchen, restrooms, and parking lots."（第七至第十一頁標示大廳、用餐區、廚房、洗手間及停車場更詳細的平面圖。）得知，(C) 項應為正選。

A **28**

What does Mr. Ames mention about Mom's Kitchen?
(A) Its restaurants can be found in different cities.
(B) All individual restaurants are identical regardless of location.
(C) It is an ideal business for a family to invest in.
(D) Owners will not have to comply with building regulations.

有關媽媽廚房，埃姆斯先生提到什麼？
(A) 在許多不同城市均有這家餐廳的分店。
(B) 不論地點，每間餐廳都是一樣的。
(C) 這對家庭來說是理想的投資企業。
(D) 業主無需遵守建築規範。

> **理由**
>
> 根據本文第一段第三句 "There are currently several Mom's Kitchens throughout Oregon, and the chain is now expanding into other states."（目前在奧勒岡州有好幾家媽媽廚房，這間連鎖餐廳正將營業範圍擴展到其他州。）得知，(A) 項應為正選。

重要單字片語

1. **prospectus** [prəˋspɛktəs] *n.*（企業）招股章程；（學校）簡章
2. **outline** [ˋaʊt͵laɪn] *n.* & *vt.* 概述
3. **detail** [ˋditel] *vt.* 詳細說明 & *n.* 細節
4. **chain** [tʃen] *n.* 連鎖店
5. **per annum** [pɚ ˋænəm] 每年
6. **diagram** [ˋdaɪə͵græm] *n.* 簡圖
7. **layout** [ˋle͵aʊt] *n.* 布局設計
8. **dimension** [dəˋmɛnʃən] *n.*（長、寬、高的）度量，大小
   We specified the dimensions of the room in the e-mail.
   我們在電子郵件中詳細說明了該房間的長、寬、高。
9. **conditions** [kənˋdɪʃənz] *n.* 環境（恆用複數）
10. **conform** [kənˋfɔrm] *vi.* 遵守（法規、習俗等）
    conform to... 遵從……
    = comply with...
    = obey...
    I feel I have no choice but to conform to the local customs.
    我感覺我別無選擇只能順從當地風俗民情。
11. **code** [kod] *n.* 法規
12. **a floor plan** 平面圖
13. **apprise** [əˋpraɪz] *vt.* 通知，告知

Questions 29-30 refer to the following text-message chain.

Siegfried Kieselbach (9:17 AM)
I just received a letter from the IRS. Apparently, we owe $20,000 in taxes.

Bonnie Rudd (9:18 AM)
Are you serious? We've paid our taxes. Our accountant, Julie, is thorough when it comes to meeting our tax obligations.

Siegfried Kieselbach (9:20 AM)
Well, that may be so, but the e-mail says if the tax bill isn't paid in 90 days, there will be severe penalties.

Bonnie Rudd (9:21 AM)
There has obviously been some kind of mistake. Let me call Julie, and I'll get right back to you.

Siegfried Kieselbach (9:23 AM)
OK. While you're doing that, I'll call Brendan to organize a meeting to discuss the matter. I'll fill you in when you get back to me.

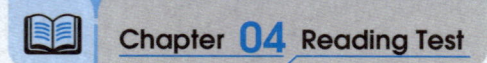

29 至 30 題請看以下簡訊討論串。

希格弗里德・基索巴赫（上午 9:17）
我剛收到一封國稅局寄來的信。看來，我們積欠了兩萬美元的稅款。

邦妮・洛德（上午 9:18）
你是認真的嗎？我們已經繳稅了。說到履行納稅義務，我們的會計師茱麗是很仔細小心的。

希格弗里德・基索巴赫（上午 9:20）
嗯，或許是這樣，但是電子郵件上表明若沒有在九十天內繳納稅款，將會給予嚴懲。

邦妮・洛德（上午 9:21）
顯然是出了某些錯誤。我先打給茱麗，再馬上回電給你。

希格弗里德・基索巴赫（上午 9:23）
好的。妳打電話時，我會打給布蘭登來安排一場會議以討論這件事。妳回電給我時，我再向妳回報狀況。

A **29**

At 9:20 AM, what does Mr. Kieselbach most likely mean when he writes, "that may be so"?
(A) He suspects that the accountant made an error.
(B) He blames Ms. Rudd for the problem.
(C) He confirms the meeting date.
(D) He believes taxes are too high.

於上午 9:20，當基索巴赫先生留言「或許是這樣」時，最有可能是什麼意思？
(A) 他懷疑會計師出錯。
(B) 他把問題怪罪於洛德女士。
(C) 他確認了會議日期。
(D) 他覺得稅收過高。

> 理由
>
> 於上午 9:18，洛德女士留言 "Our accountant, Julie, is thorough when it comes to meeting our tax obligations."（說到履行納稅義務，我們的會計師茱麗是很仔細小心的。）得知基索巴赫先生為回覆洛德女士對於會計師的評論，故可推測 (A) 項應為正選。

CH 04

C **30**

What will Mr. Kieselbach most likely do next?
(A) Reschedule a meeting
(B) Reimburse the accountant
(C) Contact a colleague
(D) Pay a tax bill

基索巴赫先生接下來最有可能做什麼？
(A) 重新排定會議
(B) 賠償會計師
(C) 聯繫同事
(D) 繳納稅款

> 理由
>
> 於上午 9:23，基索巴赫先生留言 "While you're doing that, I'll call Brendan to organize a meeting..."（妳打電話時，我會打給布蘭登來安排一場會議……）得知，(C) 項應為正選。

🔍 重要單字片語

1. **when it comes to...** 說到……
   When it comes to negotiation skills, Jane is an expert.
   說到談判技巧，阿珍是位專家。

2. **obligation** [ˌɑbləˈgeʃən] *n.*（道德上、法律上的）義務，責任

3. **severe** [səˈvɪr] *a.* 嚴重的

4. **fill sb in (on sth)**
   向某人（就某事）提供最新的狀況
   Russell will fill you in on what happened in the meeting.
   羅素會告訴你在會議上發生了什麼事。

5. **suspect** [səˈspɛkt] *vt.* 懷疑，認為，猜想
   No one suspected that Harry would get the promotion.
   沒有人料到哈利竟會獲得升遷。

6. **blame** [blem] *vt.* 指責
   blame sb for sth　把某事怪罪到某人身上
   = blame sth on sb
   We argued over who was to blame for the mistake.
   我們對誰該為這個錯誤負責而爭執。

7. **reimburse** [ˌriɪmˈbɝs] *vt.* 賠償；償還
   The company reimbursed our travel expenses.
   公司償還了我們的旅費。

Chapter 05 Listening Test

Part 1 Photographs

B **1** 🔊 113 🇨🇦

(A) A woman is distributing some documents.
(B) A woman is giving a presentation.
(C) A woman is sipping her coffee.
(D) A woman is drawing on a large screen.

(A) 一名女子正在分發文件。
(B) 一名女子正在做簡報。
(C) 一名女子正小口喝著咖啡。
(D) 一名女子正在大螢幕上繪圖。

重要單字片語

1. **distribute** [dɪˋstrɪbjʊt] *vt.* 分發，分配
   distribute sth to sb　把某物分發給某人
   The volunteers distributed hot food to the typhoon victims.
   志工分發熱食給颱風災民。

2. **sip** [sɪp] *vt.* 啜飲 & *n.* (飲料的) 一口
   My grandmother sipped a cup of hot tea.
   我阿嬤小口喝著熱茶。

C **2** 🔊 114 🇦🇺

(A) Several racks have been disassembled.
(B) Several hangers are being cleaned.
(C) Some promotional posters are being displayed.
(D) Some hoodies have been folded.

(A) 有幾組掛衣架被拆解下來。
(B) 有幾個衣架正在被清洗。
(C) 有幾張促銷海報在展示中。
(D) 有些連帽上衣已摺好。

重要單字片語

1. **rack** [ræk] *n.* 架子，掛物架
2. **disassemble** [ˌdɪsəˋsɛmbl̩] *vt.* 拆開，分解
   The clock isn't working. Disassemble it to see if any parts need to be replaced.
   這個時鐘停了，拆開看看是不是有零件需要更換。
3. **hoodie** [ˋhʊdɪ] *n.* 連帽上衣

Part 2　Question-Response

C　3　🔊 116

Where was the seminar you attended last week?
(A) It was hosted by a leading economist.
(B) It was about implementing change.
(C) It was in the convention center.

你上禮拜參加的研討會地點在哪裡？
(A) 研討會由一位頂尖經濟學家主持。
(B) 研討會的主題是如何貫徹改革。
(C) 研討會在會議中心舉行。

重要單字片語

1. **leading** [ˈlidɪŋ] *a.* 最好的；領先的；最主要的
2. **economist** [ɪˈkɑnəmɪst] *n.* 經濟學家
3. **convention** [kənˈvɛnʃən] *n.* 會議，大會

C　4　🔊 117

Do you think the company has a good reputation?
(A) Yes, I must raise my profile.
(B) Yes, I'll keep you company.
(C) Yes, it's very highly regarded.

你覺得這家公司的聲譽好嗎？
(A) 對，我必須提高我的能見度。
(B) 對，我會陪你。
(C) 是的，它的風評相當好。

重要單字片語

1. **keep sb company**　陪伴某人
   Jerry kept his girlfriend company until the taxi arrived.
   傑瑞一直陪著他女友，直到計程車來。

2. **be highly regarded**　備受推崇的
   David is highly regarded by his colleagues because of his devotion to his work.
   大衛因為對工作不遺餘力的奉獻而備受同事推崇。

Part 3　Conversations

Questions 5 through 7 refer to the following conversation.　🔊 119　M:　W:

M: I'm sorry, Melinda. On behalf of the union members, I can't accept the raise that management is proposing. The members won't be satisfied.
W: Paul, you know what the economic environment is like. We're facing decreasing sales in the industry and much steeper competition from foreign imports.
M: I know, but a 2% pay raise is hardly keeping up with inflation. Could you at least agree to increase the company's contribution to the workers' health care plan?
W: The company is already compliant with all the legal requirements in that regard.

Chapter 05 Listening Test

5 至 7 題請聽以下會話。

> 男：抱歉，梅琳達。我謹代表工會成員，無法接受管理階層所提議的加薪幅度。成員們不會感到滿意的。
> 女：保羅，你知道現在的經濟環境如何。我們正在面對產業上銷售量遞減，以及來自外國進口商品更加激烈的競爭。
> 男：我了解，但是 2% 的薪資漲幅幾乎沒有跟上通貨膨脹。妳能不能至少同意提高公司對員工醫療健保方案的繳納金？
> 女：就此方面，公司已經符合所有法律上的規定了。

A 5 📢 120 🇬🇧

What are the speakers mainly discussing?
(A) A union's request
(B) An employee's performance
(C) Customer satisfaction
(D) Foreign imports

說話者主要在討論什麼？
(A) 工會的請求
(B) 某位員工的表現
(C) 顧客滿意度
(D) 外國進口商品

A 6 📢 121 🇬🇧

What does the man request?
(A) Higher health contributions
(B) Safer working conditions
(C) Better career opportunities
(D) Shorter working hours

男子要求什麼？
(A) 更高的健保繳納金
(B) 更安全的工作條件
(C) 更好的職涯發展機會
(D) 更短的工作時數

D 7 📢 122 🇬🇧

What is mentioned about health care?
(A) The government no longer provides insurance.
(B) The union provides better coverage.
(C) The workers have changed their plan.
(D) The company complies with all the legal requirements.

關於醫療健保，文中提及下列哪一項敘述？
(A) 政府不再提供保險。
(B) 工會提供更好的保險範圍。
(C) 員工們更改了他們的方案。
(D) 公司遵循所有法律規範。

重要單字片語

1. **on behalf of sb**
 代表某人（＝ on sb's behalf）
 On behalf of everyone, I'd like to thank you for your dedication.
 我謹代表全體同仁向您的付出表達感謝之意。

2. **union** [ˋjunjən] *n.* 工會

3. **raise** [rez] *n.*（美）加薪（＝（英）rise）

4. **import** [ˋɪmpɔrt] *n.* 進口品 & [ɪmˋpɔrt] *vt.* 進口
 export [ˋɛkspɔrt] *n.* 出口品 & [ɪkˋspɔrt] *vt.* 出口

5. **inflation** [ɪnˋfleʃən] *n.* 通貨膨脹

6. **contribution** [͵kɑntrəˋbjuʃən] *n.*（醫療健保、養老金的）定期繳納金；捐獻；貢獻

7. **health care** 醫療健保
8. **be compliant with...**
   與……符合，與……一致
   The newest pension plan is compliant with all the legal requirements.
   最新的退休制度與法定規範皆一致。
9. **in that / this regard**
   在這方面，關於此事
   I have no further opinion in that regard.
   關於此事，我沒有其他意見。
10. **coverage** [ˈkʌvərɪdʒ] *n.* 保險範圍

Questions 8 through 10 refer to the following conversation. 🔊 123 M: 🇨🇦 W: 🇺🇸

M: Have you and your team had enough time to go over all the details of the contract?

W: Yes, and we're satisfied that this represents most of the conclusions we reached during our negotiations last week. However, we have one more concern with the last provision. It states that you receive a 60/40 split in your favor for the share of profits.

M: After some discussion with our team, the contract has been updated with more equitable terms. We've agreed to a 50/50 split.

W: I should think so!

M: If that satisfies your concern, please sign at the bottom of the last page. Allow me to remind you that under the terms of the contract, you are responsible for repairs to the rental properties. Also, the contract will expire in two years.

8 至 10 題請聽以下會話。

> 男：您與您的團隊有足夠時間看過合約上的所有細項嗎？
> 女：有的，這份合約表明我們上週談判達成共識的大部分結論，我們很滿意。然而，我們對於最後一項條款還是有疑慮。該條款表示，劃分收益方面，貴方可以獲得有利的六四分帳。
> 男：和我們的團隊討論後，合約已經更改為更合理的條款。我們同意五五分帳。
> 女：那是當然的！
> 男：如果那能解決您的疑慮，請在最後一頁下方簽名。容我提醒，根據合約條款，貴公司要負責出租屋的修繕。此外，此合約兩年後將會失效。

A **8** 🔊 124 🇦🇺

What are the speakers discussing?
(A) Contract terms
(B) Management concerns
(C) Sales representatives
(D) Market share

說話者在討論什麼？
(A) 合約條款
(B) 經營上的疑慮
(C) 業務員
(D) 市占率

Chapter 05 Listening Test

D **9** 🔊 125 🇦🇺

What does the woman mean when she says, "I should think so"?
(A) She thinks the man is wrong.
(B) She is hoping to discuss the matter.
(C) She is concerned about the man.
(D) She agrees with the decision.

女子說「那是當然的」時，是什麼意思？
(A) 她認為男子是錯的。
(B) 她想要討論此事。
(C) 她關心男子。
(D) 她同意該決定。

B **10** 🔊 126 🇦🇺

What does the man say about the contract?
(A) It is also available online.
(B) It will be valid for two years.
(C) It will be revised.
(D) It needs to be printed out.

關於合約，男子說了什麼？
(A) 它在網路上也可取得。
(B) 它的效期為兩年。
(C) 它會被修訂。
(D) 它需要被印出來。

重要單字片語

1. **go over...**　　審視……
   Please go over your report before you turn it in.
   繳交報告前請仔細檢查過。

2. **conclusion** [kənˋkluʒən] *n.* 結論
   reach a conclusion
   做出結論（= come to a conclusion）

3. **negotiation** [nɪˌgoʃɪˋeʃən] *n.* 協商，談判

4. **concern** [kənˋsɝn] *n.* 擔心，憂慮；關切 & *vt.* 使關心，使擔心
   be concerned about...　　擔心……
   More and more parents are concerned about school violence.
   越來越多家長擔心校園暴力的問題。

5. **provision** [prəˋvɪʒən] *n.* 條款

6. **state** [stet] *vt.* 陳述，說明
   The mayor has already stated his intention to run for re-election.
   市長已聲明他要競選連任的意圖。

7. **split** [splɪt] *n.* 配額
   a 50/50 split　　五五分
   a three-way / four-way split
   三人等分均分；四人等分均分

8. **in sb's favor**　　對某人有利
   The exchange rate is in our favor at the moment.
   目前的匯率對我們有利。

9. **share** [ʃɛr] *n.* （在若干人之間分得的）一份；股票，股份
   market share　　市占率
   Next year we hope to have a bigger share of the market.
   明年我們希望獲得更大的市場占額。

10. **profit** [ˋprɑfɪt] *n.* 利潤，利益

11. **equitable** [ˋɛkwɪtəbl̩] *a.* 公平合理的

12. **property** [ˋprɑpɚtɪ] *n.* 房產，房地產；財產（不可數）；特性（可數）

13. **valid** [ˋvælɪd] *a.* 有效的

Part 4 Talks

Questions 11 through 13 refer to the following introduction. 🔊 128

Good afternoon, ladies and gentlemen, and welcome back to the North American Entrepreneurs Conference. Our main event this afternoon is a panel discussion on securing favorable deals while you're trying to get your business off the ground. We will cover areas such as how to craft a persuasive pitch, how to negotiate better funding terms, when to compromise or stand firm, and what you should check before signing an agreement. I know you will have lots of questions for our panel, but please refrain from asking them during the discussion. Members of the panel will take questions once the main discussion is over.

11 至 13 題請聽以下開場白。

> 各位女士先生午安，歡迎回來本屆北美創業人大會。我們今天下午的重頭戲是一場專家對談，將探討如何談成條件優惠的交易來幫助公司起步。我們探討的範圍包括：怎麼講出有說服力的推銷話術、怎麼談成更佳的融資條件、何時該妥協、何時該死守，以及在簽訂合約之前該檢查哪些事項。我知道大家一定有很多問題想問我們的專家小組，但請勿在專家對談過程中發問。小組成員會在主要對談結束後開放回答問題。

C **11** 🔊 129

Who is the conference for?
(A) People nearing retirement age
(B) Members of the legal profession
(C) People starting their own company
(D) Workers moving to North America

大會是為了哪種人辦的？
(A) 接近退休年齡的人
(B) 法界人士
(C) 自行創業者
(D) 將移居北美的上班族

B **12** 🔊 130

What does the speaker say about the panel discussion?
(A) It will comprise three experts.
(B) It will cover multiple aspects.
(C) It will last for at least an hour.
(D) It will be held in an auditorium.

說話者對於專家對談有何說法？
(A) 它會有三位專家參與。
(B) 它會涵蓋多個層面。
(C) 它會持續進行至少一小時。
(D) 它會在一個禮堂舉行。

D **13** 🔊 131

What will the panel do after the discussion?
(A) Sign their autographs
(B) Hand out business cards
(C) Promote a product
(D) Answer questions

專家小組在對談結束後會做什麼？
(A) 幫觀眾簽名
(B) 發名片
(C) 推銷某項產品
(D) 回答問題

Chapter 05 Listening Test

重要單字片語

1. **entrepreneur** [ˌɑntrəprəˋnɝ] *n.* 創業家
2. **panel** [ˋpænḷ] *n.* 專題討論小組；嵌版；儀表板
3. **secure** [səˋkjʊr] *vt.* 獲得；弄牢 & *a.* 安全的
   secure a contract / job
   取得一份合約 / 工作
   Matt successfully secured a contract with a key client.
   麥特成功取得與重要客戶的合約。
4. **favorable** [ˋfevərəbḷ] *a.* 優惠的；有利的
5. **get (sth) off the ground**
   開始獲得（某事的）成功
   It took us some time to get the business off the ground, but it is now turning a profit.
   我們花了一些時間才讓生意步上軌道，但現在已經開始賺錢了。
6. **craft** [kræft] *vt.* 精心製作 & *n.* 手藝，手工藝
   These necklaces were crafted by the local women.
   這些項鍊由當地婦女所製作。
7. **refrain** [rɪˋfren] *vi.* 忍住，抑制
   refrain from + V-ing   忍住 / 不做……
   Please refrain from using your phone in the movie theater.
   請勿在電影院裡使用手機。
8. **profession** [prəˋfɛʃən] *n.* 職業（尤指需要高等教育的職業，如律師、編輯、工程師等）
   the legal profession   法律相關行業
9. **comprise** [kəmˋpraɪz] *vt.* 包括；組成
   be comprised of...   由……組成
   This drink comprises orange, guava, and milk.
   這款飲料的成分包括柳橙、芭樂和牛奶。
   The national baseball team is comprised of professional baseball players.
   這支國家棒球代表隊是由一群職業棒球選手組成的。
10. **multiple** [ˋmʌltəpḷ] *a.* 多重的，眾多的
11. **auditorium** [ˌɔdəˋtorɪəm] *n.* 禮堂
12. **autograph** [ˋɔtəˌgræf] *n.* （尤指名人的）親筆簽名 & *vt.* （名人）簽名於
    The boy asked the basketball player to autograph a T-shirt.
    這個男孩請籃球運動員在一件 T 恤上簽名。

Questions 14 through 16 refer to the following announcement. 🔊 132 🇨🇦

Thank you for that warm greeting. I would like to return the compliment our deputy director just gave me. Please give Janet a round of applause. As director of this conference, I want to remind everyone that you can pre-register for next year's conference in Kansas City, Missouri. The registration tables are near the entrance. You can't miss them. Early birds receive 50% off, so please don't hesitate to register early! Now, on behalf of the organizing committee, I officially open the conference. Please join me in welcoming our keynote speaker, Professor Daniel Everson!

14 至 16 題請聽以下公告。

> 謝謝各位的盛情相挺。我要報答副主任剛才給我的讚美。請為珍娜來點掌聲。身為這次會議的主任，我要提醒大家現在可以預先報名明年在密蘇里州堪薩斯市舉行的會議。報名處離入口處很近。你一定找得到。早鳥票打對折，所以別猶豫，趕快報名！現在，我謹代表本次會議的籌委會，宣布會議正式開始。讓我們一起來歡迎主講人丹尼爾・埃弗森教授！

D **14** 🔊 133 🇬🇧

According to the speaker, what is the advantage of pre-registration?
(A) Getting a profile
(B) Sitting at better tables
(C) Receiving free tickets
(D) Saving money

根據說話者，預先報名的好處是什麼？
(A) 得到簡要介紹
(B) 坐在好一點的桌位
(C) 收到免費入場券
(D) 省錢

C **15** 🔊 134 🇬🇧

What does the speaker imply when he says, "You can't miss them"?
(A) The listeners should register early.
(B) Lunch will be served soon.
(C) The location is easy to find.
(D) Space is limited.

說話者說「你一定找得到」時，在暗示什麼？
(A) 這些聽眾應該要早一點報名。
(B) 午餐就快要上菜了。
(C) 那個地方很容易找。
(D) 空間有限。

B **16** 🔊 135 🇬🇧

What are the listeners asked to do?
(A) Join the committee
(B) Greet a speaker
(C) Prepare a response
(D) Return their badges

這些聽眾被要求做什麼事？
(A) 參加委員會
(B) 以掌聲歡迎演講者
(C) 準備答覆問題
(D) 繳回他們的識別證

重要單字片語

1. **compliment** [ˈkɑmpləmənt] *n.* 讚美；恭維
   pay sb a compliment　對某人表示讚美
   Guests paid Rick a compliment on his newly furnished house.
   客人們對瑞克新裝潢的房子表示稱讚。

2. **deputy** [ˈdɛpjətɪ] *n.* 副手 & *a.* 副的
   As a deputy director, you will be given certain privileges.
   身為副主任，你將享有某些特權。

3. **applause** [əˈplɔz] *n.* 鼓掌；喝采
   Give the speaker a big round of applause!
   給這位演講者熱烈的掌聲吧！

4. **remind** [rɪˈmaɪnd] *vt.* 提醒；使想起
   Jack gave me a poke with his elbow, reminding me that it was time to leave.
   傑克用手肘頂了我一下，提醒我該是離開的時候了。

5. **on behalf of sb**　代表某人
   On behalf of the company I would like to thank you all.
   我謹代表公司感謝大家。

6. **join sb in + V-ing**
   參與某人一起從事……
   I'm sure you'll all join me in wishing Johnny and Rita a very happy marriage.
   我確信你們都會跟我一起來祝福強尼與麗塔新婚愉快。

7. **keynote** [ˈkinot] *n.* (書、演說等的) 要旨；主題
   We attended the keynote speech first, and then we went to our respective workshops.
   我們先去參加主題演講，然後去參加我們各自的專題研討會。

Chapter 05 Reading Test

8. **profile** [ˈprofaɪl] *n.* 簡介
   Job profiles can be found on the company's website.
   你可以在這家公司的網站找到工作簡介。

9. **badge** [bædʒ] *n.* 徽牌；徽章；證章
   All personnel are required to wear badges at work.
   所有員工上班時都需配戴證件。

Part 5 Incomplete Sentences

D **17**

We concluded from our ------- that the popularity of organic food is more than just a passing fad, so we decided to expand into this business.

(A) expiration　　　(B) relationship　　　(C) trademark　　　(D) survey

我們從調查中得出結論，有機食品受歡迎並非只是一時風行，因此我們決定將業務範圍擴展到這門生意。

理由

1. (A) **expiration** [ˌɛkspəˈreʃən] *n.* 期滿
      an expiration date　　保存期限
      Don't eat that beef sandwich! It has passed its expiration date.
      別吃那個牛肉三明治！它已經過期了。

   (B) **relationship** [rɪˈleʃənˌʃɪp] *n.* (人、團體之間的) 關係／往來
      Dora has a good relationship with her younger brother.
      朵拉和她弟弟的關係不錯。

   (C) **trademark** [ˈtredˌmɑrk] *n.* 商標 (縮寫為 TM)
      register a trademark　　去註冊一項商標
      The toy company has registered trademarks for its latest products.
      這家玩具公司已經為其最新產品註冊了商標。

   (D) **survey** [ˈsɝve] *n.* 調查 & [səˈve] *vt.* 調查；勘察
      do / conduct / carry out a survey　　進行意見調查
      The student is conducting a survey on people's opinions about the low birth rate.
      = The student is surveying people's opinions about the low birth rate.
      該學生正在進行一項調查，以了解民眾對低生育率的看法。

2. 根據語意，(D) 項應為正選。

重要單字片語

1. **popularity** [ˌpɑpjəˈlærətɪ] *n.* 受歡迎；普及
   gain in popularity　　漸受歡迎
   Organic food has gained in popularity over the past few years.
   有機食品近年來漸受歡迎。

2. **organic** [ɔrˈgænɪk] *a.* 有機的

3. **passing** [ˈpæsɪŋ] *a.* 暫時的；瞬間的

4. **fad** [fæd] *n.* 一時的風尚
   the latest / current fad　　最新潮流
   Rap music proved to be more than just a passing fad.
   事實證明，饒舌音樂並不是曇花一現。

C 18

Our headquarters are in Tokyo, but we also have ------- offices in Fukuoka, Osaka, and Sapporo.

(A) payroll　　　　(B) quota　　　　(C) branch　　　　(D) advantage

我們的總部位於東京，但我們在福岡、大阪和札幌也有分公司。

理由

1. (A) **payroll** [ˈpeˌrol] *n.* 職員名冊；發薪名單
   (be) on the payroll　　被僱用
   The company has around 100 employees on the payroll.
   公司目前約有一百名員工。

   (B) **quota** [ˈkwotə] *n.* 配額；限額
   Due to labor shortages, certain industries requested that the government increase the quota of foreign laborers.
   由於勞力短缺，某些產業請求政府增加外籍勞工的配額。

   (C) **branch** [bræntʃ] *n.* 分部，分公司；樹枝
   open a branch　　成立分部 / 公司
   The company has decided to open a branch in Tokyo next year.
   公司已決定明年要在東京成立一家分公司。

   (D) **advantage** [ədˈvæntɪdʒ] *n.* 優勢；優點；利益；益處
   have an advantage over...　　比……占有優勢
   Sarah has an advantage over Jason for the promotion because of her experience.
   莎拉比傑森在升遷上更具優勢，因為她工作經驗較豐富。

2. 根據語意，(C) 項應為正選。

A 19

The labor market ------- tight over the past two years, so we can expect some requests for salary raises from our senior employees.

(A) has been　　　　(B) had been　　　　(C) was　　　　(D) will be

勞工市場過去兩年來一直都很吃緊，所以我們能預期某些資深員工可能會要求加薪。

理由

1. 句中若有時間副詞片語 "over / during / in + the + past / last + 一段時間"（過去若干時間以來）出現時，該句的動詞應使用現在完成式或現在完成進行式。
   The city has changed a lot over the last few years.
   　　　　現在完成式
   這座城市過去幾年來改變了許多。
   The Japanese yen has been decreasing in value during the past few years.
   　　　　　　現在完成進行式
   過去幾年來日圓持續貶值。

2. 根據上述，(A) 項應為正選。

Chapter 05 Reading Test

重要單字片語

tight [taɪt] *a.* 拮据的;不寬裕的
a tight budget / schedule　　吃緊的預算 / 行程

D 20

Pre-Christmas sales are running from five to ten percent below ------- of the same period last year.

(A) this　　　　　(B) these　　　　　(C) that　　　　　(D) those

聖誕節前的銷售量比起去年同期減少了五到十個百分點。

理由

1. that 和 those 為代名詞時,可用以代替之前提到的名詞,若之前名詞為單數,則可用 that 代替;若之前名詞為複數,則用 those 代替。
   The color of this car is different from the color of that car.（可）
   = The color of this car is different from that of that car.（佳）
   這輛車的顏色和那輛車的顏色不同。
   The colors I chose were a lot brighter than those John chose.
   我選的顏色要比阿強選的顏色明亮多了。

2. 空格前子句主詞為複數 Pre-Christmas sales（聖誕節前的銷售量）,得知空格內要置 pre-Christmas sales,但因為重複,此時可用代名詞 those 代替,故 (D) 項應為正選。

B 21

Whether the two sports apparel retailers will merge or be subject to a hostile takeover bid ------- on their stock prices.

(A) depending　　　(B) depends　　　(C) depend　　　(D) depended

這兩家運動服飾零售店之間是合併還是惡意收購,要看它們的股價而定。

理由

1. 句首有 Whether（是否）所引導的名詞子句作本句主詞,視為單數,空格內應置單數動詞 depends,故 (B) 項應為正選。

2. (D) 項 depended 是過去式,而過去式須與過去未來式並用,如下列:
   John said he would come on time.
   約翰當時說他會準時到。
   因此若選 (D) 項,Whether 子句的 will 就應改成 would。

重要單字片語

1. **apparel** [ə`pærəl] *n.*（商店出售的）衣服
2. **subject** [`sʌbdʒɪkt] *a.* 取決於……;勢必受到……的
   be subject to...
   取決於……;勢必受到……的

The book is ready for printing, subject to your approval.
這本書準備發印,就等你批准了。
Flights are subject to delay because of the thick fog.
由於濃霧,班機勢必要延誤。

3. **hostile** [ˈhɑstl̩] *a.* 惡意的
4. **bid** [bɪd] *n.* 買方的出價

At the auction, the highest bid for the picture was $4,000.
這幅畫在拍賣會中的最高出價是四千美元。

📖 Part 6 Text Completion

Questions 22-25 refer to the following press release.

FastStopMart Looks to Expand into Southern India

FastStopMart is the leading convenience store chain in northern India. Over the last decade, we have established ourselves across the region as the trusted choice for food, drinks, and an array of other products. We are now seeking ------- partners to
22.
open stores in the country's southern states and union territories. We believe these areas have great commercial potential for the expansion of our operations ------- the
23.
increasing demand there for 24/7 access to quality products. Companies or individuals are invited to submit applications ------- our website at www.fast-stop-mart.in. -------.
24.   25.
We look forward to collaborating with dedicated new partners and continuing to pursue our growth strategy.

---

22 至 25 題請看以下新聞稿。

FastStopMart 計劃將業務擴展至印度南部

FastStopMart 是北印度最主要的連鎖便利商店。過去十年來，我們在整個區域建立信譽，在食物、飲料及多種其他產品上成為最可靠的選擇。我們現正尋求<u>連鎖</u>加盟主，在印度南部各邦及中央直轄區開設門市。我們相信這些地區在我們的業務擴張上有很大的商業潛力，<u>因為</u>這些區域對於全年無休購買優質產品的需求與日俱增。企業或個人均可<u>透過</u>我們的網站 www.fast-stop-mart.in 遞交加盟申請書。<u>網路上也有相關的加盟細節</u>。我們期待與全心投入的新夥伴攜手合作，持續推動我們的業務拓展策略。

D **22**

(A) obligation　　(B) strike　　(C) principle　　**(D) franchise**

理由

1. (A) **obligation** [ˌɑbləˈɡeʃən] *n.* （道德上、法律上的）義務，責任
   Young men in that country have an obligation to serve in the military.
   那個國家的年輕男性有服兵役的義務。

Chapter 05 Reading Test

(B) **strike** [straɪk] *n.* 罷工；打，擊
go on strike　　罷工
Factory workers went on strike yesterday to ask for higher wages.
工廠工人昨天罷工，以要求更高的工資。

(C) **principle** [ˈprɪnsəpl] *n.* 原則，原理；道德原則，行為準則
in principle　　原則上
While I agree with you in principle, I'm not entirely convinced your idea will work.
原則上我同意你，但並不全然認同你的想法是否會奏效。

(D) **franchise** [ˈfræn͵tʃaɪz] *n.* 連鎖事業；經銷權
Eric works for a major fast-food franchise in the US.
艾瑞克在美國的一間知名連鎖速食店上班。

2. 根據語意，可知 (D) 項應為正選。

B 23

(A) so long as　　(B) due to　　(C) whereas　　(D) no more than

理由

1. 本題測試下列固定句構：
   due to…　　因為……
   The project was abandoned due to funding shortages.
   該專案因為資金短缺而被放棄了。

2. 根據上述，(B) 項應為正選。

3. 其他選項：

   (A) **so long as + S + V**　　只要……
   So long as Anna finishes the project on time, she'll receive a bonus.
   只要安娜按時完成專案，她就會獲得獎金。

   (C) **whereas** [wɛrˈæz] *conj.* 而，然而（＝ while）
   Jenny is outgoing whereas her brother is shy.
   珍妮個性外向，而她弟弟卻很害羞。

   (D) **no more than + 數字詞**　　最多不超過……
   It takes no more than half an hour to get there by train.
   從這兒搭火車到那兒最多只要半小時。

C 24

(A) prior to　　(B) without　　(C) via　　(D) along with

理由

1. (A) **prior to…**　　在……之前
   I'd like to speak with you prior to the meeting.
   開會前我想先跟你談一下。

   (B) **without** [wɪˈðaʊt] *prep.* 沒有，無
   Kevin went to the party without his parents' permission.
   凱文沒有得到父母的允許就去參加派對。

(C) **via** [ˈvaɪə / ˈvɪə] *prep.* 透過，經由（= through）
Students can access the school library's database via the internet.
學生可以透過網路進入學校圖書館的資料庫。

(D) **along with...** 還有……；和……一起
Kelly bought pizza along with cola for the party.
凱莉為派對買了披薩和可樂。

2. 根據語意及用法，(C) 項應為正選。

A **25**

(A) Details on partnership terms can also be found online.
(B) Our flagship store is located in this southwestern city.
(C) The store's operating hours are displayed on the window.
(D) FastStopMart's best-selling product is out of stock.

理由

1. (A) 網路上也有相關的加盟細節。
   (B) 我們的旗艦店位於這座西南方的城市。
   (C) 商店的營業時間有貼在窗戶上。
   (D) FastStopMart 的熱銷商品沒有存貨了。

2. 空格前的句子 "... via our website at www.fast-stop-mart.in"（透過我們的網站 www.fast-stop-mart.in）說明某事可透過該網站進行，選項 (A) Details on partnership terms can also be found online.（網路上也有相關的加盟細節。）提及網路，得知 (A) 項置入空格後與前文語意連貫，故為正選。

重要單字片語

1. **establish oneself as...**
   確立……的地位
   Michael has established himself as an authority on 19th-century architecture.
   麥可已經確立自己在十九世紀建築領域的權威地位。

2. **array** [əˈre] *n.* 一批，一系列
   an array of... 一連串／一大堆……

3. **demand** [dɪˈmænd] *n.* 要求，請求

4. **24/7** 全年無休（= 24-7）

5. **collaborate** [kəˈlæbəˌret] *vi.* 合作
   collaborate with... 與……合作
   David collaborated with his classmates to film the video.
   大衛與他的同學合作拍攝這支影片。

6. **dedicated** [ˈdɛdəˌketɪd] *a.* 奉獻的

7. **partnership** [ˈpɑrtnɚˌʃɪp] *n.* 合夥關係

8. **flagship** [ˈflæɡˌʃɪp] *n.* （某機構的）旗艦產品，最重要理念，主建築物
   a flagship store 旗艦店

Chapter 05 Reading Test

Part 7 Reading Comprehension

Questions 26-27 refer to the following email.

From:	z.rayner@raynermc.com
To:	seth.isaacs@hour-sports-store.com
Subject:	Our Meeting

Dear Mr. Isaacs,

Thank you for meeting with me today. Here is an outline of what we discussed: Rayner Management Consultants will conduct a feasibility study into your potential merger with The Shports Company. This will evaluate the potential benefits, risks, and challenges of the merger and will include a review of the financial health of both your company and The Shports Company. It will also consider the cultural compatibility between the organizations and potential integration challenges, such as how both companies' employees will cooperate post-merger. However, as agreed, the portion of the study regarding the alignment of your IT infrastructure and software systems will be postponed for now.

Yours sincerely,

Zach Rayner
Rayner Management Consultants

26 至 27 題請看以下電子郵件。

寄件者：	z.rayner@raynermc.com
收件者：	seth.isaacs@hour-sports-store.com
主　旨：	我們的會議

親愛的艾薩克先生：

感謝您今天與我會面。以下是我們這次討論的概要：雷納管理顧問公司將對貴公司與 Shports 公司可能的合併作業進行可行性研究。此研究將評估合併的潛在利益、風險及挑戰，也將包括貴公司與 Shports 兩家公司的財務健檢。研究中還會評估兩家機構間的公司文化適配性以及整合上可能的挑戰，例如兩家公司員工在合併後的協作方式。不過我們都同意：報告中關於兩家公司資訊設備和軟體系統整合部分的評估將暫時不做。

柴克・雷納　　謹上
雷納管理顧問公司

C **26**

What is the main purpose of the email?
(A) To suggest topics for a future meeting
(B) To outline the findings of a recent report
(C) To summarize the content of a future study
(D) To review the reasons why a merger failed

這封電子郵件的主要目的是什麼？
(A) 提議未來會議要探討的主題
(B) 概述最近一份報告的研究結果
(C) 歸納一項即將進行的研究內容
(D) 檢討合併失敗的原因

> **理由**
>
> 根據本文第二句 "Here is an outline of what we discussed: Rayner Management Consultants will conduct a feasibility study into your potential merger with The Shports Company."（以下是我們這次討論的概要：雷納管理顧問公司將對貴公司與 Shports 公司可能的合併作業進行可行性研究。）得知，(C) 項應為正選。

B **27**

What is suggested about technology systems?
(A) They need to be upgraded if the merger is to go ahead.
(B) Issues surrounding them will be studied at a later date.
(C) They are the sole responsibility of The Shports Company.
(D) Questions about their practicality have already been resolved.

本文對科技系統部分有何暗示？
(A) 如果要進行合併，它們需要升級。
(B) 它們的相關問題將於日後另行研究。
(C) 它們由 Shports 公司全權負責。
(D) 它們的可行性問題已獲得解決。

> **理由**
>
> 根據本文最後一句 "... the portion of the study regarding the alignment of your IT infrastructure and software systems will be postponed for now."（……報告中關於兩家公司資訊設備和軟體系統整合部分的評估將暫時不做。）得知，(B) 項應為正選。

重要單字片語

1. **feasibility** [ˌfizəˈbɪlətɪ] *n.* 可行性
2. **merger** [ˈmɝdʒɚ] *n.*（公司）合併
3. **evaluate** [ɪˈvæljuˌet] *vt.* 評估
   It's important to evaluate every possibility before making any decision.
   在做出任何決定之前，評估每種可能性是很重要的。
4. **compatibility** [kəmˌpætəˈbɪlətɪ] *n.* 相容，並存；（電腦）相容性
5. **integration** [ˌɪntəˈgreʃən] *n.* 整合
6. **alignment** [əˈlaɪnmənt] *n.* 結盟，聯合
7. **infrastructure** [ˈɪnfrəˌstrʌktʃɚ] *n.* 基礎建設
8. **findings** [ˈfaɪndɪŋz] *n.* 研究發現（恆用複數）
9. **summarize** [ˈsʌməˌraɪz] *vt. & vi.* 摘要；總結
   The speaker summarized the main points at the end of his speech.
   演講者在其演講尾聲歸納了幾個重點。
10. **sole** [sol] *a.* 單獨的，唯一的
11. **practicality** [ˌpræktɪˈkælətɪ] *n.* 實用性

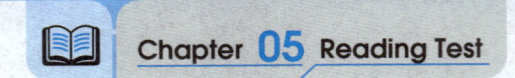

Chapter 05 Reading Test

Questions 28-30 refer to the following e-mail.

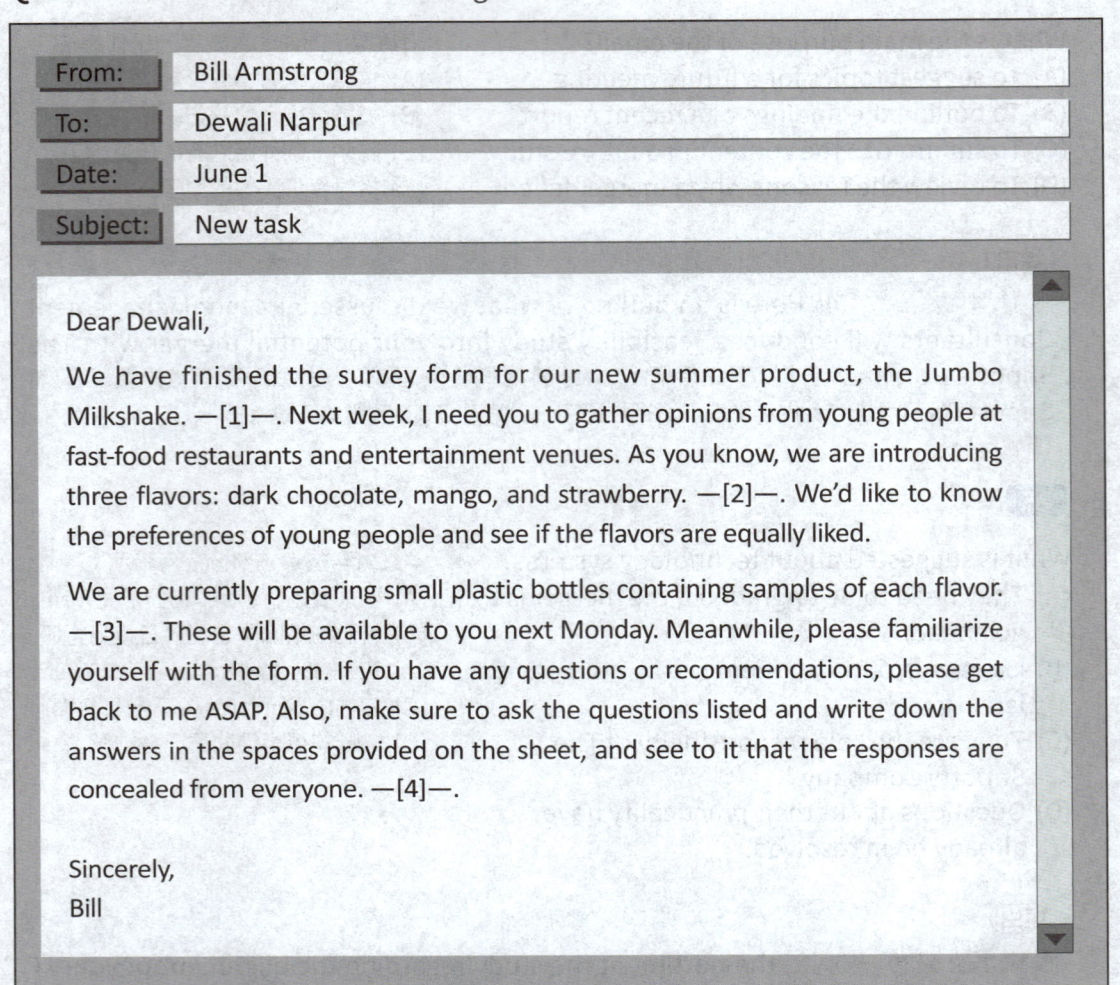

From:	Bill Armstrong
To:	Dewali Narpur
Date:	June 1
Subject:	New task

Dear Dewali,

We have finished the survey form for our new summer product, the Jumbo Milkshake. —[1]—. Next week, I need you to gather opinions from young people at fast-food restaurants and entertainment venues. As you know, we are introducing three flavors: dark chocolate, mango, and strawberry. —[2]—. We'd like to know the preferences of young people and see if the flavors are equally liked.

We are currently preparing small plastic bottles containing samples of each flavor. —[3]—. These will be available to you next Monday. Meanwhile, please familiarize yourself with the form. If you have any questions or recommendations, please get back to me ASAP. Also, make sure to ask the questions listed and write down the answers in the spaces provided on the sheet, and see to it that the responses are concealed from everyone. —[4]—.

Sincerely,
Bill

28 至 30 題請看以下電子郵件。

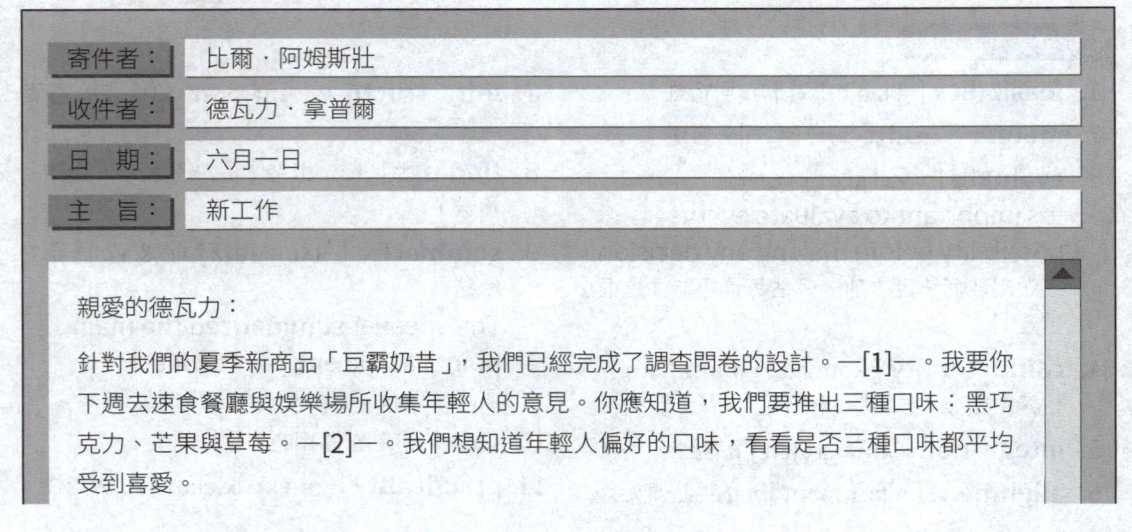

寄件者：	比爾・阿姆斯壯
收件者：	德瓦力・拿普爾
日　期：	六月一日
主　旨：	新工作

親愛的德瓦力：

針對我們的夏季新商品「巨霸奶昔」，我們已經完成了調查問卷的設計。—[1]—。我要你下週去速食餐廳與娛樂場所收集年輕人的意見。你應知道，我們要推出三種口味：黑巧克力、芒果與草莓。—[2]—。我們想知道年輕人偏好的口味，看看是否三種口味都平均受到喜愛。

104

我們目前正在準備小塑膠瓶，其內裝有各種口味的試吃品。―[3]―。下星期一就能交到你手上。在此期間，請你熟讀該問卷。若你有任何問題或建議，請儘速讓我知道。此外，切記要列在問卷上的問題，並將答覆寫在紙上的作答處，也確保答覆不被他人看見。―[4]―。

比爾　上

B 28

What is the purpose of the e-mail?
(A) To ask people's opinions of a product
(B) To explain an upcoming marketing survey
(C) To get volunteers for a project
(D) To order plastic bottles for a survey

這封電子郵件的用意為何？
(A) 詢問大家對某產品的意見
(B) 解釋即將舉辦的市場調查
(C) 徵求某計畫的志願者
(D) 為某市調訂購塑膠瓶

理由

根據本文第一段第二句 "Next week, I need you to gather opinions from young people at fast-food restaurants and entertainment venues."（我要你下週去速食餐廳與娛樂場所收集年輕人的意見。）得知有一項即將進行的市調活動，該句後文也提及市調相關的注意事項，故 (B) 項應為正選。

A 29

What will young people receive?
(A) Small portions of some drinks
(B) Free tickets to a new movie
(C) Jumbo-sized fast-food meals
(D) Samples of a chocolate bar

年輕人會拿到什麼？
(A) 小杯飲料
(B) 一部新電影的免費門票
(C) 巨無霸速食餐點
(D) 一款巧克力棒的試吃品

理由

本文第二段第一句提及 "We are currently preparing small plastic bottles containing samples of each flavor."（我們目前正在準備小塑膠瓶，其內裝有各種口味的試吃品。），本文第一段也提及要做問卷調查年輕人偏好的奶昔口味，故 (A) 項應為正選。

Chapter 05 Reading Test

D 30

In which of the positions marked [1], [2], [3], and [4] does the following sentence best belong?

"Completed forms must be returned in a sealed manila folder marked 'confidential.'"

(A) [1]
(B) [2]
(C) [3]
(D) [4]

在標記 [1]、[2]、[3]、[4] 的四個位置當中，哪一項為下列句子的最佳位置？

「填好的表格一定要放入標有『機密』的密封牛皮文件袋後繳回。」

(A) [1]
(B) [2]
(C) [3]
(D) [4]

理由

根據本文第二段第五句 "..., and see to it that the responses are concealed from everyone."（……，也確保答覆不被他人看見。），可推測市調的答覆應屬不公開文件，故與題目句子中的 confidential（機密的）相呼應，且本題句子描述完成市調後的做法，置於 (D) 項位置能承接上文，故 (D) 項應為正選。

重要單字片語

1. **venue** [ˈvɛnju] *n.* （舉辦）場所，地點

2. **preference** [ˈprɛf(ə)rəns] *n.* 偏好
   have a preference for sth
   對某物有偏好
   John has a preference for drinking chocolate milk with his breakfast.
   約翰比較偏好喝巧克力牛奶配早餐。

3. **familiarize** [fəˈmɪljəˌraɪz] *vt.* 使熟悉
   familiarize sb with sth　使某人熟悉某事
   You'll need time to familiarize yourself with our standard procedures.
   你得花些時間來熟悉我們的標準流程。

4. **recommendation** [ˌrɛkəmɛnˈdeʃən] *n.*
   建議；推薦

5. **get back to sb**　回覆某人；回電給某人
   I'll find out and get back to you.
   我查明之後再答覆你。

6. **see to it + that** 子句
   注意……，確保……
   = make sure + that 子句
   Please see to it that you turn in your financial report on time.
   請你務必要準時繳交你的財務報告。

7. **conceal** [kənˈsil] *vt.* 隱藏

8. **manila** [məˈnɪlə] *n.* 牛皮紙

Chapter 06 Listening Test

Part 1 Photographs

B **1** 🔊 137

(A) They are sanitizing their hands.
(B) They are performing surgery.
(C) A man is changing a light bulb.
(D) A man is taking off a surgical cap.

(A) 他們正在消毒雙手。
(B) 他們正在進行手術。
(C) 有個男的正在換燈泡。
(D) 某個男的正脫掉手術帽。

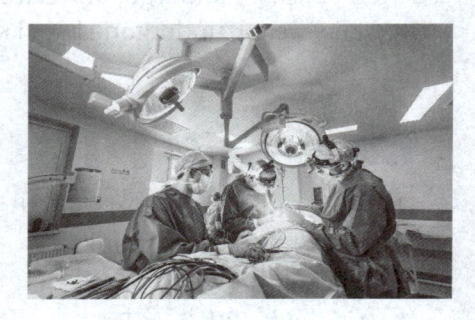

重要單字片語

bulb [bʌlb] *n.* 燈泡（= light bulb）
a 100-watt bulb　一百瓦的燈泡

C **2** 🔊 138

(A) The nurse is replacing a pillow.
(B) The doctor is using his stethoscope.
(C) The patient is lying on the bed.
(D) The nurse is delivering pajamas.

(A) 護理師正在換枕頭。
(B) 醫生正在使用聽診器。
(C) 病患正躺在床上。
(D) 護理師正拿睡衣過來。

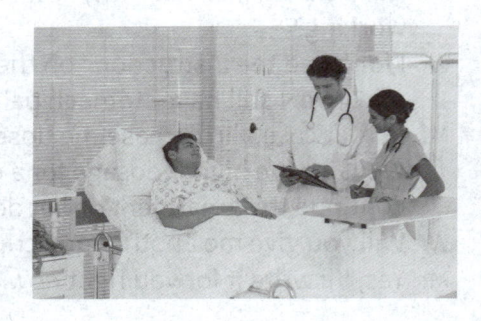

重要單字片語

1. **stethoscope** [ˈstɛθəˌskop] *n.* 聽診器
2. **pajamas** [pəˈdʒæməz] *n.* 睡衣

Part 2 Question-Response

C **3** 🔊 140

What treatment plan has your doctor suggested?
(A) The doctor will be with you soon.
(B) He says it's the best thing to do.
(C) I need to undergo physical therapy.

你的醫生建議何種治療方案？
(A) 醫生很快就會過來。
(B) 他說這樣做最好。
(C) 我得接受物理治療。

Chapter 06 Listening Test

重要單字片語

1. **undergo** [ˌʌndəˈgo] *vt.* 接受（手術）；經歷（三態為：undergo, underwent [ˌʌndəˈwɛnt], undergone [ˌʌndəˈgɔn]）

   After you undergo the operation, you'll feel a little weak for a few days.
   動完手術後，你會有幾天覺得有點虛弱。

2. **physical** [ˈfɪzɪk!] *a.* 物理的，身體的

C 　**4**　🔊 141

Have you fully recovered from the flu, Jasmine?
(A) Yes, I'm very full, thanks.
(B) No, I didn't fly there.
(C) Yes, I feel much better.

潔思敏，妳的流感完全好了嗎？
(A) 有，我吃得很飽，謝謝。
(B) 不是，我不是坐飛機去那裡的。
(C) 是的，我覺得好很多了。

Part 3 Conversations

Questions 5 through 7 refer to the following conversation. 🔊 143　M: 🇦🇺　W: 🇬🇧

M: Have a seat, Martha. Now, how is the medicine I prescribed for you last time working?
W: I followed the instructions on the bottle, but the medicine doesn't seem very effective. I still have stomach pain and occasional diarrhea.
M: In that case, I'll increase the dose. Most patients respond very well to this medicine. We'll try the higher dosage for a couple of weeks. Then, I'll assess whether to continue this treatment or not depending on your condition.
W: Will you give me another prescription?
M: Yes, I'll write it for you right now.

5 至 7 題請聽以下會話。

男：瑪莎，請坐。呃，我上次開給妳的藥有效嗎？
女：我遵照瓶子上的指示吃藥，但好像不是很有效。我的胃還是會痛，有時候還會拉肚子。
男：那樣的話，我會增加藥的劑量。大部分的病人吃了這種藥之後效果都很好。我們用多一點的劑量試個幾星期。然後我會根據妳的狀況評估是否要繼續採用這種療法。
女：您要給我另一張處方箋嗎？
男：對，我現在就開藥單給妳。

A　**5**　🔊 144 🇺🇸

Where most likely are the speakers?
(A) At a clinic
(B) At a trade show
(C) At a liquor store
(D) At a medicine factory

這些說話者最有可能在什麼地方？
(A) 診所
(B) 商展
(C) 酒舖
(D) 藥廠

B **6** 🔊 145 🇺🇸

What symptom does the woman mention?
(A) Headaches
(B) Stomach pain
(C) Back trouble
(D) Dizzy spells

這名女子提到什麼症狀？
(A) 頭痛
(B) 胃痛
(C) 背部有毛病
(D) 陣陣的暈眩

D **7** 🔊 146 🇺🇸

What will the man most likely do next?
(A) Make an assessment
(B) Decrease the dosage
(C) Take some medicine
(D) Write a prescription

這名男子接下來最有可能會做什麼事？
(A) 做個評估
(B) 減輕劑量
(C) 服用藥物
(D) 開處方箋

重要單字片語

1. **instructions** [ɪnˋstrʌkʃənz] *n.* 使用指南（恆用複數）
   Follow the instructions carefully before you operate the machine.
   你操作這臺機器之前，要先小心地照著使用指南做。

2. **effective** [ɪˋfɛktɪv] *a.* 有效的
   Aspirin is a simple but highly effective medicine.
   阿司匹靈是簡單但藥效奇佳的藥。

3. **occasional** [əˋkeʒənl̩] *a.* 偶爾的
   The weather forecast said there would be occasional showers today.
   天氣預報說今天將偶有陣雨。

4. **diarrhea** [ˌdaɪəˋriə] *n.* 腹瀉（不可數）

5. **in that case** 那樣的話；既然那樣
   In that case, I have nothing else to say.
   那樣的話，我也沒什麼話好說了。

6. **respond** [rɪˋspɑnd] *vi.* 顯出效果
   It remains to be seen whether the patient will respond to the medication.
   這種藥物是否會對那位病人發生效用還有待觀察。

7. **dosage** [ˋdosɪdʒ] *n.* 劑量（集合名詞，不可數）
   Never exceed the recommended dosage of painkillers.
   使用止痛藥千萬不要超過建議劑量。

8. **assess** [əˋsɛs] *vt.* 評估；估價
   assessment [əˋsɛsmənt] *n.* 評估
   make an assessment of...
   對……做出評估
   We are assessing the effects of these changes to our current system.
   我們正在評估這些改變對現行制度的影響。
   We should conduct a comprehensive assessment of the situation before we make any plans.
   我們在訂定任何計畫之前應該要先對情況做全盤的評估。

9. **prescription** [prɪˋskrɪpʃən] *n.* 處方
   write a prescription 開處方
   The doctor took the patient's pulse and wrote a prescription.
   那位醫生幫病人量了脈搏，然後開立處方。

10. **liquor** [ˋlɪkɚ] *n.* 蒸餾酒；烈酒（如威士忌、白蘭地、金門高粱酒）
    You have to be 21 to drink liquor in the US.
    在美國你必須滿二十一歲才能喝酒。

Chapter 06 Listening Test

11. **factory** [ˈfækt(ə)rɪ] *n.* 工廠
    There are thousands of workers in the factory.
    那家工廠有好幾千名工人。

12. **dizzy** [ˈdɪzɪ] *a.* 暈眩的
    feel dizzy　　感到暈暈的（= feel faint）
    After three glasses of beer, Jack felt slightly dizzy.
    傑克喝了三杯啤酒下肚後感到有點暈眩。

13. **spell** [spɛl] *n.* 一段時間（通常為短時間）
    Johnny had a runny nose, dizzy spells, and a persistent cough. Everyone kept their distance from him.
    強尼流鼻涕，加上陣陣的頭暈還不斷咳嗽。每個人都跟他保持距離。

Questions 8 through 10 refer to the following conversation and policy.　🔊 147
W:　　M:

W: Good morning, I'd like to purchase some health insurance. Could you tell me what you have available, please?
M: We provide a wide range of health insurance policies. Each one covers different services and has different prices. For example, the dental cover is a lot more expensive than ambulance insurance.
W: In that case, I'm afraid I can only afford hospital insurance at the moment.
M: Very well. Fill in this form and sign it, please.

Insurance Policy	
Type	**Price per Month**
Dental	$50
Vision	$30
Hospital	$25
Ambulance	$20

8 至 10 題請聽以下會話，並請看以下保單。

女：早安，我想要買些醫療保險。請問你們有哪些保險商品呢？
男：我們提供很多種醫療保險的保單。每一種保單有不同的承保範圍，保費也不一樣。舉例來說，承保牙科就會比承保救護車貴很多。
女：那樣的話，我目前恐怕只保得起住院這個項目。
男：好。請填寫這張表格，並且在上面簽名。

保單	
種類	**月費**
牙科	$50
眼科	$30
住院	$25
救護車	$20

B 8 🔊 148 🇨🇦

Why is the woman speaking to the man?
(A) To change an appointment
(B) To insure against health problems
(C) To inform him about an emergency
(D) To cancel an order

這名女子為什麼正在跟男子說話？
(A) 更改預約的時間
(B) 為健康問題投保
(C) 通知他緊急情況
(D) 取消訂單

C 9 🔊 149 🇨🇦

Look at the graphic. How much will the woman most likely pay?
(A) $50
(B) $30
(C) $25
(D) $20

請看圖表。這名女子最有可能要付多少錢？
(A) 50 美元
(B) 30 美元
(C) 25 美元
(D) 20 美元

A 10 🔊 150 🇨🇦

What does the man ask the woman to do?
(A) Complete a form
(B) Change policies
(C) Read the policy's terms
(D) Pay upfront

這名男子要求女子做什麼事？
(A) 填寫表格
(B) 變更保單
(C) 閱讀保單的條款
(D) 預先付款

🔍 **重要單字片語**

1. **cover** [ˈkʌvɚ] vt. 為……保險，承保 & n. 保險（範圍）
   cover sb for / against sth
   為某人保……的險
   Are we covered for theft and fire?
   我們保了竊盜險和火險嗎？

2. **insure** [ɪnˈʃʊr] vt. & vi.（為……）投保
   insure sth against...
   為某物保……的險
   You should insure your house against fire.
   你應為你的房子保火險。

🎧 **Part 4** Talks

Questions 11 through 13 refer to the following talk. 🔊 152 🇨🇦

OK. Please settle down. I'm Dr. Wilson from the city's Health Department. I'm here to make sure you understand how to take good care of your teeth. For the prevention of cavities, brushing your teeth after each meal is your best bet. If you don't have a toothbrush, then you should rinse your mouth with water. If you do find a cavity, you should visit your dentist for a filling. A filling keeps the cavity from getting any bigger. You can find other helpful dental hygiene tips on the Department of Health's website.

Chapter 06 Listening Test

11 至 13 題請聽以下談話。

> 好的。請安靜下來。我是本市衛生局的威爾森醫生。我來此是為了確保諸位都了解如何照顧好你們的牙齒。要避免蛀牙,最好的方式就是每餐飯後都刷牙。如果你沒有牙刷,那就應該用水漱口。假如你發現蛀牙了,就該去找牙醫補牙。補牙能讓蛀洞不再擴大。諸位可以在衛生局官方網站上找到其他有用的口腔衛生建議。

D 11 🔊 153

What is the purpose of the talk?
(A) To remind people to wash their hands
(B) To query department procedures
(C) To improve personal relationships
(D) To explain dental hygiene

這段談話的目的是什麼?
(A) 提醒大家要洗手
(B) 質疑部門程序
(C) 增進私人關係
(D) 解釋口腔衛生

A 12 🔊 154

What does the speaker mention about fillings?
(A) They are used to repair cavities.
(B) They are common procedures.
(C) They are expensive to perform.
(D) They are covered by insurance.

說話者對於補牙是怎麼說的?
(A) 補牙是用來修補蛀牙的。
(B) 補牙是常見的療程。
(C) 進行補牙的費用很貴。
(D) 補牙是由保險給付。

C 13 🔊 155

According to the speaker, where can the listeners find additional information?
(A) On toothpaste packaging
(B) At a dentist
(C) On the internet
(D) In the manual

根據說話者所述,聽眾可以在哪裡取得更多資訊?
(A) 牙膏包裝
(B) 牙醫診所
(C) 在網路上
(D) 說明書

重要單字片語

1. **settle down** 安靜下來(= calm down)
   Stop chatting and settle down. The presentation is about to begin.
   安靜下來不要再聊天了。報告即將要開始。

2. **sb's best bet** 對某人最好的辦法
   If you want to get around the city, taking the bus is your best bet.
   如果你想在這座城市四處逛逛,搭公車是你最好的辦法。

3. **rinse** [rɪns] vt. & n. 沖洗
   rinse sth out 將某物沖洗乾淨
   Can you help me rinse these cups out and put them on the counter?
   你可以幫我把這些杯子洗乾淨然後放在檯子上嗎?

4. **filling** [ˋfɪlɪŋ] n. 補牙;(補牙的)填料

5. **query** [ˋkwɪrɪ] vt. 質疑,表示疑問
   Apparently, I'm not in a position to query their decision.
   顯然地,我不夠資格去質疑他們的決定。

6. **packaging** [ˋpækɪdʒɪŋ] n. 包裝;包裝材料(不可數)

7. **manual** [ˋmænjʊəl] n. 說明書;使用手冊

Questions 14 through 16 refer to the following announcement and schedule. 🔊 156

Your attention, please. This announcement is to remind you that free flu shots are available for all department staff on Level 2 between 9 AM and 10 AM. If you haven't signed up yet, you can speak to me before we head downstairs in about 20 minutes. Also, to prevent the spread of disease, all employees must wear face masks while in the department if they are displaying any flu symptoms. The masks are located in the storage cabinet next to the water cooler. I also encourage everyone to regularly sanitize their hands using the dispensers located along walking routes and at entrances. If we work together, we can contain the illness throughout the coming flu season.

Flu Shot Schedule	
Department	Time
Administration	8 AM – 9 AM
Marketing	9 AM – 10 AM
Production	10 AM – 2 PM
Warehouse	2 PM – 4 PM

14 至 16 題請聽以下公告，並請看以下時間表。

請大家注意。本公告是為了提醒大家，免費的流感疫苗已經可以供應給位在二樓的部門全體員工，施打時間為早上九點至十點。如果有人尚未報名，可以在我們約二十分鐘後出發下樓前告訴我。另外，為了避免疾病傳染，全體員工若有流感症狀，在部門期間都必須戴上口罩。口罩放在飲水機旁的置物櫃裡。我也鼓勵大家經常使用設在走廊與入口處的乾洗手機來消毒雙手。如果大家同心協力，就能在快要到來的流感季當中控制好疫情。

疫苗施打時間表	
部門	時間
行政部	早上八點至九點
行銷部	早上九點至十點
生產部	早上十點至下午兩點
倉儲部	下午兩點至四點

B **14** 🔊 157

Look at the graphic. Which department does the speaker work in?
(A) Administration
(B) Marketing
(C) Production
(D) Warehouse

請看圖表。說話者在哪一個部門工作？
(A) 行政部門
(B) 行銷部門
(C) 生產部門
(D) 倉儲部門

113

Chapter 06 Reading Test

D **15** 🔊 158 🇬🇧

What are the listeners asked to do if they have flu-like symptoms?
(A) Take sick leave
(B) Receive a flu shot
(C) Meet at the water cooler
(D) Wear a face mask

聽眾如果有流感症狀的話被要求做什麼事？
(A) 請病假
(B) 施打流感疫苗
(C) 在飲水機旁見
(D) 戴上口罩

C **16** 🔊 159 🇬🇧

What are the listeners encouraged to do?
(A) Exit the building
(B) Drink more water
(C) Clean their hands often
(D) Work overtime

聽眾被鼓勵做什麼事？
(A) 離開大樓
(B) 喝更多水
(C) 常常清潔雙手
(D) 加班工作

重要單字片語

1. **storage** [ˈstɔrɪdʒ] *n*. 儲藏（不可數）
2. **cabinet** [ˈkæbənɪt] *n*. 櫃子
3. **water cooler** 飲水機
4. **dispenser** [dɪˈspɛnsɚ] *n*. 分發裝置，分配器
5. **contain** [kənˈten] *vt*. 抑制，控制
   The police were called to help contain the violence.
   已通知警力來幫助壓制暴力行為。
6. **warehouse** [ˈwɛrˌhaʊs] *n*. 倉庫
7. **sick leave** 病假（不可數）
   personal leave 事假
   maternity leave 產假

Part 5 Incomplete Sentences

C **17**

The nurse advised Mr. Fritsch against getting the yellow fever vaccine as he is ------- to eggs.

(A) allergy　　　(B) allergist　　　(C) allergic　　　(D) allergen

護理師建議費利奇先生不要打黃熱病疫苗，因為他對雞蛋過敏。

理由

1. 本題測試下列固定用法：
   allergic [əˈlɝdʒɪk] *a*. 過敏的（與介詞 to 並用）
   be allergic to...　　對……過敏
   Tom is allergic to peanuts.
   湯姆對花生過敏。

2. (A) **allergy** [ˈælədʒɪ] *n.* 過敏（與介詞 to 並用）
   (B) **allergist** [ˈælədʒɪst] *n.* 治療過敏的醫生
   (D) **allergen** [ˈælədʒən] *n.* 過敏原
3. 根據上述，(C) 項應為正選。

> 🔍 重要單字片語
>
> **yellow fever** [ˌjɛloˈfivɚ] *n.* 黃熱病（一種流行於熱帶及亞熱帶的傳染病）

B **18**

Taking lots of food supplements is no substitute for consuming a balanced, healthy -------.

(A) to diet　　　　　(B) diet　　　　　(C) dieted　　　　　(D) dietary

吃許多營養補充品無法取代均衡、健康的飲食。

> 理由
>
> 1. 空格前有不定冠詞 a 及形容詞 balanced（均衡的）與 healthy（健康的），得知空格內應置名詞。
> 2. 選項 (A) 為不定詞、選項 (B) 可為名詞與動詞、選項 (C) 為動詞過去式、選項 (D) 為形容詞。
> 3. 根據上述，(B) 項應為正選。

> 🔍 重要單字片語
>
> 1. **substitute** [ˈsʌbstəˌtjut] *n.* 替代品
> 2. **consume** [kənˈsum] *vt.* 吃，喝；消耗
>
> It's unhealthy to consume junk food all day.
> 整天吃垃圾食物是不健康的。

B **19**

No sooner had the doctor diagnosed Mrs. Hanson's disease ------- she started to worry about how she was going to break the bad news to her family.

(A) when　　　　　(B) than　　　　　(C) before　　　　　(D) so

醫生一診斷出韓森太太的病後，她就開始擔心要如何告訴家人這壞消息。

> 理由
>
> 1. 本題測試下列固定句構：
>   **No sooner had + 主詞 + 過去分詞 + than + 主詞 + 過去式動詞**
>   = As soon as + 主詞 + 過去式動詞，主詞 + 過去式動詞
>   = The moment / The instant + 主詞 + 過去式動詞，主詞 + 過去式動詞　　一……就……
>   No sooner had I seen Ted than I told him the truth.
>   = As soon as I saw Ted, I told him the truth.
>   = The moment I saw Ted, I told him the truth.
>   我一見到泰德，就把真相告訴他。
> 2. 根據上述，(B) 項應為正選。

Chapter 06　Reading Test

重要單字片語

break [brek] *vt.* & *vi.* 揭露（三態為：break, broke [brok], broken [ˋbrokən]）
It was the local newspaper that first broke the story.
率先揭露這則消息的是當地的報紙。

D 20

You should cover your mouth when you sneeze so you don't risk ------- other people with your germs.

(A) infect　　　(B) infected　　　(C) to infect　　　(D) infecting

打噴嚏時應該摀住嘴巴，這樣你的細菌才不會危及他人。

理由

1. 本題測試下列固定用法：

   risk + V-ing　　造成……的風險

   If you cut corners on safety, you risk endangering other people's lives.
   如果你在安全上偷工減料的話，你會危害到他人的性命。

2. 根據上述，(D) 項應為正選。

重要單字片語

1. **sneeze** [sniz] *vi.* 打噴嚏
   Don't be so rude! Cover your mouth when you sneeze.
   別這麼沒禮貌！打噴嚏時要摀住嘴。

2. **germ** [dʒɝm] *n.* 細菌，病菌（常為複數）

C 21

------- the successful surgery, Ms. Chalamet is now able to lead a happy, healthy life without the need for costly medication.

(A) Despite　　　(B) Otherwise　　　(C) Thanks to　　　(D) In order that

由於那場成功的手術，沙拉梅特女士現在能過著健康快樂的生活，而無須倚賴昂貴的藥物。

理由

1. 空格後為名詞詞組 the successful surgery（那場成功的手術），得知空格應置介詞，使之後的名詞詞組作其受詞。

2. 選項中：

   (A) **despite** [dɪˋspaɪt] *prep.* 儘管
   　Despite his hard work, John still failed the test.
   = In spite of his hard work, John still failed the test.
   　儘管他很努力，約翰還是沒通過考試。

   (B) **otherwise** [ˋʌðɚ͵waɪz] *adv.* 除此之外；否則（可修飾形容詞或整句）
   　Sam fell off his bike and bruised his knee but otherwise unhurt.
   　山姆從腳踏車上跌落，撞傷了膝蓋，除此之外沒有受傷。
   　＊ bruise [bruz] *vt.* 使瘀傷

My parents lent me the money. Otherwise, I couldn't have afforded the trip.
我爸媽借錢給我。否則，我原本是付不起這次旅費的。

(C) **thanks to...** 由於……
= because of...
= due to...
= owing to...
Thanks to Peter's full support, we finished the work as scheduled.
由於彼得全力支持，我們按預定計畫完工了。

(D) **in order that** + 主詞 + 助動詞（如：will、can、may 等）+ 原形動詞　　為了要……
= so that + 主詞 + 助動詞（如：will、can、may 等）+ 原形動詞
I got up early in order that / so that I could catch the first train.
= I got up early in order to / so as to catch the first train.
我早起是為了趕搭首班火車。

3. 選項中僅 (A)、(C) 項為介詞，根據語意，(C) 項應為正選。

重要單字片語

costly [ˈkɔstlɪ] *a.* 昂貴的（= expensive）

Part 6 Text Completion

Questions 22-25 refer to the following memo.

From:	Occupational Health & Safety Officer
To:	All Employees
Subject:	The Importance of Good Nutrition

As part of our commitment to the health and well-being of our employees, I would like to stress the importance of a sufficient intake of -------. Not only is eating food full of
22.
nutrition beneficial for your health, ------- it is vital for maintaining focus and energy in
23.
the workplace. -------. They should also contain plenty of fresh fruit and vegetables,
24.
whole grains, and healthy fats. You should eat as ------- ultra-processed foods as
25.
possible, as these have been linked to obesity and associated medical conditions. Over the next couple of days, I will be sharing more resources on healthy eating choices and recipe suggestions.

Chapter 06 Reading Test

22 至 25 題請看以下備忘錄。

> 寄件者：職場健康與安全專員
> 收件者：所有員工
> 主　旨：優質營養的重要性
>
> 本單位致力於促進所有員工的健康與福祉，其中一部分就是強調攝取足夠<u>營養素</u>的重要性。攝取富含營養的食物不僅有益健康，<u>也</u>是在職場保持專注與活力的關鍵。<u>你的三餐應該包含充分的蛋白質</u>。此外還應該有大量新鮮蔬果、全穀物與優質脂肪。你們該盡量<u>少</u>吃超加工食品，因為它們與肥胖及肥胖造成的疾病有密切關聯。在接下來的幾天當中，我會分享更多健康飲食選項與推薦食譜的資源。

D　22

(A) pharmacies　　(B) interns　　(C) flosses　　**(D) nutrients**

理由

1. (A) **pharmacy** [ˈfɑrməsɪ] *n.* 藥房
    After seeing the doctor, I had my prescription filled at the nearest pharmacy.
    看完醫生後，我把處方箋拿到最近的藥局配藥。

   (B) **intern** [ˈɪntɝn] *n.* 實習生；實習醫生
    The hospital intern assisted the doctor in examining patients.
    這位醫院實習醫生協助醫師檢查病患。

   (C) **floss** [flɔs] *n.* 牙線
    You should use mouthwash and floss on a daily basis.
    你應該每天使用漱口水和牙線。

   (D) **nutrient** [ˈnjutrɪənt] *n.* 養份（可數）
    The salad was full of nutrients and tasted delicious.
    這碗沙拉營養滿分，吃起來也很美味。

2. 根據語意，(D) 項應為正選。

B　23

(A) and　　**(B) but**　　(C) or　　(D) until

理由

1. 本題測試下列固定用法：
    not only... but (also)...　　不僅……也……
    Not only does Jim treat people well, but he (also) works hard.
    吉姆不僅待人和善，工作也很認真。

2. 根據上述，(B) 項應為正選。

D 24

(A) Getting enough exercise is likewise necessary.
(B) This recipe includes a good mix of healthy ingredients.
(C) Being able to concentrate on your work is essential.
(D) Your meals should include adequate amounts of protein.

> 理由

1. (A) 從事充足的運動也是必須的。
   (B) 這食譜綜合了多種健康食材。
   (C) 能夠專心在你的工作上很重要。
   (D) 你的三餐應該包含充分的蛋白質。

2. 空格後表示 "They should also contain plenty of fresh fruit and vegetables, whole grains, and healthy fats."（此外還應該有大量新鮮蔬果、全穀物與優質脂肪。）選項 (D) 呼應餐點應含有的養分，且置入空格後與前後文語意連貫，故 (D) 項應為正選。

A 25

(A) few　　　　　(B) a few　　　　(C) little　　　　(D) a little

> 理由

1. 本題測試下列固定用法：
   few [f ju] *a.* 沒幾個，很少（之後須接複數名詞）
   a few　　一些（之後亦須接複數名詞）
   little [ˋlɪtḷ] *a.* 沒多少（之後須接不可數名詞）
   a little　　有一些（之後亦須接不可數名詞）
   David has few friends.
   大衛沒幾個朋友。
   I have a few good friends.
   我有一些好朋友。
   Peter has little money.
   彼得沒多少錢。
   I still have a little money.
   我還有一點錢。

2. 根據上述，(A) 項應為正選。

重要單字片語

1. **commitment** [kəˋmɪtmənt] *n.* 承諾；奉獻
2. **well-being** [ˏwɛlˋbiɪŋ] *n.* 福祉（不可數）
3. **stress** [strɛs] *vt.* 強調
   My father always stresses the importance of being punctual.
   我父親一向強調準時的重要性。
4. **sufficient** [səˋfɪʃənt] *a.* 充份的，足夠的
5. **intake** [ˋɪnˏtek] *n.* （食物的）攝取
6. **adequate** [ˋædəkwət] *a.* 足夠的，合乎需要的
   be adequate for...　　合乎……的需要
   The current office space is not adequate for our needs.
   現有的辦公空間無法滿足我們的需求。
7. **resource** [ˋriˏsɔrs] *n.* 資源（常用複數）

Chapter 06 Reading Test

Part 7 Reading Comprehension

Questions 26-28 refer to the following introduction.

Dr. Michael Mosley

Dr. Michael Mosley was a renowned British doctor, writer, and broadcaster. He completed his medical degree in 1985, initially intending to become a psychiatrist. However, he soon changed course and went into broadcasting, first as a producer and then as a presenter. He hosted an array of factual programs, including *Trust Me, I'm a Doctor* and *Just One Thing*, that focused on medical issues, healthy eating, and disease prevention.

In the early 2010s, Dr. Mosley developed Type 2 diabetes, prompting him to explore ways to manage or reverse the progression of the disease. This led to his biggest claim to fame: popularizing the 5:2 diet. By promoting this fasting strategy, he helped many people to lose weight and lead healthier lives.

---

26 至 28 題請看以下簡介。

麥可・莫斯利醫師

麥可・莫斯利醫師是知名的英國醫師、作家與電視主持人。他在 1985 年讀完醫學學位，起初打算成為精神科醫師。不過他很快就轉換了跑道踏入傳播界，一開始擔任製作人，後來就當上節目主持人。他主持過多檔實境節目，包含《相信我沒錯，因為我是醫師》以及《一件事的提醒》，主要探討醫療問題、健康飲食及疾病預防等。

在 2010 年代初期，莫斯利醫師得了第二型糖尿病，促使他開始探索控制或翻轉病情的方法。他因而推廣 5：2 輕斷食法，並因此爆紅。他推廣這種斷食法，幫助許多人瘦身並且過著更健康的生活。

B **26**

What is indicated about Dr. Mosley?
(A) He studied broadcasting at university.
(B) He didn't plan to be a presenter upon graduation.
(C) He taught psychiatry during the 1980s.
(D) He quit college before he earned his degree.

本文說了莫斯利醫師的什麼事情？
(A) 他在大學學的是傳播。
(B) 他在畢業當下沒有打算當節目主持人。
(C) 他在 1980 年代教授精神病學。
(D) 他在獲得大學學位前退學了。

理由

根據本文第一段第二句 "He completed his medical degree in 1985, initially intending to become a psychiatrist."（他在 1985 年讀完醫學學位，起初打算成為精神科醫師。）得知，(B) 項應為正選。

C **27**

The word "developed" in paragraph 2, line 1, is closest in meaning to
(A) processed
(B) invented
(C) suffered
(D) emerged

第二段第一行 developed 這個字意思最接近
(A) 處理；加工
(B) 發明
(C) 患有
(D) 浮現，顯現

理由

根據本文第二段第一句 "In the early 2010s, Dr. Mosley developed Type 2 diabetes, …"（在 2010 年代初期，莫斯利醫師得了第二型糖尿病，……）得知，(C) 項應為正選。

B **28**

According to the introduction, what is Dr. Mosley most famous for?
(A) Finding a cure for a contagious disease
(B) Making an eating plan well known
(C) Working on many television dramas
(D) Losing a huge amount of weight

根據簡介，莫斯利醫師最出名的是哪件事？
(A) 找到治癒某傳染病的療法
(B) 讓某種飲食方法廣為人知
(C) 參與許多電視劇
(D) 大幅減重

理由

根據本文第二段第二句 "This led to his biggest claim to fame: popularizing the 5:2 diet."（他因而推廣 5：2 輕斷食法，並因此爆紅。）得知，(B) 項應為正選。

Chapter 06 Reading Test

重要單字片語

1. **renowned** [rɪˋnaʊnd] *a.* 著名的
2. **initially** [ɪˋnɪʃəlɪ] *adv.* 開始時，最初
3. **psychiatrist** [saɪˋkaɪətrɪst] *n.* 精神科醫師；心理治療師（等於口語中的 shrink [ʃrɪŋk] ）
4. **array** [əˋre] *n.* 一批，一系列
   an array of...　一連串 / 一大堆……
   Mary bought an array of flowers at the market.
   瑪麗在市場買了一堆花。
5. **factual** [ˋfæktʃʊəl] *a.* 事實的；與事實相關的；真實的
6. **diabetes** [ˏdaɪəˋbitiz] *n.* 糖尿病（不可數）
7. **prompt** [prɑmpt] *vt.* 促使；激勵
   prompt sb to V　驅使某人做……
   The study prompted thousands of people to stop using plastic bags.
   這項研究促使數千人停止使用塑膠袋。
8. **reverse** [rɪˋvɝs] *vt.* 翻轉，扭轉
9. **fasting** [ˋfæstɪŋ] *n.* 禁食；絕食

Questions 29-32 refer to the following online chat discussion.

Soraya Mirza　2:53 p.m.
I saw on the news today that norovirus cases are increasing rapidly across the country.

Ibrahim Faraz　2:55 p.m.
Ugh! It's so contagious that if a few people in the office get infected, it'll spread like wildfire.

Amari Diallo　2:56 p.m.
Is norovirus like Covid?

Soraya Mirza　2:56 p.m.
No, it's a stomach bug that causes vomiting and diarrhea. You've never heard of it?

Amari Diallo　2:57 p.m.
I don't keep up-to-date with health news.

Soraya Mirza　2:58 p.m.
In that case, I think we should make sure everyone in the office knows what symptoms to look out for and what to do if they catch it.

Ibrahim Faraz　3:00 p.m.
I'll get HR to create a campaign. Lina, are you online?

Lina Jaber　　　　3:01 p.m.
Yeah, I'm here. I'll get started right away. I think the key message to stress is prevention through hand hygiene: hand sanitizer doesn't kill the virus; only washing thoroughly with soap and water does.

Soraya Mirza　　　3:03 p.m.
You should also emphasize the company policy that if people catch it, they need to stay off work for 48 hours after their symptoms have gone.

29 至 32 題請看以下線上聊天討論串。

索拉雅・米爾莎　　下午 2:53
我今天在新聞上看到全國各地的諾羅病毒病例人數正在飆升。

易卜拉欣・法拉茲　下午 2:55
呃！那個傳染性是很強的，如果辦公室裡有幾個人感染，很快就會大幅擴散。

阿瑪里・迪亞洛　　下午 2:56
諾羅病毒跟新冠病毒一樣嗎？

索拉雅・米爾莎　　下午 2:56
不一樣，它是一種腸胃炎，會造成嘔吐與腹瀉。你從來沒聽過嗎？

阿瑪里・迪亞洛　　下午 2:57
我沒有在注意最新的健康報導。

索拉雅・米爾莎　　下午 2:58
如果是這樣，我們一定要確任辦公室裡每個人都知道該注意哪些症狀，還有感染後該怎麼辦。

易卜拉欣・法拉茲　下午 3:00
我去叫人資那邊弄一個活動。麗娜，妳在線上嗎？

麗娜・賈伯　　　　下午 3:01
在。我馬上就去弄。我覺得主要的訊息就是要強調手部衛生跟預防染病的關係：乾洗手是殺不死病毒的，非得用肥皂徹底洗手才行。

索拉雅・米爾莎　　下午 3:03
妳還要強調公司的規定，說染病的人必須在症狀消失的四十八小時後才能恢復上班。

Chapter 06 Reading Test

D **29**

What is mainly being discussed?
(A) A report that contains errors
(B) A fire that spreads quickly
(C) A show that focuses on health
(D) A virus that causes sickness

本文主要在討論什麼？
(A) 一份有錯誤的報告
(B) 一場快速蔓延的大火
(C) 一個以健康為主題的節目
(D) 一種致病的病毒

理由

本文主要在討論諾羅病毒的傳染與該公司的因應對策，故 (D) 項應為正選。

C **30**

Who is unfamiliar with the subject?
(A) Ms. Mirza
(B) Mr. Faraz
(C) Mr. Diallo
(D) Ms. Jaber

哪一位不熟悉本文的主題？
(A) 米爾莎女士
(B) 法拉茲先生
(C) 迪亞洛先生
(D) 賈伯女士

理由

根據下午 2:57，迪亞洛先生寫 "I don't keep up-to-date with health news."（我沒有在注意最新的健康報導。）得知，(C) 項應為正選。

C **31**

At 3:01 p.m., what does Ms. Jaber most likely mean when she writes, "I'll get started right away"?
(A) She will commence a medical procedure.
(B) She will activate an emergency protocol.
(C) She will begin working on a campaign.
(D) She will start delivering a presentation.

下午 3:01，賈伯女士寫「我馬上就去弄」時，最有可能是什麼意思？
(A) 她將進行一項醫療程序。
(B) 她將啟動一項緊急應變的標準流程。
(C) 她將開始規劃一項活動。
(D) 她將開始進行簡報。

理由

根據下午 3:00，法拉茲先生寫 "I'll get HR to create a campaign. Lina, are you online?"（我去叫人資那邊弄一個活動。麗娜，妳在線上嗎？）及下午 3:01，賈伯女士寫 "Yeah, I'm here. I'll get started right away."（在。我馬上就去弄。）得知，(C) 項應為正選。

D **32**

According to Ms. Mirza, what message should be stressed to workers?
(A) They should obtain an official doctor's note.
(B) They should use hand sanitizer liberally.
(C) They should monitor colleagues for symptoms.
(D) They should follow a company regulation.

根據米爾莎女士的說法，應該向員工強調什麼訊息？
(A) 他們應取得正式的醫師診斷書。
(B) 他們應大量使用乾洗手。
(C) 他們應關注同事的症狀。
(D) 他們應遵守公司的規定。

> 理由
> 根據下午 3:03，米爾莎女士寫 "You should also emphasize the company policy that if people catch it, ..."（妳還要強調公司的規定，說染病的人……）得知，(D) 項應為正選。

重要單字片語

1. **rapidly** [ˈræpɪdlɪ] *adv.* 迅速地，快速地
2. **spread like wildfire** （疾病或訊息）迅速傳播開來
   The rumor spread like wildfire.
   該謠言快速地傳播開來。
3. **bug** [bʌɡ] *n.* （細菌或病毒引起的）小毛病
4. **up-to-date** [ˈʌptəˈdet] *a.* 最新的
   For up-to-date news and weather, stay tuned to CNN.
   想知道最新的新聞與氣象，請鎖定 CNN 頻道。
5. **commence** [kəˈmɛns] *vi.* 開始（= begin）
   The meeting is scheduled to commence at 2 o'clock.
   該會議預定於兩點開始。
6. **protocol** [ˈprotəˌkɔl] *n.* 標準流程；議定書
7. **liberally** [ˈlɪbərəlɪ] *adv.* 大量地

Chapter 07 Listening Test

🎧 Part 1 Photographs

D 1 🔊 161 🇬🇧

(A) He is washing dishes in the sink.
(B) He is replacing a faucet.
(C) He is turning a control knob.
(D) He is installing a household appliance.

(A) 他在水槽裡洗碗盤。
(B) 他正在換水龍頭。
(C) 他正在轉動控制鈕。
(D) 他在安裝家用電器。

重要單字片語

1. **replace** [rɪˋples] *vt.* 替換，取代
   replace A with B　用 B 替換 A
   The thief replaced the real painting with a fake one.
   那名竊賊用假畫將真跡掉包。

2. **faucet** [ˋfɔsɪt] *n.* 水龍頭（= tap，英式英語）

C 2 🔊 162 🇦🇺

(A) Some cardboard boxes have been stacked along the wall.
(B) Some wooden boards have been moved outside.
(C) The room is currently being renovated.
(D) The door has been laid on the ground.

(A) 沿牆邊堆著幾個紙箱。
(B) 有幾塊木板被搬到外面。
(C) 房間正在整修。
(D) 門板被放在地上。

重要單字片語

1. **cardboard** [ˋkɑrd͵bɔrd] *n.* 硬紙板
   a cardboard box　紙箱
2. **stack** [stæk] *vt.* 把……疊起來 & *n.* 一疊；一堆

Since Kate didn't have a bookshelf, she stacked her books next to her bed.
因為凱特沒有書架，所以她把書都堆在床邊。

🎧 Part 2 Question-Response

A ③ 🔊 164 🇨🇦 🇬🇧

Is your company going to relocate from New York to Mexico?
(A) Yes, we'll reopen in January.
(B) We've been in business for ten years.
(C) We have a branch office in New York.

貴公司即將要從紐約搬遷至墨西哥嗎？
(A) 沒錯，我們會在一月重新營運。
(B) 我們已經經營十年了。
(C) 我們在紐約有分公司。

🔍 重要單字片語

1. **be in business**　經營
   The publishing company has been in business for thirty years.
   該出版社已經經營三十年了。

2. **branch** [bræntʃ] *n.* 分公司
   = a branch office

B ④ 🔊 165 🇬🇧 🇦🇺

Are you going to place a bid on that house?
(A) No, the price is quite reasonable.
(B) Yes, it's in very good condition.
(C) You can come to my place.

你要出價買那棟房子嗎？
(A) 不，房價相當合理。
(B) 是的，那棟房子屋況很好。
(C) 你可以來我家。

🔍 重要單字片語

reasonable [ˈriznəbḷ] *a.* 合理的

🎧 Part 3 Conversations

Questions 5 through 7 refer to the following conversation. 🔊 167 M: 🇨🇦 W: 🇺🇸

W: Why did the bosses decide to renovate the office building? It's not that old, is it?
M: No, it's not old, but they want to help the environment by making the building more sustainable.
W: Do you know what the work involves?
M: A large part of the renovation is fitting solar panels on the roof. The company wants to be self-sufficient in terms of energy.
W: That sounds like a lot of work. When is it going to finish?
M: Unfortunately, the contractor has fallen behind schedule due to supply problems with the solar panels.
W: That's annoying. I hope the situation gets remedied soon.

Chapter 07 Listening Test

5 至 7 題請聽以下會話。

> 女：為什麼老闆決定整修辦公室大樓？大樓還不算很老舊吧，對不對？
> 男：對，是不算老舊，但他們想要把大樓改成永續性建築，這樣對環境比較好。
> 女：你知道整修工作包含哪些東西嗎？
> 男：整修工作有很大一部份是在頂樓加裝太陽能板。公司要在能源上自給自足。
> 女：好像是大工程。整修何時會完成？
> 男：很遺憾包商因為太陽能板的供應出問題，工程進度落後了。
> 女：討厭。希望情況能盡快改善。

A 5 ◀) 168

Why is the building being renovated?
(A) To make it more environmentally friendly
(B) To ensure it complies with all local laws
(C) Because the staff have complained about it
(D) Because it is very old and falling apart

大樓為什麼在整修？
(A) 好讓大樓更環保
(B) 好確保大樓符合當地的所有法規
(C) 因為員工對大樓有所抱怨
(D) 因為大樓非常老舊且快要解體了

B 6 ◀) 169

What does the man say about the roof?
(A) It needs to be completely replaced.
(B) Solar panels will be installed there.
(C) It will feature some wind turbines.
(D) A rooftop garden will be added.

男子對屋頂有何說法？
(A) 屋頂需要全面翻新。
(B) 那裡將安裝太陽能板。
(C) 那裡將會出現幾座風力渦輪機。
(D) 那裡將要蓋個屋頂花園。

C 7 ◀) 170

What has caused the contractor's work to fall behind schedule?
(A) Structural concerns
(B) Weather problems
(C) Supply chain issues
(D) Labor shortages

造成承包商工程落後的原因是什麼？
(A) 結構問題
(B) 天候問題
(C) 供應鏈問題
(D) 勞工短缺

重要單字片語

1. **involve** [ɪnˈvɑlv] *vt.* 牽涉；包含
   This part of the test involves answering questions about a photograph.
   考試的這一部分是要就一張照片來回答相關問題。

2. **sufficient** [səˈfɪʃənt] *a.* 充份的，足夠的

3. **in terms of...** 就……而言
   In terms of comfort and design, this car is superior to that one.
   就舒適度和設計而言，這輛車優於那一輛。

4. **fall apart** 瓦解；破碎

5. **turbine** [ˈtɜbaɪn] *n.* 渦輪機

6. **shortage** [ˈʃɔrtɪdʒ] *n.* 短缺

Questions 8 through 10 refer to the following conversation with three speakers. 🔊 171
M: 🇦🇺 W1: 🇬🇧 W2: 🇺🇸

W1: We've just had a call from the tenant in 4B about a leak in his kitchen.
M: Another leak? That's the third one in the building this month.
W2: I'll contact the maintenance guy and ask him to take a look.
M: Hang fire on that for a moment, Jessica. I think we need more than just an inspection of one apartment; we need someone to maintain the water pipes throughout the building.
W1: I'll do some research on reputable plumbing firms and run them by you both.
M: Thanks, Emma.
W2: This plan of action could prove costly, though.
M: You're right, Jessica, it could. But if we can minimize damage to the property and inconvenience to the tenants, it will save money in the long run.

8 至 10 題請聽以下三人的會話。

> 甲女：4B 的租戶剛剛打電話來，說他的廚房漏水了。
> 男：又漏水？這個月大樓裡已經第三次漏水了。
> 乙女：我來聯絡維修人員，請他去看一看。
> 男：等一下，潔西卡。我想我們不只需要檢查一間公寓，我們得找人來檢修整棟大樓的水管管路了。
> 甲女：我去做點功課，篩選幾家口碑不錯的水電行，然後跟你們討論。
> 男：謝謝妳，艾瑪。
> 乙女：不過這樣做可能要花不少錢喔。
> 男：對，潔西卡，是可能很花錢。但如果我們能把大樓的損害以及租戶的不便降到最低，長遠來看還是省錢的。

D **8** 🔊 172 🇨🇦

Where most likely do the speakers work?
(A) In an insurance company
(B) In a construction company
(C) In a law faculty at a university
(D) In a property management company

說話者最有可能在哪裡工作？
(A) 在保險公司
(B) 在營造公司
(C) 在大學的法學院
(D) 在物業管理公司

C **9** 🔊 173 🇨🇦

What does the man suggest doing?
(A) Sending the maintenance man to apartment 4B
(B) Offering compensation to the affected tenant
(C) Conducting an inspection of the building's pipes
(D) Evacuating residents while the problem is being fixed

男子建議怎麼做？
(A) 派遣維修人員去 4B 公寓
(B) 給受影響的租戶提供賠償
(C) 對整棟大樓的水管進行檢修
(D) 在解決問題期間撤離租戶

Chapter 07 Listening Test

B 🔟 🔊 174 🇨🇦

What concern does Jessica raise about the plan? | 潔西卡對此做法提出何種顧慮？
(A) It might take too long. | (A) 可能很耗時。
(B) It might be expensive. | **(B) 可能很貴。**
(C) It might annoy tenants. | (C) 可能造成租戶困擾。
(D) It might be a failure. | (D) 可能失敗。

🔍 重要單字片語

1. **maintenance** [ˈmentənəns] *n.* 維護，保養（不可數）
2. **hang / hold fire** 延緩做出決定（英式英語）
3. **inspection** [ɪnˈspɛkʃən] *n.* 檢查；查驗
4. **reputable** [ˈrɛpjətəbl̩] *a.* 聲譽好的，有信譽的
5. **firm** [fɝm] *n.* 公司（= company）
6. **run sth by sb** 向某人徵求對某事物的看法

You'd better run the proposal by your manager first.
這提案你最好先看你的主管怎麼說。

7. **in the long run** 長遠地，最後
In the long run, I think that investing in the software company is a great idea.
長遠來看，我認為投資這家軟體公司是好主意。

8. **faculty** [ˈfæklti] *n.* （高等院校的）院、系
9. **evacuate** [ɪˈvækjuˌet] *vt.* 撤離；疏散

🎧 Part 4 Talks

Questions 11 through 13 refer to the following talk. 🔊 176 🇬🇧

I'd like to brief you on our search for a suitable location for our new corporate headquarters. We've narrowed the choice down to two locations. The first is two floors of the Benson Building. It's centrally located, completely refurbished, and has first-rate security. There's just one problem — the cost is beyond our budget. I bid a lower price, but the owner isn't willing to budge. The second property is on the north shore and is well within our budget. Unfortunately, it's currently occupied and requires a lot of maintenance. We'd also have to construct a reception area. I'll now present some photographs and a cost analysis of both properties.

11 至 13 題請聽以下談話。

> 有關適合我們公司總部的新地點，我想跟各位簡報研究的結果。我們已篩選出兩個地點。第一個是班森大樓裡的兩層樓。地點位處中央、完全整修過且安全措施一流。只是有個問題 ── 費用超出了我們的預算。我出了較低的價格，但屋主不願意降價。第二間房產位在北岸上，而且完全在我們的預算內。可惜的是，目前還有人在使用，而且需要大幅整修。我們還得建造接待區。我現在會展示一些照片以及兩個房產的費用分析。

B 11 🔊 177 🇨🇦

What is the purpose of the talk?
(A) To respond to complaints from customers
(B) To outline options for new headquarters
(C) To summarize a project that has finished
(D) To explain directions to a security guard

該談話的目的是什麼？
(A) 回應顧客的客訴
(B) 概述新總部的地點選項
(C) 總結已完成的專案
(D) 向警衛解釋方針

CH 07

D 12 🔊 178 🇨🇦

Which of the following is a problem with the first property?
(A) Poor reception
(B) Inadequate security
(C) Inconvenient location
(D) High price

下列哪一項是第一個房產的問題？
(A) 信號接收效果差
(B) 安全措施不足
(C) 地點不方便
(D) 價格高昂

C 13 🔊 179 🇨🇦

What will the speaker most likely do next?
(A) Drive to a property
(B) Sign a lease
(C) Show more information
(D) Display a map

說話者接下來最有可能做什麼？
(A) 開車去某房產
(B) 簽訂租約
(C) 展示更多資訊
(D) 展示地圖

重要單字片語

1. **brief** [brif] *vt.* 向（某人）做簡報
   brief sb on / about sth　向某人簡介某事
   We were briefed on what the job would include at the interview.
   我們在面試時被告知這份工作的內容。

2. **narrow sth down (to…)**
   把某件事的可能性或選擇縮小（到……）
   I've narrowed the list down to three candidates.
   我把候選人名單縮小至三人。

3. **budge** [bʌdʒ] *vi.* & *vt.* （使）改變主意；（使）移動
   I tried persuading Amy to change her mind, but she wouldn't budge.
   我嘗試說服艾咪改變主意，但是她不為所動。

4. **currently** [ˋkɝntlɪ] *adv.* 目前
   Are you currently taking any medication?
   你目前有服用任何藥物嗎？

5. **occupied** [ˋɑkjəˌpaɪd] *a.* 有人使用的；已被占用的；忙於……

6. **reception** [rɪˋsɛpʃən] *n.* 接待；（信號）接收效果
   the reception desk　接待處
   good / bad phone reception
   電話信號良好 / 差

7. **outline** [ˋaʊtˌlaɪn] *vt.* 概述 & *n.* 大綱；輪廓
   John roughly outlined his proposal at the beginning of the presentation.
   約翰在報告開頭大略講述了他的提案。

8. **inadequate** [ɪnˋædəkwət] *a.* 不足的

131

Chapter 07 Listening Test

Questions 14 through 16 refer to the following telephone message. 🔊 180

Hello, Linda. This is Don calling from Don White Real Estate. I've contacted your previous landlords, and they say you are a trustworthy tenant. Therefore, the landlord will offer you the property if you agree to the terms of the lease. The rent is $500 a month, which is due on the first of every month. Before you move in, he expects two months' rent as a deposit. The deposit will be returned when the lease expires, but <u>only after a thorough inspection</u>. I will hand over the keys when you pay the deposit and sign the lease. Oh, and the owner said to remind you that pets are strictly prohibited.

14 至 16 題請聽以下電話留言。

> 琳達，妳好。我是唐懷特不動產的阿唐。我已聯絡過妳的前房東，他們都說妳是個值得信任的房客。所以，如果妳同意租約條款的話，屋主願意租房子給妳。租金是每個月五百美金，每個月一號繳費。在妳喬遷之前，他希望的押金是兩個月的租金。租約到期時押金會歸還，但得在徹底檢查之後。妳付押金及簽合約後，我就會把鑰匙交給妳。還有，屋主說要提醒妳，嚴厲禁止飼養寵物。

C **14** 🔊 181

Who most likely is the speaker?
(A) A tenant
(B) A landlord
(C) A real estate agent
(D) A property inspector

說話者最有可能是誰？
(A) 房客
(B) 房東
(C) 房仲人員
(D) 房產稽查員

C **15** 🔊 182

What does the speaker imply when he says, "<u>only after a thorough inspection</u>"?
(A) The lease was broken by the last tenant.
(B) Inspections are conducted regularly.
(C) The return of deposits is not guaranteed.
(D) Tenants should vacate the premises.

說話者說「得在徹底檢查之後」時，在暗示什麼？
(A) 前一位租戶違約。
(B) 檢查是定期舉行的。
(C) 押金不保證能退還。
(D) 租戶得搬離該地。

A **16** 🔊 183

What does the speaker remind the listener about?
(A) Pets are not allowed.
(B) Keys must be returned to the office.
(C) A deposit will not be necessary.
(D) A witness must sign the lease.

說話者提醒聽者什麼？
(A) 不允許有寵物。
(B) 鑰匙必須歸還給辦公室。
(C) 不需要押金。
(D) 見證人必須簽租約。

Chapter 07 Reading Test

重要單字片語

1. **trustworthy** [ˈtrʌstˌwɝðɪ] *a.* 可靠的，值得信賴的
2. **expire** [ɪkˈspaɪr] *vi.* 到期，過期，失效
   My contract with the company will expire next month.
   我與該公司的合約下個月會失效。
3. **hand over sth / hand sth over**
   交出某物
   Yi-Ting handed over the red envelope to her parents.
   怡婷把紅包拿給了她的爸媽。
4. **strictly** [ˈstrɪktlɪ] *adv.* 嚴格地
5. **prohibit** [prəˈhɪbɪt] *vt.* 禁止
   prohibit sb from N/V-ing
   禁止某人……
   You are strictly prohibited from entering that section of the building.
   嚴禁諸位進入本大樓該區域。
6. **vacate** [ˈveˌket] *vt.* 搬出，空出
   Hotel guests are requested to vacate their rooms by noon.
   飯店房客須於中午之前退房。

Part 5　Incomplete Sentences

D **17**

The rental property is nicely decorated and fully -------; however, the utility bills are very expensive.

(A) furniture　　(B) furnishings　　(C) furnish　　(D) furnished

這間出租物業裝潢很不錯且傢俱齊全，不過水電費很貴。

理由

1. 空格前有副詞 fully（完整地），得知空格內應置形容詞。
2. (A) **furniture** [ˈfɝnɪtʃɚ] *n.* 傢俱（集合名詞，不可數）
   a piece of furniture　　一件傢俱
   a lot of furniture　　許多傢俱
   (B) **furnishings** [ˈfɝnɪʃɪŋz] *n.* 傢俱、窗簾等裝飾物件（恆用複數）
   (C) **furnish** [ˈfɝnɪʃ] *vt.* 配備傢俱；提供
   furnish sb with sth　　提供某人某物
   This company furnishes you with all the equipment you'll need for hiking.
   這家公司提供你健行所需的一切裝備。
   (D) **furnished** [ˈfɝnɪʃt] *a.* 配備傢俱的
   Her mansion was luxuriously furnished.
   她的豪邸裝潢奢華。
3. 根據上述，(D) 項應為正選。

D **18**

Mr. and Mrs. Metz took out an €80,000 ------- to buy the three-story house in Berlin.

(A) foundation　　(B) demolition　　(C) grid　　(D) mortgage

梅斯夫婦辦了八萬歐元的貸款買下在柏林的一間三層透天厝。

Chapter 07 Reading Test

> 理由

1. (A) **foundation** [faʊnˋdeʃən] *n.* 地基
    lay / dig the foundation　　鋪設 / 挖鑿地基
   (B) **demolition** [ˌdɛməˋlɪʃən] *n.* 拆毀，摧毀
   (C) **grid** [grɪd] *n.* 輸電網
   (D) **mortgage** [ˋmɔrgɪdʒ] *n.* 房貸（本字中 t 不發音）
    take out / pay off a mortgage　　辦理 / 清償房貸
2. 根據語意，(D) 項應為正選。

> 重要單字片語

story [ˋstɔrɪ] *n.* 樓層，層
a ten-story building　　十層樓高的大樓

C **19**

The electronics company announced that it is relocating to a smaller property to reduce its ------- expenses.

(A) outage　　　　(B) tile　　　　(C) overhead　　　　(D) resident

這間電子產品公司宣布將搬遷到較小的辦公地點，以減輕日常營運開支。

> 理由

1. (A) **outage** [ˋaʊtɪdʒ] *n.* 停電期間
    a power outage　　停電
    The severe storm struck the area, causing power outages for several days.
    劇烈的暴風雨襲擊該區，造成斷電數日。
   (B) **tile** [taɪl] *n.* 磁磚；瓦片
   (C) **overhead** [ˋovɚˌhɛd] *n.* 經常性開支，營運開支
    How can you make a profit if your overhead is so high?
    你的營運開支這麼高怎能有利潤？
   (D) **resident** [ˋrɛzədənt] *n.* 居民 & *a.* 居住的
    local residents　　當地居民
2. 根據語意，(C) 項應為正選。

A **20**

Ms. Hanson is attracted to the luxury city-center apartment because of its -------, which was inspired by classical European styles.

(A) architecture　　(B) concrete　　(C) foreman　　(D) neighbor

漢森女士深受這間市中心豪華公寓所吸引，因為公寓的建築風格有經典歐洲建築的味道。

> 理由

1. (A) **architecture** [ˈɑrkəˌtɛktʃɚ] *n.* 建築（風格）
   (B) **concrete** [ˈkɑnkrit] *n.* 混凝土
       John paved his garden with concrete.
       約翰的花園鋪設混凝土。
   (C) **foreman** [ˈfɔrmən] *n.* 工頭，領班
       The foreman oversaw the construction of the new bridge.
       該工頭監督新橋的建築工程。
   (D) **neighbor** [ˈnebɚ] *n.* 鄰居
2. 根據語意，(A) 項應為正選。

> 重要單字片語

1. **luxury** [ˈlʌkʃərɪ] *n.* 奢華（不可數）；奢侈品（可數）
   a luxury apartment　　豪華公寓
2. **inspire** [ɪnˈspaɪr] *vt.* 激發，鼓勵，啟發

   inspire sb to V　　激發某人做某事
   It was Judy who inspired me to study French in college.
   是茱蒂啟發了我在大學攻讀法文。

C **21**

Mr. Anderson doesn't like the proposed layout for the new office because it will be ------- harder for employees to interact with one another.

(A) many　　(B) all　　(C) much　　(D) very

安德森先生不喜歡所提案的新辦公室格局，因為那會讓員工之間更難與彼此溝通。

> 理由

1. 本題測試可用來修飾形容詞比較級的副詞，常見的有四個：

   much / far / a lot / a great deal + 形容詞比較級　　比……多得多
   John's English is much better than Henry's.
   約翰的英文比亨利的好太多了。
   That's a far better idea.
   那個主意好得多。
2. 原題空格後有形容詞比較級 harder（更困難的），故知 (C) 項應為正選。

> 重要單字片語

interact [ˌɪntɚˈækt] *vi.* 交流，互動
interact with sb　　與某人互動
The class is so big that the teacher has only a limited amount of time to interact with each student.
這個班級太大，因此老師只有有限的時間能與班上每位學生互動。

Chapter 07 Reading Test

Part 6 Text Completion

Questions 22-25 refer to the following article.

Tallest Building Planned

Mann Brothers Construction Company won the bid to construct the city's first-ever skyscraper on Thoreau Boulevard. The proposed 41- ------- building will become the tallest structure in the city. When ------- in two years, the building will offer both office and residential space. -------. If the proposed designs pass the strict Department of Town Planning building codes, a groundbreaking ceremony with representatives from Mann Brothers and officials from the city government ------- on October 1.

22. / 23. / 24. / 25.

---

22 至 25 題請看以下文章。

最高大樓規劃

曼恩兄弟建築公司贏得了標案，要著手在梭羅大道建造本市首座摩天大樓。擬議的四十一層大樓將成為本市最高的建築物。兩年後完工時，本大樓將提供辦公及居住空間。建築藍圖目前正在審查中。如果擬定的設計圖通過城鎮規劃署嚴格的建築法規，將會在十月一日舉行破土儀式，屆時來自曼恩兄弟建築公司的代表及市政府官員將共同參與。

D **22**

(A) stories (B) floors (C) floor **(D) story**

▍理由

1. 表示「（某建築物）有幾層樓」時，要使用 story（英式英文採 storey 的拼法），使用時可與數字及連字號並用以形成複合形容詞，之後常接 building、structure 等字，如：a five-story building（一棟五層樓大樓）；表示「在幾樓」時，則要使用 floor，如：on the fifth floor（在五樓）。
   Their new house has four stories, including the attic.
   他們的新房子有四層樓，包括閣樓。
   They're considering buying a three-story house.
   他們正在考慮買一棟三層樓的房子。
   My office is on the eighth floor.
   我的辦公室位在八樓。

2. 根據上述，空格前有 41，且之後有連字號，得知應使用 story，以形成複合形容詞 41-story（四十一層樓的），其內的名詞不可用複數，須使用單數名詞，故 (D) 項應為正選。

C **23**

(A) completion　　(B) completing　　(C) completed　　(D) completes

理由

1. 原句實等於：
   When it is completed in two years, the building will offer both office and residential space.（it 即指主要子句的主詞 the building）
2. 惟我們得知由 when 所引導的副詞子句中，該副詞子句的主詞若與主要子句的主詞相同時，可省略該主詞，並將之後的動詞改為現在分詞，若遇 be 動詞，則改為 being 後再予以省略，故此句省略主詞 it 後，可將 is 改為 being 後省略，保留過去分詞 completed。
3. 根據上述，(C) 項應為正選。

A **24**

(A) Blueprints of the structure are currently being reviewed.
(B) Residents have started to move into the building.
(C) The building was constructed in record time.
(D) Security is our top priority in the office.

理由

1. (A) 建築藍圖目前正在審查中。
   (B) 住戶已經開始搬進該棟大樓。
   (C) 該大樓以創紀錄的時間建造完成。
   (D) 在辦公室，安全是我們的首要考量。
2. 空格後的句子為 "If the proposed designs pass..."（如果擬定的設計圖通過……），而選項 (A) 中的 blueprints of the structure（建築藍圖）與空格後句子中的 proposed designs（擬定的設計圖）形成關連，且 (A) 項置入空格後與後文語意連貫，故為正選。

C **25**

(A) held　　(B) is held　　(C) will be held　　(D) holding

理由

1. 當 If 引導的條件句中副詞子句使用現在式，則主要子句使用未來式。
   If the weather is fine tomorrow, we'll go on a picnic.
   　　　　　現在式　　　　　　　未來式
   如果明天天氣好，我們就去野餐。
2. 空格前的副詞子句 "If the proposed designs pass..."（如果擬定的設計圖通過……）採現在式動詞 pass，其後主要子句中的主詞為 "a groundbreaking ceremony"（破土儀式），並有介詞片語 "with representatives from Mann Brothers..."（來自曼恩兄弟建築公司的代表……）作修飾，得知空格內應置未來式動詞，故 (C) 項應為正選。

Chapter 07 Reading Test

重要單字片語

1. **skyscraper** [ˈskaɪˌskrepɚ] *n.* 摩天大樓
2. **residential** [ˌrɛzəˈdɛnʃəl] *a.* 住宅的
   a residential area　住宅區
3. **blueprint** [ˈbluˌprɪnt] *n.* 藍圖，計畫
4. **review** [rɪˈvju] *vt.* & *n.* 審查
   be under review　審查中
   Staff performance is reviewed annually.
   員工的表現會每年接受審查。
   The terms of the contract are under review.
   合約條款正在審議。
5. **code** [kod] *n.* 法規，法則
   building codes　建築法規
6. **groundbreaking** [ˈɡraʊndˌbrekɪŋ] *n.*
   （建築工程的）破土
7. **in record** [ˈrɛkɚd] **time**
   創紀錄的時間
   The young man climbed to the peak of the mountain in record time.
   這位年輕人以創紀錄的時間攀上山峰。

Part 7 Reading Comprehension

Questions 26-27 refer to the following text-message chain.

Vance Broderick, 8:36 AM
Hi, Jacinta. I noticed a property for lease while I was driving in. It's a large warehouse with an attached office complex.

Jacinta Cassie, 8:37 AM
That used to be the headquarters of Independent Buyers. I heard there's a huge parking lot built under the offices. It would be a huge relief to solve our parking problem once and for all.

Vance Broderick, 8:38 AM
Absolutely.

Jacinta Cassie, 8:39 AM
Unfortunately, I doubt that a building that large would be in our price range.

26 至 27 題請看以下簡訊討論串。

凡斯・柏德瑞克，上午 8:36
嗨，潔辛塔。我開車來時注意到一棟要出租的房屋。它是一個大型倉庫，附有辦公區。

潔辛塔・凱西，上午 8:37
那裡曾是獨立買家的總部。我聽說辦公區下方建有大型停車場。這會是個大解脫，可以徹底解決我們的停車問題。

凡斯・柏德瑞克，上午 8:38
沒錯。

潔辛塔・凱西，上午 8:39
可惜的是，我不確定這麼大型的建築是否在我們能接受的價格範圍內。

C 26

What is most likely true about Mr. Broderick?
(A) He is a real estate agent.
(B) He owns a large warehouse.
(C) He is looking for a new office location.
(D) He works for a large manufacturer.

有關柏德瑞克先生，下列哪一項最有可能是對的？
(A) 他是房地產經紀人。
(B) 他擁有一個大型倉庫。
(C) 他正在找新的辦公室。
(D) 他為一家大型廠商工作。

理由

於上午 8:36，柏德瑞克先生留言 "I noticed a property for lease... It's a large warehouse with an attached office complex."（我注意到一棟要出租的房屋……它是一個大型倉庫，附有辦公區。），該則留言中提及 "office complex"（辦公區），可推測柏德瑞克先生應是在尋找新的辦公室，故 (C) 項應為正選。

Chapter 07 Reading Test

D **27**

At 8:38 AM, what does Mr. Broderick most likely mean when he writes, "Absolutely"?
(A) He accepts the rental fee.
(B) He promises to bargain over the price.
(C) He confirms the address of the new office building.
(D) He thinks the property can solve the parking issue.

於上午 8:38，柏德瑞克先生寫下「沒錯」時，最有可能是什麼意思？
(A) 他接受租金費用。
(B) 他保證會商談價格。
(C) 他確認了新辦公大樓的地址。
(D) 他認為該建築能解決停車問題。

理由

於上午 8:37，凱西女士留言 "I heard there's a huge parking lot built under the offices. It would be a huge relief to solve our parking problem once and for all."（我聽說辦公區下方建有大型停車場。這會是個大解脫，可以徹底解決我們的停車問題。）可推測柏德瑞克先生是在回應凱西女士提出能解決停車問題的想法，故 (D) 項應為正選。

重要單字片語

1. **warehouse** [ˈwɛr͵haʊs] *n.* 倉庫
2. **complex** [ˈkɑmplɛks] *n.* 綜合建築物，綜合區
3. **relief** [rɪˈlif] *n.* 舒解
4. **once and for all**　　徹底地，一勞永逸地
   Let's try to solve the problem once and for all.
   咱們設法把這個問題徹底搞定。
5. **doubt** [daʊt] *vt.* 懷疑
   I doubt John is competent for that job.
   我懷疑約翰能勝任那份工作。
   ＊ **competent** [ˈkɑmpətənt] *a.* 有能力的
6. **range** [rendʒ] *n.* 範圍
7. **bargain** [ˈbɑrɡən] *vi.* 商談（價格、條件等），講價

Questions 28-30 refer to the following letter.

To the Editor:

    We are outraged by your report, "Is the New City Stadium Safe Enough to Use?" (Tuesday, May 2). The "safety hazards" referred to in the apparently hastily written article will not exist by the June 1 opening.

    It goes without saying that during construction operations, electric cables must first be laid before being covered with a protective plastic layer. — [1] —. The protective coverings are scheduled to be in place by May 20. With regard to the "leaking ceiling," anyone familiar with construction sites can tell you that once the major sections of a building site are in place, they must be washed to remove leftover construction residue. — [2] —. The stadium is currently being cleaned, resulting in excess water, which will be removed long before the June 1 opening. Finally, the "empty boxes" will be fitted with proper fire safety equipment, as scheduled, on May 23.

    Your reporting on this construction site can only be called "sensationalism." Our safety record, in fact, is second to none in this state. I can assure you that the whole building will comply with fireproof and waterproof standards. — [3] —. We are also on schedule at this phase of the project. We invite your reporter to visit the stadium on May 26, the date for scheduled completion, and to write another article. We hope the reporter would then be considerate enough to include an apology, which we believe is due. — [4] —.

John Beavers
President
Altmore Construction Services

Chapter 07　Reading Test

28 至 30 題請看以下信件。

致編輯：

　　本公司對貴報社《新市立體育場使用上是否夠安全？》（五月二日星期二）的報導甚感憤怒。那篇看似草率撰寫的文章中提到的「安全隱憂」，六月一日開幕前將不會存在。

　　不用說，施工作業期間，電纜包上塑料護層之前須先行鋪設。— [1] —。保護層的作業預計在五月二十日前完成。有關「天花板漏水」，任何熟悉建築工地的人都會告訴你，一旦建築工地的主要區塊完工，建設公司就必須清洗那些區域以清除剩餘建材。— [2] —。該體育場目前正在清理，造成了多餘的積水，這些早在六月一日開幕日來臨之前便會清理乾淨。最後，那些「空箱」將按計畫於五月二十三日配備適當的消防安全設備。

　　貴報社針對此建築工地的報導只能說是「聳人聽聞」。實際上，本公司的安全紀錄在本州可說是首屈一指。我可以向你保證，整棟大樓將會符合防火、防水的標準。— [3] —。本公司也正照建案的計畫進行該階段。我們將邀請貴報社記者於預定完工日五月二十六日來本體育場參觀，並另外撰寫一份報導。本公司期盼該名記者那時能周到地附上道歉，相信那會是我們應得的。— [4] —。

阿爾特莫爾建設服務公司
總裁
約翰・比佛斯

A　28

What is indicated about the news report?
(A) It contains numerous inaccuracies.
(B) It is an unbiased account.
(C) It has caused a sensation.
(D) It is the first in a series of articles.

關於該新聞報導，本文說明了什麼？
(A) 它裡面有相當多不準確的資訊。
(B) 它是一篇公正的報導。
(C) 它造成轟動。
(D) 它是一系列文章中的第一篇。

理由
本文第二段寄信者針對該篇報導的陳述一一做出明確的指正，故 (A) 項應為正選。

C　29

What does Mr. Beavers suggest to the editor?
(A) Promoting the stadium
(B) Reading another review
(C) Writing a follow-up article
(D) Updating a schedule

比佛斯先生建議該位編輯做什麼？
(A) 推廣該體育場
(B) 讀另一份評論
(C) 寫一篇後續報導
(D) 更新行程

> 〈理由〉

根據本文第三段倒數第二句 "We invite your reporter to visit the stadium on May 26, the date for scheduled completion, and to write another article."（我們將邀請貴報社記者於預定完工日五月二十六日來本體育場參觀，並另外撰寫一份報導。）得知，(C) 項應為正選。

A 30

In which of the positions marked [1], [2], [3], and [4] does the following sentence best belong?

"The wiring for the entire structure has already been laid."

(A) [1]
(B) [2]
(C) [3]
(D) [4]

在標記 [1]、[2]、[3]、[4] 的四個位置當中，哪一項為下列句子的最佳位置？

「整棟建築的線路已經都鋪好了。」

(A) [1]
(B) [2]
(C) [3]
(D) [4]

> 〈理由〉

本文第二段第一句提及 "..., electric cables must first be laid before being covered with a protective plastic layer."（……，電纜包上塑料護層之前須先行鋪設。），得知本題的句子置入該句後方語意較為合理，故 (A) 項應為正選。

重要單字片語

1. **outrage** [ˈaʊtˌredʒ] vt. 使震怒 & n. 憤怒
   be outraged at... 對……感到震怒
   Tony was outraged at the way he had been treated.
   湯尼對所遭受的待遇感到非常憤怒。

2. **hazard** [ˈhæzɚd] n. 隱憂；危險

3. **It goes without saying that...**
   不用說，……

4. **operation** [ˌɑpəˈreʃən] n.（工商業）活動

5. **be in place**　準備妥當

6. **with regard to...**　關於……
   = in regard to...
   = regarding...

   With regard to this issue, I'd like to hear your opinions.
   關於這件事，我想聽聽諸位的意見。

7. **residue** [ˈrɛzɪˌdu] n. 剩餘物，殘留物

8. **fit** [fɪt] vt. 安置，安裝
   The rooms were all fitted with smoke alarms.
   所有的房間都安裝了煙霧報警器。

9. **sensationalism** [sɛnˈseʃənlˌɪzəm] n.
   聳人聽聞，譁眾取寵

10. **be second to none**　首屈一指

11. **due** [du] a. 應得到的

Chapter 08 Listening Test

Part 1 Photographs

B **1** 🔊 185 🇺🇸
(A) The man is pushing a car back to a garage.
(B) The worker is assembling a car.
(C) All of the doors are completely closed.
(D) The worker is opening the hood with a tool.

(A) 男子正在將車推回車庫。
(B) 工人正在組裝車子。
(C) 車門全都關緊。
(D) 工人正在用工具開啟引擎蓋。

重要單字片語

garage [gə`rɑʒ] *n.* 車庫

C **2** 🔊 186 🇬🇧
(A) The wheels are being repaired by the driver.
(B) The truck is reversing out of a warehouse.
(C) The man is operating the forklift.
(D) The man is filling up a gas tank.

(A) 司機正在修理輪胎。
(B) 卡車正在從倉庫裡倒車出來。
(C) 男子正在操作推高機。
(D) 男子正在給油箱加滿油。

重要單字片語

reverse [rɪ`vɝs] *vi.* & *vt.* 倒車
Carl carefully reversed his new sports car into a parking space.
卡爾小心翼翼地將他的新跑車倒進停車位。

144

Part 2 Question-Response

A 3 🔊 188

Why is the general manager visiting the plant?
(A) To check on their progress
(B) Once or twice a month
(C) It's on Madison Street

總經理為何要蒞臨工廠？
(A) 為檢查他們的工作進度
(B) 每個月一兩次
(C) 在麥迪森路上

重要單字片語

check on...　檢查……，查看……
I gave my neighbor a spare key to check on my pet fish while I was away on business.
我給鄰居一把備用鑰匙，在我出差時幫忙顧一下我養的魚。

A 4 🔊 189

What do you do with products that have small defects?
(A) We sell them at lower prices.
(B) In the quality control department.
(C) I want a full refund.

你們怎麼處置有細微缺陷的產品？
(A) 本公司會用較低廉的價格賣掉。
(B) 在品管部門。
(C) 我想要全額退款。

重要單字片語

refund [ˈriˌfʌnd] *n.* & [rɪˈfʌnd] *vt.* 退款
demand a refund　　要求退款

Part 3 Conversations

Questions 5 through 7 refer to the following conversation. 🔊 191 M: W:

M: You always buy the same brand of car. Don't you ever compare them with other makes and models?
W: I used to, but I found International Motors always produce quality vehicles. They have a very good reputation for paying attention to every detail during the manufacturing stage and throughout the assembly process. As a consequence, I know I will get a quality vehicle at a competitive price.
M: Would you change brands if you noticed that their quality had begun to slip?
W: If one of their cars weren't up to scratch, I would research other companies to see what else is available.

Chapter 08 Listening Test

5 至 7 題請聽以下會話。

男：妳都是買同一個廠牌的車子。難道妳不曾將妳買過的車子跟其他廠牌及車款做過比較嗎？
女：我以前曾經這麼做，但我發現國際汽車公司長久以來都生產優質好車。他們的車子之所以能深獲好評，是因為在製造階段和整個組裝過程都有注意到每個細節。所以，我知道我可以用比別家廠牌便宜的價錢買到一部品質優良的車子。
男：如果妳感覺到他們的品質開始下滑，妳會改買其他廠牌的車子嗎？
女：如果他們有車款沒有達到標準，我就會去對其他廠牌做功課，看看有沒有別的好車可買。

C **5** 192

What is most likely true about the woman?
(A) She works in a car factory.
(B) She has recently sold a car.
(C) She always buys cars from the same manufacturer.
(D) She regrets purchasing her current vehicle.

有關這名女子，下列何者最有可能是符合事實的？
(A) 她在汽車工廠上班。
(B) 她最近把車子賣掉了。
(C) 她都是買同一家廠牌的車子。
(D) 她後悔買了她現在的這部車。

A **6** 193

What does the woman mention about International Motors?
(A) It has a good reputation.
(B) Its quality has begun to slip.
(C) It no longer manufactures cars.
(D) It is under new management.

這名女子提到國際汽車的什麼事？
(A) 它的聲譽良好。
(B) 它的品質開始下滑了。
(C) 它已不再生產汽車了。
(D) 它由新的管理層管理。

B **7** 194

What does the man want to know?
(A) If the woman takes care of her car
(B) If the woman would switch to other brands
(C) If the woman likes to drive
(D) If the research is reliable

這名男子想要知道什麼？
(A) 這名女子是否有照料她的車子
(B) 這名女子是否會換其他廠牌
(C) 這名女子是否喜歡開車
(D) 那項研究是否可信賴

重要單字片語

1. **brand** [brænd] *n.* 品牌；牌子；商標
   What brand of toothpaste do you use?
   你用哪個牌子的牙膏？

2. **compare A with B**
   比較 A 與 B，將 A 與 B 做比對
   It's interesting to compare Western customs with Chinese customs.
   比較西方與中國的習俗相當有趣。

3. **make** [mek] *n.* 牌子；品牌

4. **pay attention to...**   注意……
   You should pay attention to / attend to the coach.
   你該注意教練說的話。

5. **assembly** [ə'sɛmblɪ] *n.* (機器的)裝配；組裝（不可數）
   an assembly line   生產線；裝配線

We need to build two more assembly lines to speed up production.
我們需另外建立兩條生產線以加速生產。

6. **as a consequence**
因此（= as a result / therefore）
The mayor is very popular. As a consequence, he is likely to be reelected.
這位市長非常受歡迎。因此，他很可能會連任。

7. **competitive** [kəmˋpɛtətɪv] *a.* （價格、服務等）有競爭力的；競爭的
The two banks merged in order to become more competitive in their industry.
這兩家銀行的合併是為了讓他們在銀行業更具競爭力。

8. **slip** [slɪp] *vi.* 下降；變壞；下跌
Oil prices have slipped in recent weeks.
最近幾週油價一直在下跌。

9. **be / come up to scratch**
達到應有的水準；夠得上標準
= be / come up to standard

10. **manufacturer** [ˌmænjəˋfæktʃərɚ] *n.* 製造業者；廠商
Manufacturers often introduce new products to keep their business booming.
廠商為了讓生意興隆，常推出新產品。

11. **regret** [rɪˋgrɛt] *vt.* 後悔（以動名詞作受詞）；遺憾（以不定詞作受詞）（三態為：regret, regretted [rɪˋgrɛtɪd], regretted）
There are things we regret doing and things we regret not having done.
我們會後悔做了某些事，也有些事我們後悔沒去做。
I regret to inform you that you flunked five subjects this semester.
我很遺憾要通知你，你這學期被當了五科。

12. **reliable** [rɪˋlaɪəb!̩] *a.* 可信賴的；可信的；可靠的
The weather forecast is not always reliable, so you'd better carry an umbrella with you just in case.
天氣預報並不一定可靠，所以你最好帶把傘以防萬一。

CH 08

Questions 8 through 10 refer to the following conversation. 🔊 195   W: 🇺🇸   M: 🇨🇦

W: I heard we hired ten new quality control inspectors to monitor the factory's output.
M: That's right. Over the last three months, we mechanized a lot of the manufacturing processes. We wanted to know how efficient the changes have been, so we began tests last month. Now, we're ready to take it to the next stage.
W: The manager has been smiling a lot lately.
M: I'm not surprised. We doubled production. We just need to find out if our quality has also improved.
W: Could you send me the results of the next test? I'd like to take a look.
M: I'll send you a report when it's finished.

8 至 10 題請聽以下會話。

女：我聽說我們公司僱用了十位新的品管人員來檢測工廠生產的產品。
男：沒錯。過去三個月以來，我們公司已經把許多生產過程機械化。我們想要知道這些變革的成效如何，所以我們上個月開始測試。現在，我們已經準備要進入下一個階段了。
女：經理最近一直笑容滿面。
男：我一點都不會感到意外。我們的產量增加了一倍。我們只需要弄清楚品質是否也改進了。
女：你可以把下次測試的結果寄給我嗎？我想看一下。
男：測試結束後我會寄一份報告給妳。

Chapter 08 Listening Test

B 8 🔊 196 🇬🇧

What took place last month?
(A) Employee examinations
(B) Equipment tests
(C) Job interviews
(D) Budget changes

上個月發生了什麼事？
(A) 職員考試
(B) 設備測試
(C) 求職面試
(D) 預算變動

A 9 🔊 197 🇬🇧

What does the woman imply when she says, "The manager has been smiling a lot lately"?
(A) The previous stage of mechanization went well.
(B) The factory has won an international award.
(C) The final test results were better than expected.
(D) The quality control inspector has been appointed.

這名女子說「經理最近一直笑容滿面」時，在暗示什麼？
(A) 機械化的上一個階段進行得很順利。
(B) 工廠榮獲國際獎項。
(C) 最後的測試結果優於預期。
(D) 已經指派了品管人員。

D 10 🔊 198 🇬🇧

What does the woman request?
(A) Product prices
(B) Production quotas
(C) Exam scores
(D) Test results

這名女子要求什麼？
(A) 產品的價格
(B) 產量的配額
(C) 考試的分數
(D) 測試的結果

重要單字片語

1. **output** [ˈaʊtˌpʊt] *n.* 產品；生產量
   The country's agricultural output has doubled in the past year.
   去年該國的農業生產量成長了一倍。

2. **double** [ˈdʌbḷ] *vt.* 使加倍
   The boss was surprised when Sarah asked him to double her salary.
   莎拉要求老闆把她的薪資加倍時，老闆吃了一驚。

3. **mechanization** [ˌmɛkənəˈzeʃən] *n.* 機械化（不可數）

4. **appoint** [əˈpɔɪnt] *vt.* 任命，指派
   appoint sb (as) + 職務
   任命某人擔任某職務
   Mr. Miller was appointed (as) Sales Director.
   米勒先生被任命為業務主任。

5. **quota** [ˈkwotə] *n.* 配額；限額

🎧 Part 4 Talks

Questions 11 through 13 refer to the following talk. 🔊 200 🇦🇺

I've called this meeting to discuss how to deal with a serious problem at our factory. In short, worker morale is very low. Over the past few months, employees have become less productive and taken more sick days. Since our workers are your responsibility, I'm asking you to motivate them by holding frank discussions at meetings to find out why this problem has arisen recently. Replacing our current workforce is not the answer. If the root problems are not found and corrected, the same situation will happen again. The prosperity of our company depends on how you handle this problem. Report back to me in two weeks with the results of your discussions, and I'll pass on your reports to the board.

11 至 13 題請聽以下談話。

> 我召開這個會議是要討論如何處理我們工廠的一個嚴重問題。簡單講就是，員工的士氣非常低落。過去幾個月當中，員工生產力變差而且請病假的天數增多了。既然我們的員工就是各位的責任，我要求各位找你的組員暢所欲言地開會討論，找出最近士氣低落的原因，藉此激勵他們。換掉我們目前的所有員工是解決不了問題的。如果找不出根本問題來予以矯正，同樣的情形就會再次上演。本公司的昌隆興旺就要靠各位如何處理這個問題了。兩個禮拜以後來向我報告你們跟組員商討的結果，我再將各位的報告轉給董事會。

D 11 201

What problem does the speaker mention?
(A) Manpower shortages
(B) Operational safety
(C) Low wages
(D) Low morale

說話者提到什麼問題？
(A) 人力不足
(B) 操作安全
(C) 低薪
(D) 士氣低落

A 12 202

Why is the speaker concerned?
(A) Company workers are unproductive.
(B) Company employees are on strike.
(C) He has been sick for a long time.
(D) He must hire many new workers.

說話者為什麼憂心？
(A) 公司員工的生產效益差。
(B) 公司員工在罷工。
(C) 他生病蠻久了。
(D) 他必須招聘許多新員工。

C 13 203

What are the listeners asked to do?
(A) Watch videos
(B) Read reports
(C) Hold meetings
(D) Reduce costs

聽眾被要求做什麼事？
(A) 觀看影片
(B) 閱讀報告
(C) 召開會議
(D) 減少成本

Chapter 08 Listening Test

重要單字片語

1. **call a meeting** 召開會議
   Let's call a meeting with Jessie and Jessica.
   我們找潔西和潔西卡一起來開個會吧。

2. **deal with...** 處理……（= handle...）
   It's time we took action to deal with / handle the problem.
   該是我們採取行動處裡那個問題的時候了。

3. **motivate** [ˋmotə͵vet] vt. 激勵；激發；促使
   motivate sb to V 激勵某人從事……

4. **frank** [fræŋk] a. 坦誠的，坦白的；直言不諱的
   To be frank,... 坦白說，……
   To be frank, I don't think John is a good guy.
   老實說，我覺得約翰不是好人。

5. **arise** [əˋraɪz] vi. 出現（三態為：arise, arose [əˋroz], arisen [əˋrɪzṇ]）
   arise from... 由……引起
   Should the need arise, could you work on Sundays?
   萬一有需要，你可以星期日上班嗎？

6. **workforce** [ˋwɝk͵fɔrs] n. 全體職員
   Two-thirds of the workforce in this company is female.
   這家公司有三分之二的員工是女性。

7. **root** [rut] n. 根源；起因
   the root cause 根本原因
   What do you think is the root cause of your anxiety?
   你認為你焦慮的根本原因是什麼？

8. **prosperity** [prɑsˋpɛrətɪ] n. 繁榮；興盛
   In times of economic prosperity, everyone is optimistic about the future.
   在經濟繁榮時期，每個人對未來都很樂觀。

9. **report back to sb (on sth)**
   （就某事）向某人回報
   Find out as much as you can about the new staff member and report back to me.
   盡你所能去找這個新進人員的相關資料，然後向我回報。

10. **pass on sth to sb** 轉達某事給某人知道
    I'll certainly pass on your message to our manager.
    我一定會把你的訊息轉達給我們經理知道。

11. **manpower** [ˋmæn͵paʊɚ] n. 勞動力；人力（不可數）
    We need a large amount of money and manpower for this project.
    我們需要大量的財力及人力來推動這個計畫。

Questions 14 through 16 refer to the following excerpt from a meeting and chart.
🔊 204

Spring was a great season for McAlister Woolenwear. Not only did we reach 12,000 garments, but we also signed a contract to have our clothing sold in several major international department stores. Unfortunately, we ran into problems when we upgraded our machinery during the next season. The changeover didn't go as smoothly as expected; in fact, production came to a complete standstill for more than a week while we worked on resolving several issues. By autumn, everything was back to normal, and the upgrade caused a substantial increase in production. Next winter, we expect sales to increase dramatically. In the meantime, I propose adding an afternoon shift to build up our stockpile of products.

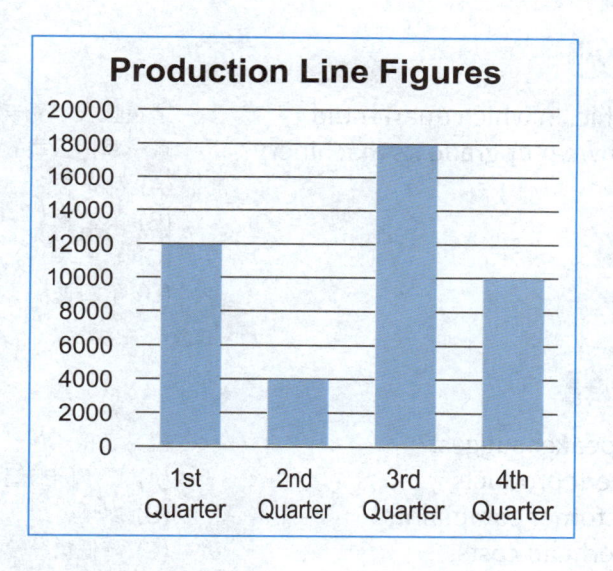

Production Line Figures

Quarter	Figure
1st Quarter	12000
2nd Quarter	4000
3rd Quarter	18000
4th Quarter	10000

14 至 16 題請聽以下會議摘錄，並請看以下圖表。

對於麥卡林斯特毛織品公司而言，春季的業績很棒。我們不但賣出了一萬兩千件衣服，而且簽了一份可以讓我們在幾家大型國際百貨公司賣衣服的合約。可惜的是，我們在第二季升級機器時遇到問題。這個轉換機器的過程並沒有預期的順利；事實上，在我們努力解決若干問題的同時，生產陷入完全停滯的狀態達一個星期之多。到了秋季，各方面都回復正常了，且機器升級也促使產量大增。我們預期明年冬季的銷量會大幅增加。在此同時，我建議增加一個下午班來擴大我們產品的存貨量。

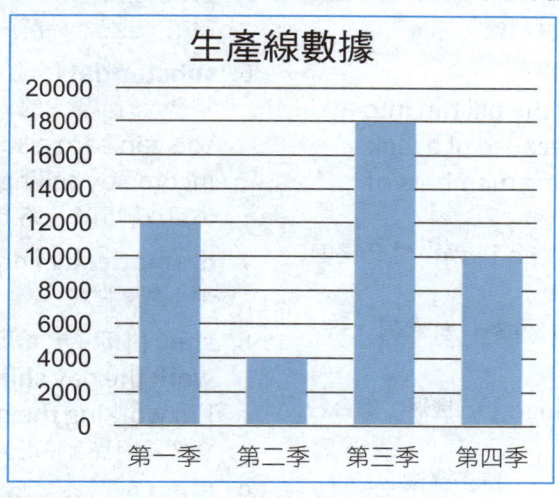

生產線數據

季	數據
第一季	12000
第二季	4000
第三季	18000
第四季	10000

C **14** 205

What happened in spring?
(A) A new product was launched.
(B) A trade show was held.
(C) A contract was signed.
(D) An agreement was canceled.

春季時發生了什麼事？
(A) 推出了一種新產品。
(B) 辦了一個商展。
(C) 簽了一份合約。
(D) 取消了一項協定。

Chapter 08 Listening Test

B 15 206 🇨🇦

Look at the graphic. In which quarter did McAlister Woolenwear upgrade its machinery?
(A) 1st quarter
(B) 2nd quarter
(C) 3rd quarter
(D) 4th quarter

請看圖表。麥卡林斯特毛織品公司在哪一季把公司的機器做了升級？
(A) 第一季
(B) 第二季
(C) 第三季
(D) 第四季

D 16 207 🇨🇦

What does the speaker suggest?
(A) Selling different products
(B) Handling customer complaints
(C) Reducing overhead costs
(D) Scheduling more work hours

說話者提議做什麼事？
(A) 賣不同的產品
(B) 處理客訴
(C) 降低營運費用
(D) 排進更多的工時

重要單字片語

1. **garment** [ˋgɑrmənt] *n.*（一件）衣服；成衣（可數）
   This garment must be hand-washed and air-dried.
   這件衣服一定要手洗並陰乾。

2. **run into...** 遇到……
   The enactment of the bill ran into trouble, mainly because of a lack of consensus among members of Congress.
   這個法案的制定過程碰上了麻煩，主因是國會議員缺乏共識。
   ＊ consensus [kənˋsɛnsəs] *n.* 意見一致；共識

3. **machinery** [məˋʃinərɪ] *n.* 機器（集合名詞，不可數）
   a lot of machinery　許多臺機器
   The general manager believes that more machinery should be bought to increase productivity.
   總經理認為應該買更多機器來增加產值。

4. **changeover** [ˋtʃendʒ͵ovɚ] *n.* 改變，轉變，變革
   The changeover to the new software has created a few problems.
   改用新軟體已經造成了一些問題。

5. **resolve** [rɪˋzɑlv] *vt.* 解決（= solve）
   resolve a problem　解決問題
   It took me five hours to resolve this problem.
   我花了五個小時解決這個問題。

6. **substantial** [səbˋstænʃəl] *a.* 大量的；相當大的；重大的
   You can earn a substantial amount of income by selling goods online.
   你可以利用在網路上賣東西來大賺一筆錢。

7. **dramatically** [drəˋmætɪklɪ] *adv.* 大幅度地；戲劇性地

8. **shift** [ʃɪft] *n.* 輪班
   work the day shift　上白天班
   I'm working the night shift this week.
   這個星期我上晚班。

9. **build up...** 擴大……

10. **stockpile** [ˋstɑk͵paɪl] *n.* 存貨量；儲備物資 & *vt.* 儲備
    They have huge stockpiles of coal.
    他們儲備了大量的煤。

11. **figure** [ˋfɪgjɚ] *n.* 數字；數據（一般用複數）；圖表
    Let's take a look at these figures before the meeting starts.
    會議開始前我們先來看一下這些數據吧。

Chapter 08　Reading Test

📖 Part 5　Incomplete Sentences

C **17**

\------- the plant has been working at full capacity, the manager wants us to find ways to accelerate our output even further.

(A) Because　　　(B) Whether　　　(C) Although　　　(D) As if

即便工廠已經產能全開，經理還是要我們找方法更進一步加快生產速度。

理由

1. (A) **because** [bɪˋkɔz] *conj.* 因為
   A new Mercedes is out of my reach because it is too expensive.
   全新賓士車對我而言遙不可及，因為太貴了。

   (B) **whether** [ˋ(h)wɛðɚ] *conj.* 是否；不論
   I wonder whether my friend will lend me money.
   不知道我朋友會不會借錢給我。

   (C) **although** [ɔlˋðo] *conj.* 雖然（= though）
   Although Karen and Dora are sisters, they barely resemble each other.
   雖然凱倫和朵拉是親姊妹，但她們倆長得只有一點點像。

   (D) **as if...** 彷彿……
   Peter loves me as if I were his own child.
   彼得愛我如同他的親生小孩。

2. 根據語意，(C) 項應為正選。

🔍 重要單字片語

1. **at full capacity**　盡全力
2. **output** [ˋaʊtˏpʊt] *n.* 生產量（不可數）

B **18**

This factory is the third- ------- manufacturer of automation equipment in the tri-state area and produces high-quality devices such as robotic arms.

(A) larger　　　(B) largest　　　(C) large　　　(D) less large

這家工廠是紐約等三州區域內的第三大自動化設備製造商，生產如機器人手臂等高品質設備。

理由

1. 本題測試下列固定用法：
   the + 序數詞（second, third, fourth, ...）+ 最高級形容詞 + 名詞單數形
   This is the fourth most popular song in the hit chart this week.
   這是本週暢銷歌曲的第四名。

2. 根據上述，空格前有 the third-（第三的），空格後有單數名詞 manufacturer（製造商），得知空格內應置最高級形容詞，故 (B) 項應為正選。

153

Chapter 08 Reading Test

D **19**

The dimensions for the product packaging ------- entered incorrectly into the sealing machine, which slowed down the process.

(A) does　　　　(B) do　　　　(C) was　　　　(D) were

在封裝機輸入的貨品包裝尺寸是錯的，導致流程被拖延。

理由

1. 本句的主詞為複數名詞 the dimensions（尺寸），後面接介詞片語 for the product packaging（貨品包裝）修飾主詞，空格後則為過去分詞 entered（被輸入），得知空格內應置 be 動詞複數型。
2. 根據上述，(D) 項應為正選。

重要單字片語

1. **enter** [ˈɛntɚ] vt.（電腦）輸入
   enter the password　輸入密碼
2. **incorrectly** [ˌɪnkəˈrɛktlɪ] adv. 不正確地

A **20**

Mr. Sklenar complained that the quality-control data is not -------; he wants the figures to be analyzed again.

(A) accurate　　　(B) accurately　　　(C) accuracy　　　(D) accumulate

斯克勒納先生抱怨說品管資料不準確，因此要求重新分析那些資料。

理由

1. 空格前有名詞 the quality-control data（品管資料）與 be 動詞 is，得知空格內應置形容詞。
2. (A) **accurate** [ˈækjərɪt] a. 精準的
   (B) **accurately** [ˈækjərɪtlɪ] adv. 精準地
   (C) **accuracy** [ˈækjərəsɪ] n. 準確性
   (D) **accumulate** [əˈkjumjəˌlet] vt. 累積 & vi. 堆積
3. 根據上述，(A) 項應為正選。

C **21**

As part of our modernization agenda, we propose ------- a faster conveyor belt system to streamline our existing procedures.

(A) preventing　　(B) downsizing　　(C) installing　　(D) measuring

我們現代化程序其中的一部份，就是建議安裝一套更快速的輸送帶系統，以提升現有流程的效率。

理由

1. (A) **prevent** [prɪˈvɛnt] vt. 防止；阻止
   prevent sb/sth from V-ing　防止某人 / 某物免於……
   The protesters prevented the workers from cutting down the old tree.
   抗議者阻止工人砍伐那棵老樹。

(B) **downsize** [ˈdaʊnˌsaɪz] *vt.* 縮小規模，裁員
　　Al was laid off because the department needed to downsize.
　　艾爾因為部門需要縮編而遭到裁員。

(C) **install** [ɪnˈstɔl] *vt.* 安裝，設置
　　The new anti-virus software has been installed on all the computers.
　　所有電腦都已安裝新的防毒軟體。

(D) **measure** [ˈmɛʒɚ] *vt.* 測量 & *vi.* 量起來有……長/寬/高
　　Cindy is being measured for her wedding dress.
　　辛蒂正為結婚禮服量尺寸。

2. 根據語意，(C) 項應為正選。

重要單字片語

modernization [ˌmɑdənəˈzeʃən] *n.* 現代化

Part 6 Text Completion

Questions 22-25 refer to the following article.

　　Essex Appliances Corporation (EAC) today announced a plan to erect two state-of-the-art manufacturing plants at its West Bridge site. When completed in six months, the factories will be able to produce ------- every one of their current major products. They
22.
will also be able to incorporate last-minute changes to any device before final production.

　　Upon completion, the two plants will provide more than 200 new jobs. Most of these jobs ------- to be filled by local residents. -------. Gordon Hardwick, CEO of EAC,
23.　　　　　　　　　　　　　　　24.
said, "In today's competitive business environment, you can't stand -------. Moving
25.
forward is the only way to survive."

22 至 25 題請看以下文章。

　　埃賽克斯電器公司（EAC）今日宣布一項計畫，將在該公司西橋廠址建造兩座最先進的廠房。工廠將在六個月後完工，之後將能生產幾乎任何一項該公司目前的主要產品。工廠也能在任何產品的最終生產前做出最後一刻的變更。
　　完工後，兩座廠房將提供兩百多個新職缺。大部分的職缺預計將由當地居民填補。職缺最終會表列於 EAC 官網。EAC 執行長高登‧哈德威克表示：「在當今這個競爭激烈的商業環境中，你不能停滯不前。勇往直前是唯一的生存之道。」

Chapter 08 Reading Test

B **22**

(A) completely　　　(B) virtually　　　(C) rarely　　　(D) really

理由

1. (A) **completely** [kəmˋplitlɪ] *adv.* 完全地
    Karen looks completely different from her sister.
    凱倫跟她的妹妹長得完全不一樣。

   (B) **virtually** [ˋvɝtʃʊ(ə)lɪ] *adv.* 幾乎（= practically [ˋpræktɪklɪ] / almost）
    It is virtually impossible to finish the report by tomorrow.
    明天完成這項計畫是幾乎不可能的事。

   (C) **rarely** [ˋrɛrlɪ] *adv.* 很少地（= seldom [ˋsɛldəm]）
    The celebrity is rarely seen in public nowadays.
    那位名人現在很少在公共場合露面。

   (D) **really** [ˋri(ə)lɪ / ˋrɪəlɪ] *adv.* 真正地
    Tell me what really happened.
    告訴我真正發生了什麼事。

2. virtually、almost、practically 及 nearly 這四個副詞皆表「幾乎」，通常用來修飾四個涵蓋性完全的詞類，即：every（每一個）、no（沒有）、all（全部）及 any（任何一個）。
    Almost everyone cried when the main character of the movie died.
    電影主角死的時候，幾乎所有人都哭了。
    I've read practically all of Neil Gaiman's books.
    尼爾．蓋曼所有的書我幾乎都看過了。

3. 根據上述，空格後有限定詞 every（每一個），得知 (B) 項應為正選。

D **23**

(A) expects　　　(B) expect　　　(C) expected　　　(D) are expected

理由

1. **expect** [ɪkˋspɛkt] *vt.* 預期，預計
    Joy's parents expect her to be a successful pianist in the future.
    喬依的父母期望她未來成為成功的鋼琴家。
    The lecture is expected to attract more than 100 people.
    該演講預計會吸引超過一百人參加。

2. expect 為主動語態時，表「期望」，主詞應為人。空格前有複數名詞詞組 Most of these jobs（大部分的職缺）作主詞，得知須使用被動語態 be expected to...（預期／預計……），故 (D) 項應為正選。

C **24**

(A) All our products come with a three-year warranty.
(B) This will cause unemployment numbers to rise.
(C) Vacancies will eventually be listed on the EAC website.
(D) We look forward to cooperating with you in the future.

理由

1. (A) 本公司所有產品皆附有三年保固。
   (B) 這將會導致失業率上升。
   (C) 職缺最終會表列於 EAC 官網。
   (D) 本公司期待未來與您合作。

2. 空格前的句子 "Most of these jobs are expected to be filled by local residents."（大部分的職缺預計將由當地居民填補。）提及 EAC 公司將釋出職缺給當地居民，選項 (C) 則進一步說明該職缺將會公布於公司官網上，置入空格後語意連貫，故應為正選。

D 25

(A) out　　　　(B) up to　　　　(C) for　　　　(D) still

理由

1. 本題測驗以下固定搭配用法：

   (A) **stand out**　　顯眼；突出
   Charlie's résumé stood out from the rest.
   查理的履歷比其他人的傑出。

   (B) **stand up to sth/sb**　　經得起……；抵抗某人
   Desert plants can stand up to heat and drought.
   沙漠植物可以承受高溫與乾旱。
   It was brave of you to stand up to those school bullies.
   你敢對抗那些校園惡霸真是勇敢。

   (C) **stand for...**　　代表……
   What does FYI stand for?
   FYI 代表什麼意思？

   (D) **stand still**　　停滯不前；站著不動（still 為副詞，表「靜止地」）
   Time seemed to have stood still as we stood on the mountaintop.
   我們站在山頂時，時間彷彿停頓了。

2. 根據上述語意，空格後的句子 "Moving forward is the only way to survive."（勇往直前是唯一的生存之道。）與選項 (D) stand still（停滯不前）形成對比，可知應為正選。

重要單字片語

1. **corporation** [ˌkɔrpəˈreʃən] *n.* 大型公司；企業集團

2. **erect** [ɪˈrɛkt] *vt.* 建立，建造
   Police have erected barriers around the Presidential Palace.
   警方在總統府周遭設立了路障。

3. **state-of-the-art** [ˌstetəvðɪˈɑrt] *a.* 最先進的

4. **incorporate** [ɪnˈkɔrpəˌret] *vt.* 使併入；包含……
   incorporate A into / in B　使 A 併入 B
   We've incorporated your suggestions into the design of the building.
   我們已將您的建議納入這棟大樓的設計中。

5. **last-minute** [ˌlæstˈmɪnɪt] *a.* 最後一刻的，臨時的
   The manager wants to make a last-minute change to the proposal.
   經理想要在提案中做臨時的修改。

Chapter 08 Reading Test

Part 7 Reading Comprehension

Questions 26-30 refer to the following email and attachment.

From:	marisa.ford-hughes@cvk-manufacturing.com
To:	plant-supervisors@cvk-manufacturing.com
Subject:	Emergency Response Procedures
Attachment:	updated.xls

Hi All,

As you are aware, an independent risk assessment of our emergency response procedures was conducted last month. The manufacturing plant was found to comply with all industry regulations and national and international safety standards. However, the risk assessment report does recommend that we make an adjustment to our standard procedure for evacuation in the event of a fire, explosion, or gas leak. Specifically, it suggests that we change the evacuation assembly area to a location further away from the plant. Please see the attachment for the updated evacuation procedure. Also, we will be performing the regular biannual testing of the emergency notification system next Monday. All workers should receive an alert on their computers and/or phones at some time during the morning.

Thank you.

Marisa Ford-Hughes
Health & Safety Manager
CVK Manufacturing

updated.xls

	Updated Emergency Procedure
Step 1	Activate the alarm; notify supervisor and emergency services
Step 2	Shut down plant machinery if safe to do so; leave your belongings behind
Step 3	Evacuate using routes marked with yellow arrows; don't use elevators
Step 4	Assemble at emergency meeting point in south parking lot

Plant supervisors are asked to hold meetings with their teams to convey this updated information at their earliest convenience. Thank you.

26 至 30 題請看以下電子郵件及附件。

寄件者：	marisa.ford-hughes@cvk-manufacturing.com
收件者：	plant-supervisors@cvk-manufacturing.com
主　旨：	緊急應變措施
附　件：	更新版.xls

大家好，

大家都知道：我們上個月針對內部的緊急應變措施找別人進行過一次風險評估。生產廠房都符合所有的產業規範以及國內外安全標準。不過，風險評估報告有建議我們調整火災、爆炸與氣體外洩發生時的標準疏散流程。更準確地說，報告建議我們將疏散時的集合地點，改成離廠房更遠一點。請參考附件中更新過後的疏散流程。此外，一年兩次的警報系統測試，將在下週一進行一次。所有員工在早上某個時間應會在電腦以及/或手機上收到警訊。

感謝，

CVK 生產實業
健康與安全主管　瑪莉莎・福特休斯

Chapter 08 Reading Test

更新版.xls

緊急措施更新版	
步驟一	啟動警報，通報主管與緊急服務機構
步驟二	在安全前提下關閉廠房的機械設備，立即疏散，勿攜帶個人物品
步驟三	遵循黃色箭頭標示的路線逃生，勿搭乘電梯
步驟四	在南端停車場的緊急集合點集合

廠區主管請儘早與團隊召開會議並傳達此更新資訊。感謝。

B 26

Why is Ms. Ford-Hughes changing a procedure?
(A) It was mandated by a law.
(B) It was suggested in a report.
(C) It was demanded by a manager.
(D) It was necessitated by a disaster.

福特休斯女士為什麼要更改一項流程？
(A) 因法律強制規定。
(B) 因某報告提出此建議。
(C) 因受到某經理的要求。
(D) 因某次災難使其變得必要。

理由

根據電子郵件第三句 "However, the risk assessment report does recommend that we make an adjustment to our standard procedure for evacuation in the event of a fire, explosion, or gas leak."（不過，風險評估報告有建議我們調整火災、爆炸與氣體外洩發生時的標準疏散流程。）得知，(B) 項應為正選。

D 27

Which step does the adjustment relate to?
(A) Step 1
(B) Step 2
(C) Step 3
(D) Step 4

變更的事項涉及哪一個步驟？
(A) 步驟一
(B) 步驟二
(C) 步驟三
(D) 步驟四

理由

根據電子郵件第四句 "Specifically, it suggests that we change the evacuation assembly area to a location further away from the plant."（更準確地說，報告建議我們將疏散時的集合地點，改成離廠房更遠一點。）及更新版的步驟四內容 "Assemble at emergency meeting point in south parking lot"（在南端停車場的緊急集合點集合）得知，(D) 項應為正選。

B **28**

What will happen on Monday?
(A) A proposal will be published.
(B) A system will be tested.
(C) A procedure will be changed.
(D) A server will be replaced.

星期一將會發生什麼事？
(A) 將會公布一項提案。
(B) 將會測試一套系統。
(C) 將會改變一項流程。
(D) 將會更換一臺伺服器。

> 理由
>
> 根據電子郵件倒數第二句 "Also, we will be performing the regular biannual testing of the emergency notification system next Monday."（此外，一年兩次的警報系統測試，將在下週一進行一次。）得知，(B) 項應為正選。

D **29**

What is NOT mentioned in the attachment?
(A) Triggering the alarm
(B) Following marked directions
(C) Turning off equipment
(D) Operating fire extinguishers

附件中未提及哪一項？
(A) 啟動警報
(B) 遵循標示的方向
(C) 關閉設備
(D) 操作滅火器

> 理由
>
> 根據更新版步驟一至四的附件內容未提及滅火器的使用，得知 (D) 項應為正選。

A **30**

According to the attachment, what are plant supervisors requested to do?
(A) Brief their staff on the new procedure
(B) Display the document in their offices
(C) Alert the authorities to potential dangers
(D) Report lack of compliance to their superiors

根據附件所述，廠區主管被要求做什麼？
(A) 向員工簡報新的流程
(B) 在辦公室裡展示該文件
(C) 向當局警示潛在的危險
(D) 向上級報告不合規的狀況

> 理由
>
> 根據附件倒數第二句 "Plant supervisors are asked to hold meetings with their teams to convey this updated information at their earliest convenience."（廠區主管請儘早與團隊召開會議並傳達此更新資訊。）得知，(A) 項應為正選。

重要單字片語

1. **assessment** [əˈsɛsmənt] *n.* 評估
   make an assessment of... 評估……
   The sales manager made an assessment of the situation.
   業務經理對此情況進行評估。

2. **evacuation** [ɪˌvækjuˈeʃən] *n.* 撤離，避難

3. **bi-** [baɪ] *prefix* 雙的
   bilingual   雙語的；通兩種語言者
   biannual   一年兩次的

Chapter 08　Reading Test

4. **activate** [ˈæktəˌvet] *vt.* 啟動，觸發
   The person on the night shift forgot to activate the security system.
   值晚班的人忘了啟動保全系統。

5. **convey** [kənˈve] *vt.* 傳達，傳遞
   convey sth to sb　傳達某事給某人
   Could you convey a message to Kate for me, please?
   可以請你幫我傳個訊息給凱特嗎？

6. **at sb's earliest convenience**
   在某人方便時儘快
   Please call me at your earliest convenience.
   請你一有空時就儘快撥電話給我。

7. **mandate** [ˈmænˌdet] *vt.* 命令

8. **necessitate** [nəˈsɛsəˌtet] *vt.* 使成必要

9. **trigger** [ˈtrɪɡɚ] *vt.* 引起，觸發
   The dust in the air triggered Kyle's allergies.
   空氣中的灰塵引發凱爾過敏。

10. **authority** [əˈθɔrətɪ] *n.* 有關當局（恆用複數）

Chapter 09 Listening Test

🎧 Part 1 Photographs

C **1** 🔊 209

(A) He is pushing an armchair.
(B) He is picking up a pencil.
(C) He is dialing a number on the phone.
(D) He is spraying some water on the window.

(A) 他正在推一張扶手椅。
(B) 他正在撿起一支鉛筆。
(C) 他正在撥電話號碼。
(D) 他正在對著窗戶噴水。

🔍 重要單字片語

1. **armchair** [ˈɑrmˌtʃɛr] *n.* 扶手椅
2. **spray** [spre] *vt.* 噴灑 & *n.* 噴霧劑

Linda sprayed water on the plants this morning.
琳達今早給植物澆水。

B **2** 🔊 210

(A) She is laying down a jacket on the table.
(B) She is pointing at some data on the bulletin board.
(C) She is carrying a small plant by hand.
(D) She is archiving some files on the shelf.

(A) 她正把外套放在桌子上。
(B) 她指著公告欄上的資料。
(C) 她手裡拿著一盆小植物。
(D) 她正把卷宗歸檔到架子上。

🔍 重要單字片語

1. **archive** [ˈɑrkaɪv] *vt.* 將……歸檔 & *n.* 檔案；檔案館 / 室；(電腦) 壓縮檔
   The files have been archived and moved to the basement.
   這些檔案已被歸檔並移至地下室。

2. **file** [faɪl] *n.* 檔案，卷宗；文件夾；(電腦) 檔案

163

Chapter 09 Listening Test

Part 2 Question-Response

B 3 🔊 212

Were you impressed by the facilities at the office?
(A) Yes, they said my résumé was excellent.
(B) Yes, the meeting rooms were spacious.
(C) Yes, it was constructed in the early 1990s.

公司裡的設施有讓你印象深刻的地方嗎？
(A) 是的，他們說我的履歷很出色。
(B) 有的，會議室很寬敞。
(C) 是的，它建於 1990 年代初期。

重要單字片語

1. **résumé** [ˈrɛzəˌme] *n.* 履歷表（亦可寫作 resume 或 resumé）
2. **spacious** [ˈspeʃəs] *a.* 寬敞的
3. **construct** [kənˈstrʌkt] *vt.* 興建，建造
   The sculpture was constructed entirely of concrete.
   這座雕像整個都是用混凝土所建造。

A 4 🔊 213

Why do you want to purchase this printer and not that one?
(A) This one best suits our needs.
(B) Yes, I'm finished with the printer.
(C) I can't retrieve my document.

你為什麼想買這臺印表機而不是那臺呢？
(A) 這臺最能滿足我們的需求。
(B) 是的，我用完印表機了。
(C) 我無法取回我的文件。

重要單字片語

1. **purchase** [ˈpɝtʃəs] *vt.* & *n.* 購買
   You can purchase the product online.
   = You can make a purchase of the product online.
   你可以在線上購買這項產品。
2. **suit** [sut] *vt.* 滿足需要
   You should choose a computer that best suits your personal needs.
   你應該選一臺最適合你個人需求的電腦。
3. **retrieve** [rɪˈtriv] *vt.* 取回，找回
   The police managed to retrieve some of the stolen money.
   警方設法取回了部分被竊款項。

Part 3 Conversations

Questions 5 through 7 refer to the following conversation. 🔊 215 M: 🇨🇦 W: 🇬🇧

M: The annual book fair is just around the corner. I need to make twenty copies of promotional flyers for that event two weeks in advance. But I just found that the copy machine is broken again.

W: Let's report this problem to the administration department. They can get it repaired.

M: I think it's beyond repair. We'd better buy a new one.
W: In that case, I'll call Tom in the purchasing office. He'll probably be able to approve a purchase order for a new machine.

5 至 7 題請聽以下會話。

> 男：一年一度的書展即將來臨。我必須為這場活動提前兩週印製二十份宣傳單。但是我剛發現影印機又故障了。
> 女：我們來向行政部門通報這個問題吧。他們可以找人來修理。
> 男：我認為那臺機器修不好。我們最好還是買一臺新的。
> 女：這樣的話，我會連絡採購室的湯姆。他應該能夠批准添購新機器的請購單。

A 5 🔊 216

According to the speaker, what will take place soon?
(A) A book fair
(B) A yard sale
(C) A technology exhibition
(D) A business conference

根據說話者所述，近期將會舉辦什麼？
(A) 書展
(B) 庭院拍賣
(C) 科技展
(D) 商務研討會

B 6 🔊 217

What is the problem?
(A) A process has been changed.
(B) A device is malfunctioning.
(C) A proposal was rejected.
(D) An inspection has been canceled.

出了什麼問題？
(A) 某作業流程被修改了。
(B) 某儀器故障了。
(C) 某提案被否決了。
(D) 某項檢查被取消了。

C 7 🔊 218

What will the woman most likely do next?
(A) Purchase some stationery
(B) Design a poster
(C) Make a telephone call
(D) Load a ream of paper

女子接下來最有可能做什麼？
(A) 採購一些文具
(B) 設計海報
(C) 打一通電話
(D) 裝放一令紙

重要單字片語

1. **annual** [ˋænjuəl] *a.* 一年一度的；年度的
2. **a book fair** 書展
3. **be around the corner** 即將來臨；轉角附近

The company trip is just around the corner.
= The company trip is coming soon.
員工旅遊即將來臨。

There is a police station just around the corner.
這附近就有警察局了。

Chapter 09 Listening Test

4. **in advance**
   預先,提前(= beforehand [bɪˋfɔrhænd])
   Please inform me of the results in advance.
   請事先告知我結果。

5. **beyond repair**　無法修復

6. **a purchase order**　請購單

7. **inspection** [ɪnˋspɛkʃən] *n.* 檢查,稽查
   a safety inspection　安全檢查

8. **ream** [rim] *n.* 令(紙張計量單位,一令為五百張紙)

Questions 8 through 10 refer to the following conversation and agenda. 🔊 219

W: 🇺🇸　M: 🇦🇺

W: So, how did the meeting go?
M: It went well! I was a bit nervous because it was the first time I'd ever chaired a meeting.
W: Were there many people in attendance?
M: Only four, plus me. I tried to stick to the agenda and give every person an equal chance to speak and share their views.
W: Did you discuss the issues with the platform we use to coordinate projects?
M: Yes, that topic was raised. You can check out the minutes for more details.

Meeting Agenda	
Chair: C. Novoa	
Attendee	**Subject**
M. Davies	Remote work policy
L. Foden	Project management system
D. Scott	Employee bonus structure
F. Lynch	Volunteering program

8 至 10 題請聽以下會話,並請看以下議程表。

女:會議開得怎麼樣?
男:很順利!我因為是第一次主持會議,有點緊張。
女:參加的人多嗎?
男:只有四個人,再加上我。我盡量照著議程走,給每個人相同的機會來發言並分享觀點。
女:我們協調專案的平臺這個議題,你們有討論到嗎?
男:有,這個主題有提出來討論。妳可以去看會議記錄,了解更多細節。

會議議程	
主席:*C.* 諾福亞	
與會者	**主題**
M. 戴維斯	遠端工作規定
L. 佛登	專案管理系統
D. 史考特	員工獎金制度
F. 林區	志工服務計畫

C **8** 🔊 220 🇬🇧

Why was the man worried?
(A) He'd never met the meeting attendees before.
(B) He was anxious about a controversial topic.
(C) He'd never been in charge of a meeting before.
(D) He was concerned about the lack of seating.

男子為何會擔心？
(A) 他以前從未見過與會者。
(B) 他對某個有爭議的主題感到焦慮。
(C) 他以前從未主持過會議。
(D) 他擔心座位不夠。

D **9** 🔊 221 🇬🇧

What did the man do?
(A) Shared snacks with the attendees
(B) Allowed the meeting to run late
(C) Invited more people to attend
(D) Followed the agenda closely

男子做了什麼？
(A) 和與會者分享點心
(B) 允許會議晚點結束
(C) 邀請更多人參加
(D) 嚴格遵循議程

B **10** 🔊 222 🇬🇧

Look at the graphic. Whose subject did the woman ask about?
(A) M. Davies'
(B) L. Foden's
(C) D. Scott's
(D) F. Lynch's

請看圖表。女子探詢到哪個人的主題？
(A) M. 戴維斯
(B) L. 佛登
(C) D. 史考特
(D) F. 林區

🔍 重要單字片語

1. **stick to...** 堅持……，堅守……
   Sarah was determined to stick to her decision to study abroad.
   莎拉下定決心堅持出國留學的決定。

2. **coordinate** [ko'ɔrdn̩,et] *vt.* 使協調 & *vt.* & *vi.* （使）相稱
   Hank was assigned to coordinate the manager's farewell party.
   漢克被指派負責協調經理的歡送會。

3. **attendee** [ə,tɛn'di] *n.* 參加者，出席者

4. **remote** [rɪ'mot] *a.* 遠端的；遠的

5. **bonus** ['bonəs] *n.* 獎金；紅利

6. **volunteer** [,vɑlən'tɪr] *vi.* 自願 & *n.* 志願者，志工
   volunteer to + V　自願做……
   Stanley volunteered to work overtime on the project.
   史丹利自願加班做專案。

7. **anxious** ['æŋkʃəs] *a.* 焦慮的

8. **controversial** [,kɑntrə'vɝʃəl] *a.* 引起爭議的

9. **seating** ['sitɪŋ] *n.* 全部座位；座次

Chapter 09 Listening Test

Part 4 Talks

Questions 11 through 13 refer to the following talk. 🔊 224 🇬🇧

Welcome to Maxim Company's training program. My name is Martha Wentworth, head of human resources. I'm speaking to you today to orient you on your duties. Since you are the first employees our clients will see when they come to visit our offices, it is important that your personal appearance and the counter be tidy and clean. You are also responsible for answering telephones, so you must take messages according to the guidelines in this booklet, which has every secretary's and executive's extensions. We look forward to your contributions to Maxim Company. Now, let's go downstairs to see what your workspace looks like and meet Ellen Spurrier, who will supervise your work. Ellen will fill you in on all the details of your job.

11 至 13 題請聽以下談話。

> 歡迎參加格言公司的培訓計畫。我是人資部主管瑪莎・溫特沃斯。今天來和諸位談話的目的是要讓大家熟悉職責。既然諸位是客戶前來公司參訪時第一眼見到的人，各位的個人形象與櫃檯的整潔乾淨就很重要。你們也要負責接聽電話，所以務必根據這本小冊子上的指導原則記錄留言，小冊子裡有每位祕書及主管的分機號碼。我們期待諸位為格言公司所做出的貢獻。我們現在下樓去看看大家的工作場所並和艾倫・斯普里爾見面，她會監督各位的工作狀況。艾倫會告訴諸位工作上的所有細節。

C **11** 🔊 225 🇦🇺

Who most likely are the listeners?
(A) Office cleaners
(B) Maxim Company's clients
(C) Receptionist trainees
(D) Security guards

聽眾最有可能是誰？
(A) 辦公室清潔工
(B) 格言公司的客戶
(C) 接待人員受訓者
(D) 保全

D **12** 🔊 226 🇦🇺

What is one purpose of the booklet?
(A) To welcome new customers
(B) To teach makeup skills
(C) To inform trainees of company benefits
(D) To provide staff members' extensions

小冊子的其中一個目的是什麼？
(A) 歡迎新的顧客
(B) 教授化妝技巧
(C) 告知受訓者公司福利
(D) 提供員工的電話分機

D **13** 🔊 227 🇦🇺

What will the listeners do next?
(A) Clean their workspace
(B) Serve clients
(C) Fill in a form
(D) See their supervisor

聽眾接下來會做什麼事？
(A) 清理工作場所
(B) 接待客戶
(C) 填寫表格
(D) 和主管見面

重要單字片語

1. **maxim** [ˈmæksɪm] *n.* 格言；箴言
2. **human resources**
   （公司的）人力資源部，人事部（縮寫為 HR）
3. **orient** [ˈɔrɪˌɛnt] *vt.* 使適應；使熟悉
   orient oneself to...
   使自己適應（= adjust oneself to...）
   be oriented to...
   以……為取向
   It took Janice a while to orient herself to her new job.
   珍妮絲花了一段時間才使自己適應新的工作。
   The course is oriented to the needs of single mothers.
   這門課是以單親媽媽的需求為取向。
4. **duty** [ˈdutɪ] *n.* 職責，任務
   My duties include setting up computer systems and installing new software.
   我的職責包含架設電腦系統以及安裝新的軟體。
5. **take a message** 記錄留言
   leave a message 留言
   John is not in at the moment. Can I take a message?
   約翰人現在不在。可以幫你記錄留言嗎？
   Would you like to leave a message?
   你要留言嗎？
6. **guideline** [ˈgaɪdˌlaɪn] *n.* 指導原則，準則
7. **booklet** [ˈbʊklət] *n.* 小冊子
8. **executive** [ɪgˈzɛkjətɪv] *n.* 行政主管
9. **look forward to N/V-ing** 期待……
   We really look forward to cooperating with your company on this project.
   我們很期待與貴公司聯手合作執行該計畫。
10. **contribution** [ˌkɑntrəˈbjuʃən] *n.* 貢獻；捐款
11. **fill sb in on sth** 讓某人了解某事
    Let me fill you in on the latest gossip in the office.
    我來告訴你辦公室最新的八卦。
12. **benefit** [ˈbɛnəfɪt] *n.* 福利；利益

CH 09

Questions 14 through 16 refer to the following telephone message. 🔊 228 🇺🇸

Hello, Mr. Larson, this is Jennifer Wilson, an editor with *Automotive World* magazine. I have dialed your number several times over the past few days. Your cell phone has been off and I haven't gotten a reply from your e-mail address. So, I'm leaving this message to see how you're doing. I'd like to touch base with you about your article that was recently accepted for publication — the one on hybrid cars. The revision of your article is due on May 5. Today is May 4. Please return my call to keep me posted on the progress. My number is 555-1892. If you're unable to meet the deadline, please inform us in advance so that we can arrange for a replacement article. Please note that the deadline will not be postponed.

14 至 16 題請聽以下電話留言。

> 你好，拉森先生，我是《汽車世界》雜誌的編輯珍妮佛‧威爾遜。過去這幾天，我撥你的電話號碼撥了好幾次。你的手機一直沒有開機，而我也未收到你電子郵件的回覆。所以我留這封語音留言，看看你狀況如何。我想與你談論關於你那篇最近接受刊載的文章 —— 就是那篇有關油電混合車的文章。修定稿的截稿日期是五月五日。今天是五月四日。請回我電話告知進展。我的號碼是 555-1892。如果你趕不上截稿期限，請提前通知我們，好讓我們能安排替代文章。請注意，截稿日期不會延後。

Chapter 09 Listening Test

B 14 229 🇨🇦

What has Ms. Wilson been trying to do?
(A) Purchase a car
(B) Contact a person
(C) Advertise a product
(D) Write an article

威爾遜女士一直在嘗試做什麼事？
(A) 購買汽車
(B) 聯絡某人
(C) 推銷商品
(D) 撰寫文章

A 15 230 🇨🇦

Why does the speaker say, "Today is May 4"?
(A) To indicate an approaching deadline
(B) To confirm the date of publication
(C) To offer more time for an article
(D) To arrange a meeting with a writer

說話者為什麼說「今天是五月四日」？
(A) 暗示即將到來的截稿日期
(B) 確認出版日期
(C) 給予更多時間來撰寫文章
(D) 安排與作家會面

B 16 231 🇨🇦

What does the speaker want to know?
(A) The name of the publication
(B) The progress of a contribution
(C) The location of an office
(D) The zip code of an address

說話者想要知道什麼？
(A) 出版品的名稱
(B) 稿件的進度
(C) 辦公室的位置
(D) 某地址的郵遞區號

重要單字片語

1. **touch base with sb**
   與某人談談；與某人聯繫
   I want to touch base with you to see if you got the e-mail from my secretary.
   我想跟你確認一下你是否有收到我祕書傳給你的電子郵件。

2. **publication** [ˌpʌbləˈkeʃən] n. 出版；出版刊物
   The book is scheduled for publication in September.
   這本書預計九月出版。
   Our latest publication is a memoir of a famous novelist.
   我們最近的出版刊物是一位知名小說家的回憶錄。

3. **hybrid** [ˈhaɪbrɪd] n. 混合物
   a hybrid car　　油電混合車

4. **revision** [rɪˈvɪʒən] n. 修訂

5. **keep sb posted (on sth)**
   向某人更新（某事的）最新狀況
   = keep sb informed (of sth)
   I want to know your progress on this case, so keep me posted.
   我想要知道你這個案件的進度，所以隨時向我報告情況。

6. **deadline** [ˈdɛdˌlaɪn] n. 截止日期
   meet / miss the deadline
   在截止日期內完成 / 錯過截止日期

7. **replacement** [rɪˈplesmənt] n. 替代物

8. **contribution** [ˌkɑntrəˈbjuʃən] n.（書、雜誌、廣播等的）稿件，作品

📖 Part 5　Incomplete Sentences

C 17

Ms. Madueke requested a ------- to the business development department, but her boss refused.

(A) maximum　　　　(B) stock　　　　(C) transfer　　　　(D) routine

馬杜凱埃小姐請調業務發展部門，但被她的上司否決了。

理由

1. (A) **maximum** [ˈmæksəməm] *n.* 最大量 & *a.* 最大量的
    a maximum of + 數字　　最多不超過……
    = at most + 數字
    You have a maximum of 90 minutes to finish the test.
    你們最多有九十分鐘的時間來完成測驗。

  (B) **stock** [stɑk] *n.* 股票；貯存，存貨 & *vt.* 貯存
    This store stocks all types of baseball gear.
    這家店有賣各種棒球裝備。

  (C) **transfer** [ˈtrænsfɚ] *n.* 調任
    Larry applied for a transfer to the company's branch office in Asia.
    賴瑞請調至亞洲的分公司。

  (D) **routine** [ruˈtin] *n.* 慣例，例行公事 & *a.* 例行公事的；常規的
    a daily routine　　每天的例行公事
    a routine checkup　　定期健康檢查

2. 根據語意，(C) 項應為正選。

重要單字片語

request [rɪˈkwɛst] *vt.* & *n.* 請求；要求
The company requests that new staff complete their training within one month.
公司要求新進員工在一個月內完成訓練。

A 18

Since Mr. Cole quit last month, no one has been managing the sales division—a fact the CEO finds ------- to believe.

(A) difficult　　　　(B) difficulty　　　　(C) difference　　　　(D) differ

自上個月柯爾先生辭職以來，業務部門一直無人管理，這讓執行長感到難以置信。

理由

1. 不完全及物動詞 find（發現……是）是加了受詞後意思仍不完全的及物動詞，因此要加形容詞做受詞補語，然後還可以接不定詞片語以表達更多細節，其句型如下：
    find + 受詞 + 形容詞 + to + V　　發現……是……
    Matt finds his new college roommate hard to get along with.
    麥特發現他的新大學室友很難相處。

Chapter 09 Reading Test

2. 選項中：
   (A) **difficult** [ˈdɪfəkəlt] *a.* 難的
   (B) **difficulty** [ˈdɪfəˌkəltɪ] *n.* 困難
   (C) **difference** [ˈdɪfərəns] *n.* 差別
   (D) **differ** [ˈdɪfɚ] *vi.* 不同，差異
      differ from... 與……不同
      Jason's political views differ considerably from those of his father.
      傑森的政治觀點和他父親的有很大的差異。
3. 根據上述，原題空格前有受詞 a fact（事實）與不完全及物動詞 find，空格後有不定詞片語 to believe（相信），得知空格內須置形容詞，故 (A) 項應為正選。

🔍 重要單字片語
   CEO 執行長（為 Chief Executive Officer 的縮寫）

D 19

The office can become unbearably hot and humid during the summer because of inadequate -------.

(A) to ventilate (B) ventilated (C) ventilate (D) ventilation

夏季時，辦公室通風不良會導致內部酷熱難耐，空氣悶溼。

理由
1. 本題測試下列固定用法：
   because of + N/V-ing 因為……
   The company went bankrupt because of poor management.
   該公司由於經營不善而破產。
2. 根據上述，空格前有形容詞 inadequate（不良的），得知空格內應置名詞與其形成名詞片語 inadequate ventilation（通風不良）。選項中惟 (D) 項 ventilation（通風）為名詞，故應為正選。

🔍 重要單字片語
1. **unbearably** [ʌnˈbɛrəblɪ] *adv.* 難耐地
2. **inadequate** [ɪnˈædəkwɪt] *a.* 不夠好的

B 20

If you are having trouble ------- your work, your line manager should be able to lend a hand.

(A) prioritize (B) prioritizing (C) to prioritize (D) priority

若你安排工作優先順序時遇到困難，你的直屬上司應該可以提供協助。

> 理由

1. 本題測試下列固定用法：
   have trouble + V-ing　　做……有困難
   Our department is having trouble finding a replacement for the manager.
   我們部門一直找不到經理的替補人選。
2. 根據上述，(B) 項應為正選。

> 重要單字片語

1. **sb's line manager**　　某人的直屬上司
2. **lend a (helping) hand**　　伸出援手，幫忙

If you need help, I'll be around to lend a hand.
如果你需要幫忙，我隨時都會伸出援手。

B **21**

The chairman addressed all the members of the board of directors, only a few of ------- were actually paying attention.

(A) that　　　　(B) whom　　　　(C) them　　　　(D) which

主席向董事會所有成員致詞，當中只有少數人認真在聽講。

> 理由

1. 空格前有完整的主要子句 "The chairman addressed all the members of the board of directors"（主席向董事會所有成員致詞），之後以逗點隔開，故空格內不得置 (C) 項的 them，因為如此一來，only a few of them 之後接 were actually paying attention，形成另一主要子句，而兩句無連接詞連接，屬於錯誤句構。
2. (B)、(D) 兩個選項皆為關係代名詞，可以連接兩句，但因空格前先行詞為 all the members of the board of directors（董事會所有成員），且空格前有 "only a few of..."，得知關係代名詞應使用 who 的受格 whom，故 (B) 項應為正選。
3. (A) 項 that 雖可作關係代名詞，等於 whom 或 which，但之前不得有介詞，但此處空格前有介詞 of，故不可選。

> 重要單字片語

address [əˋdrɛs] *vt.* 向……演說
The presidential candidate addressed an audience of 5,000 supporters.
那位總統候選人對五千名支持者發表演說。

Chapter 09 Reading Test

Part 6 Text Completion

Questions 22-25 refer to the following email.

From:	y.galanis@nisiros-insurance.gr
To:	senior.managers@nisiros-insurance.gr
Subject:	Please Check
Attachment:	draft-manual.doc

Hi All,

Please find enclosed a draft copy of the Code of Conduct & Ethics Manual. ------- 22. . We are seeking your feedback on the content, which covers areas ------- 23. acceptable behavior, conflicts of interest, and workplace ethics. Please take some time to look over the manual and submit any comments ------- 24. COB Friday, March 28. If you do not have any remarks, please at least ------- 25. receipt of the document. We will review your replies during April and distribute the manual company-wide in May.

Thank you in advance.

Yiannis Galanis
HR Director
Nisiros Insurance

22 至 25 題請看以下電子郵件。

寄件者：y.galanis@nisiros-insurance.gr
收件者：senior.managers@nisiros-insurance.gr
主　旨：請查照
附　件：手冊草案 .doc

大家好，

附件是《工作行為與倫理準則手冊》草案的副本。特別聲明：這並非最終版本。我們正徵求所有人對草案內容提出回饋意見，範圍包括可容許的行為、利益衝突以及職場倫理等等。請撥冗看一下手冊，並於三月二十八日星期五當天下班前提交意見。如果沒有任何意見，也請至少確認收悉此文件。我們會在四月閱讀大家的回覆，並於五月對全公司發放正式手冊。

在此先感謝大家的配合。

伊安尼斯・加蘭尼斯
人資部主任
尼西羅斯保險

D **22**

(A) A serious violation of the code was committed.
(B) The deadline for changes to the manual has passed.
(C) All employees received the handbook last month.
(D) I would like to make clear this is not the final version.

理由

1. (A) 某人嚴重違反了準則。
   (B) 修訂手冊的截止日期已過。
   (C) 所有員工上個月已收到手冊。
   (D) 特別聲明：這並非最終版本。
2. 空格前一句提及 "Please find enclosed a draft copy of the Code of Conduct & Ethics Manual."（附件是《工作行為與倫理準則手冊》草案的副本。），而 (D) 項的句子提及該手冊的副本並非最終版本，置入空格後與前文形成關聯，故 (D) 項應為正選。

CH 09

B **23**

(A) owing to　　　(B) such as　　　(C) prior to　　　(D) as of

理由

1. (A) **owing to...**　　由於……
   The corn crop suffered significant damage owing to the tornado.
   玉米作物因這場龍捲風損失慘重。
   (B) **such as...**　　諸如／像……（置於複數名詞之後使用）
   Fruits such as berries and apples have cancer-fighting properties.
   莓果和蘋果等水果都有抗癌功效。
   (C) **prior to...**　　在……之前
   Patients must not eat or drink anything for eight hours prior to their checkup.
   病患在體檢前八個小時絕對禁止飲食。
   (D) **as of...**　　自……起
   The new regulations will become effective as of January 1.
   新規定將自一月一日起生效。
2. 根據語意，(B) 項應為正選。

B **24**

(A) since　　　(B) by　　　(C) from　　　(D) at

理由

1. 空格前有句子 "... and submit any comments"（……提交意見），且空格後有特定時間 COB Friday, March 28（三月二十八日星期五當天下班）。根據上下文，得知空格原句應是指大家應於此時間點以前提交意見，故空格應置表「至某時間點之前」的介詞。
2. (A) 項 since 表「自……」，(B) 項 by 表「在……之前」，(C) 項 from 表「從……」，(D) 項 at 表「在……」。
3. 根據上述，(B) 項應為正選。

175

Chapter 09 Reading Test

C **25**

(A) acknowledgement (B) acknowledging
(C) acknowledge (D) to acknowledge

理由

1. 空格前有引導祈使句的 please，空格後有名詞片語 receipt of the document（收到文件）做受詞，得知空格內應置原形動詞以形成祈使句。

2. 選項中：
   (A) **acknowledgement** 為名詞，表「承認」，為動詞 acknowledge 的衍生字。
   (B) **acknowledging** 為動詞 acknowledge 的現在分詞。
   (C) **acknowledge** [əkˋnɑlɪdʒ] vt.（透過信件）確認收悉；承認
      acknowledge receipt of... 確認收到……
      We acknowledge receipt of your email dated April 1.
      我們確認已收到您四月一日寄出的電子郵件。
   (D) **to acknowledge** 為動詞 acknowledge 的不定詞片語。

3. 根據上述，(C) 項應為正選。

重要單字片語

1. **conduct** [ˋkɑndʌkt] n. 行為（不可數）
2. **ethic** [ˋɛθɪk] n. 規範；道德標準
3. **workplace** [ˋwɝkˏples] n. 職場，工作場所
4. **comment** [ˋkɑmɛnt] n. 評語，批評 & vi. 評論（與介詞 on 並用）
   make a comment on...
   對……評論／發表意見
   = comment on...
5. **COB** 下班；結束營業（為片語 close of business 的縮寫）
6. **remark** [rɪˋmɑrk] n. & vi. 評論，談論
   make a remark on... 評論／批評……
   = remark on...
7. **company-wide** [ˋkʌmpənɪˏwaɪd] adv. 全公司性地 & a. 全公司性的
8. **violation** [ˏvaɪəˋleʃən] n. 違反
9. **commit** [kəˋmɪt] vt. 犯（罪）（三態為：commit, committed [kəˋmɪtɪd], committed）
   commit a crime 犯罪
   If you commit a crime, you'd better be ready to go to jail.
   你要是犯法，最好有坐牢的心理準備。
10. **handbook** [ˋhændˏbʊk] n. 手冊，指南

📖 Part 7 Reading Comprehension

Questions 26-30 refer to the following memo and emails.

MEMO

From: Facilities Committee
To: All Department Heads
Subject: Office Furniture Upgrade

As part of the company's commitment to ensuring a comfortable work environment, funds have been allocated to comprehensively upgrade the office furniture. This will include ergonomic chairs, new desks, storage units, and cubicle dividers. A Facilities Committee has been formed to review workspace needs, consult with heads of departments, and coordinate the ordering of the new furniture. The committee is comprised of:

   Anya Peterson, who will deal with the procurement of the new furniture
   Melvin Rathbone, who will ensure the project stays within budget
   Cush Lindo, who will coordinate directly with department managers
   Rami Blofeld, who will ensure compliance with safety standards

---

From: facilities.committee@affable-artwork.com
To: kelvin.gries@affable-artwork.com
Subject: Your Furniture Order

Hi Kelvin,

Thank you for the prompt order of new furniture for your department. We have reviewed your order, cross-referenced it with the budget, and checked that none of the items will prevent people from accessing your or other departments. We are pleased to say that the order below has been approved.

Furniture Order		
Department: Accounting		
Item Code	**Item Name**	**Quantity**
TX457	Desk	12
TX188	Chair	12
TX043	Storage Unit	6
TX949	Cubicle Divider	9

Please double-check this order and confirm that it is correct. Total Xpress Furniture will deliver the new furniture on Saturday, May 31. We have hired a team that will remove the old furniture and build the new furniture, so there is no need for you to do anything. The new items will be in place when you come to the office on Monday, June 2.

Best regards,

Facilities Committee

From: kelvin.gries@affable-artwork.com
To: facilities.committee@affable-artwork.com
Subject: Re: Your Furniture Order

Hi,

The new furniture was in place this morning as promised. Unfortunately, the storage units are much smaller than we were led to believe. We expected each one to be large enough to be shared by two workers, but they can barely accommodate one worker's files. Unlike other departments, we still deal with a lot of hard copies of documents, so we require sufficient storage space. I would like these to be replaced ASAP.

Thank you.

Kelvin Gries
Head of Accounting
Affable Artwork

26 至 30 題請看以下備忘錄及電子郵件。

備忘錄

寄件者：設施委員會
收件者：全體部門主管
主　旨：辦公傢俱升級

公司承諾過要提供舒適的工作環境，兌現此承諾的其中一個部分就是撥款進行辦公傢俱的全面升級，包括人體工學椅、新辦公桌、儲物櫃以及辦公桌隔板等。公司成立了一個設施委員會，來檢討工作空間需求、諮詢各部門主管的意見以及統籌新傢俱的訂購工作。該委員會成員包括：

安雅・彼得森 ── 處理新傢俱的採購工作
馬文・拉斯本 ── 確保專案開銷在預算範圍內
庫許・林多 ── 直接與各部門經理溝通協調
拉米・布洛菲爾德 ── 確保一切符合安全標準

寄件者：facilities.committee@affable-artwork.com
收件者：kelvin.gries@affable-artwork.com
主　旨：您的傢俱訂單

凱文您好：

感謝您這麼快就幫貴部門製作好新辦公傢俱的訂購清單。我們已看過訂單，與預算做過比對，並確認所有物件都不會影響貴部門或其他部門人員的通行。我們很樂意通知您，以下的訂單已獲批准。

傢俱訂單		
部門：會計部		
物件編號	物件名稱	數量
TX457	桌子	12
TX188	椅子	12
TX043	儲物櫃	6
TX949	辦公桌隔板	9

麻煩您再看一遍這張訂單，確認是否正確。特快傢俱公司將在五月三十一日星期六把新傢俱送來。我們已找了一組人負責拆除舊傢俱並組裝新傢俱，因此您什麼事都不用做。您在六月二日星期一來上班時，就會發現新傢俱都已經就定位。

設施委員會　敬上

寄件者：kelvin.gries@affable-artwork.com
收件者：facilities.committee@affable-artwork.com
主　旨：Re: 您的傢俱訂單

您好：

今早新傢俱已經如數到位了。可惜儲物櫃比我們原先想像的小很多。我們本以為每個儲物櫃的大小是足夠兩個人共用的，但結果只勉強夠容納一個人的所有文件夾。與其他部門不同的是，我們仍然需要處理大量的紙本文件，因此需要足夠的貯存空間。我希望能盡快更換這批儲物櫃。

謝謝。

凱文‧葛瑞斯
會記部主管
迷人藝術公司

Chapter 09 Reading Test

B **26**

According to the memo, what is the purpose of the committee?
(A) To lobby bosses for funds for new equipment
(B) To assess needs and oversee furniture orders
(C) To make the office environmentally friendly
(D) To find the least expensive local suppliers

根據備忘錄，委員會的職責是什麼？
(A) 遊說老闆們撥款購買新設備
(B) 評估需求及監督傢俱訂購事宜
(C) 讓辦公室更環保
(D) 尋找價格最優惠的本地供應商

> 理由
>
> 根據備忘錄第三句 "A Facilities Committee has been formed to review workspace needs, consult with heads of departments, and coordinate the ordering of the new furniture."（公司成立了一個設施委員會，來檢討工作空間需求、諮詢各部門主管的意見以及統籌新傢俱的訂購工作。）得知，(B) 項應為正選。

C **27**

Who most likely contacted Mr. Gries?
(A) Anya Peterson
(B) Melvin Rathbone
(C) Cush Lindo
(D) Rami Blofeld

聯繫葛瑞斯先生的人最有可能是誰？
(A) 安雅・彼得森
(B) 馬文・拉斯本
(C) 庫許・林多
(D) 拉米・布洛菲爾德

> 理由
>
> 根據備忘錄倒數第二行 "Cush Lindo, who will coordinate directly with department managers"（庫許・林多 ── 直接與各部門經理溝通協調）及第二封電子郵件末尾署名處為會計部主管凱文・葛瑞斯得知，(C) 項應為正選。

A **28**

What is Mr. Gries asked to do?
(A) Verify that an order is accurate
(B) Assist with furniture construction
(C) Delay coming to the office on Monday
(D) Help to remove some unwanted items

葛瑞斯先生被要求做什麼？
(A) 確認某筆訂單是否正確
(B) 協助組裝傢俱
(C) 延後星期一到達辦公室的時間
(D) 幫忙移走一些不需要的物品

> 理由
>
> 根據第一封電子郵件第二段第一句 "Please double-check this order and confirm that it is correct."（麻煩您再看一遍這張訂單，確認是否正確。）得知，(A) 項應為正選。

180

C **29**

Which item does Mr. Gries find unsuitable?
(A) TX457
(B) TX188
(C) TX043
(D) TX949

葛瑞斯先生發現哪一項物件不合適？
(A) TX457
(B) TX188
(C) TX043
(D) TX949

> 理由
>
> 根據第二封電子郵件第二句 "Unfortunately, the storage units are much smaller than we were led to believe."（可惜儲物櫃比我們原先想像的小很多。）及第一封電子郵件中訂購清單物件名稱為 Storage Unit（儲物櫃）的物件編號為 TX043 得知，(C) 項應為正選。

CH 09

C **30**

What is indicated about the accounting department?
(A) It still lacks computers.
(B) It plans to hire more staff.
(C) It still handles a lot of paper.
(D) It hopes to move to a new area.

關於會計部，本文指出了什麼？
(A) 該部門仍然缺少電腦。
(B) 該部門打算增聘員工。
(C) 該部門依然需要處理大量的紙本文件。
(D) 該部門希望搬到新的區域。

> 理由
>
> 根據第二封電子郵件倒數第二句 "Unlike other departments, we still deal with a lot of hard copies of documents, so we require sufficient storage space."（與其他部門不同的是，我們仍然需要處理大量的紙本文件，因此需要足夠的貯存空間。）得知，(C) 項應為正選。

重要單字片語

1. **commitment** [kəˋmɪtmənt] n. 承諾；奉獻（不可數）
2. **comprehensively** [ˌkɑmprɪˋhɛnsɪvlɪ] adv. 全面地
3. **ergonomic** [ˌɝgəˋnɑmɪk] a. 人體工學的
4. **storage** [ˋstɔrɪdʒ] n. 儲藏（空間）（不可數）
5. **divider** [dəˋvaɪdɚ] n. 分隔物
6. **procurement** [proˋkjʊrmənt] n. 採購
7. **compliance** [kəmˋplaɪəns] n. 服從，遵守
   (in) compliance with...　遵守……
8. **cross-reference** [ˌkrɔsˋrɛfərəns] vt. 為……編制互相參照 & n. 互相參照
   Please cross-reference the attendance data with our client list.
   請把出席資料與客戶名單互相比對一下。

9. **unfortunately** [ʌnˋfɔrtʃənɪtlɪ] adv. 可惜的是；不幸地；倒楣地
10. **accommodate** [əˋkɑməˌdet] vt. 容納；提供膳宿
    The new stadium is big enough to accommodate forty thousand people.
    那座新體育場大到足以容納四萬人。
11. **unlike** [ʌnˋlaɪk] prep. 不像……，和……不同
12. **oversee** [ˌovɚˋsi] vt. 監督，監察（三態為：oversee, oversaw [ˌovɚˋsɔ], overseen [ˌovɚˋsin]）
    Some architects were appointed to oversee the construction project.
    幾位建築師被派來監督該營建專案。

181

Chapter 10 Listening Test

Part 1 Photographs

A **1** 🔊 233 🇬🇧

(A) The candidates are sitting on chairs next to the wall.
(B) The applicants are chatting with each other.
(C) One of the men is answering a phone call.
(D) The seats have all been occupied.

(A) 求職者坐在牆壁旁的椅子上。
(B) 應徵者正在互相聊天。
(C) 其中一位男子正在接電話。
(D) 所有的座位都有人坐。

🔍 **重要單字片語**

1. **applicant** [ˈæpləkənt] *n.* 應徵者；申請人
2. **occupied** [ˈɑkjəˌpaɪd] *a.* 被占用的，有人使用的

These seats are all occupied. I'll arrange some other ones for you.
這些座位都有人坐了。我會幫你們安排別的座位。

C **2** 🔊 234 🇺🇸

(A) A woman is taking notes on a whiteboard.
(B) A woman is leaving the meeting room.
(C) Some employees are clapping their hands.
(D) Some employees are packing up their laptops.

(A) 一名女子正在白板上做筆記。
(B) 一名女子正要離開會議室。
(C) 有些員工正在鼓掌。
(D) 有些員工正在收拾他們的筆電。

🔍 **重要單字片語**

1. **take notes** 作筆記
2. **clap** [klæp] *vt. & vi.* 拍手，鼓掌
   clap (one's) hands   拍手鼓掌

The audience clapped enthusiastically when the performers took their curtain call.
表演者謝幕時觀眾熱烈鼓掌。

3. **laptop** [ˈlæpˌtɑp] *n.* 筆電，筆記型電腦

🎧 Part 2 Question-Response

C **3** 🔊 236 🇨🇦 🇬🇧

I noticed you were absent from work yesterday, Melinda.
(A) OK, I'll take notes.
(B) Yes, I will have tomorrow off.
(C) Yes, I took personal leave.

梅琳達，我注意到妳昨天沒來上班。
(A) 好，我會作筆記。
(B) 對，我明天會休假。
(C) 對，我請事假。

🔍 **重要單字片語**

take / have tomorrow off　明天休假 / 休息一天

B **4** 🔊 237 🇺🇸 🇦🇺

How's the new recruit working out in your department?
(A) It's good for your health.
(B) She's doing just fine.
(C) In the accounting department.

那位新進員工在你們部門表現如何？
(A) 這對你的健康有益。
(B) 她表現還不錯。
(C) 在會計部門。

🔍 **重要單字片語**

accounting [əˋkaʊntɪŋ] *n.* 會計（學）（不可數）

🎧 Part 3 Conversations

Questions 5 through 7 refer to the following conversation. 🔊 239 M: 🇦🇺 W: 🇬🇧

M: Have you finished screening the candidate for the new accounting position?
W: Yes, in fact, I have his profile right here. His résumé and university transcript are very impressive. Check out these recommendation letters a professor and his former employer wrote for him. What do you think?
M: Wow! This is really something!
W: There's just one problem. We need someone to start immediately, but he can't start work until July 1.
M: Well, if we want to recruit the best person for the job, we'll have to be willing to wait for him to be available.

5 至 7 題請聽以下會話。

男：針對那位新會計職位的應徵者妳審查完畢了沒？
女：審查完了。事實上，我這裡有他的簡介。他的履歷及大學成績單讓人欽佩。瞧瞧某教授及他前任僱主替他寫的推薦信。你覺得呢？
男：哇！這真的很不簡單！

CH 10

Chapter 10 Listening Test

> 女：只是有個問題。我們需要有人馬上就能開工，但他得等到七月一號才能開始工作。
> 男：呃，如果我們要為這職位招募最適合的人，我們就得願意等到他可以到職才行。

A 5 🔊 240 🇨🇦

What are the speakers mainly discussing?
(A) A job applicant
(B) A coworker
(C) A recommendation
(D) A schedule

說話者主要在談論什麼？
(A) 一位求職者
(B) 一位同事
(C) 一項建議
(D) 一項行程

B 6 🔊 241 🇨🇦

What does the woman give the man?
(A) Records of payment
(B) Letters of reference
(C) Printed invoices
(D) Salary requirements

女子給了男子什麼？
(A) 付款記錄
(B) 推薦信
(C) 紙本發票
(D) 薪資要求

B 7 🔊 242 🇨🇦

What problem does the woman mention?
(A) A candidate's résumé is not up to date.
(B) A job applicant cannot work immediately.
(C) An employer did not write a letter of support.
(D) A suitable applicant has not been found.

女子提及了什麼問題？
(A) 求職者的履歷不是最新的。
(B) 求職者不能馬上工作。
(C) 僱主沒有寫推薦信。
(D) 合適的人選還沒找到。

重要單字片語

1. **transcript** [ˈtrænskrɪpt] *n.* 成績單；抄本，副本
2. **reference** [ˈrɛfərəns] *n.* 推薦信；推薦人
   a letter of reference　推薦信
3. **be up to date**　最新的
   The celebrity gossip on the website is not up to date.
   該網站上的名人八卦不是最新的。

Questions 8 through 10 refer to the following conversation with three speakers. 🔊 243
W: 🇺🇸　M1: 🇨🇦　M2: 🇦🇺

W: I'm worried about the first candidate. I don't think he is suitably qualified to take on such a senior role.
M1: I agree. He may be an experienced professor, but he doesn't have a suitable business degree, business experience, or any experience running a large department.
M2: But his expertise in the field of statistics makes him perfect to run the data analysis department.
W: If we employ him, I think he should be put on a three-month trial.
M1: He should also undergo a performance review every two weeks.

8 至 10 題請聽以下三人的會話。

> 女：我有些擔心第一位求職者。我認為他具備的資格並不適合擔任這樣高階的角色。
> 甲男：我同意。他或許是個經驗豐富的教授，但他沒有相關的商業學位、商業經驗、或是任何管理大部門的經驗。
> 乙男：但是他在統計學領域的專才讓他非常適合管理資料分析部。
> 女：如果我們僱用他，我認為他得歷經三個月的試用期。
> 甲男：他也得每兩個禮拜接受一次表現考評。

B **8** 🔊 244 🇬🇧

What is the woman concerned about?
(A) The interviewer's technique
(B) The applicant's qualifications
(C) The position's salary package
(D) The employment contract

女子在擔心什麼？
(A) 面試官的技巧
(B) 求職者的資格
(C) 職位的薪資待遇
(D) 受僱合約

D **9** 🔊 245 🇬🇧

What is the candidate's field of expertise?
(A) Mathematics
(B) Physics
(C) Management
(D) Statistics

求職者的專才領域是什麼？
(A) 數學
(B) 物理學
(C) 管理學
(D) 統計學

C **10** 🔊 246 🇬🇧

What does the woman suggest?
(A) Checking the candidate's application
(B) Holding a training session
(C) Placing the candidate on probation
(D) Interviewing other candidates

女子建議什麼？
(A) 檢視求職者的申請書
(B) 舉辦訓練課程
(C) 試用求職者
(D) 面試其他求職者

重要單字片語

1. **take on...** 承擔……（= undertake...）
   I'm too busy to take on any extra work.
   我太忙了，沒辦法承擔更多的工作。

2. **senior** [ˈsinjɚ] a. 高階的；年老的

3. **run** [rʌn] vt. 掌管，管理，經營（三態為：run, ran [ræn], run）
   Nancy has been running a restaurant since she graduated.
   南西畢業後一直都在經營一家餐廳。

4. **statistics** [stəˈtɪstɪks] n. 統計學（恆用複數，不可數）；統計數字（可數，單數為 statistic）
   Statistics is one of my favorite subjects.
   統計學是我最喜歡的科目之一。
   Statistics show that 65% of our customers are female.
   數據顯示本公司 65% 的顧客是女性。

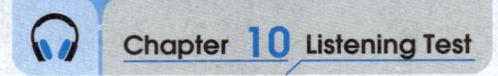

Chapter 10 Listening Test

5. **trial** [ˈtraɪəl] *n.* 試用
   a three-month trial period
   三個月的試用期
6. **undergo** [ˌʌndɚˈgo] *vt.* 經歷，接受
   （三態為：undergo, underwent
   [ˌʌndɚˈwɛnt], undergone [ˌʌndɚˈgɔn]）

   Before reaching your goal, you will undergo many hardships.
   你達成目標之前，會經歷很多困難。
7. **mathematics** [ˌmæθəˈmætɪks] *n.* 數學
   (= math [mæθ])
8. **physics** [ˈfɪzɪks] *n.* 物理學

Part 4 Talks

Questions 11 through 13 refer to the following telephone message. 🔊 248

This message is for Melissa Jones. I'm Karen Hansen from Gateway Employment Services. I received and forwarded the application you submitted for the position of midwife at St. Patrick's Private Maternity Hospital. Frankly speaking, your portfolio is very impressive, but there are many competitive applicants for the position. However, I'm sure I could quickly find you employment elsewhere should this application be unsuccessful. If you'd like to discuss this with me further, please reply via my office landline or cellphone. The numbers are on the business card I gave you.

11 至 13 題請聽以下電話留言。

> 這則留言是給梅麗莎·瓊斯。我是戈偉就業服務社的凱倫·韓森。妳應徵聖派翠克私立婦產醫院助產員一職的應徵函我已經收到並轉寄出去了。坦白講，妳的作品集是很優秀，但是本職缺有許多非常厲害的應徵者。不過，假如這次應徵不成功，我確信我能迅速幫妳找到其他地方的工作。如果妳想與我進一步地討論，請透過我的公司市話或手機回覆。電話號碼在之前給妳的名片上。

C **11** 🔊 249

Who most likely is the speaker?
(A) A trainee doctor
(B) A registered nurse
(C) A recruitment consultant
(D) An office receptionist

說話者最有可能是誰？
(A) 實習醫生
(B) 合格護理師
(C) 招募顧問
(D) 公司櫃檯人員

A **12** 🔊 250

What does the speaker say about the position?
(A) There have been many applicants.
(B) Interviews are now taking place.
(C) It has recently been filled.
(D) It provides a high salary.

關於該職缺，說話者說了什麼？
(A) 有很多應徵者。
(B) 面試正在進行。
(C) 該職缺最近已被填補了。
(D) 該職缺提供高薪水。

C **13** 🔊 251

What does the speaker ask Ms. Jones to do?
(A) Submit her portfolio
(B) Process an application
(C) Call her back if she desires
(D) Send a business card

說話者要求瓊斯女士做什麼？
(A) 提交她的作品集
(B) 審核應徵函
(C) 如果她想要的話就回電
(D) 寄一張名片

重要單字片語

1. **forward** [ˈfɔrwəd] *vt.* 轉寄；寄發
   I asked my secretary to forward all correspondence to my new e-mail address.
   我請我的助理將所有信件轉寄至我的新電子信箱。

2. **submit** [səbˈmɪt] *vt.* 提交，呈遞
   Your report needs to be submitted to the manager no later than Friday.
   你的報告最遲要在星期五前上呈給經理。

3. **midwife** [ˈmɪdˌwaɪf] *n.* 助產員，接生員

4. **maternity** [məˈtɜnətɪ] *a.* 孕婦的，產婦的

5. **Frankly speaking, ...** 坦白說，……
   = To be frank (with you), ...
   = To tell (you) the truth, ...
   Frankly speaking, I don't think this plan will work.
   坦白說，我不認為這項計畫會成功。

6. **competitive** [kəmˈpɛtətɪv] *a.* 有競爭力的

7. **landline** [ˈlændˌlaɪn] *n.* 室內電話

8. **recruitment** [rɪˈkrutmənt] *n.* 招募

Questions 14 through 16 refer to the following announcement and list. 🔊 252

Today, we say goodbye to four of our favorite coworkers. They have all decided to retire on the same day. Between them, they have chalked up over 100 years of service. I'm going to ask each of the four to say a few words. First of all, here is someone who needs no introduction. He has worked at Watson's Work Wear longer than anyone else and is indirectly responsible for much of the company's success in the protective clothing field. Before I call on him to make a short speech, I'd like to remind you that champagne and light snacks are available on the table at the back of the room. We'll definitely be raising a toast or two. Now, without further delay, let's welcome him.

Name	Length of Employment
Ron Buckingham	36 years
Cathy Stevens	27 years
Pam Ashcroft	20 years
Ian Benson	29 years

Chapter 10　Listening Test

14 至 16 題請聽以下公告，並請看以下清單。

> 今天，我們與四位大家最喜愛的同事告別。他們都決定在同一天退休。他們四人的任職年數總共超過一百年。我會請四位分別講些話。首先，這一位是不需要我來介紹的。他在華生工作服飾公司效命的時間比任何人還要長，本公司在防護衣物領域的成功也要間接歸功於他。在我請他發表短言之前，我想提醒諸位房間後方的桌上有香檳與小點心。我們肯定會舉杯慶祝一兩次。現在，不再贅言，讓我們歡迎他。

姓名	任職年數
榮恩‧柏金漢	36 年
凱西‧史蒂芬斯	27 年
潘‧阿什克羅夫特	20 年
尹恩‧班森	29 年

D 　14　 🔊 253　🇬🇧

What is being announced?
(A) Dismissals
(B) Year-end banquets
(C) Retrenchments
(D) Retirements

本公告宣布什麼事項？
(A) 解僱
(B) 尾牙
(C) 開支緊縮
(D) 退休

C 　15　 🔊 254　🇬🇧

What is provided at the event?
(A) Discounts for members
(B) Free samples
(C) Refreshments
(D) Souvenirs

活動有提供什麼？
(A) 給會員的折扣
(B) 免費試用品
(C) 茶點
(D) 紀念品

A 　16　 🔊 255　🇬🇧

Look at the graphic. Who will make the speech first?
(A) Mr. Buckingham
(B) Ms. Stevens
(C) Ms. Ashcroft
(D) Mr. Benson

請看圖表。誰會首先發表短言？
(A) 柏金漢先生
(B) 史蒂芬斯女士
(C) 阿什克羅夫特女士
(D) 班森先生

Chapter 10 Reading Test

🔍 重要單字片語

1. **chalk up...** 累積……；贏得……
   The basketball team chalked up their tenth win this season.
   那支籃球隊拿下本季第十勝。
2. **champagne** [ʃæmˋpen] *n.* 香檳（不可數）
3. **toast** [tost] *n.* 敬酒 & *vt.* 為……乾杯
   make a toast to sb　向某人敬酒
   I would like to make a toast to the bride and groom.
   我想要向新郎新娘敬酒。
4. **dismissal** [dɪsˋmɪsḷ] *n.* 解僱
5. **retrenchment** [rɪˋtrɛntʃmənt] *n.* 開支緊縮
6. **refreshments** [rɪˋfrɛʃmənts] *n.* 茶點（恆用複數）
7. **souvenir** [ˏsuvəˋnɪr] *n.* 紀念品

📖 Part 5　Incomplete Sentences

B　17

It is essential that all new starters ------- the orientation process on their first day at the company.

(A) completed　　(B) complete　　(C) to complete　　(D) completing

所有新進人員必須於到職首日就接受並完成新進人員訓練的流程。

理由

1. 本題測試表「必要的」或「適當的」的形容詞，與 that 子句的關係。
   1) 表「必要的」形容詞如下：
      essential（必要的）、necessary（必要的）、urgent（急迫的）
      表「適當的」形容詞如下：
      advisable（適當的）、desirable（合宜的）、recommendable（值得推薦的；適當的）
   2) 以上形容詞在下列句構出現時，that 子句主詞之後，恆用助動詞 should，而 should 往往予以省略，直接接原形動詞：
      It is + 上列形容詞 + that + 主詞 + (should) + 原形動詞
      It is necessary that the job (should) be finished by five.
      這個工作必須在五點前做完。
      It is advisable that we (should) get up at four tomorrow morning if we are to catch the first train.
      我們若要搭上頭班火車，最好是在明早四點就起床。
2. 根據上述，原句句首有 It is essential（那是有必要的），得知 that 子句主詞之後應置 should complete，而 should 可省略，故 (B) 項應為正選。

🔍 重要單字片語

essential [ɪˋsɛnʃəl] *a.* 有必要的；基本的

Chapter 10　Reading Test

D 18

Candidates for the ------- opened position of sales representative will in part be chosen by means of an audition.

(A) new　　　　　　(B) newest　　　　　　(C) newer　　　　　　(D) newly

新職缺的業務員應徵者有一部分將藉由試聽會來遴選。

理由

1. 空格後有過去分詞 opened 作形容詞用，表「被空出來的」，修飾名詞 position（職位），得知空格內應置副詞，以修飾 opened。

2. 選項中，(A) new（新的）、(B) newest（最新的）及 (C) newer（較新的）均為形容詞，不可選。(D) newly（最近地；剛剛地）是副詞，可修飾 opened，且合乎語意，故為正選。

重要單字片語

1. **in part**　部分
   Our success in this mission was due in part to your help.
   我們成功地完成這項任務，有部分要歸因於你的幫助。

2. **by means of...**　藉由……
   = by way of...

D 19

------- no one to apply for the vacancy, we would have to advertise the position more widely.

(A) Had　　　　　　(B) Should　　　　　　(C) If　　　　　　(D) Were

假如沒有人應徵這個職缺，我們就得透過更多管道刊登此職位的徵人廣告。

理由

1. 假設語氣的 if 子句中，若有過去完成式助動詞 had、或表「萬一」的助動詞 should、或是 were 出現時，可將這些詞置句首，而將 if 省略。
   If John had done it, he would have felt sorry.
   = Had John done it, he would have felt sorry.
   當時如果約翰做了這件事，他就會後悔。
   If Peter should tell lies, I would punish him.
   = Should Peter tell lies, I would punish him.
   萬一彼得說謊，我會處罰他。
   If I were to do it, I would certainly need your help.
   = Were I to do it, I would certainly need your help.
   我要是做這件事，肯定會需要你的協助。

2. 根據上述，若選 (A)，空格之後的 to apply 應改為 applied，而主要子句應改為 we would have had to 表「我們當時就得……」；若選 (B)，空格之後的主詞 no one 其後應刪除 to，即："Should no one apply for..."；若選 (C)，空格之後的主詞 no one 其後應置 were，即："If no one were to apply for..."；因此僅 (D) 為正選，即："Were no one to apply for..."。

> 🔍 **重要單字片語**
>
> **advertise** [ˋædvɚˌtaɪz] *vt.* 將……登廣告 & *vi.* 登廣告
> The company plans to advertise the new product on several websites.
> 公司打算在數個網站上面幫新產品打廣告。

B **20**

Due to the numerous job applications ------- for the supervisory positions, it is likely that we will have to reject over half of them.

(A) receive　　　　(B) received　　　　(C) receiving　　　　(D) receives

由於收到極多應徵管理職位者的求職信，我們很可能必須拒絕超過一半的人。

> **理由**
>
> 1. 本題測試形容詞子句化簡為分詞片語的用法，原句原為：
>   Due to the numerous job applications <u>which were received</u> for the supervisory positions, …
> 2. 此時可將關係代名詞 which 省略，之後的動詞改為現在分詞，若遇到 be 動詞則改為 being，且 being 可予以省略，故上句可改寫成：
>   Due to the numerous job applications <u>received</u> for the supervisory positions, …
> 3. 根據上述，(B) 項應為正選。

> 🔍 **重要單字片語**
>
> **numerous** [ˋnjumərəs] *a.* 很多的

C **21**

Konnektt Systems, one of the world's largest computer manufacturers, has announced ------- that will affect 8,000 of its employees.

(A) conflicts　　　　(B) diversities　　　　(C) layoffs　　　　(D) mentors

全球最大電腦製造商之一的康奈克特系統公司已宣布進行裁員，有八千名員工將受到波及。

> **理由**
>
> 1. (A) **conflict** [ˋkɑnflɪkt] *n.* 爭執，衝突 & [kənˋflɪkt] *vi.* 衝突，相抵觸
>   A conflict with B　A 和 B 衝突／相抵觸
>   What we found in the experiment conflicts with our initial assumptions.
>   我們在實驗中發現的結果與我們最初的假設相抵觸。
>
>   (B) **diversity** [daɪˋvɝsətɪ] *n.* 多樣性；差異
>   New York is a city that is known for its ethnic diversity.
>   紐約是個以種族多樣性而聞名的城市。
>   ＊ethnic [ˋɛθnɪk] *a.* 種族的
>
>   (C) **layoff** [ˋleˌɔf] *n.* 裁員（＝ lay-off）
>   The company announced layoffs affecting 20 percent of the workforce.
>   公司宣布裁員，將影響 20% 的員工。

Chapter 10 Reading Test

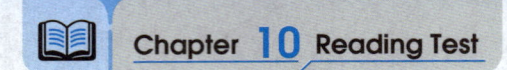

(D) **mentor** [ˈmɛntɔr] *n.* 導師，指導者
Debra is an assistant sales manager, and she will be your mentor.
黛博拉是銷售部門的協理，她會是你的指導員。

2. 根據上述，(C) 項應為正選。

重要單字片語

manufacturer [ˌmænjəˈfæktʃərɚ] *n.* 製造業者；廠商

Part 6 Text Completion

Questions 22-25 refer to the following letter.

Mr. John Burr
141 South Baker Avenue
Muncie, Indiana 47302

Dear Mr. Burr:

　　Congratulations on your retirement! We at Amalgamated Industries will miss you, but we are happy that you can now spend your time -------- you please. Since
22.
you are eligible for a pension, we urge you to visit us -------- your earliest convenience
23.
to complete the forms necessary to receive your government benefits. --------. The
24.
number for Human Resources is 848-2171. We look forward to -------- you again and
25.
helping you prepare for this next phase in your life.

Yours sincerely,

Beth Rosemary
Human Resources Director
Amalgamated Industries

192

22 至 25 題請看以下信件。

印地安納州曼西市
南貝克大街 141 號
郵遞區號 47302
約翰・伯爾先生

親愛的伯爾先生：

　　恭喜您退休了！我們在聯合產業的同仁都會很想念您，但我們仍為您感到高興的是，您現在能<u>隨心所欲地</u>利用自己的時間了。既然您有資格領取退休金，我們呼籲您<u>方便時儘早</u>來拜訪我們，以填妥讓您領取政府福利所需的表格。<u>我會親自協助您完成所有文件。</u>人資部的電話號碼為 848-2171。我們期待再次與您<u>見面</u>，並為您預備過下一個階段的生活。

聯合產業人資部主任
貝絲・羅斯瑪麗　敬上

B **22**

(A) like　　　　　　(B) as　　　　　　(C) what　　　　　(D) so

理由

1. 本句測試下列固定用法：
   as you please　　按某人喜歡的方式
   = as you like
   There were no children to cook for, so we could just do as we please.
   因為不用給孩子做飯，我們就可以自便了。
2. 根據上述，(B) 項應為正選。

A **23**

(A) at　　　　　　(B) in　　　　　　(C) with　　　　　(D) on

理由

1. 本句測試下列固定用法：
   at sb's earliest convenience　　某人方便時儘早
   at sb's convenience　　在某人方便的時候
   Give me a call at your convenience.
   你方便的時候打通電話給我。
2. 根據上述，(A) 項應為正選。

A **24**

(A) I will personally assist you with all the paperwork.
(B) A permit for the development will then be issued by the government.
(C) You will receive a refund only if you can provide documentation.
(D) Other staff members have also made the same request.

Chapter 10 Reading Test

理由

1. (A) 我會親自協助您完成所有文件。
   (B) 開發許可證接著會由政府頒發。
   (C) 只有您提供文件才能收到退款。
   (D) 其他的員工也做了相同的要求。
2. 空格前的句子提及 "…complete the forms necessary to receive your government benefits."（……以填妥讓您領取政府福利所需的表格。），得知寄件者希望收件者完成一些文件，而 (A) 項的句子提及 assist you with all the paperwork（協助您完成所有文件），可知與前句形成關聯，故應為正選。

B **25**

(A) see　　　　　(B) seeing　　　　(C) be seeing　　　(D) sees

理由

1. 本句測試下列固定句構：

   look forward to + N/V-ing　　期待……（此處 to 是介詞）
   I look forward to seeing you again.
   我期待再次與你相見。
   We look forward to your earliest reply.
   我們期待您能盡快回覆。

2. 根據上述，(B) 項應為正選。

重要單字片語

1. **urge** [ɝdʒ] *vt.* 力勸；敦促
   urge sb to + V　　力勸某人……
   = call on sb to + V
2. **paperwork** [ˈpepɚˌwɝk] *n.* 文件；文書工作
3. **phase** [fez] *n.* 階段，時期
   in the initial / final phase of the project
   專案在初始 / 最終階段
   The project is only in the initial phase, but it looks quite promising.
   這個專案只在初始階段，卻看似大有前景。

194

Part 7 Reading Comprehension

Questions 26-30 refer to the following e-mail and memo.

To:	Roger Branson
From:	Reginald Ascot
Date:	December 1
Subject:	Bonus ideas

Roger,

The board met to discuss novel ideas for the annual employee bonus, and several excellent proposals were submitted.

By far the most well-received was Colin's idea to give staff a cash bonus equivalent to one day's wage. I think this is a good idea, but in light of the immense profits made this year, Zaza suggested that staff receive an extra day of leave. I tend to agree and think this would be a great boost to morale.

Robert's suggestion, a trip to somewhere such as the Grand Canyon, was the least popular. Needless to say, it would be impossible at such short notice. Mandy's idea to raise the rate of overtime pay was almost as poorly received as Robert's.

Could you let me know your decision when you return from abroad?

Reginald Ascot

Chapter 10 Reading Test

MEMO

The executive board has decided to give all workers a holiday treat.

Due to the excellent performance of all our branches and head office departments, Mason Electronics has posted its most profitable year ever. To share this good fortune with those who made it possible — you, the employees — the executive board has decided that all staff will receive an extra day of personal leave on December 24. This includes employees at the head office, the Southridge factory, and all 12 retail outlets. It does not, however, include installation subcontractors.

Those who have already arranged personal leave on the 24th will still receive an extra day of leave. Supervisors, team leaders, and department heads must adjust their schedules and deadlines as necessary. Retail outlets should display signs to inform customers of the closure.

Finally, I'd like to take the opportunity to wish all the hard-working and selfless employees and their families a safe, loving, and happy holiday season.

Merry Christmas!

Reginald Ascot, Senior Vice President

26 至 30 題請看以下電子郵件及備忘錄。

收件者：	羅傑・布蘭森
寄件者：	雷金納德・阿斯考特
日　期：	十二月一日
主　旨：	獎金的想法

羅傑：

為了員工年終獎金，董事會開會討論一些新點子，大家提出了許多極佳的提議。

柯林建議給員工等同一天工資的現金獎金，這點子的接受度遙遙領先其他建議。我覺得這個想法不錯，不過由於今年實在賺太多錢了，扎扎則建議送員工額外一天休假。我傾向同意這項提議，覺得這可以大大提升士氣。

羅伯特建議到諸如大峽谷等地旅遊，這個想法最不受歡迎。不用說，這在短時間內是不可能的。蔓蒂提出漲加班費，這點子被嫌棄的程度跟羅伯特的點子沒差多少。

待你從國外回來後能讓我知道你的決定嗎？

雷金納德・阿斯考特

備忘錄

執行董事會已決議要給所有的員工一項假期特別款待。

由於梅森電子的分公司與總公司各部門的傑出表現，我們已公布了有史以來獲利最佳的一年。為了與使這件事得以達成的人 —— 你們，也就是諸位所有員工 —— 分享這個好成果，執行董事會已決議讓所有員工在十二月二十四日獲得一天額外的事假。這包括了總公司、南山工廠與所有十二家零售店的員工。不過，這不包括安裝分包商。

已於二十四日安排事假的人仍會獲得一天額外的假。若有需要，主管、組長與部門主管也必須調整工作行程與截止日。零售店應張貼告示以讓顧客知悉閉店的消息。

最後，我想藉此機會來祝福所有勤奮、無私的員工與其家人共同度過一個平安、有愛與快樂的假期。

聖誕節快樂！

資深副總裁
雷金納德・阿斯考特

Chapter 10 Reading Test

B **26**

In the e-mail, the word "notice" in paragraph 3, line 2, is closest in meaning to
(A) observation
(B) warning
(C) review
(D) distance

在本電子郵件裡,第三段第二行單字 notice 意思最接近下列何字?
(A) 觀察
(B) 提醒
(C) 評論
(D) 距離

理由

此行中有片語 at short notice 表示「在短時間內」,其中 notice 有表示「告知、通知」的意味,而 (B) 項 warning 具「提醒」之意,與 notice 意思最為接近,故 (B) 項應為正選。

B **27**

What is indicated about Mason Electronics?
(A) It has recovered from a financial crisis.
(B) It has multiple locations.
(C) It is expanding into overseas territories.
(D) It is on the verge of bankruptcy.

有關梅森電子,本文指出了什麼?
(A) 它已從金融危機中復原。
(B) 它有許多據點。
(C) 它正擴展到國外的地區。
(D) 它正面臨破產邊緣。

理由

根據備忘錄第二段第三句 "This includes employees at the head office, the Southridge factory, and all 12 retail outlets."(這包括了總公司、南山工廠與所有十二家零售店的員工。)可推測 (B) 項應為正選。

B **28**

Whose proposal was accepted?
(A) Colin's
(B) Zaza's
(C) Robert's
(D) Mandy's

誰的提議被採納了?
(A) 柯林
(B) 扎扎
(C) 羅伯特
(D) 蔓蒂

理由

根據電子郵件第二段第二句 "..., Zaza suggested that staff receive an extra day of leave."(……,扎扎則建議送員工額外一天休假)及備忘錄第二段第二句 "... the executive board has decided that all staff will receive an extra day of personal leave on December 24."(……執行董事會已決議讓所有員工在十二月二十四日獲得一天額外的事假。)得知,(B) 項應為正選。

D **29**

Who will NOT benefit from the proposal?
(A) Board members
(B) Department heads
(C) Factory workers
(D) Subcontractors

誰將不會受益於此提案？
(A) 董事會成員
(B) 部門主管
(C) 工廠員工
(D) 分包商

> 理由
>
> 根據備忘錄第二段最後一句 "It does not, however, include installation subcontractors."（不過，這不包括安裝分包商。）得知，(D) 項應為正選。

A **30**

What does Mr. Ascot advise middle managers to do?
(A) Alter their agendas
(B) Reduce their overheads
(C) Submit their proposals
(D) Prepare their vacations

阿斯考特先生建議中階經理做什麼？
(A) 更改工作行程
(B) 減少經常性開支
(C) 繳交提案
(D) 準備假期

> 理由
>
> 根據備忘錄第三段第二句 "Supervisors, team leaders, and department heads must adjust their schedules and deadlines as necessary."（若有需要，主管、組長與部門主管也必須調整工作行程與截止日。）得知，(A) 項應為正選。

重要單字片語

1. **novel** [ˈnɑvḷ] *a.* 新奇的，新穎的
2. **submit** [səbˈmɪt] *vt.* 繳交，遞交
   submit sth to sb　繳交某物給某人
   Sharon submitted her thesis to her professor yesterday.
   雪倫昨天繳交了論文給她的教授。
3. **equivalent** [ɪˈkwɪvələnt] *a.* 等值的；相等的；等同的
   be equivalent to...　相當於……
   The price of this dress is equivalent to that of the shoes.
   這件洋裝的價格相當於那雙鞋子。
4. **in (the) light of...**
   由於……，有鑒於……
   In light of this new evidence, the judge will certainly dismiss the case.
   由於這項新證據，法官一定會駁回此案。
5. **immense** [ɪˈmɛns] *a.* 巨大的
6. **boost** [bust] *n.* 激勵，鼓舞；促進，推動
7. **post** [post] *vt.* 公布，宣布（尤指財經訊息）
   The company posted record profits for the second fiscal quarter.
   該公司公布了第二個財政季度創紀錄的利潤。
8. **subcontractor** [ˌsʌbˈkɑntræktɚ] *n.* 分包商（contractor 則為「承包商」）
9. **crisis** [ˈkraɪsɪs] *n.* 危機

Chapter 10 Reading Test

10. **expand** [ɪk`spænd] vi. & vt. 擴大，拓展
    expand into... 擴展到……
    Mr. Wang's business has recently expanded into South America.
    王先生的事業最近擴展到南美洲。
    We've expanded our business by opening two more restaurants.
    我們擴大營業，新開了兩家餐廳。

11. **territory** [`tɛrə‚tɔrɪ] n. 地區；領土

12. **be on the verge of...**
    在……的邊緣，瀕臨……
    = be on the brink / edge of...
    As a result of poor management, the company is on the verge of bankruptcy.
    該公司因為經營不善，現在正處於破產的邊緣。

13. **bankruptcy** [`bæŋkrʌptsɪ] n. 破產

14. **alter** [`ɔltɚ] vt. 改變；修改（服裝等）

15. **agenda** [ə`dʒɛndə] n. 工作事項；會議議程

Chapter 11 Listening Test

Part 1 Photographs

B **1** 🔊 257 🇨🇦

(A) A woman is standing in line at the grocery store.
(B) A man is inspecting an item in the produce section.
(C) A man is placing a price tag on the basket.
(D) A woman is wrapping a baguette in paper.

(A) 女子在生鮮超市裡排隊。
(B) 男子在農產品區檢視一個貨品。
(C) 男子正在籃子上放置價格標籤。
(D) 女子正用紙張包裝法式長棍麵包。

重要單字片語

1. **grocery** [ˈɡrosərɪ] *n.* 食品雜貨（常用複數）
   a grocery store　　食品雜貨店；生鮮超市
2. **produce** [ˈprodjus / ˈpradjus] *n.* 農產品（不可數）
3. **wrap** [ræp] *vt.* 包裝，包（三態為：wrap, wrapped [ræpt], wrapped）
   wrap up...　　將……包起來
   Maxson is not good at wrapping up presents.
   麥克斯森對包裝禮物不在行。
4. **baguette** [bæˈɡɛt] *n.* 法式長棍麵包

C **2** 🔊 258 🇦🇺

(A) The box has been loaded on a truck.
(B) The man is purchasing some clipboards.
(C) The woman is receiving some merchandise.
(D) The woman is writing on the package.

(A) 箱子已經裝到卡車上。
(B) 男子正在買板夾。
(C) 女子正在簽收貨品。
(D) 女子正在包裹上寫字。

重要單字片語

1. **load** [lod] *vt.* 裝載
   load A into / onto B　　把 A 裝進 / 裝上 B
   We are loading motorcycles onto the truck.
   我們正把摩托車裝上卡車。
2. **receive** [rɪˈsiv] *vt.* 獲得，收到
   Did you receive that letter?
   你收到那封信了嗎？

Chapter 11 Listening Test

Part 2 Question-Response

B **3** 🔊 260 🇨🇦 🇺🇸

How can I be eligible for a 20% discount?
(A) Rectify the discrepancy.
(B) Spend more than $1,000.
(C) It cost more than I expected.

我要如何取得八折優惠的資格？
(A) 糾正有出入的部分。
(B) 消費一千美元以上。
(C) 它比我預期中還要貴。

重要單字片語

1. **discrepancy** [dɪˋskrɛpənsɪ] *n.* 差異
2. **expect** [ɪkˋspɛkt] *vt.* 預期，預料

We are expecting more than 100 applicants for this position.
我們預期該職缺會有一百多位求職者應徵。

C **4** 🔊 261 🇬🇧 🇨🇦

Management has authorized the purchase of a new printer.
(A) There is more paper in the storeroom.
(B) The printer has jammed again.
(C) Let's research what models are available.

管理階層已經批准購買新的印表機。
(A) 儲藏室有更多紙。
(B) 印表機又卡住了。
(C) 我們來研究有供應哪些機型。

重要單字片語

1. **storeroom** [ˋstɔrˌrum] *n.* 儲藏室
2. **jam** [dʒæm] *vi.* & *vt.* （使）卡住
   Holly couldn't open the window because it was jammed.
   荷麗打不開窗戶因為它被卡住了。
3. **model** [ˋmɑdḷ] *n.* 型號，樣式

Part 3 Conversations

Questions 5 through 7 refer to the following conversation. 🔊 263 M: 🇨🇦 W: 🇬🇧

M: Wow! I can't believe the protein bars are so cheap at this supermarket. They're a real bargain!
W: That's because the supermarket buys them in bulk from a wholesale supplier. The supplier distributes the protein bars to supermarkets and health food stores across the country.
M: How come you know so much about this? Do you work for them or something?
W: I watched a documentary on TV about global supply chains, and this was featured as an example.
M: Well, I'm definitely going to stock up on protein bars while I'm here!

5 至 7 題請聽以下會話。

男：哇！這家超市的蛋白棒便宜得不可思議耶！太划算了！
女：因為超市是向盤商大量購買的緣故。盤商把蛋白棒經銷到全國各地的超市與健康食品店。
男：妳怎麼這麼懂這些事？妳有在那邊上班過嗎？
女：我在電視上看過全球供應鏈的紀錄片，裡面舉了這個當範例。
男：嗯，既然來了，我絕對要把這些蛋白棒買好買滿！

A 5 ◀)264

Why is the man surprised?
(A) An item in the store is not expensive.
(B) A product he wants is not available.
(C) A supermarket sells exotic goods.
(D) A friend eats too much protein.

男子為何會驚訝？
(A) 店裡某樣商品很便宜。
(B) 他想要買的商品缺貨。
(C) 超市有賣異國風味商品。
(D) 有個朋友攝取過多蛋白質。

B 6 ◀)265

What does the woman indicate about the supplier?
(A) It deals with one specific health food store.
(B) It sends its products across the nation.
(C) It is going to raise its wholesale prices.
(D) It is based in a different country.

女子對盤商有何說法？
(A) 盤商與某特定健康食品店做生意。
(B) 盤商經銷產品遍及全國。
(C) 盤商將調漲批發價。
(D) 盤商總部在國外。

D 7 ◀)266

How did the woman find out about the supply chain?
(A) She read a news report.
(B) She asked a shop assistant.
(C) She worked for the supplier.
(D) She watched a television show.

女子是如何了解供應鏈的事？
(A) 她讀過新聞報導。
(B) 她問過商店店員。
(C) 她替盤商工作過。
(D) 她看過電視節目。

重要單字片語

1. **stock** [stɑk] *vt.* 儲存
   stock up (on sth)
   大量購買 / 囤貨（某物）
   There's a typhoon coming, so we should stock up on bottled water.
   颱風要來了，所以我們要多囤積些瓶裝水。

2. **exotic** [ɪgˋzɑtɪk] *a.* 異國風味的

203

Chapter 11 Listening Test

Questions 8 through 10 refer to the following conversation. 267 W: 🇺🇸 M: 🇦🇺

W: Steve, a large order of chemicals arrived by truck yesterday. Unfortunately, there seems to be a discrepancy between what we ordered and what we received. Milhouse is not here today, so could you check the order and help sort this mess out?

M: I'd like to, but I'm not authorized to check orders that contain chemicals. I don't have the necessary certification.

W: But we're always purchasing drums of chemicals! I would have thought everyone in this department would be certified. Surely it's a basic requirement of the position. Never mind, I'll find someone who is certified to handle chemicals to check the order.

8 至 10 題請聽以下會話。

女：史蒂夫，昨天有一大批化學物品用卡車送來了。不幸的是，我們訂購的項目跟收到的貨品似乎有出入。米爾豪斯今天不在，所以可以請你檢查那批貨，幫忙解決這個問題嗎？
男：我很樂意，但是我沒有權限查看含有化學物品的貨物。我沒有必備的專業認證。
女：可我們一向都是買桶裝化學物質的啊！我以為本部門的所有人都有處理證照耶！那該算是職務上的基本要求吧？好吧，我去找有處理化學物證照的人來檢查那批貨好了。

B **8** 268 🇨🇦

What does the woman ask the man to do?
(A) Unload a truck
(B) Check an order
(C) Take a message
(D) Complete a form

女子要求男子做什麼？
(A) 從貨車上卸下貨物
(B) 檢查一批貨
(C) 幫忙傳話
(D) 填完表單

C **9** 269 🇨🇦

What does the woman imply when she says, "But we're always purchasing drums of chemicals"?
(A) She confirms the standard operating procedure.
(B) She thinks the chemicals should be cheaper.
(C) She is surprised that the man is not certified.
(D) She personally placed the order.

女子說「可我們一向都是買桶裝化學物質的啊」時，在暗示什麼？
(A) 她認可標準操作流程。
(B) 她認為化學物品應該更便宜。
(C) 她很訝異男子沒有專業認證。
(D) 她親自下的訂單。

A **10** 270 🇨🇦

What does the woman say she will do?
(A) Ask for another colleague's help
(B) Inspect some paperwork
(C) Check the man's certification
(D) Authorize a procedure

女子說她會做什麼事？
(A) 找另一位同事來幫忙
(B) 查看一些文件
(C) 檢查男子的證照
(D) 授權某流程

重要單字片語

1. **sort sth out / sort out sth**
   處理，解決某事／某問題
   All customer complaints must be sorted out immediately.
   所有客訴都要立即解決。

2. **contain** [kənˋten] *vt.* 包含；裝有
   Cigarettes contain chemicals that contribute to lung cancer.
   香菸含有會導致肺癌的化學物質。

3. **certification** [sɚ͵tɪfəˋkeʃən] *n.* 證書，認證
   certify [ˋsɝtə͵faɪ] *vt.* 證明
   Oscar was certified as a teacher when he passed the exam last year.
   奧斯卡去年通過考試後就獲得教師認證了。

4. **drum** [drʌm] *n.*（裝油、化學用品等液體的）大桶
   an oil drum　　油桶

Part 4　Talks

Questions 11 through 13 refer to the following telephone message. 🔊 272

Hi, my name is Greg Hannon. I purchased an Astrocharge 5000 battery charger from your store a few weeks ago. When I arrived home, I noticed that the packaging was damaged, but thought no more of it. Then, yesterday, when I tried to charge some batteries for the first time, the unit wouldn't work. I think the battery recharger was probably damaged in transit. Consequently, I'd like to exchange it. Unfortunately, there's a problem: I've lost the receipt. So, I'd like to know if you could bend the store's rules and exchange it without a receipt? I'll drop by the store if I don't hear back from you.

11 至 13 題請聽以下電話留言。

> 嗨，我是葛瑞格・漢農。我幾個禮拜前從你的店裡購買了星空充電 5000 型電池充電器。我回到家時發現包裝受損，可是並沒有太留意。然後，昨天我第一次試著要將一些電池充電時，裝置卻無法使用。我想充電器應該是在運送過程中受損了。因此，我想要換掉它。不幸的是，有個問題發生了：我把收據弄丟了。所以，我想請問你是否可以放寬貴店的規定，讓我不用收據也可以換貨？如果沒有收到你的回覆，我過幾天將會順道去店裡。

C　**11**　🔊 273

What does the speaker say about the battery recharger?
(A) He should have bought it elsewhere.
(B) It stopped working after a short time.
(C) It may have been damaged.
(D) The packaging is unattractive.

關於電池充電器，說話者說了什麼？
(A) 他應該在別的地方購買。
(B) 它用沒多久就壞掉了。
(C) 它可能受損了。
(D) 包裝很不吸引人。

Chapter 11 Listening Test

D **12** 🔊 274 🇺🇸

Why is the speaker calling?
(A) To reply to an inquiry
(B) To request a refund
(C) To confirm an order
(D) To query an exchange

說話者為什麼打電話？
(A) 回覆問題
(B) 要求退款
(C) 確認訂單
(D) 詢問換貨

D **13** 🔊 275 🇺🇸

What problem does the speaker have?
(A) He accidently damaged the packaging.
(B) He forgot where the store is located.
(C) He lost the battery charger.
(D) He cannot find the receipt.

說話者有什麼問題？
(A) 他不小心毀損包裝。
(B) 他忘記店鋪的位置。
(C) 他弄丟電池充電器。
(D) 他找不到收據。

重要單字片語

1. **charger** [ˈtʃɑrdʒɚ] *n.* 充電器（= recharger [rɪˈtʃɑrdʒɚ]）
2. **consequently** [ˈkɑnsəˌkwɛntlɪ] *adv.* 因此，所以（= therefore [ˈðɛrˌfɔr]）
   Gary called in sick today; consequently, we have to take on some of his work.
   蓋瑞今天打電話請病假；因此，我們必須承擔他的一些工作。
3. **bend the rules** 放寬規定；變通，通融
4. **drop by** 順道拜訪
   I will drop by tomorrow to see how you are doing.
   我明天會順道來看看你的狀況如何。
5. **query** [ˈkwɪrɪ] *vt.* 對……提出疑問；質問 & *n.* 詢問，疑問
   Our professor always encourages us to query his statements.
   我們教授總是鼓勵我們對他的論點提出疑問。

Questions 14 through 16 refer to the following advertisement. 🔊 276 🇦🇺

We at Discount Center are proud to announce our 20th anniversary sale! And to celebrate, we're giving customers massive savings! Spend $20 or more, and you'll receive a discount of 20%. Yes, 20%! Plus, you'll go into the draw to win one of 20 round-trip airline tickets to Las Vegas! Discount Center Loyalty Card holders are also eligible to receive one of 20 gift vouchers to the value of $20,000! Don't delay; time is running out. The Discount Center's 20th anniversary sale ends at midnight on Sunday.

14 至 16 題請聽以下廣告。

本折扣中心很榮幸宣布我們將舉辦二十週年特賣會！為了慶祝週年，本公司將給予顧客大幅度的折扣！消費滿二十美元即可以獲得八折優惠。沒錯，八折！另外，您將可參加抽獎活動，有機會贏得二十張拉斯維加斯來回機票的其中一張！折扣中心忠實顧客卡的卡友還有資格獲得二十張禮券的其中一張，禮券面額是兩萬美元！別再拖了，快沒時間了。折扣中心二十週年特賣會將於星期日午夜結束。

D **14** 🔊 277 🇺🇸

What is the advertisement mainly about?
(A) A trip to an exotic country
(B) An opening of a new store
(C) A competition to win a ticket
(D) A sale to celebrate an anniversary

該廣告的主要內容是什麼？
(A) 一趟到異國的旅行
(B) 新店鋪的開幕
(C) 為了贏得某票券的競賽
(D) 為了慶祝週年的特賣會

D **15** 🔊 278 🇺🇸

How can listeners receive a discount?
(A) By shopping online
(B) By buying 20 items
(C) By applying for a store card
(D) By spending in excess of 20 dollars

聽眾要如何取得優惠？
(A) 線上購物
(B) 購買二十件商品
(C) 申請商店卡
(D) 消費金額超過二十美元

B **16** 🔊 279 🇺🇸

What does the speaker imply when he says, "Don't delay; time is running out"?
(A) The store will close very soon.
(B) The sale is on for a limited period.
(C) The loyalty scheme is nearly full.
(D) The items have almost sold out.

說話者說「別再拖了，快沒時間了」是在暗示什麼事？
(A) 該商店馬上就要打烊了。
(B) 特賣會是期間限定的。
(C) 忠實顧客的活動快要額滿。
(D) 商品快要售罄。

🔍 重要單字片語

1. **draw** [drɔ] *n.* 抽獎
2. **round-trip** [ˈraʊndˌtrɪp] *a.* 往返的
   one-way [ˈwʌnˌwe] *a.* 單程的
3. **loyalty** [ˈlɔɪəltɪ] *n.* 忠誠，忠實
4. **eligible** [ˈɛlɪdʒəbḷ] *a.* 有資格的
   be eligible to V　有資格從事……
   Only people over 18 are eligible to vote.
   只有十八歲以上的人才有資格投票。

5. **in excess** [ɪkˈsɛs / ˈɛksɛs] **of...**
   超過……
   The insurance company's profits were in excess of 10 million dollars.
   這間保險公司的盈利超過一千萬美元。

CH **11**

Chapter 11 Reading Test

Part 5 Incomplete Sentences

B **17**

It took Ms. Jeong half a day ------- the inventory, and then she spent a further two hours filing the purchase invoices.

(A) checking (B) to check (C) checked (D) check

鄭女士花了半天時間盤點庫存，然後另外花了兩小時將進貨發票歸檔。

理由

1. 本題測試表「花費」的動詞 take、cost、spend 的用法：
   a. take 須與表「時間」的名詞並用，用於下列句構中：
      sth + takes + sb + 一段時間 + to V　　從事某事花費某人若干時間
    = it + takes + sb + 一段時間 + to V
      For the most part, a foreign language takes us a few years to master.
    = For the most part, it takes us a few years to master a foreign language.
      大體而言，我們要學好一種外語得花上幾年的時間。
   b. cost 須與表「金錢」的名詞並用，用於下列句構中：
      it + costs + sb + 金錢 + to V　　從事某事花費某人若干錢
      It cost me a lot of money to buy that car.
      買那輛車花了我不少錢。
   c. spend 須以「人」作主詞，用於下列句構中：
      sb + spends + 時間 / 金錢 + V-ing　　某人花若干時間 / 錢從事……
      Mary spends a lot of money buying new clothes every month.
      瑪麗每個月會花很多錢買衣服。
2. 根據上述，原句空格前有虛主詞 it 及表花時間的過去式動詞 took，得知空格應置不定詞，故 (B) 項應為正選。

重要單字片語

file [faɪl] *vt.* 歸檔
Please file these documents in that folder.
請把這些文件歸檔在那個檔案夾內。

C **18**

As a result of exceptionally high demand and reduced supply, we regret ------- you that we are unable to dispatch your goods at this time.

(A) tell (B) telling (C) to tell (D) have told

由於需求異常高漲以及供應短缺，我們很遺憾地通知您，此刻無法幫您出貨。

理由

1. 本題測試下列動詞用法：
   regret [rɪˋgrɛt] *vt.* 抱歉；後悔

regret 後可接不定詞片語或動名詞作受詞，用法依 regret 的意思而定：
表「抱歉要……」時接不定詞片語：regret + to V
I regret to tell you that your flight has been canceled.
我很抱歉要告知您，您的班機已被取消了。
表「後悔曾經……」時接動名詞：regret + V-ing
I regret telling you the truth.
我很後悔曾告訴你真相。

2. 根據本題語意，regret 表「抱歉要……」，故 (C) 項應為正選。

> 重要單字片語

exceptionally [ɪkˋsɛpʃənəlɪ] *adv.* 異常地，格外地

B **19**

------- importing car parts, the automobile manufacturer also exports spare parts to other countries.

(A) According to　　(B) In addition to　　(C) In front of　　(D) On behalf of

除了進口車輛零件外，該汽車製造商也出口備用零件至其他國家。

> 理由

1. (A) **according to...**　根據……
   According to social convention, business people wear suits.
   依據社交傳統，商場中人得穿西裝。

   (B) **in addition to...**　除……之外（還……）
   In addition to singing, Jerry loves dancing.
   除了唱歌之外，傑瑞還喜歡跳舞。

   (C) **in front of...**　在（某物外部）的前方
   Kelly took a picture in front of the magnificent palace.
   凱莉在那座雄偉的宮殿前拍了張照片。

   (D) **on behalf of...**　代表……
   John will give a speech on behalf of his school.
   約翰將代表他的學校發表演說。

2. 根據語意，(B) 項應為正選。

D **20**

Watch Zone returned Mr. Malaban's upfront payment and offered him ------- for the shockingly poor service he received.

(A) confrontation　　(B) duplication　　(C) clearance　　(D) compensation

手錶領域公司退還了馬拉班先生的預付款，並提供賠償以彌補他受到的差勁服務。

> 理由

1. (A) **confrontation** [ˌkɑnfrʌnˋteʃən] *n.* 衝突，對峙
   Many violent and unnecessary confrontations can be avoided with communication.
   透過溝通可以避免許多暴力和無謂的衝突。

(B) **duplication** [ˌdupliˈkeʃən] *n.* 複製
(C) **clearance** [ˈklɪrəns] *n.* 清除
   a clearance sale　　清倉大拍賣
(D) **compensation** [ˌkɑmpənˈseʃən] *n.* 賠償
   claim compensation　　要求賠償
   You should claim compensation for your lost luggage.
   你該為遺失的行李要求賠償。

2. 根據語意，(D) 項應為正選。

A **21**

------- increased fuel and shipping costs, we must inform you that we cannot fill your order according to the estimate we quoted you.

(A) Due to　　　(B) In spite of　　(C) Behind　　(D) With a view to

由於燃油費及運費上漲，本公司必須通知您，我們無法用先前提供給您的報價來供貨。

> 理由

1. (A) **due to...**　　因為……
   = owing to...
   = because of...
   = as a result of...
   The project was canceled due to a lack of funds.
   這份專案因為缺乏資金而被取消。

   (B) **in spite of...**　　儘管……
   The overall situation is good in spite of some minor problems.
   儘管有些小問題，但整體情形不錯。

   (C) **behind** [bɪˈhaɪnd] *prep.* 在……之後
   Perhaps we should take a taxi since we are running behind schedule.
   因為我們的行程耽擱了，所以或許我們應該搭計程車。

   (D) **with a view to + V-ing**（此處 **to** 是介詞）　　為了……
   = with an eye to + V-ing（此處 **to** 亦是介詞）
   = for the purpose of + V-ing
   = in order to V
   Both sides met with a view to resolving their dispute.
   雙方會晤為求解決之間的爭論。

2. 根據語意，(A) 項應為正選。

> 重要單字片語

fill sb's order　　按照訂單供貨給某人

📖 Part 6　Text Completion

Questions 22-25 refer to the following e-mail.

To: All Employees
From: Martha Bennington, Department of Budgeting
Subject: New Stationery Supplies Ordering Policy

It has come to our attention that requests for stationery have become excessive over the past five months. -----22.----- items like extra paper, pens, and whiteout do not seem like much, with more than 300 employees, it all adds up. In these highly competitive times, every dollar counts. We must therefore cut costs -----23.----- we can.

In an attempt to rectify the situation, managers in each department will be required to keep track of any items purchased each month from Stationery Supplies starting on March 1. -----24.-----. Your cooperation will -----25.----- Malcolm Industries' continued success.

---

22 至 25 題請看以下電子郵件。

收件者：全體員工
寄件者：預算部瑪莎‧班寧頓
主　旨：新文具補給站訂貨規定

我們已注意到過去五個月以來文具申請已呈氾濫的現象。雖然額外的紙張、筆或立可白等用品看起來似乎不多，但以三百多位員工人數來看，加起來數量就很可觀。在這個高度競爭的時代，每一塊錢都很重要。因此在任何可行的情況下都須削減成本。

為了要整頓這樣的狀況，自三月一日起，各部門經理將被要求每個月追蹤向文具補給站購買的任何物品。因此，保留所有的收據是必要的。諸位的合作將確保馬爾科姆產業公司持續獲致成功。

A　**22**

(A) Though　　(B) Even　　(C) Despite　　(D) Even so

理由

1. 空格後有主詞 items 以及助動詞及動詞 do not seem，得知空格原句為完整子句，逗點後有 with 引導的介詞片語修飾另一完整子句 it all adds up，得知空格內應置副詞連接詞，使該子句形成副詞子句，修飾主要子句 it all adds up。選項中僅 (A) 項為連接詞，故為正選。

211

Chapter 11　Reading Test

2. 其他選項：

(B) **Even** 為副詞，表「甚至」。
This job is quite easy. Even a five-year-old boy can do it.
這工作相當簡單。甚至五歲小男孩都做得來。

(C) **Despite** 為介系詞，表「儘管」，其後只能接名詞。
Despite my warning, my son went swimming alone.
儘管我提出了警告，我兒子仍然獨自去游泳。

(D) **Even so** 為副詞片語，表「儘管如此」，常單獨使用，之後置逗點。
Mike stayed up late last night to prepare for the test. Even so, he didn't pass the test.
麥可昨晚熬夜唸書到很晚，為了要準備考試。儘管如此，他還是沒考及格。

A 23

(A) wherever　　　　(B) no matter　　　(C) what　　　　(D) how

理由

1. 空格前有完整子句 We must therefore cut costs，空格後也有主詞及助動詞 we can，得知空格內應置連接詞以連接兩句。

2. (B) 項 no matter 須與疑問詞並用，形成：no matter how（無論如何）、no matter what（無論什麼）、no matter when（無論何時）、no matter where（無論哪裡）、no matter who（無論是誰），才可作連接詞使用，故此項不可選。
No matter where you go, I'll track you down.
無論你去哪裡，我都會找到你的下落。
(C) 項的 what 為疑問詞，可引導名詞子句，置及物動詞之後時作其受詞。
I don't know what you're talking about.
我不知道你在講什麼。
(D) 項的 how 為疑問詞，可引導名詞子句，置及物動詞之後時作其受詞。
I don't know how he did it.
我不知道他怎麼做到那件事的。

3. 惟選項 (A) wherever 可作連接詞使用，表「在任何情況下」，空格置入 (A) 項後合乎語意及文法，故應為正選。此處 wherever we can 等於 in any place we can cut costs（在任何我們可省成本的地方）。

D 24

(A) Several reams of paper will be purchased instead.
(B) The quality of their service has always been a concern.
(C) Each staff member will then receive 50 new business cards.
(D) It is therefore essential to keep all the receipts.

理由

1. (A) 反而會購買好幾令紙。
(B) 他們的服務品質一直都讓人掛心。
(C) 每位員工隨後會收到五十張新名片。
(D) 因此，保留所有的收據是必要的。

2. 根據空格前的句子 "..., managers in each department will be required to keep track of any items purchased each month from Stationery Supplies..."（……，各部門經理將被要求每個月追蹤向文具補給站購買的任何物品……）得知各部門經理須掌握購買物品的動向，(D) 項句子 "It is therefore essential to keep all the receipts."（因此，保留所有的收據是必要的。）置入空格後與前文相呼應，故應為正選。

D **25**

(A) pressure　　(B) measure　　(C) reassure　　(D) ensure

理由

1. (A) **pressure** [ˈprɛʃɚ] *vt.* 對……施加壓力，強迫 & *n.* 壓力
   　　pressure sb to V　　強迫某人……
   　= pressure sb into + V-ing
   　　Don't pressure me to do things against my will.
   　= Don't pressure me into doing things against my will.
   　　別強迫我做違背我意願的事。

   (B) **measure** [ˈmɛʒɚ] *vt.* 測量（大小、長度等）；衡量（價值）
   　　I helped Kelly measure the length of this window.
   　　我幫助凱莉量這扇窗戶的長度。
   　　Don't measure a writer's success in terms of book sales.
   　　別以書籍銷售量來衡量一個作家的成就。

   (C) **reassure** [ˌriəˈʃʊr] *vt.* 使安心（之後接人作受詞）
   　　The doctor reassured Vincent that his mother would be fine.
   　　醫師安慰文森說，他母親會沒事的。

   (D) **ensure** [ɪnˈʃʊr] *vt.* 確保
   　　Please ensure that all lights are turned off before you leave.
   　　離開前請確保所有燈都關了。

2. 根據上述，選項 (A)、(B) 及 (C) 均不合乎語意，故不可選，惟 (D) 項置入空格後合乎語意及文法，故應為正選。

重要單字片語

1. **come to sb's attention**
   引起某人的注意
   It came to my attention that Judy wore sandals to work this morning.
   我今早注意到茱蒂穿涼鞋來上班。

2. **whiteout** [ˈwaɪtˌaʊt] *n.* 立可白修正液

3. **add up**　　積少成多
   Tony has to feed a family of eight. No wonder the bills soon add up.
   湯尼要養活一家八口。難怪開支很快就大起來了。

4. **count** [kaʊnt] *vi.* 重要（常與介詞 for 並用）
   It seems that my opinion doesn't count for anything around here.
   我的意見在這兒似乎不是很重要。

5. **in an attempt to V**　　為了要……
   = in order to V
   Jenny gives her children chores to do in an attempt to teach them responsibility.
   珍妮分配家務給她的孩子做，以教導他們責任感。

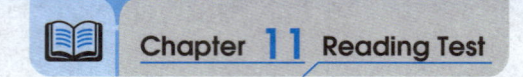

Chapter 11 Reading Test

Part 7 Reading Comprehension

Questions 26-30 refer to the following product information, online review, and response.

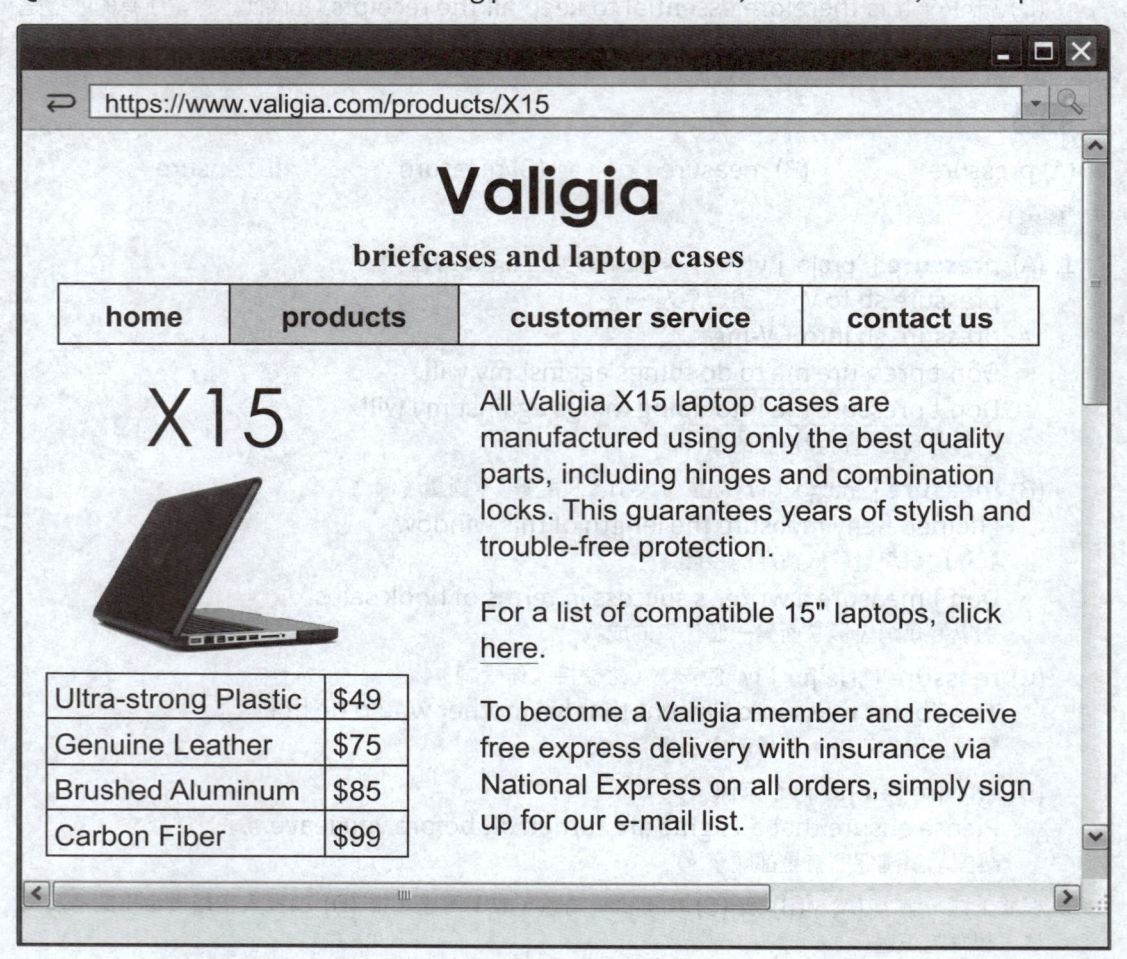

https://www.valigia.com/products/X15

Valigia
briefcases and laptop cases

| home | products | customer service | contact us |

X15

Ultra-strong Plastic	$49
Genuine Leather	$75
Brushed Aluminum	$85
Carbon Fiber	$99

All Valigia X15 laptop cases are manufactured using only the best quality parts, including hinges and combination locks. This guarantees years of stylish and trouble-free protection.

For a list of compatible 15" laptops, click here.

To become a Valigia member and receive free express delivery with insurance via National Express on all orders, simply sign up for our e-mail list.

214

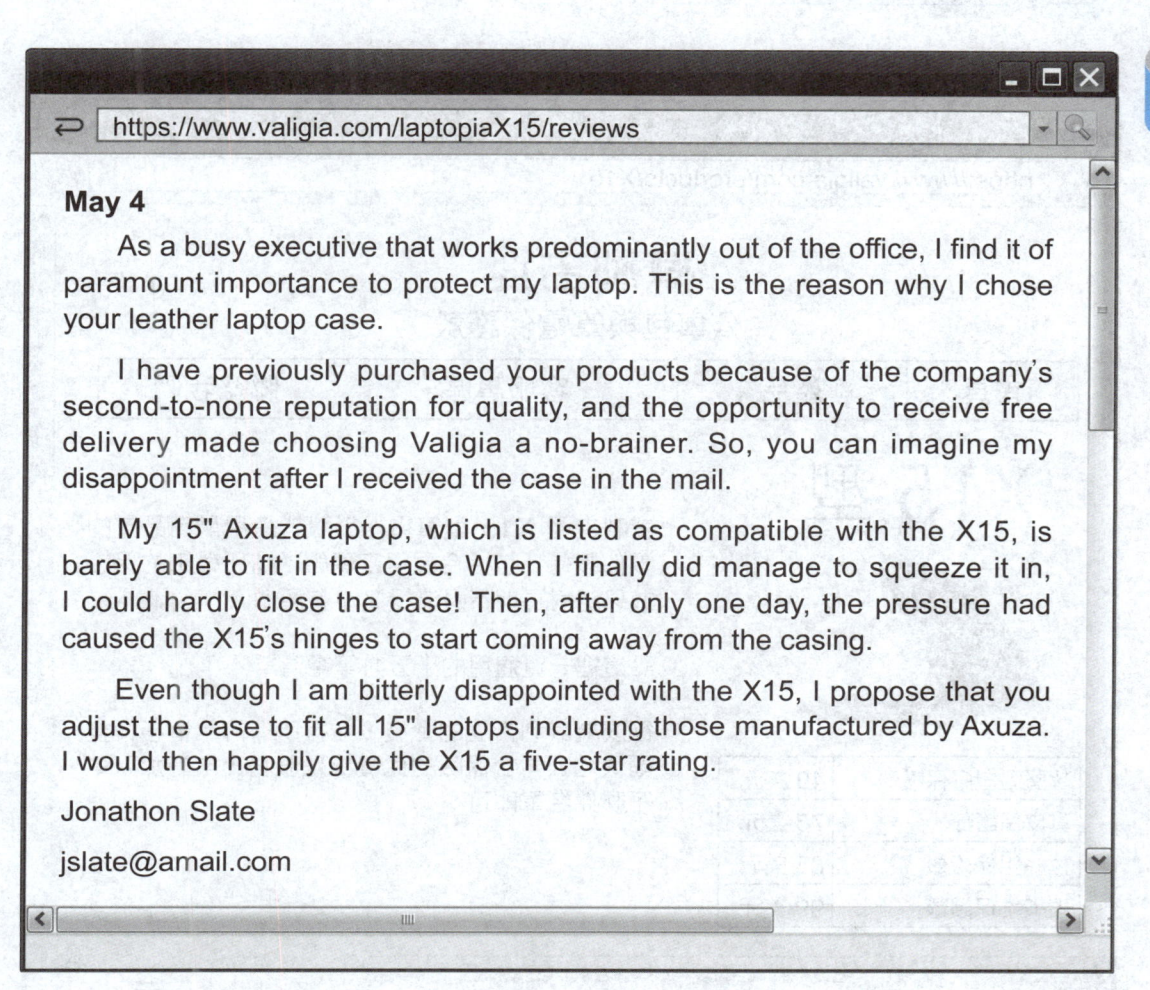

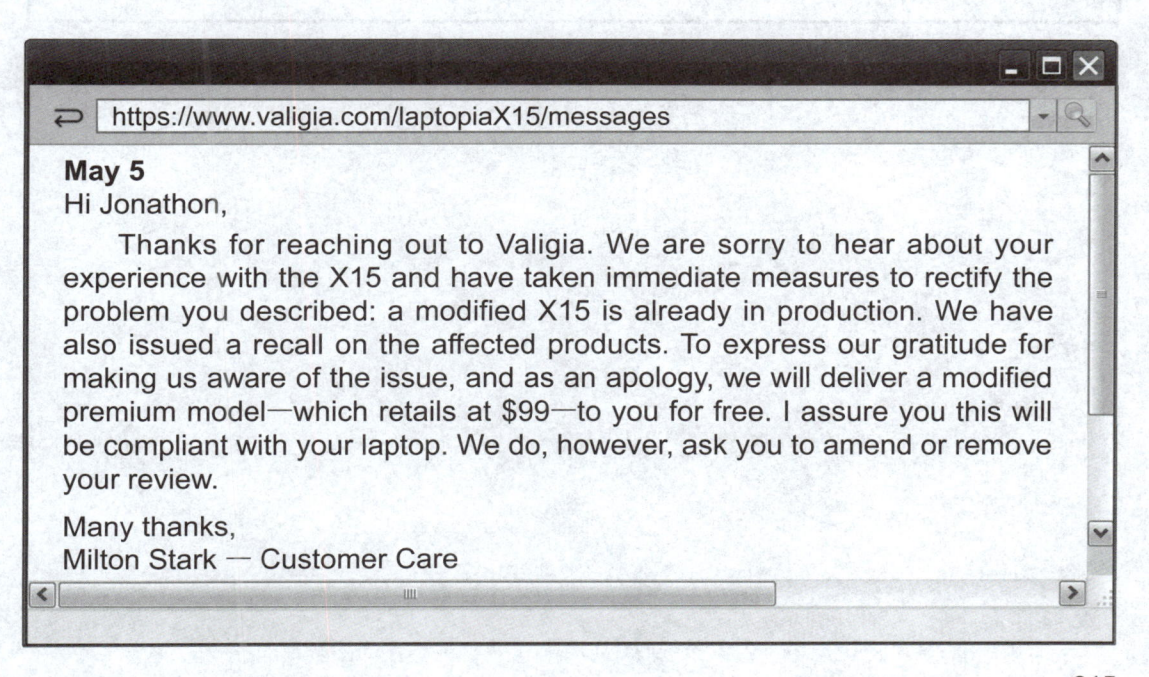

https://www.valigia.com/laptopiaX15/reviews

May 4

As a busy executive that works predominantly out of the office, I find it of paramount importance to protect my laptop. This is the reason why I chose your leather laptop case.

I have previously purchased your products because of the company's second-to-none reputation for quality, and the opportunity to receive free delivery made choosing Valigia a no-brainer. So, you can imagine my disappointment after I received the case in the mail.

My 15" Axuza laptop, which is listed as compatible with the X15, is barely able to fit in the case. When I finally did manage to squeeze it in, I could hardly close the case! Then, after only one day, the pressure had caused the X15's hinges to start coming away from the casing.

Even though I am bitterly disappointed with the X15, I propose that you adjust the case to fit all 15" laptops including those manufactured by Axuza. I would then happily give the X15 a five-star rating.

Jonathon Slate

jslate@amail.com

---

https://www.valigia.com/laptopiaX15/messages

May 5

Hi Jonathon,

Thanks for reaching out to Valigia. We are sorry to hear about your experience with the X15 and have taken immediate measures to rectify the problem you described: a modified X15 is already in production. We have also issued a recall on the affected products. To express our gratitude for making us aware of the issue, and as an apology, we will deliver a modified premium model—which retails at $99—to you for free. I assure you this will be compliant with your laptop. We do, however, ask you to amend or remove your review.

Many thanks,
Milton Stark — Customer Care

Chapter 11　Reading Test

26 至 30 題請看以下產品資訊、網路評論及回應。

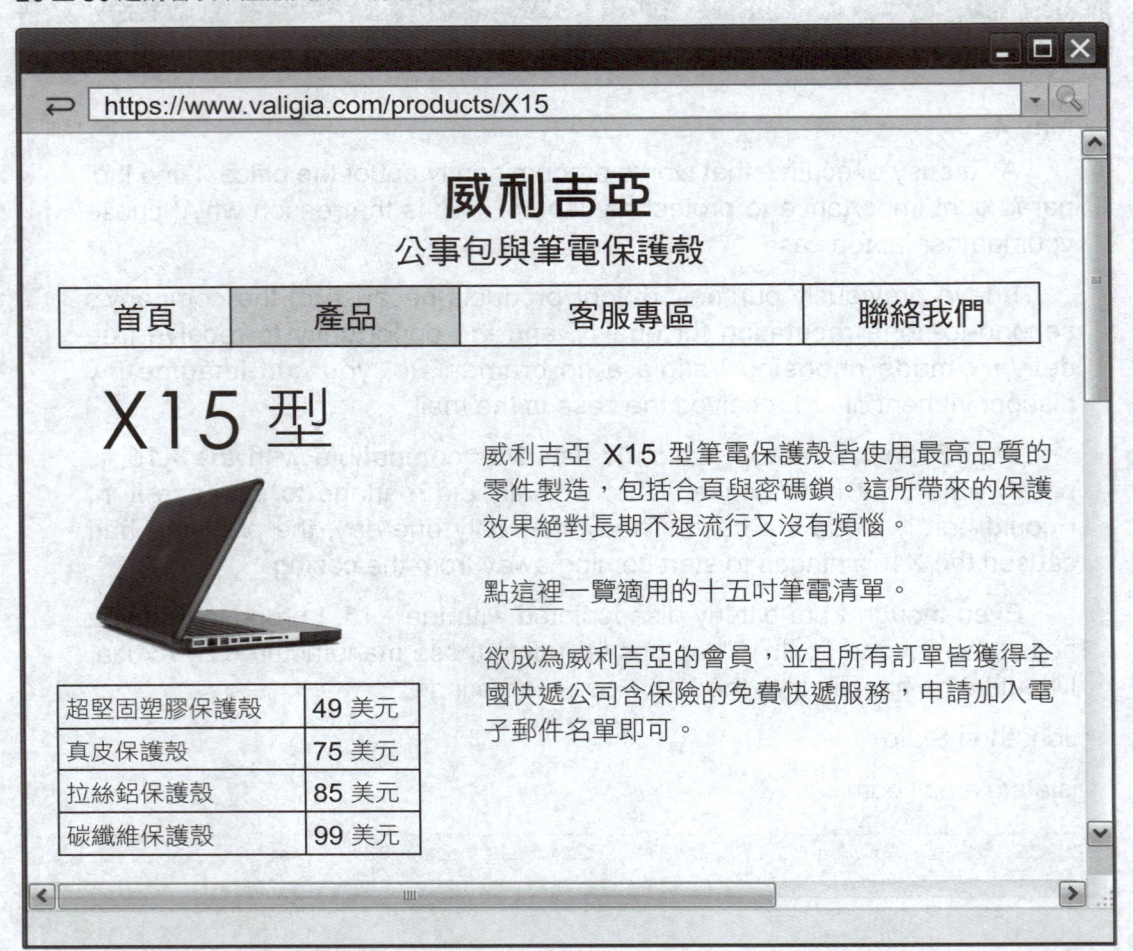

https://www.valigia.com/products/X15

威利吉亞
公事包與筆電保護殼

| 首頁 | 產品 | 客服專區 | 聯絡我們 |

X15 型

威利吉亞 X15 型筆電保護殼皆使用最高品質的零件製造，包括合頁與密碼鎖。這所帶來的保護效果絕對長期不退流行又沒有煩惱。

點這裡一覽適用的十五吋筆電清單。

欲成為威利吉亞的會員，並且所有訂單皆獲得全國快遞公司含保險的免費快遞服務，申請加入電子郵件名單即可。

超堅固塑膠保護殼	49 美元
真皮保護殼	75 美元
拉絲鋁保護殼	85 美元
碳纖維保護殼	99 美元

216

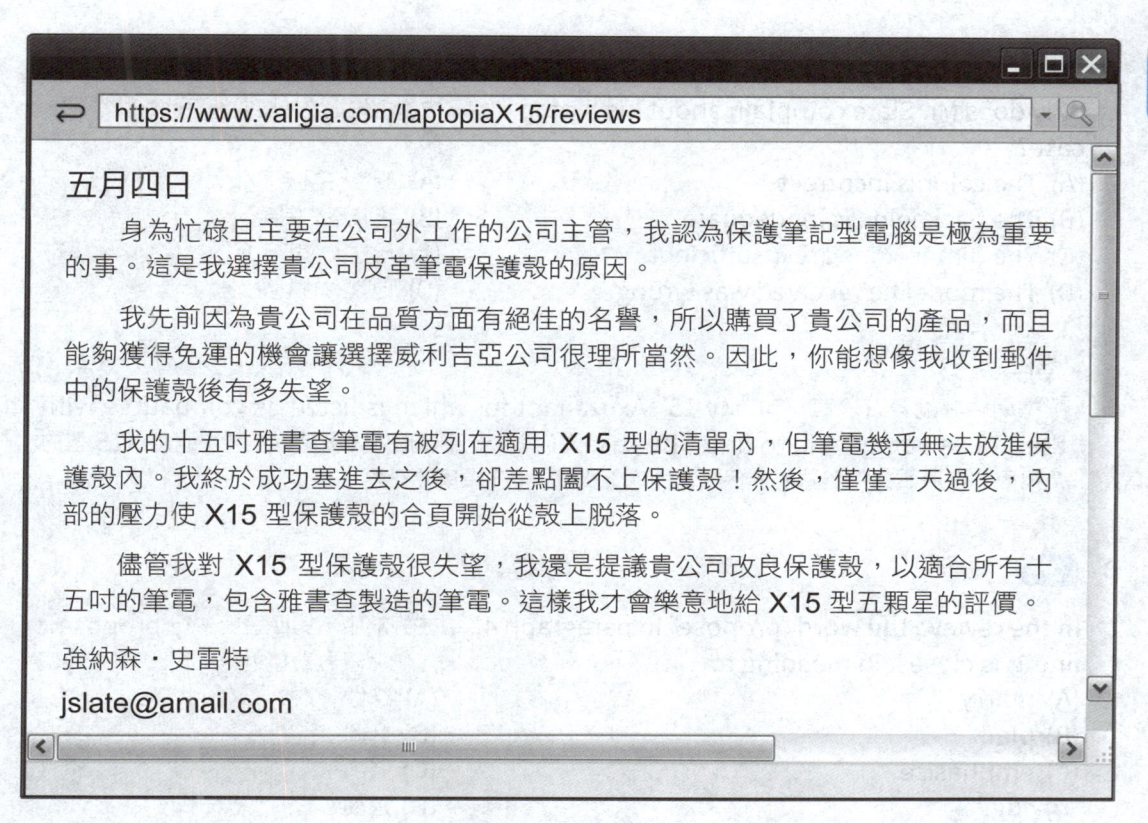

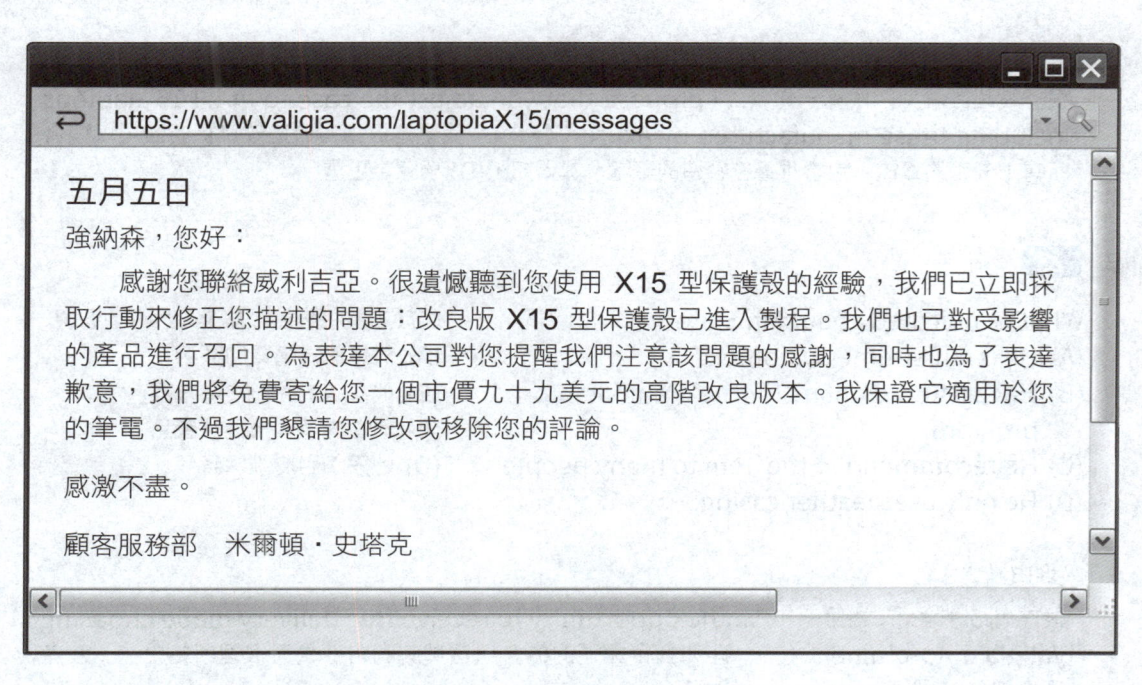

> https://www.valigia.com/laptopiaX15/reviews

五月四日

　　身為忙碌且主要在公司外工作的公司主管,我認為保護筆記型電腦是極為重要的事。這是我選擇貴公司皮革筆電保護殼的原因。

　　我先前因為貴公司在品質方面有絕佳的名譽,所以購買了貴公司的產品,而且能夠獲得免運的機會讓選擇威利吉亞公司很理所當然。因此,你能想像我收到郵件中的保護殼後有多失望。

　　我的十五吋雅書查筆電有被列在適用 X15 型的清單內,但筆電幾乎無法放進保護殼內。我終於成功塞進去之後,卻差點闔不上保護殼!然後,僅僅一天過後,內部的壓力使 X15 型保護殼的合頁開始從殼上脫落。

　　儘管我對 X15 型保護殼很失望,我還是提議貴公司改良保護殼,以適合所有十五吋的筆電,包含雅書查製造的筆電。這樣我才會樂意地給 X15 型五顆星的評價。

強納森・史雷特
jslate@amail.com

> https://www.valigia.com/laptopiaX15/messages

五月五日

強納森,您好:

　　感謝您聯絡威利吉亞。很遺憾聽到您使用 X15 型保護殼的經驗,我們已立即採取行動來修正您描述的問題:改良版 X15 型保護殼已進入製程。我們也已對受影響的產品進行召回。為表達本公司對您提醒我們注意該問題的感謝,同時也為了表達歉意,我們將免費寄給您一個市價九十九美元的高階改良版本。我保證它適用於您的筆電。不過我們懇請您修改或移除您的評論。

感激不盡。

顧客服務部　米爾頓・史塔克

Chapter 11　Reading Test

C **26**

Why does Mr. Slate complain about his laptop case?
(A) The color is incorrect.
(B) The packaging is inadequate.
(C) The dimensions are insufficient.
(D) The model he received was wrong.

史雷特先生為什麼要抱怨他的筆電保護殼？
(A) 顏色有誤。
(B) 包裝不夠完善。
(C) 尺寸上有所不足。
(D) 他收到的型號錯誤。

理由

根據網路評論第三段第一句 "My 15" Axuza laptop, which is listed as compatible with the X15, is barely able to fit in the case."（我的十五吋雅書查筆電有被列在適用 X15 型的清單內，但筆電幾乎無法放進保護殼內。）得知，(C) 項應為正選。

D **27**

In the review, the word "propose" in paragraph 4, line 1, is closest in meaning to
(A) marry
(B) plan
(C) emphasize
(D) suggest

在評論中，第四段第一行 propose 這個字意思最接近
(A) 結婚
(B) 計劃
(C) 強調
(D) 建議

理由

根據網路評論第四段第一句 "..., I propose that you adjust the case to fit all 15" laptops including those manufactured by Axuza."（……，我還是提議貴公司改良保護殼，以適合所有十五吋的筆電，包含雅書查製造的筆電。）得知，(D) 項應為正選。

B **28**

What is indicated about Mr. Slate?
(A) He is a first-time customer.
(B) He registered online for the membership program.
(C) He recommended the item to many people.
(D) He only uses leather casing.

關於史雷特先生，本文暗示了什麼？
(A) 他是首次購買的顧客。
(B) 他在線上註冊會員方案。
(C) 他向許多人推薦該產品。
(D) 他只使用皮革保護殼。

理由

根據網路評論第二段第一句 "... the opportunity to receive free delivery made choosing Valigia a no-brainer."（……能夠獲得免運的機會讓選擇威利吉亞公司很理所當然。）及產品資訊第三段 "To become a Valigia member and receive free express delivery with insurance via National Express on all orders, simply sign up for our e-mail list."（欲成為威利吉亞的會員，並且所有訂單皆獲得全國快遞公司含保險的免費快遞服務，申請加入電子郵件名單即可。）得知，(B) 項應為正選。

D 29

What model of laptop case does Mr. Stark offer Mr. Slate?
(A) Ultra-strong Plastic
(B) Genuine Leather
(C) Brushed Aluminum
(D) Carbon Fiber

史塔克先生給予史雷特先生什麼型號的筆電保護殼？
(A) 超堅固塑膠保護殼
(B) 真皮保護殼
(C) 拉絲鋁保護殼
(D) 碳纖維保護殼

> 理由
> 根據回應第四句 "..., we will deliver a modified premium model—which retails at $99—to you for free."（……，我們將免費寄給您一個市價九十九美元的高階改良版本。）得知，該型號要價九十九美元。又根據產品資訊第四項，碳纖維保護殼訂價為九十九元得知，(D) 項應為正選。

B 30

What does Mr. Stark ask Mr. Slate to do?
(A) Return the purchase
(B) Revise his review
(C) Complete a questionnaire
(D) Confirm his identification

史塔克先生要求史雷特先生做什麼？
(A) 退還購買的物品
(B) 修改他的評論
(C) 完成一份問卷
(D) 確認他的身分

> 理由
> 根據回應最後一句 "We do, however, ask you to amend or remove your review."（不過我們懇請您修改或移除您的評論。）得知，(B) 項應為正選。

重要單字片語

1. **hinge** [hɪndʒ] *n.*（門、蓋子上的）合頁，鉸鏈
2. **combination** [ˌkɑmbəˋneʃən] *n.*（密碼鎖的）數字組合
3. **guarantee** [ˌgærənˋti] *vt.* 保證，擔保 & *n.* 保證
   I guarantee you will be satisfied with our product, or we will give you a full refund.
   我保證您會滿意我們的產品，否則我們給您全額退款。
4. **compatible** [kəmˋpætəbl̩] *a.* 相容的
   be compatible with... 與……相容
   This application is not compatible with my computer.
   這個應用程式與我的電腦不相容。
5. **executive** [ɪgˋzɛkjutɪv] *n.* 主管，經理
6. **predominantly** [prɪˋdɑmənəntlɪ] *adv.* 主要地；絕大多數地
   Spain is a predominantly Catholic country.
   西班牙是以天主教為主的國家。
7. **paramount** [ˋpærəˌmaunt] *a.* 最重要的，至高無上的
   Joan's passion for her career is of paramount importance to her success.
   瓊恩對工作的熱情是她成功的重要因素。

Chapter 11 Reading Test

8. **second-to-none** [ˌsɛkəndtəˈnʌn] *a.* 首屈一指的，頂級的
   If you wish to lose weight, I recommend this second-to-none program.
   如果你想要減肥的話，我推薦這個頂級的方案。

9. **no-brainer** [ˌnoˈbrenɚ] *a.* 不費腦筋的事

10. **manage to V** 設法（完成）……
    I managed to finish my report just half an hour before the deadline.
    我設法在期限的半小時前完成報告。

11. **bitterly** [ˈbɪtɚlɪ] *adv.* 憤怒地；悲憤地

12. **adjust** [əˈdʒʌst] *vt.* 調整
    Edward took the clock off the wall to adjust the time.
    愛德華把時鐘從牆上拿下來調整時間。

13. **modified** [ˈmadəˌfaɪd] *a.* 修改過的

14. **gratitude** [ˈɡrætəˌtud] *n.* 感謝（不可數）

15. **premium** [ˈprimɪəm] *a.* 高級的，頂級的

16. **inadequate** [ɪnˈædəkwət] *a.* 不足的
    The parking facilities are inadequate for such a busy shopping center.
    對如此繁忙的購物中心而言，停車設施是不足的。

17. **insufficient** [ˌɪnsəˈfɪʃənt] *a.* 不足的，不夠的

🎧 Part 1 Photographs

D **1** 🔊 281 🇺🇸

(A) Test tubes have been scattered on the table.
(B) The woman is sealing the specimen in a container.
(C) The woman is tucking her gloves in her pocket.
(D) The woman is looking through a microscope.

(A) 試管散置於桌上各處。
(B) 女子正將樣本封在容器裡。
(C) 女子正把手套塞進口袋內。
(D) 女子正在透過顯微鏡觀察。

🔍 重要單字片語

1. **scatter** [ˈskætɚ] vt. 撒；使分散 & vi. 分散
   The old man scattered rice in the park for the pigeons to eat.
   老翁在公園裡撒米給鴿子吃。

2. **specimen** [ˈspɛsəmən] n. 樣本；標本

3. **tuck** [tʌk] vt. 把……塞入
   The principal told Alan to tuck his shirt in his trousers.
   校長要艾倫把他的襯衫塞進褲子裡。

B **2** 🔊 282 🇬🇧

(A) The man is putting a computer on top of a metal case.
(B) The technician is handling a wire.
(C) Some machinery has been unboxed.
(D) The man is pulling out a circuit board.

(A) 男子正把電腦放到金屬櫃子上方。
(B) 技術人員在弄電線。
(C) 有些機械設備已從箱子中取出。
(D) 男子正拉出一塊電路板。

🔍 重要單字片語

1. **machinery** [məˈʃinərɪ] n. 機械（集合名詞，不可數）

2. **unbox** [ʌnˈbɑks] vt. 從箱子中取出；開箱
   Please go to the warehouse and help Ted unbox the new stock.
   請去倉庫協助泰德將新進的貨物開箱。

CH 12

221

Chapter 12 Listening Test

Part 2 Question-Response

C **3** 🔊 284

Which of these laptops do you want me to take?
(A) The updated program.
(B) In the IT department.
(C) You can have the lighter one.

這幾臺筆記型電腦你要我拿哪一臺？
(A) 更新的程式。
(B) 在資訊部門。
(C) 你可以拿比較輕的。

重要單字片語

updated [ˌʌpˈdetɪd] *a.* 更新的

C **4** 🔊 285

Why is there so much static on the phone?
(A) Sales are through the roof.
(B) My number is 555-7474.
(C) Maybe the line is faulty.

為什麼電話裡有這麼多雜音？
(A) 銷售量衝破天際。
(B) 我的號碼是 555-7474。
(C) 可能是線路不良。

重要單字片語

through the roof 激增，飆升

Part 3 Conversations

Questions 5 through 7 refer to the following conversation. 🔊 287

W: Daniel, we've got a major problem. The main server has crashed and we can't access any of our files.
M: Oh, no! Do you know when the last backup was performed?
W: The system performed an automatic backup at ten o'clock this morning, so with a bit of luck we should be able to retrieve most of the critical files.
M: That's something, at least. OK, I'll call a technician now to restore operations and find the cause of the problem.

5 至 7 題請聽以下會話。

女：丹尼爾，出大事了。主伺服器當掉了，我們沒法子存取檔案。
男：糟糕！妳知道最近一次執行備份是什麼時候嗎？
女：系統今天早上十點有自動執行備份，所以如果運氣好的話，應該能夠復原大部分重要檔案。
男：有總比沒有好。我現在就去通知技術人員來修理，以恢復正常作業，並且找出是哪裡出了問題。

B 5 🔊 288 🇺🇸

What are the speakers mainly discussing?
(A) An accident involving a vehicle
(B) A system that isn't working
(C) A surgery involving a colleague
(D) A worker who hasn't arrived

說話者主要在討論什麼？
(A) 某件車禍
(B) 某個失靈的系統
(C) 某位同事的手術
(D) 某位還沒到的員工

CH 12

B 6 🔊 289 🇺🇸

What does the woman indicate about the backup?
(A) It has a critical error.
(B) It has been made recently.
(C) It has been canceled.
(D) It has failed ten times.

女子對於備份有何說法？
(A) 備份發生嚴重錯誤。
(B) 才剛做過備份。
(C) 備份已被取消。
(D) 備份已失敗十次。

C 7 🔊 290 🇺🇸

What will the man most likely do next?
(A) Reboot a system
(B) Perform an operation
(C) Contact an expert
(D) Diagnose a problem

男子接下來最有可能會做什麼？
(A) 重啟系統
(B) 施行手術
(C) 聯繫專門人員
(D) 診斷問題

重要單字片語

1. **server** [ˈsɝvɚ] *n.* 伺服器
2. **automatic** [ˌɔtəˈmætɪk] *a.* 自動的
3. **retrieve** [rɪˈtriv] *vt.* 重新找回
   The police successfully retrieved all the woman's stolen jewelry.
   警方順利地找回了這位女士所有遭竊的珠寶。
4. **critical** [ˈkrɪtɪkl̩] *a.* 至關重要的；危急的
5. **restore** [rɪˈstor] *vt.* 恢復，復原；修復；重建
   Our strategy focuses on restoring public confidence in our products.
   我們的策略著眼於恢復大眾對我們產品的信心。
6. **reboot** [riˈbut] *vt. & vi.* 重新啟動
   Please reboot your computer after installing the software.
   安裝好軟體後，請重新啟動你的電腦。

Chapter 12 Listening Test

Questions 8 through 10 refer to the following conversation and floor plan. 🔊 291

W: 🇺🇸   M: 🇨🇦

W: Al, have you finished repairing the surveillance camera at the front entrance?
M: Not yet, Betty. I had to order some spare parts from the manufacturer, including a new lens. They've been sent by courier, so they should arrive later this afternoon.
W: Is it possible to install a temporary camera? It's essential that the entrance be monitored 24/7.
M: I could, but we don't have one available.
W: Then I think you should switch the surveillance camera at the entrance with one of the non-essential cameras elsewhere in the building.
M: Which cameras are not essential?
W: The ones that are only monitoring internal rooms, not the building's entrances and exits.

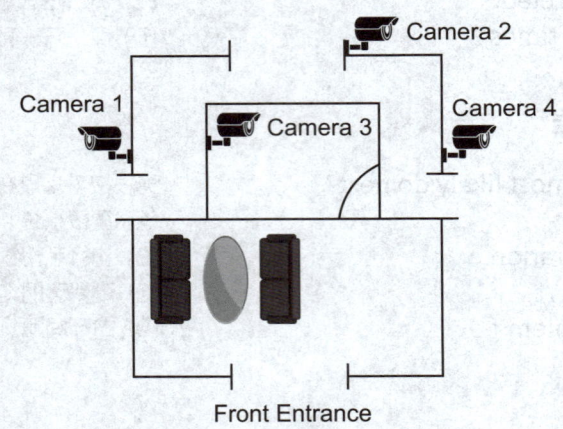

[Floor plan showing Camera 1, Camera 2, Camera 3, Camera 4, and Front Entrance]

8 至 10 題請聽以下會話，並請看以下平面圖。

女：艾爾，你把前門的那個監視攝影機修好了沒？
男：還沒耶，貝蒂。我已經去跟廠商訂購了一些備用零件，這其中包括買了一個新的攝影機鏡頭。這些零件是以快遞送貨，所以今天下午較晚的時候應該就會送來了。
女：有沒有可能架設一個臨時的監視攝影機來用呢？入口處有必要二十四小時全天候的監控。
男：可以，不過我們沒有監視攝影機可拿來用了。
女：那樣的話，我認為你應該把本大樓別處的非必要監視攝影機拿來，換到入口處來用。
男：哪一臺監視攝影機是非必要的呢？
女：那些只監控大樓房間內部的監視攝影機，而不是大樓出、入口處的監視攝影機。

```
                    二號攝影機
  一號攝影機    三號攝影機    四號攝影機



                    前門
```

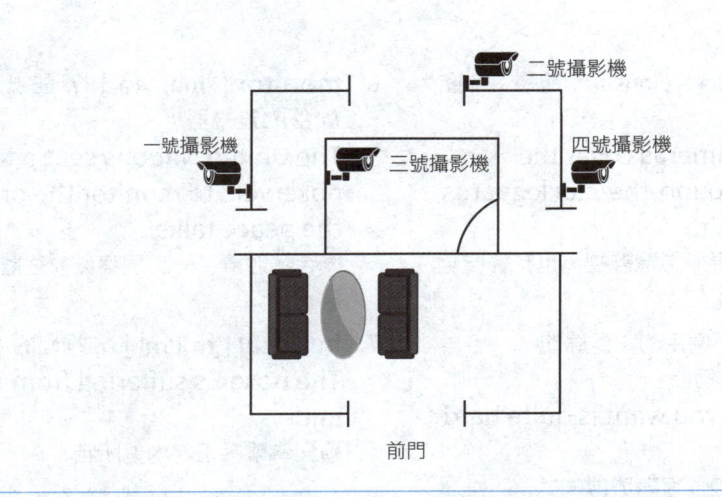

B 8 292 🍁

What did the man order?
(A) A new camera
(B) A lens
(C) A monitor
(D) A security door

男子訂購了什麼？
(A) 新的攝影機
(B) 鏡頭
(C) 監視器
(D) 安全門

C 9 293 🍁

What does the woman suggest?
(A) Canceling a scheduled appointment
(B) Filming a new advertisement
(C) Swapping a faulty device
(D) Returning an incorrect order

女子建議做什麼事？
(A) 取消已事先安排好的會面
(B) 拍攝新廣告
(C) 換掉故障的裝置
(D) 退回寄錯的訂購商品

C 10 294 🍁

Look at the graphic. Which camera will most likely be moved to the front entrance?
(A) Camera 1
(B) Camera 2
(C) Camera 3
(D) Camera 4

請看圖表。哪一臺攝影機最有可能被移到前門？
(A) 一號攝影機
(B) 二號攝影機
(C) 三號攝影機
(D) 四號攝影機

Chapter 12 Listening Test

重要單字片語

1. **surveillance** [sɚˋveləns] *n.* 監視；監督；看守
   Surveillance cameras cover the building, and round-the-clock guards protect the vault.
   整棟大樓皆有監視攝影機監控，也有警衛全天候看守金庫。

2. **spare** [spɛr] *a.* 備用的；多餘的
   a spare tire　　備胎
   The spare part you want is quite hard to get.
   你要的那種備用零件很難取得。

3. **lens** [lɛnz] *n.* 鏡頭；鏡片（此為單數，複數為 lenses [lɛnzɪz]）
   a camera lens　　相機鏡頭

4. **courier** [ˋkʊrɪɚ] *n.* 快遞員；快遞公司

5. **It is essential… that + S + (should) + V**
   ……是有必要的
   It is essential / necessary that the project (should) be finished today.
   這個計畫必須在今天完成。

6. **monitor** [ˋmɑnətɚ] *vt.* 監視；監控；監督 & *n.* 監視器
   The United Nations sent a team of observers to monitor the progress of the peace talks.
   聯合國派遣了一組觀察員前往監控和談的進展。

7. **internal** [ɪnˋtɝnḷ] *a.* 裡面的；內部的
   The boxer is suffering from an internal injury.
   這個拳擊手正為內傷所苦。

8. **swap** [swɑp] *vt.* & *vi.* & *n.* 交換（動詞三態為：swap, swapped [swɑpt], swapped）
   swap A for B　　用 A 交換 B
   Peter swapped his bicycle for his cousin's guitar.
   彼得用他的腳踏車換了他表弟的吉他。

Part 4　Talks

Questions 11 through 13 refer to the following telephone message. 🔊 296

Hi, Emma, this is Tony calling from IT. I understand from your message that you've downloaded the latest version of Super PDF Express but found that it's not compatible with our OS. At first, I found that strange as we've been using this program for years. However, when I looked into it further, I discovered that the update has some serious bugs. The company has promised to make a further update available by the end of the week, which should rectify the problem. In the meantime, if you need to convert any documents to PDFs, I suggest you revert to the previous version of the software. Let me know if you need anything else, Emma. Bye!

11 至 13 題請聽以下電話留言。

> 嗨，艾瑪，我是資訊部的湯尼。妳的訊息裡說妳下載了最新版本的 Super PDF Express，但發現它跟我們的作業系統不相容。一開始我覺得很奇怪，因為我們已經用這個程式很多年了。然而當我進一步仔細檢查後發現，更新版有幾個嚴重瑕疵。廠商承諾在週末前會提供另一個更新版本，應該可以修正這問題。在那之前，如果妳需要把文件轉檔為 PDF，我建議妳回頭使用舊版。如果妳有其他需求，隨時跟我說。掰！

B **11** 🔊 297 🇬🇧

What is indicated about Emma?
(A) She had a conflict with a client.
(B) She reported a problem to IT.
(C) She got a very strange message.
(D) She rejected advice from her boss.

本文對艾瑪有何說法？
(A) 她與某客戶發生衝突。
(B) 她向資訊部回報一個問題。
(C) 她收到一則非常奇怪的訊息。
(D) 她拒絕了上司的建議。

CH 12

A **12** 🔊 298 🇬🇧

What will be available by the end of the week?
(A) Another update for some software
(B) A vaccine for an infectious disease
(C) Another company's rival application
(D) A report on replacing hardware

週末前會有什麼東西出來？
(A) 某款軟體的另一個更新版本
(B) 某種傳染病的疫苗
(C) 另一家公司的應用程式競爭產品
(D) 關於更換硬體的一份報告

C **13** 🔊 299 🇬🇧

What does the speaker suggest?
(A) Asking a colleague to convert PDFs
(B) Contacting the manufacturer directly
(C) Using an older edition of a program
(D) Updating an operating system

說話者建議做什麼？
(A) 請同事幫忙轉 PDF 檔
(B) 直接聯繫製造商
(C) 使用舊版程式
(D) 升級作業系統

重要單字片語

1. **version** [ˋvɝʒən] *n.* 版本；譯本
2. **OS** 作業系統（為 operating system 的縮寫）
3. **bug** [bʌg] *n.*（電腦程式、機器的）毛病，缺陷；小蟲子
4. **meantime** [ˋminˌtaɪm] *n.* & *adv.* 同時，在此期間
   in the meantime 在這段時間內
5. **convert** [kənˋvɝt] *vt.* & *vi.* 轉變
   convert A to / into B 將 A 轉變成 B
   Scientists have now found a way to convert waste into usable fuel.
   科學家們已經發現了一種能夠將廢棄物轉變為可用燃料的方法。
6. **revert** [rɪˋvɝt] *vi.* 回到；恢復；重提（與介詞 to 並用）
   When the new plan failed, we decided to revert to the original one.
   新計畫失敗後，我們決定回歸最初的方案。
7. **vaccine** [vækˋsin] *n.* 疫苗
8. **infectious** [ɪnˋfɛkʃəs] *a.* 傳染（性）的
9. **rival** [ˋraɪv!] *a.* 競爭的 & *n.* 競爭者，對手 & *vt.* 與……匹敵
   It is argued that the capabilities of the human brain cannot be rivaled by computers.
   有人主張，人類大腦的能力是電腦無法匹敵的。

Chapter 12 Listening Test

Questions 14 through 16 refer to the following announcement and table. 🔊 300

I've called this meeting to make an announcement regarding the four proposed IT projects. Management has told me that there are not sufficient funds to immediately pay for all of them. There is, however, enough money to pay for the hardware upgrades for the media department. The other projects will be rolled out over the next four to six months. Many of the employees will be disappointed by this decision, especially those who still don't have Wi-Fi access. It's therefore up to all of us in the IT department to keep every device earmarked for an upgrade functioning properly until it can be replaced. All right then, I'm ready to field questions from anyone who would like to know more about the IT projects.

Project	Cost
Hardware Upgrades	$5,000
Wi-Fi Access	$10,000
Backup System	$13,000
Website Development	$21,000

14 至 16 題請聽以下宣布，並請看以下列表。

我召開這個會議是要來宣布有關擬定的四項資訊科技提案。公司高層告訴我，這四項提案沒有足夠的資金可以馬上全部支應。不過，媒體部門的電腦硬體升級是有足夠的資金可以支應。其他三項提案在未來四至六個月的期間將會開始進行。這個決定可能會使許多同仁失望，尤其是那些還沒有無線網路可用的同仁。因此，所有排定升級的設備，在更換前都仍得正常運作，這就得靠我們資訊部的人了。好，那麼，對於這四項資訊科技提案想要知道更多細節的人，我可以接受你們的提問了。

提案	金額
硬體升級	5,000 美元
使用無線網路	10,000 美元
備份系統	13,000 美元
網站研發	21,000 美元

C **14** 🔊 301

Why have some projects been postponed?
(A) Manpower issues
(B) Delivery delays
(C) Lack of money
(D) Lack of time

為何有些計畫被延遲了？
(A) 人力問題
(B) 交貨時間延遲
(C) 資金短缺
(D) 時間不夠

A **15** 🔊 302 🇺🇸

Look at the graphic. How much will the selected project cost?
(A) $5,000
(B) $10,000
(C) $13,000
(D) $21,000

請看圖表。被選中的提案將會要花多少錢？
(A) 5,000 美元
(B) 10,000 美元
(C) 13,000 美元
(D) 21,000 美元

D **16** 🔊 303 🇺🇸

What will the speaker most likely do next?
(A) Send out an e-mail
(B) Raise funds
(C) Unveil a plan
(D) Answer queries

說話者接下來最有可能做什麼事？
(A) 發電子郵件
(B) 募款
(C) 公布一項計畫
(D) 解答疑問

🔍 重要單字片語

1. **make an announcement**
   發表公告（= issue an announcement）

2. **proposed** [prə`pozd] *a.* 被提議的；建議的

3. **management** [`mænɪdʒmənt] *n.* 管理階層；資方（不可數，且多不與 the 並用）；管理
   under sb's management
   在某人的管理下
   Management decided to initiate a new marketing strategy.
   管理階層決定展開一套新的行銷策略。

4. **sufficient** [sə`fɪʃənt] *a.* 足夠的；充分的
   Please verify that there is sufficient memory available before you download any software.
   下載任何軟體前你要確認有足夠的記憶體。

5. **fund** [fʌnd] *n.* 基金；資金（複數）& *vt.* 提供資金
   The enterprise decided to inject more funds to stabilize the market.
   該企業決定投注更多資金來穩住市場。

6. **roll out...**　　推行（某運動）
   The government will roll out a series of tax cuts next year.
   政府明年將會推行一連串的減稅方案。

7. **disappoint** [ˌdɪsə`pɔɪnt] *vt.* 使失望
   disappoint sb
   使某人失望（= let sb down）
   Peter disappointed his father when he failed the college entrance exam.
   彼得大學入學考試落榜讓他爸爸失望了。

8. **be up to sb**
   由某人決定；就看某人了；隨某人
   Whether you hire him or not is up to you.
   要不要僱用他由你決定。

9. **keep** [kip] *vi.* 繼續（接現在分詞，表「進行」）
   Keep (on) working hard, and you'll be successful one day.
   繼續努力，有朝一日你就會成功。

CH 12

229

Chapter 12 Reading Test

10. **earmark** [ˈɪrˌmɑrk] vt. 指定……的用途；預先安排

11. **function** [ˈfʌŋkʃən] vi. 運作 & n. 功能；職責
    The computer stopped functioning after the power failure.
    停電之後，電腦就停止運作了。

12. **properly** [ˈprɑpɚlɪ] adv. 恰當地；適當地；正確地
    If you do it properly the first time, you won't have to do it again.
    如果你一開始就把這件事做好，就不用再做一次了。

13. **field** [fild] vt. 回答；處理；應付

14. **manpower** [ˈmænˌpaʊɚ] n. 人力，勞動力

15. **send out...** 發送……
    I must send out these letters today, but I don't have time.
    我今天必須把這些信寄出去，但是我沒時間。

16. **raise** [rez] vt. 籌集；舉起；養育
    raise funds for... 為……籌募基金
    Brian has been active in helping (to) raise money for charity.
    布萊恩一直都很主動協助慈善募款活動。

17. **unveil** [ʌnˈvel] vt. 公布；揭幕；揭開……的面紗
    Michael Jordan unveiled a magnificent statue of himself.
    邁可‧喬登為一座他自己的雄偉雕像揭幕。

18. **query** [ˈkwɪrɪ] n. 詢問，問題

Part 5 Incomplete Sentences

D **17**

The technical specifications of the solar panels can be found on this ------- energy website.

(A) to renew　　(B) renew　　(C) renewal　　(D) renewable

這個可再生能源的網站上有登載這批太陽能板的技術規格。

理由

1. 原句空格前有介詞 on（在……上）及限定詞 this（這個），空格後有名詞片語 energy website（能源網站），得知空格內只能置形容詞，作為介詞片語的一部分。

2. (A) **to renew** 為動詞 renew（更新；使展期）的不定詞片語。
   (B) **renew** [rɪˈn(j)u] vt. 更新；使展期
       Jason renewed his passport one month before its expiration date.
       傑森在護照過期前一個月去換了新的。
   (C) **renewal** [rɪˈn(j)uəl] n. 更新；展期
   (D) **renewable** [rɪˈn(j)uəbl̩] a.（能源）可再生的
       renewable energy　可再生能源

3. 根據上述，(D) 項應為正選。

重要單字片語

1. **solar** [ˈsolɚ] a. 太陽的；與太陽有關的

2. **panel** [ˈpænl̩] n. 嵌版
   a solar panel　太陽能發電板

B **18**

Ms. Shih works as a machine learning -------, advising companies on the implementation of artificial intelligence systems.

(A) consult   (B) consultant   (C) consultation   (D) consultative

施小姐是一名機器學習顧問，為導入人工智慧系統的企業提供諮詢。

理由

1. 原句空格前有不定冠詞 a 及名詞詞組 machine learning（機器學習），得知空格內應置名詞形成完整的名詞片語。

2. (A) **consult** [kənˋsʌlt] *vt.* 查閱；請教 & *vi.* 諮商
   If you have any questions, please consult this manual for guidance.
   如果您有任何問題，請查閱此手冊尋求指導。

   (B) **consultant** [kənˋsʌltənt] *n.* 顧問
   My boss asked me to schedule a meeting with our consultant.
   我的老闆要我安排與我們的顧問開會。

   (C) **consultation** [ˌkɑnsəlˋteʃən] *n.* 諮商（會）
   Through a consultation with Professor Jones, David finally determined his career path.
   經過與瓊斯教授的商討，大衛終於確立了自己的職涯方向。

   (D) **consultative** [kənˋsʌltətɪv] *a.* 諮詢的；顧問的
   A consultative group was formed to provide advice about the upcoming merger.
   公司成立了一個顧問小組，以就即將進行的合併提供建議。

3. 根據上述，(B) 項應為正選。

重要單字片語

1. **implementation** [ˌɪmpləmɛnˋteʃən] *n.*
   實施，執行

2. **artificial intelligence**
   人工智慧（縮寫為 AI）

A **19**

To increase efficiency, the president demanded that we ------- the operating system and update most of the software we use.

(A) change   (B) can change   (C) changed   (D) have changed

為了提升效率，總裁要求我們更改作業系統，並將我們使用的大部分軟體升級。

理由

1. 本題測試意志動詞的用法：
   意志動詞通常有下列四類：
   1) 建議：suggest、recommend、advise、propose
   2) 要求：ask、demand、require、request
   3) 命令：order、command
   4) 規定：rule

Chapter 12 Reading Test

2. 以上意志動詞之後接 that 子句時，that 子句中的主詞之後恆使用助動詞 should，且 should 可省略，保留之後的原形動詞。
   I proposed that the meeting (should) be postponed until next Friday.
   我提議該會議延至下星期五再舉行。

3. 根據上述，原句空格前有意志動詞 demanded，且之後接 that 子句作受詞。得知該 that 子句當中的主詞 we 之後應省略了助動詞 should，而保留原形動詞，故 (A) 項應為正選。

> 🔍 **重要單字片語**
>
> **efficiency** [ɪˋfɪʃənsɪ] *n.* 效率
> efficient [ɪˋfɪʃənt] *a.* 有效率的
> We need more efficient methods of collecting data.
> 我們需要更有效率的資料蒐集方法。

A **20**

The technician installed a signal booster in an effort to ------- the Wi-Fi signal in the office.

(A) stabilize　　　　(B) outweigh　　　　(C) interfere　　　　(D) mature

技術人員安裝了一個訊號增強器，以提升公司無線網路訊號的穩定性。

> **理由**

1. (A) **stabilize** [ˋstεblˏaɪz] *vt.* & *vi.*（使）穩固
    The government took measures to stabilize electricity prices.
    政府採取措施來穩定電價。

   (B) **outweigh** [aʊtˋwe] *vt.* 勝過；重於
    The benefits of the construction project significantly outweigh its minor drawbacks.
    這項建設計畫帶來的好處遠遠超過其微不足道的缺點。

   (C) **interfere** [ˏɪntɚˋfɪr] *vi.* 干預；妨礙
    interfere with...　　阻礙 / 妨礙……
    The company's financial problems interfered with its expansion plan.
    該公司的財務問題妨礙了其擴大營運的計畫。

   (D) **mature** [məˋtʃʊr] *vi.* 成熟 & *a.* 成熟的
    Vincent has matured into a great musician.
    文森已成長為一位優秀的音樂家。

2. 根據語意，(A) 項應為正選。

> 🔍 **重要單字片語**
>
> 1. **install** [ɪnˋstɔl] *vt.* 裝設，安裝
>   You need to restart your computer after installing the antivirus software.
>   安裝該防毒軟體後，需要重新啟動電腦。
>
> 2. **booster** [ˋbustɚ] *n.* 增強器
>   boost [bust] *vt.* 提升 & *n.* 促進，推動
>
> 3. **in an effort to + V**　　為了試著要做……
>   Larry kept making faces in an effort to entertain his daughter.
>   賴瑞不斷扮鬼臉，想要逗女兒開心。

D **21**

It's good to know that the new software, which helps reduce programming time, continues -------.

(A) enhance　　　(B) enhanced　　　(C) enhancing　　　(D) to be enhanced

知道這款有助於縮短編碼時間的新軟體還在持續優化中，很令人欣慰。

理由

1. 本題測試動詞 continue 的用法：
   continue to + V　　繼續做……
   = continue + V-ing
   The restaurant's need for part-time employees continued to grow.
   = The restaurant's need for part-time employees continued growing.
   這家餐廳對兼職員工的需求持續增長。

2. 根據語意及上述用法，因新軟體無法自我進行優化而須使用被動語態，故 (D) 項應為正選。

重要單字片語

software [ˈsɔft͵wɛr] *n.* 軟體（不可數）
a piece of software　　一件軟體（非 a software）

Part 6　Text Completion

Questions 22-25 refer to the following excerpt from an employee handbook.

Following your orientation session, you will be guided to your desk. A technician from the IT department will initiate the setup of your workstation. -------22.-. Please input a password of your choice to secure your account. The password must be -------23. ten characters long and contain both numbers and letters. The technician will also show you how to access the shared company resources, configure your email account, and navigate any software you're -------24.-. Please feel free to ask him any questions and consult him on any technical issues. -------25. everything is running smoothly, he will hand over to your line manager.

22 至 25 題請看以下員工手冊的摘錄片段。

在新進人員訓練結束後，會有人帶你去你的辦公座位。資訊部的人會幫你的電腦工作站做初始設定。他會教你怎麼登入系統。請輸入你的自選密碼以保護你的帳戶。密碼長度必須有至少十個字元，且要同時包含數字和英文字母。技術人員還會教你如何存取公司的共用資源、設定你的電子郵件帳戶，以及操作你不熟的軟體。有什麼問題都可以問他，技術上的問題也可以找他諮詢。等到一切順利運作後，他就會把接下來的時間交接給你的直屬經理。

Chapter 12　Reading Test

D **22**

(A) The program has been updated since you last used it.
(B) You must sign in at the reception desk on your first day.
(C) Downloading this software on work computers is forbidden.
(D) He will provide instructions on how to log in to the system.

理由

1. (A) 該程式自從你上次使用後已進行更新。
   (B) 報到第一天請至櫃檯簽到。
   (C) 公司禁止在公務電腦上下載此軟體。
   (D) 他會教你怎麼登入系統。

2. 根據空格前一句 "A technician from the IT department will initiate the setup of your workstation." （資訊部的人會幫你的電腦工作站做初始設定。）得知技術人員會幫新人設定專用辦公電腦，空格後又提及輸入自選密碼，(D) 項句子 "He will provide instructions on how to log in to the system."（他會教你怎麼登入系統。）置入空格後與前文相呼應，故應為正選。

D **23**

(A) in the end　　(B) for the sake of　　(C) in favor of　　(D) at least

理由

1. (A) **in the end**　　最後，終於
   We can only succeed in the end if we keep trying and learn along the way.
   唯有持續努力並從中學習，我們最終才能成功。

   (B) **for the sake of...**　　為了……的緣故
   Emma has decided to eat fewer desserts for the sake of her health.
   為了健康的緣故，艾瑪決定少吃點甜食。

   (C) **(be) in favor of sth**　　贊成某事
   Few students are in favor of going on a field trip to the zoo.
   投票要去動物園進行戶外教學的學生很少。

   (D) **at least**　　至少，起碼
   Jason needs at least 30 more minutes to get here because of the traffic.
   由於交通問題，傑森至少還需要三十分鐘才能抵達。

2. 根據上述，選項 (A)、(B) 及 (C) 均不合乎語意，故不可選，惟 (D) 項置入空格後合乎語意及文法，故應為正選。

C **24**

(A) critical of　　(B) grateful for　　(C) unfamiliar with　　(D) similar to

理由

1. 本題測試下列固定片語：
   be unfamiliar with...　　對……不熟悉
   The researcher is unfamiliar with the newly discovered virus.
   研究員對這種新發現的病毒並不熟悉。

2. 根據上述，(C) 項應為正選。

3. 其他選項：

(A) **be critical of...**　　批評……
Many parents were strongly critical of the school's new policy.
許多家長對學校的新規定提出了強烈的批評。

(B) **be grateful for...**　　對……表達感激
Kevin is grateful for his mother's love and all that she has done for him.
凱文感謝母親給他的愛，以及她為他所付出的一切。

(D) **be similar to...**　　與……相似/類似
Although the storyline of this action movie is similar to that of the other, the special effects are much better.
這部動作片的劇情雖然和另一部相似，但特效卻好很多。

B **25**

(A) Now that　　　(B) Once　　　(C) As though　　　(D) Yet

理由

1. 空格後有兩個子句且有逗號分開，且後方子句有表未來式的助動詞 will，得知含空格的子句為從屬子句，空格內應置表時間的從屬連接詞。

2. (A) **now (that)...**　　由於……；既然……
Kyle is enjoying his job now that he has more responsibility.
由於凱爾承擔了更多責任，所以他很喜歡他的工作。

(B) **once** [wʌns] *conj.* 一旦
Once the meeting is over, I'll send you a message.
一旦會議結束了，我就會傳訊息給你。

(C) **as though...**　　彷彿/似乎……
Linda treats her nephew as though he were her own son.
琳達把侄子當作親生兒子般對待。

(D) **yet** [jɛt] *conj.* 然而（= but）
The house looks great, yet we can't afford to buy it.
這棟房子看來很不錯，可是我們買不起。

3. 根據語意及用法，得知 (B) 項應為正選。

重要單字片語

1. **excerpt** [ˈɛksɝpt] *n.* 摘錄（可數）&
[ɪkˈsɝpt / ɛkˈsɝpt] *vt.* 摘錄
be excerpted from...　　從……摘錄下來
The following passage is excerpted from the Bible.
以下段落摘錄自《聖經》。

2. **session** [ˈsɛʃən] *n.* 講習會；開會

3. **configure** [kənˈfɪgjɚ] *vt.* 設定/配置（電腦或軟體等）
Andy can help you configure your laptop so it connects to the server.
安迪可以協助你設定筆電，讓它能夠連上伺服器。

Chapter 12 Reading Test

4. **navigate** [ˈnævəˌɡet] *vt.* & *vi.* 瀏覽；導航（船、飛機、車等）
The system we use is very simple and easy to navigate.
我們的系統設計簡單，很容易瀏覽。

5. **forbidden** [fɚˈbɪdn̩] *a.* 禁止的

Part 7　Reading Comprehension

Questions 26-30 refer to the following information sheet and email.

Quick-start Guide

Thank you for purchasing the X1 Electronic Secretary — the most powerful and sophisticated electronic organizer available.

To install the batteries:

✓ Hold the device with the screen facing away from you.

✓ Push down firmly on the two square depressions with your thumbs. The cover will pop up to reveal the internal battery compartment.

✓ Insert two AA batteries. Make sure to match the positive and negative ends of the batteries with the symbols inside the battery compartment.

✓ Close the cover while pressing down on the two square depressions gently at the same time.

✓ Press the power switch for approximately three seconds. The power LED light will illuminate green to indicate that the batteries are inserted properly.

Please note:

✓ Replace the batteries when the power LED flashes red.

✓ To prevent damage to the plastic case, remove the batteries if the device will not be used for an extended period of time.

Specifications subject to change without notice.

To:	Manny Jharris <mannyjharris@elsec.com>
From:	Natasha Benson <natashabenson@elsec.com>
Date:	October 3
Subject:	Electronic Secretary Prototype

Hi Manny,

 The prototype of the enhanced Electronic Secretary, the X2, has just been approved and will go into production immediately. The new model will have twice as many batteries as the X1, be 100% recyclable, and will have wireless connectivity. Furthermore, the power LED light has been modified: It will now illuminate orange to show that it is connected to Wi-Fi. Consequently, several changes must be made to the manual and quick-start guide.

 I'll let you know about any additional changes as soon as I find out about them.

Natasha Benson
Product Development

26 至 30 題請看以下資訊頁及電子郵件。

快速使用手冊

感謝您購買 X1 型電子祕書 —— 市面上最強大、最精密的電子記事本。

如何安裝電池：

- ✓ 拿起裝置，將螢幕背對您。
- ✓ 用雙手拇指用力按壓兩個正方形凹槽。蓋子會彈起，露出內部的電池槽。
- ✓ 放入兩顆三號電池。確認電池的正負極與電池槽內的正負極符號相對應。
- ✓ 將蓋子蓋起，同時輕輕按下兩個正方形凹槽。
- ✓ 按下電源開關約三秒。電源 LED 燈會亮起綠燈，表示電池已正確放入。

請注意：

- ✓ 當電源 LED 燈閃紅光時請更換電池。
- ✓ 為了避免塑膠殼受損，如果長時間不會使用到裝置，請將電池移除。

產品規格若有變更，恕不另行通知。

Chapter 12 Reading Test

收件者： 曼尼・傑利斯 <mannyjharris@elsec.com>
寄件者： 娜塔莎・班森 <natashabenson@elsec.com>
日　期： 十月三日
主　旨： 電子祕書原型機

曼尼，你好：

　　加強版的電子祕書原型機，也就是 X2 型號，剛剛被核准了，並且馬上會開始生產。新型號將會比 X1 型號需要多出一倍的電池，而且百分之百可回收，並且有無線網路連接。另外，顯示電源的 LED 燈已做過調整：連上無線網路時，它會亮橘燈。因此，說明書與快速使用手冊必須做些修改。

　　一旦我知道任何其他的改變，我會告知你。

產品研發部
娜塔莎・班森

A **26**

What is indicated about the Electronic Secretary's power LED?
(A) It changes color to show status.
(B) It flashes continually while charging.
(C) It has two square depressions.
(D) It flashes red when switched on.

關於電子祕書的電源 LED 燈，本文暗示了什麼？
(A) 它會變換顏色來顯示當前狀態。
(B) 在充電過程中，它會持續閃爍。
(C) 它有兩個正方形凹槽。
(D) 電源打開時會閃紅燈。

理由

根據資訊頁「如何安裝電池」第五項第二句 "The power LED light will illuminate green to indicate that the batteries are inserted properly."（電源 LED 燈會亮起綠燈，表示電池已正確放入。）及「請注意」第一項 "Replace the batteries when the power LED flashes red."（當電源 LED 燈閃紅光時請更換電池。）以及電子郵件中提及連上無線網路時會亮橘燈得知，(A) 項應為正選。

D **27**

How many batteries does the X2 Electronic Secretary need?
(A) One
(B) Two
(C) Three
(D) Four

電子祕書 X2 型需要多少電池？
(A) 一顆
(B) 兩顆
(C) 三顆
(D) 四顆

> 理由

根據資訊頁「如何安裝電池」第三項第一句 "Insert two AA batteries."（放入兩顆三號電池。）得知，X1 型號需要兩顆電池。又根據電子郵件第一段第二句 "The new model will have twice as many batteries as the X1,..."（新型號將會比 X1 型號需要多出一倍的電池，……）得知，X2 型號的電池需求是 X1 型號的兩倍，應需要四顆電池，故 (D) 項應為正選。

CH 12

B **28**

What Electronic Secretary X2 feature is mentioned?
(A) Portable and lightweight
(B) Recyclable parts
(C) Rechargeability
(D) Touch screen interface

文中提到了電子祕書 X2 型號的什麼特點？
(A) 輕巧好攜帶
(B) 可回收的零件
(C) 可充電
(D) 觸控介面

> 理由

根據電子郵件第一段第二句 "The new model will have twice as many batteries as the X1, be 100% recyclable, and will have wireless connectivity."（新型號將會比 X1 型號需要多出一倍的電池，而且百分之百可回收，並且有無線網路連接。）得知，(B) 項應為正選。

C **29**

In the e-mail, the word "just" in paragraph 1, line 1, is closest in meaning to
(A) only
(B) fairly
(C) recently
(D) objectively

在電子郵件中，第一段第一行 just 這個字意思最接近
(A) 唯一地
(B) 公平地
(C) 近期地
(D) 客觀地

> 理由

根據電子郵件第一段第一句 "The prototype of the enhanced Electronic Secretary, the X2, has just been approved and will go into production immediately."（加強版的電子祕書原型機，也就是 X2 型號，剛剛被核准了，並且馬上會開始生產。）得知，(C) 項應為正選。

B **30**

What does Ms. Benson indicate she will do?
(A) Confirm a booking
(B) Provide more information
(C) Approve a request
(D) Replace a broken part

班森女士表示她會做什麼事？
(A) 確認預約
(B) 提供更多資訊
(C) 批准請求
(D) 更換壞掉的零件

Chapter 12 Reading Test

> **理由**
> 根據電子郵件第二段 "I'll let you know about any additional changes as soon as I find out about them."（一旦我知道任何其他的改變，我會告知你。）得知，(B) 項應為正選。

重要單字片語

1. **firmly** [ˋfɝmlɪ] adv. 用力地
2. **depression** [dɪˋprɛʃən] n. 凹陷，坑；抑鬱
3. **pop up** 彈出；突然出現，冒出
   Click here, and a new window will pop up.
   點這裡，新的視窗就會彈出。
4. **internal** [ɪnˋtɝnl̩] a. 內部的
5. **compartment** [kəmˋpɑrtmənt] n. 隔層，隔間
6. **approximately** [əˋprɑksəmɪtlɪ] adv. 大概
   Approximately 200 people were killed in the plane crash.
   = Some 200 people were killed in the plane crash.
   = About 200 people were killed in the plane crash.
   空難中約有兩百人喪生。
7. **illuminate** [ɪˋlumə͵net] vt. 照亮
   Claire's bedside lamp dimly illuminated the room.
   克萊兒的床頭燈微微地照亮了房間。
8. **properly** [ˋprɑpɚlɪ] adv. 正確地；適當地
   My new TV isn't functioning properly, so I'm going to ask for a refund.
   我的新電視運作不正常，所以我會要求退款。
9. **flash** [flæʃ] vt. & vi. 閃光，閃亮
   Stop flashing that light in my eyes!
   別拿你的手電筒照我的眼睛！
10. **subject** [ˋsʌbdʒɛkt / ˋsʌbdʒɪkt] a. 可能受……影響的
    be subject to... 可能會受……影響
    Flights are subject to delay because of the weather.
    航班可能會因為天氣而誤點。
11. **prototype** [ˋprotə͵taɪp] n. 原型
12. **enhanced** [ɪnˋhænst] a. 改進的；增強的
13. **consequently** [ˋkɑnsə͵kwɛntlɪ] adv. 因此（= therefore）
    Tracy is always bad-tempered, and consequently she has very few friends.
    崔西總是脾氣差，因此她的朋友很少。
14. **portable** [ˋportəbl̩] a. 輕便的，方便攜帶的

Chapter 13 Listening Test

🎧 Part 1 Photographs

D **1** 🔊 305 🇨🇦

(A) She is walking across a busy street.
(B) She is rushing onto a railcar at the station.
(C) She is standing right at the edge of the track.
(D) She is paying the streetcar fare at the gate.

(A) 她正在過一條車很多的馬路。
(B) 她正衝進車站裡的列車車廂。
(C) 她站在鐵軌的邊上。
(D) 她正在閘門口付路面電車的車費。

🔍 重要單字片語

1. **railcar** [ˈrelˌkɑr] *n.* 軌道車車廂
   （= carriage，英式英語）
2. **edge** [ɛdʒ] *n.* 邊緣
3. **streetcar** [ˈstritˌkɑr] *n.* 路面電車
   （= tram，英式英語）

B **2** 🔊 306 🇦🇺

(A) Passengers are boarding the aircraft.
(B) Passengers are disembarking from the airplane.
(C) The airplane is taking off from the runway.
(D) Items of luggage are piled up next to the steps.

(A) 乘客正在登上飛機。
(B) 乘客正在下飛機。
(C) 飛機正在從跑道上起飛。
(D) 多件行李堆放在樓梯旁。

🔍 重要單字片語

take off （飛機）起飛
touch down （飛機）落地
Please turn off all electronic devices. We will soon be taking off.
請關閉所有電子產品。我們即將起飛。

Chapter 13 Listening Test

Part 2 Question-Response

A 3 🔊 308

I'd like to confirm my hotel booking for tomorrow evening.
(A) What name is your reservation under?
(B) I'm sorry I can't extend your stay.
(C) You can check in at one o'clock.

我想要確認明晚的飯店訂房。
(A) 您訂房大名是？
(B) 很抱歉我沒辦法讓您延長住宿。
(C) 您可以在一點鐘辦理入住。

重要單字片語

booking [ˈbʊkɪŋ] *n.* 預訂，預約（= reservation [ˌrɛzɚˈveʃən]）
confirm a booking　　確認預約

B 4 🔊 309

Is there a non-stop flight from London to Rome available?
(A) No, the plane flies there directly.
(B) Yes, but there's only one ticket left.
(C) That's a very famous attraction.

請問有倫敦直飛羅馬的班機嗎？
(A) 不，班機是直飛去那裡。
(B) 有，但只剩一張票了。
(C) 那是非常有名的景點。

Part 3 Conversations

Questions 5 through 7 refer to the following conversation.　🔊 311　M: 🇦🇺　W: 🇺🇸

M: Excuse me. I'm here to pick up a relative, but the train hasn't arrived yet. It's the Metroliner from Dallas. It was supposed to arrive at Track 2 at ten o'clock.
W: I'm sorry, sir, the DL226 has been delayed due to extreme weather. It's now expected to arrive in about half an hour.
M: Oh, are all the other trains delayed as well?
W: Only those from the south. The winds have really picked up because of the hurricane in the Caribbean and the Gulf of Mexico.
M: I see. Thank you.

5 至 7 題請聽以下會話。

男：不好意思。我要來這裡接我的親戚，但是火車還沒到。它是從達拉斯發車的特快列車。那班車應該要在十點時開進第二月臺才對。
女：先生，很抱歉，DL226 這班車由於極端惡劣的天氣導致誤點。目前是預計大約要半個小時以後才會到。
男：喔，是不是其他班次的火車也都誤點了？

女：只有從南部發車的北上列車誤點。由於加勒比海及墨西哥灣有颶風，南方那裡的風變得超強超大。
男：了解。謝謝妳。

D **5** 🔊 312 🇬🇧

Where does this conversation most likely take place?
(A) At a travel agency
(B) In a bus shelter
(C) At an airport
(D) In a train station

這段會話最有可能在哪裡發生？
(A) 旅行社
(B) 公車候車亭
(C) 機場
(D) 火車站

C **6** 🔊 313 🇬🇧

Who most likely is the woman?
(A) A weather reporter
(B) A taxi driver
(C) A station attendant
(D) A hotel porter

女子最有可能的身分是什麼？
(A) 氣象播報員
(B) 計程車司機
(C) 車站服務員
(D) 飯店行李搬運員

D **7** 🔊 314 🇬🇧

What is causing the delay?
(A) Traffic accidents
(B) Staffing problems
(C) Technical issues
(D) Severe weather

什麼事情造成火車誤點？
(A) 車禍事故
(B) 人員調度的問題
(C) 技術上的問題
(D) 惡劣的天氣

重要單字片語

1. **pick up sb / pick sb up**
（開車）接某人
I'll pick you up at five.
我五點鐘來接你。

2. **relative** [ˈrɛlətɪv] *n.* 親戚 & *a.* 相關的；相對的；相當的
a distant relative 遠房親戚

3. **Metroliner** [ˈmɛtroˌlaɪnɚ] *n.* 美國 Amtrak 火車公司屬下的特快列車

4. **be supposed to + 原形動詞** 應當……
You were supposed to be here an hour ago.
你在一個鐘頭前就該到這裡才對。

5. **track** [træk] *n.* 軌道；小徑 & *vt.* 追蹤；跟蹤

6. **pick up** （風）變大，變強

7. **hurricane** [ˈhɝɪˌken] *n.* 颶風；颱風

8. **the Caribbean** [ˌkærəˈbiən] **(Sea)**
加勒比海

243

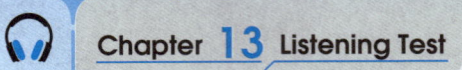

Chapter 13 Listening Test

9. **gulf** [gʌlf] *n.* 海灣；鴻溝
   The Gulf of Mexico is the ninth largest body of water in the world.
   墨西哥灣是世界第九大海域。

10. **shelter** [ˋʃɛltɚ] *n.* 遮蔽物（可數）；遮蔽（不可數） & *vt.* 遮蔽
    a bus shelter （英）公車站的候車亭
    Everyone needs food, clothing, and shelter.
    每個人都需要食物、衣服和棲身之所。

11. **porter** [ˋpɔrtɚ] *n.* 行李搬運工人；挑夫
    A porter helps carry people's suitcases.
    搬運工的工作就是幫忙人家搬運行李。

12. **staffing** [ˋstæfɪŋ] *n.* 人員配置（不可數）
    Let's discuss the staffing requirements for our thirtieth anniversary party.
    咱們來討論一下三十週年慶派對的人員配置。

13. **severe** [səˋvɪr] *a.* 嚴酷的；惡劣的；嚴重的
    We had a severe winter last year.
    去年我們度過了一個嚴冬。

Questions 8 through 10 refer to the following conversation with three speakers. 🔊 315

W: 🇬🇧　M1: 🇨🇦　M2: 🇦🇺

W: Excuse me. My husband and I just missed our flight. Is it possible to get a refund?
M1: I'm sorry, Ms. Rogers, these e-tickets are non-refundable. However, I can transfer you to the next available flight, which will be in 18 hours.
W: Well, it looks like we'll have to book a hotel for the night.
M2: Honey, we could check to see if we can get a flight on another airline.
W: But it'll be a lot more expensive than staying in a hotel.
M1: Would you like me to see what flights are available on other airlines?
W: No, thanks. I think we'll just stay in a hotel.

8 至 10 題請聽以下三人的會話。

> 女：不好意思。我和我先生沒趕上我們的飛機。可以把錢退給我們嗎？
> 甲男：很抱歉，羅傑斯太太，這些電子機票是無法退款的。不過，我可以幫您們安排換搭下一班飛機，是十八個小時之後可搭的一班飛機。
> 女：呃，看來我們必須訂個飯店房間在那裡過夜了。
> 乙男：寶貝，我們可以看看是不是有別家航空公司的飛機可搭。
> 女：但是那樣做的話會比去住飯店貴很多。
> 甲男：您要我查看看有沒有別家航空公司的飛機可搭嗎？
> 女：不用了，謝謝。我想我們會去飯店過夜。

C **8** 🔊 316 🇺🇸

What caused the couple's problem?
(A) Their passports expired.
(B) Their baggage is overweight.
(C) They missed a flight.
(D) They lost their luggage.

是什麼事情造成了這對夫妻的問題？
(A) 他們的護照過期了。
(B) 他們的行李超重了。
(C) 他們沒搭上某班機。
(D) 他們的行李掉了。

B **9** 🔊 317 🇺🇸

What does the woman ask for?
(A) A transfer
(B) A refund
(C) An exchange
(D) An upgrade

女子要求什麼事？
(A) 轉機
(B) 退款
(C) 調換
(D) 升等

CH 13

D **10** 🔊 318 🇺🇸

What does the woman's husband suggest?
(A) Extending their stay
(B) Reserving a hotel room
(C) Canceling the flight
(D) Flying with another airline

女子的丈夫建議什麼事？
(A) 延長停留的時間
(B) 預訂飯店房間
(C) 取消那班飛機
(D) 搭另一家航空公司的班機

🔍 重要單字片語

1. **non-refundable** [ˌnɑnrɪˋfʌndəb!] *a.* 不能退款的
   The travel agent pointed out that our plane tickets were non-refundable.
   旅行社的人指出，我們的機票是不能退錢的。

2. **expire** [ɪkˋspaɪr] *vi.* 到期；期滿；過期
   Your visa is about to expire, so you must have it renewed at once.
   你的簽證就快要到期了，所以你必須趕快去加簽。

3. **overweight** [ˌovɚˋwet] *a.* 過重的
   Many children in this class are overweight.
   這個班有好幾個小朋友的體重都過重。

4. **extend** [ɪkˋstɛnd] *vt.* 延長；擴大；延伸
   I'd like to extend my stay another two days.
   我想在這兒多待兩天。

5. **stay** [ste] *n.* 停留；逗留；暫住（一般用單數）& *vi.* 停留；逗留
   Peter and his wife had a good time during their stay in Bali. It was really an unforgettable experience.
   彼得和他太太在峇里島時玩得很愉快。那真是個難忘的經歷。

6. **fly** [flaɪ] *vi.* 搭飛機；飛 & *vt.* 駕駛（飛機）
   （三態為：fly, flew [flu], flown [flon]）
   Sometimes I want to fly somewhere I have never been before.
   有時候我想要搭機飛往某個我沒有去過的地方。

Chapter 13 Listening Test

Part 4 Talks

Questions 11 through 13 refer to the following announcement. 🔊 320

Good morning, ladies and gentlemen. We will soon be preparing to land. Please return your seats and tray tables to their upright positions and fasten your seatbelts. My fellow flight attendants will be checking all overhead compartments to make sure they are secure for landing. All cellphones and laptop computers should be turned off until further notice. For those passengers who need them, I will now distribute arrival cards. Thank you for your attention, and thank you for flying with Grape Airlines. We are delighted to have had you aboard.

11 至 13 題請聽以下宣布。

> 各位女士、先生早安。我們已經準備降落了。請把椅背及餐桌豎直，並繫上安全帶。機組同仁將會檢查座位上方所有的行李櫃是否都關緊，以確保降落時安全無虞。請將手機及筆記型電腦關機，並等候可再度開機的通知。我現在要發入境卡給有需要的乘客。謝謝您的合作，感謝您搭乘葡萄航空。很榮幸為您服務。

B **11** 🔊 321

According to the speaker, what will soon happen?
(A) The airplane will take off.
(B) The airplane will land.
(C) The airplane will hit turbulence.
(D) The airplane will taxi.

根據說話者，不久後將會發生什麼事？
(A) 飛機將要起飛。
(B) 飛機將要降落。
(C) 飛機將會遇到亂流。
(D) 飛機將要滑行。

A **12** 🔊 322

According to the speaker, what should be switched off?
(A) Electronic devices
(B) In-flight entertainment
(C) Overhead lights
(D) Emergency signs

依據說話者的說法，應該要把什麼關掉？
(A) 電子用品
(B) 機上娛樂設備
(C) 座位頂燈
(D) 緊急燈號

D **13** 🔊 323

What will the speaker most likely do next?
(A) Go through security
(B) Serve meals
(C) Return to her seat
(D) Distribute a form

說話者接下來最有可能做什麼事？
(A) 通過安全檢查
(B) 供應餐點
(C) 回到她的座位
(D) 分發表格

246

重要單字片語

1. **upright** [ˈʌpˌraɪt] *a.* 豎直的；直立的；挺直的 & *adv.* 垂直地
   The plane is landing. Please return your seats to an upright position.
   飛機要降落了，請將您的椅背豎直。

2. **fasten** [ˈfæsn̩] *vt. & vi.* 繫牢；扣牢；縛緊
   fasten the seat belt
   扣緊安全帶（= buckle up）
   For your safety, always fasten your seat belt while driving.
   為了安全起見，開車上路一定要繫安全帶。

3. **overhead** [ˈovɚˌhɛd] *a.* 在頭頂上方的；高架的 & [ˌovɚˈhɛd] *adv.* 頭頂上；在高空中
   an overhead bin
   機艙中頭頂上方的置物櫃

4. **secure** [sɪˈkjʊr] *a.* 關緊的；鎖牢的；安全的
   With his mother sitting beside his bed, the child felt very secure.
   有媽媽坐在床邊，那個孩子覺得很安全。

5. **distribute** [dɪˈstrɪbjut] *vt.* 分發；分送；分配
   The professor distributed the examination papers to the class.
   該教授正在把考卷發給全班。

6. **airline** [ˈɛrˌlaɪn] *n.* 航空公司
   The airline has very strict safety standards.
   該航空公司採取很嚴格的安全標準。

7. **taxi** [ˈtæksɪ] *vi.* 滑行

8. **in-flight** [ˌɪnˈflaɪt] *a.* 飛行途中提供的；飛行過程中的
   All our flights to New York offer in-flight movies.
   我們飛往紐約的所有班機上都有電影可看。

Questions 14 through 16 refer to the following talk. 🔊 324

Thank you for coming to this short meeting to confirm details of next month's business trip to our factory in New Delhi. Your total flight time will be around 19 hours, which includes a four-hour layover in London. You won't have time to visit that city, but I'm pleased to tell you that your itinerary for New Delhi has been adjusted to allow more free time there. This means you'll be able to visit some of the many fascinating attractions on offer. You'll be expected to arrange transportation such as taxis for these visits yourselves. However, a bus will be provided to shuttle you between the airport and the hotel.

14 至 16 題請聽以下短談。

> 感謝各位來開會，這個會不需要很久。我們要敲定下個月去新德里工廠出差的各項細節。整趟飛行時間大約在十九個小時左右，包含在倫敦等候轉機的四個小時。你們不會有時間去參觀倫敦市，但我很高興向各位宣布，你們在新德里的行程已經過調整，因此會有更多自由行動的時間。這意味你們可以在那邊的諸多熱門景點當中選幾個去看一看。至於自由行程的交通部分請自行安排，例如叫計程車等等。不過我們會安排巴士接送各位往返機場與飯店。

Chapter 13　Listening Test

C **14** 🔊 325 🇺🇸

What does the speaker say about the flight?
(A) It will go non-stop to New Delhi.
(B) It will be monitored at all times.
(C) It will include a stop in another place.
(D) It will be changed to a different route.

說話者對飛行歷程有何說法？
(A) 會直飛新德里。
(B) 將全程受到監控。
(C) 將包含在他處短暫停留。
(D) 將會改走不同的路線。

B **15** 🔊 326 🇺🇸

According to the speaker, what can the listeners do in New Delhi?
(A) Enjoy exotic cuisine
(B) Visit tourist sites
(C) Meet the locals
(D) Attend a sports game

根據說話者，聽眾可以在新德里做什麼？
(A) 享用異國料理
(B) 參觀旅遊景點
(C) 與當地人交流
(D) 去看運動比賽

D **16** 🔊 327 🇺🇸

What will be offered to the listeners at the airport?
(A) A city map
(B) A luggage cart
(C) An interpreter
(D) A shuttle bus

在機場會提供什麼給聽眾？
(A) 市區地圖
(B) 行李推車
(C) 口譯人員
(D) 接駁巴士

重要單字片語

1. **transportation** [ˌtrænspɚˋteʃən] *n.* （交通）運輸，運輸工具
2. **route** [rut / raʊt] *n.* 路線
3. **local** [ˋlokl] *n.* 當地人，本地人 & *a.* 當地的，本地的
4. **interpreter** [ɪnˋtɝprɪtɚ] *n.* 口譯者，口譯員
   比：translator [trænsˋletɚ] 泛指一般翻譯員，主要指筆譯，而 interpreter 則專指口譯員。

Chapter 13 Reading Test

📖 Part 5 Incomplete Sentences

C 17

The railroad company has published its fall ------- for the east coast line on its website.

(A) authority　　　(B) detector　　　(C) schedule　　　(D) belongings

鐵路公司已經在網站上公布東海岸線的秋季時刻表。

理由

1. (A) **authority** [əˈθɔrətɪ] *n.* 當局（恆用複數）；權力，權勢（不可數）
   Mr. Davis applied to the authorities for his business license.
   戴維斯先生向當局申請營業執照。

   (B) **detector** [dɪˈtɛktɚ] *n.* 探測器
   I use a metal detector to locate nails in my walls.
   我用金屬探測器來找我家牆壁裡面釘子的位置。

   (C) **schedule** [ˈskɛdʒʊl] *n.* 時間表；行程
   We came to an agreement relating to our work schedules.
   我們在工作進度上已達成共識。

   (D) **belongings** [bəˈlɔŋɪŋz] *n.* 攜帶物品；所有物（恆用複數）
   Beware of your personal belongings when you are in a crowded place.
   在人潮擁擠的地方，要留心個人隨身攜帶的物品。

2. 根據語意，(C) 項應為正選。

C 18

Compensation will be provided immediately to those passengers ------- luggage was lost in transit.

(A) that　　　(B) who　　　(C) whose　　　(D) which

行李在運送過程中遺失的那些旅客將立刻獲得補償。

理由

1. 空格前有名詞 passengers（旅客），可知空格內應置關係代名詞（who、whom）或關係代名詞所有格（whose），以引導形容詞子句，修飾 passengers。由於空格後另有名詞作形容詞子句的主詞，故此處應用 whose。

2. 根據上述，(C) 項應為正選。

B 19

By the time Mr. Tang ------- some souvenirs at a duty-free store, his flight had already been called.

(A) buys　　　(B) bought　　　(C) buying　　　(D) had bought

湯先生去到免稅店買紀念品時，他的班機早已在呼叫登機了。

Chapter 13 Reading Test

理由

1. 本題測試下列用法：
   1) by + 過去時間 → 主要子句使用過去完成式（S + had + p.p.）
   2) by + 未來時間 → 主要子句使用未來完成式（S + will + have + p.p.）
2. 空格後主要子句的動詞為過去完成式 had been called，得知空格內應置動詞過去式。故 (B) 項應為正選。

D **20**

Not until the housekeepers have finished cleaning the presidential suite ------- in.

(A) check can the guests (B) the guests check can
(C) the guests can check (D) can the guests check

直到清潔人員打掃完總統套房後，旅客才能辦理入住。

理由

1. 本題測試否定副詞、否定副詞片語或否定副詞子句置句首時，之後的主要子句要採倒裝句構。常見的否定副詞有：hardly（幾乎不）、scarcely（幾乎不）、rarely（很少，幾乎不）、little（很少）等；常見的否定副詞片語有：by no means（絕不）、on no account（絕不）、under no circumstances（絕不）等；常見的否定副詞子句有：only if（只有）、only when（只有當）、not until（直到……才）引導的副詞子句。
   Rarely does Brian tell a joke.
   布萊恩幾乎不太說笑話。
   By no means will I mention my private life.
   我絕不會提及我的私生活。
   Not until I talked to Ned did I know he was homesick.
   直到我和奈德談過，我才知道原來他想家。
2. 根據上述，本句句首有 Not until 引導的副詞子句，得知主要子句要使用倒裝句構，故 (D) 項應為正選。

A **21**

Mrs. Poilievre was at the ferry port to see her son ------- for Vancouver Island.

(A) depart (B) departs (C) to depart (D) will depart

普瓦列夫爾女士在渡輪港口目送她兒子前往溫哥華島。

理由

1. 本題測試凡表看：see（看見）、聽：hear（聽見）、感覺：feel（感覺）等的感官動詞，之後可接原形動詞、現在分詞或過去分詞的用法：
   1) 表事實時，用原形動詞作補語，譯成「……了」。
   2) 表進行狀態時，用現在分詞作補語，譯成「正在……」。
   3) 表被動狀態時，要用過去分詞作補語，譯成「被……」。
2. 根據上述，空格前有感官動詞 see，及 her son 作其受詞，因此空格應置原形動詞 depart，故 (A) 項應為正選。

📖 Part 6　Text Completion

Questions 22-25 refer to the following e-mail.

To: John Stafford
From: Julia Raymond, U-Drive Customer Service
Date: June 11
Subject: U-Drive Rental Confirmation

Dear Mr. Stafford:

This e-mail is to confirm your car rental. The pick-up date is June 28, and the return date is July 5. Please remember ------- two forms of ID and two credit
                                           22.
cards to the clerk at check-in. Also, please make sure to return the vehicle by 5 PM, ------- you may be charged a late fee. You must refill the tank prior to
        23.
returning the car to avoid refueling charges.

Finally, I'd like to invite you to join our U-Drive VIP Club. -------. Contact any
                                                              24.
U-Drive agent for ------- information. Thanks for driving with U-Drive!
                    25.

Sincerely,

Julia Raymond
Customer Service

---

22 至 25 題請看以下電子郵件。

收件者：約翰・斯塔福德
寄件者：自駕客服部茱麗亞・雷蒙德
日　　期：六月十一日
主　　旨：自駕汽車租賃確認

親愛的斯塔福德先生：

本電子郵件旨在確認您的汽車租賃事宜。您的取車日期為六月二十八日，歸還日期是七月五日。您在辦理報到手續時，請記得<u>出示</u>兩種身分證件及兩張信用卡給店員。此外，請確保您於下午五點前還車，<u>否則</u>可能會被收取逾時費用。在還車前您也必須將油箱加滿，不然就得支付加油費。

最後，我想邀請您加入自駕貴賓俱樂部。<u>會員享有不限里程的使用權益</u>。請向任何一位自駕專員聯繫以獲取<u>更多</u>資訊。再次感謝您選擇自駕的服務！

客服部
茱麗亞・雷蒙德　　敬上

251

Chapter 13 Reading Test

A 22

(A) to show　　　(B) showing　　　(C) by showing　　　(D) and show

理由

1. 動詞 remember（記得）之後可接不定詞及動名詞作受詞，惟語意不同，分述如下：
   remember to V　　記得要……
   remember + V-ing　　記得曾經……
   Remember to specify your size when placing an order for clothes.
   訂購衣服時記得要詳細說明你的尺寸。
   Do you remember switching the lights off before we left?
   你記得我們出來之前已經把燈關了嗎？

2. 空格前有動詞 remember，根據上述，得知僅 (A) 及 (B) 項可選，惟 (A) 項置入空格後符合語意，故應為正選。

C 23

(A) so　　　(B) and　　　(C) or　　　(D) if

理由

1. 空格前有完整子句 "please make sure to return the vehicle by 5 PM"（請確保您於下午五點前還車），空格後有另一完整子句 "you may be charged a late fee"（您可能會被收取逾時費用）得知空格應置連接詞，以連接兩個子句。

2. (A) **so** [so] *conj.* 所以
   I got up early, so I was able to catch the first train.
   我早起，所以我能搭上第一班火車。
   (B) **and** [ənd / ænd] *conj.* 和，及，與，並
   Sweep and mop the floor.
   把地板掃和拖一下。
   (C) **or** [ɔr] *conj.* 否則
   Study hard, or you won't pass the exam.
   用功唸書，否則你無法通過考試。
   (D) **if** [ɪf] *conj.* 如果
   If the weather is fine tomorrow, we'll go on a picnic.
   如果明天天氣好的話，我們會去野餐。

3. 根據語意，(C) 項應為正選。

D 24

(A) We have actually been in business for 20 years.
(B) All our vehicles are serviced regularly.
(C) Our customer service department is here to help you.
(D) Members are entitled to unlimited mileage.

> 理由
1. (A) 實際上我們營業已有二十年了。
   (B) 我們所有的車輛都會定期檢修。
   (C) 我們的客服部門在此為您服務。
   (D) 會員享有不限里程的使用權益。
2. 空格前的句子為 "I'd like to invite you to join our U-Drive VIP Club." （我想邀請您加入自駕貴賓俱樂部。），而 (D) 項的句子提及 Members（會員）及其可享有的權益，補述前一句提及的 U-Drive VIP Club（自駕貴賓俱樂部），且 (D) 項句子置入空格後與前後文形成關聯，故應為正選。

CH 13

C **25**

(A) far (B) much far (C) further (D) furthest

> 理由
1. 空格後有名詞 information（資訊），得知空格應置形容詞以修飾該名詞。
2. (A) **far** [fɑr] *a.* 遙遠的
   We can walk to the MRT station. It isn't far from here.
   我們可以走到捷運站。那邊離這裡不遠。
   (C) **further** [ˋfɝðɚ] *a.* 更多的，更進一步的
   Further consideration is necessary before we carry out this plan.
   在我們實施這項計畫前，必須再三考慮。
   (D) **furthest** [ˋfɝðɪst] *a.* 最遠的 & *adv.* 最遠地
3. 根據上述，僅 (C) 項合乎語意及文法，故應為正選。

🔍 重要單字片語

1. **refill** [ˌriˋfɪl] *vt.* 再裝滿 & [ˋriˌfɪl] *n.* （飲料）續杯；補充包
   The waiter refilled Jason's glass with water.
   服務生把傑森玻璃杯中的水再倒滿。
2. **prior** [ˋpraɪɚ] *a.* 在前的；優先的
   prior to... 在……之前
   Make sure you have the report ready prior to the meeting.
   務必確定你在會議之前會把報告準備好。
3. **entitle** [ɪnˋtaɪtl] *vt.* 使有權利
   entitle sb to V 使某人有權從事……
   This ticket doesn't entitle you to travel business class.
   你拿這張票不能坐商務艙。
4. **mileage** [ˋmaɪlɪdʒ] *n.* 里程數
5. **service** [ˋsɝvɪs] *vt.* （機器、車輛等）保養維修
   The car is being serviced this week and won't be ready until Friday.
   車子本週在保養，星期五前不會好。

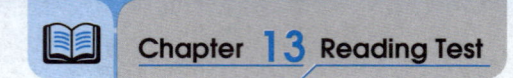

Chapter 13 Reading Test

Part 7 Reading Comprehension

Questions 26-30 refer to the following email, news report, and email.

To:	Rama Patel
From:	Emily Watkins
Date:	June 15
Subject:	Itinerary

Dear Mr. Patel:

Thank you for booking your flight through Adventure Travel.

The total cost of your tickets is US$2,300 including insurance:

Los Angeles-Seattle	$275
Seattle-New York	$550
New York-Miami	$425
Miami-Los Angeles	$1,050

I have attached a brochure from U.S. customs since you will be carrying botanical samples from overseas. Please follow the directions as the Department of Homeland Security is particularly strict on such matters.

The travel insurance policy covers flight cancellations and medical care. If you have any questions, please do not hesitate to call me at Adventure Travel. My number is 310-945-2083, extension 45.

Thank you for your business.

Ms. Emily Watkins

Airports Remain in Chaos

By Simon Phillips

(July 12) — Hurricane Patricia continues to disrupt airports around the country. All arrivals and departures have been canceled as winds exceeding 150 mph continue to batter the east of the country. Gina Washington, a spokesperson for the National Aviation Authority, issued a statement apologizing for the chaos that ensued when airports closed without warning at 9 PM on Friday evening. "The Weather Bureau upgraded the hurricane from Category 2 to Category 4, necessitating the abrupt closures," she said. "The safety of passengers and airline crew is of the utmost importance." The Federal Government will subsidize passengers affected by the cancellations with a $100 voucher. First class passengers can stay at any Highlife Hotel, business class passengers at any Harrington's Hotel, premium economy class at any Family Inn, and economy class at any budget hotel.

To:	Rama Patel
From:	Elisa Thurston
Date:	August 9
Subject:	Travel insurance claim

Dear Mr. Patel,

This e-mail is to confirm that your claim for travel insurance has been approved. A payment of US$1,050 has been credited into your West County Bank — account #332459990. However, we regret to inform you that your claim for accommodation at Harrington's Hotel was rejected as your policy does not cover such expenses. To confirm receipt of the payment, please reply to this e-mail with "confirmed" as the subject.

Yours sincerely,

Elisa Thurston

Chapter 13　Reading Test

26 至 30 題請看以下電子郵件及新聞報導。

收件者：　拉瑪・帕托
寄件者：　艾蜜莉・華特金斯
日　期：　六月十五日
主　旨：　行程表

帕托先生您好：

感謝您透過奇遇旅遊預訂機票。

您的機票（含保險）總金額為 2,300 美元：

洛杉磯 —— 西雅圖　　275 美元
西雅圖 —— 紐約　　　550 美元
紐約 —— 邁阿密　　　425 美元
邁阿密 —— 洛杉磯　　1,050 美元

因為您將會從國外攜帶植物樣本入境，所以我附寄美國海關出版的手冊給您。由於國土安全部對這類事情格外嚴格，因此請遵照手冊裡的指示。

本旅行保險承保的範圍為班機遭取消以及醫療照護的費用。如果您有任何疑問，請隨時打電話來奇遇旅遊找我。我的電話號碼是 310-945-2083，分機 45。

謝謝您的惠顧。

艾蜜莉・華特金斯女士

機場還是一片混亂

賽門・菲利普斯　報導

七月十二日電 —— 派翠西亞颶風持續打亂全國的機場作業。當它以每小時超過一百五十英里的風速持續重創我國東部時，所有起飛及降落的航班都被取消了。國家航空局發言人吉娜・華盛頓發表聲明，對星期五晚上九點無預警關閉機場所造成的混亂道歉。她說：「氣象局把該颶風的等級從二級升到四級，所以才會突然需要關閉機場。乘客及機組員的安全第一。」聯邦政府將會發一百美元的津貼給因為關閉機場而受到影響的乘客。頭等艙的乘客可去住昇活飯店，商務艙的乘客可去住哈林頓飯店，豪華經濟艙的乘客可去住家庭旅店，而經濟艙的乘客就住任一廉價旅館。

收件者： 拉瑪・帕托
寄件者： 艾莉莎・瑟斯頓
日　期： 八月九日
主　旨： 旅行保險索賠

帕托先生您好：

這封電子郵件是要來跟您確認您申請的旅遊保險理賠已被核准了。1,050 美元的理賠金已匯入您帳號 332459990 的西郡銀行帳戶。然而，我很抱歉要告知您對哈林頓飯店住宿費的理賠申請並未被核准，因為您的保險單並未承保這類費用。為了確認您確實有收到理賠金，請以主旨為「確認」的電子郵件回信給我。

艾莉莎・瑟斯頓　　敬上

CH 13

D 26

In what industry does Mr. Patel most likely work?
(A) Freight
(B) Insurance
(C) Travel
(D) Agriculture

帕托先生最有可能從事哪個行業？
(A) 貨運業
(B) 保險業
(C) 旅遊業
(D) 農業

理由

根據第一封電子郵件第三段第一句 "I have attached a brochure from U.S. customs since you will be carrying botanical samples from overseas."（因為您將會從國外攜帶植物樣本入境，所以我附寄美國海關出版的手冊給您。）得知，(D) 項應為正選。

C 27

In the first e-mail, the word "matters" in paragraph 3, line 3, is closest in meaning to
(A) results
(B) inspections
(C) situations
(D) positions

第一封電子郵件第三段第三行 matters 這個字意思最接近
(A) 結果
(B) 檢驗
(C) 情況
(D) 位置

理由

根據第一封電子郵件第三段第二句 "Please follow the directions as the Department of Homeland Security is particularly strict on such matters."（由於國土安全部對這類事情格外嚴格，因此請遵照手冊裡的指示。）得知，(C) 項應為正選。

Chapter 13 Reading Test

D **28**

Which one of Mr. Patel's flights was canceled?
(A) Los Angeles-Seattle
(B) Seattle-New York
(C) New York-Miami
(D) Miami-Los Angeles

帕托先生的哪一班飛機被取消了？
(A) 洛杉磯 —— 西雅圖
(B) 西雅圖 —— 紐約
(C) 紐約 —— 邁阿密
(D) 邁阿密 —— 洛杉磯

> 理由
>
> 根據第二封電子郵件第一、二句 "This e-mail is to confirm that your claim for travel insurance has been approved. A payment of US$1,050 has been credited into your West County Bank — account #332459990."（這封電子郵件是要來跟您確認您申請的旅遊保險理賠已被核准了。1,050 美元的理賠金已匯入您帳號 332459990 的西郡銀行帳戶。）以及第一封電子郵件第二段最後一行 "Miami-Los Angeles　　$1,050"（邁阿密 —— 洛杉磯　1,050 美元）得知，(D) 項應為正選。

B **29**

What class of ticket did Mr. Patel most likely purchase?
(A) First class
(B) Business class
(C) Premium economy class
(D) Economy class

帕托先生最有可能是買了什麼艙等的機票？
(A) 頭等艙
(B) 商務艙
(C) 豪華經濟艙
(D) 經濟艙

> 理由
>
> 根據第二封電子郵件第三句 "However, we regret to inform you that your claim for accommodation at Harrington's Hotel was rejected as your policy does not cover such expenses."（然而，我很抱歉要告知您對哈林頓飯店住宿費的理賠申請並未被核准，因為您的保險單並未承保這類費用。）以及新聞報導最後一句 "First class passengers can stay at any Highlife Hotel, business class passengers at any Harrington's Hotel, premium economy class at any Family Inn, and economy class at any budget hotel."（頭等艙的乘客可去住昇活飯店，商務艙的乘客可去住哈林頓飯店，豪華經濟艙的乘客可去住家庭旅店，而經濟艙的乘客就住任一廉價旅館。）得知，(B) 項應為正選。

A **30**

What is Mr. Patel asked to do?
(A) Acknowledge a payment
(B) Redeem a voucher
(C) Keep a receipt
(D) Return a call

帕托先生被要求做什麼事？
(A) 確認收到一筆款項
(B) 兌現代金券
(C) 保留發票
(D) 回一通電話

258

> **理由**
>
> 根據第二封電子郵件第四句 "To confirm receipt of the payment, please reply to this e-mail with 'confirmed' as the subject."（為了確認您確實有收到理賠金，請以主旨為「確認」的電子郵件回信給我。）得知，(A) 項應為正選。

重要單字片語

1. **adventure** [əd'vɛntʃɚ] *n.* 冒險；奇遇
   Peter often tells us of his many adventures in China.
   彼得常告訴我們他在中國的許多冒險經歷。

2. **botanical** [bə'tænɪkl] *a.* 植物（學）的
   a botanical garden　　植物園
   Several new botanical lotions hit the market this season and started a new trend.
   幾種新的植物性乳液於本季上市，也帶動新的風潮。

3. **homeland** ['hom,lænd] *n.* 祖國；故鄉

4. **an insurance policy**　　保險單

5. **cover** ['kʌvɚ] *vt.* 承保，涵蓋；覆蓋；掩飾 & *n.* 蓋子；掩蓋物；封面；掩護
   All employees are covered under the insurance plan.
   這項保險計畫涵蓋了所有的員工。

6. **hurricane** ['hɝɪ,ken] *n.* 颶風

7. **disrupt** [dɪs'rʌpt] *vt.* 擾亂；使混亂
   The protesters disrupted the politician's speech.
   那些抗議者擾亂該政治人物的演說。

8. **exceed** [ɪk'sid] *vt.* 超過
   Make sure our expenditure on research doesn't exceed our budget.
   要確實做到我們的研究開銷不得超過預算。

9. **mph**　　英里 / 小時；每小時英里數 (= miles per hour)

10. **batter** ['bætɚ] *vt.* & *vi.* 連續猛擊 & *n.* （棒球）打擊手

11. **aviation** [,evɪ'eʃən] *n.* 航空；航空工業
    My friend has a career in aviation as a pilot for China Airlines.
    我朋友任職航空業，擔任華航機師。

12. **issue / make / give a statement**
    發表（書面）聲明 / 作出陳述
    I'd like to issue / make / give a statement to all of you.
    本人想向諸位發表一份聲明。

13. **ensue** [ɪn'su] *vi.* 接著發生；因而產生；繼而發生
    A fire broke out in the building, and unfortunately, an explosion ensued.
    那棟大樓發生火災，不幸的是，接著還發生爆炸。

14. **bureau** ['bjʊro] *n.* （政府機構的）局；處
    the Central Weather Bureau
    中央氣象局

15. **category** ['kætə,gɔrɪ] *n.* 種類；範疇

16. **necessitate** [nə'sɛsə,tet] *vt.* 使成為必要；需要
    The manager's proposal will necessitate hiring more people.
    經理的提案會使僱用更多人員成為必要。

17. **abrupt** [ə'brʌpt] *a.* 突然的；唐突的

18. **closure** ['kloʒɚ] *n.* 關閉；倒閉；終止

19. **federal** ['fɛdərəl] *a.* 聯邦的
    the Federal Government of the United States　　（美國）聯邦政府

20. **subsidize** ['sʌbsə,daɪz] *vt.* 補貼；補助；資助

21. **premium** ['primɪəm] *a.* 高級的

22. **county** ['kauntɪ] *n.* 郡；縣
    It is said that a new university will be established in the county.
    據說一所新的大學將要設在此郡內。

23. **reply to...**　　回覆……
    Have you replied to Jimmy's letter yet?
    你回了吉米的信沒有？

24. **redeem** [rɪ'dim] *vt.* 將……兌取現金；兌換

NOTES

國家圖書館出版品預行編目（CIP）資料

NEW TOEIC 多益 13 大情境全拆解：單字‧
聽力‧閱讀一書搞定！解析本 / 賴世雄作. --
初版. -- 臺北市：常春藤數位出版股份有限公司,
2025.07　面；　公分. --（常春藤 TOEIC 多益
系列；TC13-2）
ISBN 978-626-7225-96-7（平裝）
1. CST：多益測驗
805.1895　　　　　　　　　　　　114008247

**填讀者問卷
送熊贈點**

常春藤 TOEIC 多益系列【TC13-2】
NEW TOEIC 多益 13 大情境全拆解：單字‧聽力‧閱讀一書搞定！－解析本

總 編 審	賴世雄
終　 審	梁民康
編輯小組	常春藤中外編輯群
排版設計	王玥琦‧林桂旭‧王穎緁
封面設計	林桂旭
錄　 音	林政偉
播音老師	Leah Zimmermann‧Michael Tennant‧Justine Lear
法律顧問	北辰著作權事務所蕭雄淋律師
出 版 者	常春藤數位出版股份有限公司
地　 址	臺北市忠孝西路一段 33 號 5 樓
電　 話	(02) 2331-7600
傳　 真	(02) 2381-0918
網　 址	www.ivy.com.tw
電子信箱	service@ivy.com.tw
郵政劃撥	50463568
戶　 名	常春藤數位出版股份有限公司
定　 價	699 元（2 書）
出版日期	2025 年 7 月　初版／一刷

©常春藤數位出版股份有限公司 (2025) All rights reserved.　Y000071-3592

本書之封面、內文、編排等之著作財產權歸常春藤數位出版股份有限公司所有。未經本公司書面同意，請勿翻印、轉載或為一切著作權法上利用行為，否則依法追究。

如有缺頁、裝訂錯誤或破損，請寄回本公司更換。　【版權所有　翻印必究】
服務時間：週一至週五 9：00～17：00（國定假日公休，若有其他異動，依官網公告為主）

NEW TOEIC
多益 13 大情境 全拆解
單字・聽力・閱讀一書搞定！ 學習本

TOEIC is a registered trademark of Educational Testing Service (ETS).
This publication is not affiliated with, endorsed, or approved by ETS.

Preface 序

　　Test of English for International Communication (TOEIC)「多益測驗」是以國際職場為情境的全球性英語測驗，施測於 160 個以上的國家。多益測驗分數反映受試者在職場環境中以英語溝通的能力，企業招募員工和升遷考核便經常參考測驗成績，可見其權威程度獲得高度認可。

　　多益測驗自 2018 年 3 月起更新題型後，更著重英語溝通上的實用性與整合資訊的能力。為了讓考生戰勝多益全新制，我帶領常春藤優秀的團隊編纂了這本《NEW TOEIC 多益 13 大情境全拆解：單字‧聽力‧閱讀一書搞定！》，完整囊括多益官方公布的十三項必考商業場景：企業發展、外出用餐、娛樂、財務預算、一般商業、健康、房屋／企業財產、製造業、辦公室、人事、採購、技術領域、旅遊。每一單元精選出該情境會遇到的重要單字及相關補充，並且在每單元後附上該情境的仿真迷你模擬練習題，讓讀者快速掌握必備字彙，提升聽力與閱讀的理解力。此外，本書最後另附上兩回全新撰寫的完整模擬試題，試題內容完全仿真，每題皆有詳盡解析與重點單字及其搭配詞用法，以便讀者測試學習成效、熟習考試重點。相信本書可以幫助諸位讀者在嚴苛的多益戰場中勇奪高分！

本書架構與使用說明

本書將 ETS 官方頒訂的十三種商業情境分別分為十三章（企業發展、外出用餐、娛樂、財務預算、一般商業、健康、房屋/企業財產、製造業、辦公室、人事、採購、技術領域、旅遊）：

1. 首先，你可以學習到該情境的精選字彙，每章皆列出 25 個。

重要的用法都列在這邊喔！除了有最常用的片語、搭配詞外，還會介紹用字的正確性等等相關知識。

Chapter 01　Corporate Development　企業發展

1　research [ˈrisɝtʃ] *n.* 研究（不可數）& [rɪˈsɝtʃ] *vt. & vi.* 研究

carry out / conduct / do research into / on...
對……進行研究
research into...
對……進行研究

▶ Scientists carried out extensive research into the causes of H1N1.
科學家對 H1N1 新流感的成因進行大量研究。
▶ Scientists are researching into possible cures for AIDS.
科學家正研究可能治癒愛滋病的療法。

2　equipment [ɪˈkwɪpmənt] *n.* 器材（集合名詞，不可數）

a piece of equipment　一件器材
some / a lot of equipment　一些/很多器材

▶ We need to upgrade our office equipment to improve efficiency.
我們需要升級辦公室設備以提升效率。

3　feature [ˈfitʃɚ] *n.* 特色 & *vt.* 具有

▶ One of the features of this car is that it is solar-powered.
這輛車的特色之一就是太陽能驅動。
▶ The latest model of the smartphone features an AI assistant.
這智慧手機的最新款具有人工智慧助理功能。

4　launch [lɔntʃ] *vt. & n.* 展開（活動）、發表（新作品、新產品）

launch a campaign to V
展開一項活動以……

▶ We've just launched a campaign to promote our new product.
我們剛展開促銷新產品的宣傳活動。

5　viable [ˈvaɪəbl] *a.* 可行的，可實施的

似 workable *a.* 可行的
　 feasible *a.* 可行的
反 unviable *a.* 不可行的

▶ While this proposal sounds great, it is not financially viable.
這個提案聽起來蠻好的，但在財務上行不通。

在了解補充用法後，這邊條列出實際的例句，讓你的觀念更加立體化。

除了用法外，還會有以下的體例喔：

衍 = 衍生字
補 = 補充相關要點
反 = 反義字
比 = 比較相關用字
似 = 意思近似的字詞

2. 在學習完精選字彙後，接著就可以透過單元測驗檢視學習成果，並且透過反覆練習來加深印象喔！單元測驗從聽力測驗到閱讀理解，七種題型都有練習到，讓你掌握正式考試的出題方向。

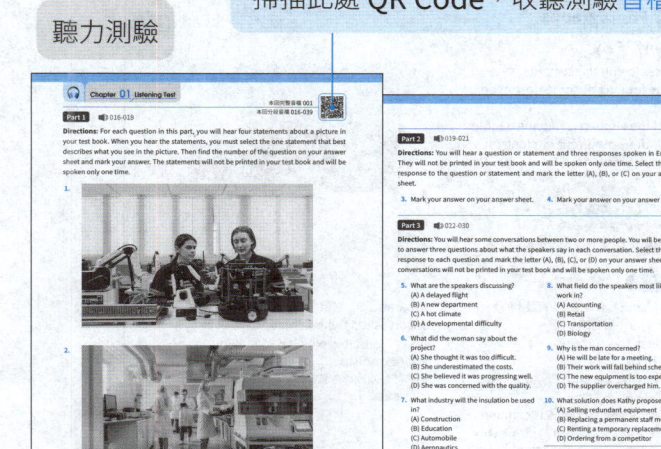

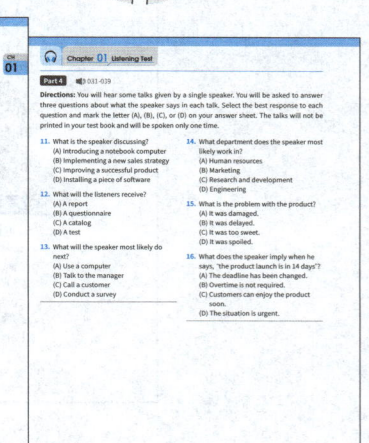

掃描此處 QR Code，收聽測驗音檔！

聽力測驗

閱讀理解

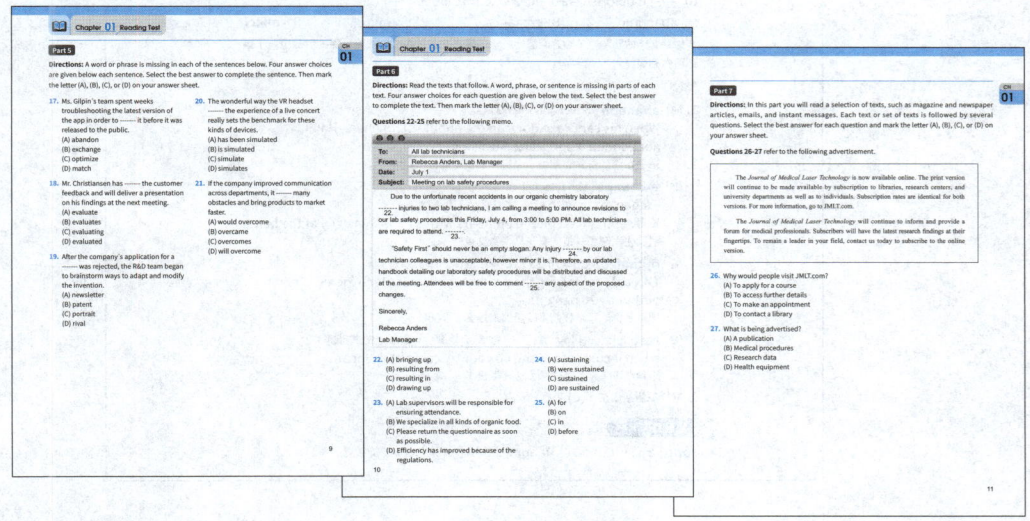

前面學習到的字彙都有實際運用到測驗內，讓你加深印象，活學活用！

3. 做完單元測驗後,馬上利用解析本訂正答案,並且檢視你所忽略的要點!

聽力測驗

Chapter 01 Listening Test

Part 1 Photographs

B 1 ◀) 017 [✦]

(A) They're closing the curtains.
(B) They're looking at some prototype devices.
(C) One of the women is moving a table.
(D) One of the women is switching on a huge machine.

(A) 他們正把窗簾拉上。
(B) 他們正看著某些裝置的原型機。
(C) 其中一個女的正在搬桌子。
(D) 其中一個女的正打開某大型機器的開關。

重要單字片語

1. **curtain** [ˈkɝtn̩] n. 窗簾;(舞臺上的)布幕 & vt. 給⋯⋯裝窗簾
   open / close the curtains
   拉開 / 拉上窗簾
   curtain sth off / curtain off sth
   用簾子遮住某物
   Part of the meeting room was curtained off, but the employees were unsure why.
   員工們不知道為何部分的會議室被簾子遮住了。

2. **look at...** 注視⋯⋯;檢查⋯⋯
   Jason asked the mechanic to look at his car's engine, which was making strange noises.
   傑森請修車師傅檢查他的汽車引擎,它發出異常的聲音。

閱讀理解

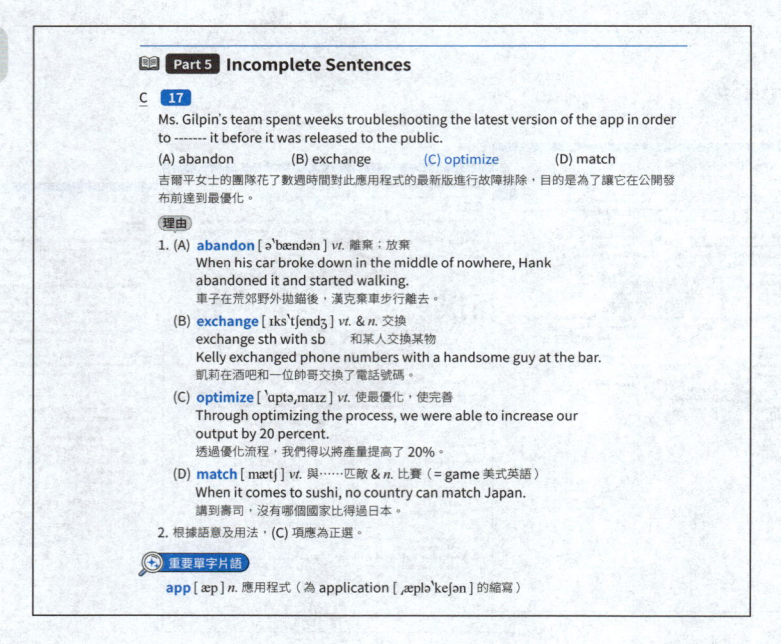

Part 5 Incomplete Sentences

C 17

Ms. Gilpin's team spent weeks troubleshooting the latest version of the app in order to -------- it before it was released to the public.
(A) abandon   (B) exchange   (C) optimize   (D) match

吉爾平女士的團隊花了數週時間對此應用程式的最新版本進行故障排除,目的是為了讓它在公開發布前達到最優化。

理由

1. (A) **abandon** [əˈbændən] vt. 離棄;放棄
   When his car broke down in the middle of nowhere, Hank abandoned it and started walking.
   車子在荒郊野外拋錨後,漢克棄車步行離去。

   (B) **exchange** [ɪksˈtʃendʒ] vt. & n. 交換
   exchange sth with sb 和某人交換某物
   Kelly exchanged phone numbers with a handsome guy at the bar.
   凱莉在酒吧和一位帥哥交換了電話號碼。

   (C) **optimize** [ˈɑptəˌmaɪz] vt. 使最優化,使完善
   Through optimizing the process, we were able to increase our output by 20 percent.
   透過優化流程,我們得以將產量提高了 20%。

   (D) **match** [mætʃ] vt. 與⋯⋯匹敵 & n. 比賽(= game 美式英語)
   When it comes to sushi, no country can match Japan.
   講到壽司,沒有哪個國家比得過日本。

2. 根據語意及用法,(C) 項應為正選。

重要單字片語

app [æp] n. 應用程式(為 application [ˌæpləˈkeʃən] 的縮寫)

4. 最後，利用本書附上的兩回完整測驗，實際模擬正式的考試。在進行測驗時，中間不要休息，因為實際考試不只測試英語能力，還考驗你的專注力以及耐力喔！

兩回完整測驗的詳解可掃描 [QR] 下載運用。

NEW TOEIC 模擬測驗 TEST 01

Part 1	Photographs	照片描述
Part 2	Question-Response	應答問題
Part 3	Conversations	簡短對話
Part 4	Talks	簡短獨白
Part 5	Incomplete Sentences	句子填空
Part 6	Text Completion	段落填空
Part 7	Single Passages	單篇閱讀
	Multiple Passages	多篇閱讀

NEW TOEIC 模擬測驗 TEST 02

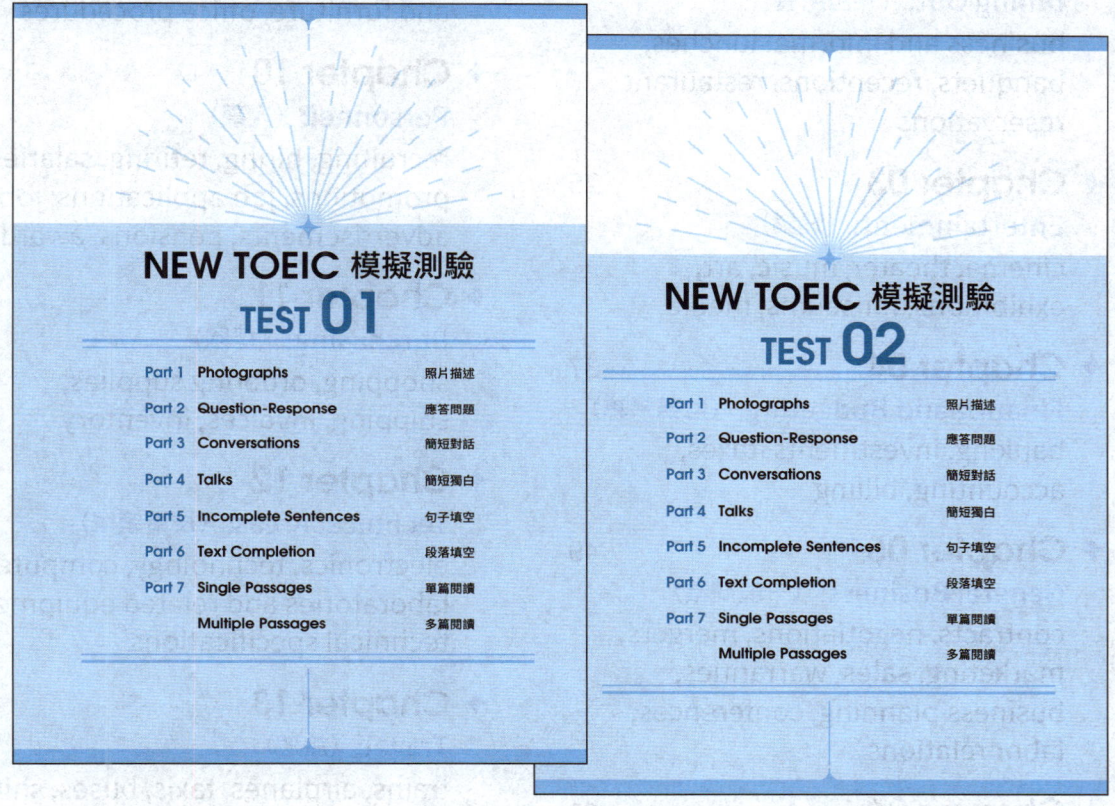

Part 1	Photographs	照片描述
Part 2	Question-Response	應答問題
Part 3	Conversations	簡短對話
Part 4	Talks	簡短獨白
Part 5	Incomplete Sentences	句子填空
Part 6	Text Completion	段落填空
Part 7	Single Passages	單篇閱讀
	Multiple Passages	多篇閱讀

5. 另外，我們特別邀請資深的 Bernice 老師分享準備多益考試的經驗與考試的作答技巧！

CONTENTS 目錄

✦ **Chapter 01** 2
Corporate Development:（企業發展）
research, product development

✦ **Chapter 02** 13
Dining Out:（外出用餐）
business and informal lunches, banquets, receptions, restaurant reservations

✦ **Chapter 03** 25
Entertainment:（娛樂）
cinema, theater, music, art, exhibitions, museums, media

✦ **Chapter 04** 37
Finance and Budgeting:（財務預算）
banking, investments, taxes, accounting, billing

✦ **Chapter 05** 49
General Business:（一般商業）
contracts, negotiations, mergers, marketing, sales, warranties, business planning, conferences, labor relations

✦ **Chapter 06** 61
Health:（健康）
medical insurance, visiting doctors, dentists, clinics, hospitals

✦ **Chapter 07** 73
Housing / Corporate Property:
（房屋／企業財產）
construction, specifications, buying and renting, electric and gas services

✦ **Chapter 08** 85
Manufacturing:（製造業）
assembly lines, plant management, quality control

✦ **Chapter 09** 97
Offices:（辦公室）
board meetings, committees, letters, memoranda, telephone, fax and e-mail messages, office equipment and furniture, office procedures

✦ **Chapter 10** 111
Personnel:（人事）
recruiting, hiring, retiring, salaries, promotions, job applications, job advertisements, pensions, awards

✦ **Chapter 11** 123
Purchasing:（採購）
shopping, ordering supplies, shipping, invoices, inventory

✦ **Chapter 12** 137
Technical Areas:（技術領域）
electronics, technology, computers, laboratories and related equipment, technical specifications

✦ **Chapter 13** 149
Travel:（旅遊）
trains, airplanes, taxis, buses, ships, ferries, tickets, schedules, station and airport announcements, car rentals, hotels, reservations, delays and cancellations

✦ **NEW TOEIC 模擬測驗 Test 01** 163

✦ **NEW TOEIC 模擬測驗 Test 02** 209

✦ 作答卡 257

全書音檔+壓縮檔+完整
模擬試題解析 PDF ▶

NEW TOEIC
13 大情境必備單字 &
單元測驗

Chapter 01 Corporate Development 企業發展

1. research ['rɪsɜtʃ] n. 研究 (不可數) & [rɪ'sɜtʃ] vt. & vi. 研究

carry out / conduct / do research into / on...
對……進行研究
research into...
對……進行研究

▶ Scientists carried out extensive research into the causes of H1N1.
科學家對 H1N1 新流感的成因進行大量研究。

▶ Scientists are researching into possible cures for AIDS.
科學家正研究可能治癒愛滋病的療法。

2. equipment [ɪ'kwɪpmənt] n. 器材（集合名詞，不可數）

a piece of equipment 一件器材
some / a lot of equipment 一些/很多器材

▶ We need to upgrade our office equipment to improve efficiency.
我們需要升級辦公室設備以提升效率。

3. feature ['fitʃɚ] n. 特色 & vt. 具有

▶ One of the features of this car is that it is solar-powered.
這輛車的特色之一就是太陽能驅動。

▶ The latest model of the smartphone features an AI assistant.
這智慧手機的最新款具有人工智慧助理功能。

4. launch [lɔntʃ] vt. & n. 展開（活動），發表（新作品、新產品）

launch a campaign to V
展開一項活動以……

▶ We've just launched a campaign to promote our new product.
我們剛展開促銷新產品的宣傳活動。

5. viable ['vaɪəbḷ] a. 可行的，可實施的

似 **workable** a. 可行的
　 feasible a. 可行的
反 **unviable** a. 不可行的

▶ While this proposal sounds great, it is not financially viable.
這個提案聽起來蠻好的，但在財務上行不通。

6. innovative ['ɪnə,vetɪv] a. 創新的

衍 **innovation** n. 創新
　 innovate vi. 創新
an innovative method / design
創新的方法/設計

▶ The manager introduced an innovative method to cut costs.
經理提出一個降低成本的創新方法。

7 obstacle [ˈɑbstəkl̩] n. 障礙；障礙物（常與介詞 to 並用）

be an obstacle / a barrier to...
對……是個障礙（物）

▶ Laziness is an obstacle to success.
懶惰是成功路上的絆腳石。

8 overcome [ˌovɚˈkʌm] vt. 克服，戰勝（三態為：overcome, overcame [ˌovɚˈkem], overcome）

▶ The staff in this department excels at working as a team to overcome obstacles.
該部門員工擅長團隊合作以克服障礙。

9 evaluate [ɪˈvæljʊˌet] vt. 評估

衍 evaluation n. 評估
似 assess vt. 評估

▶ You have to evaluate the whole situation before making any decisions.
你在做任何決定前應先評估整體情勢。

10 benchmark [ˈbɛntʃˌmɑrk] n. 水準點，基點 & vt. 以……為基點

set a benchmark 定為基點
benchmark against... 以……為基點

▶ We are confident that the product currently under development will set a benchmark for smart devices.
我們有自信目前在開發的產品將成為智慧裝置的基準。

▶ The success of all future product launches should be benchmarked against this one.
未來所有產品推出後的效益應以本次的表現當作基準。

11 version [ˈvɝʒən] n. (原物的) 變體版本

比 edition n. （每次印刷的）版本
the English version of the novel
那本小說的英文版
a paperback / hardcover edition
平裝／精裝版

▶ The updated version of the software will be released in February.
這套軟體的更新版本將於二月發行。

12 introduce [ˌɪntrəˈdjus] vt. 推出

衍 introductory a. 介紹的；
首次的（使用或經歷）
introduction n. 引進，推行

▶ The company is scheduled to introduce a new range of products next year.
公司預定於明年推出新系列產品。

13 specialize [ˈspɛʃəˌlaɪz] vi. 專精於；專攻

衍 specialized a. 專門的
specialist n. 專業人員

▶ Our organization specializes in helping children from poor families.
我們的組織專門幫助清寒家庭的孩童。

specialize in...
專攻……；專門從事……

14 simulate [ˈsɪmjəˌlet] vt. 模擬；偽裝

衍 simulated a. 模擬的
simulation n. 模擬

▶ This equipment can simulate conditions in space.
這套設備可以模擬太空中的狀況。

15 feedback [ˈfidˌbæk] n. 回饋，反應（不可數）

provide / receive positive / negative feedback
提供 / 收到正 / 反面回饋

▶ Our company welcomes any feedback from our customers.
本公司歡迎顧客提供的任何回饋。

16 result [rɪˈzʌlt] vi. 導致，造成；由……引起 & n. 結果

反 cause n. 原因
result in... 導致……
result from... 起因於……
as a result of... 由於……

▶ The car accident resulted in the death of five people.
這起車禍造成五人死亡。

▶ Millions of people died as a result of the pandemic.
數百萬人因該大流行病喪命。

17 brainstorm [ˈbrenˌstɔrm] vt. 集思廣益，腦力激盪

衍 brainstorming n. 集思廣益

▶ We need to brainstorm some ideas for our new project.
我們該為新專案腦力激盪一些點子出來。

18 propose [prəˈpoz] vt. 提議

衍 proposal n. 提案
proposed a. 提議的
propose + N/V-ing
提議……
propose sth to sb...
向某人建議某物

▶ John proposed changing the company's logo at the meeting.
約翰在會議上建議改掉公司的商標。

▶ Peter proposed a feasible solution to me.
彼得向我提議一項可行的解決方案。

19 develop [dɪˈvɛləp] vt. 開發 & vt. & vi. 發展；培養

衍 development n. 開發；發展
developed a. 已開發的
develop into sth
發展成為某事物
develop a skill
培養技能

▶ The company has spent $1 million on developing a new product.
公司已砸下一百萬美元在新產品開發之上。

▶ The mistake was ignored and later developed into a major problem.
這錯誤被忽略，後來就演變成一個大問題。

20 prototype [ˈprotəˌtaɪp] n. 雛型，樣本

▶ The engineers developed a prototype first and then refined it into a final product.
工程師先開發出一個雛型，然後再雕琢成最終的產品。

21 improve [ɪmˈpruv] vt. & vi. 改善

衍 improvement n. 改善，進步
improved a. 改良的

improve conditions / efficiency
改善環境 / 效率
improve dramatically
大幅改善

▶ Jerry did a lot to improve conditions for factory workers.
傑瑞努力改善工廠工人的工作環境。

▶ Judy's health has improved dramatically since she went on a new diet.
茱蒂的健康在採用新的飲食法後已大幅改善。

22 troubleshoot [ˈtrʌblˌʃut] vt. 排除故障，檢修；處理難題（三態為：troubleshoot, troubleshot [ˈtrʌblˌʃɑt], troubleshot）

▶ We need to get someone to troubleshoot the Wi-Fi connection.
我們要找人來檢修無線網路的連線問題。

23 optimize [ˈɑptəˌmaɪz] vt. 使優化

衍 optimization n. 優化

▶ The update will optimize the performance of our website.
此次更新將會優化我們網站的表現。

24 patent [ˈpætənt] n. 專利（權）& vt. 取得專利 & a. 專利的

apply for a patent (for...)
申請（……的）專利

▶ Polly applied for a patent for her invention to protect her intellectual property.
波莉為她的發明申請專利以保障她的智財權。

▶ You should patent your new invention as soon as possible.
你應該儘快為你的新發明取得專利。

25 product [ˈprɑdʌkt] n. 產品

衍 productive a. 多產的
production n. 生產
a dairy product   乳製品

▶ We are developing a wide range of skincare products.
我們正在研發多種護膚產品。

Chapter 01 Listening Test

Part 1 🔊 016-018

本回完整音檔 001
本回分段音檔 016-039

Directions: For each question in this part, you will hear four statements about a picture in your test book. When you hear the statements, you must select the one statement that best describes what you see in the picture. Then find the number of the question on your answer sheet and mark your answer. The statements will not be printed in your test book and will be spoken only one time.

1.

2.

Part 2 🔊 019-021

Directions: You will hear a question or statement and three responses spoken in English. They will not be printed in your test book and will be spoken only one time. Select the best response to the question or statement and mark the letter (A), (B), or (C) on your answer sheet.

3. Mark your answer on your answer sheet.
4. Mark your answer on your answer sheet.

Part 3 🔊 022-030

Directions: You will hear some conversations between two or more people. You will be asked to answer three questions about what the speakers say in each conversation. Select the best response to each question and mark the letter (A), (B), (C), or (D) on your answer sheet. The conversations will not be printed in your test book and will be spoken only one time.

5. What are the speakers discussing?
   (A) A delayed flight
   (B) A new department
   (C) A hot climate
   (D) A developmental difficulty

6. What did the woman say about the project?
   (A) She thought it was too difficult.
   (B) She underestimated the costs.
   (C) She believed it was progressing well.
   (D) She was concerned with the quality.

7. What industry will the insulation be used in?
   (A) Construction
   (B) Education
   (C) Automobile
   (D) Aeronautics

8. What field do the speakers most likely work in?
   (A) Accounting
   (B) Retail
   (C) Transportation
   (D) Biology

9. Why is the man concerned?
   (A) He will be late for a meeting.
   (B) Their work will fall behind schedule.
   (C) The new equipment is too expensive.
   (D) The supplier overcharged him.

10. What solution does Kathy propose?
    (A) Selling redundant equipment
    (B) Replacing a permanent staff member
    (C) Renting a temporary replacement
    (D) Ordering from a competitor

Chapter 01 Listening Test

Part 4 📢 031-039

Directions: You will hear some talks given by a single speaker. You will be asked to answer three questions about what the speaker says in each talk. Select the best response to each question and mark the letter (A), (B), (C), or (D) on your answer sheet. The talks will not be printed in your test book and will be spoken only one time.

11. What is the speaker discussing?
    (A) Introducing a notebook computer
    (B) Implementing a new sales strategy
    (C) Improving a successful product
    (D) Installing a piece of software

12. What will the listeners receive?
    (A) A report
    (B) A questionnaire
    (C) A catalog
    (D) A test

13. What will the speaker most likely do next?
    (A) Use a computer
    (B) Talk to the manager
    (C) Call a customer
    (D) Conduct a survey

14. What department does the speaker most likely work in?
    (A) Human resources
    (B) Marketing
    (C) Research and development
    (D) Engineering

15. What is the problem with the product?
    (A) It was damaged.
    (B) It was delayed.
    (C) It was too sweet.
    (D) It was spoiled.

16. What does the speaker imply when he says, "the product launch is in 14 days"?
    (A) The deadline has been changed.
    (B) Overtime is not required.
    (C) Customers can enjoy the product soon.
    (D) The situation is urgent.

Chapter 01 Reading Test

Part 5

Directions: A word or phrase is missing in each of the sentences below. Four answer choices are given below each sentence. Select the best answer to complete the sentence. Then mark the letter (A), (B), (C), or (D) on your answer sheet.

17. Ms. Gilpin's team spent weeks troubleshooting the latest version of the app in order to ------- it before it was released to the public.
    (A) abandon
    (B) exchange
    (C) optimize
    (D) match

18. Mr. Christiansen has ------- the customer feedback and will deliver a presentation on his findings at the next meeting.
    (A) evaluate
    (B) evaluates
    (C) evaluating
    (D) evaluated

19. After the company's application for a ------- was rejected, the R&D team began to brainstorm ways to adapt and modify the invention.
    (A) newsletter
    (B) patent
    (C) portrait
    (D) rival

20. The wonderful way the VR headset ------- the experience of a live concert really sets the benchmark for these kinds of devices.
    (A) has been simulated
    (B) is simulated
    (C) simulate
    (D) simulates

21. If the company improved communication across departments, it ------- many obstacles and bring products to market faster.
    (A) would overcome
    (B) overcame
    (C) overcomes
    (D) will overcome

9

Chapter 01 Reading Test

Part 6

Directions: Read the texts that follow. A word, phrase, or sentence is missing in parts of each text. Four answer choices for each question are given below the text. Select the best answer to complete the text. Then mark the letter (A), (B), (C), or (D) on your answer sheet.

Questions 22-25 refer to the following memo.

To: All lab technicians
From: Rebecca Anders, Lab Manager
Date: July 1
Subject: Meeting on lab safety procedures

   Due to the unfortunate recent accidents in our organic chemistry laboratory ------- injuries to two lab technicians, I am calling a meeting to announce revisions to our lab safety procedures this Friday, July 4, from 3:00 to 5:00 PM. All lab technicians are required to attend. -------.
   22.   23.

   "Safety First" should never be an empty slogan. Any injury ------- by our lab technician colleagues is unacceptable, however minor it is. Therefore, an updated
                                                                24.
handbook detailing our laboratory safety procedures will be distributed and discussed at the meeting. Attendees will be free to comment ------- any aspect of the proposed
                                                                                          25.
changes.

Sincerely,

Rebecca Anders
Lab Manager

---

22. (A) bringing up
    (B) resulting from
    (C) resulting in
    (D) drawing up

23. (A) Lab supervisors will be responsible for ensuring attendance.
    (B) We specialize in all kinds of organic food.
    (C) Please return the questionnaire as soon as possible.
    (D) Efficiency has improved because of the regulations.

24. (A) sustaining
    (B) were sustained
    (C) sustained
    (D) are sustained

25. (A) for
    (B) on
    (C) in
    (D) before

Part 7

Directions: In this part you will read a selection of texts, such as magazine and newspaper articles, emails, and instant messages. Each text or set of texts is followed by several questions. Select the best answer for each question and mark the letter (A), (B), (C), or (D) on your answer sheet.

Questions 26-27 refer to the following advertisement.

The *Journal of Medical Laser Technology* is now available online. The print version will continue to be made available by subscription to libraries, research centers, and university departments as well as to individuals. Subscription rates are identical for both versions. For more information, go to JMLT.com.

The *Journal of Medical Laser Technology* will continue to inform and provide a forum for medical professionals. Subscribers will have the latest research findings at their fingertips. To remain a leader in your field, contact us today to subscribe to the online version.

---

26. Why would people visit JMLT.com?
    (A) To apply for a course
    (B) To access further details
    (C) To make an appointment
    (D) To contact a library

27. What is being advertised?
    (A) A publication
    (B) Medical procedures
    (C) Research data
    (D) Health equipment

Chapter 01 Reading Test

Questions 28-29 refer to the following text-message chain.

Brent Fargo (10:37 AM)
Hey, I just heard back from Jayden at Jay Corp. He thinks our proposal is viable. He wants to meet with us again ASAP!

Judi Walsh (10:38 AM)
Are you serious?! What did you tell him?

Brent Fargo (10:39 AM)
I said we would meet him in his office first thing tomorrow morning. He wants to see the prototype.

Judi Walsh (10:40 AM)
Great. Then we should get together this afternoon — we can put together a brief demonstration and work out exactly what to say.

Brent Fargo (10:41 AM)
I agree. How about I come over to your place at 2:30? I'll bring the prototype.

Judi Walsh (10:41 AM)
OK. I'll see you then.

28. At 10:38 AM, what does Ms. Walsh mean when she writes, "Are you serious"?
    (A) She doesn't believe Mr. Fargo is telling the truth.
    (B) She is excited by what Mr. Fargo wrote.
    (C) She has more important matters to take care of.
    (D) She thinks Mr. Fargo has a serious problem.

29. What does Ms. Walsh indicate they should do?
    (A) Reschedule a meeting
    (B) Contact a client
    (C) Prepare a presentation
    (D) Speak to the manager

Chapter 02 Dining Out 外出用餐

1 serve [sɝv] vt. (餐廳)上菜

衍 serving n. (供一人吃的)一份食物
　　service n. 服務
serve sth to sb　　上某菜給某人
serve sb with sth　上某菜給某人

▶ Meals can be served to you in your room.
餐點能幫您送到您的房間。
▶ We arrived at the hotel and were served with a delicious lunch.
我們抵達飯店，吃了一頓美味午餐。

2 tip [tɪp] vt. 給小費 & n. 小費 (三態為：tip, tipped [tɪpt], tipped)

leave a tip
留下小費

▶ Irene tipped the waiter generously because of his good service.
= Irene left a generous tip for the waiter because of his good service.
服務生服務很好，所以艾琳給了他很多小費。

3 dine [daɪn] vi. 用餐

衍 diner n. 食客
dine with sb　與某人吃飯

▶ My girlfriend and I dined with her parents at a restaurant in town.
我、女友還有她爸媽一起在城裡某餐館吃飯。

4 invite [ɪnˋvaɪt] vt. & [ˋɪnvaɪt] n. 邀請

衍 invitation n. 邀請；請帖，邀請卡
補 RSVP n. & vi. 敬請回覆
invite sb to + 活動 / 地點
邀請某人去某活動 / 地點
invite sb to V
邀某人做……

▶ I was flattered to be invited to attend the Oscars.
我很榮幸受邀出席奧斯卡頒獎典禮。

5 silverware [ˋsɪlvɚˏwɛr] n. (銀器)餐具(集合名詞，不可數)

似 tableware n. 餐具(集合名詞，不可數)
a piece of silverware
一件(銀器)餐具

▶ Before the guests arrived, Anna polished all of the silverware and set the table.
在賓客到達前，安娜將所有餐具擦亮並布置餐桌。

13

6 entrée [ˈɑntre] n. 主菜 (= main dish / main course)

(補) 一般西餐都會有五道菜，並且依以下順序出餐：appetizer（開胃菜）、soup（湯品）、salad（沙拉）、entrée（主菜）、dessert（甜點）

▶ We had spaghetti with shrimp as an entrée.
我們叫的主菜是鮮蝦義大利麵。

7 dressing [ˈdrɛsɪŋ] n. (拌沙拉使用的) 醬料

(似) sauce n.（拌食物用的）醬
seasoning n. 調味料，佐料（鹽、胡椒粉、香料等）
condiment n. 調味品（鹽、胡椒、芥末等）

(補) 以下為常見的沙拉醬：
Thousand Island dressing（千島醬）、Caesar dressing（凱撒醬）、Italian dressing（義大利油醋醬）、ranch dressing（田園醬）、honey mustard dressing（蜂蜜芥末醬）、vinaigrette（油醋醬）、yogurt dressing（優格醬）、tartar sauce（塔塔醬）

▶ I always get Thousand Island dressing when I order a salad.
我點沙拉時總是加千島醬。

8 vegetarian [ˌvɛdʒəˈtɛrɪən] n. (蛋或奶) 素食者 & a. (蛋或奶) 素食的

(比) vegan n. 全素者 & a. 全素的
a vegetarian dish 素菜

▶ The restaurant caters to vegetarians.
這餐廳有素食者可以吃的餐點。

9 charge [tʃɑrdʒ] vt. 索費 & n. 費用

charge (sb) + 錢 + for sth
（向某人）索取某事物的費用
free of charge 免費（= for free）

▶ The restaurant charged us $200 for the bottle of wine.
那瓶酒餐廳向我們收了兩百美元。

▶ Delivery is free of charge.
送貨免運費。

10 bill [bɪl] n. 用餐帳單 (英式英語，= check 美式英語)

pay / settle the bill / check
付帳，買單

▶ David treated us to dinner and paid the bill before we left the restaurant.
大衛請我們吃晚飯，在離開餐廳前付了飯錢。

11 **flavor** [ˈflevɚ] *n.* (食物或飲料的) 味道 & *vt.* 調味

(補) 以下為常見的味道、口感形容詞：
sweet（甜的）、sour / tart（酸的）、bitter（苦的）、salty（鹹的）、savory（鮮味的）、aromatic（香氣四溢的）、rich（濃郁的）、tender（嫩的）、refreshing（爽口的）、greasy（油膩的）、fishy（腥的）、dry（乾澀的）

add / give flavor (to sth)
（為……）增添風味

▸ The tomatoes give extra flavor to the sauce.
蕃茄使這種醬汁風味更佳。

▸ The chef is well known for using exotic spices to flavor the food he makes.
那位主廚是出了名的擅用異國香料來給他做的菜調味。

12 **recipe** [ˈrɛsəpɪ] *n.* 食譜（與介詞 for 並用）

a recipe for...
料理……的食譜；導致……發生的因素

▸ Can you give me the recipe for the onion soup?
你能不能給我這道洋蔥湯的食譜？

13 **cuisine** [kwɪˈzin] *n.* 料理

▸ This restaurant offers authentic Japanese cuisine.
此餐廳供應正宗日本料理。

14 **informal** [ɪnˈfɔrml̩] *a.* 非正式的

(衍) informally *adv.* 非正式地
(反) formal *a.* 正式的

an informal meeting / visit
非正式的會議 / 拜訪

▸ The delegates of the two countries met for informal talks.
兩國代表見面進行非正式會談。

15 **signature** [ˈsɪgnətʃɚ] *a.* 為 (某人) 所特有的

the chef's signature dish
廚師的招牌菜

▸ The slow-cooked beef in chocolate sauce is that restaurant's signature dish.
這家餐廳的招牌菜是巧克力醬燉牛肉。

16 **patronize** [ˈpetrəˌnaɪz] *vt.* 經常光顧

(衍) patron *n.* 常客
patronage *n.* 惠顧，光顧

▸ The well-known restaurant is patronized by tourists and locals alike.
遊客與在地人都愛去光顧那家知名餐廳。

17. guest [gɛst] n. 客人；特別來賓，特邀嘉賓

比 host n. 男主人
　　hostess n. 女主人
guest of honor　　主客

▶ A good host always makes his guests feel at home.
好的主人總讓客人有賓至如歸的感覺。

18. toast [tost] n. 敬酒 & vt. 為……乾杯

make / have / propose a toast to sb
向某人舉杯致敬
toast A with B　　用 B 來向 A 敬酒

▶ I would like to make a toast to the bride and groom.
我想要向新郎新娘敬酒。

▶ We toasted the guests with red wine.
我們以紅酒向來賓敬酒。

19. social [ˈsoʃəl] a. 社會的；社交的

衍 socialize vi. 與人社交
　　society n. 社會
a social issue / life
社會議題 / 社交生活
social media / network
社群媒體 / 網路

▶ Aaron is so busy with work that he has hardly any social life.
艾朗工作太忙了，因此幾乎沒什麼社交生活。

20. cater [ˈketɚ] vt. & vi. 承辦酒席

衍 caterer n. 宴席承辦商，外燴公司
　　catering n. 承辦酒席服務
cater for...
承辦……的宴席，為……提供飲食

▶ Who catered your son's wedding?
令郎婚宴的酒席是哪家辦的？

▶ This company caters for private parties and small public events.
這家公司承辦私人派對和小型公開活動的外燴。

21. attire [əˈtaɪr] n. 衣著，服裝 (集合名詞，不可數)

衍 attired a. 穿著……衣服的
business attire　　商業衣著

▶ A gray suit is standard attire for men in that company.
灰色西裝是該公司男職員的標準衣著。

22. etiquette [ˈɛtɪkɛt] n. 禮儀 (不可數)

phone / social etiquette
電話 / 社交禮儀

▶ People who lack phone etiquette speak loudly on their phones in public places.
缺乏電話禮儀的人會在公共場所大聲講電話。

23 organize [ˈɔrgəˌnaɪz] vt. 籌備

衍 organizer n. 籌辦者
organize a meeting / party / trip
籌備會議 / 派對 / 旅行

▶ Kevin volunteered to organize the meeting.
凱文自願籌備這次會議。

24 banquet [ˈbæŋkwɪt] n. 宴會

a state / wedding / charity banquet
國宴 / 婚宴 / 慈善餐宴
hold a banquet 舉辦宴會

▶ Tonight we will have a state banquet in honor of the visiting president.
今晚我們將為來訪的總統舉辦國宴向他致敬。

▶ Ross promised to hold a great banquet for all his employees.
羅斯允諾為他的員工舉辦盛大的宴會。

25 venue [ˈvɛnju] n. 聚會地點（如音樂廳、體育賽場、會場）

比 avenue n. 街，道
revenue n.（公司）收益

▶ Please note the change of venue for this event.
請注意這場活動易地進行。

Chapter 02 Listening Test

Part 1 🔊 040-042

Directions: For each question in this part, you will hear four statements about a picture in your test book. When you hear the statements, you must select the one statement that best describes what you see in the picture. Then find the number of the question on your answer sheet and mark your answer. The statements will not be printed in your test book and will be spoken only one time.

本回完整音檔 002
本回分段音檔 040-063

1.

2.

18

Part 2 🔊 043-045

Directions: You will hear a question or statement and three responses spoken in English. They will not be printed in your test book and will be spoken only one time. Select the best response to the question or statement and mark the letter (A), (B), or (C) on your answer sheet.

3. Mark your answer on your answer sheet.

4. Mark your answer on your answer sheet.

Part 3 🔊 046-054

Directions: You will hear some conversations between two or more people. You will be asked to answer three questions about what the speakers say in each conversation. Select the best response to each question and mark the letter (A), (B), (C), or (D) on your answer sheet. The conversations will not be printed in your test book and will be spoken only one time.

5. Who are the main guests of the event?
   (A) Departing workers
   (B) Important clients
   (C) New employees
   (D) Workers' families

6. What does the man say about the event?
   (A) He hopes the food will be of good quality.
   (B) He wants it to be relaxed and casual.
   (C) He is unable to attend it himself.
   (D) He hopes there will be enough seats.

7. What does the woman indicate that she understands?
   (A) The invitations will be sent out very soon.
   (B) The party will be held during work hours.
   (C) The organizational challenges will be great.
   (D) The event's dress code will not be formal.

8. What does the woman say about herself?
   (A) She is a regular customer of the restaurant.
   (B) She is a committed vegetarian.
   (C) She is a part owner of the restaurant.
   (D) She is a good friend of the chef's.

9. Why does the man not order the signature dish?
   (A) He doesn't feel very hungry.
   (B) He thinks it is too expensive.
   (C) He does not really like seafood.
   (D) He wants what the woman ordered.

10. What does the man imply when he says, "tomorrow is a holiday"?
    (A) They must close the deal today.
    (B) They can enjoy some alcohol.
    (C) They must finish the meal quickly.
    (D) They don't have time for further talks.

Chapter 02 Listening Test

Part 4 🔊 055-063

Directions: You will hear some talks given by a single speaker. You will be asked to answer three questions about what the speaker says in each talk. Select the best response to each question and mark the letter (A), (B), (C), or (D) on your answer sheet. The talks will not be printed in your test book and will be spoken only one time.

11. What is the speaker mainly talking about?
    (A) The decline in table manners
    (B) The rules when dining formally
    (C) The difficulty of hosting an event
    (D) The dishes on offer at a banquet

12. According to the speaker, when can people start eating?
    (A) When others leave the table
    (B) When everyone raises their glasses
    (C) When the host has given a speech
    (D) When everyone is served their meal

13. What point does the speaker make about silverware?
    (A) It should be wiped with a napkin.
    (B) It should be taken from the left side first.
    (C) It should be used in a certain order.
    (D) It should be put on the plate after eating.

Rosebud Restaurant	
Set Menu	Price per Person
A	$29.99
B	$39.99
C	$49.99
D	$59.99

14. What has been changed for the party?
    (A) The date of the booking
    (B) The number of attendees
    (C) The start time of the event
    (D) The location of the restaurant

15. Look at the graphic. Which set menu will the speaker most likely choose?
    (A) Set Menu A
    (B) Set Menu B
    (C) Set Menu C
    (D) Set Menu D

16. What does the speaker ask the restaurant to confirm?
    (A) The total price for the booking
    (B) The availability of certain wines
    (C) The closing time on June 4th
    (D) The ability to meet dietary needs

Chapter 02 Reading Test

Part 5

Directions: A word or phrase is missing in each of the sentences below. Four answer choices are given below each sentence. Select the best answer to complete the sentence. Then mark the letter (A), (B), (C), or (D) on your answer sheet.

17. After the guests have finished ------- at the industry event, there will be ample opportunities for networking.
    (A) dine
    (B) dines
    (C) dining
    (D) dined

18. The Ocean View Restaurant, which provides a wide variety of both meat and vegetarian entrées, ------- a charming dining location.
    (A) being
    (B) be
    (C) is
    (D) are

19. The restaurant used to ------- only Japanese cuisine, but it has now branched out into Korean and Taiwanese dishes as well.
    (A) serving
    (B) served
    (C) serves
    (D) serve

20. We kindly request that you ------- by January 31 to confirm your attendance at the party.
    (A) garnish
    (B) RSVP
    (C) charge
    (D) treat

21. The celebrity couple has chosen the Bartle Hall Country Hotel as the venue ------- they will hold their wedding reception.
    (A) where
    (B) which
    (C) who
    (D) what

Chapter 02 Reading Test

Part 6

Directions: Read the texts that follow. A word, phrase, or sentence is missing in parts of each text. Four answer choices for each question are given below the text. Select the best answer to complete the text. Then mark the letter (A), (B), (C), or (D) on your answer sheet.

Questions 22-25 refer to the following memo.

From: HR Manager
To: All Employees
Subject: Cafeteria Improvements

Based on feedback from the recent staff surveys, the company is excited to announce improvements to the office cafeteria. This will primarily focus on ------- the menu. 22. Beginning on July 1, a wider range of ------- will be served to better reflect our 23. diverse workforce. -------, there will be more dishes with spicier flavors and many 24. more vegetarian options available. -------. However, we remain committed to keeping 25. our prices competitive. We appreciate your feedback and hope you enjoy the new dining experience.

---

22. (A) expansively
    (B) expansive
    (C) expanding
    (D) expansion

23. (A) ballrooms
    (B) gourmets
    (C) cuisines
    (D) allergies

24. (A) By contrast
    (B) For example
    (C) Instead
    (D) Frankly

25. (A) The renovations are due to be completed by the first week in August.
    (B) Employees voted this the tastiest dish on the cafeteria's updated menu.
    (C) The surveys are completely anonymous, and the results will be compiled by an external company.
    (D) You will notice a slight price increase to pay for the development of the new menu.

Part 7

Directions: In this part you will read a selection of texts, such as magazine and newspaper articles, emails, and instant messages. Each text or set of texts is followed by several questions. Select the best answer for each question and mark the letter (A), (B), (C), or (D) on your answer sheet.

Questions 26-27 refer to the following letter.

Chinese Women's League of San Francisco
217 Baker Street
San Francisco, CA 94117
Tel: (415) 822-4719   Fax: (415) 822-8818

To Whom It May Concern: August 28

Double Star Restaurant is one of the Chinese Women's League's favorite eateries. On September 28, we will hold our 30th anniversary celebration at our headquarters. Your restaurant has been chosen as one of the possible caterers for the banquet. Would you kindly answer the following questions?

- Do you have enough seating for a 90-person party?
- Some of our members are senior citizens with disabilities. Therefore, we require additional staff to help. We are willing to spend extra for this special service.
- We prefer Chinese cuisine. Could we meet to discuss the party's menu?
- Finally, we require an estimate of the cost.

Please respond via e-mail at kayeliao@hotwire.com.

Sincerely yours,

Kaye Liao

Kaye Liao, President
Chinese Women's League of San Francisco

---

26. What is the main purpose of the letter?
(A) To request information on a catering service
(B) To invite people to attend an annual celebration
(C) To compliment a restaurant
(D) To confirm a restaurant's invoice

27. What special request is made of Double Star Restaurant?
(A) That the banquet be held near the entrance
(B) That extra service personnel be available
(C) That a 30th anniversary discount be given
(D) That vegetarian food be provided

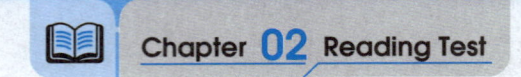

Chapter 02 Reading Test

Questions 28-30 refer to the following Web page.

Restaurate
Rate and review restaurants

| About Us | Sign Up or Log In | Read a Review | Write a Review |

For over eight years, Restaurate members' reviews and ratings have helped restaurant-goers choose the best meals at the best restaurants. — [1] —. From a humble start, operating from a laptop in Wellington, our site has grown to be an essential first stop for every serious foodie or casual diner planning to eat at an unfamiliar restaurant — no matter where they are on the planet. — [2] —. At the same time, Restaurate has become a hero for restaurants aiming for excellence and the enemy of poor-quality restaurants everywhere. — [3] —.

Restaurate is a free service. We do not charge subscription fees, sell products, or sell advertising. We do, however, pay full-time moderators. So, we ask those members that benefit from the site, and have the means, to donate through our tips page. — [4] —.

---

28. What do Restaurate members do?
    (A) Train people to cook
    (B) Comment on restaurants
    (C) Work at restaurants
    (D) Replace recipes

29. What is mentioned about Restaurate?
    (A) It advertises extensively.
    (B) It moderates reviews.
    (C) It is only available in Wellington.
    (D) It provides cooking advice.

30. In which of the positions marked [1], [2], [3], and [4] does the following sentence best belong?

    "The funds raised keep our site up and running, and 100% independent!"

    (A) [1]
    (B) [2]
    (C) [3]
    (D) [4]

Chapter 03 Entertainment 娛樂

1 audience [ˈɔdɪəns] n. 觀眾，聽眾

- 補 audience 為集合名詞，表一個群體，後面可接單數或複數動詞；若指一個以上的觀眾或聽眾群時，可加 s，後面接複數動詞。
- 比 spectator n.（比賽、活動等的）觀眾

an audience of 100　一百位觀眾
a large / small audience
一大群 / 小群觀眾或聽眾

- The professor is giving a lecture to an audience of 100 college students.
  教授正對一百位大學生進行專題演講。
- When the concert came to an end, the audience gave the singers a standing ovation.
  演唱會結束時，觀眾為這些歌手起立鼓掌。
  * give sb a standing ovation
    為某人起立鼓掌

2 popular [ˈpɑpjələ] a. 流行的，普及的；受歡迎的

- 衍 popularity n. 流行；名望

popular music　流行樂
be popular with / among...
受……的歡迎

- Hip-hop and R&B are popular with young people.
  嘻哈和 R&B 音樂受到年輕人歡迎。

3 publish [ˈpʌblɪʃ] vt. 出版

- 衍 publisher n. 出版人；出版社

publish a book / magazine
出版書籍 / 雜誌

- Our company publishes various kinds of books.
  我們公司出版多種書籍。

4 release [rɪˈlis] vt. 發行（唱片、電影、書等）& n. 發行（不可數）；新發行物（唱片、電影、書等）（可數）

- A new version of the game will be released in late July.
  這款遊戲的新版將在七月底發行。
- The rock band's first album is due for release later this month.
  這支搖滾樂團的第一張專輯預定於本月下旬發行。

5 crowded [ˈkraʊdɪd] a. 擁擠的

- 衍 crowd n. 一群人

be crowded / packed with...
擠滿了……

- The market is crowded with tourists on weekends.
  那個市集每逢週末都擠滿遊客。

25

6 entertain [ˌɛntɚˈten] vt. 款待；逗樂

衍 entertainer n. 藝人
entertainment n. 娛樂，樂趣（不可數）；娛樂節目（可數）
entertain sb with sth
以……逗樂某人

▶ My wife always does the cooking when we entertain friends.
我們招待朋友時都是由我老婆下廚。

▶ The stand-up comedian entertained the audience with hilarious jokes.
這個單口相聲演員用爆笑的笑話娛樂聽眾。

7 performance [pɚˈfɔrməns] n. 表演

衍 perform vi. 演出
performer n. 表演者
put on a performance 演出

▶ The pianist put on an excellent performance at the concert last night.
那位鋼琴家昨晚在音樂會中貢獻了精湛的演出。

8 festival [ˈfɛstəvl̩] n. 節慶；慶祝活動

衍 festive a. 節慶的，歡樂的
a music / film festival 音樂 / 電影節

▶ The film festival was a real treat for movie buffs.
那次電影節讓影癡大呼過癮。

9 review [rɪˈvju] vt. 寫（關於書籍、戲劇、電影等的）評論 & n. 影評；書評

good / bad / mixed reviews
正面的 / 負面的 / 兩極的評論

▶ Henry only goes to see movies that are reviewed favorably.
亨利只去看獲得正面評論的電影。

▶ The band's new album had mixed reviews on the internet.
該樂團新專輯的網路風評相當兩極。

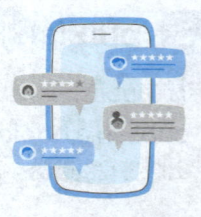

10 criticize [ˈkrɪtəˌsaɪz] vt. 批評

衍 criticism n. 批評
critic n. 評論家
be strongly / heavily criticized
受到強烈的批評
criticize sb for sth 以某事批評某人

▶ The new law has been strongly criticized by teachers.
這條新的法律受到教師們的強烈批評。

▶ The government was criticized for not taking immediate action to deal with the financial crisis.
政府被批評並未即刻採取行動處理那場金融危機。

11 exhibit [ɪɡˈzɪbɪt] n. 展覽會；展覽品 & vt. 展示，展覽

衍 exhibitor n. 參展商
exhibition n. 展覽
be on exhibit 展出
= be on display

▶ These photographs will be on exhibit until the end of the month.
這些相片將供展出至本月底為止。

▶ The artist's well-known paintings have been exhibited around the world over the past ten years.
那位藝術家的知名畫作過去十年來一直在世界各地展覽。

12 series [ˈsɪriz] n. 一系列，連續；(電視 / 廣播) 系列節目 (單複數同形)

a series of + 複數名詞　一系列的……	▶ There is a series of talk shows after the TV program.
a comedy series　喜劇連續劇	這個電視節目播完後有一連串的脫口秀。

13 collection [kəˈlɛkʃən] n. (常指同類的) 收藏品

衍 collect vt. 收集
　　collector n. 收藏家
a collection of...　……的收藏品
an art collection　藝術收藏

▶ Sammy has a large collection of antique swords.
山米收藏了大量的古劍。
＊antique [ænˈtik] a. 古董的

▶ That painting comes from a billionaire's private art collection.
那幅畫來自於某位億萬富翁的私家藝術珍藏。

14 renowned [rɪˈnaʊnd] a. 聞名的

同 famous a. 有名的
　　well-known a. 知名的
be renowned for...　因……而出名
be renowned as...
以……的身分而聞名

▶ The diplomat is renowned for his negotiation skills.
這名外交官以談判技巧高超聞名。

▶ George is renowned as a top pastry chef.
喬治是個著名的頂級糕餅師傅。

15 content [ˈkɑntɛnt] n. (書、演講的) 內容 (不可數)；內容物 (恆用複數)；目錄 (恆用複數) & [kənˈtɛnt] a. 滿意的

反 discontent a. 不滿意的 & n. 不滿意
　　(不可數)
be content with...　對……感到滿意

▶ I don't like the content of this book.
我不喜歡這本書的內容。

▶ Alex was content with his performance in the speech contest.
艾力克斯對他在演講比賽的表現很滿意。

16 stage [stedʒ] n. 舞臺

on stage　在舞臺上表演 (此意 stage 之前不置定冠詞 the)

▶ The actress was on stage for most of the play.
那位女演員幾乎整齣劇都沒有下場。

17 applause [əˈplɔz] n. 鼓掌；喝采 (不可數)

衍 applaud vi. & vt. (為某人) 鼓掌
a round of applause　一陣掌聲

▶ Give the speaker a big round of applause!
給這位演講者熱烈的掌聲吧！

18 genre [ˈʒɑnrə] n. 類型，體裁，風格

a literary / music / film genre
文學體裁 / 音樂風格 / 電影類型

▶ Rock is the music genre that Jacob likes the most, but he also enjoys listening to jazz.
搖滾樂是雅各最喜歡的音樂類型，但他也很喜歡聽爵士樂。

19 **instrument** [ˈɪnstrəmənt] *n.* 樂器 (= musical instrument)；儀器

衍 instrumental *n.* 演奏曲 & *a.* 用樂器伴奏的

▶ John's son can play several musical instruments.
約翰的兒子會演奏好幾種樂器。

20 **rehearsal** [rɪˈhɜsl] *n.* 排演，練習

衍 rehearse *vt.* & *vi.* 彩排，排演
a dress rehearsal
（正式演出前的最後一次）彩排

▶ The singer is wearing makeup for the dress rehearsal.
這位歌手正在上妝，準備最後的彩排。

21 **orchestra** [ˈɔrkɪstrə] *n.* 管弦樂團

a symphony orchestra
交響樂團
conduct an orchestra
指揮管弦樂團

▶ The orchestra's superb performance won enthusiastic applause from the audience.
那個管弦樂團的精湛演奏獲得觀眾的熱烈掌聲。

▶ Mr. Green will conduct the orchestra.
格林先生將指揮這支管絃樂團。

22 **premiere** [prɪˈmɪr] *n.* 首映；首演；首播

比 premier *a.* 最重要的 & *n.* 總理，首相

▶ Those bodyguards escorted the superstar from the movie premiere.
那些保鑣護送那名巨星從電影首映會離開。

23 **broadcast** [ˈbrɔdˌkæst] *vt.* 廣播；(電視)播送 (三態同形) & *n.* 廣播節目；電視節目

be broadcast live　被現場直播
a radio / television broadcast
廣播 / 電視節目

▶ The charity concert will be broadcast live tomorrow evening.
那場慈善音樂會將於明晚現場直播。

24 **subscribe** [səbˈskraɪb] *vi.* 訂閱 (與介詞 to 並用)

衍 subscriber *n.* 訂閱人
subscription *n.* 訂閱
subscribe to...　訂閱……

▶ With this coupon, you can subscribe to our magazine for as little as $25 per year.
有了這張優惠券，你每年能以低到二十五美元的價格訂閱本雜誌。

25 **enroll** [ɪnˈrol] *vi.* 註冊；報名

衍 enrollment *n.* 註冊
enroll in...　報名上（某課程）
= sign up for...
= register for...

▶ John enrolled in a course in Japanese at the community college.
約翰報名參加社區大學的日文課程。

Chapter 03 Listening Test

Part 1 🔊 064-066

本回完整音檔 003
本回分段音檔 064-087

Directions: For each question in this part, you will hear four statements about a picture in your test book. When you hear the statements, you must select the one statement that best describes what you see in the picture. Then find the number of the question on your answer sheet and mark your answer. The statements will not be printed in your test book and will be spoken only one time.

1.

Nazri Yaakub / Shutterstock.com

2.

29

Chapter 03 Listening Test

Part 2 🔊 067-069

Directions: You will hear a question or statement and three responses spoken in English. They will not be printed in your test book and will be spoken only one time. Select the best response to the question or statement and mark the letter (A), (B), or (C) on your answer sheet.

3. Mark your answer on your answer sheet.

4. Mark your answer on your answer sheet.

Part 3 🔊 070-078

Directions: You will hear some conversations between two or more people. You will be asked to answer three questions about what the speakers say in each conversation. Select the best response to each question and mark the letter (A), (B), (C), or (D) on your answer sheet. The conversations will not be printed in your test book and will be spoken only one time.

5. Who most likely is the woman?
   (A) An artist
   (B) An art dealer
   (C) A museum guide
   (D) A headhunter

6. What does the woman say about Jodie Dion?
   (A) She works at a local art center.
   (B) She has planned an exhibition.
   (C) She is a well-known art critic.
   (D) She is an award-winning artist.

7. What does the woman offer to do?
   (A) Present other artworks
   (B) Paint a picture
   (C) Provide a replacement
   (D) Contact the artist

Tivoli Movie Theater
Vintage Movie Festival

GENRE	MOVIE
Science fiction	War of the Planets
Bio-drama	Becoming Benjamin
Comedy	Randy Gupta's Road Trip
Horror	Monster Convention

8. What is the woman invited to do?
   (A) Have a picnic
   (B) Review a movie
   (C) Go to the movies
   (D) Perform in a play

9. Look at the graphic. Which movie will the man and woman most likely see?
   (A) *War of the Planets*
   (B) *Becoming Benjamin*
   (C) *Randy Gupta's Road Trip*
   (D) *Monster Convention*

10. What does the man suggest doing before the movie?
    (A) Downloading a schedule
    (B) Speaking to a coworker
    (C) Dining at a restaurant
    (D) Purchasing snacks

Part 4 🔊 079-087

Directions: You will hear some talks given by a single speaker. You will be asked to answer three questions about what the speaker says in each talk. Select the best response to each question and mark the letter (A), (B), (C), or (D) on your answer sheet. The talks will not be printed in your test book and will be spoken only one time.

11. Who is the speaker talking about?
    (A) An actor
    (B) A TV star
    (C) A director
    (D) A producer

12. According to the speaker, how has Mr. Almond achieved his success?
    (A) By performing in several movies
    (B) By winning numerous awards
    (C) By owning many large houses
    (D) By hosting famous shows

13. What does the speaker say will happen next Thursday?
    (A) An audition
    (B) An interview
    (C) A premiere
    (D) A lecture

14. What does the speaker thank the listener for?
    (A) Attending an opening ceremony
    (B) Donating money
    (C) Purchasing artwork
    (D) Writing an e-mail

15. What does the speaker imply when he says, "it is a Travon Santos exhibition"?
    (A) Travon Santos is a renowned artist.
    (B) It's Travon Santos's first exhibition.
    (C) He forgot to mention the artist's name.
    (D) He accidentally mispronounced the artist's name.

16. What does the speaker ask the listener to do?
    (A) Accept a gift
    (B) Join a contest
    (C) Make a speech
    (D) Arrange an exhibition

Chapter 03 Reading Test

Part 5

Directions: A word or phrase is missing in each of the sentences below. Four answer choices are given below each sentence. Select the best answer to complete the sentence. Then mark the letter (A), (B), (C), or (D) on your answer sheet.

17. Many viewers ------- the final episode of the series for failing to satisfactorily resolve the show's central mystery.
    (A) critic
    (B) criticized
    (C) criticism
    (D) critical

18. ------- by the audience's positive reaction to their music, the rock band played well past midnight at the soccer stadium.
    (A) Delight
    (B) Delights
    (C) Delighted
    (D) Delighting

19. The publishing company ------- a best seller since Mike Borton's book, *The Nightfall*, was released five years ago.
    (A) will not publish
    (B) did not publish
    (C) does not publish
    (D) has not published

20. After the fantastic performance by the renowned dance company, the audience erupted in -------.
    (A) be applauded
    (B) applauded
    (C) applaud
    (D) applause

21. Those who present a valid identification card will receive a five percent discount on tickets to all theater -------.
    (A) performances
    (B) perform
    (C) performs
    (D) performer

Part 6

Directions: Read the texts that follow. A word, phrase, or sentence is missing in parts of each text. Four answer choices for each question are given below the text. Select the best answer to complete the text. Then mark the letter (A), (B), (C), or (D) on your answer sheet.

Questions 22-25 refer to the following review.

Millie Simons has ------- an amazing voice that her phenomenal success comes
                        22.
as no surprise. And last night, she put on a concert that no one who attended will soon forget. From the flawless lights and sound to the creative staging, the concert easily ------- everyone's expectations.
        23.

Supported on stage by eight energetic dancers and four backup vocalists, Millie Simons performed all of her hits, and her banter with fans was like a conversation with friends. However, the biggest highlight was near the end of the show when the dancers and backup vocalists left the stage, and Ms. Simons performed the national anthem ------- her own. -------.
  24.   25.

---

22. (A) very
    (B) so
    (C) such
    (D) much

23. (A) went
    (B) arrived
    (C) disappointed
    (D) exceeded

24. (A) in
    (B) for
    (C) on
    (D) at

25. (A) Her solo performance received a standing ovation.
    (B) The audience waited patiently for the show to start.
    (C) Several VIPs also took to the stage.
    (D) Tickets were soon sold out before the show.

Chapter 03 Reading Test

Part 7

Directions: In this part you will read a selection of texts, such as magazine and newspaper articles, emails, and instant messages. Each text or set of texts is followed by several questions. Select the best answer for each question and mark the letter (A), (B), (C), or (D) on your answer sheet.

Questions 26-27 refer to the following email.

From: backstage@national-theater.com
To: backstage.subscribers@national-theater.com
Subject: "The Grandest Showman" Week 1

Hi!

You are receiving this email because you subscribed to the National Theater's backstage newsletter for the forthcoming production of *The Grandest Showman*. The first week of rehearsals is complete, and the cast are having a ball learning the songs. For a sneak peek at rehearsals and interviews with some of the cast members, click here. And, if you would like early access to tickets and other exclusive features, don't forget to enroll in the National Theater's VIP Membership Scheme.

See you again next week!

Malika Idrissi
Audience Engagement Coordinator
National Theater

---

26. What is indicated about *The Grandest Showman*?
 (A) It has just commenced rehearsals.
 (B) It will premiere next weekend.
 (C) It has received rave reviews.
 (D) It will contain no music.

27. According to the email, how would someone buy tickets early?
 (A) Line up at the box office
 (B) Reply to the email
 (C) Click on a link
 (D) Join a special program

Questions 28-31 refer to the following online chat discussion.

Bastien Fournier   10:05 a.m.

Good morning, Mireille. I just want to double-check that you thanked the supplier for the free concert ticket they gave you.

Mireille Dubois   10:06 a.m.

Morning, Bastien. Yes, I emailed them to say I appreciated their generosity. The concert was amazing, by the way. The band only use traditionally made instruments from their home country, so the sound they create is very special. They entertained us for over three hours!

Celeste Bianchi   10:08 a.m.

Yeah, they're renowned for their long shows.

Mireille Dubois   10:09 a.m.

Were you at the performance, too, Celeste?

Celeste Bianchi   10:10 a.m.

I wish! But I love listening to their live albums.

Bastien Fournier   10:11 a.m.

It sounds like I missed out! I hope I get to see them when they tour here next time.

Mireille Dubois   10:12 a.m.

In the meantime, Bastien, watch their encore online. They performed a song they haven't played live in ten years, and the video's gone viral.

Bastien Fournier   10:14 a.m.

Thanks, I'll check it out!

28. Who gave Ms. Dubois the concert ticket?
    (A) Her manager
    (B) Her best friend
    (C) A supplier
    (D) A colleague

29. What is suggested about the band?
    (A) They never perform abroad.
    (B) They play unique instruments.
    (C) They formed three years ago.
    (D) They typically play short concerts.

30. What does Ms. Bianchi tell Ms. Dubois?
    (A) She has no interest in the band.
    (B) She has seen the band live before.
    (C) She wishes the shows could be longer.
    (D) She wishes she could have gone to the concert.

31. At 10:14 a.m., what does Mr. Fournier most likely mean when he writes, "I'll check it out"?
    (A) He will listen to a band's new album.
    (B) He will read Ms. Dubois' email.
    (C) He will watch a video on the internet.
    (D) He will edit Ms. Dubois' report.

Chapter 04 Finance and Budgeting 財務預算

1 economic [ˌikəˈnɑmɪk / ˌɛkəˈnɑmɪk] a. 經濟的

衍 economical a. 經濟實惠的；節省的
economy n. 經濟
economic growth / development / reform　經濟成長 / 發展 / 改革

▶ According to the report, economic growth is sustainable in that country.
根據這份報告，該國家的經濟會持續成長。

2 tax [tæks] n. 稅 & vt. 課稅

income taxes　所得稅

▶ Only a minority of the voters approved of the tax increase.
只有少數選民贊成加稅。

▶ The government's declared aim was to tax the rich.
政府表明的目標是要課有錢人的稅。

3 invest [ɪnˈvɛst] vt. & vi. 投資

衍 investment n. 投資
investor n. 投資者
invest (A) in B　（以 A）投資在 B 裡

▶ We've invested a large amount of time and money in this project.
我們已在這項專案上投入了大量時間和金錢。

4 fund [fʌnd] vt. 提供資金 & n. 專款

be privately / jointly funded
私人地（民間地）/ 共同提供資金
raise funds　募資

▶ The nationwide project is privately funded by several local companies.
這項全國性的專案由許多當地公司提供民間資金。

▶ The hospital is raising funds to buy new medical equipment.
那家醫院正在募款以購買新的醫療器材。

5 profitable [ˈprɑfɪtəbḷ] a. 有利潤的

衍 profit vt. 有利於 & vi. 獲益 & n. 盈利
a highly profitable business
很賺錢的行業

▶ Buying and selling used cars is a highly profitable business.
中古車買賣是個很賺錢的行業。

6 budget [ˈbʌdʒɪt] n. 預算 & vt. & vi. (將時間、金錢) 精打細算

衍 budgetary a. 預算的
within / over budget
在預算內 / 超出預算
on a tight budget　　預算有限的
an annual budget　　年度預算

▶ The project was completed within budget.
那個專案在預算之內完成。

▶ We'll be able to afford the trip if we budget carefully.
我們若能精打細算，就能負擔這次的旅行。

7 finance [ˈfaɪnæns] n. 財政，金融 (不可數)；財力，財務狀況 (恆用複數) & [faɪˈnæns] vt. 資助

衍 financial a. 財務的；金融的
the finance department
財務部門

▶ The chairman presided over a meeting of the finance committee.
該主席主持了財務委員會的一場會議。

▶ The big project is financed by a private enterprise.
這個大案子是由一家民間企業所資助。

8 statistic [stəˈtɪstɪk] n. 統計資料，統計數據 (常用複數)

衍 statistics n. 統計學（不可數）
one statistic　　一項統計數字
two / many statistics
兩項 / 許多統計數字

▶ Those statistics show that 30% of factories shut down last year.
那些統計數字顯示 30% 的工廠去年關門大吉。

9 estimate [ˈɛstəˌmet] vt. 估算 & [ˈɛstəmɪt] n. 估計

be estimated to be / have / cost
估計為 / 有 / 花費……

▶ The deal is estimated to be worth around $2 million.
這筆交易估計價值兩百萬美元左右。

▶ It is not easy to estimate how many people have been affected by the food poisoning incident.
很難估計有多少人在這次食物中毒事件中受到影響。

10 outstanding [aʊtˈstændɪŋ] a. 未支付的

an outstanding balance
未結清的餘款

▶ I rarely have an outstanding balance on my credit card.
我的信用卡很少有未結清的餘款。

11 return [rɪˈtɜn] n. 利潤 & vt. 產生 (利潤或損失)

the return on...　　……的利潤
the returns from...
從……獲得的利潤

▶ You can get the best return on investment in AI technology nowadays.
現今你可以從投資 AI 技術中得到最大的利潤。

▶ Stockbrokers are trying to improve the returns from their stock portfolios.
股票經紀人正設法改善他們股票投資組合的報酬。

▶ Henry's investment has returned a handsome profit.
亨利的投資已經有不錯的利潤。

12 **dividend** [ˋdɪvə,dɛnd] *n.* 股息，紅利

(補) dividend 是指公司的盈餘發配給股東們的「股息」；而 bonus 則是指在固定薪水以外的「特別獎金」，通常是對員工在工作上特殊的表現給予的獎勵。

▶ Dividends will be sent to shareholders by the end of February.
股息將於二月底以前發放給各股東。

13 **inflation** [ɪnˋfleʃən] *n.* 通貨膨脹（不可數）

(衍) inflate *vt.* 使通貨膨脹
(反) deflation *n.* 通貨緊縮（不可數）

▶ Increased costs are one of the main causes of inflation.
成本上揚是通貨膨脹的主因之一。

14 **index** [ˋɪndɛks] *n.* 指數

the cost-of-living index
生活費用指數

▶ The Dow Jones index fell 10 points today.
道瓊指數今天下跌了十點。

15 **analyze** [ˋænḷ,aɪz] *vt.* 分析

(衍) analysis *n.* 分析
analyst *n.* 分析師
analytical *a.* 分析的
gather and analyze data
搜集和分析資料

▶ The job involves gathering and analyzing marketing data.
這項工作包括搜集和分析行銷數據。

▶ The stem cell samples will be analyzed by the lab department.
幹細胞檢體將由實驗部門來分析。

16 **revenue** [ˋrɛvə,n(j)u] *n.* (政府、企業) 收益，利潤，營收

tax revenues　稅收

▶ Tax revenues rose by 5.8% last year.
去年的稅收增加 5.8%。

17 **reduce** [rɪˋdjus] *vt.* 降低，減少

(衍) reduction *n.* 降低

▶ Lena reduced the amount of salt in her daily diet.
莉娜減少了她在日常飲食中的鹽分攝取量。

18 loan [lon] *n.* 貸款 & *vt.* 將……借給 (= lend)

take out / pay off a loan
辦理 / 付清貸款
    loan sb sth   借某人某物
= **lend sb sth**

▶ Frank and Clara took out a loan to buy a new house.
法蘭克和克拉拉辦理貸款買了棟新房子。

▶ Can you loan me 50 dollars?
你可以借我五十美元嗎?

19 owe [o] *vt.* 欠(債)

(補) 本字不用於進行式
    owe sb + 金額   欠某人若干金額
= **owe + 金額 + to sb**

▶ I believe you still owe me some money.
我認為你還欠我一些錢。

20 credit [ˈkrɛdɪt] *n.* 信譽(不可數);信用;賒帳

(衍) **creditor** *n.* 債權人,貸方
a credit card   信用卡
on credit   賒帳,貸款

▶ We decided to buy a new car on credit.
我們決定貸款買一部新車。

21 interest [ˈɪnt(ə)rɪst] *n.* 利益;(存款或貸款的)利息(不可數);股權,產權

It is in sb's (best) interest to V
做……對某人(最)有利
interest rates   利率

▶ It's in your best interest to invest in the bond market.
投資債券市場對你最為有利。

▶ The interest on the loan is 10% per year.
這筆貸款每年的利息為 10%。

22 withdraw [wɪðˈdrɔ] *vt.* 提(款) (三態為:withdraw, withdrew [wɪðˈdru], withdrawn [wɪðˈdrɔn])

(衍) **withdrawal** *n.* 提款
withdraw money   提款

▶ You can withdraw money from the account at any time.
你可以隨時從帳戶中提款。

23 deposit [dɪˈpɑzɪt] *n.* & *vt.* 存款

make a deposit of $500 into...
把五百美元存入……
= **deposit $500 into...**

▶ I'd like to make a deposit of $500 into my savings account.
= I'd like to deposit $500 into my savings account.
我想在儲蓄戶頭存入五百美元。

24 penalty [ˈpɛnḷtɪ] n. 處罰；罰金

衍 penalize vt. 處罰
the penalty for... ……的處罰
incur penalties 遭到罰款

▶ They asked for the maximum penalty for assault to be increased to ten years.
他們要求企圖傷害罪的最高量刑應提高至十年。

▶ Anyone who fails to pay taxes on time will incur financial penalties.
任何人延誤繳稅將被處以罰款。

25 bankruptcy [ˈbæŋkrʌptsɪ] n. 破產

衍 bankrupt vt. 使破產 & a. 破產的
on the edge / verge of bankruptcy
瀕臨破產
file for / declare bankruptcy
申請 / 宣布破產

▶ Because of poor management, the company is on the verge of bankruptcy.
由於管理不善，該公司瀕臨破產的邊緣。

Chapter 04 Listening Test

本回完整音檔 004
本回分段音檔 088-111

Part 1 🔊 088-090

Directions: For each question in this part, you will hear four statements about a picture in your test book. When you hear the statements, you must select the one statement that best describes what you see in the picture. Then find the number of the question on your answer sheet and mark your answer. The statements will not be printed in your test book and will be spoken only one time.

1.

2.

42

Part 2 🔊 091-093

Directions: You will hear a question or statement and three responses spoken in English. They will not be printed in your test book and will be spoken only one time. Select the best response to the question or statement and mark the letter (A), (B), or (C) on your answer sheet.

3. Mark your answer on your answer sheet.
4. Mark your answer on your answer sheet.

Part 3 🔊 094-102

Directions: You will hear some conversations between two or more people. You will be asked to answer three questions about what the speakers say in each conversation. Select the best response to each question and mark the letter (A), (B), (C), or (D) on your answer sheet. The conversations will not be printed in your test book and will be spoken only one time.

5. What are the speakers mainly discussing?
   (A) Broker fees
   (B) Inflation
   (C) Interest rates
   (D) Investment strategies

6. What did the broker suggest the man do?
   (A) Save more money
   (B) Find another broker
   (C) Sell his stocks and bonds
   (D) Vary his investments

7. What does the woman imply about the new strategy?
   (A) It will probably save time.
   (B) It will probably have more risk.
   (C) It will probably be profitable.
   (D) It will probably reduce the service fees.

8. What does Indira point out about the company's revenue?
   (A) It has gone down sharply.
   (B) It has increased significantly.
   (C) It has not been analyzed.
   (D) It has not changed.

9. What has Alyssa noted down as fixed assets?
   (A) Billing systems
   (B) New printing presses
   (C) Brand-new computers
   (D) Book-binding machines

10. What does the man say he will do tomorrow?
    (A) Allocate resources to a department
    (B) Talk about another subject
    (C) Collect a package from a depot
    (D) Read the latest magazine issue

Chapter 04 Listening Test

Part 4 🔊 103-111

Directions: You will hear some talks given by a single speaker. You will be asked to answer three questions about what the speaker says in each talk. Select the best response to each question and mark the letter (A), (B), (C), or (D) on your answer sheet. The talks will not be printed in your test book and will be spoken only one time.

11. What does the speaker want to focus on this year?
    (A) Minimizing tax
    (B) Reducing overheads
    (C) Marketing online
    (D) Purchasing equipment

12. What does the speaker request help with?
    (A) Producing a business plan
    (B) Researching rivals
    (C) Preparing a presentation
    (D) Solving an accounting problem

13. What will the listeners receive by e-mail?
    (A) A budget
    (B) An application form
    (C) An invoice
    (D) A spreadsheet

| Northern Region Economic Forum ||
Speaker	Topic
Ilya Morozov	Cutting the deficit
Kenji Takahashi	How to curb inflation
Sofia Márquez	Investment opportunities
Leila Farouk	Tax system reforms

14. How does the speaker start the announcement?
    (A) By outlining the order of speeches
    (B) By offering his gratitude to a sponsor
    (C) By introducing a keynote speaker
    (D) By mentioning some security concerns

15. Look at the schedule. Whose speech is most eagerly awaited?
    (A) Ilya Morozov
    (B) Kenji Takahashi
    (C) Sofia Márquez
    (D) Leila Farouk

16. What does the speaker remind the listeners?
    (A) That IDs must be worn at all times
    (B) That the minor hall is not accessible
    (C) That lunch will be served at 1:00 p.m.
    (D) That free food and drink is available

Part 5

Directions: A word or phrase is missing in each of the sentences below. Four answer choices are given below each sentence. Select the best answer to complete the sentence. Then mark the letter (A), (B), (C), or (D) on your answer sheet.

17. If you have a single source of income independent of interest or -------, you can fill out form W2EZ.
    (A) divide
    (B) dividends
    (C) divided
    (D) divine

18. You are able to ------- money from your personal savings account using an ATM.
    (A) deduct
    (B) fluctuate
    (C) benefit
    (D) withdraw

19. Please ask the accounting department to chase up the ------- payment from AlphaSource Industries.
    (A) economic
    (B) wealthy
    (C) risky
    (D) outstanding

20. Mr. Kwarteng advised Ms. Scott on the best investment ------- in which to place her money.
    (A) funds
    (B) installments
    (C) hazards
    (D) transactions

21. The national cost-of-living index increased only 1.5% last year, ------- that inflation is now within an acceptable range.
    (A) shows
    (B) showing
    (C) to show
    (D) will show

Chapter 04 Reading Test

Part 6

Directions: Read the texts that follow. A word, phrase, or sentence is missing in parts of each text. Four answer choices for each question are given below the text. Select the best answer to complete the text. Then mark the letter (A), (B), (C), or (D) on your answer sheet.

Questions 22-25 refer to the following memo.

From: Head of Finance
To: All Heads of Department
Subject: Next Year's Budget

For internal distribution only.

As you are aware, the country is experiencing economic challenges. Many businesses are struggling, and we are not immune to these difficulties. We have ------- decided to freeze departmental budgets for the next financial year. Despite this, departments will still be expected to ------- their operational commitments. Please submit proposals outlining how you intend to fund these commitments and if you plan to make cuts. -------. Late submissions may ------- a penalty. For any queries, please contact me or any senior manager on the finance team.

---

22. (A) moreover
(B) although
(C) therefore
(D) even though

23. (A) meet
(B) fail
(C) live
(D) catch

24. (A) I went through the documents myself last night.
(B) We sincerely hope that next year is more profitable.
(C) These proposals are due by the end of next week.
(D) Many other countries are in a similar situation.

25. (A) agree with
(B) result in
(C) give up
(D) glance at

Part 7

Directions: In this part you will read a selection of texts, such as magazine and newspaper articles, emails, and instant messages. Each text or set of texts is followed by several questions. Select the best answer for each question and mark the letter (A), (B), (C), or (D) on your answer sheet.

Questions 26-28 refer to the following document.

Angel Seed Company, Ltd.
Prospectus for Mom's Kitchen

Outline:

Welcome to Angel Seed Company, Ltd. The prospectus you are holding details a retail restaurant chain called Mom's Kitchen. There are currently several Mom's Kitchens throughout Oregon, and the chain is now expanding into other states. We believe that once our proposed funding goal is reached, all participants will achieve returns of at least 20% per annum. If you are interested in this exciting and profitable project after reading this prospectus, please fill out the form on page 17 and return it to us as quickly as possible.

Pages 3-6 show architecture diagrams for the layout of the standard Mom's Kitchen, though actual dimensions may be adjusted according to local conditions. All layouts conform to building, safety, and parking lot codes in the state of Oregon.

Pages 7-11 show more detailed floor plans for the lobby, dining areas, kitchen, restrooms, and parking lots.

Pages 12-16 show the monthly operating costs of each unit. We estimate a maximum number of guests at 120 per location, making each a medium-sized restaurant. We also estimate an entire staff of 20, including servers and chefs. These operating expenses include food and beverage costs, salaries, taxes, and other essential payments that a wise investor should be apprised of before investing.

We look forward to receiving your application and investment.

Brandon Ames
Senior Investment Consultant
Angel Seed Company, Ltd.

---

26. What is the purpose of the prospectus?
(A) To improve kitchen hygiene
(B) To train restaurant personnel
(C) To attract business partners
(D) To finalize a business loan

27. What will probably be found on page ten?
(A) An investment form
(B) Oregon state building codes
(C) Restroom floor plans
(D) Expected salaries for employees

28. What does Mr. Ames mention about Mom's Kitchen?
(A) Its restaurants can be found in different cities.
(B) All individual restaurants are identical regardless of location.
(C) It is an ideal business for a family to invest in.
(D) Owners will not have to comply with building regulations.

Chapter 04 Reading Test

Questions 29-30 refer to the following text-message chain.

Siegfried Kieselbach (9:17 AM)
I just received a letter from the IRS. Apparently, we owe $20,000 in taxes.

Bonnie Rudd (9:18 AM)
Are you serious? We've paid our taxes. Our accountant, Julie, is thorough when it comes to meeting our tax obligations.

Siegfried Kieselbach (9:20 AM)
Well, that may be so, but the e-mail says if the tax bill isn't paid in 90 days, there will be severe penalties.

Bonnie Rudd (9:21 AM)
There has obviously been some kind of mistake. Let me call Julie, and I'll get right back to you.

Siegfried Kieselbach (9:23 AM)
OK. While you're doing that, I'll call Brendan to organize a meeting to discuss the matter. I'll fill you in when you get back to me.

29. At 9:20 AM, what does Mr. Kieselbach most likely mean when he writes, "that may be so"?
    (A) He suspects that the accountant made an error.
    (B) He blames Ms. Rudd for the problem.
    (C) He confirms the meeting date.
    (D) He believes taxes are too high.

30. What will Mr. Kieselbach most likely do next?
    (A) Reschedule a meeting
    (B) Reimburse the accountant
    (C) Contact a colleague
    (D) Pay a tax bill

Chapter 05 General Business 一般商業

1 contract ['kɑntrækt] n. 合約

sign a contract with sb
與某人簽訂合約

▶ The record company signed a contract with the singer.
唱片公司跟那位歌手簽訂了合約。

2 revise [rɪ'vaɪz] vt. 修正 (= modify ['mɑdə,faɪ])

衍 revision n. 修正

▶ I'll have my lawyer revise the contract based on our negotiation.
我會請我的律師根據我們的協商修正合約。

3 expire [ɪk'spaɪr] vi. 到期，過期，失效

衍 expired a. 過期的
expiration n. 過期
反 validate vt. 使有效

▶ The contract between our company and the supplier will expire at the end of May.
我們公司和那家供應商之間的合約五月底即將到期。

4 confidential [,kɑnfə'dɛnʃəl] a. 機密的，保密的

衍 confidentially adv. 機密地
confidential information / document 機密資訊 / 文件
keep sth confidential 將某事保密

▶ All patients' medical records and personal information will be kept confidential.
所有患者的就醫紀錄與個人資料都將保密。

5 persuasive [pɚ'swesɪv] a. 有說服力的

衍 persuasively adv. 有說服力地
persuade vt. 說服
persuasive arguments / evidence
有說服力的論點 / 證據

▶ David made a powerful and persuasive speech at the meeting.
大衛在會議中發表了一篇措詞有力且具說服力的演說。

6 negotiate [nɪ'goʃɪ,et] vt. & vi. 協商，談判 (與介詞 with 並用)

衍 negotiation n. 協商
negotiable a. 可協商的
negotiate with sb about / on sth
就某事物與某人協商

▶ The salesman negotiated with the customer about the price of the car.
業務員與顧客協商車價。

49

7 agreement [əˋgrimənt] n. 協定，協議

衍 agree vi. 同意
agreeable a. 令人愉快的
sign an agreement　簽訂協定
come to / reach an agreement
達成協議
break the terms of the agreement
違反協定條款

▶ The government signed an international arms-control agreement during a meeting at the UN.
該政府在聯合國會議上簽署了一份國際限武協定。

▶ Action has to be taken to punish the country that broke the terms of the agreement on human rights.
吾人應採取行動以制裁違反人權協定條款的國家。

8 terms [tɝmz] n. 條款

under the terms of...
按照……條款
the terms and conditions of...
……的條款與條件

▶ Under the terms of their contract, employees must give two months' notice if they want to quit.
按照合約條款，打算離職的員工必須於兩個月前提出申請。

▶ These are the terms and conditions of your employment.
這些是你的僱用條款與條件。

9 comply [kəmˋplaɪ] vi. 遵守

衍 compliance n. 遵守
compliant a. 順從的
comply with...　遵守……

▶ There are heavy penalties for failure to comply with the regulations.
若未遵守這些規定將遭受嚴格處分。

10 cooperate [koˋɑpəˏret] vi. 合作（與介詞 with 並用）

衍 cooperation n. 合作
cooperative a. 合作的
cooperate with...　和……合作

▶ The two companies cooperated with each other on this project.
這兩家公司在該計畫上彼此合作。

11 headquarters [ˋhɛdˏkwɔrtɚz] n. 總部（單複數同形，縮寫為 HQ，本字後可接單數或複數動詞）

衍 headquartered a. 總部設在……的

▶ The new recruits were sent to the headquarters in New York for training.
新員工被送去紐約的總部接受訓練。

12 branch [bræntʃ] n. 分部，分店，分公司

open a branch　成立分部 / 公司

▶ They're planning to open a branch in Bangkok next month.
他們計劃下個月在曼谷成立一家分公司。

13 expand [ɪkˋspænd] vt. & vi. 擴張 (業務)

衍 expansion n. 擴展
expand into... （業務）擴張至……

▶ We expanded our business by setting up two branch offices in Japan.
我們在日本成立兩家分公司以擴大事業規模。

▶ Our business has recently expanded into South America.
本公司的事業最近擴展到南美洲。

14 franchise [ˋfræn,tʃaɪz] n. 連鎖事業；經銷權 & vt. 給予經銷權

a franchise holder
連鎖事業擁有者
a fast-food franchise
速食連鎖企業

▶ That coffee shop is an international franchise.
那間咖啡店是一家國際連鎖事業。

▶ IBM has franchised our company to market its products in Japan.
IBM 授權本公司在日本行銷他們的產品。

15 merge [mɝdʒ] vi. & vt. (機構或企業的) 合併

衍 merger n. （機構或企業的）合併

▶ John's department will merge with mine.
約翰的部門將和我的部門合併。

16 takeover [ˋtek,ovɚ] n. 收購

a hostile takeover　惡意收購
make a takeover bid for...
出價收購……

▶ A multinational company made a takeover bid for a local engineering firm.
某跨國公司出價收購當地的某家工程公司。

17 conference [ˋkɑnfərəns] n. 大型會議

衍 confer vi. 商討
a press / news conference
記者會
a conference room　會議室

▶ The press conference is scheduled for 2 p.m. this afternoon.
記者會預定在今天下午兩點召開。

18 seminar [ˋsɛmə,nɑr] n. 研討會，講座

attend / hold a seminar
出席 / 舉辦研討會
a seminar on...
關於……的研討會 / 講座

▶ We attended a seminar on how to improve efficiency yesterday.
我們昨天參加一場如何提升效率的研討會。

CH 05

19 presentation [ˌprɛznˈteʃən] n. 簡報，口頭報告

make / give a presentation on...
就……發表簡報

▶ I'm going to ask each of you to make a short presentation.
我要各位每個人都發表簡短的口頭報告。

▶ The sales manager is going to give a presentation on our new products.
業務經理將進行簡報，介紹本公司的新產品。

20 competition [ˌkampəˈtɪʃən] n. 競爭；競賽

衍 compete vi. 競爭
　competitor n. 競爭對手
in competition with... 與……競爭
fierce / stiff / intense competition
競爭激烈

▶ We are in competition with three other companies for the contract.
我們和另外三家公司競爭那份合約。

▶ You don't need to eat so quickly! It's not a competition.
你不用吃那麼快！又不是在比賽。

21 survey [ˈsɝve] n. 意見調查 & [səˈve] vt. 進行意見調查

補 questionnaire 是印有一連串問題的書面問卷，而 survey 是指進行意見調查的活動。
a market survey 市場調查
do / conduct / carry out a survey
進行意見調查

▶ We're conducting a survey of people's opinions about credit card interest rates.
我們正在進行一項調查，以了解民眾對信用卡利率的看法。

22 conduct [kənˈdʌkt] vt. 執行，進行

conduct a survey / an experiment
進行調查 / 實驗

▶ We conducted a survey to find out consumer attitudes towards organic food.
我們進行一項調查，好了解消費者對有機食物的態度。

23 representative [ˌrɛprɪˈzɛntətɪv] n. 代表（人）& a. 代表的

a sales representative
業務代表，業務員（常簡稱為 a sales rep）

▶ Judy's good interpersonal skills and outgoing personality make her a great sales representative.
茱蒂良好的人際關係技巧以及外向的個性，使她成為優秀的業務代表。

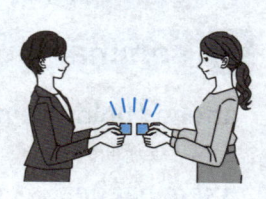

24 promotional [prəˋmoʃən!] *a.* 推銷的

衍 promotion *n.* 促銷活動
promote *vt.* 促銷；使升遷

▶ Giant recently released a promotional video for its new carbon fiber bike.
日前，捷安特公司為了他們新的碳纖維腳踏車公布了一部促銷影片。

25 reputation [ˌrɛpjəˋteʃən] *n.* 名譽

acquire / gain / earn a reputation for... 因……獲得名聲
establish a reputation as... 建立……的名聲

▶ In his last job, Mike acquired a reputation for being late.
邁可在上一份工作中得到了愛遲到的名聲。

▶ Canon has established a good reputation as a consumer electronics manufacturer.
佳能公司樹立了良好的消費電子製造商的聲譽。

Chapter 05 Listening Test

本回完整音檔 005
本回分段音檔 112-135

Part 1 112-114

Directions: For each question in this part, you will hear four statements about a picture in your test book. When you hear the statements, you must select the one statement that best describes what you see in the picture. Then find the number of the question on your answer sheet and mark your answer. The statements will not be printed in your test book and will be spoken only one time.

1.

2.

54

Part 2 🔊 115-117

Directions: You will hear a question or statement and three responses spoken in English. They will not be printed in your test book and will be spoken only one time. Select the best response to the question or statement and mark the letter (A), (B), or (C) on your answer sheet.

3. Mark your answer on your answer sheet.

4. Mark your answer on your answer sheet.

Part 3 🔊 118-126

Directions: You will hear some conversations between two or more people. You will be asked to answer three questions about what the speakers say in each conversation. Select the best response to each question and mark the letter (A), (B), (C), or (D) on your answer sheet. The conversations will not be printed in your test book and will be spoken only one time.

5. What are the speakers mainly discussing?
   (A) A union's request
   (B) An employee's performance
   (C) Customer satisfaction
   (D) Foreign imports

6. What does the man request?
   (A) Higher health contributions
   (B) Safer working conditions
   (C) Better career opportunities
   (D) Shorter working hours

7. What is mentioned about health care?
   (A) The government no longer provides insurance.
   (B) The union provides better coverage.
   (C) The workers have changed their plan.
   (D) The company complies with all the legal requirements.

8. What are the speakers discussing?
   (A) Contract terms
   (B) Management concerns
   (C) Sales representatives
   (D) Market share

9. What does the woman mean when she says, "I should think so"?
   (A) She thinks the man is wrong.
   (B) She is hoping to discuss the matter.
   (C) She is concerned about the man.
   (D) She agrees with the decision.

10. What does the man say about the contract?
    (A) It is also available online.
    (B) It will be valid for two years.
    (C) It will be revised.
    (D) It needs to be printed out.

Chapter 05 Listening Test

Part 4 🔊 127-135

Directions: You will hear some talks given by a single speaker. You will be asked to answer three questions about what the speaker says in each talk. Select the best response to each question and mark the letter (A), (B), (C), or (D) on your answer sheet. The talks will not be printed in your test book and will be spoken only one time.

11. Who is the conference for?
    (A) People nearing retirement age
    (B) Members of the legal profession
    (C) People starting their own company
    (D) Workers moving to North America

12. What does the speaker say about the panel discussion?
    (A) It will comprise three experts.
    (B) It will cover multiple aspects.
    (C) It will last for at least an hour.
    (D) It will be held in an auditorium.

13. What will the panel do after the discussion?
    (A) Sign their autographs
    (B) Hand out business cards
    (C) Promote a product
    (D) Answer questions

14. According to the speaker, what is the advantage of pre-registration?
    (A) Getting a profile
    (B) Sitting at better tables
    (C) Receiving free tickets
    (D) Saving money

15. What does the speaker imply when he says, "You can't miss them"?
    (A) The listeners should register early.
    (B) Lunch will be served soon.
    (C) The location is easy to find.
    (D) Space is limited.

16. What are the listeners asked to do?
    (A) Join the committee
    (B) Greet a speaker
    (C) Prepare a response
    (D) Return their badges

Part 5

Directions: A word or phrase is missing in each of the sentences below. Four answer choices are given below each sentence. Select the best answer to complete the sentence. Then mark the letter (A), (B), (C), or (D) on your answer sheet.

17. We concluded from our ------- that the popularity of organic food is more than just a passing fad, so we decided to expand into this business.
    (A) expiration
    (B) relationship
    (C) trademark
    (D) survey

18. Our headquarters are in Tokyo, but we also have ------- offices in Fukuoka, Osaka, and Sapporo.
    (A) payroll
    (B) quota
    (C) branch
    (D) advantage

19. The labor market ------- tight over the past two years, so we can expect some requests for salary raises from our senior employees.
    (A) has been
    (B) had been
    (C) was
    (D) will be

20. Pre-Christmas sales are running from five to ten percent below ------- of the same period last year.
    (A) this
    (B) these
    (C) that
    (D) those

21. Whether the two sports apparel retailers will merge or be subject to a hostile takeover bid ------- on their stock prices.
    (A) depending
    (B) depends
    (C) depend
    (D) depended

CH 05

57

Chapter 05 Reading Test

Part 6

Directions: Read the texts that follow. A word, phrase, or sentence is missing in parts of each text. Four answer choices for each question are given below the text. Select the best answer to complete the text. Then mark the letter (A), (B), (C), or (D) on your answer sheet.

Questions 22-25 refer to the following press release.

FastStopMart Looks to Expand into Southern India

FastStopMart is the leading convenience store chain in northern India. Over the last decade, we have established ourselves across the region as the trusted choice for food, drinks, and an array of other products. We are now seeking ------- partners to open stores in the country's southern states and union territories. We believe these areas have great commercial potential for the expansion of our operations ------- the increasing demand there for 24/7 access to quality products. Companies or individuals are invited to submit applications ------- our website at www.fast-stop-mart.in. -------. We look forward to collaborating with dedicated new partners and continuing to pursue our growth strategy.

---

22. (A) obligation
    (B) strike
    (C) principle
    (D) franchise

23. (A) so long as
    (B) due to
    (C) whereas
    (D) no more than

24. (A) prior to
    (B) without
    (C) via
    (D) along with

25. (A) Details on partnership terms can also be found online.
    (B) Our flagship store is located in this southwestern city.
    (C) The store's operating hours are displayed on the window.
    (D) FastStopMart's best-selling product is out of stock.

Part 7

Directions: In this part you will read a selection of texts, such as magazine and newspaper articles, emails, and instant messages. Each text or set of texts is followed by several questions. Select the best answer for each question and mark the letter (A), (B), (C), or (D) on your answer sheet.

Questions 26-27 refer to the following email.

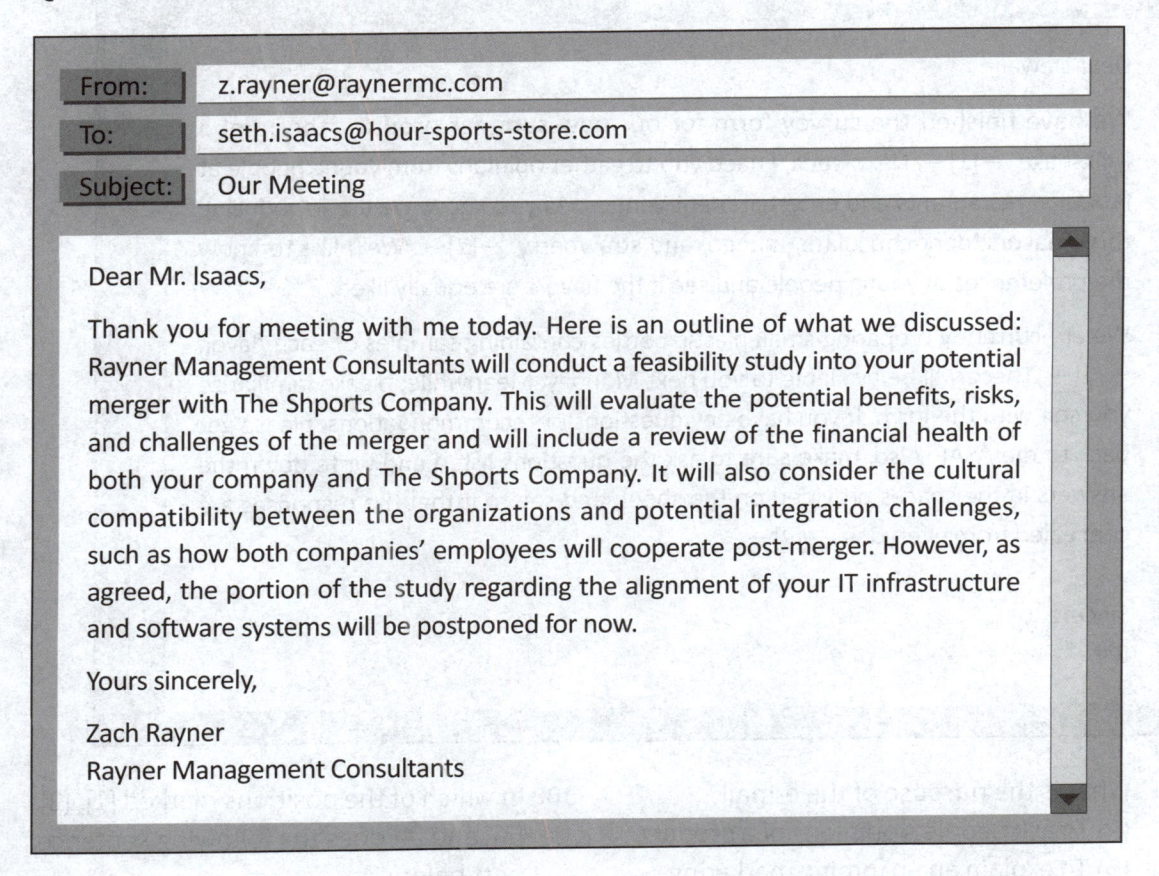

From:	z.rayner@raynermc.com
To:	seth.isaacs@hour-sports-store.com
Subject:	Our Meeting

Dear Mr. Isaacs,

Thank you for meeting with me today. Here is an outline of what we discussed: Rayner Management Consultants will conduct a feasibility study into your potential merger with The Shports Company. This will evaluate the potential benefits, risks, and challenges of the merger and will include a review of the financial health of both your company and The Shports Company. It will also consider the cultural compatibility between the organizations and potential integration challenges, such as how both companies' employees will cooperate post-merger. However, as agreed, the portion of the study regarding the alignment of your IT infrastructure and software systems will be postponed for now.

Yours sincerely,

Zach Rayner
Rayner Management Consultants

26. What is the main purpose of the email?
    (A) To suggest topics for a future meeting
    (B) To outline the findings of a recent report
    (C) To summarize the content of a future study
    (D) To review the reasons why a merger failed

27. What is suggested about technology systems?
    (A) They need to be upgraded if the merger is to go ahead.
    (B) Issues surrounding them will be studied at a later date.
    (C) They are the sole responsibility of The Shports Company.
    (D) Questions about their practicality have already been resolved.

59

Chapter 05 Reading Test

Questions 28-30 refer to the following e-mail.

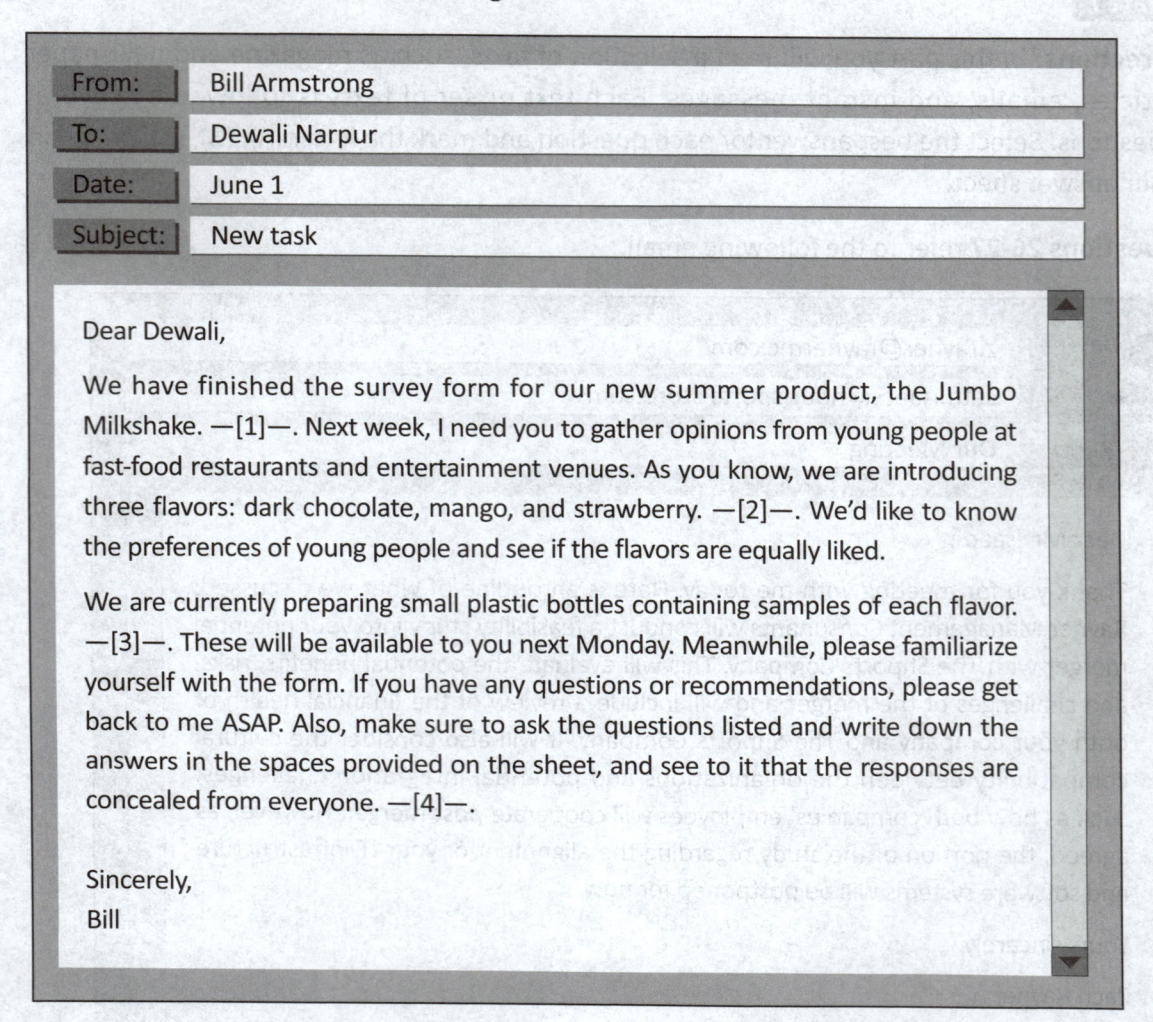

From: Bill Armstrong
To: Dewali Narpur
Date: June 1
Subject: New task

Dear Dewali,

We have finished the survey form for our new summer product, the Jumbo Milkshake. —[1]—. Next week, I need you to gather opinions from young people at fast-food restaurants and entertainment venues. As you know, we are introducing three flavors: dark chocolate, mango, and strawberry. —[2]—. We'd like to know the preferences of young people and see if the flavors are equally liked.

We are currently preparing small plastic bottles containing samples of each flavor. —[3]—. These will be available to you next Monday. Meanwhile, please familiarize yourself with the form. If you have any questions or recommendations, please get back to me ASAP. Also, make sure to ask the questions listed and write down the answers in the spaces provided on the sheet, and see to it that the responses are concealed from everyone. —[4]—.

Sincerely,
Bill

---

28. What is the purpose of the e-mail?
    (A) To ask people's opinions of a product
    (B) To explain an upcoming marketing survey
    (C) To get volunteers for a project
    (D) To order plastic bottles for a survey

29. What will young people receive?
    (A) Small portions of some drinks
    (B) Free tickets to a new movie
    (C) Jumbo-sized fast-food meals
    (D) Samples of a chocolate bar

30. In which of the positions marked [1], [2], [3], and [4] does the following sentence best belong?

    "Completed forms must be returned in a sealed manila folder marked 'confidential.'"

    (A) [1]
    (B) [2]
    (C) [3]
    (D) [4]

Chapter 06 Health 健康

1 healthy [ˈhɛlθɪ] a. 健康的

- 衍 health n. 健康
- 反 unhealthy a. 不健康的

▶ Gordon offered me some useful tips on healthy eating.
高登提供我一些關於健康飲食的祕訣。

2 diet [ˈdaɪət] n. (為特殊目的而設計的) 飲食

- go / be on a diet　進行節食 / 在節食
- have a balanced / healthy diet
有均衡 / 健康的飲食

▶ To lose some weight, many of my colleagues are going on a diet.
為了減重，我有許多同事都在節食。

3 obesity [oˈbisətɪ] n. 肥胖 (症) (不可數)

- 衍 obese a. 過胖的

▶ Obesity is a major problem in the United States.
在美國，肥胖症是一大問題。

4 hygiene [ˈhaɪdʒin] n. 衛生 (不可數)

- 衍 hygienic a. 衛生的
- hygienically adv. 衛生地

▶ It was the poor standards of hygiene at that restaurant that caused Neil to fall ill.
就是那家餐廳差勁的衛生水準才導致尼爾生病的。

5 nutrient [ˈn(j)utrɪənt] n. 養分，營養物 (可數)

- 比 nutrition n. 營養（不可數）
- 衍 nutritious a. 營養的
- an essential nutrient　必要的養分

▶ Plants absorb essential nutrients from the soil.
植物從土壤中吸收必要的養分。

6 protein [ˈprotiɪn] n. 蛋白質

- 補 以下列舉常見的營養素：
carbohydrate（碳水化合物）、
fat（脂肪）、vitamin（維生素）、
mineral（礦物質）、fiber（纖維質）、
antioxidant（抗氧化物）

▶ The nutritionist emphasized the importance of eating a diet rich in protein.
該營養師強調攝取蛋白質豐富的飲食很重要。

7 disease [dɪˈziz] n. 疾病

- 補 disease 通常指的是較嚴重、特定的病症以及有關器官的病，如 Parkinson's / liver disease（帕金

▶ The chain-smoker died of lung disease.
這名老菸槍死於肺病。

61

森氏症 / 肝病）；illness 則通常指身體的大小不適，以及心理疾病，如 a minor / mental illness（小病 / 心理疾病）。

an acute / a chronic disease
急性 / 慢性病

a contagious / an infectious disease　傳染病

8　vaccine [ˋvæksin] n. 疫苗

衍 vaccinate vt. 為……接種疫苗

▶ The results show that the vaccine is effective.
研究結果顯示該疫苗有效。

9　infect [ɪnˋfɛkt] vt. 使感染（疾病）（常用被動語態）；（電腦病毒）感染

衍 infection n. 感染
　infectious a. 傳染性的
be infected with + 疾病
感染某疾病

▶ A large number of people around the globe were infected with the coronavirus after the outbreak of COVID-19.
新冠肺炎爆發後，全球有許多人都感染了冠狀病毒。

10　contagious [kənˋtedʒəs] a. 傳染性的

▶ The contagious disease spread rapidly throughout the village.
該傳染病迅速地在那個村莊蔓延開來。

11　prevention [prɪˋvɛnʃən] n. 預防

衍 prevent vt. 預防
　preventive a. 預防的

▶ This campaign aims to promote the prevention of lung cancer.
該活動旨在宣導肺癌的預防。

12　therapy [ˋθɛrəpɪ] n. 療法

衍 therapist n. 治療師
occupational / physical / speech therapy　職能 / 物理 / 語言治療

▶ The cost of multi-drug therapies may run as high as US$8,000 annually.
綜合藥物療法的支出每年可能要花上高達八千美金。

13　insurance [ɪnˋʃurəns] n. 保險（不可數）

衍 insure vt. & vi.（為……）投保

▶ Is dental care covered in your insurance?
你的保單有涵蓋牙醫險嗎？

14 dentist [ˈdɛntɪst] n. 牙醫

- 衍 dental a. 牙齒的
- 補 以下為常見的醫師：surgeon（外科醫師）、physician（內科醫師）、cardiologist（心臟病醫師）、pediatrician（小兒科醫師）、psychiatrist（精神科醫師）

the dentist / dentist's 牙醫診間；牙科診所

▶ The dentist replaced my bad tooth with an artificial one.
牙醫拔掉我那顆爛牙並裝上假牙。

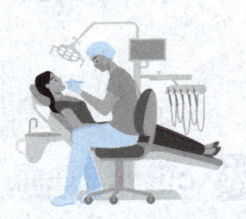

15 cavity [ˈkævətɪ] n. 蛀牙（洞）

▶ Marcy made an appointment with her dentist to have all her cavities filled.
瑪西和她的牙醫約好把所有的蛀牙都補好。

16 symptom [ˈsɪmptəm] n. 症狀

- 補 以下為常見的症狀：fever（發燒）、cough（咳嗽）、sore throat（喉嚨痛）、runny nose（流鼻水）、stuffy nose / nasal congestion（鼻塞）、sneezing（打噴嚏）、headache（頭痛）、dizziness（頭暈）、fatigue（疲累）、muscle pain / body aches（肌肉痛 / 全身酸痛）、chills（發冷）、nausea（噁心）、vomiting（嘔吐）、diarrhea（腹瀉）

▶ Richard had all the typical flu symptoms: fever, tiredness, dry cough, a sore throat, and a runny nose.
理察符合所有典型的流感症狀：發燒、疲憊、乾咳、喉嚨痛、流鼻水。

17 flu [flu] n. 流行性感冒

flu shot 流感疫苗
have the flu 得到流感

▶ Billy was infected with the flu at school.
比利在學校被傳染了流感。

18 allergic [əˈlɝdʒɪk] a. 過敏的（與介詞 to 並用）

- 衍 allergy n. 過敏（與介詞 to 並用）

be allergic to... 對……過敏

▶ Tom is allergic to animal hair.
湯姆對動物的毛過敏。

19 patient [ˈpeʃənt] n. 病人

▶ The patient finally recovered from his illness.
那位病人最後終於痊癒了。

20. treatment [ˈtritmənt] n. 治療

- 衍 treat vt. 治療
- the treatment for... ……的治療
- get / receive treatment 接受治療

▶ The medicine was regarded as a breakthrough in the treatment for cancer.
這種藥被認為是治療癌症的一項突破。

▶ Some patients in that country have to wait for weeks to receive the treatment they need.
該國有些病患要等待幾星期才能得到所需的治療。

21. clinic [ˈklɪnɪk] n. 診所；門診部

- 衍 clinical a. 臨床的
- a dental clinic 牙科診所

▶ The rich man founded a free medical clinic for the poor.
這位有錢人替窮人成立免費的醫療診所。

22. diagnose [ˈdaɪəɡˌnos] vt. 診斷

- 衍 diagnosis n. 診斷
- diagnostic a. 診斷的
- be diagnosed as sth 被診斷出是某疾病
- diagnose sb with sth 診斷某人患有……

▶ The patient's condition was diagnosed as some sort of eating disorder.
那位病患的病況被診斷為某種飲食失調症。

▶ Ted's aunt was diagnosed with breast cancer at the age of 50.
泰德的阿姨五十歲時被診斷出患有乳癌。

23. prescribe [prɪˈskraɪb] vt. 給……開（處方）

- 衍 prescription n. 處方箋
- prescribe sb sth 給某人開立……
- prescribe sth for... 為……開立……

▶ If this medicine doesn't work, I may have to prescribe you something stronger.
如果這種藥沒效，我可能得開些更強的藥給你。

▶ The doctor prescribed some painkillers for my stomach pains.
醫生替我的胃痛開了些止痛藥。

24. surgery [ˈsɝdʒərɪ] n. 外科手術（不可數）

- 衍 surgical a. 外科手術的
- undergo surgery on... 進行……的手術

▶ The basketball player underwent minor surgery on his left knee.
那位籃球選手進行了左膝的小手術。

25. dose [dos] n. （藥物的）一劑

- 衍 dosage n. 劑量（集合名詞，不可數）

▶ The label says you should take one dose four times a day.
標籤上寫著每天要服用四次，每次一劑。

Part 1 🔊 136-138

Directions: For each question in this part, you will hear four statements about a picture in your test book. When you hear the statements, you must select the one statement that best describes what you see in the picture. Then find the number of the question on your answer sheet and mark your answer. The statements will not be printed in your test book and will be spoken only one time.

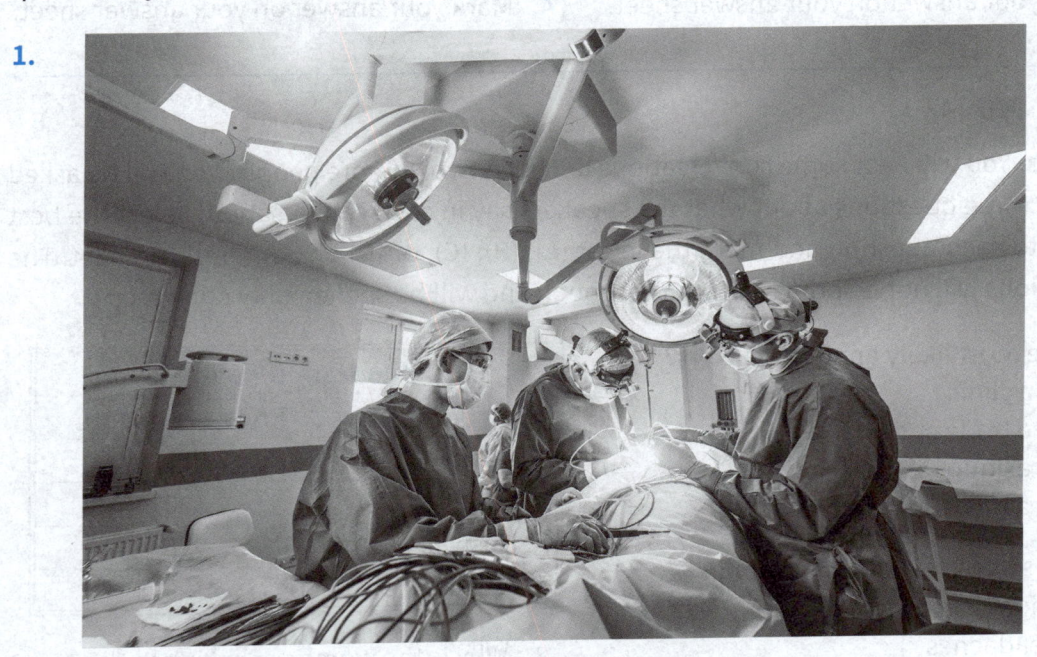

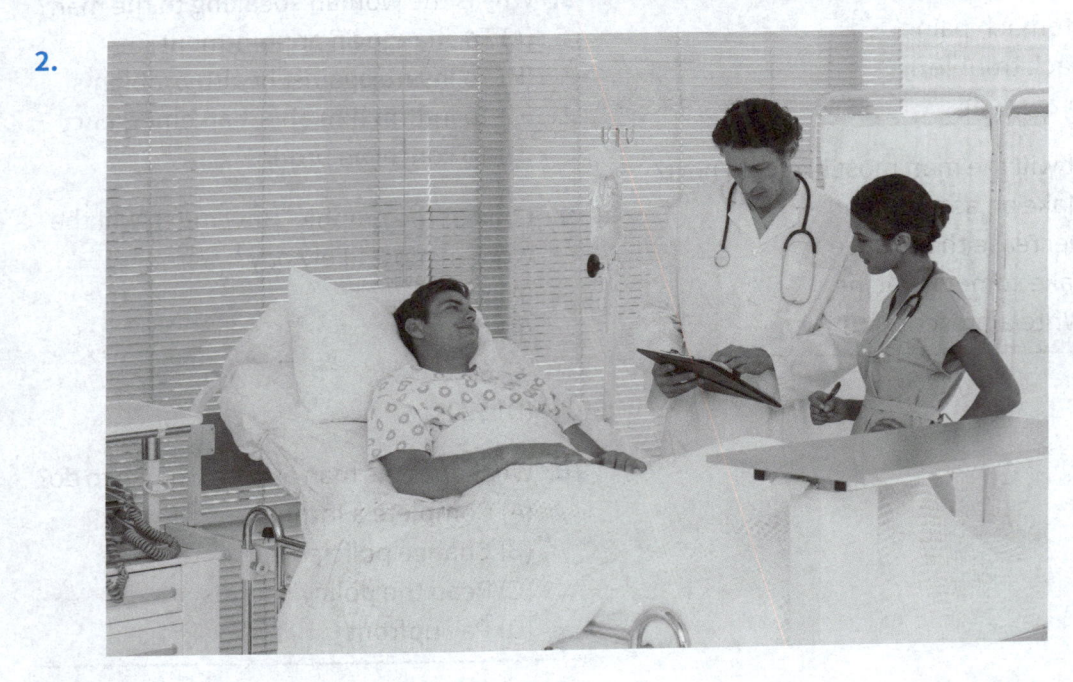

1.

2.

65

Chapter 06 Listening Test

Part 2 🔊 139-141

Directions: You will hear a question or statement and three responses spoken in English. They will not be printed in your test book and will be spoken only one time. Select the best response to the question or statement and mark the letter (A), (B), or (C) on your answer sheet.

3. Mark your answer on your answer sheet.

4. Mark your answer on your answer sheet.

Part 3 🔊 142-150

Directions: You will hear some conversations between two or more people. You will be asked to answer three questions about what the speakers say in each conversation. Select the best response to each question and mark the letter (A), (B), (C), or (D) on your answer sheet. The conversations will not be printed in your test book and will be spoken only one time.

5. Where most likely are the speakers?
   (A) At a clinic
   (B) At a trade show
   (C) At a liquor store
   (D) At a medicine factory

6. What symptom does the woman mention?
   (A) Headaches
   (B) Stomach pain
   (C) Back trouble
   (D) Dizzy spells

7. What will the man most likely do next?
   (A) Make an assessment
   (B) Decrease the dosage
   (C) Take some medicine
   (D) Write a prescription

Insurance Policy	
Type	**Price per Month**
Dental	$50
Vision	$30
Hospital	$25
Ambulance	$20

8. Why is the woman speaking to the man?
   (A) To change an appointment
   (B) To insure against health problems
   (C) To inform him about an emergency
   (D) To cancel an order

9. Look at the graphic. How much will the woman most likely pay?
   (A) $50
   (B) $30
   (C) $25
   (D) $20

10. What does the man ask the woman to do?
    (A) Complete a form
    (B) Change policies
    (C) Read the policy's terms
    (D) Pay upfront

Part 4 🔊 151-159

Directions: You will hear some talks given by a single speaker. You will be asked to answer three questions about what the speaker says in each talk. Select the best response to each question and mark the letter (A), (B), (C), or (D) on your answer sheet. The talks will not be printed in your test book and will be spoken only one time.

11. What is the purpose of the talk?
    (A) To remind people to wash their hands
    (B) To query department procedures
    (C) To improve personal relationships
    (D) To explain dental hygiene

12. What does the speaker mention about fillings?
    (A) They are used to repair cavities.
    (B) They are common procedures.
    (C) They are expensive to perform.
    (D) They are covered by insurance.

13. According to the speaker, where can the listeners find additional information?
    (A) On toothpaste packaging
    (B) At a dentist
    (C) On the internet
    (D) In the manual

| Flu Shot Schedule ||
Department	Time
Administration	8 AM – 9 AM
Marketing	9 AM – 10 AM
Production	10 AM – 2 PM
Warehouse	2 PM – 4 PM

14. Look at the graphic. Which department does the speaker work in?
    (A) Administration
    (B) Marketing
    (C) Production
    (D) Warehouse

15. What are the listeners asked to do if they have flu-like symptoms?
    (A) Take sick leave
    (B) Receive a flu shot
    (C) Meet at the water cooler
    (D) Wear a face mask

16. What are the listeners encouraged to do?
    (A) Exit the building
    (B) Drink more water
    (C) Clean their hands often
    (D) Work overtime

Chapter 06 Reading Test

Part 5

Directions: A word or phrase is missing in each of the sentences below. Four answer choices are given below each sentence. Select the best answer to complete the sentence. Then mark the letter (A), (B), (C), or (D) on your answer sheet.

17. The nurse advised Mr. Fritsch against getting the yellow fever vaccine as he is ------- to eggs.
    (A) allergy
    (B) allergist
    (C) allergic
    (D) allergen

18. Taking lots of food supplements is no substitute for consuming a balanced, healthy -------.
    (A) to diet
    (B) diet
    (C) dieted
    (D) dietary

19. No sooner had the doctor diagnosed Mrs. Hanson's disease ------- she started to worry about how she was going to break the bad news to her family.
    (A) when
    (B) than
    (C) before
    (D) so

20. You should cover your mouth when you sneeze so you don't risk ------- other people with your germs.
    (A) infect
    (B) infected
    (C) to infect
    (D) infecting

21. ------- the successful surgery, Ms. Chalamet is now able to lead a happy, healthy life without the need for costly medication.
    (A) Despite
    (B) Otherwise
    (C) Thanks to
    (D) In order that

Part 6

Directions: Read the texts that follow. A word, phrase, or sentence is missing in parts of each text. Four answer choices for each question are given below the text. Select the best answer to complete the text. Then mark the letter (A), (B), (C), or (D) on your answer sheet.

Questions 22-25 refer to the following memo.

From:	Occupational Health & Safety Officer
To:	All Employees
Subject:	The Importance of Good Nutrition

As part of our commitment to the health and well-being of our employees, I would like to stress the importance of a sufficient intake of -------. Not only is eating food full of nutrition beneficial for your health, ------- it is vital for maintaining focus and energy in the workplace. -------. They should also contain plenty of fresh fruit and vegetables, whole grains, and healthy fats. You should eat as ------- ultra-processed foods as possible, as these have been linked to obesity and associated medical conditions. Over the next couple of days, I will be sharing more resources on healthy eating choices and recipe suggestions.

22. (A) pharmacies
    (B) interns
    (C) flosses
    (D) nutrients

23. (A) and
    (B) but
    (C) or
    (D) until

24. (A) Getting enough exercise is likewise necessary.
    (B) This recipe includes a good mix of healthy ingredients.
    (C) Being able to concentrate on your work is essential.
    (D) Your meals should include adequate amounts of protein.

25. (A) few
    (B) a few
    (C) little
    (D) a little

69

Chapter 06 Reading Test

Part 7

Directions: In this part you will read a selection of texts, such as magazine and newspaper articles, emails, and instant messages. Each text or set of texts is followed by several questions. Select the best answer for each question and mark the letter (A), (B), (C), or (D) on your answer sheet.

Questions 26-28 refer to the following introduction.

Dr. Michael Mosley

Dr. Michael Mosley was a renowned British doctor, writer, and broadcaster. He completed his medical degree in 1985, initially intending to become a psychiatrist. However, he soon changed course and went into broadcasting, first as a producer and then as a presenter. He hosted an array of factual programs, including *Trust Me, I'm a Doctor* and *Just One Thing*, that focused on medical issues, healthy eating, and disease prevention.

In the early 2010s, Dr. Mosley developed Type 2 diabetes, prompting him to explore ways to manage or reverse the progression of the disease. This led to his biggest claim to fame: popularizing the 5:2 diet. By promoting this fasting strategy, he helped many people to lose weight and lead healthier lives.

---

26. What is indicated about Dr. Mosley?
(A) He studied broadcasting at university.
(B) He didn't plan to be a presenter upon graduation.
(C) He taught psychiatry during the 1980s.
(D) He quit college before he earned his degree.

27. The word "developed" in paragraph 2, line 1, is closest in meaning to
(A) processed
(B) invented
(C) suffered
(D) emerged

28. According to the introduction, what is Dr. Mosley most famous for?
(A) Finding a cure for a contagious disease
(B) Making an eating plan well known
(C) Working on many television dramas
(D) Losing a huge amount of weight

Questions 29-32 refer to the following online chat discussion.

Soraya Mirza 2:53 p.m.
I saw on the news today that norovirus cases are increasing rapidly across the country.

Ibrahim Faraz 2:55 p.m.
Ugh! It's so contagious that if a few people in the office get infected, it'll spread like wildfire.

Amari Diallo 2:56 p.m.
Is norovirus like Covid?

Soraya Mirza 2:56 p.m.
No, it's a stomach bug that causes vomiting and diarrhea. You've never heard of it?

Amari Diallo 2:57 p.m.
I don't keep up-to-date with health news.

Soraya Mirza 2:58 p.m.
In that case, I think we should make sure everyone in the office knows what symptoms to look out for and what to do if they catch it.

Ibrahim Faraz 3:00 p.m.
I'll get HR to create a campaign. Lina, are you online?

Lina Jaber 3:01 p.m.
Yeah, I'm here. I'll get started right away. I think the key message to stress is prevention through hand hygiene: hand sanitizer doesn't kill the virus; only washing thoroughly with soap and water does.

Soraya Mirza 3:03 p.m.
You should also emphasize the company policy that if people catch it, they need to stay off work for 48 hours after their symptoms have gone.

Chapter 06 Reading Test

29. What is mainly being discussed?
    (A) A report that contains errors
    (B) A fire that spreads quickly
    (C) A show that focuses on health
    (D) A virus that causes sickness

30. Who is unfamiliar with the subject?
    (A) Ms. Mirza
    (B) Mr. Faraz
    (C) Mr. Diallo
    (D) Ms. Jaber

31. At 3:01 p.m., what does Ms. Jaber most likely mean when she writes, "I'll get started right away"?
    (A) She will commence a medical procedure.
    (B) She will activate an emergency protocol.
    (C) She will begin working on a campaign.
    (D) She will start delivering a presentation.

32. According to Ms. Mirza, what message should be stressed to workers?
    (A) They should obtain an official doctor's note.
    (B) They should use hand sanitizer liberally.
    (C) They should monitor colleagues for symptoms.
    (D) They should follow a company regulation.

72

Chapter 07 Housing / Corporate Property 房屋 / 企業財產

1 rent [rɛnt] vt. 租借，出租 & n. 租金

rent sth (out) to sb
將某物租給某人

- Mrs. Johnson makes ends meet by renting rooms to college students.
  強森太太把房間租給大學生以維持生計。
- The rent for this house is cheap compared with others in the neighborhood.
  這棟房子的租金和附近的其它房子相比算是便宜的。

2 leak [lik] vi. & vt. 漏（水、油、瓦斯等）& n. 洩漏

a gas leak　瓦斯外洩

- Oil was leaking out of that bus.
  那輛巴士正在漏機油。
- There is a gas leak in the kitchen.
  廚房裡有瓦斯外洩。

3 -proof [pruf] suffix 防……的（多用於「名詞 -proof」的複合字）

（補）以下為常見的複合字：soundproof（隔音的）、waterproof（防水的）、fireproof（防火的）、rustproof（防鏽的）、bulletproof（防彈的）

- The soundproof concert hall blocks out all outside noise.
  有做隔音的音樂廳可阻隔外頭所有的噪音。

4 landlord [ˈlændˌlɔrd] n. 房東；地主

- Emma signed a one-year lease with the landlord.
  艾瑪與房東簽了一年租約。

5 tenant [ˈtɛnənt] n. 房客，租戶

- The tenants in this apartment are not allowed to keep pets.
  本公寓的房客禁止養寵物。

6 lease [lis] n. （房屋、土地、設備的）租約 & vt. 租借

take out a lease
簽租約

lease sth to sb
將某物租借給某人

- Mr. Johnson took out a lease on a ten-acre field.
  強森先生簽約租下十英畝土地。
- We've decided to lease the factory to that company.
  我們決定將這間工廠出租給那家公司。

7 resident [ˈrɛzədənt] n. (某地的) 居民，住戶 & a. 居住的

衍 residential a. 住宅的
be resident in...　居住於……

▶ Some residents woke up immediately when the fire broke out last night.
昨晚火災發生時，有些居民立即就醒來了。

▶ Ralph used to live in Germany, but he is now resident in the UK.
勞夫以前住在德國，現在定居於英國。

8 appliance [əˈplaɪəns] n. (家用) 電器

a household / domestic appliance
家用電器

▶ The store sells a wide range of household appliances—washing machines, dishwashers, and so on.
那家店出售各種家用電器，如洗衣機、洗碗機等等。

9 utility [juˈtɪlətɪ] n. (水電瓦斯等) 公共服務 (常用複數)；效用 (不可數)

衍 utilize vt. 利用

▶ The rent for this apartment does not include utilities.
這間公寓的租金不含水電瓦斯費。

▶ Tests have proved the utility of this new product.
測試結果證實這項新產品的效用。

10 furnished [ˈfɝnɪʃt] a. 含有傢俱的

衍 furnish vt. 配備傢俱；提供

▶ Jason moved into a partially furnished apartment last week.
傑森上週搬進了一間只有部分傢俱的公寓。

11 mortgage [ˈmɔrgɪdʒ] n. (以房地產為抵押品的) 貸款；房貸 & vt. 抵押 (字母 t 不發音)

mortgage rates　房貸利率

▶ Mortgage rates are set to rise again this spring.
房貸利率將於今春再次上漲。

▶ Frank had to mortgage his house to pay off his debts.
法蘭克必須抵押他的房子以償還債務。

12 real estate [ˈrɪəl ɪsˈtet] n. 房地產；不動產 (不可數)

▶ By investing in real estate, David made a huge fortune.
大衛投資房地產賺了很多錢。

13 bid [bɪd] n. 投標；(在拍賣會上) 出價 & vt. & vi. 競價；投標 (動詞三態同形)

make a bid 投標出價
bid + 金額 + for sth 出價若干金額買某物

▶ The manager gave the job to the contractor who made the lowest bid.
經理把工作給了投標價格最低的承包商。

▶ Bruce bid $10,000 for an antique vase at the auction.
布魯斯在拍賣會出價一萬美元競標一個古董花瓶。

14 property [ˈprɑpɚtɪ] n. 房地產 (可數或不可數)；財產 (不可數)

personal property 個人動產 / 財產

▶ Property prices have risen sharply over the past decade.
過去十年來，房地產價格狂飆。

▶ Keep an eye on your personal property when you're in public places.
在公眾場所要留意你的個人財物。

15 layout [ˈleˌaʊt] n. (空間的) 格局；(刊物的) 版面編排 (常為單數)

▶ Emma doesn't like the layout of the old apartment.
艾瑪不喜歡這間老公寓的格局。

▶ The fashion magazine's attractive new page layout boosted its sales.
該時尚雜誌吸引人的新穎版面設計刺激了銷售量。

16 structure [ˈstrʌktʃɚ] n. 建築物；結構 & vt. 構成，組織

衍 structural a. 結構的

▶ Taipei 101 used to be the tallest structure in the world.
臺北 101 曾是世上最高的建築物。

▶ Kevin carefully structured his presentation to outline the project's goals clearly.
凱文仔細構思他的簡報內容以求清楚概述專案的目標。

17 premises [ˈprɛmɪsɪz] n. 建築物及周圍所屬土地，場所 (恆用複數)

on / off (the) premises 在場所內 / 外

▶ Eating and drinking are strictly prohibited on the premises.
本場所內嚴禁飲食。

18 construct [kənˈstrʌkt] vt. 建造 (= build)

衍 construction n. 建造；結構
be constructed of sth
……由某物建造成的

▶ The residents remained bitterly opposed to the plan to construct a nuclear power plant on the beachfront.
當地居民依然憤怒抵制那個要在濱海地區興建核電廠的計畫。

▶ The tall building was constructed entirely of concrete, steel, and glass.
這棟高樓全是由混凝土、鋼鐵和玻璃建造而成。

19 overhead [ˈovɚˌhɛd] n. (公司) 經常性開支 (不可數)

▶ We need to improve sales because the overhead is rising.
由於日常開支增加，我們得提升銷售量。

20 maintain [menˈten] vt. 維修保養；維持 (某個狀況)

衍 maintenance n. 維修，保養；維持（皆不可數）
be well / poorly maintained
維修保養良好 / 不善

▶ The report found that the safety equipment installed in that building had been poorly maintained.
該報導發現安裝於那棟大樓內的安全器材維修不善。

▶ Our company puts special emphasis on maintaining high-quality service.
本公司特別強調維持高品質服務。

21 relocate [ˌriloˈket] vi. & vt. (公司、工人) 搬遷

relocate to + 地方
遷址到某地
relocate A to B
將 A 搬遷至 B

▶ A lot of factories are relocating to Vietnam because of cheaper labor costs.
許多工廠因較廉價的勞動成本而遷至越南。

▶ The company relocated its head office to northern Paris.
該公司將總部搬遷至巴黎北部。

22 renovate [ˈrɛnəˌvet] vt. 整修，翻修

衍 renovation n. 整修，翻修

▶ It will take over two years to renovate the art museum.
這座美術館要花兩年多的時間整修。

23 sustainable [səˈstenəbl̩] a. 可持續的；可維持的

衍 sustainability [sə͵stenəˈbɪlətɪ] n. 持續性

sustainable energy resources
永續能源資源

▶ Solar and wind power are two examples of sustainable energy resources that have been promoted by the government in recent years.
太陽能和風能是這幾年來政府推廣的兩個永續能源例子。

▶ According to this report, economic growth is sustainable in that country.
根據這份報告，那個國家的經濟會持續成長。

24 architecture [ˈɑrkə͵tɛktʃɚ] n. 建築（風格）；建築學（不可數）

衍 architectural a. 建築（學）的
architect n. 建築師

modern / medieval architecture
現代 / 中世紀建築

▶ Chicago is known for its architecture, especially its skyscrapers.
芝加哥以建築風格聞名，尤其是摩天大樓。

25 condition [kənˈdɪʃən] n. 狀況；條件

be in good / bad condition
狀況良好 / 不佳

on (the) condition that...
條件是……

▶ The apartment has been well maintained and is in good condition.
這間公寓屋況維護頗佳，整體狀況不錯。

▶ I can lend you my car on condition that you return it on time.
你若能準時把車還我，我就借給你。

Chapter 07 Listening Test

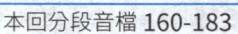

Part 1　160-162

Directions: For each question in this part, you will hear four statements about a picture in your test book. When you hear the statements, you must select the one statement that best describes what you see in the picture. Then find the number of the question on your answer sheet and mark your answer. The statements will not be printed in your test book and will be spoken only one time.

1.

2.

Part 2 🔊 163-165

Directions: You will hear a question or statement and three responses spoken in English. They will not be printed in your test book and will be spoken only one time. Select the best response to the question or statement and mark the letter (A), (B), or (C) on your answer sheet.

3. Mark your answer on your answer sheet.

4. Mark your answer on your answer sheet.

Part 3 🔊 166-174

Directions: You will hear some conversations between two or more people. You will be asked to answer three questions about what the speakers say in each conversation. Select the best response to each question and mark the letter (A), (B), (C), or (D) on your answer sheet. The conversations will not be printed in your test book and will be spoken only one time.

5. Why is the building being renovated?
   (A) To make it more environmentally friendly
   (B) To ensure it complies with all local laws
   (C) Because the staff have complained about it
   (D) Because it is very old and falling apart

6. What does the man say about the roof?
   (A) It needs to be completely replaced.
   (B) Solar panels will be installed there.
   (C) It will feature some wind turbines.
   (D) A rooftop garden will be added.

7. What has caused the contractor's work to fall behind schedule?
   (A) Structural concerns
   (B) Weather problems
   (C) Supply chain issues
   (D) Labor shortages

8. Where most likely do the speakers work?
   (A) In an insurance company
   (B) In a construction company
   (C) In a law faculty at a university
   (D) In a property management company

9. What does the man suggest doing?
   (A) Sending the maintenance man to apartment 4B
   (B) Offering compensation to the affected tenant
   (C) Conducting an inspection of the building's pipes
   (D) Evacuating residents while the problem is being fixed

10. What concern does Jessica raise about the plan?
    (A) It might take too long.
    (B) It might be expensive.
    (C) It might annoy tenants.
    (D) It might be a failure.

Chapter 07 Listening Test

Part 4 🔊 175-183

Directions: You will hear some talks given by a single speaker. You will be asked to answer three questions about what the speaker says in each talk. Select the best response to each question and mark the letter (A), (B), (C), or (D) on your answer sheet. The talks will not be printed in your test book and will be spoken only one time.

11. What is the purpose of the talk?
    (A) To respond to complaints from customers
    (B) To outline options for new headquarters
    (C) To summarize a project that has finished
    (D) To explain directions to a security guard

12. Which of the following is a problem with the first property?
    (A) Poor reception
    (B) Inadequate security
    (C) Inconvenient location
    (D) High price

13. What will the speaker most likely do next?
    (A) Drive to a property
    (B) Sign a lease
    (C) Show more information
    (D) Display a map

14. Who most likely is the speaker?
    (A) A tenant
    (B) A landlord
    (C) A real estate agent
    (D) A property inspector

15. What does the speaker imply when he says, "only after a thorough inspection"?
    (A) The lease was broken by the last tenant.
    (B) Inspections are conducted regularly.
    (C) The return of deposits is not guaranteed.
    (D) Tenants should vacate the premises.

16. What does the speaker remind the listener about?
    (A) Pets are not allowed.
    (B) Keys must be returned to the office.
    (C) A deposit will not be necessary.
    (D) A witness must sign the lease.

Chapter 07 Reading Test

Part 5

Directions: A word or phrase is missing in each of the sentences below. Four answer choices are given below each sentence. Select the best answer to complete the sentence. Then mark the letter (A), (B), (C), or (D) on your answer sheet.

17. The rental property is nicely decorated and fully -------; however, the utility bills are very expensive.
    (A) furniture
    (B) furnishings
    (C) furnish
    (D) furnished

18. Mr. and Mrs. Metz took out an €80,000 ------- to buy the three-story house in Berlin.
    (A) foundation
    (B) demolition
    (C) grid
    (D) mortgage

19. The electronics company announced that it is relocating to a smaller property to reduce its ------- expenses.
    (A) outage
    (B) tile
    (C) overhead
    (D) resident

20. Ms. Hanson is attracted to the luxury city-center apartment because of its -------, which was inspired by classical European styles.
    (A) architecture
    (B) concrete
    (C) foreman
    (D) neighbor

21. Mr. Anderson doesn't like the proposed layout for the new office because it will be ------- harder for employees to interact with one another.
    (A) many
    (B) all
    (C) much
    (D) very

Chapter 07 Reading Test

Part 6

Directions: Read the texts that follow. A word, phrase, or sentence is missing in parts of each text. Four answer choices for each question are given below the text. Select the best answer to complete the text. Then mark the letter (A), (B), (C), or (D) on your answer sheet.

Questions 22-25 refer to the following article.

Tallest Building Planned

Mann Brothers Construction Company won the bid to construct the city's first-ever skyscraper on Thoreau Boulevard. The proposed 41- ------- building will become the tallest structure in the city. When ------- in two years, the building will offer both office and residential space. -------. If the proposed designs pass the strict Department of Town Planning building codes, a groundbreaking ceremony with representatives from Mann Brothers and officials from the city government ------- on October 1.

---

22. (A) stories
    (B) floors
    (C) floor
    (D) story

23. (A) completion
    (B) completing
    (C) completed
    (D) completes

24. (A) Blueprints of the structure are currently being reviewed.
    (B) Residents have started to move into the building.
    (C) The building was constructed in record time.
    (D) Security is our top priority in the office.

25. (A) held
    (B) is held
    (C) will be held
    (D) holding

Part 7

Directions: In this part you will read a selection of texts, such as magazine and newspaper articles, emails, and instant messages. Each text or set of texts is followed by several questions. Select the best answer for each question and mark the letter (A), (B), (C), or (D) on your answer sheet.

Questions 26-27 refer to the following text-message chain.

Vance Broderick, 8:36 AM
Hi, Jacinta. I noticed a property for lease while I was driving in. It's a large warehouse with an attached office complex.

Jacinta Cassie, 8:37 AM
That used to be the headquarters of Independent Buyers. I heard there's a huge parking lot built under the offices. It would be a huge relief to solve our parking problem once and for all.

Vance Broderick, 8:38 AM
Absolutely.

Jacinta Cassie, 8:39 AM
Unfortunately, I doubt that a building that large would be in our price range.

---

26. What is most likely true about Mr. Broderick?
    (A) He is a real estate agent.
    (B) He owns a large warehouse.
    (C) He is looking for a new office location.
    (D) He works for a large manufacturer.

27. At 8:38 AM, what does Mr. Broderick most likely mean when he writes, "Absolutely"?
    (A) He accepts the rental fee.
    (B) He promises to bargain over the price.
    (C) He confirms the address of the new office building.
    (D) He thinks the property can solve the parking issue.

Chapter 07 Reading Test

Questions 28-30 refer to the following letter.

To the Editor:

We are outraged by your report, "Is the New City Stadium Safe Enough to Use?" (Tuesday, May 2). The "safety hazards" referred to in the apparently hastily written article will not exist by the June 1 opening.

It goes without saying that during construction operations, electric cables must first be laid before being covered with a protective plastic layer. — [1] —. The protective coverings are scheduled to be in place by May 20. With regard to the "leaking ceiling," anyone familiar with construction sites can tell you that once the major sections of a building site are in place, they must be washed to remove leftover construction residue. — [2] —. The stadium is currently being cleaned, resulting in excess water, which will be removed long before the June 1 opening. Finally, the "empty boxes" will be fitted with proper fire safety equipment, as scheduled, on May 23.

Your reporting on this construction site can only be called "sensationalism." Our safety record, in fact, is second to none in this state. I can assure you that the whole building will comply with fireproof and waterproof standards. — [3] —. We are also on schedule at this phase of the project. We invite your reporter to visit the stadium on May 26, the date for scheduled completion, and to write another article. We hope the reporter would then be considerate enough to include an apology, which we believe is due. — [4] —.

John Beavers
President
Altmore Construction Services

28. What is indicated about the news report?
    (A) It contains numerous inaccuracies.
    (B) It is an unbiased account.
    (C) It has caused a sensation.
    (D) It is the first in a series of articles.

29. What does Mr. Beavers suggest to the editor?
    (A) Promoting the stadium
    (B) Reading another review
    (C) Writing a follow-up article
    (D) Updating a schedule

30. In which of the positions marked [1], [2], [3], and [4] does the following sentence best belong?

    "The wiring for the entire structure has already been laid."

    (A) [1]
    (B) [2]
    (C) [3]
    (D) [4]

Chapter 08 Manufacturing 製造業

1. assemble [əˋsɛmbḷ] vt. 組裝，裝配 & vi. 集合

衍 assembly n. 裝配；集會

▶ Those electric cars will be assembled in the US.
那批電動車將在美國組裝完成。

▶ All department heads were asked to assemble in the conference room after lunch.
所有部門主管被要求午餐後在會議室集合。

2. production [prəˋdʌkʃən] n. 生產；產量（皆不可數）

衍 produce vt. 生產
producer n. 生產者
product n. 產品

補 a production line 指的是工廠裡的生產線，而 a product line 則指的是公司的產品系列。

▶ It takes only 10 hours to manufacture a car on the production line at this factory.
這家工廠的生產線僅需十小時即可生產出一輛汽車。

▶ The increase in production has been achieved through the use of technology.
科技的運用成功增加了生產量。

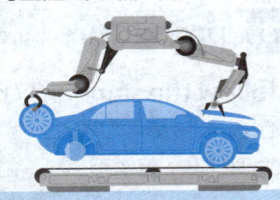

3. productive [prəˋdʌktɪv] a. 多產的，有生產力的

衍 productivity n. 生產力

▶ Our factory must become more productive, or it will soon close down.
我們的工廠必須增加生產力，否則很快就會關門大吉。

4. manufacture [ͺmænjəˋfæktʃɚ] n. & vt. (用機器大量) 生產，製造

衍 manufacturer n. 廠商；製造商

▶ The manufacture of clothing requires a lot of fabric.
製造衣物需要大量的布料。

▶ John's father runs a company that manufactures bicycles.
約翰的父親經營一家生產自行車的公司。

5. install [ɪnˋstɔl] vt. 裝設，安裝

衍 installation n. 安裝，設置（不可數）

▶ Several technicians are coming to install air conditioners in our new office.
幾位師傅會來我們的新辦公室安裝冷氣機。

85

6 progress [ˈprɑgrɛs] n. 進展；進步（皆不可數）

衍 progressive a. 進步的
make progress 有進展／進步
in progress 正在進行中的

▶ The two companies are trying to finalize a deal, but little progress has been made.
這兩間公司想敲定一筆交易，但尚未有任何進展。

▶ Work on the office building is still in progress.
辦公大樓的施工仍在進行中。

7 process [ˈprɑsɛs] vt. 加工；處理 & n. 製作方法；過程

▶ One thousand workers were employed to process materials for the electronics factory.
該電子工廠僱有一千名工人進行原料加工。

▶ The company is working on a more efficient process to produce paper.
該公司正研發更高效的造紙流程。

8 procedure [prəˈsidʒɚ] n. 程序，步驟，手續（與介詞 for 並用）

follow the standard / normal procedure
遵循標準／正常程序

▶ All chemical factories must follow the standard procedure for getting rid of toxic waste.
所有化學工廠都必須遵守處理有毒廢棄物的標準程序。

▶ What is the procedure for applying for a work permit?
申請工作許可證的手續為何？

9 standard [ˈstændɚd] n. 標準，水平 & a. 標準的

meet / reach a standard
達到標準

standard practice
標準作法

▶ Some snack stands at that night market fail to meet a certain standard of cleanliness.
那個夜市有若干小吃攤未能符合某一項清潔標準。

▶ It is standard practice to search travelers as they go through customs.
在旅客通關時對其進行搜查是標準作業。

10 defect [ˈdifɛkt] n. (東西的) 缺點，缺陷

衍 defective a. 有缺陷的（= faulty）
比 drawback n. (事情的) 缺點

▶ A few design defects in the aircraft caused the crash.
飛機設計上的幾處缺陷導致這場空難。

11 efficient [ɪˈfɪʃənt] a. 高效能的；有效率的

衍 efficiently adv. 有效率地
   efficiency n. 效率
反 inefficient a. 沒效率的

▶ Household appliances are now much more energy efficient than in the past.
現在的家電比以往更加節能。

| energy efficient 節能的 | ▶ We need an efficient manager to ensure the smooth operation of the office.
我們需要一位有效率的經理來確保辦公室運作順暢。 |

12 quality [ˈkwɑlətɪ] n. 品質 (不可數) & a. 優質的

| be of high / low quality
品質好 / 差
quality control
品管 | ▶ This pair of jeans is of high quality, and the price is reasonable.
這條牛仔褲品質很好，價格又合理。
▶ The shoes in the store are all made of quality leather.
這家店裡的鞋子都是用高級皮革製成。 |

13 inspector [ɪnˈspɛktɚ] n. 檢查員；督察員

| 衍 inspect vt. 檢查；視察
inspection n. 檢查；查驗 | ▶ The city government inspector deemed the playground unsafe for children.
市政府稽查員認為這遊樂場對兒童來說不安全。 |

14 standstill [ˈstændˌstɪl] n. 停頓，停滯

| come to a standstill / halt
停擺，停頓 | ▶ The factory came to a standstill because of the workers' strike.
工廠因工人罷工而陷於停工的狀態。 |

15 automation [ˌɔtəˈmeʃən] n. 自動化 (不可數)

| 衍 automate vt. & vi. (使) 自動化
automated a. 自動化的 | ▶ We are living in an era of advanced technology and automation.
我們正生活在一個高科技與自動化的時代。 |

16 adjustment [əˈdʒʌstmənt] n. 調整

| 衍 adjust vt. 調整
make an adjustment 調整 | ▶ Jason needs to make a few adjustments to his essay before submitting it.
傑森在繳交他的短篇論文前還須做些許調整。 |

17 device [dɪˈvaɪs] n. 裝置，設備

| | ▶ Emma just bought a device that can control all the appliances in her apartment remotely.
艾瑪剛買了一個能從遠端操控她公寓所有電器的裝置。 |

18 **dimension** [dəˈmɛnʃən] *n.* 尺寸，大小 (常為複數)

衍 dimensional *a.* 尺寸的

▶ David specified the dimensions of the living room in an email to his interior designer.
大衛在寄給室內設計師的電子郵件中詳述了客廳的尺寸。

19 **accelerate** [ækˈsɛləˌret] *vt.* & *vi.* (使) 加速 (= speed up)

衍 acceleration *n.* 加速

▶ The marketing department has developed new strategies to accelerate our business growth.
行銷部門已經制定了新的策略來加速我們業務的成長。

20 **operate** [ˈɑpəˌret] *vt.* 操作 & *vi.* 運轉；經營，營運

衍 operation *n.* 操作；運轉
operational *a.* 操作上的；運作中的

▶ You'd better read the instructions carefully before operating the device.
你在操作這臺設備前最好仔細閱讀使用說明。

▶ The factory is operating around the clock to complete all the orders.
工廠為了完成所有訂單而日夜不停地運作。

21 **warehouse** [ˈwɛrˌhaʊs] *n.* 倉庫

▶ The goods are usually sent directly from the warehouse to the convenience stores.
商品通常會從倉庫直接運送到便利商店。

22 **packaging** [ˈpækɪdʒɪŋ] *n.* 包裝 (工作)；包裝材料 (集合名詞，不可數)

衍 package *n.* 包裝；包裹；組/套 & *vt.* 打包，包裝

▶ The email states that the cost of packaging is included in the price.
電子郵件中說明包裝費用已包含在價格當中。

▶ The new packaging at this fast-food restaurant is eco-friendly.
這家速食餐廳的新包材很環保。

23 **plant** [plænt] *n.* 工廠，廠房

a power / steel / coal plant
發電 / 鋼鐵 / 煤礦廠

▶ All villagers voted against the construction of the nuclear power plant.
所有的村民都投票反對蓋核電廠。

24 **warranty** [ˈwɔrəntɪ] *n.* 保固書，保證書 (= guarantee [ˌgærənˈti])

be under warranty / guarantee
在保固期內

▶ If your broken smartphone is still under warranty, you can get it repaired for free.
如果你那支壞掉的智慧型手機還在保固期間內，你就可以免費送修。

25 **accurate** [ˈækjərət] *a.* 準確的，精準的

衍 accuracy *n.* 準確性
反 inaccurate *a.* 不準確的

▶ The instrument should enable scientists to be more accurate in predicting earthquakes.
這個儀器應該可以讓科學家更準確地預測地震。

Chapter 08 Listening Test

Part 1 🔊 184-186

Directions: For each question in this part, you will hear four statements about a picture in your test book. When you hear the statements, you must select the one statement that best describes what you see in the picture. Then find the number of the question on your answer sheet and mark your answer. The statements will not be printed in your test book and will be spoken only one time.

1.

Dizfoto / Shutterstock.com

2.

90

Part 2 🔊 187-189

Directions: You will hear a question or statement and three responses spoken in English. They will not be printed in your test book and will be spoken only one time. Select the best response to the question or statement and mark the letter (A), (B), or (C) on your answer sheet.

3. Mark your answer on your answer sheet.

4. Mark your answer on your answer sheet.

Part 3 🔊 190-198

Directions: You will hear some conversations between two or more people. You will be asked to answer three questions about what the speakers say in each conversation. Select the best response to each question and mark the letter (A), (B), (C), or (D) on your answer sheet. The conversations will not be printed in your test book and will be spoken only one time.

5. What is most likely true about the woman?
   (A) She works in a car factory.
   (B) She has recently sold a car.
   (C) She always buys cars from the same manufacturer.
   (D) She regrets purchasing her current vehicle.

6. What does the woman mention about International Motors?
   (A) It has a good reputation.
   (B) Its quality has begun to slip.
   (C) It no longer manufactures cars.
   (D) It is under new management.

7. What does the man want to know?
   (A) If the woman takes care of her car
   (B) If the woman would switch to other brands
   (C) If the woman likes to drive
   (D) If the research is reliable

8. What took place last month?
   (A) Employee examinations
   (B) Equipment tests
   (C) Job interviews
   (D) Budget changes

9. What does the woman imply when she says, "The manager has been smiling a lot lately"?
   (A) The previous stage of mechanization went well.
   (B) The factory has won an international award.
   (C) The final test results were better than expected.
   (D) The quality control inspector has been appointed.

10. What does the woman request?
    (A) Product prices
    (B) Production quotas
    (C) Exam scores
    (D) Test results

CH 08

91

Chapter 08 Listening Test

Part 4 🔊 199-207

Directions: You will hear some talks given by a single speaker. You will be asked to answer three questions about what the speaker says in each talk. Select the best response to each question and mark the letter (A), (B), (C), or (D) on your answer sheet. The talks will not be printed in your test book and will be spoken only one time.

11. What problem does the speaker mention?
    (A) Manpower shortages
    (B) Operational safety
    (C) Low wages
    (D) Low morale

12. Why is the speaker concerned?
    (A) Company workers are unproductive.
    (B) Company employees are on strike.
    (C) He has been sick for a long time.
    (D) He must hire many new workers.

13. What are the listeners asked to do?
    (A) Watch videos
    (B) Read reports
    (C) Hold meetings
    (D) Reduce costs

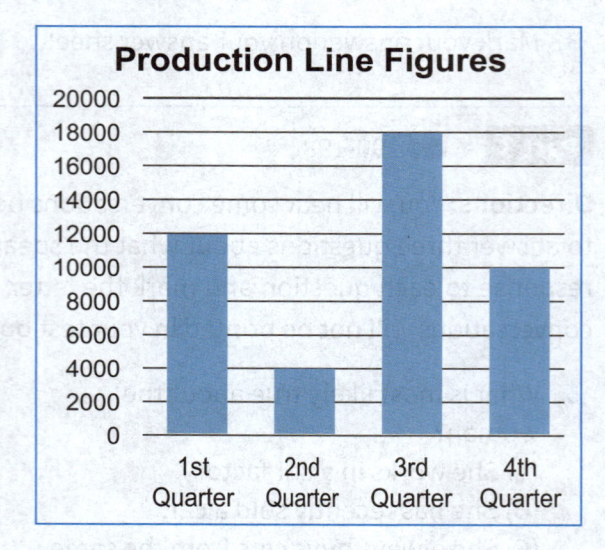

Production Line Figures

1st Quarter	12000
2nd Quarter	4000
3rd Quarter	18000
4th Quarter	10000

14. What happened in spring?
    (A) A new product was launched.
    (B) A trade show was held.
    (C) A contract was signed.
    (D) An agreement was canceled.

15. Look at the graphic. In which quarter did McAlister Woolenwear upgrade its machinery?
    (A) 1st quarter
    (B) 2nd quarter
    (C) 3rd quarter
    (D) 4th quarter

16. What does the speaker suggest?
    (A) Selling different products
    (B) Handling customer complaints
    (C) Reducing overhead costs
    (D) Scheduling more work hours

Chapter 08 Reading Test

Part 5

Directions: A word or phrase is missing in each of the sentences below. Four answer choices are given below each sentence. Select the best answer to complete the sentence. Then mark the letter (A), (B), (C), or (D) on your answer sheet.

17. ------- the plant has been working at full capacity, the manager wants us to find ways to accelerate our output even further.
    (A) Because
    (B) Whether
    (C) Although
    (D) As if

18. This factory is the third- ------- manufacturer of automation equipment in the tri-state area and produces high-quality devices such as robotic arms.
    (A) larger
    (B) largest
    (C) large
    (D) less large

19. The dimensions for the product packaging ------- entered incorrectly into the sealing machine, which slowed down the process.
    (A) does
    (B) do
    (C) was
    (D) were

20. Mr. Sklenar complained that the quality-control data is not -------; he wants the figures to be analyzed again.
    (A) accurate
    (B) accurately
    (C) accuracy
    (D) accumulate

21. As part of our modernization agenda, we propose ------- a faster conveyor belt system to streamline our existing procedures.
    (A) preventing
    (B) downsizing
    (C) installing
    (D) measuring

Chapter 08 Reading Test

Part 6

Directions: Read the texts that follow. A word, phrase, or sentence is missing in parts of each text. Four answer choices for each question are given below the text. Select the best answer to complete the text. Then mark the letter (A), (B), (C), or (D) on your answer sheet.

Questions 22-25 refer to the following article.

Essex Appliances Corporation (EAC) today announced a plan to erect two state-of-the-art manufacturing plants at its West Bridge site. When completed in six months, the factories will be able to produce ------- every one of their current major products. They
22.
will also be able to incorporate last-minute changes to any device before final production.

Upon completion, the two plants will provide more than 200 new jobs. Most of these jobs ------- to be filled by local residents. -------. Gordon Hardwick, CEO of EAC,
23.   24.
said, "In today's competitive business environment, you can't stand -------. Moving
25.
forward is the only way to survive."

---

22. (A) completely
    (B) virtually
    (C) rarely
    (D) really

23. (A) expects
    (B) expect
    (C) expected
    (D) are expected

24. (A) All our products come with a three-year warranty.
    (B) This will cause unemployment numbers to rise.
    (C) Vacancies will eventually be listed on the EAC website.
    (D) We look forward to cooperating with you in the future.

25. (A) out
    (B) up to
    (C) for
    (D) still

Part 7

Directions: In this part you will read a selection of texts, such as magazine and newspaper articles, emails, and instant messages. Each text or set of texts is followed by several questions. Select the best answer for each question and mark the letter (A), (B), (C), or (D) on your answer sheet.

Questions 26-30 refer to the following email and attachment.

From:	marisa.ford-hughes@cvk-manufacturing.com
To:	plant-supervisors@cvk-manufacturing.com
Subject:	Emergency Response Procedures
Attachment:	updated.xls

Hi All,

As you are aware, an independent risk assessment of our emergency response procedures was conducted last month. The manufacturing plant was found to comply with all industry regulations and national and international safety standards. However, the risk assessment report does recommend that we make an adjustment to our standard procedure for evacuation in the event of a fire, explosion, or gas leak. Specifically, it suggests that we change the evacuation assembly area to a location further away from the plant. Please see the attachment for the updated evacuation procedure. Also, we will be performing the regular biannual testing of the emergency notification system next Monday. All workers should receive an alert on their computers and/or phones at some time during the morning.

Thank you.

Marisa Ford-Hughes
Health & Safety Manager
CVK Manufacturing

Chapter 08 Reading Test

---

updated.xls

	Updated Emergency Procedure
Step 1	Activate the alarm; notify supervisor and emergency services
Step 2	Shut down plant machinery if safe to do so; leave your belongings behind
Step 3	Evacuate using routes marked with yellow arrows; don't use elevators
Step 4	Assemble at emergency meeting point in south parking lot

Plant supervisors are asked to hold meetings with their teams to convey this updated information at their earliest convenience. Thank you.

---

26. Why is Ms. Ford-Hughes changing a procedure?
    (A) It was mandated by a law.
    (B) It was suggested in a report.
    (C) It was demanded by a manager.
    (D) It was necessitated by a disaster.

27. Which step does the adjustment relate to?
    (A) Step 1
    (B) Step 2
    (C) Step 3
    (D) Step 4

28. What will happen on Monday?
    (A) A proposal will be published.
    (B) A system will be tested.
    (C) A procedure will be changed.
    (D) A server will be replaced.

29. What is NOT mentioned in the attachment?
    (A) Triggering the alarm
    (B) Following marked directions
    (C) Turning off equipment
    (D) Operating fire extinguishers

30. According to the attachment, what are plant supervisors requested to do?
    (A) Brief their staff on the new procedure
    (B) Display the document in their offices
    (C) Alert the authorities to potential dangers
    (D) Report lack of compliance to their superiors

Chapter 09 Offices 辦公室

1 board [bɔrd] n. 董事會

a board member / meeting
董事會成員 / 會議

▶ The board of directors approved the proposal to open a branch office in Taipei.
董事會批准了在臺北設立分公司的提案。

2 chair [tʃɛr] n. (會議 / 協會的) 主席 & vt. 主持 (會議)

chair a meeting　　主持會議

▶ Sarah asked the chair if she could say a few words about the issue.
莎拉詢問主席是否可以就該議題發表幾句話。

▶ Bruce is going to chair the meeting tomorrow morning.
布魯斯明早要主持會議。

3 agenda [əˋdʒɛndə] n. 議程；工作事項

on the agenda
在議程 / 工作事項內

be high on the agenda
……很重要

▶ This important issue should be placed on the agenda.
這個重要議題應該列入議程。

▶ In our company, quality control is high on the agenda.
品管是本公司的首要之務。

4 minute [ˋmɪnɪt] n. 會議記錄 (恆用複數，與 the 並用)

take the minutes　　作會議記錄

▶ It is Irene's turn to take the minutes at the staff meeting.
這次輪到艾琳在員工會議上作會議記錄。

5 document [ˋdɑkjəmənt] n. (書面或電腦) 文件 & vt. 記錄

a(n) official / confidential / legal document
正式 / 機密 / 法律文件

▶ Please store these confidential documents in a safe place.
請把這些機密文件存放在安全的所在。

6 attendance [əˋtɛndəns] n. 出席；出席人數

衍 attend vt. 參加
　　attendee n. 出席者

in attendance　　出席

▶ Emma was happy because all of her friends were in attendance at her wedding.
艾瑪很高興，因為她所有的朋友都出席了自己的婚禮。

▶ Attendance at the conference was low because people were occupied with other projects.
研討會的出席人數很少，因為大夥兒都忙於其他專案。

7 postpone [postˋpon] vt. 延期，延緩 (= put off)

postpone + N/V-ing
將……延期，暫緩……

postpone sth until...
將某事延至……

▶ Emily postponed her vacation because her son got sick.
因為兒子生病了，艾蜜莉暫緩去度假。

▶ The tennis match has been postponed until next Friday because of the storm.
這場網球比賽因為暴風雨的關係而延期到下週五。

8 division [dəˋvɪʒən] n. 部門

(補) division 與 department 皆可指公司結構中的部門，一般而言，division 所表達的規模可能比 department 還大，但還是取決於公司內的定義，有時兩者可以互換。

sales / marketing division
銷售 / 行銷部門

▶ The sales division has performed very well over the past five years.
過去五年來，業務部門表現相當出色。

9 facility [fəˋsɪlətɪ] n. 設備；設施（常用複數）

(衍) facilitate vt.
促進，使便利

▶ The office facilities are being upgraded to include a gym and a bar.
辦公室設施正在進行更新，要增加健身房跟吧檯。

10 access [ˋæksɛs] n. 接近或使用的權利或方法（不可數，與介詞 to 並用）& vt. 存取（電腦資料）；使用

(衍) accessible a.（地或物）可到達的，可進入的

(比) assess vt. 評估，評價

have access to sth
可以接近 / 取得某物

▶ Only the CEO has access to the company's computer database.
只有執行長可以進入公司的電腦資料庫。

▶ Members of the online store have to enter their passwords to access their personal shopping records.
該網店的會員必須輸入密碼才能取得自己的購物紀錄。

11 malfunction [mælˋfʌŋkʃən] n. & vi. 故障

(反) function n. 功能 & vi. 運作

▶ The captain reported a malfunction in the aircraft's navigation system.
機長通報飛機的導航系統發生故障。

▶ The driver was severely injured in the accident because the airbags malfunctioned.
該名駕駛在事故中受了重傷，因為安全氣囊故障了。

12 extension [ɪkˈstɛnʃən] n. 分機號碼；電話分機

衍 extend vt. & vi. 延長；延期

▶ If you have any questions, feel free to call me at 1357910, extension 9.
如果你有任何問題，儘管撥打 1357910 轉分機 9 與我聯繫。

13 dial [ˈdaɪəl] vt. 撥，按（電話號碼）

dial a number
撥電話號碼

▶ Please dial this number if you want to file a complaint about poor service.
若您覺得服務不周想要投訴，請撥打此電話。

14 transfer [trænsˈfɝ] vt. & vi. 調離（三態為：transfer, transferred [trænsˈfɝd], transferred) & [ˈtrænsfɝ] n. 調任

transfer sb to + 地方
轉調某人至某地

▶ The company has transferred Chris to the Chicago office.
公司已把克里斯調去芝加哥分公司。

▶ Jennifer requested a transfer to the marketing department.
珍妮佛申請調任行銷部門。

15 stationery [ˈsteʃənˌɛrɪ] n. 文具（集合名詞，不可數）

補 本字與 stationary（固定的，不動的）發音相同。

a stationery store 文具店

▶ Please pick up some pens from the stationery store on your way back to the office.
麻煩在回辦公室的路上去文具店買幾支筆回來。

16 ventilation [ˌvɛntəˈleʃən] n. 通風（設備）（不可數）

衍 ventilate vt. 使通風

▶ Good ventilation is essential for factory workers.
良好的通風對工廠工人來說是不可或缺的。

17 memo [ˈmɛmo] n. 備忘錄；備忘便條（為 memorandum [ˌmɛməˈrændəm] 的縮寫）

▶ The manager issued a memo about the updated office policies.
關於更新過後的辦公室規定，經理發布了一份備忘錄。

CH 09

18 bulletin board [ˈbulətɪn ˈbɔrd] n. 布告欄

▶ You can stick the poster on the bulletin board so people passing by will notice it.
你可以把海報張貼在布告欄上，這樣經過的人都會注意到。

19 enclose [ɪnˈkloz] vt. (隨函) 附上

衍 enclosure n. (信函) 附件
Please find enclosed...
請查收……（商業書信常用語）

▶ Please return the completed form and enclose a copy of your ID.
請將填好的表格寄回，並附上您的身分證影本。

▶ Please find enclosed an agenda for the meeting.
茲附上那場會議的議程，請查收。

20 acknowledge [əkˈnɑlɪdʒ] vt. (透過信件) 確認收悉

衍 acknowledgment n. 收悉通知
(= acknowledgement)
acknowledge receipt of...
確認收悉……

▶ Kindly acknowledge receipt of this email at your earliest convenience.
收到此電子郵件請盡快回信確認。

21 colleague [ˈkɑlig] n. 同事

▶ Karen has been working overtime frequently ever since one of her colleagues suddenly quit.
自從凱倫的一位同事突然辭職以來，她便經常加班。

22 approve [əˈpruv] vt. 批准 & vi. 同意

衍 approval n. 贊成，同意
approve of sth
同意 / 贊成某事

▶ After an intense discussion, the committee finally approved David's proposal.
經過一番激烈的討論，委員會終於批准了大衛的提案。

▶ Linda doesn't approve of her daughter's habit of skipping meals.
琳達不認同她女兒經常不吃飯的習慣。

23 manage [ˈmænɪdʒ] vt. 管理；經營 & vt. & vi. 成功做到

衍 management n. 管理；經營；資方，管理階層
manager n. 經理
manage to + V 成功做到……

▶ Mike used to assist his parents in managing the restaurant.
麥克以前曾協助他父母管理餐廳。

▶ If you can manage to review my report by tomorrow, I'd appreciate it.
您若能在明天之前撥冗看一下我的報告，我將感激不盡。

24 **prioritize** [praɪˋɔrəˌtaɪz] *vt.* 按優先順序列出 & *vi.* 確定（事項的）優先順序

衍 prioritization *n.* 確定優先順序
priority *n.* 優先事項

▶ Sam has too many tasks to carry out; he needs to prioritize them.
山姆有太多任務要執行，他需要先排定它們的優先順序。

25 **supervise** [ˋsupɚˌvaɪz] *vt.* 監督，管理

衍 supervision *n.* 監督，管理（不可數）
supervisor *n.* 監督者，主管

▶ The marketing manager was appointed to supervise the ad campaign.
行銷經理被指派控管這項廣告活動。

CH 09

Chapter 09 Listening Test

Part 1 🔊 208-210

Directions: For each question in this part, you will hear four statements about a picture in your test book. When you hear the statements, you must select the one statement that best describes what you see in the picture. Then find the number of the question on your answer sheet and mark your answer. The statements will not be printed in your test book and will be spoken only one time.

1.

2.

本回完整音檔 009
本回分段音檔 208-231

102

Part 2 🔊 211-213

Directions: You will hear a question or statement and three responses spoken in English. They will not be printed in your test book and will be spoken only one time. Select the best response to the question or statement and mark the letter (A), (B), or (C) on your answer sheet.

3. Mark your answer on your answer sheet.
4. Mark your answer on your answer sheet.

Part 3 🔊 214-222

Directions: You will hear some conversations between two or more people. You will be asked to answer three questions about what the speakers say in each conversation. Select the best response to each question and mark the letter (A), (B), (C), or (D) on your answer sheet. The conversations will not be printed in your test book and will be spoken only one time.

5. According to the speaker, what will take place soon?
   (A) A book fair
   (B) A yard sale
   (C) A technology exhibition
   (D) A business conference

6. What is the problem?
   (A) A process has been changed.
   (B) A device is malfunctioning.
   (C) A proposal was rejected.
   (D) An inspection has been canceled.

7. What will the woman most likely do next?
   (A) Purchase some stationery
   (B) Design a poster
   (C) Make a telephone call
   (D) Load a ream of paper

| Meeting Agenda ||
| Chair: C. Novoa ||
Attendee	Subject
M. Davies	Remote work policy
L. Foden	Project management system
D. Scott	Employee bonus structure
F. Lynch	Volunteering program

8. Why was the man worried?
   (A) He'd never met the meeting attendees before.
   (B) He was anxious about a controversial topic.
   (C) He'd never been in charge of a meeting before.
   (D) He was concerned about the lack of seating.

9. What did the man do?
   (A) Shared snacks with the attendees
   (B) Allowed the meeting to run late
   (C) Invited more people to attend
   (D) Followed the agenda closely

10. Look at the graphic. Whose subject did the woman ask about?
    (A) M. Davies'   (B) L. Foden's
    (C) D. Scott's   (D) F. Lynch's

CH 09

103

Chapter 09 Listening Test

Part 4 🔊 223-231

Directions: You will hear some talks given by a single speaker. You will be asked to answer three questions about what the speaker says in each talk. Select the best response to each question and mark the letter (A), (B), (C), or (D) on your answer sheet. The talks will not be printed in your test book and will be spoken only one time.

11. Who most likely are the listeners?
    (A) Office cleaners
    (B) Maxim Company's clients
    (C) Receptionist trainees
    (D) Security guards

12. What is one purpose of the booklet?
    (A) To welcome new customers
    (B) To teach makeup skills
    (C) To inform trainees of company benefits
    (D) To provide staff members' extensions

13. What will the listeners do next?
    (A) Clean their workspace
    (B) Serve clients
    (C) Fill in a form
    (D) See their supervisor

14. What has Ms. Wilson been trying to do?
    (A) Purchase a car
    (B) Contact a person
    (C) Advertise a product
    (D) Write an article

15. Why does the speaker say, "Today is May 4"?
    (A) To indicate an approaching deadline
    (B) To confirm the date of publication
    (C) To offer more time for an article
    (D) To arrange a meeting with a writer

16. What does the speaker want to know?
    (A) The name of the publication
    (B) The progress of a contribution
    (C) The location of an office
    (D) The zip code of an address

Chapter 09 Reading Test

Part 5

Directions: A word or phrase is missing in each of the sentences below. Four answer choices are given below each sentence. Select the best answer to complete the sentence. Then mark the letter (A), (B), (C), or (D) on your answer sheet.

17. Ms. Madueke requested a ------- to the business development department, but her boss refused.
    (A) maximum
    (B) stock
    (C) transfer
    (D) routine

18. Since Mr. Cole quit last month, no one has been managing the sales division—a fact the CEO finds ------- to believe.
    (A) difficult
    (B) difficulty
    (C) difference
    (D) differ

19. The office can become unbearably hot and humid during the summer because of inadequate -------.
    (A) to ventilate
    (B) ventilated
    (C) ventilate
    (D) ventilation

20. If you are having trouble ------- your work, your line manager should be able to lend a hand.
    (A) prioritize
    (B) prioritizing
    (C) to prioritize
    (D) priority

21. The chairman addressed all the members of the board of directors, only a few of ------- were actually paying attention.
    (A) that
    (B) whom
    (C) them
    (D) which

105

Chapter 09 Reading Test

Part 6

Directions: Read the texts that follow. A word, phrase, or sentence is missing in parts of each text. Four answer choices for each question are given below the text. Select the best answer to complete the text. Then mark the letter (A), (B), (C), or (D) on your answer sheet.

Questions 22-25 refer to the following email.

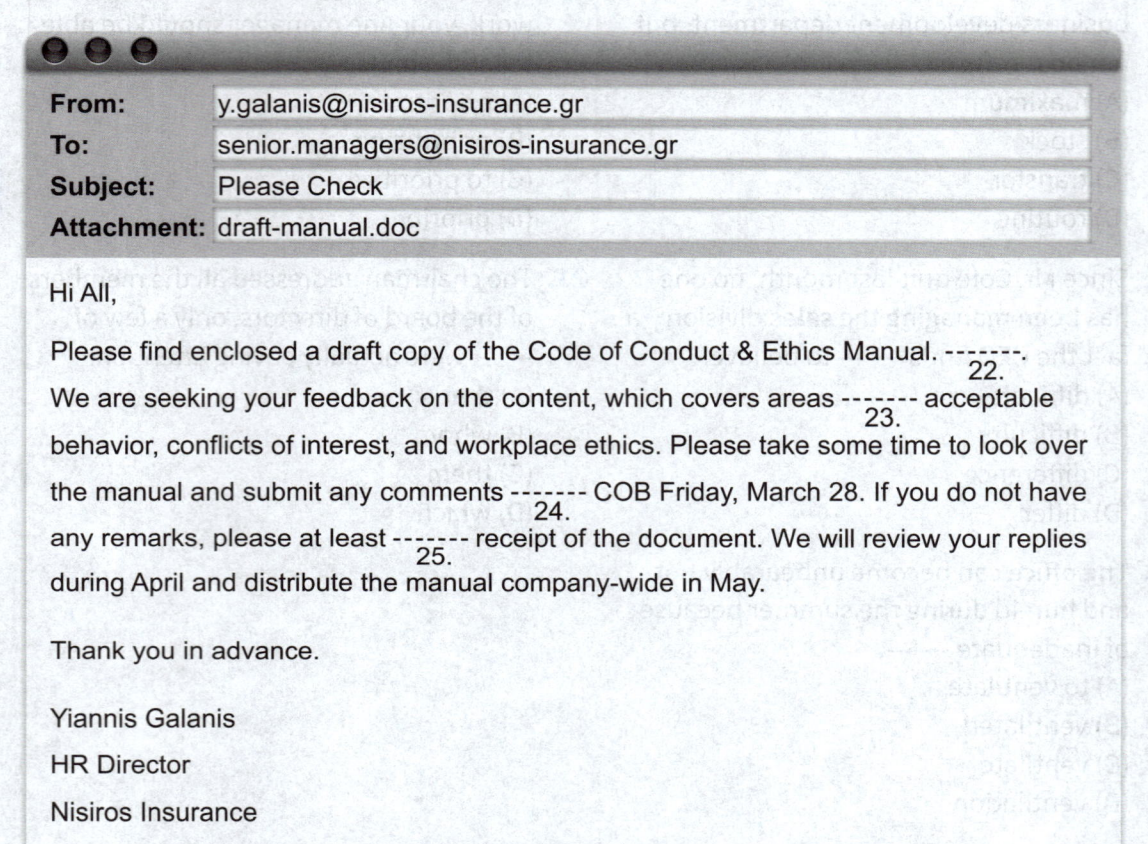

From: y.galanis@nisiros-insurance.gr
To: senior.managers@nisiros-insurance.gr
Subject: Please Check
Attachment: draft-manual.doc

Hi All,

Please find enclosed a draft copy of the Code of Conduct & Ethics Manual. ------- 22. We are seeking your feedback on the content, which covers areas ------- 23. acceptable behavior, conflicts of interest, and workplace ethics. Please take some time to look over the manual and submit any comments ------- 24. COB Friday, March 28. If you do not have any remarks, please at least ------- 25. receipt of the document. We will review your replies during April and distribute the manual company-wide in May.

Thank you in advance.

Yiannis Galanis
HR Director
Nisiros Insurance

---

22. (A) A serious violation of the code was committed.
    (B) The deadline for changes to the manual has passed.
    (C) All employees received the handbook last month.
    (D) I would like to make clear this is not the final version.

23. (A) owing to
    (B) such as
    (C) prior to
    (D) as of

24. (A) since
    (B) by
    (C) from
    (D) at

25. (A) acknowledgement
    (B) acknowledging
    (C) acknowledge
    (D) to acknowledge

Part 7

Directions: In this part you will read a selection of texts, such as magazine and newspaper articles, emails, and instant messages. Each text or set of texts is followed by several questions. Select the best answer for each question and mark the letter (A), (B), (C), or (D) on your answer sheet.

Questions 26-30 refer to the following memo and emails.

MEMO

From: Facilities Committee
To: All Department Heads
Subject: Office Furniture Upgrade

As part of the company's commitment to ensuring a comfortable work environment, funds have been allocated to comprehensively upgrade the office furniture. This will include ergonomic chairs, new desks, storage units, and cubicle dividers. A Facilities Committee has been formed to review workspace needs, consult with heads of departments, and coordinate the ordering of the new furniture. The committee is comprised of:

Anya Peterson, who will deal with the procurement of the new furniture
Melvin Rathbone, who will ensure the project stays within budget
Cush Lindo, who will coordinate directly with department managers
Rami Blofeld, who will ensure compliance with safety standards

---

From: facilities.committee@affable-artwork.com
To: kelvin.gries@affable-artwork.com
Subject: Your Furniture Order

Hi Kelvin,

Thank you for the prompt order of new furniture for your department. We have reviewed your order, cross-referenced it with the budget, and checked that none of the items will prevent people from accessing your or other departments. We are pleased to say that the order below has been approved.

Furniture Order		
Department: Accounting		
Item Code	Item Name	Quantity
TX457	Desk	12
TX188	Chair	12
TX043	Storage Unit	6
TX949	Cubicle Divider	9

107

Please double-check this order and confirm that it is correct. Total Xpress Furniture will deliver the new furniture on Saturday, May 31. We have hired a team that will remove the old furniture and build the new furniture, so there is no need for you to do anything. The new items will be in place when you come to the office on Monday, June 2.

Best regards,

Facilities Committee

From: kelvin.gries@affable-artwork.com
To: facilities.committee@affable-artwork.com
Subject: Re: Your Furniture Order

Hi,

The new furniture was in place this morning as promised. Unfortunately, the storage units are much smaller than we were led to believe. We expected each one to be large enough to be shared by two workers, but they can barely accommodate one worker's files. Unlike other departments, we still deal with a lot of hard copies of documents, so we require sufficient storage space. I would like these to be replaced ASAP.

Thank you.

Kelvin Gries
Head of Accounting
Affable Artwork

---

26. According to the memo, what is the purpose of the committee?
    (A) To lobby bosses for funds for new equipment
    (B) To assess needs and oversee furniture orders
    (C) To make the office environmentally friendly
    (D) To find the least expensive local suppliers

27. Who most likely contacted Mr. Gries?
    (A) Anya Peterson
    (B) Melvin Rathbone
    (C) Cush Lindo
    (D) Rami Blofeld

28. What is Mr. Gries asked to do?
    (A) Verify that an order is accurate
    (B) Assist with furniture construction
    (C) Delay coming to the office on Monday
    (D) Help to remove some unwanted items

29. Which item does Mr. Gries find unsuitable?
    (A) TX457
    (B) TX188
    (C) TX043
    (D) TX949

30. What is indicated about the accounting department?
    (A) It still lacks computers.
    (B) It plans to hire more staff.
    (C) It still handles a lot of paper.
    (D) It hopes to move to a new area.

Chapter 10 Personnel 人事

1 résumé [ˈrɛzəˌme / ˈrɛzjʊˌme] *n.* 履歷

(補) 本字也作 resume 或 resumé，等於英式英語裡的 CV（curriculum vitae [kəˈrɪkjʊləm ˈvitaɪ]）

▶ Applicants for the job should submit their résumés no later than July 31.
應徵本工作者應於七月三十一日前交出履歷。

2 candidate [ˈkændəˌdet / ˈkændədət] *n.* 求職應徵者；候選人

▶ There are quite a few candidates for this position.
有相當多的求職者應徵這個職位。

3 recruit [rɪˈkrut] *vt. & vi.* 招募（員工、新兵）& *n.* 新成員；新兵

(衍) recruitment *n.* 招募
recruiter *n.* 招募人員；徵兵人員

▶ The real estate agency recruited Ruth to head its sales team.
該房屋仲介公司招募了露絲擔任其業務團隊的主管。

▶ All the recruits have to complete a three-month training course.
所有新進員工都必須完成為期三個月的培訓課程。

4 vacancy [ˈvekənsɪ] *n.* 空位，空缺

(衍) vacant *a.* 空缺的
a job vacancy 職缺

▶ There are currently no vacancies in our company.
我們公司目前沒有職缺。

5 apply [əˈplaɪ] *vi.* 應徵，申請

apply for + 工作 / 許可
應徵某工作 / 申請某許可
apply to + 機關 向某機關申請

▶ Mike is applying to Harvard to study law.
邁可正向哈佛大學申請入學研習法律。

6 application [ˌæpləˈkeʃən] *n.* 申請 / 應徵（表格）

(衍) applicant *n.* 應徵者，申請者
make / submit an application to V...
應徵 / 申請從事……

▶ Jason submitted an application to join the CNN news team.
傑森送出應徵 CNN 新聞團隊的文件。

111

7 recommendation [ˌrɛkəmɛnˈdeʃən] n. 推薦信；推薦

衍 recommend vt. 推薦，建議
a letter of recommendation
推薦信

▶ Monica asked the manager to write a letter of recommendation for her.
莫妮卡請經理幫她寫一封推薦信。

8 interview [ˈɪntɚˌvju] n. & vt. 面試；採訪

衍 interviewer n. 面試官；採訪者
interviewee n. 被面試者；受訪者
a job interview
工作面試

▶ The HR manager asked the candidate many tough questions during the interview.
人資經理在面試期間問了該應試者許多難以回答的問題。

▶ Jerry interviewed the director and cast of the film for his YouTube video.
傑瑞為他的 YouTube 影片採訪了這部電影的導演及卡司。

9 qualify [ˈkwɑləˌfaɪ] vt. & vi. (使) 有資格 (三態為：qualify, qualified [ˈkwɑləˌfaɪd], qualified)

衍 qualification n. 資格，條件
qualify as / for...
有……的身分資格 / 有資格做……

▶ Anthony qualified as a professional architect last year.
安東尼去年取得了專業建築師資格。

10 impressive [ɪmˈprɛsɪv] a. 令人印象深刻的

衍 impress vt. 使印象深刻
impression n. 印象；想法，感覺

▶ The second interviewee's résumé was quite impressive.
第二位面試應徵者的履歷令人印象深刻。

11 requirement [rɪˈkwaɪrmənt] n. 要求，必要條件 (常為複數)

衍 require vt. 需要；要求
meet / satisfy / fulfill the requirements 符合要求

▶ It's not easy for Phoebe to meet the requirements of the position.
對菲比來說，要符合這職位的要求並不容易。

12 experienced [ɪkˈspɪrɪənst] a. 有經驗的

衍 experience n. 經驗（不可數）；經歷（可數）& vt. 體驗，經歷
反 inexperienced a. 無經驗的，經驗不足的
be experienced in + N/V-ing
對……有經驗

▶ John is an experienced surgeon who has performed countless operations.
約翰是一名經驗老到的外科醫生，動過無數次的手術。

▶ Owen is very experienced in fixing roofs.
歐文在修理屋頂方面非常有經驗。

13 employ [ɪmˋplɔɪ] vt. 僱用 (= hire)

衍 employer n. 僱主
employee n. 受僱者
employment n. 僱用；就業，在職；工作

employ sb as sth　　僱用某人當……
employ sb to + V　　僱用某人去做……

▶ The manager employed Eric as an engineer in our lab.
經理僱用艾瑞克來當我們實驗室的工程師。

▶ The expert was employed to develop strategies for improving productivity.
這位專家受僱來研擬出提高生產力的方法。

14 reject [rɪˋdʒɛkt] vt. 不錄用；拒絕接受

衍 rejection n. 拒絕（求職者等）；排斥

▶ Tom was rejected by most of the companies he applied to.
湯姆去應徵的公司大部分都沒有錄用他。

▶ The president rejected all of our ideas for reforming the social welfare system.
總統拒絕了我們為了改革社會福利體系而提出的所有想法。

15 human resources　（公司的）人力資源部，人事部（縮寫為 HR）(= personnel [ˌpɝsnˋɛl])

▶ Jennifer transferred from the accounting department to human resources last month.
珍妮佛上個月從會計部轉調人力資源部。

16 probation [proˋbeʃən] n. (工作) 試用 (期)；(留任) 察看期

a probation period　（工作）試用期
on probation　　　　在試用期中

▶ Once the probation period is completed, employees will be offered a one-year contract.
一旦試用期結束，員工將獲得一年的合約。

17 orientation [ˌɔrɪənˋteʃən, ˌorɪɛnˋ-] n. 職前培訓會；迎新會

衍 orient vt. 使適應
an orientation session
新人訓練課程

▶ New employees will attend a brief orientation session on their first day.
新進員工報到當天會參加一場簡短的新人訓練課程。

18 raise [rez] n. 加薪

比 promotion n. 職位升遷
a pay raise　加薪

▶ Stephen will receive a pay raise as a reward for his hard work.
史蒂芬將獲得加薪，以獎勵他的辛勤工作。

CH 10

19 salary [ˈsælərɪ] n. (按月發放的) 薪水

比 wage n. （按小時、日、週所計的）工資
an annual / a monthly / a starting salary　年 / 月 / 起薪

▶ Scott declined the job offer because the salary was too low.
史考特婉拒了這個工作機會，因為薪資太低了。

20 absent [ˈæbsn̩t] a. 缺勤的，缺席的

衍 absence n. 缺席
be absent from...　缺席……

▶ Dana was absent from work for a week because she had the flu.
黛娜因為得了流感而一個禮拜沒去上班了。

21 overtime [ˈovɚˌtaɪm] adv. 超時 & n. 加班 (時數)；加班費 (= overtime pay / earnings)

do / work overtime
加班工作

▶ Paul worked overtime to meet his project's deadline.
保羅為了趕上專案的截止日期而加班。

▶ Sarah's salary last month was $1,500, including overtime.
莎拉上個月的薪水含加班費為一千五百美元。

22 layoff [ˈleˌɔf] n. 裁員 (= lay-off)

▶ With another wave of layoffs approaching, all the staff members are afraid of losing their jobs.
另一波的裁員逼近，所有員工都很怕飯碗不保。

23 leave [liv] n. 休假 (不可數)

personal / sick / annual leave
事 / 病 / 年假
take leave　請假

▶ Sophia took personal leave to take care of her sick son.
蘇菲亞為了照顧生病的兒子而請了事假。

24 retire [rɪˈtaɪr] vi. 退休

衍 retired a. 已退休的
retirement n. 退休
retire from...　從……退休

▶ Kevin was forced to retire because of ill health.
凱文因為身體健康不佳而被迫退休。

25 pension [ˈpɛnʃən] n. 退休金，養老金

a pension plan　退休金計畫
receive a pension　領退休金

▶ Mrs. Johnson receives her pension on the first day of each month.
強森太太每個月的第一天都會領退休金。

Chapter 10 Listening Test

Part 1 🔊 232-234

本回完整音檔 010
本回分段音檔 232-255

Directions: For each question in this part, you will hear four statements about a picture in your test book. When you hear the statements, you must select the one statement that best describes what you see in the picture. Then find the number of the question on your answer sheet and mark your answer. The statements will not be printed in your test book and will be spoken only one time.

1.

2.

CH 10

115

Chapter 10 Listening Test

Part 2 🔊 235-237

Directions: You will hear a question or statement and three responses spoken in English. They will not be printed in your test book and will be spoken only one time. Select the best response to the question or statement and mark the letter (A), (B), or (C) on your answer sheet.

3. Mark your answer on your answer sheet.

4. Mark your answer on your answer sheet.

Part 3 🔊 238-246

Directions: You will hear some conversations between two or more people. You will be asked to answer three questions about what the speakers say in each conversation. Select the best response to each question and mark the letter (A), (B), (C), or (D) on your answer sheet. The conversations will not be printed in your test book and will be spoken only one time.

5. What are the speakers mainly discussing?
    (A) A job applicant
    (B) A coworker
    (C) A recommendation
    (D) A schedule

6. What does the woman give the man?
    (A) Records of payment
    (B) Letters of reference
    (C) Printed invoices
    (D) Salary requirements

7. What problem does the woman mention?
    (A) A candidate's résumé is not up to date.
    (B) A job applicant cannot work immediately.
    (C) An employer did not write a letter of support.
    (D) A suitable applicant has not been found.

8. What is the woman concerned about?
    (A) The interviewer's technique
    (B) The applicant's qualifications
    (C) The position's salary package
    (D) The employment contract

9. What is the candidate's field of expertise?
    (A) Mathematics
    (B) Physics
    (C) Management
    (D) Statistics

10. What does the woman suggest?
    (A) Checking the candidate's application
    (B) Holding a training session
    (C) Placing the candidate on probation
    (D) Interviewing other candidates

Part 4 🔊 247-255

Directions: You will hear some talks given by a single speaker. You will be asked to answer three questions about what the speaker says in each talk. Select the best response to each question and mark the letter (A), (B), (C), or (D) on your answer sheet. The talks will not be printed in your test book and will be spoken only one time.

11. Who most likely is the speaker?
    (A) A trainee doctor
    (B) A registered nurse
    (C) A recruitment consultant
    (D) An office receptionist

12. What does the speaker say about the position?
    (A) There have been many applicants.
    (B) Interviews are now taking place.
    (C) It has recently been filled.
    (D) It provides a high salary.

13. What does the speaker ask Ms. Jones to do?
    (A) Submit her portfolio
    (B) Process an application
    (C) Call her back if she desires
    (D) Send a business card

Name	Length of Employment
Ron Buckingham	36 years
Cathy Stevens	27 years
Pam Ashcroft	20 years
Ian Benson	29 years

14. What is being announced?
    (A) Dismissals
    (B) Year-end banquets
    (C) Retrenchments
    (D) Retirements

15. What is provided at the event?
    (A) Discounts for members
    (B) Free samples
    (C) Refreshments
    (D) Souvenirs

16. Look at the graphic. Who will make the speech first?
    (A) Mr. Buckingham
    (B) Ms. Stevens
    (C) Ms. Ashcroft
    (D) Mr. Benson

Chapter 10 Reading Test

Part 5

Directions: A word or phrase is missing in each of the sentences below. Four answer choices are given below each sentence. Select the best answer to complete the sentence. Then mark the letter (A), (B), (C), or (D) on your answer sheet.

17. It is essential that all new starters ------- the orientation process on their first day at the company.
    (A) completed
    (B) complete
    (C) to complete
    (D) completing

18. Candidates for the ------- opened position of sales representative will in part be chosen by means of an audition.
    (A) new
    (B) newest
    (C) newer
    (D) newly

19. ------- no one to apply for the vacancy, we would have to advertise the position more widely.
    (A) Had
    (B) Should
    (C) If
    (D) Were

20. Due to the numerous job applications ------- for the supervisory positions, it is likely that we will have to reject over half of them.
    (A) receive
    (B) received
    (C) receiving
    (D) receives

21. Konnektt Systems, one of the world's largest computer manufacturers, has announced ------- that will affect 8,000 of its employees.
    (A) conflicts
    (B) diversities
    (C) layoffs
    (D) mentors

Part 6

Directions: Read the texts that follow. A word, phrase, or sentence is missing in parts of each text. Four answer choices for each question are given below the text. Select the best answer to complete the text. Then mark the letter (A), (B), (C), or (D) on your answer sheet.

Questions 22-25 refer to the following letter.

Mr. John Burr
141 South Baker Avenue
Muncie, Indiana 47302

Dear Mr. Burr:

Congratulations on your retirement! We at Amalgamated Industries will miss you, but we are happy that you can now spend your time ------- you please. Since
          22.
you are eligible for a pension, we urge you to visit us ------- your earliest convenience
                                                   23.
to complete the forms necessary to receive your government benefits. -------. The
                                                                       24.
number for Human Resources is 848-2171. We look forward to ------- you again and
                                                              25.
helping you prepare for this next phase in your life.

Yours sincerely,

Beth Rosemary
Human Resources Director
Amalgamated Industries

---

22. (A) like
    (B) as
    (C) what
    (D) so

23. (A) at
    (B) in
    (C) with
    (D) on

24. (A) I will personally assist you with all the paperwork.
    (B) A permit for the development will then be issued by the government.
    (C) You will receive a refund only if you can provide documentation.
    (D) Other staff members have also made the same request.

25. (A) see
    (B) seeing
    (C) be seeing
    (D) sees

119

Chapter 10 Reading Test

Part 7

Directions: In this part you will read a selection of texts, such as magazine and newspaper articles, emails, and instant messages. Each text or set of texts is followed by several questions. Select the best answer for each question and mark the letter (A), (B), (C), or (D) on your answer sheet.

Questions 26-30 refer to the following e-mail and memo.

To:	Roger Branson
From:	Reginald Ascot
Date:	December 1
Subject:	Bonus ideas

Roger,

The board met to discuss novel ideas for the annual employee bonus, and several excellent proposals were submitted.

By far the most well-received was Colin's idea to give staff a cash bonus equivalent to one day's wage. I think this is a good idea, but in light of the immense profits made this year, Zaza suggested that staff receive an extra day of leave. I tend to agree and think this would be a great boost to morale.

Robert's suggestion, a trip to somewhere such as the Grand Canyon, was the least popular. Needless to say, it would be impossible at such short notice. Mandy's idea to raise the rate of overtime pay was almost as poorly received as Robert's.

Could you let me know your decision when you return from abroad?

Reginald Ascot

MEMO

The executive board has decided to give all workers a holiday treat.

Due to the excellent performance of all our branches and head office departments, Mason Electronics has posted its most profitable year ever. To share this good fortune with those who made it possible — you, the employees — the executive board has decided that all staff will receive an extra day of personal leave on December 24. This includes employees at the head office, the Southridge factory, and all 12 retail outlets. It does not, however, include installation subcontractors.

Those who have already arranged personal leave on the 24th will still receive an extra day of leave. Supervisors, team leaders, and department heads must adjust their schedules and deadlines as necessary. Retail outlets should display signs to inform customers of the closure.

Finally, I'd like to take the opportunity to wish all the hard-working and selfless employees and their families a safe, loving, and happy holiday season.

Merry Christmas!

Reginald Ascot, Senior Vice President

---

26. In the e-mail, the word "notice" in paragraph 3, line 2, is closest in meaning to
(A) observation
(B) warning
(C) review
(D) distance

27. What is indicated about Mason Electronics?
(A) It has recovered from a financial crisis.
(B) It has multiple locations.
(C) It is expanding into overseas territories.
(D) It is on the verge of bankruptcy.

28. Whose proposal was accepted?
(A) Colin's
(B) Zaza's
(C) Robert's
(D) Mandy's

29. Who will NOT benefit from the proposal?
(A) Board members
(B) Department heads
(C) Factory workers
(D) Subcontractors

30. What does Mr. Ascot advise middle managers to do?
(A) Alter their agendas
(B) Reduce their overheads
(C) Submit their proposals
(D) Prepare their vacations

NOTES

Chapter 11 Purchasing 採購

1. purchase [ˈpɝtʃəs] vt. & n. 購買 (物)

purchase sth　　購買某物
= make a purchase of sth

▶ Jenny went to the store and purchased some stationery for the office.
= Jenny went to the store and made a purchase of some stationery for the office.
珍妮去商店購買了一些辦公室用的文具。

2. item [ˈaɪtəm] n. (物品) 項目，商品

衍 itemize vt. 列出清單

▶ I'd like to pay for each item separately, please.
我想把每樣東西分開結帳，謝謝。

3. refund [ˈriˌfʌnd] n. 退款 & [rɪˈfʌnd] vt. 退還

衍 refundable a. 可退款的
demand a (full) refund
要求（全額）退款

▶ Monica returned her faulty phone to the store and demanded a refund.
莫妮卡將她有瑕疵的手機退回店家，並要求退錢。

▶ The travel agency refunded the customers after the trip was canceled.
行程取消後，旅行社便退款給客人。

4. retail [ˈritel] n. 零售生意 (不可數) & vt. & vi. 零售 & a. 零售的 & adv. 以零售方式

衍 retailer n. 零售商；零售店
a retail outlet / price　　零售店 / 價
retail at / for + 金額　　零售價格為……

▶ The retail price of this microwave oven is $110.
= This microwave oven retails at $110.
這個微波爐的零售價是一百一十美元。

5. wholesale [ˈholˌsel] n. 批發生意 (不可數) & vt. & vi. 批發 (貨物) & a. 批發的 & adv. 批發地

衍 wholesaler n. 批發商
a wholesale price　　批發價
wholesale at / for + 金額
批發價格為……

▶ Evelyn bought her gown for the party at a wholesale price.
伊芙琳以批發價買了要穿去參加派對的禮服。

▶ Our company wholesales wine to restaurants and bars.
我們公司批發葡萄酒給餐廳與酒吧。

6 discount [ˈdɪskaʊnt] n. 折扣 & vt. 打折

give / offer sb a 20% discount on sth
就某物幫某人打八折

- We'll offer a 20% discount on the refrigerator if you buy it now.
  您若現在就把冰箱買下來，我們會給您打八折。
- The vendor discounted the apples that had bruises on them.
  小販把碰傷的蘋果打折出售。

7 compliant [kəmˈplaɪənt] a. 合規的，一致的；順從的

衍 **comply** vi. 遵守，順從
compliance n. 遵守（不可數）
be compliant with... 遵照……

- The latest version of this software is compliant with industry standards.
  該軟體的最新版本符合業界標準。

8 deliver [dɪˈlɪvɚ] vt. & vi. 遞送

衍 **delivery** n. 運送，交貨

- You have to sign for the package in person when it is delivered.
  當包裹送達時，你必須親自簽收。

9 shipping [ˈʃɪpɪŋ] n. (航空、船、車)運輸 (不可數)

衍 **ship** vt. & vi.（用飛機、船或卡車等）運送

- Please transfer a payment of $47, plus $9 for shipping.
  請轉帳四十七美元另加九美元運費。

10 import [ˈɪmpɔrt] n. 進口；輸入品 & [ɪmˈpɔrt] vt. 進口，輸入

import sth from + 地方
從某地進口某物

- The government placed restrictions on the import of beef from foreign countries.
  政府對外國牛肉的進口施加限制。
- This batch of chocolate was imported from Switzerland.
  這一批巧克力是從瑞士進口的。

11 export [ˈɛkspɔrt] n. 出口；輸出品 & [ɪkˈspɔrt] vt. 出口，輸出

export sth to + 地方
出口某物至某地

- Wool is one of New Zealand's major exports.
  羊毛是紐西蘭的主要輸出品之一。
- Their fruits are exported to many Asian countries.
  他們的水果外銷到許多亞洲國家。

12 distribute [dɪˋstrɪbjut] *vt.* 經銷；分發

衍 distribution *n.* 經銷；分發

▶ The company is authorized to distribute our products in some South American countries.
這家公司獲得授權在某些南美洲國家經銷我們的產品。

▶ The charity distributes food and clothes to earthquake victims.
那間慈善機構把食物和衣服分發給地震災民。

13 order [ˋɔrdɚ] *vt.* 訂購；訂製 & *n.* 訂單；訂購

place an order
下訂單購買

▶ The company has ordered several computers to replace the old ones.
公司已訂購數臺電腦來替換舊的。

▶ Carol placed an order for kitchenware a week ago.
卡蘿在一個禮拜前下訂單購買了廚房用具。

14 quote [kwot] *vt.* & *n.* 報價

▶ The agent quoted us $500 for shipping and handling.
代辦人員給我們報價的運費加手續費為五百美元。

▶ If I were you, I would ask them for a written quote before they start work.
換做我是你，我會在他們開工之前向他們索取書面報價。

15 merchandise [ˋmɝtʃənˌdaɪz] *n.* 商品（集合名詞，不可數）& *vt.* 促銷

衍 merchant *n.* 商人
a piece of merchandise
一件商品

▶ The candy bars were merchandised at the counter to encourage impulse purchases.
糖果棒被擺放在櫃檯做促銷，以刺激顧客衝動買下來。

16 bargain [ˋbɑrgən] *n.* 划算的東西；協議 & *vi.* 講價，討價還價

a real bargain 物超所值
bargain with sb 與某人討價還價

▶ The scooter Ryan bought yesterday was a real bargain.
萊恩昨天買的那臺機車真是超值。

▶ Linda is bargaining with a street vendor over the price of a handbag.
琳達正在就一個手提包的價格和街頭攤販討價還價。

17 **inventory** [ˈɪnvənˌt(ɔ)rɪ] *n.* 存貨（清單）；盤點（存貨）（後者不可數）

make an inventory of...
將……列成存貨清單
take inventory 盤點（存貨）

▶ We made an inventory of everything in the storage room.
我們將儲藏室內的所有東西都列入存貨清單。

▶ The store's staff takes inventory of the stock every season.
店員每季都會盤點庫存。

18 **supply** [səˈplaɪ] *vt.* 提供，供應（三態為：supply, supplied [səˈplaɪd], supplied）& *n.* 供應量

（反）demand *vt.* 要求 & *n.* 需要，需求
supply sb with sth 提供某人某物
supply and demand 供需

▶ The water towers on the roof supply the residents with all the water they need.
屋頂上的水塔為住戶提供所需的用水。

19 **invoice** [ˈɪnvɔɪs] *n.* 費用清單

（補）invoice 通常指商品或服務供應商提供給顧客的費用清單，而 bill 則指餐廳、酒吧或飯店的帳單，或水電等費用的帳單。

▶ Please sign your name at the bottom of the invoice.
麻煩在費用清單的底下簽上您的姓名。

20 **receipt** [rɪˈsit] *n.* 收據（可數）；收到（不可數）

（補）本字的 p 不發音。
on / upon receipt of... 一收到……

▶ On receipt of your order, goods will be delivered within three days.
商品在接獲您訂單的三天內會出貨。

21 **inquiry** [ɪnˈkwaɪrɪ / ˈɪnkwərɪ] *n.* 詢問（= enquiry，英式英語）

（衍）inquire *vi.* 詢問（= enquire，英式英語）
make an inquiry about / into...
詢問……

▶ Many people called to make inquiries about our new product.
許多人來電詢問我們的新產品。

22 **excessive** [ɪkˈsɛsɪv] *a.* 過度的

（衍）excess *n.* 超過，過量 & *a.* 過多的

▶ Buy-one-get-one-free deals at supermarkets can make shoppers buy excessive amounts of food.
超市買一送一的優惠會促使消費者買過量的食物。

126

23 **bulk** [bʌlk] *n.* 大量；大部分

衍 bulky *a.* 體型龐大的；笨重的
in bulk　大量地

▶ Can you offer me a discount on those boxes of tissues if I buy in bulk?
我如果大批購買那些盒裝面紙，你可以給我折扣嗎？

24 **compensation** [ˌkɑmpənˈseʃən] *n.* 補償，賠償 (不可數)

衍 compensate *vt.* 賠償 & *vi.* 彌補
claim / demand / seek compensation for...
為……要求補償 / 賠償

▶ You should claim compensation for your damaged goods.
你應該為受損的商品申請要求賠償。

25 **upfront** [ʌpˈfrʌnt] *a.* 預付的

▶ The salesman suggested that we pay a certain amount of money as an upfront fee.
業務員建議我們付一定額度的錢作為預付款。

Chapter 11 Listening Test

本回完整音檔 011
本回分段音檔 256-279

Part 1 🔊 256-258

Directions: For each question in this part, you will hear four statements about a picture in your test book. When you hear the statements, you must select the one statement that best describes what you see in the picture. Then find the number of the question on your answer sheet and mark your answer. The statements will not be printed in your test book and will be spoken only one time.

1.

2.

Part 2 🔊 259-261

Directions: You will hear a question or statement and three responses spoken in English. They will not be printed in your test book and will be spoken only one time. Select the best response to the question or statement and mark the letter (A), (B), or (C) on your answer sheet.

3. Mark your answer on your answer sheet.
4. Mark your answer on your answer sheet.

Part 3 🔊 262-270

Directions: You will hear some conversations between two or more people. You will be asked to answer three questions about what the speakers say in each conversation. Select the best response to each question and mark the letter (A), (B), (C), or (D) on your answer sheet. The conversations will not be printed in your test book and will be spoken only one time.

5. Why is the man surprised?
   (A) An item in the store is not expensive.
   (B) A product he wants is not available.
   (C) A supermarket sells exotic goods.
   (D) A friend eats too much protein.

6. What does the woman indicate about the supplier?
   (A) It deals with one specific health food store.
   (B) It sends its products across the nation.
   (C) It is going to raise its wholesale prices.
   (D) It is based in a different country.

7. How did the woman find out about the supply chain?
   (A) She read a news report.
   (B) She asked a shop assistant.
   (C) She worked for the supplier.
   (D) She watched a television show.

8. What does the woman ask the man to do?
   (A) Unload a truck
   (B) Check an order
   (C) Take a message
   (D) Complete a form

9. What does the woman imply when she says, "But we're always purchasing drums of chemicals"?
   (A) She confirms the standard operating procedure.
   (B) She thinks the chemicals should be cheaper.
   (C) She is surprised that the man is not certified.
   (D) She personally placed the order.

10. What does the woman say she will do?
    (A) Ask for another colleague's help
    (B) Inspect some paperwork
    (C) Check the man's certification
    (D) Authorize a procedure

Chapter 11 Listening Test

Part 4 271-279

Directions: You will hear some talks given by a single speaker. You will be asked to answer three questions about what the speaker says in each talk. Select the best response to each question and mark the letter (A), (B), (C), or (D) on your answer sheet. The talks will not be printed in your test book and will be spoken only one time.

11. What does the speaker say about the battery recharger?
    (A) He should have bought it elsewhere.
    (B) It stopped working after a short time.
    (C) It may have been damaged.
    (D) The packaging is unattractive.

12. Why is the speaker calling?
    (A) To reply to an inquiry
    (B) To request a refund
    (C) To confirm an order
    (D) To query an exchange

13. What problem does the speaker have?
    (A) He accidently damaged the packaging.
    (B) He forgot where the store is located.
    (C) He lost the battery charger.
    (D) He cannot find the receipt.

14. What is the advertisement mainly about?
    (A) A trip to an exotic country
    (B) An opening of a new store
    (C) A competition to win a ticket
    (D) A sale to celebrate an anniversary

15. How can listeners receive a discount?
    (A) By shopping online
    (B) By buying 20 items
    (C) By applying for a store card
    (D) By spending in excess of 20 dollars

16. What does the speaker imply when he says, "Don't delay; time is running out"?
    (A) The store will close very soon.
    (B) The sale is on for a limited period.
    (C) The loyalty scheme is nearly full.
    (D) The items have almost sold out.

Chapter 11 Reading Test

Part 5

Directions: A word or phrase is missing in each of the sentences below. Four answer choices are given below each sentence. Select the best answer to complete the sentence. Then mark the letter (A), (B), (C), or (D) on your answer sheet.

17. It took Ms. Jeong half a day ------- the inventory, and then she spent a further two hours filing the purchase invoices.
    (A) checking
    (B) to check
    (C) checked
    (D) check

18. As a result of exceptionally high demand and reduced supply, we regret ------- you that we are unable to dispatch your goods at this time.
    (A) tell
    (B) telling
    (C) to tell
    (D) have told

19. ------- importing car parts, the automobile manufacturer also exports spare parts to other countries.
    (A) According to
    (B) In addition to
    (C) In front of
    (D) On behalf of

20. Watch Zone returned Mr. Malaban's upfront payment and offered him ------- for the shockingly poor service he received.
    (A) confrontation
    (B) duplication
    (C) clearance
    (D) compensation

21. ------- increased fuel and shipping costs, we must inform you that we cannot fill your order according to the estimate we quoted you.
    (A) Due to
    (B) In spite of
    (C) Behind
    (D) With a view to

Chapter 11 Reading Test

Part 6

Directions: Read the texts that follow. A word, phrase, or sentence is missing in parts of each text. Four answer choices for each question are given below the text. Select the best answer to complete the text. Then mark the letter (A), (B), (C), or (D) on your answer sheet.

Questions 22-25 refer to the following e-mail.

To: All Employees
From: Martha Bennington, Department of Budgeting
Subject: New Stationery Supplies Ordering Policy

It has come to our attention that requests for stationery have become excessive over the past five months. -------- items like extra paper, pens, and whiteout do not seem like
                                                    22.
much, with more than 300 employees, it all adds up. In these highly competitive times, every dollar counts. We must therefore cut costs -------- we can.
                                                                                        23.

In an attempt to rectify the situation, managers in each department will be required to keep track of any items purchased each month from Stationery Supplies starting on March 1. --------. Your cooperation will -------- Malcolm Industries' continued success.
               24.   25.

---

22. (A) Though
    (B) Even
    (C) Despite
    (D) Even so

23. (A) wherever
    (B) no matter
    (C) what
    (D) how

24. (A) Several reams of paper will be purchased instead.
    (B) The quality of their service has always been a concern.
    (C) Each staff member will then receive 50 new business cards.
    (D) It is therefore essential to keep all the receipts.

25. (A) pressure
    (B) measure
    (C) reassure
    (D) ensure

132

Part 7

Directions: In this part you will read a selection of texts, such as magazine and newspaper articles, emails, and instant messages. Each text or set of texts is followed by several questions. Select the best answer for each question and mark the letter (A), (B), (C), or (D) on your answer sheet.

Questions 26-30 refer to the following product information, online review, and response.

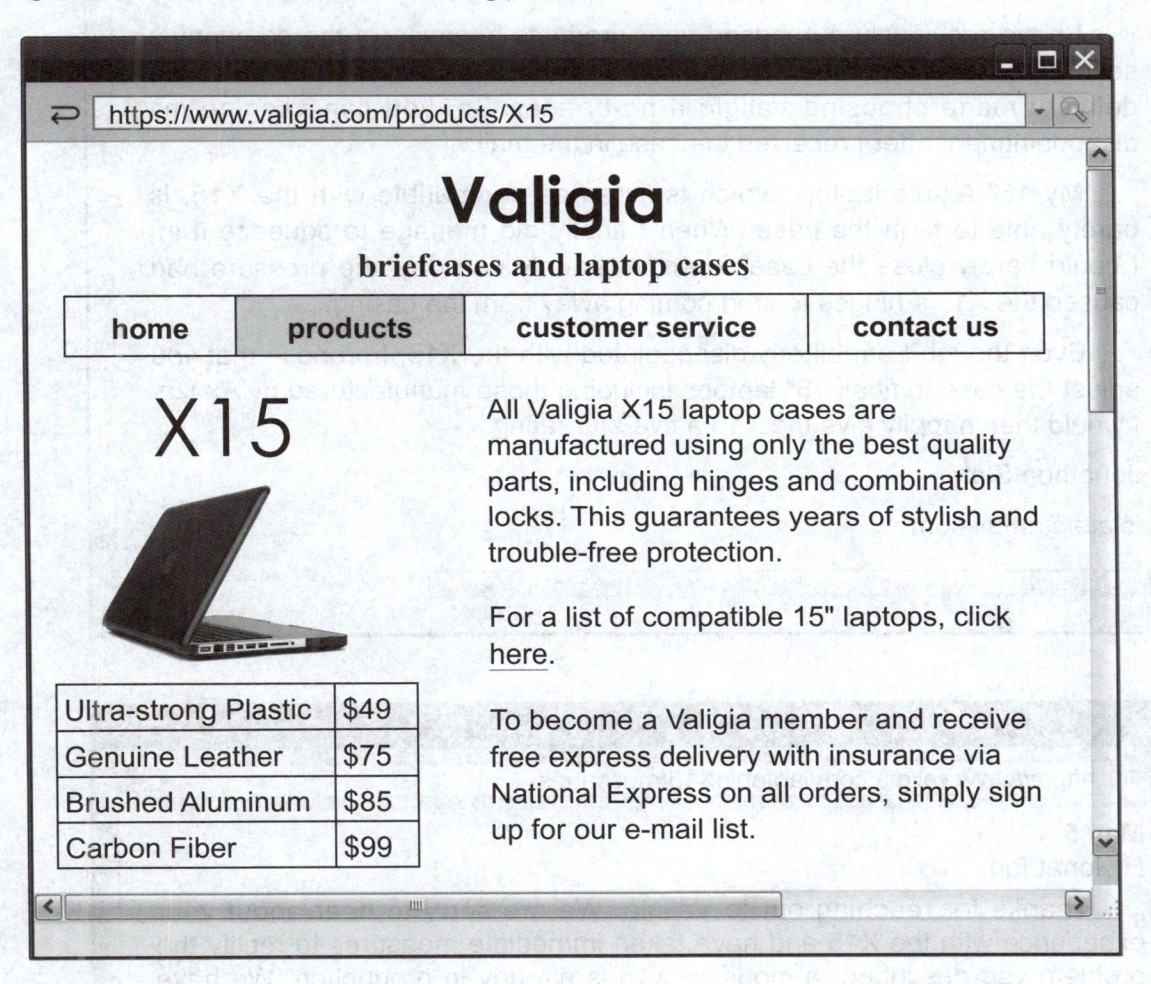

---

https://www.valigia.com/products/X15

Valigia
briefcases and laptop cases

| home | products | customer service | contact us |

X15

Ultra-strong Plastic	$49
Genuine Leather	$75
Brushed Aluminum	$85
Carbon Fiber	$99

All Valigia X15 laptop cases are manufactured using only the best quality parts, including hinges and combination locks. This guarantees years of stylish and trouble-free protection.

For a list of compatible 15" laptops, click here.

To become a Valigia member and receive free express delivery with insurance via National Express on all orders, simply sign up for our e-mail list.

133

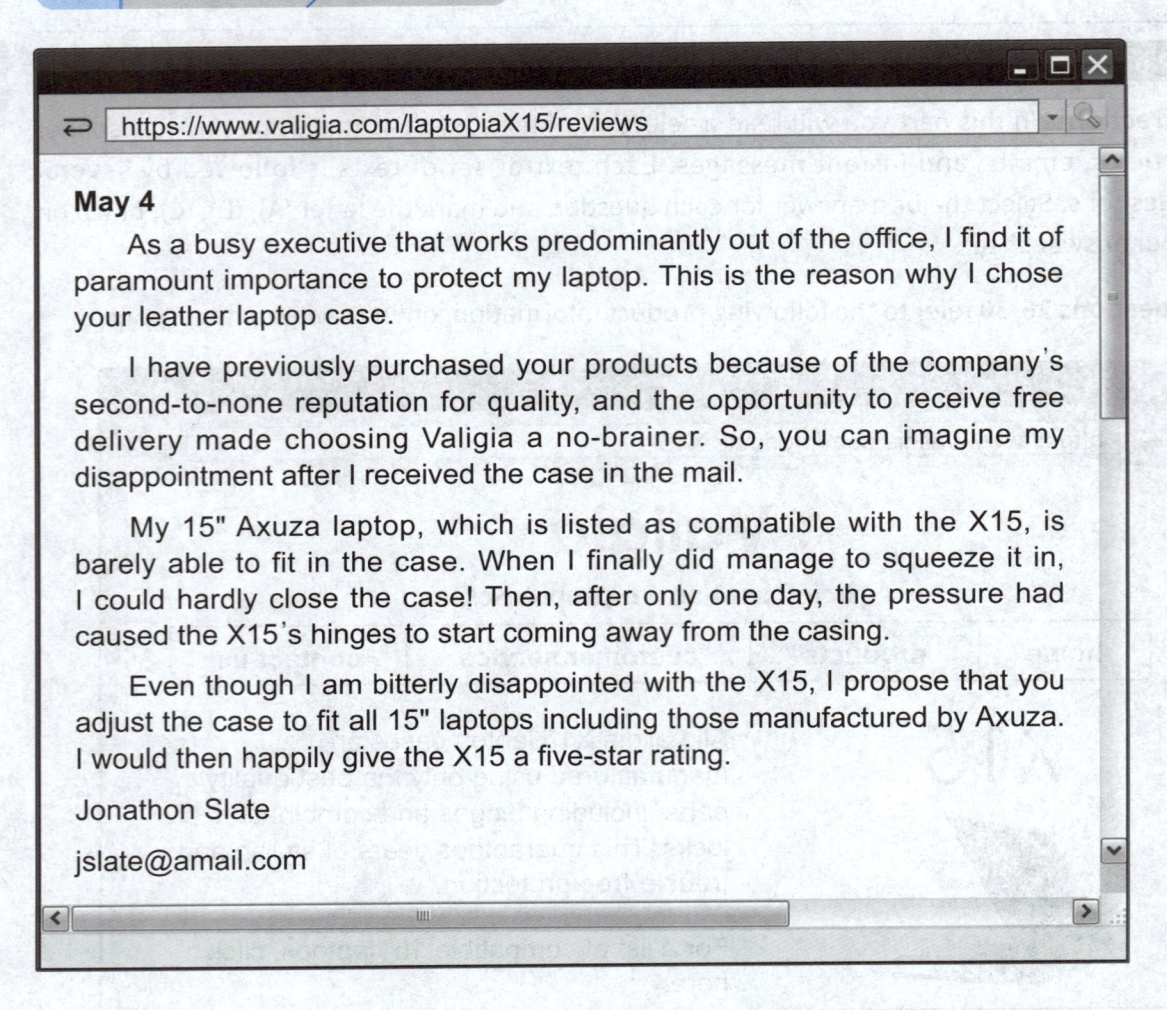

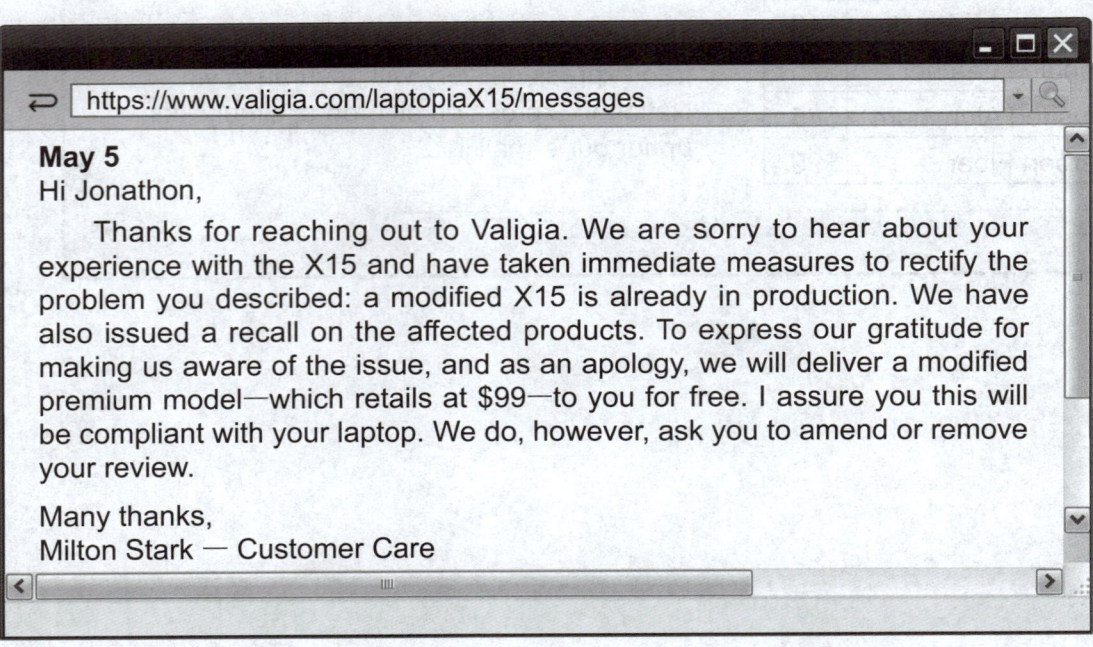

https://www.valigia.com/laptopiaX15/reviews

May 4

As a busy executive that works predominantly out of the office, I find it of paramount importance to protect my laptop. This is the reason why I chose your leather laptop case.

I have previously purchased your products because of the company's second-to-none reputation for quality, and the opportunity to receive free delivery made choosing Valigia a no-brainer. So, you can imagine my disappointment after I received the case in the mail.

My 15" Axuza laptop, which is listed as compatible with the X15, is barely able to fit in the case. When I finally did manage to squeeze it in, I could hardly close the case! Then, after only one day, the pressure had caused the X15's hinges to start coming away from the casing.

Even though I am bitterly disappointed with the X15, I propose that you adjust the case to fit all 15" laptops including those manufactured by Axuza. I would then happily give the X15 a five-star rating.

Jonathon Slate

jslate@amail.com

---

https://www.valigia.com/laptopiaX15/messages

May 5

Hi Jonathon,

Thanks for reaching out to Valigia. We are sorry to hear about your experience with the X15 and have taken immediate measures to rectify the problem you described: a modified X15 is already in production. We have also issued a recall on the affected products. To express our gratitude for making us aware of the issue, and as an apology, we will deliver a modified premium model—which retails at $99—to you for free. I assure you this will be compliant with your laptop. We do, however, ask you to amend or remove your review.

Many thanks,
Milton Stark — Customer Care

26. Why does Mr. Slate complain about his laptop case?
    (A) The color is incorrect.
    (B) The packaging is inadequate.
    (C) The dimensions are insufficient.
    (D) The model he received was wrong.

27. In the review, the word "propose" in paragraph 4, line 1, is closest in meaning to
    (A) marry
    (B) plan
    (C) emphasize
    (D) suggest

28. What is indicated about Mr. Slate?
    (A) He is a first-time customer.
    (B) He registered online for the membership program.
    (C) He recommended the item to many people.
    (D) He only uses leather casing.

29. What model of laptop case does Mr. Stark offer Mr. Slate?
    (A) Ultra-strong Plastic
    (B) Genuine Leather
    (C) Brushed Aluminum
    (D) Carbon Fiber

30. What does Mr. Stark ask Mr. Slate to do?
    (A) Return the purchase
    (B) Revise his review
    (C) Complete a questionnaire
    (D) Confirm his identification

NOTES

Chapter 12 Technical Areas 技術領域

1　IT [ˋaɪˋti] *n.* 資訊科技（為 information technology 的縮寫）

▶ Chloe works as a programmer in the IT department of the company.
克洛伊在公司的資訊部擔任程式設計師。

2　wire [waɪr] *n.* 電線；金屬絲 & *vt.* 接電線

衍 wiring *n.* 線路系統
　 wired *a.* 有連上網路的
比 cable *n.* 電纜，纜線
a telephone wire　　電話線

▶ The technician connected the blue wire to the red one, and the phone worked again.
技師將藍線與紅線相接，然後電話又通了。

▶ The building is so remote that it's not even wired (up) to a power grid.
這棟建築位置過於偏僻，以致於甚至沒有接通電力系統。

3　switch [swɪtʃ] *n.* (電源) 開關 & *vt.* 開或關 (電器等的開關)；轉換

switch / turn on...
打開……的電源
switch / turn off...
關掉……的電源

▶ The switch on the heater was broken, so it wouldn't work.
暖氣的開關壞了，所以無法運作。

▶ Switch off the air conditioner before you leave the office.
把冷氣機關掉後再離開辦公室。

4　download [ˋdaʊnˌlod] *vt.* (電腦) 下載 & *n.* 下載的檔案；下載 (過程)

反 upload *vt.* 上傳 & *n.* 上傳的檔案

▶ It took Emma ten minutes to download the software from the official website.
艾瑪花了十分鐘從官方網站下載這款軟體。

▶ Harry accidentally deleted all the downloads in this folder.
哈利不小心刪除了這個資料夾裡所有下載的檔案。

5　input [ˋɪnˌpʊt] *vt.* 輸入 (三態為：input, input / inputted [ˋɪnˌpʊtɪd], input / inputted) & *n.* 輸入 (電腦等的) 資料 (不可數)

input A into B
將 A 輸入 B

▶ Kevin input his data into the computer so it could be analyzed.
凱文把他的數據輸入電腦好進行分析。

▶ The employees have access to the input data in our database.
員工可以存取我們資料庫裡輸入的資料。

6 crash [kræʃ] vi. & vt. (使)(電腦)當機 & n. (電腦)當機

▶ Dora's computer crashed after she installed the new software.
朵拉在她的電腦上安裝新軟體後，電腦就當機了。

▶ David needs to buy a new computer because his old one has experienced many crashes.
大衛需要買新電腦，因為舊的電腦當機了許多次。

7 program [ˈproɡræm] n. (電腦)程式 & vt. & vi. (為……)編寫程式

(衍) programmer n. 程式設計師
(補) 此單字的英式拼法為 programme。

▶ The program wasn't working properly, so the computer had to be restarted.
這個程式無法正常運作，因此電腦需要重新開機。

▶ Frank is the engineer responsible for programming the computers in our department.
法蘭克是專為本部門的電腦編寫程式的工程師。

8 backup [ˈbækˌʌp] n. 備份；後備

(衍) back sth up　　備份……

▶ Make sure to dispose of these files and destroy any backup copies you have.
請務必處理掉這些檔案，並銷毀你手上任何備份副本。

9 technician [tɛkˈnɪʃən] n. 技術人員，技師

▶ The technician will inspect your phone to ensure you can get online.
技師會檢查您的手機，以確保您可以上網。

10 instruction [ɪnˈstrʌkʃən] n. (電腦)指令；(機器等)使用說明(恆用複數)

(衍) instruct vt. 教導；指示
instructor n. 教練；大學講師

▶ There is an issue with the computer processor that's causing it to execute instructions incorrectly.
該電腦的處理器出問題，導致它執行指令錯誤。

▶ You must read the instructions carefully before using the device.
你務必仔細閱讀說明後再使用此裝置。

11 rectify [ˈrɛktəˌfaɪ] vt. 糾正，改正（三態為：rectify, rectified [ˈrɛktəˌfaɪd], rectified）

似 correct vt. 修正，改正
rectify an error / a fault　糾正錯誤

▶ The engineers worked overtime to rectify the faults in the control panel.
工程師加班修正控制板裡的錯誤。

12 modify [ˈmɑdəˌfaɪ] vt. 改造；修改；更改（三態為：modify, modified [ˈmɑdəˌfaɪd], modified）

衍 modification n. 修改

▶ Kyle modified his computer to improve its speed.
凱爾改裝他的電腦，讓它運作得更快。

13 renewable [rɪˈnjuəbḷ] a. （能源）可再生的；可延長有效期的，可續期的

衍 renew vt. 更新；使展期
　　renewal n.（對合約等的）有效期延長
renewable energy sources
可再生能源，永續能源

▶ We should cherish renewable energy sources such as wind and solar power.
我們應該珍惜諸如風能和太陽能之類的可再生能源。

▶ Your work permit is renewable.
您的工作許可證是可展延的。

14 upgrade [ˌʌpˈgred] vt. & [ˈʌpgred] n. 升級

a software / system upgrade
軟體 / 系統升級

▶ Could you please help me upgrade the operating system on my computer?
可以麻煩你幫忙我升級我電腦的作業系統嗎？

▶ Due to a tight budget, the company has to put its system upgrade plan on hold.
由於預算緊縮，公司不得不暫緩實施系統的升級計畫。

15 update [ʌpˈdet] vt. 更新 & [ˈʌpdet] n. 更新（軟體）

▶ It is necessary to update our company's computer software system.
我們公司的電腦軟體系統有必要更新。

▶ There is a free update for the antivirus software that you can download online.
網路上有該防毒軟體的免費更新供你下載。

16 initiate [ɪˈnɪʃɪˌet] vt. 開始實施，發起

衍 initiative n. 計畫；措施
　　initial a. 起初的

▶ The technician will initiate the system reboot to update the computer.
技術人員將會重啟系統以更新電腦。

17 enhance [ɪnˈhæns] vt. 加強，提升

衍 enhancement n. 增強，提升

▶ This app can greatly enhance the image resolution on your phone.
這個應用程式可以大大提升你手機上的圖片解析度。

18 electronic [ɪˌlɛkˈtrɑnɪk] a. 電子的

衍 electronics n. 電子學
比 electric a. 用電的
electrical a. 與電有關的

an electronic book / keyboard / gadget　電子書 / 鍵盤樂器 / 裝置

▶ Some readers prefer electronic books to printed ones because they are more convenient.
有些讀者因較為方便之故捨棄紙本書而偏愛看電子書。

19 circuit [ˈsɝkɪt] n. 電路

an electrical circuit　電路
a short circuit　短路

▶ The big fire was caused by a short circuit in the wiring.
這場大火是由電線短路引發的。

20 microscope [ˈmaɪkrəˌskop] n. 顯微鏡

衍 scope n. 觀測器
under a / the microscope
在顯微鏡下
through a / the microscope
透過顯微鏡

▶ The scientist was examining a virus under a microscope.
這位科學家正在顯微鏡下仔細觀察某種病毒。

21 static [ˈstætɪk] n. 靜電干擾；靜電 (= static electricity)（不可數）& a. 靜電的；靜止的

▶ It is a high-quality radio with no static at all.
這是一部品質極高的收音機，完全不受靜電干擾。

▶ Gold prices have remained static for a while.
金價已經原地打轉很久了。

22 compatible [kəmˈpætəbl̩] a.（電腦）相容的

反 incompatible a.（電腦）不相容的
be compatible with sth
（電腦）可和某物相容

▶ The application is not compatible with my computer system.
這個應用程式與我的電腦系統不相容。

23 faulty [ˈfɔltɪ] *a.* 有故障的；有缺陷的；有缺點的

衍 fault *n.* 缺點；過失（不可數）

▶ Customers may request a refund if our appliances are faulty.
如果我們的家電有問題，顧客可以要求退款。

24 consultant [kənˈsʌltənt] *n.* 顧問

衍 consult *vt.* 請教，求教 & *vi.* 諮商，研討
consultation *n.* 諮詢；就診

▶ Alice is currently working part-time as a software consultant.
愛麗絲目前擔任兼職軟體顧問。

25 stabilize [ˈstebḷˌaɪz] *vt.* & *vi.* (使)穩固，(使)穩定

衍 stable *a.* 穩定的
stability *n.* 穩定（性）

▶ The engineer installed a cooling system to stabilize the device's temperature.
工程師安裝了冷卻系統，以穩定裝置的溫度。

Chapter 12 Listening Test

Part 1 🔊 280-282

Directions: For each question in this part, you will hear four statements about a picture in your test book. When you hear the statements, you must select the one statement that best describes what you see in the picture. Then find the number of the question on your answer sheet and mark your answer. The statements will not be printed in your test book and will be spoken only one time.

1.

2.

Part 2 🔊 283-285

Directions: You will hear a question or statement and three responses spoken in English. They will not be printed in your test book and will be spoken only one time. Select the best response to the question or statement and mark the letter (A), (B), or (C) on your answer sheet.

CH
12

3. Mark your answer on your answer sheet.

4. Mark your answer on your answer sheet.

Part 3 🔊 286-294

Directions: You will hear some conversations between two or more people. You will be asked to answer three questions about what the speakers say in each conversation. Select the best response to each question and mark the letter (A), (B), (C), or (D) on your answer sheet. The conversations will not be printed in your test book and will be spoken only one time.

5. What are the speakers mainly discussing?
   (A) An accident involving a vehicle
   (B) A system that isn't working
   (C) A surgery involving a colleague
   (D) A worker who hasn't arrived

6. What does the woman indicate about the backup?
   (A) It has a critical error.
   (B) It has been made recently.
   (C) It has been canceled.
   (D) It has failed ten times.

7. What will the man most likely do next?
   (A) Reboot a system
   (B) Perform an operation
   (C) Contact an expert
   (D) Diagnose a problem

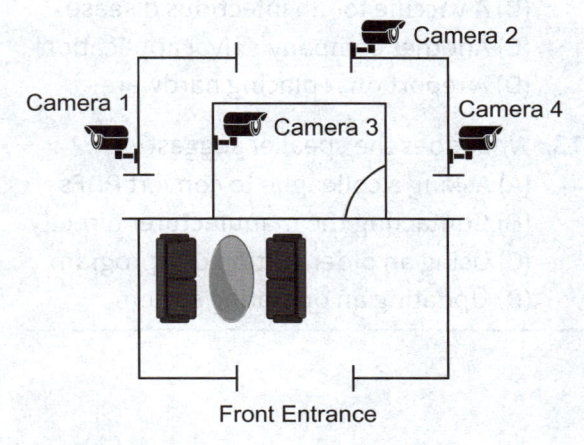

8. What did the man order?
   (A) A new camera   (B) A lens
   (C) A monitor   (D) A security door

9. What does the woman suggest?
   (A) Canceling a scheduled appointment
   (B) Filming a new advertisement
   (C) Swapping a faulty device
   (D) Returning an incorrect order

10. Look at the graphic. Which camera will most likely be moved to the front entrance?
    (A) Camera 1   (B) Camera 2
    (C) Camera 3   (D) Camera 4

143

Chapter 12 Listening Test

Part 4 🔊 295-303

Directions: You will hear some talks given by a single speaker. You will be asked to answer three questions about what the speaker says in each talk. Select the best response to each question and mark the letter (A), (B), (C), or (D) on your answer sheet. The talks will not be printed in your test book and will be spoken only one time.

11. What is indicated about Emma?
    (A) She had a conflict with a client.
    (B) She reported a problem to IT.
    (C) She got a very strange message.
    (D) She rejected advice from her boss.

12. What will be available by the end of the week?
    (A) Another update for some software
    (B) A vaccine for an infectious disease
    (C) Another company's rival application
    (D) A report on replacing hardware

13. What does the speaker suggest?
    (A) Asking a colleague to convert PDFs
    (B) Contacting the manufacturer directly
    (C) Using an older edition of a program
    (D) Updating an operating system

Project	Cost
Hardware Upgrades	$5,000
Wi-Fi Access	$10,000
Backup System	$13,000
Website Development	$21,000

14. Why have some projects been postponed?
    (A) Manpower issues
    (B) Delivery delays
    (C) Lack of money
    (D) Lack of time

15. Look at the graphic. How much will the selected project cost?
    (A) $5,000
    (B) $10,000
    (C) $13,000
    (D) $21,000

16. What will the speaker most likely do next?
    (A) Send out an e-mail
    (B) Raise funds
    (C) Unveil a plan
    (D) Answer queries

Chapter 12 Reading Test

Part 5

Directions: A word or phrase is missing in each of the sentences below. Four answer choices are given below each sentence. Select the best answer to complete the sentence. Then mark the letter (A), (B), (C), or (D) on your answer sheet.

17. The technical specifications of the solar panels can be found on this ------- energy website.
    (A) to renew
    (B) renew
    (C) renewal
    (D) renewable

18. Ms. Shih works as a machine learning -------, advising companies on the implementation of artificial intelligence systems.
    (A) consult
    (B) consultant
    (C) consultation
    (D) consultative

19. To increase efficiency, the president demanded that we ------- the operating system and update most of the software we use.
    (A) change
    (B) can change
    (C) changed
    (D) have changed

20. The technician installed a signal booster in an effort to ------- the Wi-Fi signal in the office.
    (A) stabilize
    (B) outweigh
    (C) interfere
    (D) mature

21. It's good to know that the new software, which helps reduce programming time, continues -------.
    (A) enhance
    (B) enhanced
    (C) enhancing
    (D) to be enhanced

Chapter 12 Reading Test

Part 6

Directions: Read the texts that follow. A word, phrase, or sentence is missing in parts of each text. Four answer choices for each question are given below the text. Select the best answer to complete the text. Then mark the letter (A), (B), (C), or (D) on your answer sheet.

Questions 22-25 refer to the following excerpt from an employee handbook.

Following your orientation session, you will be guided to your desk. A technician from the IT department will initiate the setup of your workstation. -------. Please input a
22.
password of your choice to secure your account. The password must be ------- ten
23.
characters long and contain both numbers and letters. The technician will also show you how to access the shared company resources, configure your email account, and navigate any software you're -------. Please feel free to ask him any questions and
24.
consult him on any technical issues. ------- everything is running smoothly, he will
25.
hand over to your line manager.

---

22. (A) The program has been updated since you last used it.
    (B) You must sign in at the reception desk on your first day.
    (C) Downloading this software on work computers is forbidden.
    (D) He will provide instructions on how to log in to the system.

23. (A) in the end
    (B) for the sake of
    (C) in favor of
    (D) at least

24. (A) critical of
    (B) grateful for
    (C) unfamiliar with
    (D) similar to

25. (A) Now that
    (B) Once
    (C) As though
    (D) Yet

Part 7

Directions: In this part you will read a selection of texts, such as magazine and newspaper articles, emails, and instant messages. Each text or set of texts is followed by several questions. Select the best answer for each question and mark the letter (A), (B), (C), or (D) on your answer sheet.

Questions 26-30 refer to the following information sheet and email.

Quick-start Guide

Thank you for purchasing the X1 Electronic Secretary — the most powerful and sophisticated electronic organizer available.

To install the batteries:

- ✓ Hold the device with the screen facing away from you.
- ✓ Push down firmly on the two square depressions with your thumbs. The cover will pop up to reveal the internal battery compartment.
- ✓ Insert two AA batteries. Make sure to match the positive and negative ends of the batteries with the symbols inside the battery compartment.
- ✓ Close the cover while pressing down on the two square depressions gently at the same time.
- ✓ Press the power switch for approximately three seconds. The power LED light will illuminate green to indicate that the batteries are inserted properly.

Please note:

- ✓ Replace the batteries when the power LED flashes red.
- ✓ To prevent damage to the plastic case, remove the batteries if the device will not be used for an extended period of time.

Specifications subject to change without notice.

Chapter 12 Reading Test

To: Manny Jharris <mannyjharris@elsec.com>
From: Natasha Benson <natashabenson@elsec.com>
Date: October 3
Subject: Electronic Secretary Prototype

Hi Manny,

   The prototype of the enhanced Electronic Secretary, the X2, has just been approved and will go into production immediately. The new model will have twice as many batteries as the X1, be 100% recyclable, and will have wireless connectivity. Furthermore, the power LED light has been modified: It will now illuminate orange to show that it is connected to Wi-Fi. Consequently, several changes must be made to the manual and quick-start guide.

   I'll let you know about any additional changes as soon as I find out about them.

Natasha Benson
Product Development

26. What is indicated about the Electronic Secretary's power LED?
    (A) It changes color to show status.
    (B) It flashes continually while charging.
    (C) It has two square depressions.
    (D) It flashes red when switched on.

27. How many batteries does the X2 Electronic Secretary need?
    (A) One
    (B) Two
    (C) Three
    (D) Four

28. What Electronic Secretary X2 feature is mentioned?
    (A) Portable and lightweight
    (B) Recyclable parts
    (C) Rechargeability
    (D) Touch screen interface

29. In the e-mail, the word "just" in paragraph 1, line 1, is closest in meaning to
    (A) only
    (B) fairly
    (C) recently
    (D) objectively

30. What does Ms. Benson indicate she will do?
    (A) Confirm a booking
    (B) Provide more information
    (C) Approve a request
    (D) Replace a broken part

Chapter 13 Travel 旅遊

1 flight [flaɪt] *n.* 班機，航班；飛行

a flight attendant / flight crew
空服員 / 全體機組人員
a non-stop / red-eye flight
直飛 / 紅眼班機

▶ The flight from Taipei to Kyoto takes about three hours.
臺北到京都的班機大約要飛三個小時。

▶ If you feel sick on the plane, you can ask the flight attendants for help.
如果你在飛行途中感到不適，可以向空服員求助。

2 passenger [ˋpæsn̩dʒɚ] *n.* 乘客

a passenger plane
客機

▶ Only a few passengers survived the fatal bus crash on the highway.
在高速公路上的那場致命巴士車禍中，只有少數乘客倖存。

3 luggage [ˋlʌgɪdʒ] *n.* 行李（集合名詞，不可數）（= baggage [ˋbægɪdʒ]，美式英語）

a piece / an item of luggage
一件行李（非 a luggage）
claim one's luggage　　領取行李

▶ Remember to claim your luggage after you go through customs.
記得在過海關後領取你的行李。

4 board [bɔrd] *vt.* & *vi.* 登上（飛機、船、公車等）

▶ The passengers waited in a long line at the gate to board the plane.
乘客們在登機口大排長龍，準備登機。

5 depart [dɪˋpɑrt] *vi.* 啟程，出發

衍 **departure** *n.* 出發，離開
depart for + 地方　　前往某地
depart from + 地方　　離開某地

▶ A shuttle bus departs for the baseball stadium every 10 minutes.
每十分鐘就有一班接駁公車開往棒球場。

▶ Trains to Taipei depart from this station every 30 minutes.
自本站開往臺北的列車每三十分鐘發一班車。

6. disembark [ˌdɪsɪmˈbɑrk] vi. (旅途結束後) 下（船、飛機等）& vt. 使上岸；卸（貨）

- 衍 disembarkation n. 下（船、飛機等）；上岸（不可數）
- 反 embark vi. & vt. 登（船、飛機等）

disembark from... 從……下……

▶ Don't forget to take all your belongings with you when you disembark from the plane.
下飛機時請記得帶走您所有的隨身物品。

7. aboard [əˈbɔrd] prep. & adv. 在船 / 飛機 / 火車上；上船 / 飛機 / 火車

- 比 abroad adv. 在國外

go aboard + 交通工具
登上某交通工具

▶ Dennis went aboard the train just before it left the platform.
丹尼斯在火車就快要駛離月臺時才上車。

▶ The tourists aboard the ship were surprised to see whales swimming around it.
船上的遊客看到鯨魚在船的周遭游動時感到非常驚訝。

8. fare [fɛr] n. 交通費

- 補 fare 專指搭乘交通工具的費用，fee 則指其他專業服務上的費用。

air / bus / taxi fare 飛機 / 公車票價 / 計程車車資
half / full fare 半票 / 全票票價

▶ International air fares have increased dramatically in recent months due to rising fuel prices.
由於燃料價格上漲，國際機票票價在最近幾個月大幅上漲。

▶ Children under six travel for free, while children aged six to 16 pay half fare.
六歲以下孩童搭乘免票，六至十六歲半票。

9. delay [dɪˈle] n. 延期，延遲，耽擱 & vi. & vt. (使) 延誤 / 延期

delay sth for + 一段時間 將某事延後一段時間
delay + N/V-ing 延誤 / 期……

▶ The flight was delayed for an hour due to the heavy rain.
該航班因為大雨而被延後了一個小時。

▶ The manager decided to delay holding the meeting until next Monday.
經理決定把會議延到下禮拜一再開。

10. cancelation [ˌkænslˈeʃən] n. 取消（= cancellation，英式拼法）

- 衍 cancel vt. 取消

a cancelation fee 辦取消的手續費

▶ The snowstorm led to the cancelation of the flights.
暴風雪導致多架班機取消。

11. check in 辦理住房手續 / 登機

- 反 check out 辦理退房手續

▶ Please inform us in advance if you wish to check in after 11 p.m.
您若希望於晚間十一點之後辦理住房手續，請事先告知我們。

12 customs [ˈkʌstəmz] *n.* 海關（恆用複數）

go through customs 通關

▶ Travelers have to present their passports as they go through customs.
遊客通過海關時必須出示護照。

13 transit [ˈtrænsɪt] *n.* 運輸（不可數）

in transit 運送途中
a mass / public transit system
大眾 / 公共運輸系統
Mass Rapid Transit
捷運（簡稱 MRT）

▶ Emma filed an insurance claim for her luggage that was lost in transit.
艾瑪的行李在運送途中遺失了，所以她去申請保險理賠。

▶ The city government has proposed several measures to improve the public transit system.
市政府已提出多項措施來改善公共運輸系統。

CH 13

14 overseas [ˌovɚˈsiz] *adv.* 在海外 & [ˈovɚˌsiz] *a.* 來自海外的；外國來的

▶ Richard studied overseas for a year and earned a master's degree.
理查出國深造一年，取得碩士學位。

▶ Miranda has returned to her hometown from a long overseas trip.
米蘭達已經結束了一趟漫長的海外旅行回到了故鄉。

15 turbulence [ˈtɝbjələns] *n.* （氣體的）亂流；（水的）湍流（不可數）

▶ We might experience unexpected turbulence, so please ensure your seat belt remains fastened.
我們可能會遇到突如其來的亂流，請務必確保安全帶繫緊。

16 rental [ˈrɛntl̩] *n.* 租用費；租用的物品；出租

衍 **rent** *n.* 租金 & *vt.* 出租
a rental car
租賃汽車
a car rental company
租車公司

▶ The package tour we chose includes airfare, accommodations, and car rental.
我們挑選的套裝行程包含機票、住宿及租車費用。

17 layover [ˈleˌovɚ] *n.* （尤指飛行途中的）短暫停留（= stopover，英式英語）

a four-hour / brief layover
四小時 / 短暫的停留

▶ We have a brief layover in Bangkok before continuing to London.
在繼續飛往倫敦前，我們中途會在曼谷短暫停留。

151

18 suite [swit] n. 套房

a honeymoon suite
蜜月套房

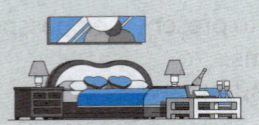

▶ The honeymoon suites at the luxurious hotel offer great views of the sea.
這家豪華飯店的蜜月套房可以很清楚地觀賞海景。

19 reservation [͵rɛzɚˋveʃən] n. 預訂，訂位

衍 reserve vt. 預訂
make a reservation for...
預訂……

▶ Brenda always makes reservations for her flights through the internet.
布蘭達一向透過網路預訂機票。

20 brochure [broˋʃur] n. 資料（或廣告）小冊子

補 brochure 與 pamphlet 皆可指小冊子，惟 brochure 常用在宣傳商品、活動的廣告上，而 pamphlet 則多用在宣傳對某主題的意見或觀點上。另外，leaflet 則指單張的傳單，與 brochure 相同，多用在宣傳商品、活動上。

a travel brochure　　旅遊小冊子

▶ The beautiful pictures in the travel brochure tempted me to go on vacation.
旅行手冊上的美麗照片讓我很想去度假。

21 souvenir [͵suvəˋnɪr] n. 紀念品；紀念物

keep sth as a souvenir
保存某物當作紀念品

▶ Sarah kept the key chain her boyfriend bought for her as a souvenir.
莎拉把男朋友買給她的鑰匙圈留作紀念。

22 itinerary [aɪˋtɪnə͵rɛrɪ] n. 旅遊行程，預定行程

a detailed itinerary
詳細的旅遊行程

▶ A visit to Tokyo must be included in the itinerary for our Asian vacation.
東京之行一定要排進我們亞洲之旅的行程中。

23 confirm [kənˋfɝm] vt. 確認；證實

衍 confirmation n. 證實；認可
confirm a booking / reservation
確認預約

▶ I'm calling to confirm a booking for a single room for August 15.
我來電是要確認八月十五日一間單人房的預約。

24 schedule [ˈskɛdʒʊl] *vt.* 安排，計劃 & *n.* 日程表，行程表

be scheduled to + V 預定做……
on schedule 按預定時間
ahead of / behind schedule
比預定時間提前 / 落後

▶ The bus is scheduled to depart at 3:30 p.m.
這班公車預定在下午三點三十分發車。

▶ The construction of the new train station is running two months behind schedule.
新火車站的工程進度比預定的要落後兩個月。

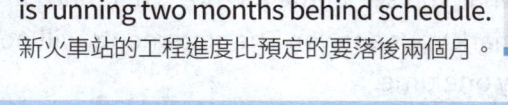

25 attraction [əˈtrækʃən] *n.* 吸引力；吸引人的事物

衍 attract *vt.* 吸引
　　attractive *a.* 有吸引力的；誘人的
hold no attraction for sb
對某人沒有吸引力
a tourist attraction 旅遊景點

▶ Hiking holds no attraction for Jerry; he's the indoor type.
健行對傑瑞沒有吸引力，他喜歡室內活動。

▶ The Statue of Liberty is a major tourist attraction in the United States.
自由女神像是美國一個主要的旅遊景點。

CH 13

153

Chapter 13　Listening Test

Part 1　🔊 304-306

Directions: For each question in this part, you will hear four statements about a picture in your test book. When you hear the statements, you must select the one statement that best describes what you see in the picture. Then find the number of the question on your answer sheet and mark your answer. The statements will not be printed in your test book and will be spoken only one time.

1.

2.

154

Part 2 🔊 307-309

Directions: You will hear a question or statement and three responses spoken in English. They will not be printed in your test book and will be spoken only one time. Select the best response to the question or statement and mark the letter (A), (B), or (C) on your answer sheet.

3. Mark your answer on your answer sheet.
4. Mark your answer on your answer sheet.

Part 3 🔊 310-318

Directions: You will hear some conversations between two or more people. You will be asked to answer three questions about what the speakers say in each conversation. Select the best response to each question and mark the letter (A), (B), (C), or (D) on your answer sheet. The conversations will not be printed in your test book and will be spoken only one time.

5. Where does this conversation most likely take place?
   (A) At a travel agency
   (B) In a bus shelter
   (C) At an airport
   (D) In a train station

6. Who most likely is the woman?
   (A) A weather reporter
   (B) A taxi driver
   (C) A station attendant
   (D) A hotel porter

7. What is causing the delay?
   (A) Traffic accidents
   (B) Staffing problems
   (C) Technical issues
   (D) Severe weather

8. What caused the couple's problem?
   (A) Their passports expired.
   (B) Their baggage is overweight.
   (C) They missed a flight.
   (D) They lost their luggage.

9. What does the woman ask for?
   (A) A transfer
   (B) A refund
   (C) An exchange
   (D) An upgrade

10. What does the woman's husband suggest?
    (A) Extending their stay
    (B) Reserving a hotel room
    (C) Canceling the flight
    (D) Flying with another airline

Chapter 13 Listening Test

Part 4 🔊 319-327

Directions: You will hear some talks given by a single speaker. You will be asked to answer three questions about what the speaker says in each talk. Select the best response to each question and mark the letter (A), (B), (C), or (D) on your answer sheet. The talks will not be printed in your test book and will be spoken only one time.

11. According to the speaker, what will soon happen?
    (A) The airplane will take off.
    (B) The airplane will land.
    (C) The airplane will hit turbulence.
    (D) The airplane will taxi.

12. According to the speaker, what should be switched off?
    (A) Electronic devices
    (B) In-flight entertainment
    (C) Overhead lights
    (D) Emergency signs

13. What will the speaker most likely do next?
    (A) Go through security
    (B) Serve meals
    (C) Return to her seat
    (D) Distribute a form

14. What does the speaker say about the flight?
    (A) It will go non-stop to New Delhi.
    (B) It will be monitored at all times.
    (C) It will include a stop in another place.
    (D) It will be changed to a different route.

15. According to the speaker, what can the listeners do in New Delhi?
    (A) Enjoy exotic cuisine
    (B) Visit tourist sites
    (C) Meet the locals
    (D) Attend a sports game

16. What will be offered to the listeners at the airport?
    (A) A city map
    (B) A luggage cart
    (C) An interpreter
    (D) A shuttle bus

Chapter 13 Reading Test

Part 5

Directions: A word or phrase is missing in each of the sentences below. Four answer choices are given below each sentence. Select the best answer to complete the sentence. Then mark the letter (A), (B), (C), or (D) on your answer sheet.

17. The railroad company has published its fall ------- for the east coast line on its website.
    (A) authority
    (B) detector
    (C) schedule
    (D) belongings

18. Compensation will be provided immediately to those passengers ------- luggage was lost in transit.
    (A) that
    (B) who
    (C) whose
    (D) which

19. By the time Mr. Tang ------- some souvenirs at a duty-free store, his flight had already been called.
    (A) buys
    (B) bought
    (C) buying
    (D) had bought

20. Not until the housekeepers have finished cleaning the presidential suite ------- in.
    (A) check can the guests
    (B) the guests check can
    (C) the guests can check
    (D) can the guests check

21. Mrs. Poilievre was at the ferry port to see her son ------- for Vancouver Island.
    (A) depart
    (B) departs
    (C) to depart
    (D) will depart

Chapter 13 Reading Test

Part 6

Directions: Read the texts that follow. A word, phrase, or sentence is missing in parts of each text. Four answer choices for each question are given below the text. Select the best answer to complete the text. Then mark the letter (A), (B), (C), or (D) on your answer sheet.

Questions 22-25 refer to the following e-mail.

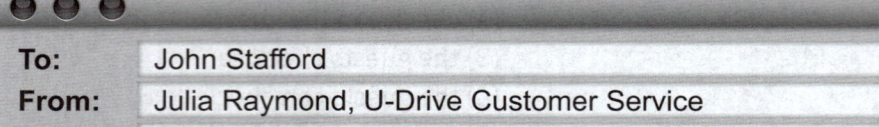

To: John Stafford
From: Julia Raymond, U-Drive Customer Service
Date: June 11
Subject: U-Drive Rental Confirmation

Dear Mr. Stafford:

This e-mail is to confirm your car rental. The pick-up date is June 28, and the return date is July 5. Please remember -------- two forms of ID and two credit
22.
cards to the clerk at check-in. Also, please make sure to return the vehicle by 5 PM, -------- you may be charged a late fee. You must refill the tank prior to
23.
returning the car to avoid refueling charges.

Finally, I'd like to invite you to join our U-Drive VIP Club. --------. Contact any
24.
U-Drive agent for -------- information. Thanks for driving with U-Drive!
25.

Sincerely,

Julia Raymond
Customer Service

---

22. (A) to show
    (B) showing
    (C) by showing
    (D) and show

23. (A) so
    (B) and
    (C) or
    (D) if

24. (A) We have actually been in business for 20 years.
    (B) All our vehicles are serviced regularly.
    (C) Our customer service department is here to help you.
    (D) Members are entitled to unlimited mileage.

25. (A) far
    (B) much far
    (C) further
    (D) furthest

Part 7

Directions: In this part you will read a selection of texts, such as magazine and newspaper articles, emails, and instant messages. Each text or set of texts is followed by several questions. Select the best answer for each question and mark the letter (A), (B), (C), or (D) on your answer sheet.

Questions 26-30 refer to the following email, news report, and email.

To:	Rama Patel
From:	Emily Watkins
Date:	June 15
Subject:	Itinerary

Dear Mr. Patel:

Thank you for booking your flight through Adventure Travel.

The total cost of your tickets is US$2,300 including insurance:

Los Angeles-Seattle	$275
Seattle-New York	$550
New York-Miami	$425
Miami-Los Angeles	$1,050

I have attached a brochure from U.S. customs since you will be carrying botanical samples from overseas. Please follow the directions as the Department of Homeland Security is particularly strict on such matters.

The travel insurance policy covers flight cancellations and medical care. If you have any questions, please do not hesitate to call me at Adventure Travel. My number is 310-945-2083, extension 45.

Thank you for your business.

Ms. Emily Watkins

Airports Remain in Chaos

By Simon Phillips

(July 12) — Hurricane Patricia continues to disrupt airports around the country. All arrivals and departures have been canceled as winds exceeding 150 mph continue to batter the east of the country. Gina Washington, a spokesperson for the National Aviation Authority, issued a statement apologizing for the chaos that ensued when airports closed without warning at 9 PM on Friday evening. "The Weather Bureau upgraded the hurricane from Category 2 to Category 4, necessitating the abrupt closures," she said. "The safety of passengers and airline crew is of the utmost importance." The Federal Government will subsidize passengers affected by the cancellations with a $100 voucher. First class passengers can stay at any Highlife Hotel, business class passengers at any Harrington's Hotel, premium economy class at any Family Inn, and economy class at any budget hotel.

To: Rama Patel
From: Elisa Thurston
Date: August 9
Subject: Travel insurance claim

Dear Mr. Patel,

This e-mail is to confirm that your claim for travel insurance has been approved. A payment of US$1,050 has been credited into your West County Bank — account #332459990. However, we regret to inform you that your claim for accommodation at Harrington's Hotel was rejected as your policy does not cover such expenses. To confirm receipt of the payment, please reply to this e-mail with "confirmed" as the subject.

Yours sincerely,

Elisa Thurston

26. In what industry does Mr. Patel most likely work?
    (A) Freight
    (B) Insurance
    (C) Travel
    (D) Agriculture

27. In the first e-mail, the word "matters" in paragraph 3, line 3, is closest in meaning to
    (A) results
    (B) inspections
    (C) situations
    (D) positions

28. Which one of Mr. Patel's flights was canceled?
    (A) Los Angeles-Seattle
    (B) Seattle-New York
    (C) New York-Miami
    (D) Miami-Los Angeles

29. What class of ticket did Mr. Patel most likely purchase?
    (A) First class
    (B) Business class
    (C) Premium economy class
    (D) Economy class

30. What is Mr. Patel asked to do?
    (A) Acknowledge a payment
    (B) Redeem a voucher
    (C) Keep a receipt
    (D) Return a call

CH 13

NEW TOEIC 模擬測驗
TEST 01

Part 1	Photographs	照片描述
Part 2	Question-Response	應答問題
Part 3	Conversations	簡短對話
Part 4	Talks	簡短獨白
Part 5	Incomplete Sentences	句子填空
Part 6	Text Completion	段落填空
Part 7	Single Passages	單篇閱讀
	Multiple Passages	多篇閱讀

TEST 01 Listening Test

本回完整音檔 014
本回分段音檔 328-454

LISTENING TEST

In the Listening test, you will be asked to demonstrate how well you understand spoken English. The entire Listening test will last approximately 45 minutes. There are four parts, and directions are given for each part. You must mark your answers on the separate answer sheet. Do not write your answers in your test book.

Part 1 🔊 328-334

Directions: For each question in this part, you will hear four statements about a picture in your test book. When you hear the statements, you must select the one statement that best describes what you see in the picture. Then find the number of the question on your answer sheet and mark your answer. The statements will not be printed in your test book and will be spoken only one time.

Statement (D), "A man is pointing to his computer screen," is the best description of the picture, so you should select answer (D) and mark it on your answer sheet.

1.

2.

3.

4.

5.

6.

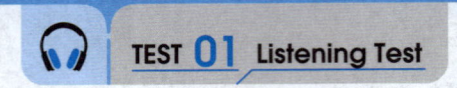

TEST 01 Listening Test

Part 2 🔊 335-360

Directions: You will hear a question or statement and three responses spoken in English. They will not be printed in your test book and will be spoken only one time. Select the best response to the question or statement and mark the letter (A), (B), or (C) on your answer sheet.

7. Mark your answer on your answer sheet.
8. Mark your answer on your answer sheet.
9. Mark your answer on your answer sheet.
10. Mark your answer on your answer sheet.
11. Mark your answer on your answer sheet.
12. Mark your answer on your answer sheet.
13. Mark your answer on your answer sheet.
14. Mark your answer on your answer sheet.
15. Mark your answer on your answer sheet.
16. Mark your answer on your answer sheet.
17. Mark your answer on your answer sheet.
18. Mark your answer on your answer sheet.
19. Mark your answer on your answer sheet.
20. Mark your answer on your answer sheet.
21. Mark your answer on your answer sheet.
22. Mark your answer on your answer sheet.
23. Mark your answer on your answer sheet.
24. Mark your answer on your answer sheet.
25. Mark your answer on your answer sheet.
26. Mark your answer on your answer sheet.
27. Mark your answer on your answer sheet.
28. Mark your answer on your answer sheet.
29. Mark your answer on your answer sheet.
30. Mark your answer on your answer sheet.
31. Mark your answer on your answer sheet.

Part 3 🔊 361-413

Directions: You will hear some conversations between two or more people. You will be asked to answer three questions about what the speakers say in each conversation. Select the best response to each question and mark the letter (A), (B), (C), or (D) on your answer sheet. The conversations will not be printed in your test book and will be spoken only one time.

32. What is indicated about the woman?
    (A) She got a serious injury.
    (B) She has never skied before.
    (C) She rented the wrong item.
    (D) She has won a sports medal.

33. Who most likely is the man?
    (A) A tour guide
    (B) A clothing model
    (C) A ski store clerk
    (D) A professional athlete

34. What will the woman most likely do next?
    (A) Hit the slopes
    (B) Try on some gear
    (C) Ride in a ski lift
    (D) Check a map

35. Who does the woman want to employ?
    (A) More young people
    (B) Qualified teachers
    (C) Some tech experts
    (D) Skilled lecturers

36. What does the man suggest doing?
    (A) Placing ads on social media
    (B) Attending various job fairs
    (C) Promoting internal staff
    (D) Advertising in newspapers

37. What does the man ask the woman to do?
    (A) Approve a budget
    (B) Check a résumé
    (C) Proofread a job ad
    (D) Provide a schedule

TEST 01

GO ON TO THE NEXT PAGE ➔ 169

TEST 01 Listening Test

38. What will the man do this weekend?
(A) Take an educational course
(B) Enter a gaming competition
(C) Join a training exercise
(D) Watch a basketball game

39. What is the man looking forward to the most?
(A) Watching a speech
(B) Meeting a celebrity
(C) Wearing a costume
(D) Purchasing a console

40. How will the man travel to New York?
(A) He will drive himself.
(B) He will get a ride.
(C) He will go by train.
(D) He will take a plane.

41. Why do the fire extinguishers need to be replaced?
(A) They have rusted.
(B) They are low in pressure.
(C) They have become blocked.
(D) They are dented and cracked.

42. Why is the woman relieved?
(A) The fire is under control.
(B) The factory will close soon.
(C) She has a lot of experience.
(D) She has relevant insurance.

43. What does the man mention about the replacements?
(A) They are a different color.
(B) They are out of stock.
(C) They will arrive today.
(D) They will last for years.

44. What are the speakers discussing?
(A) Adding specific product lines for the elderly
(B) Merging operations with a Dutch company
(C) Introducing a special service for old people
(D) Extending business hours for a trial period

45. When will the new scheme start?
(A) Immediately
(B) After a holiday
(C) Next year
(D) Before a vacation

46. What does the woman propose to do?
(A) Clean the checkout area
(B) Train the full-time staff
(C) Promote the system online
(D) Set up signs at the entrance

47. Why is the man making the call?
(A) To transfer a large sum of money
(B) To report a card that has been lost
(C) To open a new savings account
(D) To report some irregular charges

48. What does the woman ask the man to provide?
(A) His first and last name
(B) His account number
(C) His date of birth
(D) His password

49. What does the man inquire about?
(A) The status of a complaint
(B) The possibility of a new card
(C) The likelihood of a refund
(D) The length of a process

50. Who most likely is the man?
    (A) A designer
    (B) An actor
    (C) A historian
    (D) A director

51. What was the woman's opinion of the movie?
    (A) She thought it was well paced.
    (B) She found it very entertaining.
    (C) She felt it didn't match the hype.
    (D) She struggled to understand it.

52. What does the man intend to do?
    (A) Check out an alternative movie
    (B) Consult some online resources
    (C) Correspond with a filmmaker
    (D) Contribute to a documentary

53. Why does the woman need to reschedule the meeting?
    (A) A room is not available.
    (B) A prototype is not ready.
    (C) An event conflicts with it.
    (D) A colleague is overseas.

54. Why does the man say, "Mark's the expert on automation"?
    (A) To explain Mark's visit to Australia
    (B) To suggest that Mark should be promoted
    (C) To introduce Mark to an unfamiliar audience
    (D) To stress that Mark must attend the meeting

55. What does the man suggest doing?
    (A) Canceling the meeting altogether
    (B) Inviting others to attend the meeting
    (C) Moving the meeting to a different time
    (D) Proceeding with the meeting as planned

56. Where most likely are the speakers?
    (A) In a liquor store
    (B) In a home kitchen
    (C) At a farmers' market
    (D) At a café bar

57. What does the woman imply when she says, "I'm only making slow-cooked beef"?
    (A) The meal will be very easy to make.
    (B) Using expensive wine is unnecessary.
    (C) The dish is the man's all-time favorite.
    (D) Adding spices is a waste of time.

58. What will the man buy at the store?
    (A) Some vegetables
    (B) More alcohol
    (C) Some beef
    (D) More garlic

59. What does the man say about the refrigerator?
    (A) It has no freezer compartment.
    (B) It was replaced quite recently.
    (C) It has been leaking periodically.
    (D) It contains some spoiled items.

60. What happened at Krista's old company?
    (A) The carpets were cleaned often.
    (B) The photocopier kept breaking down.
    (C) The leaking dishwasher caused a lot of damage.
    (D) The break room was closed due to lack of use.

61. What will the man most likely do next?
    (A) Try to fix an appliance
    (B) Contact a repairman
    (C) Move the refrigerator
    (D) Check the room for damage

TEST 01

GO ON TO THE NEXT PAGE   171

TEST 01 Listening Test

Supreme Salon—Price List	
Regular Cut	$25
Regular Cut & Wash	$28
Regular Cut & Beard Trim	$35
Beard Trim	$15

35th Annual Bakery Exhibition	
Area 1	Baking Tools & Equipment
Area 2	Packaging Machinery & Materials
Area 3	Frozen Dough & Baking Ingredients
Area 4	Finished Baked Goods: Bread & Pastries

62. Look at the graphic. How much will the man most likely pay?
    (A) $25
    (B) $28
    (C) $35
    (D) $15

63. What is the man doing on Friday?
    (A) Attending a wedding
    (B) Voting in an election
    (C) Meeting with a manager
    (D) Giving a tour of a site

64. What is mentioned about the man's company?
    (A) It is growing at present.
    (B) It sells electrical products.
    (C) It imports lots of goods.
    (D) It is laying off staff.

65. What did the speakers just purchase?
    (A) Cooling racks
    (B) Dough mixers
    (C) Baking trays
    (D) Flour sifters

66. Look at the graphic. Where will the man and woman go next?
    (A) Area 1
    (B) Area 2
    (C) Area 3
    (D) Area 4

67. What is the woman eager to do?
    (A) Sample baked goods
    (B) Discover new equipment
    (C) Sell her own pastries
    (D) Learn new techniques

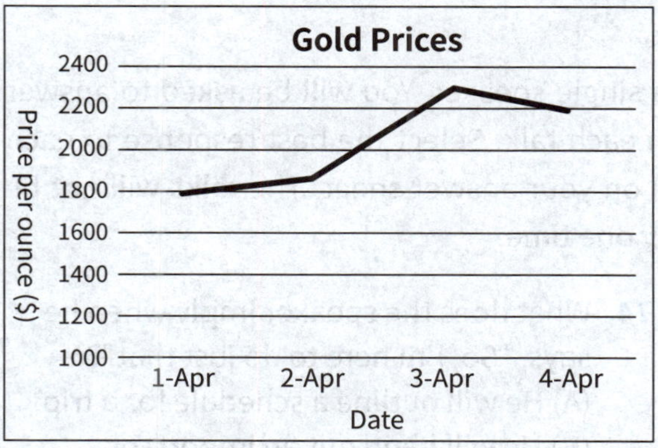
Gold Prices
2400
2200
2000
1800
1600
1400
1200
1000
Price per ounce ($)
1-Apr
2-Apr
3-Apr
4-Apr
Date

68. Why did the man invest in gold?
(A) To fund his retirement
(B) To keep his savings secure
(C) To diversify his portfolio
(D) To make a huge profit

69. Look at the graphic. When did the man make his investment?
(A) On April 1
(B) On April 2
(C) On April 3
(D) On April 4

70. What does the woman plan to do?
(A) Buy some stocks and shares
(B) Make an investment in gold
(C) Seek some professional advice
(D) Put more money into savings

TEST 01

TEST 01 Listening Test

Part 4 414-454

Directions: You will hear some talks given by a single speaker. You will be asked to answer three questions about what the speaker says in each talk. Select the best response to each question and mark the letter (A), (B), (C), or (D) on your answer sheet. The talks will not be printed in your test book and will be spoken only one time.

71. What problem does the speaker mention?
    (A) Striking drivers
    (B) Torrential storms
    (C) Canceled trains
    (D) Significant delays

72. According to the speaker, what is the train company waiting for?
    (A) The weather to improve
    (B) The specialists to arrive
    (C) The union to agree to terms
    (D) The train car to be fixed

73. How are the listeners advised to travel?
    (A) By bus
    (B) By scooter
    (C) By taxi
    (D) By bike

74. What does the speaker imply when he says, "So, I'm here to do just that"?
    (A) He will outline a schedule for a trip.
    (B) He will hand out an important document.
    (C) He will clarify some details of a policy.
    (D) He will apologize for a last-minute change.

75. Why can the listeners no longer travel first class?
    (A) The airline scrapped a rewards program.
    (B) The company wants to save money.
    (C) The perk was abused by workers in the past.
    (D) The firm wants to treat all staff fairly.

76. What are the listeners invited to do?
    (A) Pay for their own upgrade
    (B) Give feedback on a policy
    (C) Attend a planning session
    (D) Pose potential scenarios

77. Where most likely is the speaker?
    (A) In a bistro
    (B) In a supermarket
    (C) In a wellness seminar
    (D) In a cooking class

78. What does the speaker stress about kimchi?
    (A) Its special jars
    (B) Its long history
    (C) Its sour flavor
    (D) Its health benefits

79. How does the speaker try to reassure the listeners?
    (A) By referring to a limited special offer
    (B) By mentioning the low cost of the product
    (C) By informing them that they can return the item
    (D) By telling them different spice levels are available

80. What is the company doing this year?
    (A) Organizing a company-wide trip
    (B) Reimbursing staff for travel costs
    (C) Presenting long-service awards
    (D) Canceling a staff holiday party

81. Why should the listeners check an email?
    (A) To find out how much money they get
    (B) To check examples of acceptable receipts
    (C) To vote for their preferred destination
    (D) To consult an itinerary for a vacation

82. What does the speaker imply when he says, "this is a step in the right direction"?
    (A) The company will cut more costs this year.
    (B) The leave rules will be the next to be updated.
    (C) The new policy will better meet employees' needs.
    (D) The staff will enjoy socializing together more often.

83. What situation is the speaker addressing?
    (A) A power outage
    (B) A medical emergency
    (C) A suspicious item
    (D) A fire alarm

84. Where are the listeners asked to go?
    (A) To a parking lot
    (B) To a sports field
    (C) To an arena's lobby
    (D) To an alternative stadium

85. Who will arrive at the stadium soon?
    (A) First-aid responders
    (B) Security specialists
    (C) Fire service personnel
    (D) Maintenance teams

86. Why does the speaker say, "A mutual friend gave me your number"?
    (A) To justify an unexpected call
    (B) To submit a painting
    (C) To recommend a candidate
    (D) To ensure the number is correct

87. Why is the speaker leaving the message?
    (A) To ask for an autograph
    (B) To arrange a delivery
    (C) To criticize an article
    (D) To request an interview

88. What does the speaker ask the listener to do?
    (A) Send him a manuscript
    (B) Fill out a questionnaire
    (C) Suggest a location
    (D) Call him back

TEST 01

GO ON TO THE NEXT PAGE → 175

TEST 01 Listening Test

89. What is the main purpose of the announcement?
    (A) To ask workers to wear protective gear
    (B) To remind people of a scheduled operation
    (C) To announce an unexpected safety inspection
    (D) To tell staff to help unpack a delivery

90. What does the speaker ask the listeners to do?
    (A) Place orders online
    (B) Gather in the loading bay
    (C) Put tanks onto a truck
    (D) Stay away from an area

91. What will the speaker be doing tomorrow?
    (A) Supervising the refill
    (B) Visiting another site
    (C) Upgrading some facilities
    (D) Taking a gas safety course

92. Who most likely is speaking?
    (A) A travel agent
    (B) A check-in officer
    (C) A cruise ship entertainer
    (D) An animal rights campaigner

93. What is unique about the trip?
    (A) It involves sailing to different islands.
    (B) It includes a special cooking course.
    (C) It involves seeing a rare animal breed.
    (D) It includes a mountain trek with local guides.

94. What does the speaker ask the listeners to provide?
    (A) Details of preferred accommodations
    (B) Information on selected excursions
    (C) Details of dietary requirements
    (D) Feedback on an itinerary

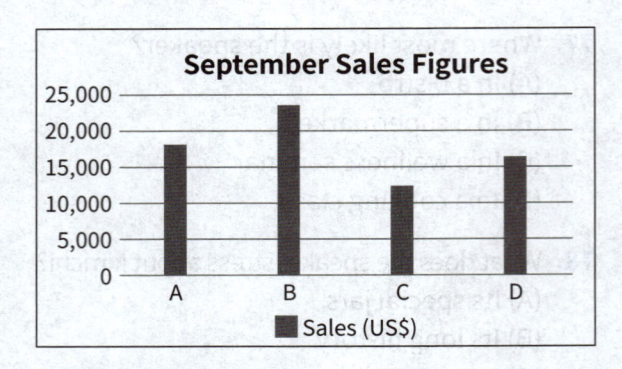

September Sales Figures

	A	B	C	D
Sales (US$)	18,000	24,000	12,500	16,500

95. What does the speaker say about September's sales figures?
    (A) They are missing some data.
    (B) They are still being analyzed.
    (C) They are better than average.
    (D) They are unexpectedly poor.

96. What did the company do in September?
    (A) Restructured a department
    (B) Weathered a downturn
    (C) Streamlined a procedure
    (D) Released a new item

97. Look at the graphic. Which bar most likely represents Barry's sales?
    (A) Bar A
    (B) Bar B
    (C) Bar C
    (D) Bar D

176

BAGGAGE CLAIM		
Flight	Origin	Carousel
328	Dallas, TX	3
412	Atlanta, GA	4
226	Tampa, FL	6
818	Charlotte, NC	8

98. What problem is the speaker addressing?
    (A) Issues with screens
    (B) Weather conditions
    (C) Crew availability
    (D) Security concerns

99. Look at the graphic. Which flight's passengers should now use Carousel 4?
    (A) Flight 328
    (B) Flight 412
    (C) Flight 226
    (D) Flight 818

100. What are all passengers advised to do?
    (A) Follow updates on the airline's app
    (B) Visit the customer service desk
    (C) Keep an eye on the arrivals board
    (D) Ensure they take the correct bags

This is the end of the Listening test. Turn to Part 5 in your test book.

NO TEST MATERIAL ON THIS PAGE

TEST 01 Reading Test

READING TEST

In the Reading test, you will read a variety of texts and answer several different types of reading comprehension questions. The entire Reading test will last 75 minutes. There are three parts, and directions are given for each part. You are encouraged to answer as many questions as possible within the time allowed.

You must mark your answers on the separate answer sheet. Do not write your answers in your test book.

Part 5

Directions: A word or phrase is missing in each of the sentences below. Four answer choices are given below each sentence. Select the best answer to complete the sentence. Then mark the letter (A), (B), (C), or (D) on your answer sheet.

101. Ms. Bertrand thanked Mr. Schneider for his ------- advice about making lucrative investments.
    (A) value
    (B) valuable
    (C) valueless
    (D) valuation

102. The manager rejected every single one of the designs for the new paperweight because he did not like ------- of them.
    (A) all
    (B) some
    (C) many
    (D) any

103. The amount of money Ms. Goldstein inherited ------- sufficient for her to open her own art restoration studio.
    (A) is
    (B) are
    (C) be
    (D) being

104. Mr. Okonkwo liked the first group's presentation, but he preferred the second group's because ------- was more detailed.
    (A) them
    (B) themselves
    (C) theirs
    (D) they

105. No matter how persistent the salesman was, he could not ------- Ms. Hoxha to buy the designer purse.
    (A) to convince
    (B) convince
    (C) convincing
    (D) convincingly

106. Ms. Chang knew there was ------- chance of a promotion while the company was struggling to stay profitable.
    (A) few
    (B) a few
    (C) little
    (D) a little

GO ON TO THE NEXT PAGE 179

107. Relaxton Industries' latest growth ------- is to expand into the booming Southeast Asia market.
(A) individual
(B) prevention
(C) strategy
(D) personality

108. The boardwalk will be closed for an extra week because the repairs to the damaged boards ------- taking longer than initially thought.
(A) are
(B) is
(C) will
(D) have

109. Ms. Efendi was instructed to ------- the human resources manager on her first day at the office.
(A) switch off
(B) pile up
(C) die down
(D) report to

110. Global Renewal Tech is ------- a big company that it requires tens of thousands of employees to keep it running smoothly.
(A) further
(B) much
(C) so
(D) such

111. The convenience store employee saw the line ------- longer and asked her colleague to man another cash register.
(A) to grow
(B) growing
(C) grows
(D) grew

112. If the restaurant served less expensive meals, Ms. Thwaytes ------- there on a more regular basis.
(A) dines
(B) dined
(C) could dine
(D) had dined

113. When Mr. Drummond went to see the dentist -------, she informed him that his teeth were in perfect condition.
(A) someday
(B) everyday
(C) the other day
(D) every day

114. Ms. Albanese has been unemployed ------- she was made redundant by her employer six months ago.
(A) since
(B) before
(C) while
(D) then

115. The pastry chef instructed his assistant to cut the cake ------- in half to ensure fairness.
    (A) vividly
    (B) accidentally
    (C) precisely
    (D) fortunately

116. It is about time that the company ------- to take advantage of the immense benefits offered by AI.
    (A) start
    (B) started
    (C) starting
    (D) starts

117. The company's executive leadership will ------- negotiations with representatives of a rival firm regarding a potential merger.
    (A) speak to
    (B) apply to
    (C) recover from
    (D) engage in

118. The survey results indicate that most users prefer the old version of the messaging software ------- the new one.
    (A) or
    (B) than
    (C) to
    (D) and

119. Mr. Hsu knew that he had made a bad impression when he did not arrive ------- time for the interview.
    (A) at
    (B) for
    (C) under
    (D) on

120. Ms. Walker couldn't help ------- what her colleagues from her old company were up to these days.
    (A) wonder
    (B) wondering
    (C) to wonder
    (D) wondered

121. Tech support can offer advice if you experience any issues ------- to the new version of the operating system.
    (A) ensuring
    (B) migrating
    (C) inhabiting
    (D) exploiting

122. There were ------- reasons why Mr. Hieronymus turned down the job offer, but the chief one was the low pay.
    (A) numerous
    (B) delightful
    (C) regretful
    (D) tedious

GO ON TO THE NEXT PAGE → 181

123. Employees are reminded that those ------- will work overtime this evening must first obtain permission from their supervisor.
(A) which
(B) where
(C) whom
(D) who

124. The construction project will be put on hold this weekend ------- the approaching hurricane impacts the island badly.
(A) so long as
(B) even if
(C) except for
(D) in case

125. Being stricken with the flu this winter does not guarantee ------- from the virus next winter.
(A) immune
(B) immunity
(C) immunize
(D) immunization

126. The costume designer is incredibly artistic, but she struggles to ------- her ideas clearly during pre-production meetings.
(A) articulation
(B) articulated
(C) articulate
(D) articulately

127. Only when the scented candles have sold out ------- signing a new contract with the supplier.
(A) can we contemplate
(B) we can contemplate
(C) can contemplate we
(D) contemplate can we

128. Mr. Yamamoto opened the ramen restaurant ------- the fact that there were already two similar establishments on the same street.
(A) from
(B) within
(C) despite
(D) until

129. Two vehicles were involved in a serious ------- on the southbound highway at three o'clock this morning.
(A) benchmark
(B) collision
(C) friction
(D) certification

130. It is imperative that Ms. Sanchez ------- the meeting on finding a new brand ambassador as that is her field of expertise.
(A) to attend
(B) attended
(C) attends
(D) attend

Part 6

Directions: Read the texts that follow. A word, phrase, or sentence is missing in parts of each text. Four answer choices for each question are given below the text. Select the best answer to complete the text. Then mark the letter (A), (B), (C), or (D) on your answer sheet.

Questions 131-134 refer to the following notice.

**ATTENTION: CUSTOMERS OF
GLOBAL-SPEND DEPARTMENT STORE**

Please note that the elevators at Global-Spend Department Store are intended first and foremost for ------- users. This group includes the elderly, the disabled, pregnant
131.
women, and people with strollers. Please yield to these users and anyone else with limited mobility. -------. These are located at every corner on each floor of the
132.
department store. There are also stairs at the north and south sides of each floor for those customers who want to be more -------. We thank you for your ------- in this
133.   134.
matter and wish you a pleasant shopping experience at Global-Spend Department Store.

---

131. (A) gym
 (B) reservation
 (C) privilege
 (D) priority

132. (A) The elevator at the Church Street entrance is currently under maintenance.
 (B) Remember that not all disabilities are visible, so please be considerate and understanding.
 (C) We kindly ask that general users consider taking the escalators whenever possible.
 (D) This policy is designed to be fair to all customers of Global-Spend Department Store.

133. (A) serious
 (B) active
 (C) demanding
 (D) sympathetic

134. (A) cooperate
 (B) cooperative
 (C) cooperatively
 (D) cooperation

GO ON TO THE NEXT PAGE → 183

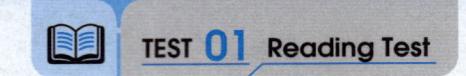

Questions 135-138 refer to the following advertisement.

> **Got dust mites?**
> **We'll send 'em packing!**
>
> Dust mites are an invisible menace in our homes. These tiny creatures live in household dust and love warm, humid -------. -------. They can also make asthma
>   135.   136.
> and allergies worse. That's where Mighty Mite Removers comes in! We offer an expert cleaning service that targets dust mites at the source! Our powerful vacuums ------- HEPA filters will capture the dust mites. And our high-heat steam cleaning
> 137.
> system will deep clean your mattresses, pillows, carpets, and curtains. Our service comes with a no-fuss 90-day money-back guarantee if you are not -------. Trust
>   138.
> Mighty Mite Removers to send your dust mites packing!

135. (A) movements
(B) environments
(C) regulations
(D) circulations

136. (A) High levels of dust mites can lower the air quality in your home.
(B) For independent reviews of our service, check out this website.
(C) We recommend dusting your apartment at least once a week.
(D) An average-size room will be cleaned within sixty minutes.

137. (A) off
(B) into
(C) with
(D) as

138. (A) satisfy
(B) satisfied
(C) satisfying
(D) satisfaction

Questions 139-142 refer to the following news report.

Albescu and Forta Drinks Part Ways

By David Jones
Tennis Correspondent

Soft drinks giant Forta Drinks has officially ended its sponsorship deal with tennis star Ella Albescu. In a statement ------- yesterday, the company thanked Ms. Albescu for her professionalism during their five-year partnership but added that it was "time for a change of direction." However, industry insiders ------- that the decision is connected to Ms. Albescu's performance on the court. -------. This makes her less attractive to major sponsors. Ms. Albescu will be $100,000 a year worse off ------- the cancelation of the Forta Drinks deal. She will no doubt be concerned her other sponsorship deals may go the same way.

139. (A) releases
(B) releasing
(C) had released
(D) released

140. (A) praise
(B) appeal
(C) suspect
(D) confront

141. (A) She easily won her first match after returning from a training camp.
(B) The former world number one has dropped to 57th in the rankings.
(C) Ms. Albescu has also signed a deal with a leading sportswear brand.
(D) Her coach welcomed the decision and thanked her long-time fans.

142. (A) instead of
(B) rather than
(C) in line with
(D) thanks to

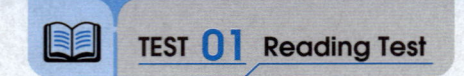

TEST 01 Reading Test

Questions 143-146 refer to the following email.

From: c.kryten@sophe-securities.com
To: a.pernot@sophe-securities.com
Subject: Expenses Claim SS2564

Dear Ms. Pernot,

We have reviewed the expenses claim for your business trip to Bangkok from April 24 to May 1. While the vast ------- (143) of your expenses have been approved, we are unable to approve one item. -------- (144). The company travel policy does not cover costs associated with excess baggage. The only exception would be ------- (145) you were transporting company-related material. Your line manager has confirmed that this was not the case. As such, you will need to cover the $95 cost ------- (146). We respectfully suggest that you follow the airline's standard baggage rules in future.

Thank you.

Chris Kryten
Finance Officer
Sophe Securities

---

143. (A) majority
(B) minority
(C) manuscript
(D) deposit

144. (A) You are permitted to spend $40 per day on meals and snacks.
(B) We are sorry for the inconvenience caused by the cancellation of your flight.
(C) All funds should be in your bank account within three workdays.
(D) This relates to a few extra kilograms carried on your return flight.

145. (A) still
(B) if
(C) once
(D) total

146. (A) manually
(B) sincerely
(C) personally
(D) publicly

Part 7

Directions: In this part you will read a selection of texts, such as magazine and newspaper articles, emails, and instant messages. Each text or set of texts is followed by several questions. Select the best answer for each question and mark the letter (A), (B), (C), or (D) on your answer sheet.

Questions 147-148 refer to the following notice.

NOTICE

Visitors are reminded that this neighborhood is not only for tourists; people live, work, and raise their families here, too. We kindly ask that while you enjoy visiting our beautiful community, you show respect to its residents. Please avoid making loud noise near homes, do not take pictures of people without their permission, and keep driveways to homes and businesses clear at all times. Your cooperation helps to preserve the character that makes this place worth visiting. Thank you.

---

147. What is the main purpose of the notice?
 (A) To tell drivers to follow national laws
 (B) To ask travelers not to disturb locals
 (C) To tell residents to respect their neighbors
 (D) To ask companies to follow building rules

148. What instruction is NOT mentioned in the notice?
 (A) Don't take photos of residents
 (B) Don't block people's entrances
 (C) Don't leave litter in the area
 (D) Don't make excessive noise

GO ON TO THE NEXT PAGE → 187

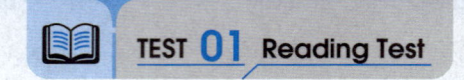

Questions 149-150 refer to the following email.

From: c.wagner@liebe-fritsch-tech.com
To: l.bauer@liebe-fritsch-tech.com
Subject: Job Ad Ref: LFT651

Dear Mr. Bauer,

I'm writing with regard to the recently posted job ad for a Diversity and Inclusion Manager. The new CEO believes that this role heavily duplicates duties already being performed by other members of Human Resources. He has therefore requested that the ad be immediately pulled from all relevant platforms. We will not proceed with recruitment at this time. First thing in the morning, please get in touch with anyone who has already applied for the position and offer our apologies for the error.

Thank you.

Clara Wagner
Executive Assistant
Liebe Fritsch Tech

---

149. What is indicated about the job ad?
 (A) It does not promote diversity.
 (B) It needs to be withdrawn now.
 (C) It is for an assistant to the CEO.
 (D) It must be checked thoroughly.

150. What does Ms. Wagner ask Mr. Bauer to do in the morning?
 (A) Meet with an HR manager
 (B) Interview any candidates
 (C) Post a revised job ad
 (D) Contact any applicants

Questions 151-152 refer to the following text-message chain.

Jalen Scott 9:55 p.m.
Hi, Yara. I'm sorry to bother you so late, but I forgot to ask a question about the trip to Cuba.

Yara Alvarado 9:57 p.m.
Don't worry about it.

Jalen Scott 9:58 p.m.
What is the best method of payment when we're there?

Yara Alvarado 10:00 p.m.
Well, cash is king in Cuba. In practice, most businesses accept US dollars. You should bring plenty of small bills because you'll get change back in the local currency.

Jalen Scott 10:01 p.m.
And how about US credit cards?

Yara Alvarado 10:03 p.m.
You can't use them in Cuba, so you may as well leave them at home.

Jalen Scott 10:04 p.m.
Got it—thanks for your replies.

---

151. At 9:57 p.m., what does Ms. Alvarado most likely mean when she writes, "Don't worry about it"?
(A) She is not bothered about a delay.
(B) She is willing to provide information.
(C) She hopes Mr. Scott will enjoy the trip.
(D) She doesn't care about a late payment.

152. What does Ms. Alvarado mention about US dollars?
(A) They can only be used if they're large bills.
(B) They must be converted to the local currency.
(C) They will actually be accepted at most places.
(D) They are less useful than US credit cards.

GO ON TO THE NEXT PAGE   189

TEST 01 Reading Test

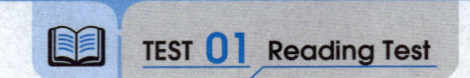

Questions 153-154 refer to the following email.

From: omar.al-farsi@al-farsi-manufac.com
To: sonya.ivanova@ipt.com
Subject: Order No. IPT9865

Dear Ms. Ivanova,

It is with regret that I must inform you of my decision to cancel the above order for height gauges. Please note that this is in no way reflective of the quality of your products or the service you have provided over the years. It is simply due to the recent unexpected increase in import tariffs. These have significantly impacted our bottom line, and I have no choice but to source the height gauges from a local supplier. As soon as the trade conditions become more favorable, I fully intend to acquire the goods once again from your company. Thank you for your understanding, and I look forward to working with you in the future.

Yours sincerely,

Omar Al-Farsi
Owner & Founder
Al-Farsi Manufacturing

---

153. Why has Mr. Al-Farsi canceled the order?
(A) The quality of the precision tools has declined.
(B) A customer has reported several faults with an item.
(C) The service received from the supplier has worsened.
(D) An increased tax has driven up costs and hit his profits.

154. What is Mr. Al-Farsi's intention for the future?
(A) That he will build a more profitable company
(B) That he will order from Ms. Ivanova again
(C) That he will make the required gauges himself
(D) That he will meet Ms. Ivanova in person

Questions 155-157 refer to the following press release.

For Immediate Release:
NorwegTech and Marine Core Systems Announce Partnership

NorwegTech, one of the world's leading cloud computing service providers, and Marine Core Systems, an innovator in ocean engineering, have announced a partnership to develop a network of underwater data centers. These will be positioned in the Norwegian Sea, where conditions are considered highly favorable in terms of temperature and minimizing environmental disturbance. "Data centers use huge amounts of electricity, much of which is needed for cooling," said Astrid Bakken, CEO of NorwegTech. "Placing them in the ocean will vastly improve cooling efficiency, thereby reducing energy consumption." Marine Core Systems is a relatively new player in the field of subsea engineering but has quickly gained a reputation for developing innovative, green, sustainable solutions. "Our primary objective is to help the planet," said its CEO, Zane Novak. "This partnership allows us to achieve that aim."

---

155. What is the purpose of the partnership?
(A) To clean up the world's oceans
(B) To promote tours to Norway
(C) To establish many computing facilities
(D) To make cloud storage more affordable

156. What does Ms. Bakken mention about data centers?
(A) They consume a lot of power.
(B) They are expensive to produce.
(C) They take years to engineer.
(D) They are vulnerable to hacking.

157. What is indicated about Marine Core Systems?
(A) It is trying to improve its image.
(B) It hopes to expand into Europe.
(C) It has existed for several decades.
(D) It wants to help the environment.

GO ON TO THE NEXT PAGE →

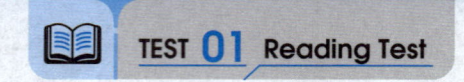

Questions 158-160 refer to the following social media post.

Bess Smithson is **feeling energized** at **Birmingham, Alabama**.

Good morning! I'm full of energy today, and that's because I just used avocado oil in my morning smoothie! —[1]— Avocados are well known for their health benefits: they're a superb source of key vitamins and minerals, full of heart-healthy fats, and high in fiber. —[2]— Their oil can be drizzled on salads, used while roasting veggies, and added to smoothies. But not all avocado oils are created equal. In my opinion, the best on the market is Ava's Avocado Oil. —[3]— Its main advantage is that Ava only uses surplus avocados in her oil. That is, she takes avocados that would otherwise have been thrown away and gives them a new purpose! Why not try out Ava's Avocado Oil yourself? —[4]— I've teamed up with Ava to offer my followers a twenty-percent discount on a bottle of her oil. Head over to avas-avocado-oil.com and quote AvaBess123 to get your exclusive discount!

👍 Like   💬 Comment   ➡ Share

158. What benefit of Ava's Avocado Oil does Ms. Smithson mention?
(A) It contains the finest avocados from a specific region.
(B) It contains more vitamins than most avocado oils.
(C) It is made from avocados that would have been wasted.
(D) It is less expensive than other oils on the market.

159. Why would a follower use the code AvaBess123?
(A) To receive a free bottle of oil
(B) To obtain Ms. Smithson's smoothies
(C) To be sent an avocado recipe book
(D) To get a reduction on a bottle

160. In which of the positions marked [1], [2], [3], and [4] does the following sentence best belong?

"Not only that, but these tropical fruits can help you stay fuller for longer."

(A) [1]
(B) [2]
(C) [3]
(D) [4]

Questions 161-163 refer to the following advertisement.

Moving to another country—whether temporarily or permanently—can be a stressful experience. You've got a million and one things to organize, from accommodations to employment to education. Why not let DirectPath Immigration Services take away at least some of the pressure? Whether you're grappling with visa applications, work permits, green cards, or citizenship forms, we are here to guide you through the process. We provide step-by-step support to make sure you do not miss any vital information or paperwork that could upset your long-term plans.

Why else should you choose DirectPath Immigration Services? Our advisors have years of experience in the immigration field and are available 24/7 to answer any of your questions. Our personable staff offer services in languages from every corner of the globe, including Spanish, Arabic, and Vietnamese. And our prices are transparent and affordable. Head over to direct-path-immigration.com for a list of our prices, broken down by country and immigration type. DirectPath Immigration Services—we're your path toward a new life.

161. Who most likely is the intended audience for the advertisement?
(A) Short-term tourists
(B) Vacation rental owners
(C) Study-abroad students
(D) International migrants

162. The word "guide" in paragraph 1, line 6, is closest in meaning to
(A) affix
(B) show
(C) influence
(D) register

163. What is NOT mentioned as a reason for choosing the service?
(A) Clear and cheap rates
(B) Knowledgeable advisors
(C) Free appeals process
(D) Multilingual assistance

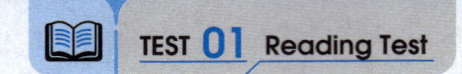

Questions 164-167 refer to the following online chat discussion.

Hugo Morales   2:12 p.m.
I've got an update on the office renovations. Unfortunately, the whole project has gone over budget. It means the phase involving the renovation of the bathrooms has been put on hold until at least next year.

Mira Popescu   2:14 p.m.
Does that affect the timeline for the current phase?

Hugo Morales   2:15 p.m.
It does, Mira. We should be able to wrap things up around one week earlier than planned.

Mira Popescu   2:16 p.m.
Would you like me to communicate that to the staff?

Hugo Morales   2:18 p.m.
Hang fire on that for now. Let's get a definitive completion date first.

Mira Popescu   2:19 p.m.
Got it.

Hugo Morales   2:20 p.m.
Also, we've had some complaints from the PR firm on the 4th floor.

Finn Jensen   2:21 p.m.
Here we go again. What is it now?

Hugo Morales   2:22 p.m.
They're saying that workmen are taking up all the space in the elevators.

Finn Jensen   2:24 p.m.
Well, there's not much we can do about that. We've already scheduled as much of the work as possible for the weekend. Plus, there hasn't been a peep of complaint from the tech startup on the 6th floor.

Hugo Morales   2:25 p.m.
Nevertheless, let's do what we can to keep disturbances to a minimum for others in the office building.

164. What does Mr. Morales mention about the bathrooms?
    (A) They were refurbished last year.
    (B) They won't be renovated yet.
    (C) They will cost less to revamp.
    (D) They will take a week to redecorate.

165. What does Mr. Morales ask Ms. Popescu to do?
    (A) Announce a change immediately
    (B) Prepare a fully updated budget
    (C) Wait before informing the staff
    (D) Distribute a revised timeline

166. At 2:21 p.m., what does Mr. Jensen most likely imply when he writes, "Here we go again"?
    (A) The elevators are often out of order.
    (B) The PR firm has made other criticisms.
    (C) The 4th floor requires additional renovations.
    (D) The deadline has been changed frequently.

167. What is indicated about the office building?
    (A) Its elevators are inspected annually.
    (B) It was constructed within the last decade.
    (C) It includes some residential floors.
    (D) It contains different companies.

GO ON TO THE NEXT PAGE 195

Questions 168-171 refer to the following email.

From: jiho.park@jeong-lee-pharma.com
To: operations.team@jeong-lee-pharma.com
Subject: E-Signatures Training Session
Attachment: QuickStartGuide.doc

Hi All,

We will be holding a training session on using electronic signatures (e-signatures) for documents. I've sent this email to the entire department, but it is specifically for those who prepare, sign, or send internal or external business-related documents. These include but are not restricted to contracts, informed consent forms, and non-disclosure agreements. The training session will take place on Thursday, August 14, from 2:00 p.m. to 4:00 p.m. in Conference Room C. Remote workers can join via Zoom, a link for which will be provided nearer the time.

Having recently attended an outside training course on the use of e-signatures and been awarded a certificate for doing so, I shall lead our training session myself. I will use real-world examples to ensure that it won't be just a dry, academic session. Please respond to this email to tell me whether you will be able to attend, and please specify whether that attendance will be in person or remotely.

Best regards,
Jiho Park
Operations Manager
Jeong-Lee Pharma

---

168. According to the email, who is the training session for?
(A) Every member of one department
(B) All senior managers in a company
(C) Only workers who deal with clients
(D) Anyone who deals with documents

169. What does Mr. Park suggest about the Zoom link?
(A) It is broken and will be fixed.
(B) It can be found in an attachment.
(C) It requires a secure password.
(D) It will be provided later.

170. Why will Mr. Park run the training session?
(A) He has obtained the relevant knowledge.
(B) He must step in to replace an instructor.
(C) He uses e-signatures most frequently.
(D) He is a world-renowned academic.

171. What does Mr. Park ask the recipients to do?
(A) Avoid signing contracts before the session
(B) Forward the email to interested parties
(C) Send a reply indicating attendance
(D) Review an attached document

Questions 172-175 refer to the following news report.

CITY SUBWAY TO CUT THE NOISE

By Saeed Mirza
Transportation Editor

The Springfield Public Transit Authority (SPTA) announced yesterday that it will reduce the number of "unnecessary" in-station announcements in a bid to improve the customer experience. —[1]— The move follows a three-month consultation process in which an overwhelming majority of passengers expressed frustration at the frequent and repetitive nature of the announcements.

SPTA spokesperson Peter Mourad stressed that all announcements relating to safety and security would remain. These will include service changes, emergency instructions, and public health alerts. —[2]— However, Mr. Mourad added that "non-critical messages, such as those related to the imposition of fines for drinking and eating in subway stations, will be repeated less frequently. We want our announcements to have purpose."

Many passengers welcomed the news. —[3]— "It will be nice to have some peace and quiet," regular commuter Zara Khan told *The Springfield Daily Express*. "Everyone knows they should remember their belongings; we don't need to be told about it every ten seconds like children."

However, the National Transportation Safety Board has expressed caution, noting that it will follow the implementation of the policy closely. —[4]— The "non-critical" announcements will be curtailed at Red Line stations beginning May 1, with the other lines following suit at weekly intervals.

---

172. What is the main topic of the news report?
(A) The introduction of quiet cars on subway trains
(B) The decrease in messages at subway stations
(C) The enforcement of rules about speaking softly
(D) The reduction in availability of subway staff

173. According to the news report, why might passengers receive a penalty?
(A) For carrying restricted items
(B) For failing to pay the fare
(C) For smoking cigarettes
(D) For consuming food

174. What is suggested about the new policy?
(A) It will be vetoed by a safety group.
(B) It will be reviewed in one month.
(C) It will be implemented in stages.
(D) It will be publicized on notices.

175. In which of the positions marked [1], [2], [3], and [4] does the following sentence best belong?

"We spoke to several yesterday evening as they were entering or exiting major stations."

(A) [1]
(B) [2]
(C) [3]
(D) [4]

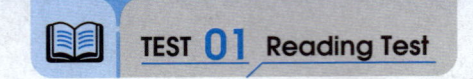

Questions 176-180 refer to the following excerpt from a handbook and email.

Company Guidelines for Sick Leave

This section of the handbook relates to the company's sick leave policy. It is designed to ensure clarity and consistency in application and to promote employee well-being. The following points apply to both full-time and part-time staff. Interns and other temporary workers should consult with their direct supervisor or manager for guidance.

- Employees are entitled to ten days of paid sick leave per calendar year.
- They are permitted to take off up to three consecutive days of sick leave without needing to submit a medical certificate.
- A medical certificate must be provided for absences longer than this.
- Sick leave that has not been used cannot be rolled over to the following year or cashed out; it will expire at the end of each year.

From: nahla.osman@m-a-enterprises.com
To: elvin.bakari@m-a-enterprises.com
Subject: Sick Leave

Dear Mr. Bakari,

It has come to my attention that during your recent absence, you exceeded the amount of sick leave allowed without the provision of medical documentation by one day.

Please be aware that a medical certificate is required for absences of this length. According to our records, you have seldom taken sick leave during your five years at the company, so I presume this is a simple oversight on your part. I therefore suggest that you visit your doctor to obtain a retrospective medical certificate to cover the absence. Please submit this within the next five workdays.

Please feel free to reply to this email if you have any questions.

Kind regards,

Nahla Osman
Human Resources Manager
Mensah-Abassi Enterprises

176. In the handbook, who are instructed to speak to their supervisors?
(A) Part-time workers
(B) Temporary staff
(C) Full-time employees
(D) All unwell personnel

177. What will happen to unused sick leave?
(A) It will be paid to the employee in cash.
(B) It will be added to the following year's total.
(C) It will be converted into store points.
(D) It will be forfeited at the close of the year.

178. What is indicated about Mr. Bakari?
(A) He was rarely ill in the past.
(B) He is a new recruit to the firm.
(C) He has been promoted to manager.
(D) He is taking medication for his vision.

179. Where is Mr. Bakari advised to go?
(A) To the onsite infirmary
(B) To a doctor's office
(C) To the HR department
(D) To a local pharmacy

180. How long was Mr. Bakari absent from work recently?
(A) Two days
(B) Three days
(C) Four days
(D) Five days

TEST 01

GO ON TO THE NEXT PAGE 199

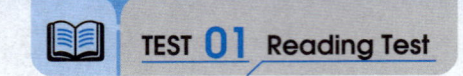

TEST 01 Reading Test

Questions 181-185 refer to the following email and advertisement.

From: henrietta.bush@coniston-tech.com
To: ben.smithers@coniston-tech.com
Subject: Overseas Posting

Dear Mr. Smithers,

First of all, thank you for accepting the international assignment to Germany. When we acquired the factory in Munich, we knew we would have to spend significant time optimizing its robotics infrastructure and combining its systems with ours. You're clearly the best person for the job.

Secondly, I would like to mention a language-learning app called Lingo Leveler. You're unlikely to need to speak German in the factory because the team there all speak English fluently. However, being able to communicate with the locals about everyday topics will undeniably enhance your cultural experience. The app is compatible with both iOS and Android systems. The company will be happy to pay for the premium service. Just send a copy of the invoice to Mark in Finance, and he will reimburse you.

Best regards,

Henrietta Bush
Global Mobility Coordinator
Coniston Tech

Level-up your German language skills with…

LINGO LEVELER

Want to improve your language abilities? Our fantastically flexible app allows you to do so in whichever way you desire. Simply select the course that meets your needs:

- **LL101**: Business Writing in German
- **LL102**: Daily Conversation in German
- **LL103**: Negotiation Skills in German
- **LL104**: Reading Comprehension in German

All of our courses feature material inspired by real-world situations, so you can be sure they're indispensable to your business or travel needs. Download the app for free today. Why not upgrade to our premium service for only $100 per annum and enjoy ad-free lessons and bonus exercises? Lingo Leveler—level-up your skills today!

181. Why will Mr. Smithers travel to Germany?
    (A) To improve his manufacturing knowledge
    (B) To oversee the opening of a new branch
    (C) To teach English to the local staff
    (D) To assist with robotics integration

182. What does Ms. Bush ask Mr. Smithers to provide?
    (A) A flight ticket
    (B) A business plan
    (C) Proof of payment
    (D) Language test results

183. According to the advertisement, what will all courses include?
    (A) Scenarios based on the real world
    (B) Material written by native speakers
    (C) Lessons that include lots of games
    (D) Content suitable for adults and children

184. What is suggested about the premium version of the app?
    (A) It works on only one operating system.
    (B) It requires a payment every month.
    (C) It does not contain any commercials.
    (D) It provides real-time feedback for the exercises.

185. Which language course will Mr. Smithers most likely choose?
    (A) LL101
    (B) LL102
    (C) LL103
    (D) LL104

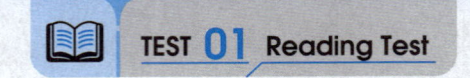

Questions 186-190 refer to the following notice, email, and news report.

NOTICE: DISRUPTION TO BUS SERVICES

The Fairview City Transit Authority would like to notify residents about disruption to some bus services next week. This is due to the installation of new solar-powered digital displays at several bus stops. The work will take place from Monday 2 March to Wednesday 4 March and will be restricted to the northern district. The specific schedule is as follows:

Bus Stop	Date & Time
Vine Street	Mon. 2 March, 9 a.m. to 12 p.m.
Ashton Road	Mon. 2 March, 1 p.m. to 4 p.m.
Oak Street	Tue. 3 March, 9 a.m. to 12 p.m.
Main Road	Wed. 4 March, 1 p.m. to 4 p.m.

Alternate boarding points will be clearly marked but may require a short walk for safety reasons. We appreciate your patience.

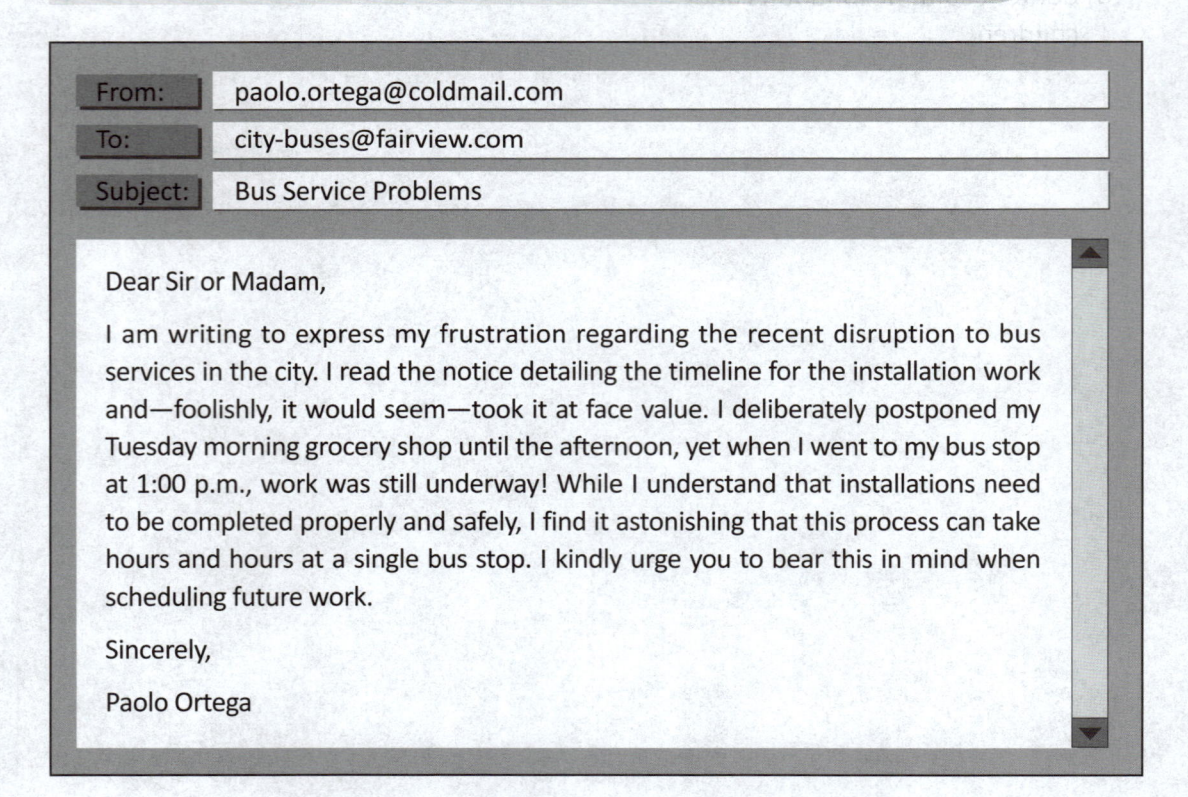

From: paolo.ortega@coldmail.com
To: city-buses@fairview.com
Subject: Bus Service Problems

Dear Sir or Madam,

I am writing to express my frustration regarding the recent disruption to bus services in the city. I read the notice detailing the timeline for the installation work and—foolishly, it would seem—took it at face value. I deliberately postponed my Tuesday morning grocery shop until the afternoon, yet when I went to my bus stop at 1:00 p.m., work was still underway! While I understand that installations need to be completed properly and safely, I find it astonishing that this process can take hours and hours at a single bus stop. I kindly urge you to bear this in mind when scheduling future work.

Sincerely,

Paolo Ortega

All Change for Fairview Buses

By Missy Anderson
Staff Reporter

Fairview City has announced the completion of its project to install solar-powered displays at the city's bus stops. The final stops in the eastern and western districts were upgraded yesterday morning, April 6. The work is part of a larger drive to make the city and its facilities more sustainable. According to Matt Fring of the Fairview City Transit Authority, the new displays will "save hundreds of kilowatt hours of electricity every year, helping to reduce carbon emissions and bring down bills."

186. Why are bus services being disrupted?
    (A) Roadwork is taking place in the area.
    (B) Eco-friendly displays are being installed.
    (C) Additional routes are being added to timetables.
    (D) Maintenance work is underway on the fleet of buses.

187. Which bus stop does Mr. Ortega most likely live nearby?
    (A) Vine Street
    (B) Ashton Road
    (C) Oak Street
    (D) Main Road

188. What does Mr. Ortega express shock about?
    (A) The long length of an installation process
    (B) The unsuitability of an alternative stop
    (C) The lack of clarity on a bus stop display
    (D) The absence of information from a city

189. What is implied about the work undertaken by the city?
    (A) It cost less money than initially projected.
    (B) It was expanded to cover a larger area.
    (C) It will lead to many extra city jobs.
    (D) It might include the subway, too.

190. The word "drive" in paragraph 1, line 3, of the news report is closest in meaning to
    (A) road
    (B) event
    (C) device
    (D) effort

Questions 191-195 refer to the following menu, email, and review.

JESSY'S BAR & LOUNGE

Signature Cocktails

Scary Sunset
Rum, blood orange juice, cinnamon syrup, salt

Cool as a Cucumber
Vodka, cucumber purée, mint, cucumber tonic

Relaxing Refresher
Gin, lime juice, lavender syrup, edible flowers

Smokin' Session
Bourbon whisky, brown sugar syrup, smoked honey

*All the above cocktails are priced at £12.
Jessy is proud to only use ingredients from within a 30-mile radius of the bar.
For food pairings with our cocktails, please ask your waiter.*

From:	gavin.southgate@southgate-and-son.co.uk
To:	jessy@jessysbarandlounge.co.uk
Subject:	Supply Issue

Dear Jessy,

I hope you are well. I need to inform you that, due to a bottling machine breakdown at Lixora Solutions, we will be unable to include lavender syrup in this week's regular Thursday delivery to your bar. We will, however, include some elderflower syrup in the delivery. My recommendation would be to use this as a substitute in your drinks to add a similar floral taste. I am pleased to say that we are expecting replenishment of the out-of-stock syrup next Tuesday. I would therefore like to offer you a special delivery of the item next Wednesday to apologize for the hassle.

Warm regards,

Gavin Southgate
Southgate & Son Suppliers

Jessy's Bar & Lounge
Customer Reviews
★★★★

At first, I struggled to find this bar. It's located down an unassuming side street, and its sign isn't exactly obvious. However, I'm glad I persevered and went inside because I had a great night. There was a superb live pianist playing jazz classics, which was the undoubted highlight. The drinks were delicious, too, albeit expensive. I had a couple of beers and then opted for one of Jessy's signature cocktails. Apparently, one of its ingredients was different from normal. Jessy said she'd be reverting to the original recipe the day after my visit, but my advice would be to keep the modified version! My only complaint was that the bar was a little quiet. Next time, I'll visit on a Friday so there's a bit more of an atmosphere.

—Maya Whiting

191. What is indicated about Jessy's Bar & Lounge?
(A) Its signature drinks all have different prices.
(B) Its cocktail ingredients are locally sourced.
(C) It does not provide food for its customers.
(D) It closes every night before midnight.

192. Which cocktail was impacted by the supply issue?
(A) Scary Sunset
(B) Cool as a Cucumber
(C) Relaxing Refresher
(D) Smokin' Session

193. What does Mr. Southgate suggest that Jessy do?
(A) Seek a substitute supplier
(B) Use an alternative ingredient
(C) Remove a drink temporarily
(D) Reduce the price on a cocktail

194. What does Ms. Whiting praise about Jessy's Bar & Lounge?
(A) The location
(B) The waiters
(C) The music
(D) The décor

195. When did Ms. Whiting visit Jessy's Bar & Lounge?
(A) On Tuesday
(B) On Wednesday
(C) On Thursday
(D) On Friday

GO ON TO THE NEXT PAGE

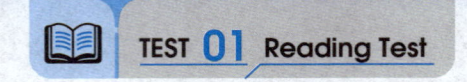

Questions 196-200 refer to the following report, website, and form.

Tourism Report: Isla Compasión

Isla Compasión experienced significant growth in tourism this year. This has been predominantly ascribed to improvements in the island's transportation infrastructure and a boom in dive tourism. Most visitors stayed on the island for one week, with peak arrivals in July and August. It is clear that many tourists enjoy coming back to the island year after year. Visitor data for the island's main towns is as follows:

Town	No. of Visitors	% Increase on Last Year
Punta Zuri	113,300	44
Marina Clara	66,600	20
Pueblo Estrella	207,450	68
Es Mirador	188,950	95

---

www.dereksdivecenter.com/dives

DÉRÉK'S DIVE CENTER

Dérék's Dive Center is located in one of Isla Compasión's major tourist-friendly towns, which has seen visitor numbers increase by almost 100% this year compared with last year. We therefore advise you to pre-book your dives as early as possible. Choose from these underwater adventures, depending on your skill level:

Level	Dive
Beginner	The Turtles Dive allows you to see these beautiful creatures in shallow water. It's ideal for first-timers.
Intermediate	The Coral Dive lets you explore the island's underwater caves. It requires some previous diving experience.

Advanced	The Twilight Dive allows you to experience the ocean as night sets in. You must have at least 20 dives under your belt to take part in this dive.
Professional	The Shipwreck Dive lets you visit a famous wreck in the ocean. It's our most challenging dive and requires 50+ previous dives.

Whichever dive you choose, you will be accompanied by our expert instructors. We are particularly proud to have been awarded five stars by the Isla Compasión Dive Safety Board, which signifies that we have never been involved in an incident that compromises the well-being of our customers.

DÉRÉK'S DIVE CENTER—CUSTOMER FEEDBACK FORM	
Name	Chul Park
Which dive did you take part in?	☐ Turtles ☑ Coral ☐ Twilight ☐ Shipwreck
Please rate the following (1 = poor, 5 = excellent):	
Dive site experience	4
Equipment quality	5
Safety and briefing	5
Friendliness of staff	4
What did you enjoy most?	I liked the small size of the dive group. It made the whole experience feel more personal and less stressful.
Was there anything we could improve?	The dive center restrooms are cramped and outdated. This is in stark contrast to the modern, spacious environment in the rest of the center.
Would you recommend us to others?	☑ Yes ☐ No

TEST 01 Reading Test

196. What is suggested about Isla Compasión?
(A) It has a poor road network.
(B) It is located in the Caribbean.
(C) It gets many repeat visitors.
(D) It is less popular in August.

197. Where is Dérék's Dive Center most likely located?
(A) Punta Zuri
(B) Marina Clara
(C) Pueblo Estrella
(D) Es Mirador

198. According to the website, what is Dérék's Dive Center especially pleased about?
(A) Its personalized service
(B) Its stunning location
(C) Its novel experiences
(D) Its safety record

199. What is Mr. Park's diving skill level?
(A) Beginner
(B) Intermediate
(C) Advanced
(D) Professional

200. What would Mr. Park like Dérék's Dive Center to do?
(A) Modernize its pre-booking system
(B) Offer a greater variety of dives
(C) Upgrade its bathroom facilities
(D) Include more rest periods in dives

Stop! This is the end of the test. If you finish before time is called, you may go back to Parts 5, 6, and 7 and check your work.

NEW TOEIC 模擬測驗
TEST 02

Part 1	**Photographs**	照片描述
Part 2	**Question-Response**	應答問題
Part 3	**Conversations**	簡短對話
Part 4	**Talks**	簡短獨白
Part 5	**Incomplete Sentences**	句子填空
Part 6	**Text Completion**	段落填空
Part 7	**Single Passages**	單篇閱讀
	Multiple Passages	多篇閱讀

TEST 02 Listening Test

本回完整音檔 015
本回分段音檔 455-581

LISTENING TEST

In the Listening test, you will be asked to demonstrate how well you understand spoken English. The entire Listening test will last approximately 45 minutes. There are four parts, and directions are given for each part. You must mark your answers on the separate answer sheet. Do not write your answers in your test book.

Part 1 🔊 455-461

Directions: For each question in this part, you will hear four statements about a picture in your test book. When you hear the statements, you must select the one statement that best describes what you see in the picture. Then find the number of the question on your answer sheet and mark your answer. The statements will not be printed in your test book and will be spoken only one time.

Statement (D), "A man is pointing to his computer screen," is the best description of the picture, so you should select answer (D) and mark it on your answer sheet.

1.

2.

GO ON TO THE NEXT PAGE 211

TEST 02 Listening Test

3.

4.

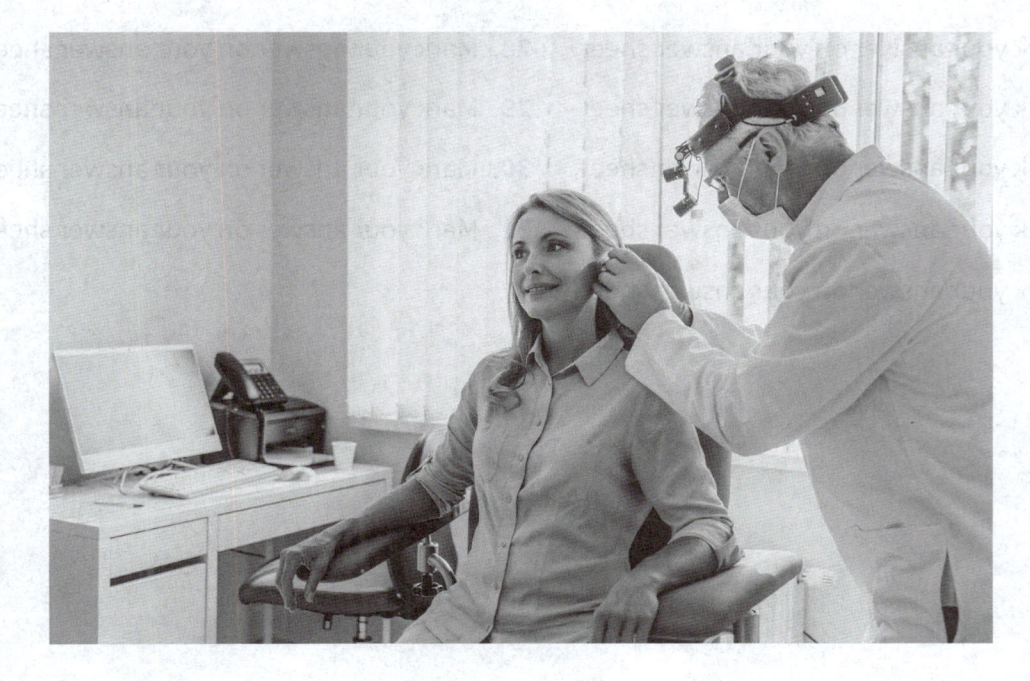

5.

6.

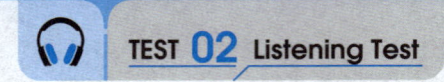

TEST 02 Listening Test

Part 2 462-487

Directions: You will hear a question or statement and three responses spoken in English. They will not be printed in your test book and will be spoken only one time. Select the best response to the question or statement and mark the letter (A), (B), or (C) on your answer sheet.

7. Mark your answer on your answer sheet.
8. Mark your answer on your answer sheet.
9. Mark your answer on your answer sheet.
10. Mark your answer on your answer sheet.
11. Mark your answer on your answer sheet.
12. Mark your answer on your answer sheet.
13. Mark your answer on your answer sheet.
14. Mark your answer on your answer sheet.
15. Mark your answer on your answer sheet.
16. Mark your answer on your answer sheet.
17. Mark your answer on your answer sheet.
18. Mark your answer on your answer sheet.
19. Mark your answer on your answer sheet.
20. Mark your answer on your answer sheet.
21. Mark your answer on your answer sheet.
22. Mark your answer on your answer sheet.
23. Mark your answer on your answer sheet.
24. Mark your answer on your answer sheet.
25. Mark your answer on your answer sheet.
26. Mark your answer on your answer sheet.
27. Mark your answer on your answer sheet.
28. Mark your answer on your answer sheet.
29. Mark your answer on your answer sheet.
30. Mark your answer on your answer sheet.
31. Mark your answer on your answer sheet.

Part 3 🔊 488-540

Directions: You will hear some conversations between two or more people. You will be asked to answer three questions about what the speakers say in each conversation. Select the best response to each question and mark the letter (A), (B), (C), or (D) on your answer sheet. The conversations will not be printed in your test book and will be spoken only one time.

32. What is unique about the deodorant?
    (A) It is entirely natural.
    (B) It is for men and women.
    (C) It is extra-long-lasting.
    (D) It is activated by body heat.

33. How does the woman obtain the deodorant?
    (A) She buys it online.
    (B) She makes it herself.
    (C) She imports it from abroad.
    (D) She gets it from a local supplier.

34. What concerns the woman?
    (A) Dealing with business paperwork
    (B) Creating original marketing ideas
    (C) Training the new staff in her company
    (D) Making sufficient quantities of a product

35. What are the man's plans for the weekend?
    (A) He is giving a guided tour.
    (B) He is starting a long vacation.
    (C) He is booking a spa break.
    (D) He is visiting another city.

36. What cost saving does the man mention?
    (A) Transportation
    (B) Accommodations
    (C) Insurance
    (D) Visas

37. What does the man want to do the most?
    (A) Learn about the past
    (B) Try some typical food
    (C) Ride along waterways
    (D) See a historic palace

GO ON TO THE NEXT PAGE → 215

TEST 02 Listening Test

38. What is the man training to be?
    (A) A weatherman
    (B) A bus driver
    (C) An airline pilot
    (D) A travel agent

39. Why does the man think the training is useful?
    (A) It leads to more promotions.
    (B) It saves money in the long run.
    (C) It helps prepare for emergencies.
    (D) It takes less time than other courses.

40. What does the woman hope the man will do?
    (A) Fly a plane she is on
    (B) Get full credit on a test
    (C) Avoid a serious incident
    (D) Receive a raise in pay

41. Why is the company relocating?
    (A) It requires a larger building.
    (B) It needs to save money on rent.
    (C) It is downsizing its workforce.
    (D) It wants to be more accessible.

42. Where will the new office be?
    (A) In a park in the suburbs
    (B) In a central shopping area
    (C) In an old industrial zone
    (D) In a waterfront district

43. What does the man ask the woman to do?
    (A) Create a timeline for the move
    (B) Brief the workers on the details
    (C) Hire a specialist moving company
    (D) Make a list of the impacted staff

44. Who most likely is the woman?
    (A) A restaurant hostess
    (B) A bank manager
    (C) A hotel receptionist
    (D) An office secretary

45. What does the man wish to do?
    (A) Cancel his reservation
    (B) Shorten his stay
    (C) Upgrade his room
    (D) Extend his trip

46. What does the woman inform the man of?
    (A) He will receive a call.
    (B) He must pay a penalty.
    (C) He will need to rebook.
    (D) He must reply to an email.

47. What are the speakers mainly discussing?
    (A) The advantages of a company
    (B) The difficulty of finding work
    (C) The vacancies in a department
    (D) The status of a job application

48. According to the man, what is the company now doing?
    (A) Narrowing down the candidates list
    (B) Finalizing the job requirements
    (C) Adjusting the wording of a job ad
    (D) Discussing the potential salary

49. What does the man advise the woman to do?
    (A) Make a list of her qualifications
    (B) Prepare for tough questions
    (C) Research the company
    (D) Check her emails

50. Why is the man calling?
    (A) To rent a vehicle
    (B) To query a bill
    (C) To cancel a transaction
    (D) To admit an error

51. What mistake did the company make?
    (A) It mislaid a driver's license.
    (B) It charged for the wrong car.
    (C) It debited an account twice.
    (D) It billed the wrong person.

52. What will the man receive tomorrow?
    (A) A note from the manager
    (B) An amended receipt
    (C) A money-off coupon
    (D) A better vehicle

53. What does the man indicate about the presentation?
    (A) It will be difficult to deliver.
    (B) It contains confidential data.
    (C) It will be done by Friday.
    (D) It is essentially complete.

54. What does the woman imply when she says, "Mr. Ford's attention can easily wander"?
    (A) Mr. Ford is suffering from a medical issue.
    (B) Mr. Ford will be unable to attend the meeting.
    (C) The presentation should be postponed.
    (D) The presentation should be concise.

55. What will the man most likely do tomorrow morning?
    (A) Rewrite a proposal
    (B) Rearrange a consultation
    (C) Practice a presentation
    (D) Add visuals to slides

56. What is the woman's problem?
    (A) She is unable to send files.
    (B) She can't download an app.
    (C) She is not receiving messages.
    (D) She can't access the internet.

57. What does the woman say that she tried doing?
    (A) Checking a manual
    (B) Restarting a laptop
    (C) Updating an app
    (D) Asking a supervisor

58. Why does the man say, "I've got a meeting with my manager in five"?
    (A) To provide a reason for a delay
    (B) To indicate a potential solution
    (C) To reschedule a training session
    (D) To invite his colleague to attend

59. What is the meeting about?
    (A) Demonstrating a product
    (B) Renewing an agreement
    (C) Handling a complaint
    (D) Reviewing a timeline

60. What problem does Aimee mention?
    (A) Roadwork on the nearby highway
    (B) Tech issues in the boardroom
    (C) Construction work in the parking lot
    (D) Renovation work in the meeting room

61. Where do the speakers decide to meet?
    (A) A fancy restaurant
    (B) A conference center
    (C) A new coffee shop
    (D) A hotel meeting room

TEST 02

GO ON TO THE NEXT PAGE   217

TEST 02 Listening Test

Appleby's Restaurant—Salads	
Club Salad	Lettuce, tomatoes, chicken, eggs...
Italian Salad	Lettuce, mozzarella cheese, olives...
Sautéed Salad	Kale, sautéed shrimp, halloumi cheese...
Appleby's Salad	Lettuce, carrots, red onions, nuts...

62. Why is the woman concerned?
    (A) She has little money.
    (B) She has some allergies.
    (C) She is not very hungry.
    (D) She is in a hurry.

63. Look at the graphic. Which salad will the woman most likely order?
    (A) Club Salad
    (B) Italian Salad
    (C) Sautéed Salad
    (D) Appleby's Salad

64. What does the man say about the dressing?
    (A) It is unavailable today.
    (B) It contains complex ingredients.
    (C) It is served on the side.
    (D) It costs additional money.

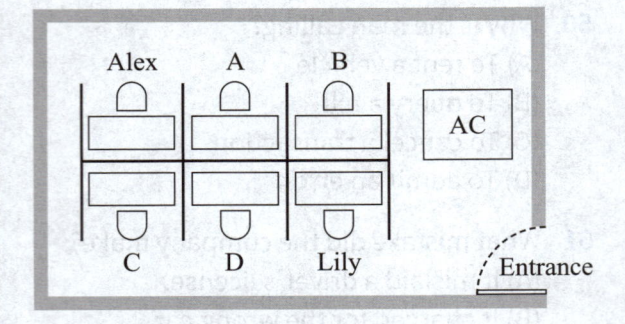

65. Who most likely is the woman?
    (A) An environmental inspector
    (B) A human resources manager
    (C) A temporary worker
    (D) A junior intern

66. Look at the graphic. Where is the man's desk located?
    (A) Point A
    (B) Point B
    (C) Point C
    (D) Point D

67. What does the man inquire about?
    (A) A room where he can have meetings
    (B) A zone where he can take a break
    (C) An area where he can socialize
    (D) A place where he can focus in peace

Customer Survey Results

- Arctic White 16%
- Titanium Silver 33%
- Forest Green 27%
- Midnight Blue 24%

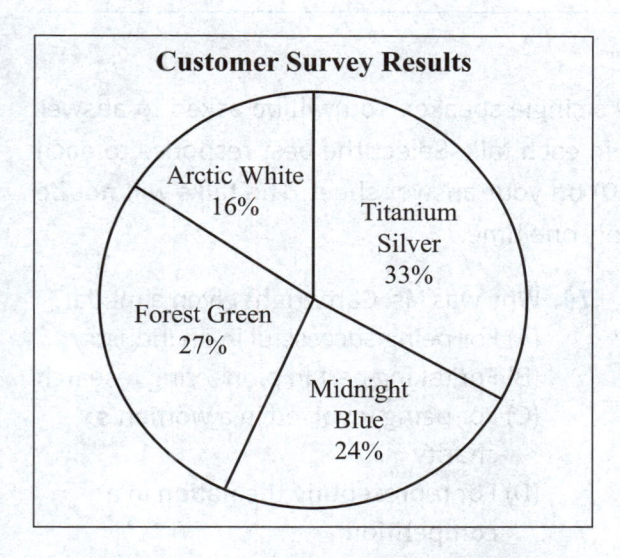

68. What product are the speakers discussing?
    (A) Laptop bags
    (B) Phone cases
    (C) Water bottles
    (D) Training shoes

69. Look at the graphic. Which color will the company most likely stop producing?
    (A) Titanium Silver
    (B) Midnight Blue
    (C) Forest Green
    (D) Arctic White

70. What does the woman propose doing?
    (A) Interviewing a wider range of customers
    (B) Checking product samples more carefully
    (C) Seeking an alternative color pigment
    (D) Manufacturing more of the other colors

GO ON TO THE NEXT PAGE

TEST 02 Listening Test

Part 4 🔊 541-581

Directions: You will hear some talks given by a single speaker. You will be asked to answer three questions about what the speaker says in each talk. Select the best response to each question and mark the letter (A), (B), (C), or (D) on your answer sheet. The talks will not be printed in your test book and will be spoken only one time.

71. Who would most likely give this talk?
    (A) A dentist
    (B) A nutritionist
    (C) A pharmacist
    (D) A fitness instructor

72. What does the speaker mention about inflammation?
    (A) It can be reduced by exercise.
    (B) It is strongly linked to our diets.
    (C) It can lead to heart disease.
    (D) It is worsened by smoking.

73. What does the speaker encourage listeners to do?
    (A) Get frequent check-ups
    (B) Try some new equipment
    (C) Research a topic online
    (D) Subscribe to a mailing list

74. Why was Ms. Cartwright given a medal?
    (A) For being successful in an industry
    (B) For taking part in pioneering research
    (C) For being involved in a women's charity
    (D) For representing the nation in a competition

75. What does the speaker imply when he says, "who accepted the award on her behalf"?
    (A) Ms. Cartwright fell ill during the event.
    (B) The ceremony had been postponed once before.
    (C) Ms. Cartwright didn't receive the award in person.
    (D) The ceremony was held entirely online.

76. What will Ms. Cartwright do in New Jersey tonight?
    (A) Sign copies of a new record
    (B) Perform with another singer
    (C) Give a speech about her career
    (D) Auction a medal to raise money

77. Where would you most likely hear this announcement?
    (A) In a railroad station
    (B) In a ferry terminal
    (C) In a bus station
    (D) In an airport

78. According to the speaker, what has recently happened?
    (A) Some travelers have been injured.
    (B) Some workers have found illegal items.
    (C) Some countries have changed rules.
    (D) Some passengers have received fines.

79. Why would the listeners most likely check a leaflet?
    (A) To look at a map of the facility
    (B) To discover the latest travel advisories
    (C) To consult a list of banned items
    (D) To learn about evacuation procedures

80. What has the company been doing for the past decade?
    (A) Researching green technologies
    (B) Making a lot of electric cars
    (C) Investing in infrastructure
    (D) Creating a new type of fuel

81. What does the speaker mean when she says, "That is the reality"?
    (A) The business must stick by its original decision.
    (B) The electric vehicles are the best on the market.
    (C) The regulations have forced the company to act.
    (D) The company has encountered several challenges.

82. What will the speaker most likely do next?
    (A) Test drive a car
    (B) Display a blueprint
    (C) Present findings
    (D) Take questions

83. What does the speaker say about ride-hailing apps?
    (A) Only one is accessible in the region.
    (B) They are being increasingly regulated.
    (C) Some are more reliable than others.
    (D) Many different ones are available.

84. What is unique about the app being advertised?
    (A) It allows real-time ride sharing.
    (B) It detects users' preferred languages.
    (C) It offers drivers based on their character.
    (D) It guarantees the lowest price at all times.

85. What is provided to first-time users?
    (A) A promotion code
    (B) A discount for referrals
    (C) A day of unlimited rides
    (D) Access to a premium service

86. How should customers input their license plate?
    (A) By giving it to a security guard
    (B) By entering it into a machine
    (C) By providing it via an app
    (D) By filling it out on a form

87. Why does the speaker say, "please bear with us"?
    (A) To highlight that a system is very new
    (B) To express regret for a slow-moving line
    (C) To indicate they are trying to fix a problem
    (D) To apologize for the staff's lack of expertise

88. What does the speaker mention about the payment procedure?
    (A) It also has a technical issue.
    (B) It can be followed as normal.
    (C) It has been suspended for today.
    (D) It will be updated in the future.

GO ON TO THE NEXT PAGE → 221

TEST 02 Listening Test

89. Why should workers hold fewer meetings?
(A) Because they cost a lot of money
(B) Because they occupy too much time
(C) Because there is a shortage of rooms
(D) Because there are many employees offsite

90. What should the listeners do before scheduling a meeting?
(A) Modify the list of attendees
(B) Consider whether it is necessary
(C) Get permission from a manager
(D) Check the room booking system

91. What does the speaker suggest doing instead of holding a meeting?
(A) Making a phone call
(B) Distributing a newsletter
(C) Sending out an email
(D) Using a shared document

92. Who is most likely making this announcement?
(A) A trained electrician
(B) An organic farmer
(C) A chilled food salesman
(D) A supermarket manager

93. Why are smart refrigerators being installed?
(A) To comply with a rule
(B) To lower energy costs
(C) To ensure food quality
(D) To tackle shoplifting

94. What does the speaker ask the listeners to do?
(A) Contribute their views about the decision
(B) Be patient during the installation process
(C) Check the use-by dates on chilled products
(D) Return any damaged goods for a refund

Inventory Check—Low Stock Report		
Section	Product	Units
A	Graphic T-shirts	20
B	Denim Jeans	3
C	Puffer Vests	18
D	Leather Belts	5

95. What did the speaker do the previous night?
(A) Attended a meeting
(B) Treated his staff
(C) Went to a sale
(D) Counted stock

96. Look at the graphic. According to the speaker, which section requires urgent action?
(A) Section A
(B) Section B
(C) Section C
(D) Section D

97. What does the speaker ask Marian to do after the meeting?
(A) Welcome customers to the store
(B) Speak to another division
(C) Label products with discounts
(D) Set up a promotional display

Weekly Smartphone Usage (%)

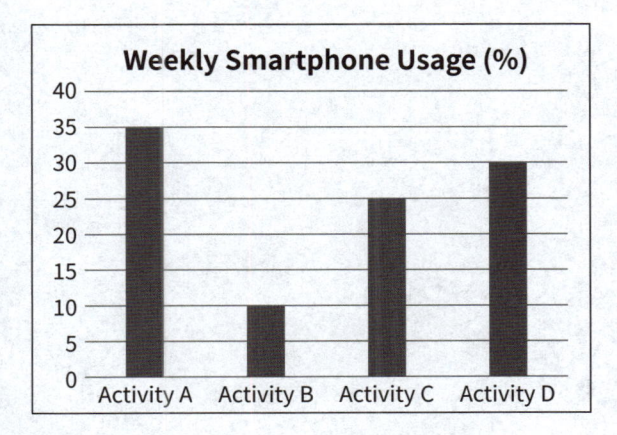

(Bar chart: Activity A = 35, Activity B = 10, Activity C = 25, Activity D = 30)

98. According to the speaker, what was the listener's concern?
    (A) His fingers were aching.
    (B) His screen was broken.
    (C) His eyes were painful.
    (D) His phone was old.

99. Look at the graphic. Which bar represents video games?
    (A) Bar A
    (B) Bar B
    (C) Bar C
    (D) Bar D

100. What does the speaker recommend doing?
    (A) Switching to a new smartphone
    (B) Going to bed at an earlier time
    (C) Reducing phone usage at night
    (D) Reading fewer news articles

This is the end of the Listening test. Turn to Part 5 in your test book.

GO ON TO THE NEXT PAGE → 223

NO TEST MATERIAL ON THIS PAGE

TEST 02 Reading Test

READING TEST

In the Reading test, you will read a variety of texts and answer several different types of reading comprehension questions. The entire Reading test will last 75 minutes. There are three parts, and directions are given for each part. You are encouraged to answer as many questions as possible within the time allowed.

You must mark your answers on the separate answer sheet. Do not write your answers in your test book.

Part 5

Directions: A word or phrase is missing in each of the sentences below. Four answer choices are given below each sentence. Select the best answer to complete the sentence. Then mark the letter (A), (B), (C), or (D) on your answer sheet.

101. Mr. Dlamini prefers this applicant for the position because she is a forensic science ------- from the top university in the country.
    (A) graduated
    (B) graduation
    (C) graduate
    (D) gradual

102. Given the amount of money riding on the contract, Ms. Giannopoulos ------- that she have final approval.
    (A) assisted
    (B) persisted
    (C) resisted
    (D) insisted

103. During the meeting, most people spoke in support of the client acquisition plan, but the finance director spoke out ------- it.
    (A) without
    (B) against
    (C) under
    (D) along

104. The lights in the office are hurting the call center operators' eyes because they are ------- brighter than necessary.
    (A) more
    (B) so
    (C) some
    (D) far

105. The suitable age range for the puzzle must be amended because the rules are too ------- for young children.
    (A) complexity
    (B) complicated
    (C) complicate
    (D) complication

106. Before you fill out the passport renewal form, please ensure that you have ------- a photo taken recently.
    (A) had
    (B) have
    (C) has
    (D) to have

GO ON TO THE NEXT PAGE → 225

TEST 02 Reading Test

107. With a background in infectious diseases, Dr. Murphy is the ideal candidate to lead the international health -------.
(A) organize
(B) organization
(C) organizational
(D) organizationally

108. Due to its sensitive content, the paperwork needs to ------- in a secure location.
(A) store
(B) stored
(C) be stored
(D) storing

109. Rather than asking an assistant to write the report, Ms. Kaur decided to do it -------.
(A) she
(B) her
(C) hers
(D) herself

110. Most of the younger employees supported the idea of moving to a fully remote work model, ------- the older workers were less enthusiastic.
(A) whereas
(B) in addition
(C) now that
(D) meanwhile

111. The new drone comes with a high-definition camera, so it is clearly ------- to the previous model.
(A) better
(B) worse
(C) superior
(D) inferior

112. All managers and assistant managers in the company are expected to ------- the leadership training course.
(A) suffer from
(B) give up
(C) take part in
(D) take over

113. Mr. Miyagi will travel to the Boston International Trade Fair ------- Seattle, a major city in the Pacific Northwest.
(A) via
(B) into
(C) minus
(D) till

114. The marketing manager instructed his team to stop ------- outdated methods of customer acquisition, such as advertising in newspapers.
(A) to use
(B) using
(C) used
(D) use

115. Ms. Cameron considers the situation with the client to be urgent and wishes her manager ------- more responsive to her emails asking for support.
    (A) be
    (B) is
    (C) being
    (D) were

116. Our new website features bold colors, strong visuals, and exciting animations, ------- reflecting the company's energy.
    (A) initially
    (B) unfortunately
    (C) vibrantly
    (D) rapidly

117. Ms. Jacobson compiled a shortlist of insurance brokers and forwarded it to ------- had the authority to make the final selection.
    (A) whichever
    (B) however
    (C) whatever
    (D) whoever

118. The opening of the fishing charter business will ------- more people to connect with the region's maritime history.
    (A) able
    (B) enable
    (C) disable
    (D) capable

119. Ms. Mbatha was called to a meeting with the logistics coordinator, but she had no idea what it was -------.
    (A) above
    (B) regarding
    (C) though
    (D) otherwise

120. Mr. Sutherland neglected to set his alarm, so he ------- when his boss called.
    (A) still sleeps
    (B) is still sleeping
    (C) still slept
    (D) was still sleeping

121. The document attached to the email is only relevant to senior managers, so everyone else can ------- it.
    (A) ignore
    (B) ignorance
    (C) ignorant
    (D) ignorantly

122. A fire broke out at the warehouse ------- the goods were stored, but thankfully, none of the items were damaged.
    (A) who
    (B) whom
    (C) in which
    (D) whenever

GO ON TO THE NEXT PAGE   227

123. Mr. Mason does not tolerate people questioning his decisions; he expects absolute ------- from his employees.
(A) welfare
(B) obedience
(C) popularity
(D) limitation

124. According to the property appraiser, if the house ------- earlier, it could have commanded a much higher price.
(A) is sold
(B) were sold
(C) has been sold
(D) had been sold

125. The Board of Directors appointed Mr. Greenberg, ------- background is in regulatory compliance, to head the Financial Oversight Commission.
(A) which
(B) that
(C) who
(D) whose

126. Ms. Lai has worked for the educational company for forty years because she truly ------- its mission.
(A) copes with
(B) believes in
(C) let alone
(D) other than

127. During the annual maintenance review, Mr. Silva discovered the photocopiers ------- on the second floor were in desperate need of replacement.
(A) locate
(B) located
(C) locating
(D) are located

128. At the end of the appointment, Dr. Riviera advised that the patient ------- more fiber to aid digestion.
(A) consume
(B) consumes
(C) consumed
(D) consuming

129. Employees working on the large corporate campus who fall ill can visit the on-site -------.
(A) jewelry
(B) pottery
(C) infirmary
(D) gallery

130. ------- little prior experience in public relations, Ms. Chang consulted a senior colleague on the matter.
(A) Have
(B) Had
(C) Having
(D) To have

Part 6

Directions: Read the texts that follow. A word, phrase, or sentence is missing in parts of each text. Four answer choices for each question are given below the text. Select the best answer to complete the text. Then mark the letter (A), (B), (C), or (D) on your answer sheet.

Questions 131-134 refer to the following excerpt from a brochure.

There are many reasons to visit Portugal, -------- the mouthwatering food and the
131.
fascinating culture. This tour gives you three more, as you step back in time to stay in three stunning *pousadas*. --------. They allow you to experience the thrill of the past
132.
while enjoying the conveniences of the present. The accommodations for this tour are a monastery, a palace, and a fortress. So, whether you want to live like a monk, a king, or a --------, we've got you covered. What's more, each of the hotels is situated
133.
near one of Portugal's major -------- areas, providing you with the opportunity to
134.
sample city life. Book today to secure your place.

131. (A) as if
 (B) ever since
 (C) such as
 (D) in advance

132. (A) The complete itinerary for the trip can be found in the travel packet you received.
 (B) Single, double, twin, and family rooms are available at this particular location.
 (C) These are historic buildings that have been carefully converted into luxury hotels.
 (D) Portugal's monarchy ended over a century ago, and the country is now a republic.

133. (A) soldier
 (B) athlete
 (C) cruiser
 (D) physician

134. (A) dreadful
 (B) rigid
 (C) wild
 (D) urban

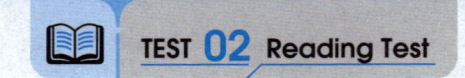

TEST 02 Reading Test

Questions 135-138 refer to the following invitation.

Dear Residents,

You are invited to a town hall meeting on Sunday, June 8, at 6:00 p.m. to discuss a crucial issue impacting our community: social media bans. This meeting provides a platform for open discussion ------- many aspects of the bans. These ------- reducing cyberbullying to safeguarding the younger generation to protecting free speech. -------. This is your opportunity to question them, so we encourage you to come prepared. To make it easier for everyone to attend, free ------- will be provided from several subway stations to the town hall. Further details and timings of this service can be found on the reverse of this invitation. We hope to see you there.

John Finch
Mayor of Rivertown

135. (A) by
 (B) on
 (C) at
 (D) to

136. (A) look up
 (B) pencil in
 (C) pick up
 (D) range from

137. (A) We will be joined by representatives from the tech industry.
 (B) However, many people agree that restrictions are necessary.
 (C) Refreshments will be provided courtesy of a local bakery.
 (D) Unfortunately, national policymakers are unable to attend.

138. (A) tuition
 (B) subscription
 (C) transportation
 (D) registration

Questions 139-142 refer to the following letter.

NRSM National Bank
123 Main Street
Washington, D.C.

Dear Sir or Madam,

I am writing to express my frustration with your extremely slow ATMs. Over the past few months, I have noticed them becoming progressively slower. -------. ------- I
 139.   140.
completed this on my most recent visit to one of your branches, a line of ten people had already formed behind me. This can be especially ------- during peak hours.
 141.
I hope you will urgently look into this matter and service or replace your machines. Otherwise, I will be forced to take my money and business -------. I look forward to
 142.
your response.

Yours sincerely,

Kelvin Maxwell

139. (A) I read in the press that cases of bank fraud have increased recently.
(B) The failure of the contactless payment system is quite embarrassing.
(C) Closing local branches is particularly unfair to your elderly customers.
(D) Basic transactions such as withdrawing cash can take several minutes.

140. (A) These days
(B) Over time
(C) By the time
(D) Over the years

141. (A) pleasant
(B) hospitable
(C) annoying
(D) efficient

142. (A) accordingly
(B) elsewhere
(C) afterwards
(D) furthermore

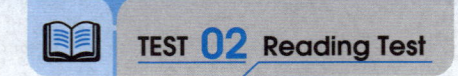

TEST 02 Reading Test

Questions 143-146 refer to the following press release.

For Immediate Release:
Alstonville Racecourse to Open Next Month

Alstonville Racecourse will open its gates to the public next month, further boosting the sporting opportunities ------- in New South Wales. The racecourse will boast a
143.
first-rate flat track, grandstand ------- with unrivalled views, and amenities to suit a
144.
variety of budgets. -------. There will also be live music from the band Tame Koala
145.
after that day's racing has concluded. Racecourse Director Kyle Donovan said that he hopes to offer "an unforgettable experience to racing fans both new and old."

The facility is expected to ------- the best horses, jockeys, owners, and trainers from
146.
around the country.

---

143. (A) at first
 (B) on offer
 (C) at length
 (D) by no means

144. (A) sit
 (B) sitting
 (C) seated
 (D) seating

145. (A) We are currently advertising for part-time hospitality staff.
 (B) The inaugural race will set off at 2:00 p.m. on Saturday, May 17.
 (C) A full circuit of the flat track covers around two thousand meters.
 (D) General racecourse admission prices will start from $10.

146. (A) concede
 (B) attach
 (C) draw
 (D) undergo

Part 7

Directions: In this part you will read a selection of texts, such as magazine and newspaper articles, emails, and instant messages. Each text or set of texts is followed by several questions. Select the best answer for each question and mark the letter (A), (B), (C), or (D) on your answer sheet.

Questions 147-148 refer to the following memo.

Memo

From: Shirley Marsden—Project Manager
To: Project Team
Subject: Project Kick-Off Meeting

Please be advised that the kick-off meeting for Project Agile, originally scheduled for December 12, has been postponed. This is due to the fact that Agile will now be integrated with Project Beacon, and the joint project will commence at a later date. A revised calendar invite will be sent in due course. In the meantime, please retain any paperwork related to Agile; hopefully, this can still be used going forward.

---

147. Why has the kick-off meeting been postponed?
(A) The project has been canceled by the manager.
(B) One of the key stakeholders is unable to attend.
(C) The project will be combined with another one.
(D) A piece of equipment will not be ready in time.

148. What does Ms. Marsden ask the team to do?
(A) Attend a briefing next week
(B) Keep hold of their documents
(C) Brainstorm ideas for an initiative
(D) Mark a new date on their calendars

Questions 149-150 refer to the following email.

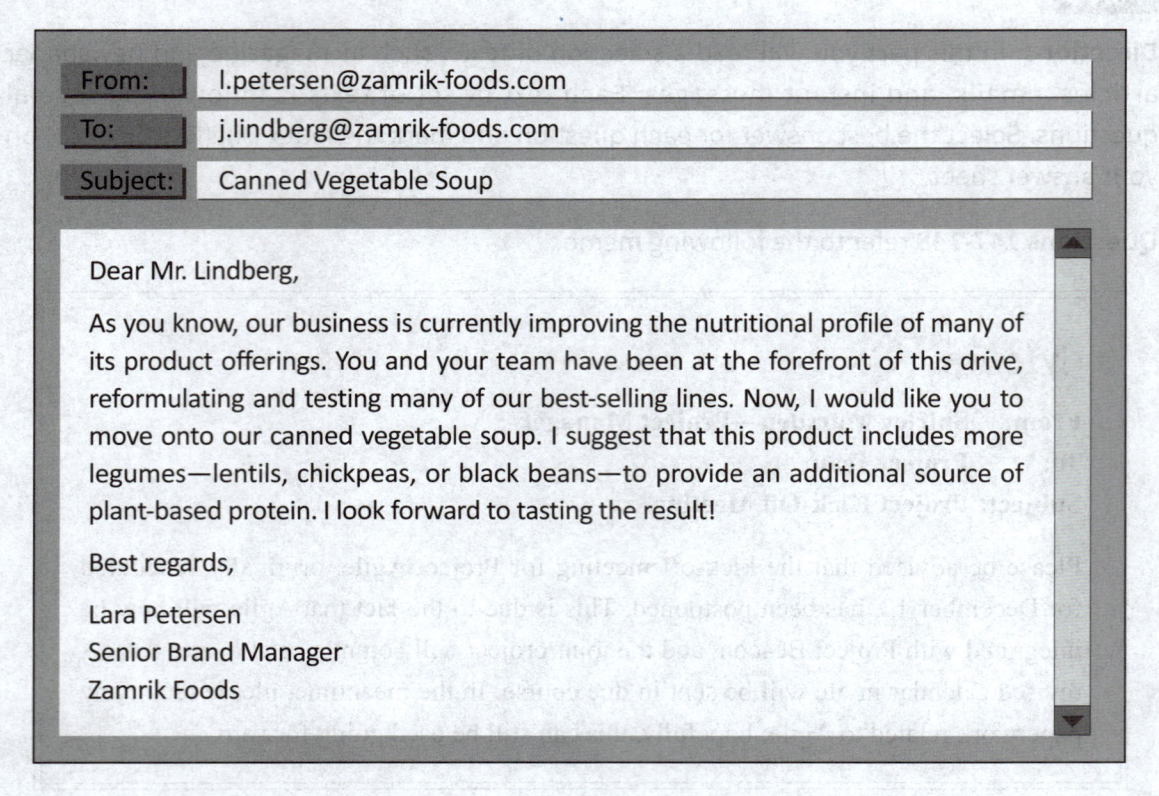

From: l.petersen@zamrik-foods.com
To: j.lindberg@zamrik-foods.com
Subject: Canned Vegetable Soup

Dear Mr. Lindberg,

As you know, our business is currently improving the nutritional profile of many of its product offerings. You and your team have been at the forefront of this drive, reformulating and testing many of our best-selling lines. Now, I would like you to move onto our canned vegetable soup. I suggest that this product includes more legumes—lentils, chickpeas, or black beans—to provide an additional source of plant-based protein. I look forward to tasting the result!

Best regards,

Lara Petersen
Senior Brand Manager
Zamrik Foods

---

149. Who most likely is Mr. Lindberg?
    (A) A top-performing salesperson
    (B) A research and development manager
    (C) A customer services representative
    (D) An information technology supervisor

150. What does Ms. Petersen suggest doing to the canned soup?
    (A) Removing artificial ingredients
    (B) Increasing its shelf life
    (C) Reducing the salt content
    (D) Adding more plant foods

Questions 151-152 refer to the following text-message chain.

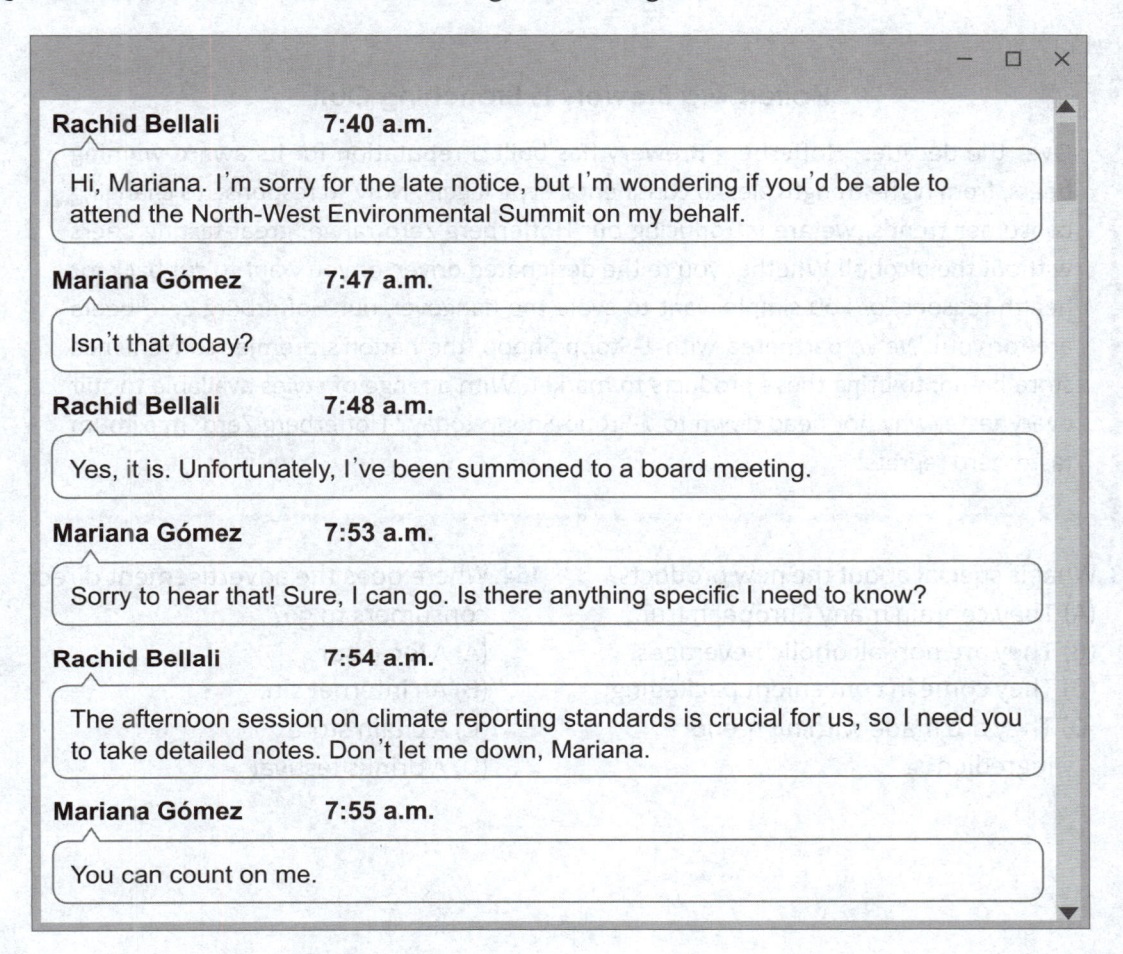

Rachid Bellali   7:40 a.m.

Hi, Mariana. I'm sorry for the late notice, but I'm wondering if you'd be able to attend the North-West Environmental Summit on my behalf.

Mariana Gómez   7:47 a.m.

Isn't that today?

Rachid Bellali   7:48 a.m.

Yes, it is. Unfortunately, I've been summoned to a board meeting.

Mariana Gómez   7:53 a.m.

Sorry to hear that! Sure, I can go. Is there anything specific I need to know?

Rachid Bellali   7:54 a.m.

The afternoon session on climate reporting standards is crucial for us, so I need you to take detailed notes. Don't let me down, Mariana.

Mariana Gómez   7:55 a.m.

You can count on me.

---

151. What does Mr. Bellali want Ms. Gómez to do?

(A) Go to an event instead of him
(B) Send a summit schedule to him
(C) Accompany him to a conference
(D) Give his apologies to the board

152. At 7:55 a.m., what does Ms. Gómez most likely mean when she writes, "You can count on me"?

(A) She will represent the company on the global stage.
(B) She will gather information on an important subject.
(C) She will deliver a speech in front of a large audience.
(D) She will ensure others follow reporting standards.

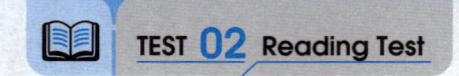

Questions 153-154 refer to the following advertisement.

Hofferberg Brewery is Branching Out!

Over the decades, Hofferberg Brewery has built a reputation for its award-winning beers, from high-strength ales to continental-style lagers. Now, in response to changing consumer trends, we are introducing our Hofferberg Zero range: great-tasting beers without the alcohol! Whether you're the designated driver, or you want to cut back for health reasons, or you simply want to avoid the hangover, our Hofferberg Zero beers are for you! We've partnered with 1-Stopp-Shopp, the nation's premier convenience store brand, to bring these products to market. With a range of styles available to suit every taste, why not head down to 1-Stopp-Shopp today? Hofferberg Zero: maximum taste; zero regrets!

153. What is special about the new products?
(A) They contain many European fruits.
(B) They are non-alcoholic beverages.
(C) They come in convenient packaging.
(D) They are made with high-end ingredients.

154. Where does the advertisement direct consumers to go?
(A) A local bar
(B) An internet site
(C) A chain store
(D) A drinks festival

Questions 155-157 refer to the following excerpt from some guidelines.

For most employees, going on vacation is the highlight of the year. What's less appealing is returning to the workplace after a relaxing week or two in a tropical location. But don't worry: we're here to help you make that transition smoothly. On that first morning back in the office, make sure your top priority is to catch up with your coworkers and tell them about your trip. This will help you to reconnect with them, and it also promotes a friendly and happy work environment. Eventually, though, you'll have to check that mountain of emails waiting for you. What you'll probably discover is that the majority of these messages have already been dealt with while you were away and are no longer relevant. So, don't feel intimidated by the size of that inbox!

155. What is the main purpose of the guidelines?
(A) To assist employees covering for their colleagues
(B) To provide instructions for working while abroad
(C) To help vacationers deal with returning to work
(D) To give advice to workers looking to change jobs

156. According to the guidelines, what should people do first when going into the office?
(A) Deal with very urgent tasks
(B) Share stories with colleagues
(C) Prioritize their heavy workload
(D) Set clear goals for the first week

157. What is suggested about work emails?
(A) It is best to filter them by subject.
(B) Many of them can likely be ignored.
(C) They should be filed in a separate inbox.
(D) All of them are equally important.

TEST 02

GO ON TO THE NEXT PAGE   237

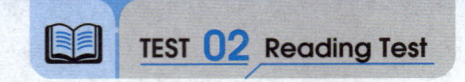

Questions 158-160 refer to the following email.

From: cardiology-appointments@nr-hospital.com
To: gilbert.gill@zmail.com
Subject: Change to Your Upcoming Appointment

Dear Mr. Gilbert,

We are writing to inform you that your consultation with Dr. Raya Rowling, originally scheduled for January 19, has been rescheduled. —[1]— This is due to the fact that Dr. Rowling will be carrying out surgery on the afternoon of the original date. —[2]— The new appointment details are as follows:

Date:	February 1
Time:	2:00 p.m.
Room:	12B, Cardiology Department (as previous)

If the new time is inconvenient, please don't hesitate to contact us at 555-1935 to arrange an alternative appointment. —[3]— If, however, the time is suitable, you do not need to do anything. Please remember to bring any medications you are currently taking to the appointment. —[4]— We look forward to seeing you soon.

Warm regards,

Pippa Reynolds
Appointments Coordinator
Cardiology Department
National Royal Hospital

---

158. Why has Mr. Gilbert's appointment been rescheduled?
(A) The patient will be unable to attend.
(B) The hospital will be refurbished.
(C) The doctor will be performing an operation.
(D) The department will be undergoing an inspection.

159. What is indicated about the new appointment?
(A) It will be held later the same month.
(B) It might be with a different doctor.
(C) It will be in the same location.
(D) It must be confirmed via email.

160. In which of the positions marked [1], [2], [3], and [4] does the following sentence best belong?

"Having these will allow Dr. Rowling and her colleagues to better assess your medical needs."

(A) [1]
(B) [2]
(C) [3]
(D) [4]

Questions 161-163 refer to the following press release.

Horizon SecureForce Achieves Major Milestone

Horizon SecureForce, a highly respected leader in information security solutions, is proud to announce that it has obtained certification from the International Organization for Standardization (ISO). The certification relates to ISO 27001, which provides a basis for handling and securing sensitive company data. This marks a major breakthrough in the company's continuing efforts to promote the importance of managing confidential data.

"This was attained following a grueling audit process and confirms our commitment to our customers' security," said Dorian Boateng, CEO of Horizon SecureForce. "It will allow us to pursue contracts with government agencies, multinational corporations, and international financial institutions, massively expanding our potential customer base."

For media queries and background on Horizon SecureForce, please contact Sasha Volkova at sasha.v@hsf.com or 555-7626.

161. What has recently happened to Horizon SecureForce?
 (A) It has entered a partnership with a former competitor.
 (B) It has released a huge new range of security products.
 (C) It has achieved record-breaking annual sales figures.
 (D) It has been officially certified by a global body.

162. According to Mr. Boateng, what can the company now do?
 (A) Relocate its headquarters overseas
 (B) Seek other clients worldwide
 (C) Offer physical security services
 (D) Stop performing internal audits

163. Why might readers contact Ms. Volkova?
 (A) To obtain further information about Horizon SecureForce
 (B) To learn about the International Organization for Standardization
 (C) To find out how to send their data to her in a secure fashion
 (D) To discover more details about an authorization process

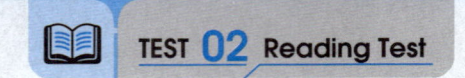

Questions 164-167 refer to the following online chat discussion.

Olivia Tremblay 11:21 a.m.
Thank you both for joining this online discussion. Theo, I believe you've got a situation that needs addressing.

Theo Bouchard 11:22 a.m.
That's right. My staff have received multiple complaints—from both stores and shoppers—over the last week about some of our garments, namely our midi sundresses and maxi skirts.

Olivia Tremblay 11:23 a.m.
What do the complaints relate to?

Theo Bouchard 11:24 a.m.
They're all about sizing discrepancies. Medium dresses labeled as small; large skirts labeled as medium—that kind of thing.

Logan Cloutier 11:26 a.m.
I think the roots of this problem go back to last month, when we were short of two members of the quality control team. Quite simply, my remaining guys had too little time to check all the garments thoroughly.

Olivia Tremblay 11:28 a.m.
I understand your frustration, Logan, but you're the QC Manager—it was your responsibility to find a solution and make sure things like this didn't happen.

Logan Cloutier 11:29 a.m.
Message received.

Olivia Tremblay 11:30 a.m.
The urgent issue now, though, is how to deal with the affected inventory. In my opinion, we need to identify the specific batches and pull them from sale immediately.

Theo Bouchard 11:31 a.m.
Agreed.

164. What industry do the people most likely work in?
(A) Cosmetics
(B) Fashion
(C) Electronics
(D) Furniture

165. What problem are the speakers discussing?
(A) Faded garment colors
(B) Poorly stitched patterns
(C) Incorrect sizes on labels
(D) Missing buttons and zippers

166. At 11:29 a.m., what does Mr. Cloutier most likely imply when he writes, "Message received"?
(A) He has resolved a technical issue.
(B) He knows he should be held accountable.
(C) He has gotten an important company email.
(D) He realizes he must attend a meeting in person.

167. What does Ms. Tremblay propose doing?
(A) Investing in some new machinery
(B) Boosting resources for quality control
(C) Adjusting a standard operating procedure
(D) Withdrawing some products from stores

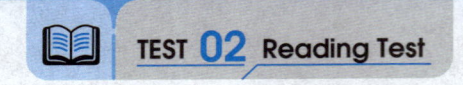

Questions 168-171 refer to the following business proposal.

Proposal for Vertical Integration with Southward Logistics

From: Vincent Hsiao—Director of Strategy
To: Executive Team

Following a thorough analysis of our supply chain and related logistical operations, I would like to propose an initiative. Specifically, this is the acquisition of Southward Logistics, our key distributor in the Australasia region. We currently depend on Southward for the bulk of our shipping and handling in that region. The fact that it also has transshipment offices in Malaysia, Singapore, and Indonesia makes it even more vital to our interests.

By bringing activities such as shipping and handling in-house, we can simplify our order management system; improve our negotiating power with distributors in other regions, such as Scott-Lewis Logistics; and slash distribution expenses by an estimated ten percent. We will also establish greater control over the quality of our service.

It is widely rumored that Southward Logistics is open to acquisition talks. We would, of course, need to commission a feasibility study into this matter, which I could set in motion prior to next quarter's strategy meeting. However, if you all approve of the proposal in principle, I can discuss the matter informally with my sources at Southward Logistics during my regular trip to their Perth branch next week.

Please let me know your thoughts.

168. What does Mr. Hsiao propose doing?
    (A) Finding an alternative supplier
    (B) Merging with a competitor
    (C) Relocating to Australia
    (D) Buying another company

169. What is implied about Southward Logistics?
    (A) Its service reaches many different countries.
    (B) Its facilities require significant modernization.
    (C) It used to be known by another name.
    (D) It employed Mr. Hsiao in the past.

170. The word "control" in paragraph 2, line 4, is closest in meaning to
    (A) calm
    (B) switch
    (C) power
    (D) dial

171. What will Mr. Hsiao do next week?
    (A) Attend a strategic meeting
    (B) Visit a major distributor
    (C) Publish a feasibility study
    (D) Sign an important contract

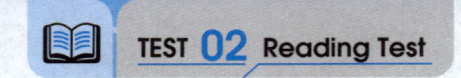

TEST 02 Reading Test

Questions 172-175 refer to the following email.

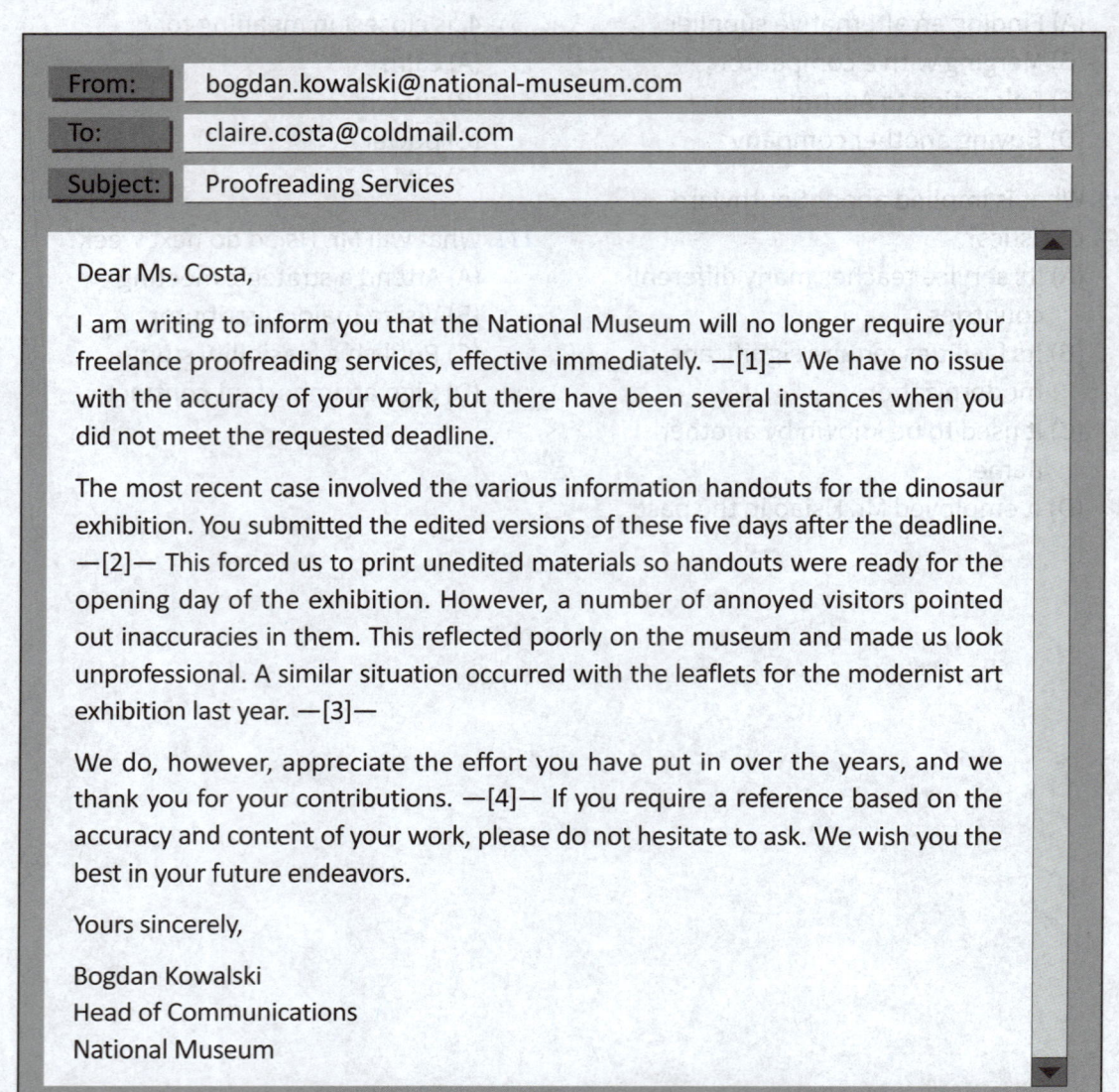

From:	bogdan.kowalski@national-museum.com
To:	claire.costa@coldmail.com
Subject:	Proofreading Services

Dear Ms. Costa,

I am writing to inform you that the National Museum will no longer require your freelance proofreading services, effective immediately. —[1]— We have no issue with the accuracy of your work, but there have been several instances when you did not meet the requested deadline.

The most recent case involved the various information handouts for the dinosaur exhibition. You submitted the edited versions of these five days after the deadline. —[2]— This forced us to print unedited materials so handouts were ready for the opening day of the exhibition. However, a number of annoyed visitors pointed out inaccuracies in them. This reflected poorly on the museum and made us look unprofessional. A similar situation occurred with the leaflets for the modernist art exhibition last year. —[3]—

We do, however, appreciate the effort you have put in over the years, and we thank you for your contributions. —[4]— If you require a reference based on the accuracy and content of your work, please do not hesitate to ask. We wish you the best in your future endeavors.

Yours sincerely,

Bogdan Kowalski
Head of Communications
National Museum

172. Why does the museum no longer require Ms. Costa's services?
    (A) They are expanding their team internally.
    (B) There are no new exhibitions planned.
    (C) She made several errors while editing.
    (D) She regularly submitted work late.

173. What is implied about the dinosaur exhibition?
    (A) It involved realistic, life-size models.
    (B) It was less popular than expected.
    (C) It received some complaints.
    (D) It is still running at present.

174. What does Mr. Kowalski offer Ms. Costa?
    (A) A severance package
    (B) A letter of recommendation
    (C) A free ticket to an exhibition
    (D) A chance to work together again

175. In which of the positions marked [1], [2], [3], and [4] does the following sentence best belong?

    "Ultimately, the materials for both exhibitions had to be reprinted at great expense."

    (A) [1]
    (B) [2]
    (C) [3]
    (D) [4]

GO ON TO THE NEXT PAGE 245

Questions 176-180 refer to the following meeting minutes and advertisement.

MEETING MINUTES

Project:	Teeny Tiny Air Purifier
Date:	Monday, May 26
Attendees:	Luis Barreto
	Dario Ventura
	Minji Kim
	Carla Jimenez

Key Points: Promotional Direction

- LB proposed hiring influencer to endorse product on their YouTube channel.
- DV countered with idea of using medical professional to emphasize health benefits.
- MK suggested using celebrity mom to show product suitable for those from all walks of life.
- CJ advocated using well-known entrepreneur to lend product an air of quality.

Other Points Raised

- LB talked about need to keep logo clean and understated—all attendees agreed.
- DV to hold meeting with marketing next week to ensure product launch on schedule.
- MK to instruct designers to come up with logo concepts right away.
- CJ to work on ad copy once dehumidifier project complete.

Meet the Teeny Tiny Air Purifier!

Sleek and compact, the Teeny Tiny Air Purifier fits in the palm of your hand but makes a big impact on the quality of your air. Whether you're in the car, the bedroom, or the office, this portable purifier will deliver powerful results. A single charge via the supplied USB-C cable will allow it to purify continuously for twelve hours. Buy it before the end of this month and get a free filter refill with every purchase! Want to find out more about how the Teeny Tiny Air Purifier is beneficial for your body? Head over to our YouTube channel, where the famous Dr. Sheila Roberts will explain all! The Teeny Tiny Air Purifier: it's teeny; it's tiny; it's too good to refuse!

176. What did the meeting attendees reach a consensus about?
    (A) That the product logo should be simple
    (B) That the YouTube videos should be short
    (C) That the air purifier should be reasonably priced
    (D) That the product launch should be delayed

177. What will most likely happen immediately after the meeting?
    (A) Some marketing assistants will meet.
    (B) The design team will be briefed.
    (C) A product manager will send an email.
    (D) More copywriters will be hired.

178. What is mentioned about the air purifier?
    (A) It is supplied with a small carrying case.
    (B) It can be used in 12 different locations.
    (C) It should be plugged in while purifying.
    (D) It can operate for half a day once charged.

179. Why would a customer most likely buy the air purifier before a deadline?
    (A) To get a limited-edition color
    (B) To obtain a special guarantee
    (C) To get 20 percent off the product
    (D) To receive an additional filter

180. Whose idea has been used to promote the product?
    (A) Mr. Barreto
    (B) Mr. Ventura
    (C) Ms. Kim
    (D) Ms. Jimenez

GO ON TO THE NEXT PAGE

Questions 181-185 refer to the following invoice and email.

Forever Furniture World

Email: customerservice@ffw.com Phone: 555-90802

Invoice No.: 7193A
Order Date: August 19
Payment Due Date: September 2
Billed To: Ines Althoff Publishing, Meridian, Idaho, 83642

Code	Description	Quantity	Unit Price	Total
FFW801	Standard Office Desk—Gray	22	$350	$7,700
FFW748	Ergonomic Office Chair—White	22	$200	$4,400
FFW438	Tall Storage Unit—Wood	10	$120	$1,200
FFW432	Mobile Filing Cabinet—Black	12	$150	$1,800

Subtotal: $15,100
Sales Tax (6%): $906
Total Due: $16,006

Free delivery on all orders exceeding $10,000

Please make payment via bank transfer to NRSM National Bank, Account Number 77222870, Routing Number 81924857, or pay online at www.ffw.com

---

From: jed.pellegrini@iap.com
To: customerservice@ffw.com
Subject: Re: Order 7193A

Hi,

I placed the above order on August 19, but I have just realized that I need to make some urgent corrections to it. My company now requires two fewer of item FFW432. In addition, we need ten more of the storage units. I apologize for the errors and for any inconvenience these may cause. I hope that the requested corrections can be made at this late stage.

I'd also like to use this opportunity to ask about the assembly of the items. I understand that they won't be delivered assembled, but please can you confirm that each box will come with instructions? I've asked the maintenance guys to be on standby on delivery day, and I want to ensure everything runs smoothly.

Thank you in advance.

Jed Pellegrini
Operations Coordinator
Ines Althoff Publishing

181. What is indicated about the order?
(A) It contains items of different colors.
(B) It necessitates an extra fee for delivery.
(C) It requires payment within one week.
(D) It involves more chairs than desks.

182. Why is a link to a website included in the invoice?
(A) To give the purchaser a way to complain
(B) To allow the customer to track the delivery
(C) To give more background about the company
(D) To provide an alternative method of payment

183. How many of the tall storage units does Mr. Pellegrini now require?
(A) Twenty-two
(B) Ten
(C) Twelve
(D) Twenty

184. The word "stage" in paragraph 1, line 5, of the email is closest in meaning to
(A) circuit
(B) phase
(C) theater
(D) sphere

185. What does Mr. Pellegrini ask for?
(A) Assistance when unloading a delivery
(B) Confirmation about assembly directions
(C) Recommendations for a maintenance contract
(D) Updates on an outstanding bank transfer

GO ON TO THE NEXT PAGE 249

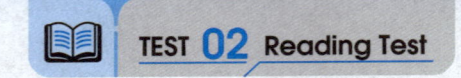

TEST 02 Reading Test

Questions 186-190 refer to the following emails and form.

From: melanie.atwell@glistening-gifts.com
To: judith.rhames@glistening-gifts.com
Subject: Restaurant Options

Hi Judith,

As you requested, I have been reviewing restaurant possibilities for the ten-year anniversary party. The options below all meet the non-negotiable criteria: they're centrally located in the city; they have space for all fifty of us; and they provide somewhere to park. However, they all have pluses and minuses, so I'll leave the final decision up to you.

Restaurant	Pro	Con
Alberto's	We can use their music system	Some reviews say noisy
Silver Fork	Large outdoor space available	Cancelation penalty
Theater Street	Most reviews have five stars	Limited wine list
Cherry & Oak	Many reviews praise the service	Dated interior

Kind regards,

Melanie

Telephone Message	
Date:	Tue, September 2
Time:	14:45
Caller:	Eddie Simpson
For:	Judith Rhames
Message taken by:	Reception
Message details:	

Restaurant called re. anniversary party
Need to confirm menu choice today:
 ➢ 3-course meal: $45/person
 ➢ 3-course meal with drinks: $65/person
 ➢ Buffet: $30/person
 ➢ Buffet with drinks: $50/person
Whichever option selected, transfer 10% of total cost to restaurant by end of workweek

250

From: judith.rhames@glistening-gifts.com
To: all.staff@glistening-gifts.com
Subject: 10-Year Anniversary Party

Hi All,

I hope everyone is looking forward to our ten-year anniversary party—I certainly am! I'd like to take this opportunity to address a few questions that various people have raised. First of all, there is no need to select your meals; the restaurant will be serving a buffet comprising a range of vegetarian and non-vegetarian international cuisines. There will also be free-flowing house wines, bottled beers, and soft drinks.

Secondly, we have booked the entire terrace area of the restaurant, so we will be able to enjoy the balmy fall temperatures. The restaurant has confirmed that the terrace has an awning to protect us in the unlikely event of rain. Thirdly, you will soon receive a formal invitation to the event—please RSVP as instructed. And finally, there will probably be an after-party in one of the clubs in the city, so remember to wear your dancing shoes!

Thanks, everyone!

Judith

---

186. What is NOT mentioned in the first email as essential for each restaurant?
(A) It can accommodate 50 people.
(B) It is located in the city center.
(C) It provides vegan options.
(D) It has a parking lot.

187. According to the form, what should Ms. Rhames do before Friday?
(A) Return a call
(B) Pay a deposit
(C) Confirm a date
(D) Book some transport

188. How much will the company most likely spend per head?
(A) Forty-five dollars
(B) Sixty-five dollars
(C) Thirty dollars
(D) Fifty dollars

189. Which restaurant did Ms. Rhames most likely choose?
(A) Alberto's
(B) Silver Fork
(C) Theater Street
(D) Cherry & Oak

190. According to the second email, what will employees soon get?
(A) An official invitation
(B) A sample menu
(C) A dress code
(D) A song list

GO ON TO THE NEXT PAGE ➔ 251

Questions 191-195 refer to the following proposal, news report, and email.

Proposal: Ensuring Greenhaven Lives up to its Name

<u>Objective</u>: To increase the amount of green space in four main districts of the city.

<u>District breakdown</u>:

- North District: expand North Park by 20%; convert disused parking lot on Burbank Avenue into urban park.
- South District: plant 80 native trees along Bluebell Road and 50 along Somerset Street; surround industrial area with green buffer zone.
- Central District: add rooftop gardens on municipal buildings; transform disused railway line into green walkway.
- West District: add nature play area to Butterfly Park; offer incentives for installing vertical gardens on private buildings.

<u>Timeline</u>: Phase 1 to begin Q2 this year; full implementation by close of Q4 next year.

AMBITIOUS GREEN PLAN LAUNCHED BY CITY

By Ali Rostov
Environment Editor

Greenhaven City Council has announced an ambitious plan to vastly increase the amount of green space in multiple districts of the city. Environmental groups reacted enthusiastically to the plans, which will see the transformation of vacant lots, major thoroughfares, and neglected areas into vibrant green spaces. The project will commence in early April with the conversion of Bluebell Road into a tree-lined street, before expanding across the city.

The landscaping firm EnvoRise Solutions has been awarded the contract for this first phase of the project. However, Greenhaven Mayor, Richard Draper, told this newspaper that the city would need to hire an additional contractor. "This is a huge project with a suitably large budget," he said. "We are determined to utilize all resources at our disposal and make this city a better place to live for all of its residents."

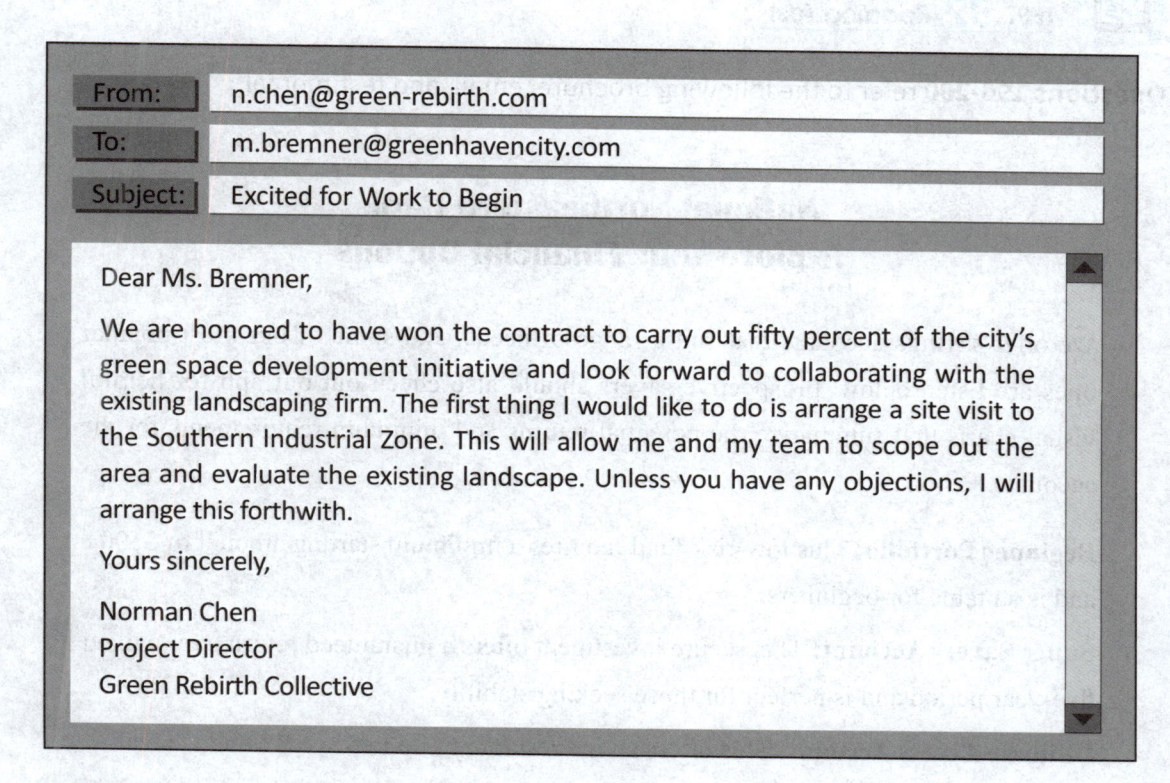

From: n.chen@green-rebirth.com
To: m.bremner@greenhavencity.com
Subject: Excited for Work to Begin

Dear Ms. Bremner,

We are honored to have won the contract to carry out fifty percent of the city's green space development initiative and look forward to collaborating with the existing landscaping firm. The first thing I would like to do is arrange a site visit to the Southern Industrial Zone. This will allow me and my team to scope out the area and evaluate the existing landscape. Unless you have any objections, I will arrange this forthwith.

Yours sincerely,

Norman Chen
Project Director
Green Rebirth Collective

---

191. According to the proposal, what will happen to buildings owned by the city?
(A) They will have gardens added to their roofs.
(B) They will be forced to install solar panels.
(C) They will have plants placed in their interiors.
(D) They will get rainwater harvesting systems.

192. What is suggested about the work to increase green space?
(A) It has faced some opposition due to high costs.
(B) It is expected to take over a year to complete.
(C) It was initially proposed several years ago.
(D) It is funded by the national government.

193. Which area of the city will the project start in?
(A) North District
(B) South District
(C) Central District
(D) West District

194. What is indicated about Green Rebirth Collective?
(A) It will specialize in adding nature play areas.
(B) It will work on only one district of the city.
(C) It will not take part in press conferences.
(D) It will work with EnvoRise Solutions.

195. What does Mr. Chen want to do straight away?
(A) Visit a former railway line
(B) Confirm the details of a budget
(C) Meet with a city representative
(D) Check out a manufacturing area

GO ON TO THE NEXT PAGE ➔ 253

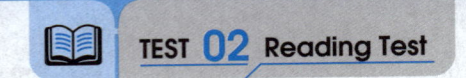

Questions 196-200 refer to the following brochure, email, and testimonial.

National Northeastern Bank
Explore Your Financial Options

We offer savings accounts that suit a range of needs, and some of our most popular ones are listed below. Prospective savers should also check out our app for helpful visual charts that summarize the potential returns and minimum requirements for the accounts.

Beginner Portfolio: This low-risk fund requires a minimum starting amount of $500 and is suitable for beginners.

Super Savers Account: This secure investment offers a guaranteed return over a fixed five-year period and is perfect for those seeking stability.

Ultimate Access Account: This offers an interest rate of up to 5% APY and is ideal for those wanting easy access to their funds while earning more interest.

Silver Savings Plan: This long-term savings solution is perfect for individuals planning a comfortable old age in their 60s, 70s, and 80s.

From:	levi.klein@national-northeastern.com
To:	rosemary.reeves@coldmail.com
Subject:	The Right Savings Plan for You

Dear Ms. Reeves,

It was a pleasure to meet you in the branch earlier today, and I thank you for your interest in opening a savings account with the National Northeastern Bank. You indicated that you value security and would like an account that offers a guaranteed return over a set period of time. It is clear to me that one of our accounts can fulfill your criteria, but I would like to ask you to attend a consultation with one of our financial advisors so they can explain the preferred option in more detail. These sessions can be booked here. They are free and are available in the branch on weekdays or online seven days a week. After the consultation, you are under no obligation to open an account.

Kind regards,

Levi Klein
Customer Representative
National Northeastern Bank

National Northeastern Bank
Customer Testimonials

The staff at my local branch of this bank could not have been more helpful. From Mr. Klein, whom I met in the branch, to the financial advisor, who explained my savings account to me in detail on a Sunday morning, I rate them all highly. Mr. Klein even showed me how to configure automatic monthly transfers using the app—something I really should've been able to figure out myself! I'll definitely recommend this bank to my friends and family. – Rosemary Reeves

196. According to the brochure, what should potential savers use the app to do?
(A) View frequently asked questions
(B) Record their saving progress
(C) Read customer profiles
(D) Look at useful graphics

197. Which account is most suitable for Ms. Reeves?
(A) Beginner Portfolio
(B) Super Savers Account
(C) Ultimate Access Account
(D) Silver Savings Plan

198. What is the main purpose of the email?
(A) To request more details from an account holder
(B) To outline the benefits of a specific product
(C) To invite a customer to meet an advisor
(D) To offer a promotional rate of interest

199. What is suggested about Ms. Reeves?
(A) She attended an appointment via the internet.
(B) She previously closed an account with the bank.
(C) She felt compelled to open a savings account.
(D) She was recommended the bank by a friend.

200. What did Mr. Klein give Ms. Reeves?
(A) Assistance with a relative's retirement planning
(B) Instructions for setting up regular payments
(C) Details on how to use online banking securely
(D) Help with choosing a life insurance policy

Stop! This is the end of the test. If you finish before time is called, you may go back to Parts 5, 6, and 7 and check your work.

NEW TOEIC Simulated Tests 1-5
ANSWER SHEET

Chapter 1

Part 1		Part 4		Part 6	
1	Ⓐ Ⓑ Ⓒ Ⓓ	11	Ⓐ Ⓑ Ⓒ Ⓓ	22	Ⓐ Ⓑ Ⓒ Ⓓ
2	Ⓐ Ⓑ Ⓒ Ⓓ	12	Ⓐ Ⓑ Ⓒ Ⓓ	23	Ⓐ Ⓑ Ⓒ Ⓓ
Part 2		13	Ⓐ Ⓑ Ⓒ Ⓓ	24	Ⓐ Ⓑ Ⓒ Ⓓ
3	Ⓐ Ⓑ Ⓒ	14	Ⓐ Ⓑ Ⓒ Ⓓ	25	Ⓐ Ⓑ Ⓒ Ⓓ
4	Ⓐ Ⓑ Ⓒ	15	Ⓐ Ⓑ Ⓒ Ⓓ	**Part 7**	
Part 3		16	Ⓐ Ⓑ Ⓒ Ⓓ	26	Ⓐ Ⓑ Ⓒ Ⓓ
5	Ⓐ Ⓑ Ⓒ Ⓓ	**Part 5**		27	Ⓐ Ⓑ Ⓒ Ⓓ
6	Ⓐ Ⓑ Ⓒ Ⓓ	17	Ⓐ Ⓑ Ⓒ Ⓓ	28	Ⓐ Ⓑ Ⓒ Ⓓ
7	Ⓐ Ⓑ Ⓒ Ⓓ	18	Ⓐ Ⓑ Ⓒ Ⓓ	29	Ⓐ Ⓑ Ⓒ Ⓓ
8	Ⓐ Ⓑ Ⓒ Ⓓ	19	Ⓐ Ⓑ Ⓒ Ⓓ		
9	Ⓐ Ⓑ Ⓒ Ⓓ	20	Ⓐ Ⓑ Ⓒ Ⓓ		
10	Ⓐ Ⓑ Ⓒ Ⓓ	21	Ⓐ Ⓑ Ⓒ Ⓓ		

Chapter 2

Part 1		Part 4		Part 6	
1	Ⓐ Ⓑ Ⓒ Ⓓ	11	Ⓐ Ⓑ Ⓒ Ⓓ	22	Ⓐ Ⓑ Ⓒ Ⓓ
2	Ⓐ Ⓑ Ⓒ Ⓓ	12	Ⓐ Ⓑ Ⓒ Ⓓ	23	Ⓐ Ⓑ Ⓒ Ⓓ
Part 2		13	Ⓐ Ⓑ Ⓒ Ⓓ	24	Ⓐ Ⓑ Ⓒ Ⓓ
3	Ⓐ Ⓑ Ⓒ	14	Ⓐ Ⓑ Ⓒ Ⓓ	25	Ⓐ Ⓑ Ⓒ Ⓓ
4	Ⓐ Ⓑ Ⓒ	15	Ⓐ Ⓑ Ⓒ Ⓓ	**Part 7**	
Part 3		16	Ⓐ Ⓑ Ⓒ Ⓓ	26	Ⓐ Ⓑ Ⓒ Ⓓ
5	Ⓐ Ⓑ Ⓒ Ⓓ	**Part 5**		27	Ⓐ Ⓑ Ⓒ Ⓓ
6	Ⓐ Ⓑ Ⓒ Ⓓ	17	Ⓐ Ⓑ Ⓒ Ⓓ	28	Ⓐ Ⓑ Ⓒ Ⓓ
7	Ⓐ Ⓑ Ⓒ Ⓓ	18	Ⓐ Ⓑ Ⓒ Ⓓ	29	Ⓐ Ⓑ Ⓒ Ⓓ
8	Ⓐ Ⓑ Ⓒ Ⓓ	19	Ⓐ Ⓑ Ⓒ Ⓓ	30	Ⓐ Ⓑ Ⓒ Ⓓ
9	Ⓐ Ⓑ Ⓒ Ⓓ	20	Ⓐ Ⓑ Ⓒ Ⓓ		
10	Ⓐ Ⓑ Ⓒ Ⓓ	21	Ⓐ Ⓑ Ⓒ Ⓓ		

Chapter 3

Part 1		Part 4		Part 6	
1	Ⓐ Ⓑ Ⓒ Ⓓ	11	Ⓐ Ⓑ Ⓒ Ⓓ	22	Ⓐ Ⓑ Ⓒ Ⓓ
2	Ⓐ Ⓑ Ⓒ Ⓓ	12	Ⓐ Ⓑ Ⓒ Ⓓ	23	Ⓐ Ⓑ Ⓒ Ⓓ
Part 2		13	Ⓐ Ⓑ Ⓒ Ⓓ	24	Ⓐ Ⓑ Ⓒ Ⓓ
3	Ⓐ Ⓑ Ⓒ	14	Ⓐ Ⓑ Ⓒ Ⓓ	25	Ⓐ Ⓑ Ⓒ Ⓓ
4	Ⓐ Ⓑ Ⓒ	15	Ⓐ Ⓑ Ⓒ Ⓓ	**Part 7**	
Part 3		16	Ⓐ Ⓑ Ⓒ Ⓓ	26	Ⓐ Ⓑ Ⓒ Ⓓ
5	Ⓐ Ⓑ Ⓒ Ⓓ	**Part 5**		27	Ⓐ Ⓑ Ⓒ Ⓓ
6	Ⓐ Ⓑ Ⓒ Ⓓ	17	Ⓐ Ⓑ Ⓒ Ⓓ	28	Ⓐ Ⓑ Ⓒ Ⓓ
7	Ⓐ Ⓑ Ⓒ Ⓓ	18	Ⓐ Ⓑ Ⓒ Ⓓ	29	Ⓐ Ⓑ Ⓒ Ⓓ
8	Ⓐ Ⓑ Ⓒ Ⓓ	19	Ⓐ Ⓑ Ⓒ Ⓓ	30	Ⓐ Ⓑ Ⓒ Ⓓ
9	Ⓐ Ⓑ Ⓒ Ⓓ	20	Ⓐ Ⓑ Ⓒ Ⓓ	31	Ⓐ Ⓑ Ⓒ Ⓓ
10	Ⓐ Ⓑ Ⓒ Ⓓ	21	Ⓐ Ⓑ Ⓒ Ⓓ		

Chapter 4

Part 1		Part 4		Part 6	
1	Ⓐ Ⓑ Ⓒ Ⓓ	11	Ⓐ Ⓑ Ⓒ Ⓓ	22	Ⓐ Ⓑ Ⓒ Ⓓ
2	Ⓐ Ⓑ Ⓒ Ⓓ	12	Ⓐ Ⓑ Ⓒ Ⓓ	23	Ⓐ Ⓑ Ⓒ Ⓓ
Part 2		13	Ⓐ Ⓑ Ⓒ Ⓓ	24	Ⓐ Ⓑ Ⓒ Ⓓ
3	Ⓐ Ⓑ Ⓒ	14	Ⓐ Ⓑ Ⓒ Ⓓ	25	Ⓐ Ⓑ Ⓒ Ⓓ
4	Ⓐ Ⓑ Ⓒ	15	Ⓐ Ⓑ Ⓒ Ⓓ	**Part 7**	
Part 3		16	Ⓐ Ⓑ Ⓒ Ⓓ	26	Ⓐ Ⓑ Ⓒ Ⓓ
5	Ⓐ Ⓑ Ⓒ Ⓓ	**Part 5**		27	Ⓐ Ⓑ Ⓒ Ⓓ
6	Ⓐ Ⓑ Ⓒ Ⓓ	17	Ⓐ Ⓑ Ⓒ Ⓓ	28	Ⓐ Ⓑ Ⓒ Ⓓ
7	Ⓐ Ⓑ Ⓒ Ⓓ	18	Ⓐ Ⓑ Ⓒ Ⓓ	29	Ⓐ Ⓑ Ⓒ Ⓓ
8	Ⓐ Ⓑ Ⓒ Ⓓ	19	Ⓐ Ⓑ Ⓒ Ⓓ	30	Ⓐ Ⓑ Ⓒ Ⓓ
9	Ⓐ Ⓑ Ⓒ Ⓓ	20	Ⓐ Ⓑ Ⓒ Ⓓ		
10	Ⓐ Ⓑ Ⓒ Ⓓ	21	Ⓐ Ⓑ Ⓒ Ⓓ		

Chapter 5

Part 1		Part 4		Part 6	
1	Ⓐ Ⓑ Ⓒ Ⓓ	11	Ⓐ Ⓑ Ⓒ Ⓓ	22	Ⓐ Ⓑ Ⓒ Ⓓ
2	Ⓐ Ⓑ Ⓒ Ⓓ	12	Ⓐ Ⓑ Ⓒ Ⓓ	23	Ⓐ Ⓑ Ⓒ Ⓓ
Part 2		13	Ⓐ Ⓑ Ⓒ Ⓓ	24	Ⓐ Ⓑ Ⓒ Ⓓ
3	Ⓐ Ⓑ Ⓒ	14	Ⓐ Ⓑ Ⓒ Ⓓ	25	Ⓐ Ⓑ Ⓒ Ⓓ
4	Ⓐ Ⓑ Ⓒ	15	Ⓐ Ⓑ Ⓒ Ⓓ	**Part 7**	
Part 3		16	Ⓐ Ⓑ Ⓒ Ⓓ	26	Ⓐ Ⓑ Ⓒ Ⓓ
5	Ⓐ Ⓑ Ⓒ Ⓓ	**Part 5**		27	Ⓐ Ⓑ Ⓒ Ⓓ
6	Ⓐ Ⓑ Ⓒ Ⓓ	17	Ⓐ Ⓑ Ⓒ Ⓓ	28	Ⓐ Ⓑ Ⓒ Ⓓ
7	Ⓐ Ⓑ Ⓒ Ⓓ	18	Ⓐ Ⓑ Ⓒ Ⓓ	29	Ⓐ Ⓑ Ⓒ Ⓓ
8	Ⓐ Ⓑ Ⓒ Ⓓ	19	Ⓐ Ⓑ Ⓒ Ⓓ	30	Ⓐ Ⓑ Ⓒ Ⓓ
9	Ⓐ Ⓑ Ⓒ Ⓓ	20	Ⓐ Ⓑ Ⓒ		
10	Ⓐ Ⓑ Ⓒ Ⓓ	21	Ⓐ Ⓑ Ⓒ Ⓓ		

TOEIC is a registered trademark of the Educational Testing Service (ETS). This publication is not affiliated with, endorsed, or approved by ETS.

NEW TOEIC Simulated Tests 6-9
ANSWER SHEET

Chapter 6

Part 1	Part 4	Part 6
1 Ⓐ Ⓑ Ⓒ Ⓓ	11 Ⓐ Ⓑ Ⓒ Ⓓ	22 Ⓐ Ⓑ Ⓒ Ⓓ
2 Ⓐ Ⓑ Ⓒ Ⓓ	12 Ⓐ Ⓑ Ⓒ Ⓓ	23 Ⓐ Ⓑ Ⓒ Ⓓ
Part 2	13 Ⓐ Ⓑ Ⓒ Ⓓ	24 Ⓐ Ⓑ Ⓒ Ⓓ
3 Ⓐ Ⓑ Ⓒ	14 Ⓐ Ⓑ Ⓒ Ⓓ	25 Ⓐ Ⓑ Ⓒ Ⓓ
4 Ⓐ Ⓑ Ⓒ	15 Ⓐ Ⓑ Ⓒ Ⓓ	**Part 7**
Part 3	16 Ⓐ Ⓑ Ⓒ Ⓓ	26 Ⓐ Ⓑ Ⓒ Ⓓ
5 Ⓐ Ⓑ Ⓒ Ⓓ	**Part 5**	27 Ⓐ Ⓑ Ⓒ Ⓓ
6 Ⓐ Ⓑ Ⓒ Ⓓ	17 Ⓐ Ⓑ Ⓒ Ⓓ	28 Ⓐ Ⓑ Ⓒ Ⓓ
7 Ⓐ Ⓑ Ⓒ Ⓓ	18 Ⓐ Ⓑ Ⓒ Ⓓ	29 Ⓐ Ⓑ Ⓒ Ⓓ
8 Ⓐ Ⓑ Ⓒ Ⓓ	19 Ⓐ Ⓑ Ⓒ Ⓓ	30 Ⓐ Ⓑ Ⓒ Ⓓ
9 Ⓐ Ⓑ Ⓒ Ⓓ	20 Ⓐ Ⓑ Ⓒ Ⓓ	31 Ⓐ Ⓑ Ⓒ Ⓓ
10 Ⓐ Ⓑ Ⓒ Ⓓ	21 Ⓐ Ⓑ Ⓒ Ⓓ	32 Ⓐ Ⓑ Ⓒ Ⓓ

Chapter 7

Part 1	Part 4	Part 6
1 Ⓐ Ⓑ Ⓒ Ⓓ	11 Ⓐ Ⓑ Ⓒ Ⓓ	22 Ⓐ Ⓑ Ⓒ Ⓓ
2 Ⓐ Ⓑ Ⓒ Ⓓ	12 Ⓐ Ⓑ Ⓒ Ⓓ	23 Ⓐ Ⓑ Ⓒ Ⓓ
Part 2	13 Ⓐ Ⓑ Ⓒ Ⓓ	24 Ⓐ Ⓑ Ⓒ Ⓓ
3 Ⓐ Ⓑ Ⓒ	14 Ⓐ Ⓑ Ⓒ Ⓓ	25 Ⓐ Ⓑ Ⓒ Ⓓ
4 Ⓐ Ⓑ Ⓒ	15 Ⓐ Ⓑ Ⓒ Ⓓ	**Part 7**
Part 3	16 Ⓐ Ⓑ Ⓒ Ⓓ	26 Ⓐ Ⓑ Ⓒ Ⓓ
5 Ⓐ Ⓑ Ⓒ Ⓓ	**Part 5**	27 Ⓐ Ⓑ Ⓒ Ⓓ
6 Ⓐ Ⓑ Ⓒ Ⓓ	17 Ⓐ Ⓑ Ⓒ Ⓓ	28 Ⓐ Ⓑ Ⓒ Ⓓ
7 Ⓐ Ⓑ Ⓒ Ⓓ	18 Ⓐ Ⓑ Ⓒ Ⓓ	29 Ⓐ Ⓑ Ⓒ Ⓓ
8 Ⓐ Ⓑ Ⓒ Ⓓ	19 Ⓐ Ⓑ Ⓒ Ⓓ	30 Ⓐ Ⓑ Ⓒ Ⓓ
9 Ⓐ Ⓑ Ⓒ Ⓓ	20 Ⓐ Ⓑ Ⓒ Ⓓ	
10 Ⓐ Ⓑ Ⓒ Ⓓ	21 Ⓐ Ⓑ Ⓒ Ⓓ	

Chapter 8

Part 1	Part 4	Part 6
1 Ⓐ Ⓑ Ⓒ Ⓓ	11 Ⓐ Ⓑ Ⓒ Ⓓ	22 Ⓐ Ⓑ Ⓒ Ⓓ
2 Ⓐ Ⓑ Ⓒ Ⓓ	12 Ⓐ Ⓑ Ⓒ Ⓓ	23 Ⓐ Ⓑ Ⓒ Ⓓ
Part 2	13 Ⓐ Ⓑ Ⓒ Ⓓ	24 Ⓐ Ⓑ Ⓒ Ⓓ
3 Ⓐ Ⓑ Ⓒ	14 Ⓐ Ⓑ Ⓒ Ⓓ	25 Ⓐ Ⓑ Ⓒ Ⓓ
4 Ⓐ Ⓑ Ⓒ	15 Ⓐ Ⓑ Ⓒ Ⓓ	**Part 7**
Part 3	16 Ⓐ Ⓑ Ⓒ Ⓓ	26 Ⓐ Ⓑ Ⓒ Ⓓ
5 Ⓐ Ⓑ Ⓒ Ⓓ	**Part 5**	27 Ⓐ Ⓑ Ⓒ Ⓓ
6 Ⓐ Ⓑ Ⓒ Ⓓ	17 Ⓐ Ⓑ Ⓒ Ⓓ	28 Ⓐ Ⓑ Ⓒ Ⓓ
7 Ⓐ Ⓑ Ⓒ Ⓓ	18 Ⓐ Ⓑ Ⓒ Ⓓ	29 Ⓐ Ⓑ Ⓒ Ⓓ
8 Ⓐ Ⓑ Ⓒ Ⓓ	19 Ⓐ Ⓑ Ⓒ Ⓓ	30 Ⓐ Ⓑ Ⓒ Ⓓ
9 Ⓐ Ⓑ Ⓒ Ⓓ	20 Ⓐ Ⓑ Ⓒ Ⓓ	
10 Ⓐ Ⓑ Ⓒ Ⓓ	21 Ⓐ Ⓑ Ⓒ Ⓓ	

Chapter 9

Part 1	Part 4	Part 6
1 Ⓐ Ⓑ Ⓒ Ⓓ	11 Ⓐ Ⓑ Ⓒ Ⓓ	22 Ⓐ Ⓑ Ⓒ Ⓓ
2 Ⓐ Ⓑ Ⓒ Ⓓ	12 Ⓐ Ⓑ Ⓒ Ⓓ	23 Ⓐ Ⓑ Ⓒ Ⓓ
Part 2	13 Ⓐ Ⓑ Ⓒ Ⓓ	24 Ⓐ Ⓑ Ⓒ Ⓓ
3 Ⓐ Ⓑ Ⓒ	14 Ⓐ Ⓑ Ⓒ Ⓓ	25 Ⓐ Ⓑ Ⓒ Ⓓ
4 Ⓐ Ⓑ Ⓒ	15 Ⓐ Ⓑ Ⓒ Ⓓ	**Part 7**
Part 3	16 Ⓐ Ⓑ Ⓒ Ⓓ	26 Ⓐ Ⓑ Ⓒ Ⓓ
5 Ⓐ Ⓑ Ⓒ Ⓓ	**Part 5**	27 Ⓐ Ⓑ Ⓒ Ⓓ
6 Ⓐ Ⓑ Ⓒ Ⓓ	17 Ⓐ Ⓑ Ⓒ Ⓓ	28 Ⓐ Ⓑ Ⓒ Ⓓ
7 Ⓐ Ⓑ Ⓒ Ⓓ	18 Ⓐ Ⓑ Ⓒ Ⓓ	29 Ⓐ Ⓑ Ⓒ Ⓓ
8 Ⓐ Ⓑ Ⓒ Ⓓ	19 Ⓐ Ⓑ Ⓒ Ⓓ	30 Ⓐ Ⓑ Ⓒ Ⓓ
9 Ⓐ Ⓑ Ⓒ Ⓓ	20 Ⓐ Ⓑ Ⓒ Ⓓ	
10 Ⓐ Ⓑ Ⓒ Ⓓ	21 Ⓐ Ⓑ Ⓒ Ⓓ	

TOEIC is a registered trademark of the Educational Testing Service (ETS). This publication is not affiliated with, endorsed, or approved by ETS.

NEW TOEIC Simulated Tests 10-13
ANSWER SHEET

Chapter 10

Part 1	Part 4	Part 6
1 Ⓐ Ⓑ Ⓒ Ⓓ	11 Ⓐ Ⓑ Ⓒ Ⓓ	22 Ⓐ Ⓑ Ⓒ Ⓓ
2 Ⓐ Ⓑ Ⓒ Ⓓ	12 Ⓐ Ⓑ Ⓒ Ⓓ	23 Ⓐ Ⓑ Ⓒ Ⓓ
Part 2	13 Ⓐ Ⓑ Ⓒ Ⓓ	24 Ⓐ Ⓑ Ⓒ Ⓓ
3 Ⓐ Ⓑ Ⓒ	14 Ⓐ Ⓑ Ⓒ Ⓓ	25 Ⓐ Ⓑ Ⓒ Ⓓ
4 Ⓐ Ⓑ Ⓒ	15 Ⓐ Ⓑ Ⓒ Ⓓ	**Part 7**
Part 3	16 Ⓐ Ⓑ Ⓒ Ⓓ	26 Ⓐ Ⓑ Ⓒ Ⓓ
5 Ⓐ Ⓑ Ⓒ Ⓓ	**Part 5**	27 Ⓐ Ⓑ Ⓒ Ⓓ
6 Ⓐ Ⓑ Ⓒ Ⓓ	17 Ⓐ Ⓑ Ⓒ Ⓓ	28 Ⓐ Ⓑ Ⓒ Ⓓ
7 Ⓐ Ⓑ Ⓒ Ⓓ	18 Ⓐ Ⓑ Ⓒ Ⓓ	29 Ⓐ Ⓑ Ⓒ Ⓓ
8 Ⓐ Ⓑ Ⓒ Ⓓ	19 Ⓐ Ⓑ Ⓒ Ⓓ	30 Ⓐ Ⓑ Ⓒ Ⓓ
9 Ⓐ Ⓑ Ⓒ Ⓓ	20 Ⓐ Ⓑ Ⓒ Ⓓ	
10 Ⓐ Ⓑ Ⓒ Ⓓ	21 Ⓐ Ⓑ Ⓒ Ⓓ	

Chapter 11

Part 1	Part 4	Part 6
1 Ⓐ Ⓑ Ⓒ Ⓓ	11 Ⓐ Ⓑ Ⓒ Ⓓ	22 Ⓐ Ⓑ Ⓒ Ⓓ
2 Ⓐ Ⓑ Ⓒ Ⓓ	12 Ⓐ Ⓑ Ⓒ Ⓓ	23 Ⓐ Ⓑ Ⓒ Ⓓ
Part 2	13 Ⓐ Ⓑ Ⓒ Ⓓ	24 Ⓐ Ⓑ Ⓒ Ⓓ
3 Ⓐ Ⓑ Ⓒ	14 Ⓐ Ⓑ Ⓒ Ⓓ	25 Ⓐ Ⓑ Ⓒ Ⓓ
4 Ⓐ Ⓑ Ⓒ	15 Ⓐ Ⓑ Ⓒ Ⓓ	**Part 7**
Part 3	16 Ⓐ Ⓑ Ⓒ Ⓓ	26 Ⓐ Ⓑ Ⓒ Ⓓ
5 Ⓐ Ⓑ Ⓒ Ⓓ	**Part 5**	27 Ⓐ Ⓑ Ⓒ Ⓓ
6 Ⓐ Ⓑ Ⓒ Ⓓ	17 Ⓐ Ⓑ Ⓒ Ⓓ	28 Ⓐ Ⓑ Ⓒ Ⓓ
7 Ⓐ Ⓑ Ⓒ Ⓓ	18 Ⓐ Ⓑ Ⓒ Ⓓ	29 Ⓐ Ⓑ Ⓒ Ⓓ
8 Ⓐ Ⓑ Ⓒ Ⓓ	19 Ⓐ Ⓑ Ⓒ Ⓓ	30 Ⓐ Ⓑ Ⓒ Ⓓ
9 Ⓐ Ⓑ Ⓒ Ⓓ	20 Ⓐ Ⓑ Ⓒ Ⓓ	
10 Ⓐ Ⓑ Ⓒ Ⓓ	21 Ⓐ Ⓑ Ⓒ Ⓓ	

Chapter 12

Part 1	Part 4	Part 6
1 Ⓐ Ⓑ Ⓒ Ⓓ	11 Ⓐ Ⓑ Ⓒ Ⓓ	22 Ⓐ Ⓑ Ⓒ Ⓓ
2 Ⓐ Ⓑ Ⓒ Ⓓ	12 Ⓐ Ⓑ Ⓒ Ⓓ	23 Ⓐ Ⓑ Ⓒ Ⓓ
Part 2	13 Ⓐ Ⓑ Ⓒ Ⓓ	24 Ⓐ Ⓑ Ⓒ Ⓓ
3 Ⓐ Ⓑ Ⓒ	14 Ⓐ Ⓑ Ⓒ Ⓓ	25 Ⓐ Ⓑ Ⓒ Ⓓ
4 Ⓐ Ⓑ Ⓒ	15 Ⓐ Ⓑ Ⓒ Ⓓ	**Part 7**
Part 3	16 Ⓐ Ⓑ Ⓒ Ⓓ	26 Ⓐ Ⓑ Ⓒ Ⓓ
5 Ⓐ Ⓑ Ⓒ Ⓓ	**Part 5**	27 Ⓐ Ⓑ Ⓒ Ⓓ
6 Ⓐ Ⓑ Ⓒ Ⓓ	17 Ⓐ Ⓑ Ⓒ Ⓓ	28 Ⓐ Ⓑ Ⓒ Ⓓ
7 Ⓐ Ⓑ Ⓒ Ⓓ	18 Ⓐ Ⓑ Ⓒ Ⓓ	29 Ⓐ Ⓑ Ⓒ Ⓓ
8 Ⓐ Ⓑ Ⓒ Ⓓ	19 Ⓐ Ⓑ Ⓒ Ⓓ	30 Ⓐ Ⓑ Ⓒ Ⓓ
9 Ⓐ Ⓑ Ⓒ Ⓓ	20 Ⓐ Ⓑ Ⓒ Ⓓ	
10 Ⓐ Ⓑ Ⓒ Ⓓ	21 Ⓐ Ⓑ Ⓒ Ⓓ	

Chapter 13

Part 1	Part 4	Part 6
1 Ⓐ Ⓑ Ⓒ Ⓓ	11 Ⓐ Ⓑ Ⓒ Ⓓ	22 Ⓐ Ⓑ Ⓒ Ⓓ
2 Ⓐ Ⓑ Ⓒ Ⓓ	12 Ⓐ Ⓑ Ⓒ Ⓓ	23 Ⓐ Ⓑ Ⓒ Ⓓ
Part 2	13 Ⓐ Ⓑ Ⓒ Ⓓ	24 Ⓐ Ⓑ Ⓒ Ⓓ
3 Ⓐ Ⓑ Ⓒ	14 Ⓐ Ⓑ Ⓒ Ⓓ	25 Ⓐ Ⓑ Ⓒ Ⓓ
4 Ⓐ Ⓑ Ⓒ	15 Ⓐ Ⓑ Ⓒ Ⓓ	**Part 7**
Part 3	16 Ⓐ Ⓑ Ⓒ Ⓓ	26 Ⓐ Ⓑ Ⓒ Ⓓ
5 Ⓐ Ⓑ Ⓒ Ⓓ	**Part 5**	27 Ⓐ Ⓑ Ⓒ Ⓓ
6 Ⓐ Ⓑ Ⓒ Ⓓ	17 Ⓐ Ⓑ Ⓒ Ⓓ	28 Ⓐ Ⓑ Ⓒ Ⓓ
7 Ⓐ Ⓑ Ⓒ Ⓓ	18 Ⓐ Ⓑ Ⓒ Ⓓ	29 Ⓐ Ⓑ Ⓒ Ⓓ
8 Ⓐ Ⓑ Ⓒ Ⓓ	19 Ⓐ Ⓑ Ⓒ Ⓓ	30 Ⓐ Ⓑ Ⓒ Ⓓ
9 Ⓐ Ⓑ Ⓒ Ⓓ	20 Ⓐ Ⓑ Ⓒ Ⓓ	
10 Ⓐ Ⓑ Ⓒ Ⓓ	21 Ⓐ Ⓑ Ⓒ Ⓓ	

TOEIC is a registered trademark of the Educational Testing Service (ETS). This publication is not affiliated with, endorsed, or approved by ETS.

NEW TOEIC Simulated Test 1

ANSWER SHEET

LISTENING SECTION

Part 1

No.	ANSWER A B C D
1	Ⓐ Ⓑ Ⓒ Ⓓ
2	Ⓐ Ⓑ Ⓒ Ⓓ
3	Ⓐ Ⓑ Ⓒ Ⓓ
4	Ⓐ Ⓑ Ⓒ Ⓓ
5	Ⓐ Ⓑ Ⓒ Ⓓ
6	Ⓐ Ⓑ Ⓒ Ⓓ
7	Ⓐ Ⓑ Ⓒ
8	Ⓐ Ⓑ Ⓒ
9	Ⓐ Ⓑ Ⓒ
10	Ⓐ Ⓑ Ⓒ

Part 2

No.	ANSWER A B C
11	Ⓐ Ⓑ Ⓒ
12	Ⓐ Ⓑ Ⓒ
13	Ⓐ Ⓑ Ⓒ
14	Ⓐ Ⓑ Ⓒ
15	Ⓐ Ⓑ Ⓒ
16	Ⓐ Ⓑ Ⓒ
17	Ⓐ Ⓑ Ⓒ
18	Ⓐ Ⓑ Ⓒ
19	Ⓐ Ⓑ Ⓒ
20	Ⓐ Ⓑ Ⓒ

No.	ANSWER A B C
21	Ⓐ Ⓑ Ⓒ
22	Ⓐ Ⓑ Ⓒ
23	Ⓐ Ⓑ Ⓒ
24	Ⓐ Ⓑ Ⓒ
25	Ⓐ Ⓑ Ⓒ
26	Ⓐ Ⓑ Ⓒ
27	Ⓐ Ⓑ Ⓒ
28	Ⓐ Ⓑ Ⓒ
29	Ⓐ Ⓑ Ⓒ
30	Ⓐ Ⓑ Ⓒ

No.	ANSWER A B C
31	Ⓐ Ⓑ Ⓒ
32	Ⓐ Ⓑ Ⓒ Ⓓ
33	Ⓐ Ⓑ Ⓒ Ⓓ
34	Ⓐ Ⓑ Ⓒ Ⓓ
35	Ⓐ Ⓑ Ⓒ Ⓓ
36	Ⓐ Ⓑ Ⓒ Ⓓ
37	Ⓐ Ⓑ Ⓒ Ⓓ
38	Ⓐ Ⓑ Ⓒ Ⓓ
39	Ⓐ Ⓑ Ⓒ Ⓓ
40	Ⓐ Ⓑ Ⓒ Ⓓ

Part 3

No.	ANSWER A B C D
41	Ⓐ Ⓑ Ⓒ Ⓓ
42	Ⓐ Ⓑ Ⓒ Ⓓ
43	Ⓐ Ⓑ Ⓒ Ⓓ
44	Ⓐ Ⓑ Ⓒ Ⓓ
45	Ⓐ Ⓑ Ⓒ Ⓓ
46	Ⓐ Ⓑ Ⓒ Ⓓ
47	Ⓐ Ⓑ Ⓒ Ⓓ
48	Ⓐ Ⓑ Ⓒ Ⓓ
49	Ⓐ Ⓑ Ⓒ Ⓓ
50	Ⓐ Ⓑ Ⓒ Ⓓ

No.	ANSWER A B C D
51	Ⓐ Ⓑ Ⓒ Ⓓ
52	Ⓐ Ⓑ Ⓒ Ⓓ
53	Ⓐ Ⓑ Ⓒ Ⓓ
54	Ⓐ Ⓑ Ⓒ Ⓓ
55	Ⓐ Ⓑ Ⓒ Ⓓ
56	Ⓐ Ⓑ Ⓒ Ⓓ
57	Ⓐ Ⓑ Ⓒ Ⓓ
58	Ⓐ Ⓑ Ⓒ Ⓓ
59	Ⓐ Ⓑ Ⓒ Ⓓ
60	Ⓐ Ⓑ Ⓒ Ⓓ

No.	ANSWER A B C D
61	Ⓐ Ⓑ Ⓒ Ⓓ
62	Ⓐ Ⓑ Ⓒ Ⓓ
63	Ⓐ Ⓑ Ⓒ Ⓓ
64	Ⓐ Ⓑ Ⓒ Ⓓ
65	Ⓐ Ⓑ Ⓒ Ⓓ
66	Ⓐ Ⓑ Ⓒ Ⓓ
67	Ⓐ Ⓑ Ⓒ Ⓓ
68	Ⓐ Ⓑ Ⓒ Ⓓ
69	Ⓐ Ⓑ Ⓒ Ⓓ
70	Ⓐ Ⓑ Ⓒ Ⓓ

Part 4

No.	ANSWER A B C D
71	Ⓐ Ⓑ Ⓒ Ⓓ
72	Ⓐ Ⓑ Ⓒ Ⓓ
73	Ⓐ Ⓑ Ⓒ Ⓓ
74	Ⓐ Ⓑ Ⓒ Ⓓ
75	Ⓐ Ⓑ Ⓒ Ⓓ
76	Ⓐ Ⓑ Ⓒ Ⓓ
77	Ⓐ Ⓑ Ⓒ Ⓓ
78	Ⓐ Ⓑ Ⓒ Ⓓ
79	Ⓐ Ⓑ Ⓒ Ⓓ
80	Ⓐ Ⓑ Ⓒ Ⓓ

No.	ANSWER A B C D
81	Ⓐ Ⓑ Ⓒ Ⓓ
82	Ⓐ Ⓑ Ⓒ Ⓓ
83	Ⓐ Ⓑ Ⓒ Ⓓ
84	Ⓐ Ⓑ Ⓒ Ⓓ
85	Ⓐ Ⓑ Ⓒ Ⓓ
86	Ⓐ Ⓑ Ⓒ Ⓓ
87	Ⓐ Ⓑ Ⓒ Ⓓ
88	Ⓐ Ⓑ Ⓒ Ⓓ
89	Ⓐ Ⓑ Ⓒ Ⓓ
90	Ⓐ Ⓑ Ⓒ Ⓓ

No.	ANSWER A B C D
91	Ⓐ Ⓑ Ⓒ Ⓓ
92	Ⓐ Ⓑ Ⓒ Ⓓ
93	Ⓐ Ⓑ Ⓒ Ⓓ
94	Ⓐ Ⓑ Ⓒ Ⓓ
95	Ⓐ Ⓑ Ⓒ Ⓓ
96	Ⓐ Ⓑ Ⓒ Ⓓ
97	Ⓐ Ⓑ Ⓒ Ⓓ
98	Ⓐ Ⓑ Ⓒ Ⓓ
99	Ⓐ Ⓑ Ⓒ Ⓓ
100	Ⓐ Ⓑ Ⓒ Ⓓ

READING SECTION

Part 5

No.	ANSWER A B C D
101	Ⓐ Ⓑ Ⓒ Ⓓ
102	Ⓐ Ⓑ Ⓒ Ⓓ
103	Ⓐ Ⓑ Ⓒ Ⓓ
104	Ⓐ Ⓑ Ⓒ Ⓓ
105	Ⓐ Ⓑ Ⓒ Ⓓ
106	Ⓐ Ⓑ Ⓒ Ⓓ
107	Ⓐ Ⓑ Ⓒ Ⓓ
108	Ⓐ Ⓑ Ⓒ Ⓓ
109	Ⓐ Ⓑ Ⓒ Ⓓ
110	Ⓐ Ⓑ Ⓒ Ⓓ

No.	ANSWER A B C D
111	Ⓐ Ⓑ Ⓒ Ⓓ
112	Ⓐ Ⓑ Ⓒ Ⓓ
113	Ⓐ Ⓑ Ⓒ Ⓓ
114	Ⓐ Ⓑ Ⓒ Ⓓ
115	Ⓐ Ⓑ Ⓒ Ⓓ
116	Ⓐ Ⓑ Ⓒ Ⓓ
117	Ⓐ Ⓑ Ⓒ Ⓓ
118	Ⓐ Ⓑ Ⓒ Ⓓ
119	Ⓐ Ⓑ Ⓒ Ⓓ
120	Ⓐ Ⓑ Ⓒ Ⓓ

No.	ANSWER A B C D
121	Ⓐ Ⓑ Ⓒ Ⓓ
122	Ⓐ Ⓑ Ⓒ Ⓓ
123	Ⓐ Ⓑ Ⓒ Ⓓ
124	Ⓐ Ⓑ Ⓒ Ⓓ
125	Ⓐ Ⓑ Ⓒ Ⓓ
126	Ⓐ Ⓑ Ⓒ Ⓓ
127	Ⓐ Ⓑ Ⓒ Ⓓ
128	Ⓐ Ⓑ Ⓒ Ⓓ
129	Ⓐ Ⓑ Ⓒ Ⓓ
130	Ⓐ Ⓑ Ⓒ Ⓓ

Part 6

No.	ANSWER A B C D
131	Ⓐ Ⓑ Ⓒ Ⓓ
132	Ⓐ Ⓑ Ⓒ Ⓓ
133	Ⓐ Ⓑ Ⓒ Ⓓ
134	Ⓐ Ⓑ Ⓒ Ⓓ
135	Ⓐ Ⓑ Ⓒ Ⓓ
136	Ⓐ Ⓑ Ⓒ Ⓓ
137	Ⓐ Ⓑ Ⓒ Ⓓ
138	Ⓐ Ⓑ Ⓒ Ⓓ
139	Ⓐ Ⓑ Ⓒ Ⓓ
140	Ⓐ Ⓑ Ⓒ Ⓓ

Part 7

No.	ANSWER A B C D
141	Ⓐ Ⓑ Ⓒ Ⓓ
142	Ⓐ Ⓑ Ⓒ Ⓓ
143	Ⓐ Ⓑ Ⓒ Ⓓ
144	Ⓐ Ⓑ Ⓒ Ⓓ
145	Ⓐ Ⓑ Ⓒ Ⓓ
146	Ⓐ Ⓑ Ⓒ Ⓓ
147	Ⓐ Ⓑ Ⓒ Ⓓ
148	Ⓐ Ⓑ Ⓒ Ⓓ
149	Ⓐ Ⓑ Ⓒ Ⓓ
150	Ⓐ Ⓑ Ⓒ Ⓓ

No.	ANSWER A B C D
151	Ⓐ Ⓑ Ⓒ Ⓓ
152	Ⓐ Ⓑ Ⓒ Ⓓ
153	Ⓐ Ⓑ Ⓒ Ⓓ
154	Ⓐ Ⓑ Ⓒ Ⓓ
155	Ⓐ Ⓑ Ⓒ Ⓓ
156	Ⓐ Ⓑ Ⓒ Ⓓ
157	Ⓐ Ⓑ Ⓒ Ⓓ
158	Ⓐ Ⓑ Ⓒ Ⓓ
159	Ⓐ Ⓑ Ⓒ Ⓓ
160	Ⓐ Ⓑ Ⓒ Ⓓ

No.	ANSWER A B C D
161	Ⓐ Ⓑ Ⓒ Ⓓ
162	Ⓐ Ⓑ Ⓒ Ⓓ
163	Ⓐ Ⓑ Ⓒ Ⓓ
164	Ⓐ Ⓑ Ⓒ Ⓓ
165	Ⓐ Ⓑ Ⓒ Ⓓ
166	Ⓐ Ⓑ Ⓒ Ⓓ
167	Ⓐ Ⓑ Ⓒ Ⓓ
168	Ⓐ Ⓑ Ⓒ Ⓓ
169	Ⓐ Ⓑ Ⓒ Ⓓ
170	Ⓐ Ⓑ Ⓒ Ⓓ

No.	ANSWER A B C D
171	Ⓐ Ⓑ Ⓒ Ⓓ
172	Ⓐ Ⓑ Ⓒ Ⓓ
173	Ⓐ Ⓑ Ⓒ Ⓓ
174	Ⓐ Ⓑ Ⓒ Ⓓ
175	Ⓐ Ⓑ Ⓒ Ⓓ
176	Ⓐ Ⓑ Ⓒ Ⓓ
177	Ⓐ Ⓑ Ⓒ Ⓓ
178	Ⓐ Ⓑ Ⓒ Ⓓ
179	Ⓐ Ⓑ Ⓒ Ⓓ
180	Ⓐ Ⓑ Ⓒ Ⓓ

No.	ANSWER A B C D
181	Ⓐ Ⓑ Ⓒ Ⓓ
182	Ⓐ Ⓑ Ⓒ Ⓓ
183	Ⓐ Ⓑ Ⓒ Ⓓ
184	Ⓐ Ⓑ Ⓒ Ⓓ
185	Ⓐ Ⓑ Ⓒ Ⓓ
186	Ⓐ Ⓑ Ⓒ Ⓓ
187	Ⓐ Ⓑ Ⓒ Ⓓ
188	Ⓐ Ⓑ Ⓒ Ⓓ
189	Ⓐ Ⓑ Ⓒ Ⓓ
190	Ⓐ Ⓑ Ⓒ Ⓓ

No.	ANSWER A B C D
191	Ⓐ Ⓑ Ⓒ Ⓓ
192	Ⓐ Ⓑ Ⓒ Ⓓ
193	Ⓐ Ⓑ Ⓒ Ⓓ
194	Ⓐ Ⓑ Ⓒ Ⓓ
195	Ⓐ Ⓑ Ⓒ Ⓓ
196	Ⓐ Ⓑ Ⓒ Ⓓ
197	Ⓐ Ⓑ Ⓒ Ⓓ
198	Ⓐ Ⓑ Ⓒ Ⓓ
199	Ⓐ Ⓑ Ⓒ Ⓓ
200	Ⓐ Ⓑ Ⓒ Ⓓ

TOEIC is a registered trademark of Educational Testing Service (ETS). This publication is not affiliated with, endorsed, or approved by ETS.

NEW TOEIC Simulated Test 2

ANSWER SHEET

LISTENING SECTION

Part 1

No.	ANSWER A B C D
1	A B C D
2	A B C D
3	A B C D
4	A B C D
5	A B C D
6	A B C D
7	A B C
8	A B C
9	A B C
10	A B C

Part 2

No.	ANSWER A B C
11	A B C
12	A B C
13	A B C
14	A B C
15	A B C
16	A B C
17	A B C
18	A B C
19	A B C
20	A B C

No.	ANSWER A B C
21	A B C
22	A B C
23	A B C
24	A B C
25	A B C
26	A B C
27	A B C
28	A B C
29	A B C
30	A B C

Part 3

No.	ANSWER A B C D
31	A B C
32	A B C D
33	A B C D
34	A B C D
35	A B C D
36	A B C D
37	A B C D
38	A B C D
39	A B C D
40	A B C D

No.	ANSWER A B C D
41	A B C D
42	A B C D
43	A B C D
44	A B C D
45	A B C D
46	A B C D
47	A B C D
48	A B C D
49	A B C D
50	A B C D

No.	ANSWER A B C D
51	A B C D
52	A B C D
53	A B C D
54	A B C D
55	A B C D
56	A B C D
57	A B C D
58	A B C D
59	A B C D
60	A B C D

No.	ANSWER A B C D
61	A B C D
62	A B C D
63	A B C D
64	A B C D
65	A B C D
66	A B C D
67	A B C D
68	A B C D
69	A B C D
70	A B C D

Part 4

No.	ANSWER A B C D
71	A B C D
72	A B C D
73	A B C D
74	A B C D
75	A B C D
76	A B C D
77	A B C D
78	A B C D
79	A B C D
80	A B C D

No.	ANSWER A B C D
81	A B C D
82	A B C D
83	A B C D
84	A B C D
85	A B C D
86	A B C D
87	A B C D
88	A B C D
89	A B C D
90	A B C D

No.	ANSWER A B C D
91	A B C D
92	A B C D
93	A B C D
94	A B C D
95	A B C D
96	A B C D
97	A B C D
98	A B C D
99	A B C D
100	A B C D

READING SECTION

Part 5

No.	ANSWER A B C D
101	A B C D
102	A B C D
103	A B C D
104	A B C D
105	A B C D
106	A B C D
107	A B C D
108	A B C D
109	A B C D
110	A B C D

No.	ANSWER A B C D
111	A B C D
112	A B C D
113	A B C D
114	A B C D
115	A B C D
116	A B C D
117	A B C D
118	A B C D
119	A B C D
120	A B C D

No.	ANSWER A B C D
121	A B C D
122	A B C D
123	A B C D
124	A B C D
125	A B C D
126	A B C D
127	A B C D
128	A B C D
129	A B C D
130	A B C D

Part 6

No.	ANSWER A B C D
131	A B C D
132	A B C D
133	A B C D
134	A B C D
135	A B C D
136	A B C D
137	A B C D
138	A B C D
139	A B C D
140	A B C D

Part 7

No.	ANSWER A B C D
141	A B C D
142	A B C D
143	A B C D
144	A B C D
145	A B C D
146	A B C D
147	A B C D
148	A B C D
149	A B C D
150	A B C D

No.	ANSWER A B C D
151	A B C D
152	A B C D
153	A B C D
154	A B C D
155	A B C D
156	A B C D
157	A B C D
158	A B C D
159	A B C D
160	A B C D

No.	ANSWER A B C D
161	A B C D
162	A B C D
163	A B C D
164	A B C D
165	A B C D
166	A B C D
167	A B C D
168	A B C D
169	A B C D
170	A B C D

No.	ANSWER A B C D
171	A B C D
172	A B C D
173	A B C D
174	A B C D
175	A B C D
176	A B C D
177	A B C D
178	A B C D
179	A B C D
180	A B C D

No.	ANSWER A B C D
181	A B C D
182	A B C D
183	A B C D
184	A B C D
185	A B C D
186	A B C D
187	A B C D
188	A B C D
189	A B C D
190	A B C D

No.	ANSWER A B C D
191	A B C D
192	A B C D
193	A B C D
194	A B C D
195	A B C D
196	A B C D
197	A B C D
198	A B C D
199	A B C D
200	A B C D

TOEIC is a registered trademark of Educational Testing Service (ETS). This publication is not affiliated with, endorsed, or approved by ETS.